A Sparrow Among Stars

CELESTIAL DESTINY
BOOK ONE

SARA PUISSEGUR

A Sparrow Among Stars is a work of fiction. All names, places, characters, and incidents are the product of the author's imagination and used fictitiously. Any resemblance to actual persons, living or deceased, events, or locations is entirely coincidental.

A Sparrow Among Stars: Celestial Destiny Book One by Sara Puissegur

Published by Sara Puissegur

www.sarapuissegur.com

Copyright © 2024 by Sara Puissegur

All rights reserved. No portion of this book may be reproduced in any form without permission from the publisher, except as permitted by U.S. copyright law. For permissions, contact: sarapuissegur@gmail.com

Cover design by she_cr0w.

Edited by Samantha Carpenter/Jack Clarie (Verse & Vine Publishing).

ISBN: 979-8-9906556-0-7 (paperback)
979-8-9906556-1-4 (hard cover)
979-8-9906556-2-1 (ebook)

Printed in the United States of America

First Edition

*For everyone who needs to escape,
and for everyone we lost too soon.*

KINGDOM OF DENORFIA

KINGDOM OF NYZENARD

Graynor

Lettras

Jessirae

Marlto River

KINGDOM OF HYROSENCIA

Murmont

Axys

Morl

ELJICOY LAKE

Ramdemoi

Eldawia River

Kypno

CELESTIAL DESTINY SERIES

Ewiajoy

Durm

THAMAR
OUNTAINS

Silvermane Symptee

NEW HYROSENCIA

Lexilor

Avoika River

Faswyn

LESTERA SEA

Estivor

Lei'wana

Noomi   Envyre

**VALLEY
OF
NORLEE**   **ORD
               METSIILVA**   Sarklii

Monteris

CONTENTS

Chapter 1: The Rabbit's Snare 1
Chapter 2: The Weight of a Crown 11
Chapter 3: Unexpected Company 21
Chapter 4: Midnight Menace 35
Chapter 5: The Prisoner 45
Chapter 6: Enchanted 55
Chapter 7: Royal Rendezvous 67
Chapter 8: Guarded 77
Chapter 9: Old Friends 91
Chapter 10: Wicked Plans 103
Chapter 11: Embers & Ashes 111
Chapter 12: Fresh Blood 123
Chapter 13: Dark Corners 139
Chapter 14: Counting the Days 153
Chapter 15: The Well 165
Chapter 16: Crimson Tears 175
Chapter 17: Predators & Prey 185
Chapter 18: The Crags of Vigilance 199
Chapter 19: Secrets 211
Chapter 20: Reputation 225
Chapter 21: Reflections 239
Chapter 22: Exposed 253
Chapter 23: Warm Welcome 265
Chapter 24: The Steel Fortress 277
Chapter 25: Something Blue 287
Chapter 26: Daylight 301
Chapter 27: The Heir's Blade 315
Chapter 28: Masquerade 333
Chapter 29: Traitors 351
Chapter 30: Perilous Path 367
Chapter 31: Haunted 379
Chapter 32: Hard Lessons 391
Chapter 33: Mercy 407
Chapter 34: United At Last 419

THE RABBIT'S SNARE

The wooden gate creaked open as Serena Finch slipped out of her family's cottage with an iron bowl of kitchen scraps nestled against her hip. The sunrise bathed the farm in shades of gold. She rubbed her arms, her spotted frock doing little to dull the cold bite in the air. Gravel crunched under her boots as she fetched the full bucket of corn and grains.

Emptying the scraps into the bucket, she set the bowl on the dew-kissed ground and squinted at the horizon. The rising sun reached across the land, painting the sky in hues of pink and orange. Feeding the family's hens had grown to be her favorite part of the day, and she often paused to ponder the warmth of the dawning day and what it might yet bring. A frown flashed across her face as she thought about her father, but she quickly set it aside to focus on her task.

She had just turned eighteen the month before. As the oldest remaining child in the Finch family household, she took her responsibilities seriously. She began each day by feeding the flock, often before her mother could even ask. Now she flicked her wrist, chicken feed peppering the yard before her. The hens rustled awake, sauntering sleepily to their breakfast. With the nests now vacant, Serena carefully slipped the previous day's eggs into the hem of her frock, humming along with the cooing doves.

When Serena stepped back into the kitchen, Mary Finch greeted her daughter with a kiss on the cheek as she placed the fresh eggs into a basket on the counter. Noticing the other ingredients Mama had taken out, Serena stepped up to the counter, brushing shoulders with her mother.

"Let me try again today," Serena said, determined to finally master her mother's special bread recipe. "I still haven't gotten it perfect."

"It tasted fine last time," Mama said with a chuckle, passing a brown sack of flour to her daughter. "The key is to knead it well." Serena nodded as she carefully dumped flour into a large bowl.

She glanced toward the hall that led to their bedrooms and narrowed her eyes. "It's too quiet. Are the boys still asleep?"

"No, they're getting ready," Mama said. "They both have tests today. After breakfast, we're going to review their notes. At this rate, it will take divine intervention to keep Daniel in school another two years."

Serena tried to hide her smirk as she began forming a dough with water and eggs. She was grateful to have completed her advanced lessons the previous year, finishing a year early, with her brother Cameron's class. Graduating early had given her the opportunity to help her mother more at home since her father and elder brother had left. She closed her eyes and pictured their faces as she mixed the dough with her bare hands. They both had black hair and chiseled jaws, with creases etched across their foreheads from stubbornness. It was no surprise to her when Cameron left first; she knew his longing to leave Durmak grew stronger each day, though she wasn't certain why.

She and Cameron were always close. Even as they grew older, they would play hide and seek together in the woods and caves around Durmak. He was a natural hunter; he could quickly find Serena even in the trickiest places. One morning long ago, Serena had decided to go out and hide deep in the woods, nearly all the way to Ewiajoy, the next town over. She thought it would take him till noon to find her, but within an hour he had tracked her down.

"You shouldn't be out here, Rena," he had said. "It's dangerous."

"What makes it dangerous?" It wasn't often that he showed concern.

"They say the king's soldiers pass this way," Cameron said.

Serena shuddered. Though they had never seen any soldiers, their village feared them. The reputation of King Rexton's army hung in the corners of their imaginations, a shadowy fear from far off lands. "How'd you find me?"

"I always find you, Serena. You're far from home, so I knew you'd keep the road in sight." Just as Cameron gestured toward the road, a troop of soldiers came down it. The two of them crept up to the edge of the trees to get a closer look. Serena was frightened by their fierce appearance; the look in their eyes was ruthless and cold. But she saw that Cameron was in awe of them.

After that day, Cameron began to ask their father about Rexton and his soldiers. But Papa was always short; he never spoke much about it, but he made it clear he thought them no good. That did nothing for Cameron's curiosity. As soon as he turned seventeen, he started talking about enlisting in the king's army. Though their father, John, wanted him to apprentice at the forge, Cameron argued that he wanted to forge his own path. Finally, the summer after he turned eighteen, he packed his rucksack and left. The sound of her mother's sobs rang through the back of her mind; the walls of the cottage had never been as thin as they were that night.

"I miss Cameron," Serena said. "Papa, too."

Mama froze midway through pouring oats into a pot of hot water. She nodded and sighed. "As do I."

"Any word from Papa lately?" Serena asked, glancing sidelong at her mother.

Her mother plopped the brown sack on the counter haphazardly, sending dry oats trickling across the counter. "No," she said, grinding her teeth. "I'm afraid not."

It had been five months since Papa left in search of supplies for the forge. Despite Mama's objections, he left as the harshest days of winter descended. Nearly five months had passed, and he had yet to write or return home. Mama wiped stray oats from the counter with her hand, brushing them off into the bag. Then she began mixing the oatmeal with a wooden spoon.

"You don't think something happened to Papa, do you?" Serena asked, bracing herself for her mother's answer. They had expected him to return in just a few weeks. After that, Mama would tell the children, "Any day now." But after two months with no letters, she had stopped saying it. They were all scared of asking the question aloud, scared of what they might have to imagine or accept. But Serena couldn't push the thoughts down anymore. She remembered how the stern look on Papa's face always melted away when he saw her.

Mama stiffened, watery oatmeal dripping off the wooden spoon onto the floor as she stared at her daughter. Before she could answer, they were interrupted by a lanky boy who raced through the kitchen, bumping into her as he avoided the younger boy at his heels. "Watch it," she said, glancing over her shoulder. Daniel dangled something over Samuel's head and cackled.

"Sorry, Ma! He took my lucky rabbit's foot," Samuel said. His voice cracked as he jumped, trying in vain to reach the small object. He was small in stature, still waiting for a growth spurt that would catch him up to his tormentor.

"Look at you, hopping like a bunny," Daniel said with a grin.

"Give it back, Daniel," Samuel said.

"What's so lucky about this smelly old thing?" the older boy asked, dodging his brother's flailing arms. "Maybe I could use some luck, too."

Samuel's feet landed hard on the stone floor; his shoulders slumped in defeat. "Papa gave it to me," he said.

"Daniel, that's enough," Mama scolded. She whipped around to face her sons, wiping her hands on the front of her apron. "Hand it over now."

"Yes, Ma," Daniel said, avoiding her eyes. Dropping his arm, he reluctantly held out the rabbit's foot, and Samuel snatched it greedily, petting the matted gray fur with his fingers.

Mama turned back to the counter and aggressively scooped oatmeal into bowls. "Breakfast is ready," she said without looking up.

Daniel and Samuel shuffled toward her, each grabbing a bowl off the counter and taking it to the dining table. "Thanks, Ma," they said in unison.

"Dough's wrapped and resting," Serena said, beaming at her mother. "I'll go prepare the pit."

"I started the fire for you," Daniel said with his mouth full.

Serena wrinkled her nose. "Thanks."

"It's the least you could do since you've wasted so much time this morning," Mama said.

"I'm sorry, Ma," he muttered with a frown.

She sighed. "And now you won't have time to check the snares before school. Suppose we'll just have to have plain bread for lunch."

"I can check them, Mama," Serena offered, finishing off her breakfast.

"By yourself? Do you know where they are?" Mama asked, shifting uncomfortably in her seat.

"Of course," Serena said, pushing back her chair. She stooped to kiss her mother on the cheek. "I used to go with Cameron all the time. I'll be fine. I know the woods."

Mama reached out and brushed a hand through her daughter's wavy hair. Serena had braided a small section on one side of her head, pulling the hair back from her face. Locking eyes with her cheerful girl, her mother gleamed with pride. "All right, if you insist," she said, patting her daughter on the cheek. She pushed back her chair and followed Serena to the front door, calling back, "Boys, get out your notes. It's time to study."

Serena glanced back at her brothers while they grumbled, pulling out their books. She grinned as Samuel carefully tucked his lucky rabbit's foot inside his rucksack. "See you later, boys," she called over her shoulder. "Good luck at school today."

"Yeah, yeah," Daniel muttered, urging her to leave with the flick of his hand.

"Thanks, Sis," Samuel said with a wave.

On the porch, Mama grabbed Serena by the arm and pulled her into a tight hug. "Thank you for all your help, sweet girl. I know it's been hard, but you've been the biggest blessing."

"Anything for you, Mama," Serena said, stepping back. "Oh! What about the bread?"

"I'll finish up the bread," Mary said, shaking her head. "Go. Take your time and enjoy the walk. There will be many other days for you to make bread."

Serena smiled as she walked around her family's home and into the woods behind it. The sunlight shone from its high place through the trees, painting her body in a kaleidoscope of light and dark stripes. She listened to the sound of twigs splitting beneath her boots as she trekked deeper into the wilderness. She enjoyed the smell of the grass and wandering the woods, appreciating the first blooms of spring.

The breeze blew through her hair, making her shiver. She stepped into a small clearing between the trees. She breathed in the cool air and welcomed the sunbeams as they warmed her skin. She closed her eyes and listened to the crisp chirping of the rare red crickets, which were usually most active at night. Then she continued searching for snares.

The first trap had been fruitless. Serena rose from the ground and sighed. Turning, she was surprised to see William Burroughs, his dark hair disheveled, walking toward her with a pile of logs in his arms. Will was only a year older than she and had always been close to her brother Cameron. The two boys apprenticed together under her father. When John left Durmak, he asked Will to work the forge, assuring him they would resume his apprenticeship when he returned.

During winter, Will's father fell ill, and he had to step away from the forge to help with his family's farm. With the added load of his father's work, his days of joking around with the other boys in town were long over. Gone was the brazen boy who went to school with the Finch children. He had been replaced with this muscular young man with sweat on his brow and a smile that made Serena's heart flutter. She smiled shyly. Though he was not known for his brawn in his youth, she noticed the large pile of firewood he was carrying. She shook the unusual thought from her mind and tore her eyes off his biceps.

"Good morn, Serena," he said, pausing beside her. "Out early today, aren't you?"

"Somebody has to be," she said. "I'm checking the traps since the boys have tests today."

"I don't miss those days," he said with a laugh.

"Neither do I," she said. "Are you always out this early?"

Will shook his head. "I'm always somewhere early, but today I need to catch up at the forge. Mind if I walk with you on the way?"

Serena smiled coyly. "Of course not." Where were these butterflies in her stomach coming from? It was just Will after all. They continued deeper into the forest, and Will paused with her when she stopped to inspect a snare. "You don't have to wait for me, you know," she said, dropping to her knees excitedly when she found one trap had ensnared a plump rabbit. She pulled a small knife from one of her boots and grabbed the brown rabbit by the ears, then released its hind leg from the trap. Staring into the creature's eyes, she raked her teeth over her lip. "My brothers usually do this part."

Will crouched down next to her and dropped the pile of logs onto the grass beside them. "This is no task for a lady. Let me do it," he said, extending his hand.

Carefully, she placed the handle of the blade on his palm, their fingertips brushing against each other as she pulled back her hand. Then she looked back at the rabbit and muttered, "Don't look at me like that. We have to eat something."

Will laughed and reached for the rabbit. Noticing her discomfort, he said, "You don't have to watch. Death is unsightly."

Serena stood and turned away as he dispatched the animal. "Thanks for the help, Will. I suppose I'm not much of a hunter."

"It's no trouble," he said. He wiped the bloody blade against the grass, leaving a crimson streak against the green pasture.

"You are too kind," Serena said. She held out an empty canvas bag, and he deposited their catch in it.

She reached for a log on the ground, but Will put out a hand to stop her. "I can handle these. Don't worry about me."

"I want to help you," Serena replied, grabbing two logs near her feet. "It's the least I can do. You stopped what you were doing to help me."

"It's fine," he insisted. When she had finished piling the logs in his arms, he asked, "Have you heard from your father lately? Any idea when he'll be back?"

Serena pressed her lips together and shook her head. "No," she said, "and I don't suppose we will. It's been too long."

Will frowned, looking down at the logs in his arms. After a solemn silence settled over them, he asked, "Are you all right out here alone?"

"I am always out here alone. I like it—the quiet. 'Tis nice," Serena said as she handed the last log to Will, looking around. Taking notice of a figure running toward them, she added, "Well, some days are quiet, but not all are spent alone."

Will furrowed his brow and turned to see another teenage girl running in their direction. Her strawberry blonde hair flapped in the wind as she ran quickly between the trees, her eyes glimmering with a hint of mischief.

"Mornin', Serena," called Talitha Vise loudly, sending several birds flying. Noticing Will, she stopped next to Serena and elbowed her. "Your mum said I could find you here. I'm surprised to see you out here now—and with Burroughs of all people." She laughed heartily.

"Pure coincidence," Serena said quickly.

"Morn, Tal," he said. "I will leave you ladies to your gossip." Glancing sideways at Serena, he added, "Tell the boys good luck. I'm sure I'll see you all at the bonfire tonight."

"Of course," Serena said.

As he turned and headed back toward town, Talitha shouted, "We will be there!"

When Will was far enough away, Talitha peered back at the young man and teased, "He is looking handsome as ever. Are you going to go after him? Because if you aren't..."

"He looks at me like a sister," Serena argued, cursing the stars for the way her burning cheeks betrayed her feelings.

"I don't know about that," Talitha said. "He seems much friendlier with you than either of his sisters."

Serena stooped down to check another trap and tried to hide her smile. She excitedly pulled another rabbit out by the ears. "My father would have killed any boy he caught looking at me like that."

"Fathers are always like that, but your mother—she would be thrilled," Talitha said. "Besides, when Will apprenticed for your father, he liked him very much! I am sure he would be pleased with such a match."

The girls giggled at the possibilities, and Serena shoved her uneasy thoughts about her father away. They chattered about the boys in Durmak for over an hour as Serena moved from trap to trap.

"Serena!" Will's shouting startled the girls, and a flight of pigeons fluttered their way out of the trees. "Serena! Talitha! Where are you?"

"Over here," she called back.

"Serena?" Will confirmed.

"We're over here!" Alarmed, the girls started in the direction of his voice. When they found each other, his face was paler than before, his eyes wide in panic. "Will, what's wr—"

"Serena," Will said again, the faintest hint of relief flashing across his face. The young man hunched over, gasping for air. "You're all right," he inhaled sharply. "You're all right," he said again, more to himself this time. He took a few more breaths before he continued speaking. "Your family," he rasped. "I don't know why," he paused. "I don't know. I had to make sure you were—"

"My family? Will, breathe." Serena placed a hand on his shoulder. "What happened? What is it?"

He looked up at her, and the worry creased into his brows made her heart sink. "I don't know. I heard screams. From your house. I ran. I ran to see. When I got there..." Will shook his head. "I don't know what happened. Your family's been attacked."

Serena dropped the rabbit in the grass at his feet and took off running toward home, with Will and Talitha at her heels. Fierce flames consumed their stable, but the animals were no longer inside. Some were roaming about the area, while others fled for shelter in the woods. Before she reached the front door of the cottage, she stumbled upon her younger brother, Samuel, lying still in the grass. His shirt was bloody, his eyes wide and empty.

"No!" she screeched, clutching at her brother's lifeless body. Will and Talitha tried to pull her away from him but failed.

Serena groaned, "Who?" She sobbed as her eyes fell on the rabbit's foot clutched in one of his pale hands. "Why?"

Talitha stepped back, tears sliding down her freckled cheeks. Never in their lifetime had they seen a murder in Durmak, and Samuel Finch was just a twelve-year-old boy.

Will wrapped an arm around Serena's waist and attempted to pull her away from the body. Shoving his arm away, she screamed, "Find the healer. Please! I must find my mother. I must be the one to tell her."

As she pushed herself onto her feet, Will tried to stop her. "Don't go in there, Serena," he pleaded, reaching to support her.

"Don't treat me like a child," she snapped as angry tears welled violently within her eyes. "If you want to help me, get out of my way! Go find the Elders and bring them here."

Will staggered back a few steps. "Stop, Serena. I've checked. They're gone. You don't need to go in there." Then he turned and raced toward the center of town to find the Elders.

Talitha reached for her friend, shaking her head. "Listen to him, Serena. Wait for an Elder."

Talitha's words barely registered in Serena's mind. She jerked her arm out of Talitha's grasp, turned, and ran up the steps into the cottage. As she entered, her heart staggered. Blood covered the wall, and Daniel was slumped over in the hallway in a pool of his own blood.

There was no sign of her mother in the kitchen or sitting area. Three bowls of oatmeal sat abandoned on the dining table. Serena trembled as she stepped past her brother's body in search of her mother. Serena found her in her parents' bedroom, sprawled out on the floor beside the bed. She stumbled to her knees and brushed the hair from her mother's face. Though her eyes were closed, Serena could feel the faintest breath escape from her mother's parted lips. "Mama? Are you there?" Serena asked as tears flowed down her bright red cheeks.

"Oh, thank the stars. You're alive," whispered her mother, trying to lift an unsteady hand toward Serena's face.

"Mama!" Startled, Serena took a shaky breath and gripped her mother's hand tightly. "Oh, Mama! What's happened to you? Who did this? Where are you hurt? Tell me how to mend your wound. I can do it. I can..."

Mama's lips quivered in a half smile, and she murmured, "There is so much I need to tell you, Serena. You were the daughter I always wanted. We tried so hard to keep you safe."

"I am safe, Mama. I am unharmed. Please tell me what to do. Please," Serena begged, shaking as she examined the rips in her mother's frock, determining that under all the blood there must be a severe wound to her abdomen.

"You cannot help me, child," whispered Mama. "I need you to go to the wardrobe. In the back, Papa's sword..."

"What? What's going on?"

"Serena. The wardrobe—take the sword."

Serena crawled over to the large wooden structure and began sifting through its contents. She pulled out a massive sword in a leather sheath.

Mama nodded. "Good. And in his old boots, there is a gold ring... Take it. These will protect you."

Serena reached inside one boot, and finding nothing, tossed it aside. She reached into the other and pulled out a small gold band. "What's going on?"

"The ring—It was mine... from Queen Elara Garrick," Mama told her.

Serena stared in disbelief. She had never heard her parents speak of the runaway princess, the last of the Garrick royal line. Surely her mother was mistaken. She crawled back over to where her mother lay dying and asked, "Who did this?"

"Rexton. He has searched for us for a long time." She coughed violently, gasping for air. Serena laced her fingers through her mother's. Mama sputtered, "Hide the ring. Only wear it when you're alone. When you're safe. Promise me."

"I don't understand."

"Go to the City of Mercy."

"We can't cross the valley, Mama. Papa said it's not safe."

"Serena, promise me you will go to her."

"To who?"

"Elara. Go before he finds you."

With her last words, Mama's head drooped to the side, and her eyes clouded. Serena wept, placing her mother's hands over her chest. Then, composing herself as best she could, she rose to her feet. Realizing she had blood on her hands and clothes, she ran across the hall to her own bedroom, quickly changing her dress. With shaky hands, she picked up the rucksack her parents made them keep for emergencies. This was what they meant.

She attached the sword's sheath to her belt and carefully climbed through her bedroom window. She took one final glance of her home through tears, then raced for the edge of the forest, evading any more tearful farewells and disappearing into the shadows.

THE WEIGHT OF A CROWN

Queen Elara Garrick of Hyrosencia stood on her balcony overlooking Symptee, the last refuge of her fractured kingdom. With the aid of the dwarfs, the humans who survived the brutal journey across the Athamar Mountains were able to build a grand city around the citadel that came to be her home. Past the castle grounds and brick homes, Elara watched members of the Garrick Guard march along the top of the towering stone wall that offered the Hyrosencian refugees protection from aggressors.

When word spread of the siege of Lettras and Graynor, hundreds of her loyal subjects fled their homes seeking refuge from Antoine Rexton's wrath. Though the fortress was ill-equipped to house such an incredible volume of guests, her people worked tirelessly for years, building up two new cities in the shadows east of the Athamar Mountains. For seventeen years, her people called Symptee the City of Mercy, and it matched what Graynor had once been. Still, Elara's heart yearned for the home of her youth, despite having spent nearly as many years of her life within the walls of the eastern citadel.

One of Elara's many guardsmen knocked on the door to her private chambers before nudging it open. "Your Majesty, the oracle and the herbalist wish to speak with you."

"Tell them I shall meet them in the gardens," the queen replied with a nod. Turning from her balcony, she returned to her chambers. One of her maidservants offered a cream silk scarf, which she draped over her shoulders.

Flanked by four guardsmen with swords at their hips, Elara walked down the steps to the lower level of the citadel. At the bottom of the steps stood Commander Alexander Stanton, one of the oldest remaining members of the Garrick Guard. The uniformed man bowed before the monarch, and she nodded her head in acknowledgment.

"To what do I owe the pleasure of this visit, Commander?"

The middle-aged man smiled at her, his golden eyes contrasted against dark skin. "Your betrothed requested that I ensure you remain in high spirits during his time abroad."

"How considerate. I can assure you I am well," she replied, returning a smile. "Gerard needed this trip. It shall be his final visit to the Isles before we wed, and he has not seen his homeland in two years. I know the ache of longing for home all too well." Silence settled between the two before she added, "I know visits will be scarce after our nuptials. It's why I encouraged him to go."

"Aye, milady, but that does not mean you shan't miss him."

"Oh, I miss him terribly! But I am not discouraged. We shall be reunited soon."

Alexander walked alongside Queen Elara as her guards escorted her down a long hallway made of gray stone walls. Glancing sideways at her companion, Elara asked, "Have you received word from your daughter?"

"Not yet, Your Majesty," he replied. "The guardians have been gone but ten days. If their journey goes according to our plans, they should enter Norlee within the week. We expect their return in two months' time."

"That day cannot come soon enough," she said, looking weary. She smiled as a servant curtsied and passed them in the hallway. "We witnessed their incredible abilities in person. They were the most exceptional warriors in the Tournament of Guardians—far greater than any before them. I believe Divinity selected the four of them for this task, despite two being non-believers. This is their sacred destiny. They cannot fail."

"The guardians shall succeed, Your Majesty. The Estrelles have prayed for a turn in the war for many years. I have full faith in the warriors we selected—my daughter included. They shall succeed in retrieving those who are important to you. I daresay we shall have the advantage by year's end."

Elara's heels clacked against the hard floor, echoing throughout the grand structure. "I have prayed Divinity would bless Hyrosencia in such a way," she said, clasping her hands in front of her midsection. "Our faith has been tested for many years, but our people are resilient. They look to the sky and cry out for justice. We all hope this war will end in our favor—that we may one day return to our homeland."

"Undoubtedly, Divinity hears our cries and knows of the unwavering faith of the Hyrosencians," Alexander said. "Our people are devoted to Divinity and those chosen by the heavens to lead us. I had never seen such deep devotion to Estrellogy before we fled here. The people pray so fervently for peace and believe so fiercely in the oracle's prophecy."

"As do I," she whispered, clutching the deep blue silk of her skirt in her hands. "I pray each night that Divinity shall favor us—that the true heir of Hyrosencia shall finally free our people of the evil which reigns over our land."

"We all do, milady," said the commander as they turned the corner. "I have confidence that the guardians will find the lost heir. Then we shall have an advantage in this war at last."

"You have been a crucial ally all these years, Alexander," the queen said, pausing just outside a cased opening in the stone wall to their right. Out of the corner of her eye, Elara glimpsed the lush green gardens and wavered. Turning to face the commander, she added, "All know Idonea's words, though only the wise can recognize their ambiguity. As she professed, our fate is yet undecided. Only the true heir has a chance of defeating Antoine, but only when the heir is ready for the task. Should they not be—"

"They shall be ready, Your Majesty," the commander replied, bowing his head. "The guardians have accepted their responsibility. They will achieve that which has been impossible for so long."

"I pray our trust is well placed," the queen said, curtsying. "Thank you for checking in, Commander, but I must excuse myself. The Cinderfells await me."

"Of course. Enjoy your visit," Alexander said with a bow. Then, turning on his heels, he strode down the hall in the direction from which they came.

When Elara and her entourage emerged in the garden, two women of ebony complexion stood awaiting her near a grand fountain. Approaching the center of the garden, Elara smiled at the Cinderfell sisters, raised a hand, and signaled for her guards to fall back.

"Idonea, Ismenia, it is wonderful to see you on such a lovely day," the queen said, bowing her head.

"Indeed, it is, milady. The flowers bloom early this year," Ismenia noted, dipping her head to inhale the sweet scent of a white star-shaped flower. "I hope the chilly night air shall not ruin this blessing for us."

"Be it hardly March, the last of winter shall surely kill the blossoms, but all shall be fertile when your betrothed returns," Idonea said, and her lips curled in a knowing smile.

Both women had the same dark eyes and raven hair. Idonea's hair, however, was cut close to her scalp, and Ismenia's locks cascaded down her back and over her shoulders. All three women were in their early thirties yet walked divergent paths. Though they had all resided in the citadel since the start of the war, the queen remained intrigued by the sisters' differing natures. Ismenia, an herbalist, was ever the optimist; her cheerful smile made her a magnet at court. Idonea was often somber and less sociable. As the only oracle of her generation, she preferred to spend most nights studying the stars in solitude.

"And do you know when I should expect my betrothed to return?"

"It shall be a month or more before you receive the guests you long for," Idonea said.

"Always such vague answers," Elara said, rolling her eyes. "I should hope it is before the days of blistering heat return."

"Come now, Idonea," Ismenia said, placing a hand on her sister's shoulder. "You said you had good news to relay to our queen."

"Good news? Please tell me at once," Elara said, extending a hand toward each of the Cinderfell sisters. Her pale hands were a sharp contrast against their chocolate skin as she squeezed their hands eagerly.

Idonea glanced at her sister and smirked. "For once, the stars shine in Hyrosencia's favor," she said to the queen.

"Idonea, you are the only Estrelist among us. Please stop speaking in riddles and tell me what you have read in the stars," Elara urged.

"My apologies, Your Majesty. I cannot control what the stars reveal. However, the sky was clear last night. I saw it, and I knew. Several souls ascended into the skies. As the flying stars rose to their rightful place, I sensed a great unrest. Then I envisioned a young lady with brown hair and tear-filled green eyes. She is alive, and the archer approaches. I am optimistic."

"You have never been an optimist," Elara said. "Are you certain of this? That the guardians are close?"

"I saw the girl—Serena, I believe—quite plainly. Wherever she is, your archer shall find her. Have faith in your guardians, milady. They are on the right path."

"That is excellent news, if you are correct," Elara said.

"I am certain of this, Your Majesty."

Ismenia beamed and patted Elara's hand. "Is that not pleasing news?"

"It really is," the queen said. "How I have longed for Marjorie and her family to finally join us here."

Idonea turned and walked toward the perimeter of the citadel grounds, where vibrant purple wisteria trees lined the edge of the lush garden. Elara and Ismenia watched as the tall woman in a plain black dress sashayed away from them. "Sister, don't be rude!" Ismenia called out. She rushed after her sister, her simple cream frock blowing in the breeze.

Turning toward Elara, Ismenia said, "I apologize, Your Majesty. You know very well my sister is not one for prolonged company."

Elara was close behind her. She hiked up her skirt and walked quickly in Idonea's direction, leaving her shoes behind on the stone path as they ventured into the yard. The blades of grass tickled the bottom of Elara's feet, a sensation she had long forgotten. As the queen entered the shade of the wisteria trees, she took a deep breath, inhaling the sweet scent of her favorite flowers.

"Milady, what are you doing?" Idonea asked, alarmed by her uncharacteristic behavior.

"I have just received good news, and now I intend to enjoy this beautiful morning with two dear friends," Elara said, taking a seat in the grass. Her blue skirt flowed out in all directions, covering much of the green landscape.

Ismenia sat beside the monarch and asked, "Do you not have more important matters to attend to this morning?"

"None so important they cannot wait a few hours," Elara replied, propping herself up as she leaned back on both of her arms. The grass itched her palms through her skirt. A canopy of lilac flowers shielded their faces from the sunlight.

"It's an honor to be a friend of the crown," Ismenia said, picking up some of the purple flowers that had fluttered to the ground. "It has been a while since we last spoke. Have you been well?"

"I am well, though I wish everyone would stop worrying over me," Elara confessed. "I was starting to forget how it felt to be outdoors. I have been spending far too much time locked in meetings with the War Council. It's tiring, but I know it's vital to our safety."

"I can only imagine your burdens, milady," Idonea said, running her fingertips through the purple flowers that hung down near her head. "'Tis why I prefer the privacy of the observatory at night. The Estrelists know not to speak unless there is something worth sharing."

"If only the generals could abide by such a rule," Elara said, flopping onto her back and chuckling at the thought. "As queen, I cannot be afforded the luxury of solitude for long."

"We can leave if you would prefer," Idonea said, exchanging a look with her sister.

Ismenia added, "As queen, you should be able to take time for yourself. You are a Garrick. If you need a break from the Council, tell the commanders to take care of their duties and report to you once a week."

"I should," the queen said, making a mental note. "You're right, Ismenia. I would gladly see you both more frequently. Good company is rare, especially within the citadel. Most of the nobles have such political motivations it deters me from going near their wives."

"That sounds quite lonely, milady," Ismenia said, glancing down at her hands. Four rings adorned her fingers, two of which were decorative, while the other two held healing herbs.

"I have told you before—please call me Elara when it's just us. I have grown tired of being called 'Your Majesty' all day. Let us speak as true friends," the queen said as she played with her long dark curls.

"Yes, Elara," the sisters said in unison, both of their faces uneasy.

"I propose we meet again tomorrow. Should you like to join me for morning tea?"

"Do you not have ladies-in-waiting who join you for tea?" Idonea asked.

Elara sighed and said, "No. My ladies are too busy doting on their children and chasing their husbands around the castle. I have no place among them anymore."

Without looking at her, Idonea said, "You shall have your own children one day. Quite soon, in truth."

Elara sat up, her wide eyes darting from Idonea to Ismenia. A wide grin spread across the queen and the herbalist's faces, and they squealed in delight. Ismenia exclaimed, "Oh, a royal baby! What a joyous prediction!"

The queen laughed heartily. "Gerard would surely hasten his return if he heard that prediction."

Then her smile faded as fear crept into her heart. Elara placed a hand on top of her stomach and said, "As you know, I had a miscarriage during my first marriage. I was devastated. But when Caspian died suddenly, I was relieved we had no children. I'd always feared your prophecy could fall onto them."

"By the stars," whispered Ismenia. She placed a reassuring hand on Elara's arm.

"You cannot live in fear of what could be," Idonea said, stepping toward the queen. Bending her knees and squatting beside her, the dark-skinned beauty reached out a hand and caressed the queen's cheek. "Is that why you refused to remarry for so long?"

Elara looked away from them, staring at the stone wall which separated them from the Hyrosencian refugees. She took a deep breath and locked eyes with the oracle. "Can you tell me whether my firstborn will be the true heir from your prophecy?"

Rising, Idonea said, "This insight has always been vague, but I sensed Divinity's meaning. The prophecy referred to a child of Prince Stellan—may he rest in eternal peace."

Elara pressed her hands to her face for a moment, squeezing her eyes shut. After seventeen years, she found it hard to picture her brother's face. "It's been months since anyone has spoken his name before me. I thought everyone was forgetting him, as I, myself, am." She opened her eyes and sighed. Her eyes held no tears, for after all this time, she was no longer in mourning. All that remained of her grief was the constant heaviness in her chest, a relentless reminder that she was the only Garrick to escape Antoine Rexton's invasion of Hyrosencia.

"We have not forgotten him," Idonea said, observing the guardsmen who paced far above them on the innermost wall.

"Perhaps we should organize a festival or a starlight service, something in honor of your loved ones?" Ismenia said.

Elara turned toward Ismenia, who offered a warm smile, and nodded. "I should like to honor my kin once more. Perhaps when the guardians return, we shall finally have reason for such a celebration."

"Aye, milady, we shall all have great cause for celebration then," Ismenia said.

Idonea turned her back to them; crumpled purple flowers cascaded from her hands and drifted to rest on the ground. "The true heir will endure many trials before facing Antoine. I pray Divinity gives them the strength to bear the weight of their destiny."

"The weight of a crown," Elara whispered.

THE SUN SHONE BRIGHTLY in Graynor, but the servants kept their eyes down, focusing on the floor as they rushed along the walls. King Antoine Rexton stormed through the castle hallways, angrier than usual. Throwing open the dining hall doors, Antoine yelled, "Where is my son? Find him at once!"

Several terrified servants scurried out of the room as Antoine strode to the far end of the dining table and sat across from his wife, Chelsea. They had been passionate lovers while the youngest prince of Nyzenard was distantly betrothed to Princess Elara. While Chelsea was the only woman to give him a son, Antoine held no love for her in his eyes as he glared past her at the doorway. Though she had quietly served beside him for nearly two decades, he had never granted her the title of queen she so desperately coveted. He believed no woman worthy of a crown, scoffing when he heard Elara's people over the mountains called her queen. In his mind, she was a princess without a kingdom, her survival merely giving her people hope that the Garrick family might one day sit upon his throne.

Each morning, the Rexton family would gather for breakfast. Chelsea and their daughter Sabine knew to eat in silence while the king informed Anteros of his duties for the day. Over the years, Prince Anteros stood quietly by his father's side for every meeting and every execution. He was an arrogant boy with black hair that nearly covered his hazel eyes, an athletic build from weapons training, and a reputation for causing scandals at court. He was typically found skulking behind his father's right shoulder during the interrogation and torture of those who were suspected loyalists—those who remained devoted to the Garrick royal line despite Rexton's conquest.

For his seventeenth birthday, Anteros asked his father to allow him to take an excursion with three friends. The young prince often enjoyed drinking and indulging in the debaucheries of the nobles and their sons. Luckily for them, the city of Jessiraé was known for entertaining wealthy and privileged men with insatiable habits, and his father begrudgingly agreed to send him on holiday. For over a week, their party indulged in spirits, gambled their fathers' coins, and admired the beautiful courtesans who were eager to please them.

Antoine had expected his son to return from his getaway two days prior. It was now the second morning of his son's absence, and Antoine's eyes were wide in astonishment. His nostrils flared as he let out a deep, hot breath. "If I had another son, that brat's title would be in jeopardy," Antoine said.

Chelsea attempted to reassure her husband that their son would be home soon. "He's only doing the things you did at that age," she reminded him.

Antoine slammed his fists on the table, stood, and yelled, "I wasn't the crown prince! I had to fight for what I have, as will he. I gave him a week for his fun. That wretch shall not inherit my throne if he doesn't work to retain it."

Chelsea flinched and hung her head. As she closed her eyes, expecting a plate or silverware to fly by her at any moment, the door flung open once more, drawing Antoine's attention. Sabine declared, "Good morning, Father! Look who I found sleeping in the carriage this morning."

In walked his nearly sixteen-year-old daughter in a gaudy pink dress with frills, her shiny black hair pinned up in curls. Beside her was her ghastly-looking older brother in an unkempt dark gray ensemble. He pulled the chair across from his mother out from the table and plopped down on it. Chelsea wrinkled her nose in displeasure and asked, "Anteros, are you drunk?"

Antoine slammed a fist on the table, making the dishes clatter violently.

Anteros glanced sideways at his father. Smirking, he said, "It was an excellent trip, Father. You really should travel more often for pleasure. You could use some loosening up, and obviously Mother is not doing the trick."

Sabine gasped, covering her delighted smile with a white-gloved hand. "Oh, how vulgar, Anteros! You cannot say such things! Those are our parents." She muffled her giggling and seated herself in the chair next to him.

Their mother's mouth hung open as she looked at her son in disgust. As a burning blush spread through her cheeks, Chelsea pushed back from the table and stormed out of the room.

"Hold your tongue, or I will cut it out," declared his father without moving. Leaning back into his chair, Antoine sighed, rubbing the bridge of his nose between his fingers. "Elara and her loyalists are out there plotting to attack us any day, and my son is a drunken imbecile. This is my heir. My only son! It's time you grow up. We cannot continue living in complacency. Tensions have been rising in the North. As long as the Garrick line lives on, their people have hope. We must crush it before rebellion overtakes us."

Anteros rolled his eyes, scraping his fork against his plate. "I know, Father," he said icily. "I know. 'Elara and her loyalists must be eliminated.' I have heard this all before. You have been saying it my entire life."

Glaring at his son's slouched body, Antoine tossed his silverware across the table and screamed, "Get out of here! Go to your room until you learn some respect."

Anteros stood promptly and swiped a pastry from the plentiful tray on the table as he swaggered toward the exit. He saluted his sister with a satisfied grin on his face as he left them. He was not drunk—perhaps mildly hungover.

ENTERING HIS PRIVATE CHAMBERS, Anteros locked the door and approached the wall on the far side of the room. He grasped the heavy drapes in both hands and flung them to the side to let the blazing sunlight brighten the space. Basking in the sunshine, he unbuttoned his wrinkled gray vest and dropped it onto the floor.

He turned to a cart in the corner of the room and poured himself half a glass of liquor. Attempting to untie the front of his dusty blue shirt one-handed, he walked out onto his balcony. Peering down at the castle grounds, he observed who was coming and going. With each passing minute, he grew less interested in his monotonous surroundings as he sipped from his glass. Then he noticed Captain Thurwynn of the Enforcing Army exiting a large black carriage at the castle's entrance. Behind him, three soldiers were removing an agitated young woman from the carriage. Her hands were bound tightly behind her back with rope, and her ginger hair clung to her forehead, covering her eyes. She attempted to flee in vain. One of the soldiers lifted her off the ground and tossed her over his shoulder. This did not please the young lady, who shrieked and thrashed about in his arms as the men were received by the castle guards.

Anteros took a swig from his glass and leaned lazily against the stone edge of the balcony. He watched as the men proceeded into the castle carrying the spirited girl. "Finally, things are getting interesting around here," Anteros said to himself and turned to reenter his chambers.

Anteros stripped out of his disheveled attire and changed into fresh clothes. His father would be summoning him for a meeting with the heads of the Enforcing Army any moment now. Soon he would learn more about the mysterious prisoner with the vibrant red hair. He grinned at the thought.

UNEXPECTED COMPANY

Serena woke suddenly, paralyzed by fear. Her body was covered with her old brown cloak, which she had carefully concealed with dirt and leaves before going to sleep. Something was poking at her leg. She could not decipher whether it was a bird or a blade. Holding her breath, Serena waited and listened.

She felt it again, something rustling in the leaves and jabbing at her knee. If it was an animal, she had a chance of catching something to eat. She waited a moment, then abruptly propelled her body upright, sending a crow flying and squawking angrily.

Rays of sunlight hit her face, and she draped an arm over her brow to block it from her eyes. Serena had been rotating the location of her camp outside of the town of Ewiajoy, the next town north of Durmak, every day for weeks. She had taken a small animal trap from the forest near her home on the day her family was slaughtered. Each day, she would check the trap in hopes she had caught something to eat, and if she did, she would cook it and feast greedily on her prize. Whenever she had to, she went into Ewiajoy early in the morning to trade extra animal meat or skins for bread.

Her mother's final words never stopped ringing in Serena's ears as she sat alone in the woods. Though she often considered traveling toward the Valley of Norlee, she could not bring herself to go alone. Her parents had always said the valley was dangerous, overrun by raiders and rogues who pledged loyalty to no one.

And despite her ache to return home, Serena could not go back to Durmak for fear that her mother and brothers' killers were still there. If someone was willing to kill an innocent, unarmed boy, they would have no problem harming her as well, and she could not risk it.

Her father had once told her the safest thing to do if she was scared was to hide and carefully observe her surroundings. So with no map and little knowledge of the kingdom, Serena hid and waited in the woods. She knew Papa wouldn't come—she accepted the harsh truth Mama never uttered—but maybe Cameron would? When training ended, he'd be granted leave. Mama had said that, hadn't she? He'd find her. He'd know what to do. She just had to wait.

Serena shook the leaves from her cloak and fastened it at her throat. Then she went to the base of the nearest tree, dropped to her knees and shoved her hands deep in the leaves, digging around until she uncovered her rucksack. Just under the grimy bag was her father's sword, which she halfheartedly carried. Serena rose to her feet, slung the bag over her shoulder with the sword sticking out of the top, and trudged to the edge of the Eldawia River. After following the river north for nearly an hour, Serena stopped and scrutinized the area. There was no sign of any others around. When she was this far from town, she never encountered others in the woods. People in Hyrosencia were inclined to stay close to their homes, something she appreciated weeks after going into hiding.

Feeling safe for a moment, Serena dropped her rucksack and exhaled. Sitting on the ground, she unlaced her boots and pulled off her socks for the first time in three days, wiggling her toes. Wincing, Serena said to herself, "I have got to clean myself up. I smell like a dead animal!"

Removing her cloak and trousers, Serena tossed them on top of her bag and ran for the river. The cold water made her shiver at first as she trudged forward until the water was waist deep. Bending her knees, she inhaled sharply and pulled her entire body under the cool water, running her fingers through her grungy hair. She swam against the current with her eyes closed, focused on the cold flow around her. When she came up for air, she tossed her long brown tresses away from her face.

After swimming and bathing, Serena worked her way back toward the riverbank. Her feet sank into the squishy, sandy mud at the bottom of the river as she trekked onward. When the water was just below her knees, she paused, closed her eyes, and basked in the warmth of sunlight on her skin.

"Serena."

Her eyes snapped open, and she looked up at the sky in alarm. "Mama?"

A moment later, Serena heard, "Refreshing, isn't it?"

She whipped her head around, looking toward the bank where she had left her things. There stood a young woman holding John Finch's sword in her hands and admiring it. Her eyes shimmered like sapphires set perfectly on her pale, delicate face, and her blonde hair spilled over her shoulders, brushing against her thin, toned arms. Everything about this stranger stood out against the dark green hues of the forest that matched her cloak. Serena had never seen someone so beautiful. The strange woman studied her without a hint of emotion in her eyes.

"Who are you?" asked Serena, glaring at the stranger. "What do you want?"

"My name is Crystal Windaef. I was sent to find the Finch family."

"I don't know anyone by the name Finch, miss. Please leave me be."

"You're smart, lying about your name," Crystal said. "But you need not lie to me. You cannot hide your identity with this in your possession." Crystal dropped down to a knee and gently placed the sword on the grass next to Serena's cloak.

Locking eyes with Crystal, Serena scrutinized her more closely. It was then that she noticed the bow and quiver of arrows over her shoulder. "Mary Finch is dead. You must already know that," Serena said. "Who are you really?"

Crystal remained poised, her face unchanged by the news. "You cannot hide in the woods forever, Serena. Get out of the river. We don't have time to waste."

Serena clenched her jaw. "How do you know my name?"

"You're on my list," Crystal said.

Serena gulped. "List? Were you sent to kill me?"

For the first time, Serena spied a glimmer of sadness in Crystal's eyes, but only for a second. "No. My weapons are solely for protection."

Seeing no way of eluding the stranger, Serena approached cautiously, hoping she could get close enough to snatch the sword and run. Water trickled profusely from her arms as she made her way up the bank, her eyes never leaving Crystal's. When she was in the grass a few yards away, Crystal rose from her knee and said, "I mean you no harm. Please, sit. I'll make a fire. You can dry off while we chat."

Then Crystal turned her back on the girl to begin building a fire. Without looking back at Serena, she said, "I must apologize for not finding your family sooner. What happened to them?"

Serena sat on top of her cloak and pulled half of it over her lap. "They were massacred. I was not home at the time. I couldn't save any of them."

Crystal turned to look at Serena. "Somehow I don't think you possess the skills required to save anyone." She looked down her nose at the glowering girl. "If you had been there, you would be dead as well."

"Maybe I would be better off dead!" Serena yelled. Looking toward the river, she wiped at the tears brimming in her eyes. She felt anger course through her veins as she looked back at the stranger. "You don't know me. You know nothing but my name."

"Did your parents ever tell you with whom their allegiance lied?"

Serena looked down at her father's sword and remembered her mother's dying words. "I never thought they had any loyalty to Rexton or the Runaway Queen, but now—"

"Don't call her that," Crystal interrupted. "Elara Garrick is the rightful queen of Hyrosencia. Have some respect for your sovereign."

"Why should I call her my queen? She abandoned her people to the wrath of a tyrant," Serena said, her chest swelling as her heartbeat accelerated. She thought about Cameron but pushed the thought away just as fast. "We were stupid to think Durmak was ever safe. No one is safe under King Rexton's reign. Look at my family. They're dead, and I don't even know why." Serena blinked back tears as she grabbed her trousers and hastily thrust her legs into them. "He didn't protect us, but neither has she."

Crystal stared at the tiny dancing flames and exhaled deeply. As she murmured something indecipherable, the flames kicked up higher and hotter. Once fully clothed, Serena plopped back down on top of her rumpled cloak. They sat in silence for several minutes until Serena's stomach grumbled. Crystal smiled faintly and reached into her bag. "Are you hungry?"

When Serena nodded, Crystal withdrew a generous hunk of bread and offered it in her outstretched hand. "I can feed myself," Serena grumbled, eyeing the loaf suspiciously.

One corner of Crystal's lips quirked up in a slight grin. "If I wanted you dead, I would have shot you in the river," she said, locking eyes with the girl. "Just take it." She ripped a bite off with her teeth and ate it, showing Serena the truth in her words.

Serena flushed as she reached out and accepted the offering, mumbling, "Thank you." She gorged herself on the loaf without taking a breath. When she was nearly finished, she stopped, carefully wrapping the last few bites in a cloth.

"You don't have to do that. We can buy more," Crystal said.

Serena stuffed it in her rucksack for later. "Maybe you can. I don't have any coins left."

"I have plenty enough to feed both of us," Crystal assured her.

Serena studied the blonde woman with the solemn face. Crystal's high cheekbones and piercing blue eyes made her look foreign. She wore dark brown pants and a matching fitted vest over a cream blouse. Her cloak was fastened at her throat with a stunning gold brooch that resembled her bow. Her clothes were crisp and clean compared to the other nomads Serena had seen from afar.

"I don't even know you," said Serena. "Where are you from?"

Smirking a bit, Crystal locked eyes with her and said, "Not from Hyrosencia. That's all I shall say for now. Just know I am a friend." Crystal tossed a handful of dirt over the fire, and it began dying out. It was still early in the day. Standing, Crystal said, "I'm traveling north to Morlerae, where I have companions waiting for me. I must insist you join us."

"Why?"

"Because you are important to someone I work for," Crystal answered, offering her a hand. "Trust me. I have traveled all this way to find your family and bring you to Symptee. It's the only place you will be safe."

Serena exhaled and pushed herself up onto her feet. Her mother had urged her to seek refuge in the City of Mercy, after all, and Crystal did have weapons, which meant both food and protection. Shoving an arm through her rucksack and slinging it onto her back, she said, "I suppose it would not hurt to go with you. If you wanted me dead, I would already be dead."

"You are right about that," Crystal chuckled. "Let us leave Ewiajoy behind. I assume you have been in this area a while?"

"It has been near a month."

"Then let us move on to Kypno. The journey should only take a couple days."

Smiling a bit, Serena nodded. Surprisingly, she was less afraid of journeying farther from home now that she had made a new acquaintance. They gathered their belongings and started following the Eldawia River north. She wondered what Cameron would think. Would he be proud of her courage to brave the valley and mountains? Or would he just think her a fool? She wondered then if she'd ever see her older brother again. Aloud, she said, "I have never been to Kypno. How does it compare to Ewiajoy?"

Crystal laughed. "It's bigger than the towns you have seen, but not nearly as grand as Morlerae. You shall see both soon enough if you stay with me."

They worked their way downriver, picking their way along the pebbly bank. At times, Crystal would lead them just inside the tree line to stay out of sight of any boats coming up the river to Ewiajoy. The strange woman paced swiftly through the brambles, and Serena fought off pain and weariness to keep up. She did not want to appear weak. The thought kept creeping up on her that someday soon she might have to use her father's sword. And what strength beyond her own must she gain to wield it? She tightened her sack, drew deep breaths, and pushed her legs on. They went on like this for two days.

On the second day at sunset, as they made camp, Crystal said they would reach Kypno early the next morning. She seemed to have the lay of the land committed to memory. "Kypno is a mile northeast," Crystal said. "When we wake, we should wash up in the river. It may be our last chance for a while. Then we can go into town for horses and supplies."

"Horses? Do you truly have enough shillings for such a long journey?"

"Aye," Crystal replied. "You need not worry about coins, Serena. If you would like, we can see if the inn has a room available for a night. You look as if you could use a proper night's sleep."

Serena scowled, dropping her bag onto the ground. "I have not slept well since the day I lost my family. When I close my eyes, all I see is red."

Crystal looked away from her and busied herself by gathering sticks for a fire. "I am terribly sorry, Serena. That must have been traumatic for you."

Serena crossed her arms in front of her chest. "I found my mother in time to hear her final words. There was nothing I could do to save her."

For the first time during their journey together, Serena spoke about the worst day of her life. Crystal asked, "And what did she say?"

"Nothing I could comprehend." Serena frowned.

"What of your father? I assume the sword you carry belonged to him."

Serena nodded. "I suppose it did." The fire rapidly ignited between them, startling her and taking her back to the day the stable was on fire. Staring at the flames, Serena told her, "My father left months ago. He needed supplies for the forge. We have not heard from him ."

"And what of your other siblings? John and Mary had three children, or four?"

Scrunching her nose, Serena blinked back tears. "Five, actually. My little sister took ill and passed before her fourth birthday. And Cameron, my eldest brother... He joined the king's army last year, much to my father's protest. The younger two..." She paused, looking grim. "You seem to know so much yet so little about us."

"Your father knew my commander long ago. The queen was aware they had several children, though there were no official records."

"My dad's been a blacksmith all my life, but I've never seen this sword. It was hidden away, along with the truth. How could it protect us in the back of a closet? How could he? He left and never came back." Serena felt the lump rising in her throat and became silent, covering her eyes with one hand. Red specks exploded behind her eyelids, and she opened her eyes in anger. "When I came home, my brothers Samuel and Daniel were dead. Nothing could have prepared us for this. It was dreadful. There was blood everywhere." She hugged her arms tightly, trying to contain her trembling limbs.

Crystal walked around the fire and put an arm around Serena. "Perhaps you should sit. You don't have to tell me everything." She helped Serena take a seat on the ground. Then, placing a hand on Serena's shoulder, Crystal said, "I am sorry you had to see them in such a way. I wish I would have made it to Durmak sooner." Tears slipped down Serena's cheeks. Crystal pat Serena on the top of her head. The gesture was unexpected but oddly comforting, reminding the girl of her mother. "There is nothing you could have done. Surely anyone else who encountered the attackers would have ended up dead," Crystal said.

Sniffling, Serena looked up at her and asked, "Do you know who would do this? Why someone would want to kill us? Even the boys... Mama helped women birth their babies, and Papa was a blacksmith. Our neighbors were like family. I cannot understand it."

Crystal came onto her knees and sat back on top of her calves. She stared at the dancing flames in thought. "When you learn the truth, it shall help you move past your grief. I cannot give you the answers myself, but I can help you seek them. You could find all the answers in the City of Mercy."

Serena nodded, leaning her head onto Crystal's shoulder, and said, "Is this what having an older sister is like?" She smiled, thinking of her older brother.

Crystal cleared her throat and said, "Or a good friend. Now get some sleep. Tomorrow, we venture into a new day."

Serena laid flat on the ground and covered her arms and legs with her cloak. Crystal moved a few feet away and propped her back up against a tree. Serena watched her, wondering what the strange woman knew and hadn't said as she drifted to sleep.

THE BUNKHOUSE DOOR SLAMMED open. Cameron Finch and eleven other young soldiers scrambled off their beds to stand at attention. Captain Marcus Pelham stepped through the doorway. He scratched his scruffy black beard as he barked, "At ease, men." His eyes scanned their faces until he stopped on Cameron's.

Cameron froze, staring down at his socks with wide eyes as the stocky man approached him. Nearly twenty years old, the Finch boy stood two inches taller than the captain, his once lanky frame now filled out by the swell of muscles developed during his basic training. Despite his stature, Cameron knew where he fell in the food chain; his superiors had made it clear that he was neither the best nor the worst of Horde 12.

"Yes, Captain?" Cameron asked hesitantly. He clasped his clammy hands behind his back, his stomach twisting in confusion at the surprise visit.

"You have a visitor, Finch," Pelham stated, lifting his chin. "Follow me."

Cameron was bewildered by his vague statement. A visitor? No one visited the barracks in Murmont. It was against Enforcing Army rules to have family and friends visit during the initial training period. They rarely even allowed the soldiers to post letters to their kin, claiming the army was their new family. "Is it my father? Has something happened?" the young man questioned, hopping on one leg as he thrust the other foot into one of his issued boots.

Pelham turned and clomped toward the door without answering, and Cameron hopped after him, pulling his second boot on in the process. When he caught up to his captain outside, the young man slowed, remaining two steps behind his superior until they reached the administrative building. The only time he had gone in there was six months prior, when he was scolded for writing too many letters home. The captain had thrust a handful of his letters into his arms and told him to burn them. Without a second thought, Cameron tossed them into the fireplace, watching his words disappear in a cloud of ash and smoke. He had not written another letter since.

As they mounted the steps and entered a gray brick building, Cameron breathed in the musty smell of cigar smoke and wondered if he might ever rank high enough to join the officers in this building. Pelham nodded his head to other officers as they passed in the hall, and the young man kept his head down, his eyes focused on his captain's boots.

"In here," Pelham said. He gestured with his hand toward an open doorway, and Cameron peered inside. Sitting at a small table facing the doorway was a familiar face framed by dark, unkempt waves.

"Will!" Cameron exclaimed, instinctively stepping closer, but his captain's arm shot out, preventing him from entering.

Pelham leaned closer, his breath hot against Cameron's cheek as his deep voice whispered, "Recruitment in the South is pitifully low. Do make sure this unauthorized visit is worthwhile."

He swallowed hard, nodding slowly in acknowledgment. Cameron knew recruitment was one of the king's greatest concerns, so it was no surprise that the captain wanted him to charm his best friend into enlisting.

The captain motioned for Cameron to enter the room, and Will stood abruptly to greet his friend. "Cam, it's been a while," Will said, outstretching a hand.

Cameron glanced back at Pelham and decided a simple handshake would be acceptable. Will raised his brows as his friend squeezed his hand firmly before stuffing his hands into his pockets. "I never thought I'd see you in Murmont. What brings you here, Will?" He noticed the purple bags under his friend's eyes and wondered what misfortune could have made him lose sleep.

Will swallowed, his eyes taking in the radical change in his friend's physical appearance. "Maybe we should sit," he suggested, motioning to the table. The chair scraped loudly as Will dragged it across the tile floor, the sound making him wince.

"What's going on?" Cameron demanded; his eyes narrowed. He did not move to sit at the table, though his superior had already made himself comfortable.

Will sighed, dragging his hands over his face. "There was an attack in Durmak," he began, forcing his tired eyes to meet his friend's. "Your mum and your brothers—well, they're gone. They were murdered. We don't know who is responsible. No one saw what happened."

Cameron blinked at him, every muscle in his body limp. Will was serious—as serious as Cameron had ever seen him outside of the forge. "Who? Why would anyone? This doesn't make sense," he stuttered, shaking his head. "They would never hurt anyone," he muttered, stumbling back into a chair that Pelham had pulled out. His cheeks burned as he fought back tears, the heaviness in his heart nearly unbearable.

His captain planted two heavy hands on his shoulders and squeezed, though the motion felt anything but supportive. "Such a shame that the valley's riffraff have taken to killing innocents," the man offered, no hint of pity in his voice. "We shall have to increase our numbers at the border to ensure our citizens' protection."

"We don't know if it was ravagers," Will declared, his eyes barely narrowing as he looked the stocky middle-aged man in the face. "All we know is someone killed them, and we don't know why. It didn't seem like anything was taken."

"You said Mum and the boys?" Cameron asked, suddenly snapped out of his trance. "But what of my father and Serena? Where are they?"

Will paused, pressing his lips into a thin line as he twiddled his hands together on the table. "Your father left for supplies before winter and never returned," he said, unable to look at his friend.

"What do you mean he left?" Cameron demanded, slamming his hands on the table. "He would never leave them unprotected. That's not like him. Not at all!" His friend pulled his lips to one side and hummed to himself. "So, is Serena home all by herself then?" Cameron asked, his tears dried up and replaced by something familiar—a bitterness he often felt when asked to take care of his younger siblings. He did not want to abandon the last of his training and return to a boring life on the farm or at the forge babysitting what remained of the Finch family. He was finally making a name for himself as a soldier.

"No," Will said, leaning his chest into the table. "When we found... your brothers... she insisted on going in the house to find your mum. She sent me for the Elders. I begged her not to go into that house, but you know how your sister is."

"Yes, I do." Cameron scoffed, picturing her ferocious laugh and determined grin. She was a gentle soul, though she'd always been prone to wandering where she shouldn't. The young soldier planted his palms on the wooden table and leaned forward. "Where is she, Will? Where is my sister?"

"I don't know," his friend replied quietly. "When I returned with the Elders, she was gone. We found your mother's body in her bedroom, along with some bloody handprints, but no sign of Serena. It's like she vanished."

Cameron cursed as he slammed his fist on the table. "Damn that girl! She is going to get herself killed," he growled, glaring at his friend. "How could you let her run off like that?"

"I didn't let her do anything," Will argued, leaning back in his chair. "The entire town searched the area for a week—me included. There was no sign of her. I had hoped she might have come here looking for you, but clearly she has not."

The captain pushed back his chair and stood. "This really is terrible news, young man," he offered. "I will draw up some paperwork, and hopefully some of our men down south will be able to uncover her whereabouts."

Cameron nodded, and the captain exited the room, leaving them alone. Turning back to his childhood friend, Cameron cleared his throat and wrung his hands together in his lap. "I'm sorry, Will. I know this isn't your fault," he muttered as tears filled his eyes at the overwhelming thought that he might be the last living Finch in Hyrosencia. "If I had known this would happen, I would have—"

"There was no way to know," Will interrupted, reaching over to pat Cameron on his arm. "I saw Serena checking traps that morning while I was chopping firewood. If she took off, I'm sure she had a plan. She knows those woods as well as you and I do."

The soldier nodded, rubbing his hands over his damp face. "I wish I could go looking for her," he muttered, knowing he would never ask his superiors for the leave. Training was too fast paced, too important. If he left now, he would fall behind.

"I will keep looking for her," Will promised.

"I appreciate you coming all this way, Will," Cameron began, looking nervously from Will's hope-filled eyes to his calloused hands. "What if you join the army?

You're strong. You've experience in heavy lifting. Surely the king could use more hands forging weapons in Murmont."

Will's face went blank, staring at his friend as though he were looking at a stranger. "Cam," he started cautiously, "You know I don't want to be one of the king's men. That was always your dream."

"But it could be yours, too!" the soldier declared. His chair scraped against the floor as he stood unexpectedly, casting his shadow over the weary traveler from Durmak. "Just think, Will. The two of us together again taking on a bigger city. There's nothing left for you in Durmak. For either of us."

"I said no, Cam," Will said, projecting his voice louder as he rose to face his friend. Eye to eye, Will was two inches taller, and Cameron puffed out his chest, craning his neck in a vain effort to match his stature.

"You really can't let go of that silly town to make something more of yourself?" Cameron asked.

"That silly town is my home, and I never once have thought about abandoning it to be one of the king's lackeys," Will snapped. Cameron's nostrils flared, and his eyes flicked toward the door in fear someone might have heard him. "Our dreams aren't the same, Cam. Stop trying to force it."

Cameron clicked his tongue against the top of his mouth and nodded as he took a step back, smoothing down the front of his shirt. "Then you'd best be getting back to your farm," he spat, whirling around and storming out of the building. If his friend wanted to stay behind in an antiquated town, there was nothing he could do but let him go. He had new friends, and even better, he had a purpose. Just as his superiors wanted, he would push his old life to the recesses of his mind and work toward being the best soldier he could be. The old life was gone now anyway.

SERENA AND CRYSTAL ENTERED the small city of Kypno early the following morning. Serena was amazed by how many merchants had stands lined up along the main road. She trailed closely behind Crystal, who marched into an inn and took a seat at a small table next to a window. She slid into the opposite chair, stretching her tired feet under the table.

A rotund woman in a plain dress with a revealing bodice walked over to their table. "Welcome to The Cardinal. Today we be serving venison stew for five shillings a plate. What will ye be having?"

"We shall take two plates of stew and some water, please," Crystal answered before tossing a shiny gold coin on the table, which the woman eagerly snatched up.

"Thanking ye kindly, miss."

When the woman sauntered off toward the kitchen, Serena whispered, "A gold piece? That seems too much! Better not flash around coins like that."

"Tosh, none but the barmaid saw it. She'll bring back the extra shillings." Crystal surveyed the room discreetly. There were only a few other patrons seated at tables across the room.

The barmaid returned to the table with two mugs of water and Crystal's spare shillings. As she placed the food in front of them, Crystal asked, "Is there a vacancy at the inn today?"

"Yes, miss. There almost always is," the woman said. "Will ye be needing a room?"

"Yes."

"Excellent. See me when ye finish your meal, and I can show you upstairs."

"Thank you, miss." Crystal nodded, and they dug into their hot meal.

"Are we to delay our journey until tomorrow then?" Serena asked.

"Yes," answered Crystal. "We are at least two days from the reservoir, and about three days more to Morlerae. We both need to rest well while we can. We'll have to sleep in shifts the rest of the journey."

After their meal, Crystal found the barmaid and said, "We're going into town for a few things and will return for the room within the hour."

As they exited The Cardinal, Crystal looked at Serena's ragged clothes and said, "We should buy you some new clothes before we leave. Your boots are quite worn, and we have only just begun. Your cloak needs replacing as well."

"They function just fine," Serena protested. "My boots are comfortable, and my cloak can be mended. Why should you waste money on that?"

Crystal groaned, stopping just short of the marketplace to look at her. Keeping her voice low, she said, "Anyone who may be looking for you will expect you to look ragged. They shall expect you to be starving, sleeping in the woods, alone, begging for scraps. My duty is to ensure you remain safe and hidden."

"Why is that?" Serena asked, cocking her head to one side.

Crystal's eyes widened a bit. "Keep your voice down. We can discuss it further in privacy. For now, let's purchase what we need."

Crystal fished out three gold pieces, dropped them in Serena's hand, and pointed at the nearest merchant. "Go in there and ask them for the best boots for travelers. With your spare coins, pick out a cloak." Crystal pointed across the road at the market and added, "I'm going to purchase food for the journey. When you're done, come find me in the market."

"If you insist," Serena muttered.

Serena strolled into a shop named The River Swan. She spoke to a tall, slender man with a mustache about purchasing new leather boots. The man informed her that he would measure her feet and custom make a pair, which typically took a few weeks of labor.

Hesitantly, she said, "We are but travelers passing through. We still have a long journey ahead. Would you have anything already made?"

The man paused for a moment, scratching his chin. "I may have just the thing." He went behind a closed door and fumbled around a bit. "Ah, here they are." He emerged with two pairs of brown boots and said, "I made these for my daughters, but I can make more. See if either suits you."

Sitting on a small bench, Serena tried on the larger of the two pairs and found they fit well. The leather was a rich caramel brown and went up to the middle of her calf. "How much for these and new stockings, sir?"

"Eighteen shillings, miss," said the merchant.

"You undervalue your wares, sir. And do you have any cloaks available? Something dark and simple?"

Perusing his selection, the man pulled a deep blue cloak from the bottom of a stack. "This is the perfect one for a traveler. The inside is lined with silk, which will keep you warm at night."

Serena held the material between her hands, feeling the velvet and the smooth silk. "It is unlike anything I have seen."

"You must be from the South," he said with a chuckle. "Yes, the silk is quite rare, but it shall keep you comfortable in all conditions—guaranteed."

"And the cost?"

"Another fifteen shillings, miss. 'Tis ten for a simpler cloak. Which would ye prefer?"

"I should like this one, sir. There shall be many cold nights ahead."

Serena reached into her pocket and pulled out two of the gold coins. She handed them to the merchant, whose eyes widened.

"We do not see gold pieces every day, and here ye have two!"

"It is nothing, sir," Serena said, her eyes shifting to the floor. "My father was a blacksmith. I sold his tools to an apprentice in Ewiajoy. He paid handsomely for everything I had. Please make no fuss over it."

The man nodded. "Very well, young lady. I appreciate your patronage." He pocketed the two gold pieces and handed her several shillings, adding, "May the stars guide your journey."

"Thank you kindly. May the sun light your day."

Stepping out of the shop, Serena peered down the road at the outdoor vendors. The sun shone high in the sky, and many people filled the streets, patronizing the merchants selling eggs and produce. Next door there was a sizable bakery with customers standing in line outside the front door. Serena was tempted to spend the last of Crystal's coins on extra bread for the journey.

As Serena scanned her surroundings, movement drew her attention to a nearby alley, and she caught a glimpse of someone standing in the shade between two buildings, a dark hooded cloak concealing their face. Even though she could not see their eyes, she shuddered at the eerie feeling she was being watched.

"There you are," Crystal said, carrying two apples in her left hand. Serena averted her gaze from the alleyway to look at her travel companion. When Crystal was close enough, she tossed one to Serena and said, "Store this in your bag for later. There's plenty more of that and bread for the days ahead."

Serena smiled and admired the ripe red apple. She had not eaten fruit in over a week. Today was turning out to be the best day since she had been forced to flee Durmak. She peered back at the alley, but the figure was no longer there. She looked around at the merchants on the road one last time, unable to shake the goosebumps creeping up through her arms and back. She shivered and shook her head, pulling her new cloak around her body.

Crystal led them back to The Cardinal, where the barmaid showed them upstairs to a small room with two single beds. Crystal filled the woman's hand with coins and said, "We shall be gone quite early in the morn. Thank you for your hospitality." Then she flopped onto the bed nearest the door and sighed.

"You look pleased," Serena said, closing the door to their quarters. She laid her bag on the floor and perched on the end of the second bed.

"That I am," said Crystal, folding her arms behind her head and staring at the ceiling. "I have been away from home for a long time, Serena, and beds are a luxury."

"That I can agree with," Serena said, laying back. "This place is nicer than I expected." Closing her eyes, she added, "Thank you for your kindness, Crystal."

Serena looked away as the foreigner replied, "I am your guardian now. No thanks are required."

Although it was early afternoon, the tired travelers nestled into their beds for a much-needed rest. When Serena finally drifted off to sleep, she dreamed of the hooded stranger lurking in the shadows and wondered who he could be.

MIDNIGHT MENACE

When Serena opened her eyes around dawn, Crystal was awake and ready to leave. Serena sat up sluggishly and stretched her arms above her head, a sleepy smile crossing her face. "Good morn," she said, covering her mouth to muffle a loud yawn.

"The sun shines on us this day," Crystal said as she peered out the window. "You must have slept well. You were snoring."

"I do not snore," Serena said with a laugh, hopping off the bed. Crystal tossed an off-white ball of fabric at her, and Serena jumped back, barely catching it. "What's this?"

"A clean blouse. Yours is looking quite pitiful. Take it. We can buy more clothes along the way."

Serena unrolled the blouse. When she compared it to the top she was wearing, her eyes widened as she realized her blouse was no longer the beautiful cream color it had once been. Yanking the tattered, stained garment over her head, she pulled on the new one. The fabric smelled of pine needles.

"Thank you... again."

"Don't mention it. You look much better than how I found you!" Crystal chuckled. "Now hurry up. We really should be going before the rest of the town awakens."

"Just one moment." Serena sat on the edge of her bed to lace up her new boots. Then she stood and fastened her new cloak.

"I quite like that," Crystal said. "Good choice."

When they opened the door, they found two flower sprigs set at the threshold. Bending down, Crystal picked one up to get a closer look at the flowers, which changed from black to purple in the dim light as she inspected them. "How unusual," Crystal said. "I have never seen such an interesting bloom."

Serena studied the dark flowers for a moment. "It's Midnight Mystica—quite common in the southern woods. They only bloom in moonlight."

Crystal clenched her teeth and rose to her feet. "Suspicious," she said, glancing each way down the hall. "We should move quickly. Someone may be watching us."

They descended the stairs two at a time and made their way through the empty dining hall. Once outside the inn, a beautiful burst of muted hues peaked over the trees, greeting the travelers as they set out. The girls silently walked down the main road, passing a few merchants who were busy setting up their goods for the day. Serena's gaze lingered on the hands carefully stacking plump, red apples in a large basket.

When they were nearly out of town, she glanced back at the marketplace and thought she saw a dark figure slip into the shadows. Shaking her head, she turned back to Crystal and said, "Let's go. This place has left me feeling uneasy."

"I have an idea which may help ease your worries," said Crystal.

She turned and walked down a side street until they came to a large stable. Crystal motioned for Serena to follow her inside. There were several horses in individual stalls. A young boy, busy feeding them, glanced over and yelled, "Oy, what be ye business? 'Tis early. Me master is not here."

"My apologies," said Crystal, stepping toward the boy. "I was hoping to purchase a couple of horses for my friend and me. We are leaving for Morlerae this morn."

"Horses?" Serena asked. "Are you sure? I don't mind walking."

"Nor do I, but 'tis a long, hard journey. Best to preserve our strength when we can," Crystal said. Turning back to the boy, she crouched down so they were eye level. "Are you permitted to sell horses in your master's absence?"

"No, miss, but if ye got enough coins, I could help," said the boy, who could not have been over ten years old. "I know he would want at least thirty shillings for each."

"Oh, I do not doubt that," Crystal said, ruffling the boy's hair. "How would four gold pieces be for both?"

The boy's eyes lit up as he burst into a large smile. "You have four? Must be from the capital, eh? You a lord's wife?"

Crystal laughed, and it was a melodic sound, songlike, causing Serena to smile. She hadn't heard such a joyful noise since meeting her guardian. Crystal pulled coins from the bag attached to her belt and counted them out for the little boy, who beamed in awe. "I am afraid not," Crystal said, grinning at Serena. "Now which of these beautiful steeds are for sale?"

The boy ran several feet from them and stopped in front of a black stallion. "This one's my favorite. Midnight, we call 'im."

Crystal said, "We shall take him. This one will be my friend's." She glanced back at Serena, who was watching the horse. Then she pointed to the stall next to Midnight and added, "I think I should like this one. What say you of him?"

The boy shuffled to the next stall, which held a large brown stallion, and said, "This here is Cinnamon. He is me master's favorite. I oughta not sell 'im without his say."

"What do we have here?" The trio turned to see a tall, thin man with a thick beard approaching them. He wrung his hands together as he said, "Good morn, ladies. How can I help you?"

Crystal opened her palm to show him the gold pieces. "We need two horses for travel. Would these be available? This young man has been immensely helpful while we awaited your arrival."

The man searched Crystal's face. "Where be ye traveling? It's dangerous for two women to travel alone."

"We are not alone. We are simply tasked with picking up the horses before we meet our brothers," Crystal said. Her eyes flicked over to Serena, who nodded without hesitation. "We should like two strong steeds—capable of carrying two riders at once."

"I see you have gold," the merchant said. He reached toward her hand, and Crystal closed it, smiling.

"We can always buy in Morlerae if you do not wish to sell to women," she said.

"No, that is no issue, miss," he said, his eyes scrutinizing their attire. Serena pulled her cloak closed and scowled. "But it shall be six gold pieces for these two, including the saddles. They are my prize stallions, after all. I am sure your brothers shall be most pleased."

Crystal smiled victoriously. "Excellent." Pulling two more coins from her money pouch, she handed the pieces to the merchant and said, "Thank you for your help, sir. We shall send our friends your way when they pass through Kypno."

"Much obliged," the man said, pocketing the coins. He ordered the stable hand to bring Midnight out of his stall, while he saddled Cinnamon.

Serena followed the boy. When he opened the stall, she stepped forward to get a closer look at the black stallion and placed a hand gently on his snout. "I suppose you're mine now. Best you learn my face."

The stable hand balanced on a stool and carefully lugged a saddle up onto the majestic steed. Serena combed her fingers through the horse's mane while the boy secured the saddle. He attached a harness to Midnight's face, carefully adjusting the brown leather straps on its cheeks before handing Serena the reins.

Pleased with their purchase, Crystal and Serena led their horses toward the exit of the stable. Before leaving, Crystal discreetly handed the stable hand two shillings and said, "Thank you for your help. These are for you, not your master. Pocket them. Buy with them whatever you wish. You earned it." She ruffled the boy's messy hair before turning away.

Crystal nodded for Serena to follow her toward the edge of Kypno. Serena spared a final glance toward the stables. The little boy beamed as he got to work sweeping Midnight's stall out, no longer paying any attention to them. Serena squinted at Crystal, who was smiling, despite the determination on her face, as they made their way out of Kypno. She wondered where her mysterious escort could have gotten so many coins and why she would hand them out so freely. Generosity was scarce in the South; people needed every last coin to keep their families warm and well-fed. As they cantered down the quiet dirt road, Serena hoped she might one day have enough coins to care for herself and share with others.

AS THE SUN BEGAN to set, Crystal steered off the main path, guiding Serena a short distance into the forest until she felt a fire could not be spotted from the road. They tied the horses to a nearby tree, and Serena began building a fire. Crystal stiffened and raised her head. Her eyes scoured the tree line lit by their small campfire.

"You look so tense," Serena said. "You should eat something. It has been a long day." Crystal exhaled, then froze. Serena heard it then, the hushed sound of something rustling in the grass nearby. She wasn't alarmed, having spent many nights in the forest alone. "It's probably an animal, Crystal," she said. "The forest never sleeps."

"You can never be too careful, Serena." Moments later, the guardian shook her head, lifting a finger to her lips and pulling a small dagger from her belt. Serena froze where she knelt by the fire. When she felt the increasing heat of the flames near her left cheek, she turned her torso away and peered out into the dark abyss beyond the firelight. Crystal was only a few steps away from their grazing horses, and there was but a couple of yards between Serena and the guardian. They remained still, listening carefully to their surroundings. All Serena could hear were the mosquitos buzzing near her face and crickets chirping in the distance. But she could sense Crystal's tension. What had she heard?

As if in answer to her question, Serena heard the faintest sound of twigs crunching under cautious feet. Serena darted her eyes to Crystal, who nodded in the direction where the sound originated. They were dangerously close to its source. Serena stiffened, realizing she had only a small dagger on her. Her bag was on the ground next to them, where the gleaming hilt of her father's sword jutted out and lay partly on the grass.

Out of nowhere, there was a silver flash that shot out of the darkness. It hit Serena before she knew it was coming, knocking the air out of her lungs. Crystal cursed and shrieked, "Get down!" Serena stumbled backward with a small dagger sticking out from the front of her left shoulder. She winced as she reached her shaky fingers toward the blade, drops of blood trickling from the bottom of the knife wound.

"Wait. Leave it, or you'll bleed out," Crystal yelled, her eyes fixed on the dark figure in the shadows as she lifted her bow level with her chin. She loosed the first arrow, and her ears perked up at the slightest rustling in the grass. The guardian grinned as she reached for another arrow from the quiver. Drawing back her left hand to the corner of her lips, she paused for a second before releasing the arrow into the darkness.

There was a loud cracking sound as someone rushed through the dark, concealed by the trees, and Crystal quickly grabbed another arrow from her quiver. "There you are," she whispered. She held the bow low with the arrow nocked, breathing steadily. She swung around, lifting the bow and drawing back the arrow, and let it loose into the dark. The figure yelped as the arrow struck. The leaves crunched under his weight as he collided with the ground. "Stay here," Crystal ordered Serena, pulling another arrow and racing in his direction.

She returned a few minutes later and dropped onto her knees beside Serena, casting her bow and quiver onto the ground. Serena's eyes streamed with tears.

She hoped Crystal could somehow ease her pain. The raw wound on her shoulder was deep. The sting of the sharp metal made even the tiniest breaths agonizing. "Help me," Serena whispered. "I don't want to die."

"You will not die this night, that I can promise," Crystal said, inhaling deeply. "I'm going to remove it now. Take a deep breath for me. Three, two..."

Serena cried out as Crystal yanked the blade out of her shoulder; blood splattered across both as the guardian discarded the weapon, immediately applying pressure to the gushing wound. As Crystal muttered, her hands glowed, and Serena blinked in disbelief, her vision blurring from blood loss. Laying her head back in the damp grass, Serena closed her weary eyes and listened to the incoherent words Crystal rattled off. She could not tell if the guardian was speaking another language or if her ears were playing tricks on her as she lay dying in the woods that had once been her haven.

"Serena, can you hear me?" Crystal asked, her voice much calmer than Serena expected. "You're going to live. Just keep breathing. I will take care of you."

Serena nodded, the back of her throat too dry for her to reply. The guardian continued muttering indistinguishable words, and a burning sensation spread through Serena's shoulder before she slipped out of consciousness.

WHEN SERENA WOKE, SHE was flat on her back. The grass was cool against her fingertips. She blinked a few times until she began to make out faint stars against the cerulean sky and tree limbs hanging overhead. She tried to sit up, but it sent her coughing. Crystal put a hand on her arm, stopping her.

"Stay put for a moment. I need to treat your wound again," said Crystal, peeling back a piece of blood-soaked fabric from Serena's shoulder.

Serena winced. "Blazing fires, it burns." She could see Crystal in the faint light. But it still seemed dark, for it was not yet dawn. "I was out all night?"

Crystal paused and looked at her with grave concern. "Not quite," she said. Averting her eyes, the guardian took a handful of a green, squishy mixture and smeared the fresh-smelling blend onto Serena's wound, causing her to cringe in pain. "You were unconscious all night... Then you were in and out all day while we traveled. It was not easy to care for you while riding."

"I slept all day?"

"Yes. I suppose your body was in shock."

Serena took a deep breath, peering down at her injured shoulder. "What is that?"

"A poultice. It will help. Just stay still." Crystal put a hand on Serena's unharmed shoulder, holding her down against the ground as she continued treating the wound.

Serena grimaced. "Thank you. I suppose I should not be complaining."

"No, you really should not," Crystal said, looking directly into Serena's eyes. "If you had been with anyone else, you would be cold in the ground."

"My memory is hazy. What happened?"

"We were ambushed. Our assailant stabbed you. The wound was quite deep. Luckily for you, I am learned in the arts of healing."

Serena tried to swallow but found her mouth was dry. "Could I have some water?" Crystal swiped a canteen and offered it to her. She took it with one hand and slowly brought it to her lips, closing her eyes as the cool water rushed over her parched lips and dribbled out of the corner of her mouth. She gulped until the canteen was empty. Holding the bottle out to Crystal, Serena said, "Thanks."

"Of course," the guardian said with a curt nod. "You'll need plenty of fluids to build your strength back up."

"I could use more than water," Serena said, feeling an ache in her empty stomach.

"When I'm done here, you can eat," Crystal said as she wrapped Serena's shoulder with a fresh strip of torn fabric. "At least I was able to put your old shirt to good use."

When Crystal was finished wrapping Serena's wound, she helped her sit up. Then, she said sternly, "I will bring you food. You rest and let me do everything. Your wound will take quite some time to heal. Do not make it worse."

Serena nodded.

Crystal stood and tied her bags to her horse's saddle. "We will have to take things slow while you recover," she said, a hint of vexation in her tone. "I knew this journey would be perilous, but that was far too close for my taste. I have taken us far out of the usual path to Morlerae, but who knows who else could be lurking out here?"

"Do you know who attacked us?" Serena asked.

The guardian looked at Serena with pity. She sighed, then said, "I suspect he was one of Rexton's spies. He must have spotted us in Kypno. We shall have to be more careful in Morlerae."

"Do you know who killed my family? You must know! You knew my name; you found me in the woods. What's going on, Crystal? I deserve to know."

Pain flickered across Crystal's face, but she regained her bearing just as fast. "We mustn't speak about these things now, Serena."

"You called yourself a friend when we first met. A friend would tell me what happened to my family. A friend would tell me why I was almost killed." Serena narrowed her eyes at the guardian. When she realized the woman would reveal nothing, she resigned. "If it is so dangerous, then let us go while there is still light." She tried to roll herself onto her knees but winced in pain, throwing down her right hand in the damp grass to catch herself.

"I told you not to move without help," Crystal said, rushing over to her. She lifted Serena's right arm around her shoulders and helped Serena to her feet with little difficulty.

Serena took two unsteady steps and said, "It's a good thing you thought to get horses. I would not have made it far walking."

Crystal helped Serena lean against Midnight, who sat in the grass resting next to Cinnamon. Then she fished half a loaf of bread out of her bag and handed it to her. "Eat this. You'll need a full stomach to push through the pain."

Serena was ravenous. She ate the bread slowly, careful not to move her left arm. After a few bites, she asked, "Have we any water left?" Crystal nodded, unscrewed the lid from a second canteen, and handed it to her. She gulped from it; small beads of water escaped from the corners of her mouth and dripped onto her shirt. She felt as though she would never be able to quench her thirst. When Serena had finished off the water, she looked at Crystal and said, "I'm sorry. I didn't think to save you any."

Crystal took the empty canteen from her. "I brought us away from the main trail. It's safest to stay near the river, then go the long way around the reservoir, instead of the shorter path." She patted Cinnamon on the cheek and coaxed the horse to stand. Then she tossed the saddle over the steed, ran her fingers through its mane, and fastened the wide strap underneath it. Her knuckles white against the reins, she led him toward the river.

Serena used her right arm to ease herself back onto her feet. "I wish I were a horse right now. They don't seem phased by the danger we faced." She gently pulled on Midnight's reins until he willingly rose to his feet.

Crystal glanced back at her and rolled her eyes. "You are a stubborn one, Serena Finch." The guardian left Cinnamon at the water and marched over to Serena, snatching Midnight's reins from her. "I can take care of both horses. Just sit by the water."

Serena followed Crystal to the river and sat a few feet away from the horses. She took deep breaths while watching the guardian refill their canteens. When the first was full, Crystal offered it to Serena, who drank from it eagerly. When she had emptied it again, Crystal laughed and said, "That's enough for now. You can have more later."

The guardian took a long swig from her own canteen, then topped off the rest of the containers. Packing them into their bags, she placed one hand on Midnight's chest while helping Serena mount him. Then Crystal stepped into the stirrup and gracefully swung her left leg over the back end of the horse, settling onto the saddle behind Serena. She held onto Cinnamon's torn-up reins and turned to Serena, asking, "Are you sure you feel up for riding right now?"

"Yes, I am awake. I can manage for a while." Serena gave her a grim half smile.

"Very well. Let me know if you grow tired, and we can stop," said Crystal. As they urged the horses to start walking, Crystal added with a smirk, "And try not to fall off."

Noticing the heavy bags under Crystal's eyes, she asked, "Have you slept since the attack?"

The archer was silent for a moment. Pinching the bridge of her nose, Crystal said, "There will be time to rest soon enough. I'll be fine."

Serena looked forward as Midnight carried them along the edge of the winding Eldawia River. Though Crystal kept the horses walking at a slow pace, Serena winced at nearly every step and willed the days ahead to pass faster.

THE PRISONER

Antoine reread the report from Captain Levraea numerous times each day. The captain's initial report revealed that a recent recruit's parents were listed as John and Mary Finch, who were not recorded in any census records. The captain suspected John Finch could be Nathan Fritz, a knight of the Garrick Guard who had eluded capture during the initial siege of Graynor. Cameron Finch's enlistment papers gave him everything. The eldest Finch boy's birthdate matched the records from Graynor, along with the birthdates of both parents. What Antoine found most suspicious was Serena Finch; the Fritzes had no reported daughter. They had been hiding under Antoine's nose all this time in the southernmost town in Hyrosencia—Durmak. The discovery was astounding. The last of Elara's loyalists had escaped his reach.

Without hesitation, the king had ordered High Commander Nesdel to select the four best lieutenants in Murmont to discreetly infiltrate the town and eliminate the hiding loyalists and their offspring. The people in Durmak were trusting and friendly, gladly giving his men directions to the Finch home. In the early hours of a chilly March morning, they struck, silencing the two youngest sons and the woman. To their dismay, they found that John Finch and his daughter were not home, a fact that made the king even more wary.

The soldiers scoured the woods to no avail. On their journey north, they came across a fiery teenage girl alone in the woods north of Kypno. They suspected she was hiding something. It seemed as if she was wandering aimlessly, searching for someone. Despite their prolonged search, she was the only girl they encountered in the woods during their two-week hunt. Due to her hostility toward them, they decided to take her into the king's custody.

Over a week had passed since the arrival of the mysterious young lady at Graynor Castle, yet Antoine was no closer to the information he so desperately desired. The girl did not resemble anyone in any of the old portraits of the Fritz or Garrick families. Despite enduring the most grueling torture for days, she refused to give her name. The men informed the king that none of their tactics drew any useful information from her, only screaming and swearing. When she was exhausted from the usual means of torture, Prince Anteros suggested they lock the girl in the dungeon and give her time to recover from the trauma. The king was infuriated with the lack of progress but did not want her dead before he gained answers. He insisted her proximity to Durmak was too close to be coincidental.

The girl knelt in the center of the room with her hands and feet bound by chains. The four members of the Enforcing Army who had captured her stood close behind, looking smug. Their presence put the prisoner on edge. Despite spending a week in the dungeon, her breathing remained haggard, and her arms were quivering. However, her pale face, freckled with bits of dried blood, remained full of tenacity as her piercing eyes glared at the king.

Another uniformed man entered the room and bowed. Levraea had arrived in Graynor only a few hours prior. When the soldiers had first arrived with the unnamed girl, Antoine sent word to the captain to come to Graynor. He had been impatiently awaiting the captain's arrival, knowing he was the recruiting officer who enlisted Cameron Finch into the king's service.

"The firstborn son, Cameron, is in Enforcement Horde 12 in Murmont. He remains compliant and unaware of what has occurred," Levraea said. "He joined your army willingly. We believe he was unaware of his parents' allegiance."

The girl scoffed and spat a mouthful of blood on the floor between Antoine and his officers. The king clenched his jaw, then pulled a broadsword from his hip. Antoine grabbed the girl by a handful of her fiery hair and yanked her upward to get a better look at her face. His hot breath burned her cheeks as he tugged her hair tighter and bellowed, "Answer your king! Is Cameron Finch your brother?"

The girl flinched; her face twisted in anguish as his spit peppered her cheeks. "No!" Tears pooled in the corners of her eyes as she raised her chained hands a few inches, only to drop them back onto her lap. "Let me go... Please... I have done you no wrong."

The room fell quiet, and the tyrant drew back from the girl, taking in the pathetic sight. Lifting his eyes to Levraea, he asked, "Captain, does this girl resemble the son of the loyalists? You've seen his face."

The stocky man straightened up, clasped his hands behind his back, and declared, "No, Your Majesty. Cameron Finch has dark hair and dark eyes."

Pointing his sword at the soldiers looming behind the prisoner, Antoine asked, "And what of those who were slain in Durmak?"

The soldiers floundered, their wide eyes lowering to the floor. As the king glared pointedly at them, one stuttered, "Well, Your Majesty, they—the sons—their hair was dark as yours, but the woman, hers was lighter, graying."

Antoine lowered his sword, nodding his head slowly. Looking down at the girl, he said, "You are of no use to me." Then, with one quick movement, he swung the sword, slashing the closest lieutenant's throat. Blood splattered over the girl, and she stared at the king's feet with wide eyes as the soldier's head plopped onto the floor beside her. The other men stepped back in surprise and genuflected before their king; their armor clanked against the floor as they trembled.

Antoine exhaled loudly, leaning over her to wipe both sides of the bloodied blade on her dirty blouse. Her eyes wandered over his shoulder and locked on a boy around her age. Anteros straightened his black jacket with gold embellishments, cocking his head to the side to study her.

The king stood and asked her calmly, "You are not the daughter of John and Mary Finch then?"

The frightened girl looked at him with wide eyes as she shook her head. Antoine asked, "Then who are you? Why were you wandering the woods with no papers?"

"I was looking for my friend," the girl sputtered, tears streaking her dirty cheeks. "She ran away from home. I just wanted to find her. I feared she was in danger."

Anteros stepped forward, stopped by his father's side, and crouched down in front of the girl. Reaching a hand toward her, he brushed some of the oily ginger hair back from her face and wiped at the fresh blood that painted her cheek. Studying the helpless girl, he said, "Tell us your name."

She stared at him for a moment. Then, slumping her head to one side, she studied the young prince. Scrunching her eyebrows, the girl said, "You first."

"You are not in the position to ask questions," Antoine said, shoving his sword into its leather scabbard at his hip.

Anteros turned and glanced up at his father. Smirking, he said, "She's in shock. It's unlikely we'll learn anything more from her today." He turned back to their captive, and her forehead creased as she scowled at him. Tracing a thumb along her jawline, he said, "Such a lovely face. A shame to keep it confined to a grimy dungeon—especially if you're not the girl he's looking for."

"That's enough," Antoine growled, clutching his son's shoulder.

Anteros rose and shrugged his father's hand off. "Yes, Father."

The girl's eyes widened as she looked from the young man to the cruel dictator. Antoine stared past his son at the wretched, wounded girl. Waving one hand, Antoine said, "Return her to the dungeon. Interrogation shall resume tomorrow."

Two of the soldiers lifted the girl by her upper arms, and her feet dragged the floor as they hurried from the room. The rhythmic sound of chains clinking against the floor echoed faintly, the noise fading with each step until the room finally fell silent.

Antoine pointed from the last soldier to the corpse between them and demanded, "Clean up this mess. I trust you shall not disappoint me again." The skittish soldier grabbed his fallen comrade by the arms and began dragging his body out of the room, leaving a trail of blood in their wake. Turning to the uniformed man beside him, the king said, "Come, Captain. We must convene with Thurwynn at once."

Anteros fell in step behind his father and the captain as they entered the hallway. When they reached the stairwell, Antoine whipped around and placed a strong hand on his son's shoulder. His lips curled in a devious smile as he leaned closer and said, "I have other plans for you, my son. Are you up for a challenge?"

Anteros bowed his head. Breaking eye contact, he asked, "What do you require, Father?"

"I hear you're quite good at charming the young ladies at court," Antoine said, throwing an arm around his son's shoulders.

The prince shifted his feet. "Have I charmed the wrong lady?" he asked with a smirk, no hint of remorse in his voice.

Antoine chuckled, tightening his grip on the boy's shoulder. "I am not concerned with your dalliances," the king said. "But I should like to put that charming smile to good use."

THE PRINCE STRODE DOWN a spiraling stairwell, tossing a deep red apple in the air and catching it without looking away from the steps. With each step, he descended further into the damp darkness of the dungeons below the castle. As he reached the last step, the prince met four lethargic guards, who immediately scrambled to stand in a row and bow.

"No need for that, men," he said, waving his free hand. "As you were."

"What brings you down here, Your Royal Highness?" one asked.

"Give me the key to the girl's cell," said Anteros, holding out a hand.

The oldest of the guards unhooked a large ring of chunky keys from his belt and handed it over to the prince, looking uneasy. As Anteros headed down the hall, the guard called out, "She is in the last cell. Be warned: She is quite feisty!" Their laughter echoed down the hall.

"I am well aware," Anteros said, peering over his shoulder at the guards. "Remain at your post. This situation calls for privacy." The men snickered, leaning back against the rough stone walls.

The farther Anteros walked down the hall, the narrower the path became. He passed dozens of cells, several of which imprisoned multiple men suspected of menial crimes against his father. Glancing through the bars, he noticed many were unmoving, some on the verge of starvation. He tossed the apple up and caught it again, turning his eyes away from the cells.

When he neared the end of the hall, Anteros paused in front of a wooden door with a small slat at eye level. The prince stepped up to the door and peered through the opening. Huddled in the corner of the room was the prisoner he sought.

"Good morning, Red."

The girl stirred, turning her head to blink up at the hazel eyes watching her. "What?" she asked, rubbing one eye with her wrist.

Anteros shoved the key into the lock and turned it until the metal clicked. Pushing the thick wooden door inward, he stepped into the cell. "I said good morning, Red."

"Red? You mean my hair?" she asked. She sat up, touched her tangled tresses, and tensed as the prince closed the door behind him.

When Anteros started walking toward her, she pressed her back into the corner, eyes wide. Her breath caught. Then, she asked, "Wait... What are you doing?"

Seeing the fear in her eyes, Anteros stopped in the middle of the room. "I am not here to hurt you," he said, holding up both of his hands. "You need not be afraid. I am merely here to speak with you."

"I do not wish to speak to you."

"Then I shall sit here and wait until you are ready." Anteros lowered himself onto the cold stone floor and stretched out his legs. He placed the apple on the floor next to him before leaning back on his arms.

The girl scrambled to adjust her position, propping her back against one of the walls. Pulling her legs close to her body, she rested her chin on top of her knees and stared at him. They sat in silence for what felt like an hour, stealing glances at each other, and the girl averted her gaze each time their eyes met.

Finally, she asked, "You are the son of King Rexton?"

Anteros leaned forward as his lips curled up in a smirk. "You are quite perceptive." Her eyes darted to the apple for a second, and she licked her cracked lips. The prince picked it up and tossed it back and forth between his hands. "This is for you," he said as he gently tossed it underhand to the girl, who jumped but managed to catch it. She inspected the apple from all angles as her stomach grumbled, but she hesitated to sink her teeth in. Anteros said, "It's fresh from the tree. I picked it myself. Eat."

She took a large bite out of the fruit. Juice dribbled down her chin as she closed her eyes and sighed in delight. Taking another bite, her crunching hastened, hunger taking over as she ravenously consumed the sweet red fruit.

"Slow down, Red," Anteros said with a chuckle. "There's more where that came from—if you cooperate."

She stopped chewing. Lowering her hand, she narrowed her eyes and asked, "Cooperate with what?"

"First, I should like to know your name."

The girl took another bite, slower now, while she pondered the request. With her mouth full, she mumbled something indistinguishable.

Anteros shook his head and frowned. "What was that?"

She swallowed the chewed-up apple, and her face softened. "I said thank you."

The corners of his mouth twitched up in a smile. "My pleasure, Red."

"Stop calling me that."

"I will, gladly, when you tell me your name."

"You are persistent," she noted, rolling her eyes.

"I believe that is a compliment." One corner of his mouth quirked up, and the girl huffed, shifting her body to face the far wall.

"Right now, it is bothersome."

"Why do you refuse to answer?" Anteros asked, his gaze tracing a deep chasm that cut through the floor between them and up the wall.

"I have seen the horror your father's men leave behind. They slaughtered an innocent woman and children," she replied, staring at the small sliver of sky visible through the iron bars within a window. She sighed as she turned back to him and added, "I won't place my own family in danger."

Her sorrowful look caused a tight pang in the prince's chest. "I can understand your fear," Anteros said, "but you are not the person my father wants. We know you're from Durmak, though. You must have known the Finches, even in passing. We're looking for John Finch and his missing daughter. The king has no reason to keep you alive unless you speak."

"There is nothing to tell," she said bitterly. "My kin have no quarrels with the king, nor affiliation with any loyalists. I should rather die in silence than see my own family butchered."

"Your situation shall improve if you speak to me. I shall make sure your family is spared. We could even find a place for you in the kitchen or as a maid."

"No, thank you," she said, waving one hand in protest. "I do not need the pity of a spoiled prince."

"Spoiled? Suppose I should be insulted," he said. The girl continued to glower at him, her eyes reminding him of the sky before a midday storm.

Anteros rose to his feet, pushing himself off the ground with both hands. Stepping forward, the girl shrank back in fear, and he paused. Scrutinizing her face, he asked, "Are you sure you're all right?"

The prisoner crossed her arms and looked down at the floor. Her eyes glazed over, as if recalling something. "I am alive," she whispered as she traced a small white scar on her cheek with delicate fingertips.

"What happened to you? Did the men—"

"Stop," she said abruptly. "You have no right to ask such things."

He stared at her as a sinking feeling crept into his chest. He knew from the look on her face she must have endured unspeakable pain while his father's men dragged her north to Graynor. Clenching his fists, Anteros bent his knees and squatted a few feet away from her. "I shall ask but once. Who hurt you? If you can identify him—"

"Your father disposed of one wretch, and I'm sure the other wet himself," she said, her voice cold. She stole a glance at the prince. "Why do you care?"

"I would not wish any harm to my sister or mother. You do not deserve to be mistreated either. None should feel they have such authority."

"Except your father. He has such authority, enough to terrorize the entire kingdom, should he wish," the prisoner said, rolling her eyes. "I trust you have the same freedoms."

"You are mistaken," he said. "I am not my father, though he so wishes I was."

"I am to believe you do not take after your father?"

"I should hope so," Anteros said. "I did not come here to hurt or scare you. My only aim is to understand your silence."

"What is there to understand? I am a prisoner of the king, taken by force, far from my home, with no cause. I do not know you, and I have nothing to offer you."

"We believe you knew the Finch family. Can you tell me anything which would not be a betrayal of your neighbors?"

"I have known them all my life. They were good people. I never knew them to speak against the king. Not once," she said. "I cannot fathom why they should deserve the fate they received."

"This must come as a shock to you, so I shall be candid. Mary Finch was a former maidservant to Elara Garrick, and John, a knight of the Garrick Guard."

"By the stars! That cannot be. If that were true, they would have gone with her."

"Yet many who were loyal did not follow her," Anteros said. "Over the years, my father has captured many who worked for the Garricks, particularly those who once lived in Graynor, and assembled a list of others who were devoted to them. The Finches were high on that list. My father believed even their eldest children should have known the truth, for a couple were born before his siege."

"I can assure you, their children knew nothing of that. I was quite close to their daughter. Her parents told the story of how they met in Durmak. All their children were born there."

"You were lied to," the prince said.

"If that is true, they lied to their own children as well."

Anteros exhaled, rubbing his forehead. "Is your friend worth your silence?"

"Yes. Wherever she is, I do not know, and I am thankful you do not know either."

"I can appreciate your candor, Red. You seem like a loyal friend. But if you truly do not know anything, why stay silent? The only person who can save you is yourself."

"Oh, so the handsome prince has no intention of saving the damsel in distress? I suppose they don't teach gallantry in the North."

"Handsome, huh?" Anteros said, lips parting in a devilish grin, and her cheeks turned deep red as she averted her eyes. "As amusing as this is, I can only help you if you talk to me."

Anteros turned and walked toward the cell door. When he glanced back at her, she stared at him with the saddest eyes he had ever seen. He paused with the door half-open and said, "Besides, I don't think you're a damsel in distress at all. You're stronger than you appear."

He grasped the metal handle and started pulling the heavy door closed behind him. It was nearly closed when she asked, "Would you bring another apple tomorrow?"

The prince smiled, glancing through the small opening at the hopeful detainee. "Perhaps I could be persuaded."

Her face fell as she contemplated the meaning of his words.

"Don't fret. I didn't mean anything nefarious," Anteros said, running a hand through his hair. When she did not reply, he heaved the door closed, inserted the key into the lock, and turned it all the way to the left.

"Talitha."

Anteros looked up and found her staring back through the slot on the door. Leaning closer, he asked, "What was that?"

"My name. It's Talitha."

"Talitha," he repeated, his eyes locked on hers as he tested her name on his lips. "That's a good start. Perhaps you'll have more to share when I return." Winking at her, Anteros turned and marched in triumph down the hall.

At the dungeon's exit, he ordered the most trustworthy of the guards to bring the girl fresh water and bread from the kitchen. Then, turning to face the others, he pulled the sword from his belt and pointed it toward each man's face, one by one.

"As I am the only person that girl has spoken to all week, she is now my ward. Bring her food and water and leave her be. I will return for further questioning. If I learn that any of you have touched her, you will lose your head. Is that clear?"

The soldiers swallowed and nodded, falling in line and bowing before their prince. Anteros stuffed the sword back in its sheath and bounded up the stairs, feeling a surge of confidence knowing he was the only person in the castle who knew Talitha's name.

ENCHANTED

Crystal and Serena traveled in silence as songbirds called in the branches overhead.

"We are close to the reservoir. I can smell the water," Crystal said at last. The journey took longer than Crystal had anticipated. Due to Serena's weakened condition, she needed frequent breaks from riding. Each time they stopped, Crystal kept a watchful eye on their surroundings while Serena ate, drank, and slept.

"Are you sure it's safe here?" Serena asked as they rode into the clearing at the reservoir's edge.

"Nowhere in the open is safe, Serena. You should know that." Crystal leapt down from her horse and led him toward the water. "We should fill our bottles and continue to the shelter. We'll be safe there for the night. The rest of my comrades should be waiting at the cabin or in Morlerae. They'll join us as we make our way to Symptee."

"There are other guardians here? How many are there?"

"I am the unit lead," Crystal said. "I chose three others to come on this mission. We parted ways in Morlerae to track down different families. We hoped to safely get a dozen loyalists out of Hyrosencia, but those hopes are dwindling."

"I'm sure Her Majesty would have preferred to see one of my parents over me," Serena said, looking down. "Who else did you hope to find?"

"While I traveled south, the men were to go to Axys," she said. "They were to keep an eye out for any of Elara's missing guardsmen."

"The men?"

"Yes, Cole and Rigel," she said. "The final member of our party, Xandra, was to wait in Morlerae for everyone to return."

"Xandra? That's an odd name," Serena said. "Why did she not travel south with you?"

"She's named after her father, Alexander. He's the commander of the Garrick Guard now," Crystal told her. "They crossed with Elara when Rexton first besieged the capital. The commander was friends with your father before the war. Should we not return within a month, she is to report back to Symptee."

"Wait—How did he know my father?"

Crystal slowly turned toward Serena but stopped short of facing her. Looking toward the water, she explained, "When Rexton invaded, your parents were living in Graynor. John was a member of the Garrick Guard stationed in the castle when Rexton attacked. The Garricks told those with children to flee east or south to safety." Crystal glanced at Serena. She sighed and muttered to herself, "I shouldn't have said anything. Had I realized you did not know—"

"No," Serena said. "It's my family. I should know. After everything I've been through, I deserve the truth. Tell me what else you know. From the beginning."

Crystal nodded hesitantly and said, "Your parents chose to stay in Hyrosencia. They feared their children would not survive the journey east. As they went south, they warned people of Rexton's invasion, giving others time to flee east before his forces reached the South. When your family arrived in Durmak, a family living there decided to cross Norlee while the borders were still unguarded. They left their home to your family."

"My parents said we were all born in Durmak," Serena said, her brow furrowed. "But Rexton did not invade until the year after my birth. Does that mean I was born in Graynor?"

"Yes, as was your elder brother," Crystal said. "It was crucial that everyone in town say your family had lived there for generations, and all the Elders agreed. It was the only way to keep you all safe." After a moment, Crystal added, "Elara knows them as Sir Nathan and Marjorie Fritz."

"Fritz," Serena said quietly, turning from Crystal and walking a few feet away. Plopping on the ground, Serena covered her eyes with her hands. "How could they lie to us about our family name? And their ties to the Garricks? What else did they keep from us?" Serena felt a hand rest on her shoulder but shrugged it off. Everything she had been told growing up was a lie. The small truth Crystal had revealed—and Serena trusted the guardian's words, for it explained the sword hidden in the wardrobe—weighed Serena down, and her mind churned with new questions.

"I didn't know your parents, nor do I envy their struggles," said Crystal. "It was dangerous to live in Hyrosencia if you had been affiliated with the royal family; it still is. These secrets were meant to protect you. Elara spoke so highly of Marjorie and Sir Nathan. She trusted them both, and she was desperate to find a way to bring you all to Symptee. My comrades and I were sent to retrieve your family for her. Every attempt prior had failed until I found you."

"Why?" Serena asked through clenched teeth. She turned toward her guardian in an unsteady motion. "Why did my parents never mention they were loyal to the Garricks? I mean, blazing embers, I am eighteen! I am not a child anymore."

"I only know what Queen Elara told us before we left Symptee. I am sorry."

"If Elara has sent others to retrieve us, why did none make it to Durmak? Why did her guards never find us?"

"Because Rexton is clever. He built Murmont into a stronghold for his army. Set up a blockade so it's nearly impossible to pass through Norlee unnoticed," Crystal said in exasperation. "We have lost countless guards in attempts to get to you."

Murmont. That's where Cameron was training as one of Rexton's soldiers. The thought sickened her. "Surely she needn't waste her resources for one knight! Why continue to send her people?"

"This was not only about retrieving your father," Crystal said, mounting her horse and taking a deep breath. "Your mother was one of Elara's maidservants for several years. She also helped care for the infants in the nursery when needed."

"My mother was the queen's maid? That's why Elara wanted her rescued? Is there a shortage of maids in Symptee?"

"She was more than a maid to Elara. She was like an older sister. All the knights and servants, everyone who worked for the royal family, Elara loved them all," Crystal said. "King Scorpius was good for this kingdom, and Prince Stellan would have been, too."

Serena slowly pushed herself off the ground, using her right arm to stabilize herself. She mounted Midnight without aid, grimacing aloud, and said, "We should go. It's not safe to dwell here."

Crystal nodded and nudged her horse with her heel. When their horses were side-by-side, the guardian glanced over at Serena, who stared forward with her jaw clenched.

"I did not mean to upset you," Crystal said. "Please try to understand. Your parents kept secrets for your safety. They could not risk the truth reaching the wrong people."

"My mother knew that we would never do anything to endanger our family. And look! None of her children knew the truth, yet someone discovered their allegiance to Elara anyway. Rexton came after us because of it. That's why they're dead, isn't it?"

Crystal nodded.

Serena glared into the darkness of the forest beyond them, contemplating the cause of her family's demise. "My father was the only one who knew how to wield a sword, and he wasn't there when Rexton's men came for us," Serena said, a bitter bite in her voice. "I don't see why they continue to come after me. I knew nothing of my parents' ties to Elara. I can't even fend for myself!"

"Rexton's pride. It's not enough to see all of Elara's loyal followers fall. There's a bounty on their children as well. His generals were ordered to show no mercy. If anyone has a tie to the Garricks, he intends to snuff out their entire family."

"And my brother Cameron willingly fights for that twisted bastard," Serena said, adding, "if the king has not already killed him." After a moment, she said, "I wish there were a way to reach him."

"Serena, I wish it were possible for us to save him, but we cannot linger in search of him. It's too dangerous," Crystal said. "If it helps, I believe Rexton will have kept Cameron alive. He cannot slaughter his own soldiers if he wishes to eradicate the Hyrosencian loyalists. Your brother is likely far north, where he won't discover your family's fate."

"Even as I held my mother as she took her last breath, I did not feel such anger as I do now," Serena said. "All I felt before was sadness and fear. Now, I am angry enough that I could kill Antoine Rexton myself."

"Good," the guardian said. "You'll need that anger soon enough."

"What do you mean?"

Crystal shook her head. "It has been a long and gruesome war, but we must believe that it shall be ended soon."

"I hope it ends in our favor, with Rexton hanged for his crimes."

They traveled in silence for the next hour until Crystal took a sharp turn between a pair of massive oak trees. There was no dirt pathway nor sign of a trail. Puzzled, Serena asked, "How are you so sure of where we are?"

"Because I have been here before, and I never forget my way," said Crystal with a satisfied smile. "Trust me."

By midday, they reached a clearing in the forest with a small cabin at the far end. "It looks abandoned," Serena said. She grasped the reins tightly in her right hand, swung her leg around Midnight's rear, and carefully dismounted. She approached a window and attempted to look inside, but the windows were frosted.

Crystal led both horses to the far side of the cabin and tied them securely where they had plenty of grass to graze and a small stream for water. Then she walked up to a large thick set of wooden shutters and said, "This is our entrance." Serena tugged at the shutters, but they did not budge. "How do we get in?"

The archer grinned as she said, "It's enchanted. You must know a password to access it."

"Enchanted? But I thought magic had all but died out among humans."

"Not quite." Crystal stepped closer to the cabin and whispered something indecipherable. There was a popping sound, followed by the shutters creaking as they opened slightly. Serena stepped back in surprise. Crystal thrust the shutters out of the way and pushed up the glass, giving them an opening.

Serena's jaw dropped. "What did you say?"

"I told it to open in the ancient language. Anyone could open it, human or otherwise, if they know the phrase." Crystal sat on the edge of the open window and swung her legs inside. Hopping off the ledge, she reached out a hand to help Serena step through.

The inside of the cabin was nothing like Serena expected. The ornate room featured several armchairs and a wooden table with benches that could seat six. Crystal reached through the window and closed the shutters. With a quick hand motion, she muttered under her breath.

Serena had already sunk deep into the softest chair she had ever felt with a huge smile on her face.

"Wait until you see the beds," Crystal said with a smirk.

Crystal disappeared through a doorway into another room. Serena chased after her, coming to an abrupt stop when she saw them. There were four single beds with fluffy feather pillows and warm wool blankets. Crystal had flopped down onto the bed closest to the door, chuckling as the girl gawked. Serena's eyes clouded as she laid on the bed next to her.

"Did I die?" Serena asked, hugging a pillow to her chest.

"I have worked very hard to keep you alive," Crystal said, and they both laughed. "I cannot wait for you to finally see Symptee. It has grown into quite a wondrous city over the years."

"I wish I could have seen Hyrosencia in its prime, before everything changed," said Serena, staring at the wooden panels overhead.

"Change is not all bad," Crystal said. "People respond to the heaviness of change in different ways. Some collapse under it, but others are molded into something else entirely—sometimes something greater."

"How has the war impacted your family?"

"My village was attacked when I was a child, and my mother died," Crystal said. "That's why I became a warrior. I never wanted to feel useless like that again. I chose to give my life to this cause because Hyrosencia needs fighters, and I wanted to help those who cannot fight for themselves."

"People like me," Serena muttered to herself. "How long have you been a warrior?"

"Well over a decade," the blonde woman said, staring at the opposite wall.

"A decade?" Serena sat up and stared at her acquaintance. "How old are you?"

"I've always felt much older than I look," Crystal grinned. "I started my training quite young."

"I'm most surprised you have such advanced skills at your age. You cannot be older than what? Twenty-five?"

"Of course," Crystal said, picking at a strand of her long hair. "It's quite common for children to enroll in the Academy due to the war. The queen requires at least ten years of training before joining her service. I spent most of my youth perfecting my skills."

Serena thought for a moment and frowned. "I turned eighteen mere days before the attack. I wish I had learned to fight somehow. Not that it matters anymore."

"It's never too late to learn how to protect yourself," Crystal said. "And you should."

"Perhaps one day," Serena said, thinking of how her mother had died. Her father's sword was right there in the wardrobe, and her mother still had no chance against her attacker. "I don't want to die the way my mother did. She must have been so afraid."

"You will know peace again, Serena," Crystal said, locking eyes with her. "You have always been cared for by others. Now you need to learn how to protect yourself. Once you're sure of your ability to defend yourself, that peace will return. You'll see."

"I thought if I could stay hidden, at least I would be safe, but you still found me. Thank heavens it was you and no one else," Serena said, pulling her feet up and resting her chin on her knees. "I've known the woods my whole life, yet for the first time, I was terrified of them. I hid for so long I lost count of the days. Do you know what day it is?"

"I believe it's the end of April. Or perhaps the first of May?" Crystal said with uncertainty. "Why do you ask?"

"My mother always said the first of May was important, but I never knew why. It was not any of our birthdays."

Crystal pondered the date for a moment before her face lit up in realization. "That may be Queen Elara's birthday! I wonder why Mary would have mentioned that to you without context."

Serena placed a hand over her pocket and patted. She could still feel the little gold ring Mary had given to her tucked safely in the small pocket of her trousers. Her mother had not gotten the chance to tell her why she had held onto this ring for seventeen years. Serena racked her brain but could not recall her mother ever wearing it, even in the privacy of their home. "Why do you think my parents chose to remain in Hyrosencia, despite their allegiance to the queen? I cannot fathom why they didn't try to cross the valley when my brother Samuel was older. If they had, we would have all been safe."

Crystal rolled onto her side, facing Serena, and said, "In wartime, everyone must make difficult decisions. Every choice you make—even the smallest ones—can impact your loved ones, even the fate of an entire realm."

The room fell silent while Serena wondered what difficult choices her parents were forced to make when they fled the capital with two young children in tow.

"Rexton decided to invade Hyrosencia and slay the royal family," Crystal said. "The guards evacuated Elara for the sake of their people. Elara is no warrior, and she certainly knows it. But she has been a symbol of hope for her people since Rexton seized Graynor. She will be until the true heir is ready to face their destiny."

"The true heir? Of Hyrosencia? Does Elara have a son?"

Crystal sat up and looked out the window at their horses grazing outside. "Elara does not have any children yet. She married a Denorfian prince some years ago, but he died of illness before they could produce an heir," she explained. "But she will soon be wed again. Perhaps soon enough there will be another child of the Garrick bloodline."

"But if she does not have children yet, it could be another 20 years before there is an heir old enough to lead an army," Serena sighed.

"Not necessarily," said Crystal without looking at Serena. "Elara had an older brother, Prince Stellan. He had two children, Elyse and Ansel. It is our belief that at least one of their children was evacuated safely. Stellan's eldest living child is the true heir to the throne."

"I never knew Elara had a brother." Serena rubbed the bridge of her nose. "Honestly, my parents were terrible tutors. I hardly know the history of our kingdom or our family." She crossed her arms over her chest and watched Crystal braid a tiny portion of her hair with a somber expression on her face. "No one spoke of old Hyrosencia in Durmak. It was all quite secretive. There were rumors years ago that Elara was collecting children and having them trained to be members of her army. Cameron and Will used to joke about the child armada." She smiled, remembering her brother and his friend.

Crystal's eyes darted toward Serena. She said slowly, emphasizing each word, "That is false. There has never been a child armada. Such a thought would offend your queen greatly." Crystal stood and walked over to a cushioned bench on the far side of the room. Unclasping her bow-and-arrow pin, she removed her cloak and flung it over an empty bed, setting the pin down on the end of the bench. Then she sat, looking directly at Serena, and said, "Those who began training as children did so by choice. Most do not begin training for combat before the age of twelve. Elara has never accepted anyone under the age of seventeen into the Guard, and no one is forced to join. We volunteered. Even with her father's permission, my friend Xandra still had to wait until she was old enough and had trained hard enough to become a guardian."

Serena bit the inside of her lip, glanced away from the guardian, and said, "I did not mean to offend you or the queen. I just—I have been in the dark all this time. I don't know what is true and what is not."

Crystal sighed and said, "I cannot hold that against you. I understand how you feel, being in the dark about important things. I was not unlike you when I was younger."

Serena wanted to hear more, but she could see that Crystal was exhausted from the dark bags under her eyes. The guardian had barely slept since they left Kypno, and Serena wanted her to rest while they were safeguarded.

"You should sleep, Crystal. You look ghastly," she joked.

Crystal's chuckle gave way to a noisy yawn. "I do not doubt it. It has been a long week," she said, laying back on the bed. "You should rest as well."

"I will in a moment," said Serena. "I think I shall sit up a bit longer. I have a lot to think about, but don't let me keep you awake."

"Oh, you won't." Crystal said as she closed her eyes. She smiled faintly, nestling into the bed under a warm blanket. "Whatever you do, stay inside."

"I will. I promise," Serena said.

CAMERON FINCH DISMOUNTED FROM his horse and peered up at the expanse of cream-colored brick that stretched toward the sky. Graynor Castle was larger than he had expected, making even the tallest men feel small as they stood in its shadow. He swallowed, casting his eyes forward as his captain led him toward the front entrance.

His head was still reeling from the revelation that half his family had been murdered—the other half missing—when Captain Pelham informed him that King Antoine had requested an audience with them. Though the young man had the greatest respect for the king, he was unnerved by this sudden invitation, having never laid eyes upon the monarch. After all, he was just a lowly recruit. Staring at the back of his captain's burgundy jacket, Cameron watched the way the sun reflected off the gold epaulets on his shoulders and pictured himself wearing an officer's uniform.

"Finch," Pelham barked, snapping the soldier out of his trance. His captain had paused in the doorway and turned toward him. Lowering his chin, the man said in a low voice, "You are to conduct yourself with the utmost care while we are here. You will address the king as 'Your Majesty' and refrain from asking foolish questions. Understood?"

Cameron nodded, wiping his sweaty hands against his thighs. Without another word, the captain turned and continued into the castle with Cameron trailing him like a shadow. They weaved their way down cobblestone halls, past open doorways and busy servants whose curious stares followed them. The soldier peered down at his simple black uniform and adjusted his shirt. He had heard of the king's fluctuating moods, how his anger came in waves like the tide of the Lestern Sea, and he did not want to make a poor impression.

Pelham stopped, turning on his heels to face a massive doorway. "Here we are. Chin up, Finch."

The young man's eyes widened as he followed the captain through the doorway into a large conference room. A massive mahogany table encircled by a dozen hand-carved wooden chairs filled the open space, and seated at the head of the table was King Antoine Rexton, his ruby-encrusted crown glinting in the sunlight streaming through the window.

"Marcus, you've made it," Antoine said, nodding his head to the man before his gaze shifted to the boy. "This must be the Finch boy you've told me about."

Cameron swallowed, his throat feeling dry as he bowed his head low and said, "Your Majesty, it is an honor to meet you."

As he raised his head, Cameron found the king studying him, his lips curled in a sinister grin. "Come, sit, boy." Antoine motioned to the empty chair beside him, and Pelham nudged Cameron toward it. "Cameron, was it?"

"Yes, Your Majesty," he replied sheepishly. "How may I serve you?"

The king examined the young soldier, the intensity of his gaze making Cameron feel like a small boy cornered by a black bear in the woods. Then Antoine laughed, his deep voice reverberating through the small space and disarming Pelham and Cameron. His left hand came down hard on the soldier's shoulder. "My boy, that's not why you are here." When the soldier frowned, uncertain why he would be summoned, Antoine added, "Your captain informed me of the terrible news you received last week. Such a shame to hear. I wanted to offer my heartfelt condolences for your losses and inquire whether you need any assistance from the crown."

Cameron blinked at the king, his chest tightening as he pictured his brothers' faces. "Thank you," he barely managed to stutter, clearing his throat. Somehow, having his loss recognized by the king made his chest swell with pride, easing the painful memories that flashed through his mind.

"As soon as I heard the news, I sent men to Durmak to investigate their murders. We cannot sit on this information and wait for the next time Elara's assassins strike," the king said.

"Elara? The Garrick princess?" Cameron asked, two deep lines forming a chasm on his forehead. "What has she to do with my family?"

"Everything," Antoine said, squeezing Cameron's forearm. "We've received reports of her spies crossing the mountains. They will stop at nothing to take my throne. They must have been looking for supplies or loyalists when they came across your kin. Their work was sloppy, as though the attack was not planned."

"I don't know what my mother or brothers could have done to deserve—"

"Nothing, dear boy," Antoine interrupted, pursing his lips. "They are ruthless fighters, incapable of respecting innocent life. That's why it is imperative we track them down."

"I can help," Cameron said, perking up at the prospect. "I've always been an excellent tracker."

Antoine glanced over his shoulder at the captain, and Pelham shrugged. "Of my men, he is one of the best in that art."

The king nodded, raising his eyebrows as he turned back to the boy. "I appreciate your commitment to the cause, but surely you must have family matters to attend to following your mother's death?"

Cameron shook his head firmly. The Elders would have already buried his loved ones, as was customary to do within three days of death. There was nothing he could do for corpses. "I appreciate your concern, Your Majesty. Truly," Cameron said, brazenly staring the king head on. "But I assure you, I am fit for duty. I do not need leave; I only want to be useful to you."

Antoine's eyes flicked toward Pelham, who stood a few paces behind the young man, and smacked his lips together tentatively. "Do you not have any other kin you need to contact?"

Cameron flinched, the muscles in his jaw tightening. He could feel his pulse in a vein on the side of his neck as he remembered arguing with his father before he left to join the Enforcing Army. Now, he didn't know where his father was—or if he was alive. They had never seen eye to eye, so part of him didn't want to go looking for more heartbreak. "My friend said my father left Durmak months ago and never returned," he said with a shrug.

Antoine lifted his chin, nodding slowly. "My men can make inquiries for you. Perhaps they can track him down," the king said, taking a sip from a gold goblet. "Anyone else?"

Cameron sank his teeth into his bottom lip, thinking about Serena's disappearance. According to Will, she was alive the last time he had seen her, and they suspected she had run off on her own. What a fool. She was always wandering off in the woods by herself. One day she was going to run into the wrong type of people—slave traders, or worse. "My sister is missing. She has a knack for running off, and I've always been the one sent after her," he noted, not meeting the king's eyes. Cameron clenched his fists in his lap, knowing it would not bode well to ask for leave to go after her. He was the king's man now. He should not worry about his younger sister anymore.

"Your sister, how old is she?" Antoine asked, his tone lightening. "Perhaps she is out searching for your father on her own. She must be terribly frightened."

"If I know Serena, she isn't as scared as she should be," he admitted.

"Hmm," Antoine hummed thoughtfully, weighing his next words. "Cameron. I'm a family man myself, you know. I have two beautiful children not much younger than you. If anything were to happen to my daughter, I know my son Anteros would be quick to go looking for her."

Cameron looked down at his calloused hands. His knuckles had turned stark white as he wrung them together. "Serena is eighteen," he said. "I've pledged my life to your service, Your Majesty. I will not abandon that promise to look for a runaway."

Pelham clapped his hands together and said, "I must commend your dedication, Finch. Most would jump at the chance to take leave in your situation."

"Yes, you're right about that, Marcus," the king said, narrowing his eyes. "My greatest concern is my people's safety. There is no kingdom without subjects, after all. Should you have any idea where your sister may have gone, I could send someone to look for her in your stead."

"I have not the slightest idea," Cameron said, frowning. "I just hope she wasn't found by the monsters who killed the rest of our family."

"As do I." Antoine traced his finger in a circle around the rim of his chalice. "It's a shame we don't know where she is. She could have critical information on the enemy if she witnessed anything. I should very much like to speak with her."

"I must apologize for her disappearance," Cameron said, gritting his teeth. Once again, Serena's foolish tendency to wander off in the woods was causing him trouble. "She's reckless, prone to getting into trouble. If I knew where she was—"

"You are a tracker, are you not?" Antoine asked loudly, staring down the soldier. "It would please your king if you would track her down and bring her here, where we can ensure her safety until the assassins are captured. See if she knows anything. Do you think you could do that?"

Cameron gaped at the king, his lips parted as he struggled to form his thoughts into words. The king wanted him to go looking for Serena? Was this a trick? A test of some sort? He pushed back his chair and knelt in front of the king, striking his breast. "I shall go wherever you see fit, Your Majesty. The choice is yours alone."

Antoine chuckled, leaning back in his chair and watching the boy. "I like you, Cameron. You're a devoted soldier." The king beckoned with a hand for the soldier to stand, and he slowly rose to his feet. Antoine stood a few inches taller than him and grinned. Clapping him hard on the back, the king said, "Consider this your first major assignment. I know you shall do well." Then he glanced at Pelham, adding, "Let it be known at Murmont that Finch here has completed training. In fact, I am personally promoting him to Private First Class—Corporal Finch upon his successful return."

The soldier jolted forward a step, barely catching himself. As he found his balance, he clasped his hands behind his back and bowed his head. "Thank you for your trust, Your Majesty. I will not disappoint you."

"I know you won't," Antoine said, a sly smile barely visible under his thick beard. "And before you go, I have a lead for you to look into."

ROYAL RENDEZVOUS

When Serena was sure her companion was fast asleep, she fished around in her pocket until she found the ring from Elara. Taking a close look at it for the first time, she noticed there were minuscule engravings on the outside of the ring which matched those etched on the blade of her father's sword. After staring at the gold band for some time, Serena placed her fingertips around it and shoved it onto the middle finger of her left hand. In the blink of an eye, she was somewhere else. Serena looked around in panic. She could feel the bed she laid on, but she could not see it. Though she raised her hands out in front of her body, there were no hands in her line of sight.

"Thank the stars! Where have you been Mary? I have been waiting for hours!" a strange woman's voice said.

Serena jumped at the sound of the unfamiliar voice and her mother's name. She sat up on her bed. "What is this? Who are you? Why can I not see—"

"You are not Mary," the woman said. "This ring was given to Mary Finch. How did you acquire it?"

Serena felt faint as she whispered, "Elara? Are you Queen Elara?"

"I shall not answer that until I know who you are. Do you have a mirror? I should like to see who I am speaking with at once."

Trying to look around, Serena said, "I don't know this place. Where am I?"

"Stop moving your head so much," the faceless woman said. "Remove the ring for a moment and go in search of a mirror. Water will do, if necessary. Look at your reflection, and then return the ring to your finger."

"Yes, miss."

Serena yanked the ring off and at once could see she was still seated on the same bed as before. Crystal remained asleep in the bed next to hers. Quietly creeping into the cabin's parlor, Serena found no mirror. She did not want to waste their water supply but was growing desperate as the seconds ticked by. She knew she needed answers, and Elara might be the key.

She had an idea. Pulling her father's sword from its sheath, she smiled triumphantly into her reflection on the smooth side of the blade. Carefully, she took a seat on one of the plush chairs. Laying the sword across her legs, she released it to push the gold ring back onto her finger. Instantly, she was back inside the strange room with high stone walls and deep purple drapery pulled back from tall windows. The room was illuminated by the faint glimmer of several candles, and she wondered if the woman was in New Hyrosencia.

The voice asked again, "Who are you? I still cannot see your face."

Serena looked down at the sword on her lap, though her view of a stone wall did not change. "My name is Serena Finch. I am the daughter of John and Mary Finch. Now please tell me your name."

Although Serena remained seated on the chair in the cabin, her view shifted as the woman stepped in front of a large oval mirror with an embellished frame made of gold. Serena peered into a pair of fierce green eyes bearing a striking resemblance to her own.

The beautiful woman said, "I have waited many years to meet you, Serena. I am Elara Garrick, Queen of Hyrosencia. First, I must know, are you somewhere safe? Somewhere no one will find you or overhear you?"

"Your Majesty, it's an honor," Serena stuttered, closing her eyes and bowing her head. "I am in a cabin near a reservoir. It's protected by magic. One of your guardians brought me here—Crystal Windaef."

"Excellent. I am glad to hear it," Elara said, smiling at her reflection. "There be no need for formalities tonight. We both have many questions."

"Yes," Serena agreed. "Many. Is this the City of Mercy? How am I seeing you? Is this magic?"

Elara laughed, and Serena observed the queen's reflection. Elara had a petite frame with delicate facial features, and her laugh caused small wrinkles to appear in the corners of her eyes. Her eyes seemed weary as her smile faded. She must have been around the same age as Mary Finch, maybe a few years younger. "It is," she said. "A sorcerer created this set of rings many years ago as a precaution. I have used them to stay in contact with Mary and John. When two sundered souls wear these rings, they may see through each other's eyes and hear each other's voices."

Elara held up one hand in the mirror to show Serena a matching band on her finger.

"You were close to my mother then? That is what Crystal said."

"Crystal," Elara said, her eyes glancing side to side. "And where is she?"

"She's asleep, milady. I'm afraid it's been a brutal week. Someone tried to kill us."

Elara's eyes widened, and she planted her hands on the nearest wall to stabilize herself. "Heavens, are you all right? What of the others?"

Serena wondered why Elara suddenly looked pale and thought she even saw tears welling in the queen's eyes. "We're all right, milady. Crystal is as skilled at healing as she is with her bow. She saved me."

Elara's breath caught, and she blinked back her emotions. "Thank the heavens, indeed! I shall give extra hours of prayer in thanksgiving for your welfare."

"You sound relieved," Serena said. "I am surprised you care so greatly when we have never met."

Elara stared at the girl's reflection in the cold steel. "Of course I care. Your parents are very important to me, as are you. I cannot wait to be reunited with Mary and meet all of her beautiful children at last."

Serena froze. "But milady, my mother—she is not with us." She closed her eyes and whispered, "She was murdered two months ago. As were my two younger brothers."

Serena blinked and watched as Elara's cheeks deflated, her relieved smile replaced by a wave of horror. Elara's bottom lip began quivering. She closed her eyes, placing her hands over them. "No. That cannot be. We were so close. They were nearly there."

Serena heard Elara struggle to suppress her tears. Serena said, "When I found her, I begged her to tell me how to mend her wounds. She said I couldn't help her. She told me to go to the City of Mercy, to find you. Made me promise. She gave me this ring and Papa's sword. Then I held her hand as her soul slipped from this world."

Elara sniffled loudly and blinked, wiping at her cheeks. She was no longer looking into the mirror. Instead, Serena could see the top of the mountains peeking over Elara's balcony. Elara took a haggard breath and said, "Oh, child, I am so sorry you had to witness such an injustice. Mary deserved a better life and a more peaceful death."

"I'd like to think she had a good life," said Serena, remembering her mother's gentle laugh. "We were happy until we were attacked—and now I know it was for their loyalty to you. Something I knew nothing of at the time. Why would they keep such a thing from me?"

"You were so young when the siege occurred," Elara said quietly.

"And now I am grown. They could have told me the truth," Serena spit out.

Elara exhaled, shaking her head in agreement. "You're right. But there is no changing the past," she whispered. "How did you manage to survive the attack?"

And so Serena told the queen every detail of the horrid events, from baking bread with Mama that morning to changing her blood-soaked blouse, fetching her emergency rucksack, and sneaking away before the Elders arrived.

"Serena," the queen said, "I would have given anything to save them from such a fate."

"Really? Then why did it take seventeen years to send for us?" Serena snapped.

Elara stepped back in front of the mirror and blinked into it, her brows knit together in aggravation. Long had it been since anyone had addressed her with such hostility. "We tried many times to send guards for you, but Rexton's men have been ruthless. Crystal's unit is the first to make it across Norlee and into Hyrosencia undetected."

"She found me in the forest last week," said Serena. "It's unfortunate she did not arrive sooner. Perhaps my family would not have suffered such a grim demise."

The queen swallowed hard, displeased to see such bitterness in Serena's glare. "Perhaps," she said with a sigh. "But I am thankful you have survived."

"Barely," Serena replied, biting her bottom lip.

"Have you been injured?" Elara asked in alarm.

"I was stabbed in the shoulder. I could have died, Crystal said. Luckily, she is a skilled healer, as she put it," Serena mocked, one corner of her mouth turning upward in a half smile.

Elara took a deep breath. Serena could see the despair on the queen's face as she said, "You must trust Crystal and the rest of the guardians with everything in you. Listen to them. They will protect you with their lives. When you are healed, you should learn how to defend yourself with the sword you have. I fear this shall not be the last time your life is in danger."

Serena nodded. "Crystal said as much."

Elara blotted a handkerchief at the corner of her red, puffy eyes. Her irises glowed even brighter than before. Serena said, "You grieve as if you have lost a sister."

"I have," said Elara. "We have both lost so many to this war. I wish to save everyone we can before Rexton burns the rest of our kingdom to the ground."

Serena gripped the hilt of the sword in her right hand and held it up so that Elara could see her reflection again. Looking into Elara's eyes in the mirror, Serena said, "I should like to be a part of that. I have nothing left to lose."

"You still have your life, and that is everything. Please do all you can to hold onto it," said Elara, a glimmer of hope twinkling in her sad eyes.

Serena nodded, reminded of her mother's final words. She wondered what it must have been like for her mother, an ordinary woman, to have worked for the royal family. Could they truly have been so close that Elara wept for her?

The queen asked the girl if she would answer a few questions, and Serena agreed, proceeding to tell Elara in detail about her life in Durmak. Then she told her what little Crystal had revealed about her parents' relationship with the Garrick family and how she had been born in Graynor and not in Durmak, as she grew up believing. To Serena's dismay, Elara offered no further information about Sir Nathan and Marjorie Fritz, but she didn't press the issue either. She was still trying to process all she had already learned.

"I should like to speak to you again if ever you are safe and willing," the queen said after Serena had answered her questions.

Serena nodded.

Elara bowed her head briefly. "Please give Crystal my regards. I hope by now you trust her. She and the other guardians, they are our finest warriors. I have no doubt that we shall be together soon. Until we are united, move quickly and be cautious."

"Until we are united," Serena whispered. The words echoed through her mind in her mother's voice, as it had been Mary's favorite way to say goodbye, and Serena knew then that Crystal must have spoken the truth. Queen Elara and her mother must have known each other long ago.

Slipping the enchanted ring off her finger, Elara's face blurred out of view, and Serena blinked as her eyes refocused on her own reflection in the blade of the sword. The girl stared at her reflection for a moment; a feeling of déjà vu swelled in her chest as she remembered the queen's face. Then she thrust the blade back into the leather scabbard. Rising from her seat, Serena shuffled back toward the room where Crystal slumbered peacefully and slipped into her own bed. Her forehead wrinkled crossly as she remembered that her mother had used the same phrase to bid her father farewell months ago.

"Until we are united," she said to no one as she clenched her right hand into a fist. The enchanted ring pressed into the palm of her hand as she finally drifted to sleep.

ELARA SPRAWLED ACROSS HER bed but could not sleep. Her eyes were tired, and her cheeks were streaked following her discussion with Serena. When the queen closed her eyes, she pictured her friend Marjorie's cheerful face, and she could hear her voice reassuring her that although they had lost their homes, they would win the final battle. After so many years, Elara had expected to speak to Marjorie on her birthday, as they had throughout years past.

The Finch family had survived seventeen years in hiding, concealed from Rexton and his growing army. As time passed, Elara came to believe that Sir Nathan, Marjorie, and the children were safe. She had been wrong. The Finches were never truly safe because they had remained in Hyrosencia. The queen wished she could have done more to bring them to the City of Mercy.

Rolling onto her side, Elara looked out her window into the darkness of the midnight sky. The moon cast a bright white light over the city, illuminating her room through the open window. Her chambers were several stories off the ground, and all she could see from her bed were the hundreds of stars shining above the peaks of the Athamar Mountains.

For hundreds of years, her people believed that the stars represented the souls of those who had left this world. She always wondered which were her father, mother, and brother. Focusing on a star twinkling above the crest of the mountains, Elara muttered, "Each day Antoine has ruled my kingdom, I have failed my people. But my gravest mistake was failing you, Marjorie. I thought you were secure. I thought we had time."

Tears cascaded down her cheeks. When she could no longer make out the stars, she rolled onto her back and squinted at the lavender canopy draped over her bed. She was not fond of the color—it felt too cheerful for these difficult times—but she allowed her ladies to decorate after the evacuation because it brought them joy. Most people would feel fortunate to live in as grand a palace as she did, and she was thankful her father had built this sanctuary before they knew she would need one. However, the citadel served as a constant reminder that Antoine Rexton had fooled them both, and she had lost everything because of it.

The City of Mercy, as her people called it, had quickly expanded thanks to her allies. Hundreds of brave Hyrosencians who were strong enough to follow her across the mountains arrived within the first month of the war. Within a year, she had recruited the aid of the dwarfs, and together they had built an immense stone wall around the perimeter of their new capital. Elara now found herself trapped behind the wall that protected her, and this life of exile reminded her each day of the man she was once betrothed to, the man who had become her greatest enemy. She shivered and pulled a thick blanket up to her chin.

Suddenly, there were three quick knocks on her door. It was late. She did not expect anyone to come by her chambers. The visitor knocked on her door twice more, so she shot up.

It was improper to have visitors to her personal chambers at such a late hour, but many nights she longed for company while she lay awake. A decade after her first husband's death, Elara began allowing noblemen to pursue her hand in marriage, but most suitors were transactional and unromantic. When Lord Gerard Stirling of the Eastern Isles arrived in Symptee, however, they immediately established a connection which exceeded diplomacy. Gerard proved himself to be an ally to her struggling nation, offering the support of his king and his personal estate. What began as a friendship built on mutual respect flourished into something more. Elara knew her betrothed was the one knocking at her door. It was not the first time she had quickly tip-toed to her door late at night, the stone floor cold and coarse against her bare feet. When she reached the threshold, she asked, "Who calls at this hour?"

A deep voice murmured from the other side of her door, "It is Lord Stirling, Your Majesty. I should like to present you with a gift before the day's end, if I may?"

"Yes, of course. One moment," she said, relieved at the sound of his voice. She turned the lock until it clicked and opened the door to her betrothed. She nodded to the silent guardsman who stood watch outside her chamber.

"I could not fall sleep without seeing you," Gerard said, brushing his fingertips across her damp cheek. "Are you not well, my darling?"

She shushed him and felt the color flush her face as she grabbed his arm and pulled him through the doorway. Gently, she pushed the door closed and locked it. As soon as she turned, Gerard wrapped his arms around her waist and kissed her. Elara relaxed and pressed her lips to his for a moment, one hand in his hair while the other pressed against his chest. Without warning, Gerard scooped her up in both arms and carried her toward the bed.

"Gerard, put me down at once!" she said.

"Forgive me, but you should be in bed at this hour," he said, laying her down and stooping to kiss her on the cheek. "Surely you must be exhausted."

"You are being ridiculous," she said, sitting up. "How can I sleep when there is so much to think about?"

"Elara, you overburden yourself," Gerard said. "There is no cause to fret on this day. There is no indication of Rexton's forces advancing into your territory."

"That day shall be here soon enough, but first will come the arrival of a very special guest."

"Your friend Marjorie?" he asked as he sat on the edge of her bed. "Did you have a pleasant chat this evening?"

She buried her face into a pillow as her sorrow swelled. Gerard shifted to lay beside her and rubbed her back in consolation. She turned toward him. "I'm glad you are here," she said, wiping the tears from her eyes.

Gerard ran his fingers through her hair and kissed the top of her head. "What has happened? What did she say?"

"I did not speak to Marjorie. She has left us for the stars."

"She is dead? Who told you such a thing?"

"I spoke to Serena." Elara looked into his steady gray eyes and took a deep breath. "Crystal Windaef has found her."

"That is assuring news, at least! You must be relieved to have spoken to her directly."

"Yet I am not," Elara hissed. "Marjorie and two of her sons lost their lives because she once served me. She was kind and loyal—a true friend. And now she is dead. There is no assurance in that." Elara turned away from Gerard, but he wrapped an arm around her anyway. She knew he couldn't understand her affection for her maidservant.

"Darling, they made the choice to stay behind. For seventeen years, Antoine Rexton could not find them. They stayed because they felt secure. Their deaths do not fall on you."

She wriggled free of his hold, swung her feet over the edge of the bed, and leapt off. Her satin gown dragged the floor as she walked out onto her balcony and gazed out at the city. She tried to hold the image of Marjorie's face in her mind. A cold gust of wind hit her and shook the image, as if to carry her friend away. She shuddered and rubbed her bare arms.

"You are going to catch cold, my bride. Please come inside," he pleaded, walking toward the balcony. He stopped in the doorway. "I have a gift for you."

"You already gifted me a necklace this morning," Elara said.

"I did. But this could be better," he said and fished a folded letter from his pocket. He held it above her head and stepped backward into the room. "You must come inside to read it, and you must promise to sleep after."

"We are not wed yet, and you already try ordering me about." Elara rushed forward and snatched the parchment from him with a victorious smile. "Who is it from?" she asked as she unfolded the letter.

"My cousin—the crown prince of the Eastern Isles."

Elara's eyes danced back and forth across the paper as she devoured the words. She looked up at Gerard with wide eyes. "He has accepted the terms of the new treaty! The Eastern Isles shall send soldiers to our aid." The queen threw her arms around Gerard's neck and hugged him tightly, breathing a sigh of relief. "How long have you known?"

He wrapped his arms around her. "As I said upon my arrival, the Eastern Isles have always been your allies. Our people shall win this war together. I know it."

Elara trusted he was right. The Treaty of the Five Realms became null when Rexton overthrew the Garricks, and trade between the human nations ceased. The Islander King wished to aid the Hyrosencian refugees but had lost the resources to do so. After many years of recovering and rebuilding, they were able to negotiate the trade of fish from the sea in exchange for grain and produce. The relationship between New Hyrosencia and the Eastern Isles expanded, and the two small kingdoms began to flourish. Now, the Islanders were willing to fight by their side in the war for Hyrosencia, and this was the greatest gift Elara could have ever received from her allies—beside the return of her betrothed.

"Thank you, Gerard," she said, pecking him repeatedly on his cheek. "I do not know what Hyrosencia would have done without the Islanders these recent years. It brings me such peace knowing we have their support."

"I hope to always bring you such peace, my queen."

"I told you to stop calling me that, my lord," Elara said with a smirk.

"As you wish," he laughed. "Would you prefer it if I called you what you truly are to me?"

"And what would that be?"

"My greatest treasure."

Elara closed her eyes and stood on her toes to kiss him once more. When they pulled apart, Elara blinked in a daze, beaming at him.

"Perhaps this news shall finally help you sleep," her husband-to-be said. "And perhaps it would help if you were to change attire? Surely you are not comfortable."

Looking down at her golden gown, Elara laughed halfheartedly. "I had not even noticed. On this day, I always dismiss the maids early for some privacy."

Gerard stepped back to admire her. "Do you need my assistance?"

"Gerard!" Elara said. Her face flushed as she pushed him back playfully. "You are such a scoundrel."

"I only mean to help you, however I can," he said, taking her hand and spinning her.

Elara shook her head but allowed him to begin unlacing her corset. As it fell to the floor, she took a slow, deep breath. "Thank you," she said, feeling the tightness in her chest dissipate as her lungs filled with the cold mountain air. "Sometimes I forget how easy it should be to breathe."

Gerard then took his time unfastening the back of her dress, beginning at her neck and moving slowly down to her lower back. Elara stepped away and ducked behind a panel to finish disrobing. She changed into a floor-length yellow night dress. The color reminded her of a daffodil. Her long dark curls cascaded down her back and over her bare shoulders. Gerard perched on the edge of her bed waiting. The queen approached him slowly as his eyes raked over her. He placed his hands on her waist and bent forward to kiss Elara on her shoulder.

"How is it possible you are even more beautiful now? I suppose I should leave you to your dreams." He stood and turned as if to leave, but Elara reached out her hand and grabbed his arm.

"Please stay. It has been an emotional day, and I don't wish to be alone."

Gerard smiled and said, "If the queen so demands it."

He grasped the blankets on her bed and pulled them back. Then, he lifted Elara off her feet and laid her in the center of the bed. Climbing up next to her, he pulled the pile of blankets up to their chests.

"I thought you wanted me to sleep," Elara said between playful kisses.

Gerard chuckled, then reluctantly pulled away. "I do. You need it." He sighed, placed a hand on her cheek, and stole one final kiss. His body radiated with warmth, and she nestled closer, resting her cheek against his chest.

"I'm glad you are here, Gerard. I only rest well when you are by my side."

"I shall always be here for you, Elara, and soon I shall be able to spend every night beside you."

She yawned rather loudly, then said, "I so look forward to that. I love you."

"And I love you," he said, holding her close as she drifted to sleep in his arms.

GUARDED

The enchanted ring remained hidden in Serena's pocket, and she couldn't stop thinking about her conversation with the queen the night before, even as Crystal prattled on about the weather. Warm rays of sunlight reached through the tree limbs overhead as they continued their trek forward. Serena closed her eyes and imagined what it would be like to enter the gates at the City of Mercy and at last meet Queen Elara Garrick in person.

"Serena, did you hear me?"

She opened her eyes and looked at Crystal, who had dismounted and was stroking Cinnamon's mane. Serena pulled back on her horse's reins, and Midnight came to a halt. "Oh, no, sorry," she said, blinking. "I was lost in thought. What were you saying?"

"We near Morlerae. We should walk from here," Crystal said. She lifted the hood of her dark green cloak and draped it over her head. "It's best we use the utmost caution while we're in town." Serena could no longer see Crystal's hair, and most of the guardian's face was concealed by her hood. A stranger could have mistaken her for a man. "Your turn," Crystal said, taking Midnight's reins in her hands and steadying the horse.

Serena dismounted; her boots slammed onto the hard ground and sent a cloud of dirt into the air. She pulled the hood of her cloak over her head until she could barely see under it. Crystal nodded and handed back her horse's bridles. They guided the animals on foot until they reached a clearing that had been trodden by many before them.

"This is the trail between the reservoir and Morlerae," the guardian said. "We are close." She led them to the left, and Serena followed her down the worn path.

After a short distance, Serena barely glimpsed a smile from under Crystal's hood as she turned to her and said, "We are here at last." Serena squinted ahead. She caught a glimpse of a stone wall between the trees and could hear the buzzing of many voices nearby.

"If we are stopped," Crystal said, "let me do the talking. There will be soldiers everywhere, some of whom may be on the lookout for you. We must be careful."

Serena nodded.

When they emerged from the edge of the forest, she was in awe of the vast city before them. As far as she could see to both sides, there was a thick stone wall surrounding the city, with several soldiers pacing along the top.

"There are but three ways to enter and exit Morlerae—all heavily guarded," Crystal said. "If asked, your name is Bianca George. Do you understand?"

"Bianca George," Serena repeated, her heartbeat quickening. "Perhaps we should not have come here."

"We have no choice." Crystal led them toward the nearest entrance. "The rest of the guardians await our arrival, although they will be expecting a much larger group." The guardian's gaze dropped to the ground, her expression heavy.

Serena sighed. "It's all right. My mum would be relieved to know I am under Elara's protection. I have only made it this far because of you."

Neither spoke as they approached the gate. The steady clopping of hooves against gravel mocked Serena's frantic heart beating against her ribcage. Peeking through grated bars, Serena swallowed hard as she saw four guards jesting with one another. The men snapped to attention, and their laughter ceased when the women reached the gate.

The man closest to the gate inquired about their business entering Morlerae. Looking through the slatted entrance at the uniformed man, Crystal said, "I am Cordelia Espenza, daughter of the innkeeper Francis. I was sent to retrieve my cousin Bianca from Kypno. She is to work for us as a barmaid."

Serena nodded to confirm the blonde's story, but she remained silent.

"Which inn is that?" a guard with a thick beard growled, scowling at Serena as two of the guards cranked open the steel gate.

"The Mocking Fox, of course," Crystal said with a wink. She stepped closer to the soldier, blocking his view of her charge.

"Remove your hoods," demanded another soldier, stepping closer to Serena. Crystal nonchalantly tossed her hood back and flashed a dazzling smile, gaining the attention of all the men. "My father will be very displeased if you don't let me in. He's expecting us." The guardian's coy flirtations were a perfect diversion, as none of the men could look away from her. In the meantime, Serena removed her own hood and shuffled to hide behind Crystal in unease.

The men glanced at each other for validation. Then a much younger soldier approached and said, "The innkeeper reported this to the brigade some weeks ago. Long journey for a young lady to take alone. Are you quite all right, miss?"

Crystal chuckled and said, "Of course! This is my home. I am quite familiar with these woods. It was an arduous journey, but I rested well in my aunt's home before we departed."

The soldiers accepted her answer and stepped aside, allowing them to enter the city. Just when they believed they were in the clear, the youngest soldier ran up behind them and said, "Please allow me to escort you. Which inn did you say it was again?"

Crystal glanced over her shoulder, once again feigning delight. "That is terribly kind of you, sir. It's The Mocking Fox." Giving Serena a look, the guardian took hold of both horses by the straps and nodded for her to step aside for the soldier.

"Ah, that one remains quite busy. There are hardly ever rooms available, but we enjoy the ale at the tavern." The soldier sauntered past Serena and joined Crystal a few steps ahead.

She touched his arm and said, "Yes, there is hardly ever a vacancy. We are blessed, indeed." The soldier continued with the pleasantries, clearly enamored by Serena's beautiful travel companion.

Serena remained a few feet behind them, glancing around nervously as she replaced her hood. She peered back at the soldiers guarding the gated entrance and wondered how Crystal would cleverly explain their departure in the coming days.

Dozens of vendors and customers lined the main road through Morlerae. Serena observed the merchants' wares, eventually stopping to admire some embroidered blouses in the window of one shop. In its reflection, she thought she caught sight of a hooded figure lurking behind her, but when she turned around, no one was there. Then she realized Crystal and the soldier had also disappeared.

"She is going to kill me," Serena muttered. She ducked into the clothing shop and asked a voluptuous red-haired woman, "How would I find The Mocking Fox? I'm afraid I have lost my way."

"The inn be just down the main road to yer left. Before ye go... I see ye have need of a new blouse. Did ye find trouble in the woods, miss?"

Serena looked down and realized her dirty, bloodstained shirt was partially visible under her cloak. Pulling the cloak to the center to cover it, she smiled and said, "Oh, it's nothing. I cut up my hand on thorns while picking berries." She pretended to look at the blouses and cloaks on display. "These are quite beautiful."

"Do ye have any coin on ye?" the woman asked. "If not, ye need not lurk about here."

Serena pulled two coins from her pocket and flashed them at the woman. "What can I get for two silver pieces?"

The woman perked up. "Any of these," she said as she motioned to two tables in the center of the store. The tables were covered in blouses in any color she could imagine. Serena handed both coins to the woman, who greedily stuffed them into the top of her dress. Smiling, the woman said, "Chose whichever ye like, miss."

The shopkeeper stepped out into the road, and Serena watched her through the window. The woman was baiting other consumers to enter her shop by pointing out damage to their attire. Taking advantage of her moment alone, Serena lifted a cornflower blue blouse made of thicker material. The long sleeves would be useful when they journeyed north into the mountains.

"That would look quite fetching on you," a raspy, unfamiliar voice said from behind her.

Startled, Serena spun and nearly ran into a man whose oversized black cloak concealed his eyes. Immediately, goosebumps swept over her arms, and her spine tingled. "Oh, thank you, sir. I should be going."

The man's lips curled in an unnerving smirk as he chuckled. "So polite. I am surprised a pretty little thing like you has eluded me for this long."

She stepped backward and bumped into a table. Her eyes darted around, searching for anything she could use as a weapon. "Are you the man who attacked me?" she asked, her heartbeat pounding in her ears. She reached a shaking hand toward her belt and realized in horror that her sword was not attached. Her bag was still draped over her horse, and Crystal was nowhere near.

"Not I. But it doesn't surprise me that you have other admirers. I did leave you some pretty little flowers, though." The man stepped toward her, and she ducked underneath the wooden table covered in colorful blouses. As she scrambled, trying to crawl away, the man stooped down and grabbed her by the ankles, dragging her back toward him. "What's the rush, young lady?" he asked with an exasperated expression.

A piercing pain shot through Serena's left arm as she rolled on the floor. Wincing, she clutched at her injured shoulder. For a moment, she thought she had been stabbed a second time. "Let me go!" Serena shrieked, kicking her attacker hard in the chest.

He stumbled backward and hit a table with such force that it flipped. "I will get you good for that," the man spat, his breath haggard as he struggled back onto his feet.

Fighting the wave of pain, Serena slid under the table. Without looking back, she stumbled onto her feet and yanked open the shop door. She ran into town, her eyes raking the streets for her guardian. Just as she passed a second building, someone reached out and grabbed her by the waist, pulling her into a dark alley. She gasped when the figure pinned her against a wall. As she tried to scream, he quickly covered her mouth with his hand.

"Shhh," he whispered, leaning close and locking eyes with her. "It's me, Will. You're safe. Don't panic." He removed the hand from her mouth and leaned his shoulder against the wall, blocking her view of the street.

Her eyes widened as she yanked off his hood, revealing the familiar disheveled waves and warm eyes of her friend from Durmak. "Will!" she gasped. "What are you doing here? How—"

He wrapped his arms around her waist before she could finish her question. Serena gasped, pressing her palms against his chest. He had never shown her such affection before. When Will released her, he said, "My stars, Serena, what is going on? You left without warning. We didn't know what to think. The Elders dared question if you had—"

"Don't finish that sentence!" Serena shoved him away in anger, breathing heavily, and furrowed her brows. "What are you doing here? You should be in Durmak." She went to shove past Will, but he seized her by the wrist.

"You left without a word. Talitha said you went in the house, but you were gone when I got there with the Elders. Everyone was upset."

"And you think I wasn't?" She yanked her arm out of his grasp and stepped back, crossing them over her chest. "How did you find me? It's been weeks since I left."

"Talitha, the Elders, the whole town searched for you for a week with no luck. We couldn't fathom how you could just vanish," Will said, his eyes locking on hers with intensity. Serena's gaze flickered uneasily between Will and the bustling street behind him. "I went to Murmont. I spoke with Cameron. He was shocked, of course. I wish I hadn't had to tell him what happened."

Serena hung her head and pressed her lips together, fighting the ache in her chest. "You told him I was missing?"

"He's your brother," Will said. "I hoped he'd help me search for you."

"He left us behind. He and our father," Serena said, her voice rising. "I don't need either of them anymore."

Will scoffed. "I checked every town from Durmak to Murmont for you. Imagine my surprise when I stopped to speak with the blacksmith and spotted you entering the shop across the street."

Her mouth hung open in surprise. "Were you looking for work here?" Serena asked. "You're not returning home?"

"I don't know yet," he admitted. "If I could find someone to finish my apprenticeship, that would be nice. I could return home and take over your father's forge when I complete my training."

"Papa would be proud if you did. He enjoyed working with you," she said quietly.

"And what would he think about you running off on your own? It's not safe for a young woman to be out here alone."

She fidgeted, avoiding his impatient gaze. "Mama told me to leave with her dying breath. To get out before it's too late. I had no choice but to run."

"You should have gone to Murmont. At least Cameron could have protected you," he argued. His shirt sleeves strained against his biceps as he crossed his arms, and Serena quickly looked away.

"Showing up at the stronghold would have been a terrible idea," she snapped.

"Seeing you alive isn't enough, Rena. I need answers," he said as he stepped closer. "What am I supposed to tell everyone back home? They all want to know why you left. They'd want to know where you were going."

Serena held her hands up and shrugged. She exhaled and realized her knuckles were white. She loosened her grip on her new blouse, feeling the blood rush to her fingers. "I really must find the inn," she said.

As she tried to walk past Will, he reached out an arm to block her path. "So that's it? You're just going to walk away?" Serena sighed and scrunched her face. No answer was going to satisfy him.

"I can't go back to Durmak, Will. This is for the best." Will protested, but she ignored him and pulled her hood over her head. "I must go."

"Would you just let me help you?" He grabbed her arm, and his touch set her skin ablaze. Her mind raced with entangled memories of Will with her dear brothers. "I swear! You're even more stubborn than my sister," he groaned.

There was once a day when she'd have basked in his attention; she would have swooned to see him demonstrate such care for her. But gone were those carefree days. Now she needed to survive, and she had no time for silly childhood crushes. "You can't help me, Will," she said, wishing he could. He uttered a guttural growl and pulled his hand back from her. Peering into the street, Serena paused and said quietly, "I hear The Mocking Fox has good ale. Perhaps I'll see you later."

Serena returned to scanning the area for Crystal. She had only gone a few feet up the crowded street when she made eye contact with her. When Serena reached her, the guardian grasped her by the shoulders and examined her, asking, "Are you all right? Were you injured?" Her eyes darted over Serena.

Serena looked away but tried to assure her. "I'm fine. I just got distracted in the market, and then a creepy man got in my face."

"Creepy man?" Crystal repeated, her narrowed eyes glancing back toward the market.

"I'm fine," Serena said again. "He had no weapon. Just put his hands on me."

"Blazing embers," Crystal muttered. Yanking the blouse from Serena's hands, the guardian pushed her right shoulder and said, "Don't wander off again!"

Serena rubbed her sore arm. "It wasn't intentional. The market distracted me. I've never seen such a grand market."

"You say that in every city, but there are far greater sights ahead," Crystal laughed. When she tossed the shirt back at Serena, the ball of blue fabric hit her in the face and fell into her hands.

"Well, it is the greatest I have seen so far," Serena corrected, folding the blouse over her uninjured arm. "Where's the inn? You must be tired. I certainly am."

Turning, Crystal pointed to a sizable building made of red-brown brick off in the distance and to the right. "There," the guardian said. They maneuvered their way through the crowded street until they reached the front door, above which hung a rusting iron cutout of a fox. Crystal pushed open the door, and Serena followed her into the teeming tavern, taken aback by the boisterous patrons crammed inside. Crystal steered them through several tables and past a doorway on the left, beyond which lay a small kitchen. Leading them down a hallway to the right, she stopped before a flight of stairs with a sign boasting: "Fox Family Only." Smiling at the sign, Crystal began to ascend the narrow stairway with purpose and determination, like a hunter who had cornered her prey.

"Are you sure we can go up there?" Serena asked. She took a few hesitant steps and peered back down the empty hall.

"Yes, of course. I am Cordelia Espenza, after all." Crystal winked over her shoulder at Serena.

On the second floor was a small passage with six closed doors. Crystal walked straight ahead and opened the door at the end of the hall without knocking. Serena's eyes widened, and she froze in the middle of the hallway.

Crystal took a few steps into the room and asked, "Have you lot missed me?"

A woman squealed, "Crystal! You're back!" Metal clanked against the floor then, causing Serena to jump in surprise.

Seconds later, a glowing young woman rushed forward and threw her arms around the blonde archer. "We were beginning to wonder if something had happened to you."

Crystal laughed and hugged her friend back. "You cannot get rid of me so easily."

"Did you make it to Durmak? Did you find them?" her friend asked.

Curious, Serena stepped closer to the doorway to get a better look at the young woman. She was tall and lean with a wide, dazzling smile. Her raven hair cascaded over her shoulders in large, loose curls. Her arms were bare, her bronzed muscles on full display, and a short sword was strapped to one of her thighs over black pants. Though sweat dripped down her temples, Serena found her striking. The beautiful stranger must have been around Crystal's age, she thought.

"No and yes." Crystal glanced back at girl in the hallway. "Serena, I want you to meet Xandra." She gestured for her to join them.

Xandra. Serena remembered Crystal mentioning her name. Xandra was another guardian from the Garrick Guard. Serena walked through the doorway and extended a hand. Xandra shook it and grinned, a twinkle in her eyes. "You found the Finches after all! What glorious news!"

Serena bit her lip and looked down at their hands. Xandra gave a firm handshake, her callouses like sandpaper against Serena's palm. She pulled back her hand and wondered what would cause these beautiful young women to join the queen's service in the height of a brewing war.

"I'm afraid I did not make it in time," Crystal said. "Mary Finch and the younger boys were killed before I arrived. I was lucky enough to find Serena before anyone else. She has been through a great ordeal these past few weeks."

Xandra gently squeezed Serena's shoulder and frowned. "Oh, I am terribly sorry."

"Serena Finch is in the care of the Garrick Guard now," said Crystal. "We promised the queen to bring whoever we can to safety, and that we shall."

"That we shall!" a voice boomed from across the room. Serena realized a pasty young man with lightly freckled skin and copper hair had been watching them. He stood near the window with a sword hanging down by his side. His shirt was tinged with splotches of sweat, as if he had just been running. After a final glance at the busy street below, he sheathed his weapon and sauntered toward them with a smirk on his face. "Good to see you again, Crys."

"Rigel DeVarr," Crystal said as she crossed her arms and looked him over. "I half expected you to get distracted and stay in Axys."

"How you doubt my loyalty," Rigel said with a scoff. "We had no luck finding anyone the queen was looking for. Cole said there was no reason to linger, so we came back. What took you so long? I am quite tired of being cooped up here." He narrowed his eyes, deep and blue as the sea. "This is Serena Finch?" he asked. When she nodded, he reached for her hand, bending his head to kiss her knuckles.

"I'm nobody, really," Serena stuttered, drawing back her hand. "My parents knew the queen long ago. I knew nothing of it. I'm not sure I was worth all this trouble."

"Nonsense! We came for the Finches, and even saving just one of you makes this journey worth it," Xandra assured Serena with a smile.

"And the queen shall be quite pleased to see you," Rigel added.

"Thank you. For helping me, I mean." Serena glanced between the three guardians. She could not fathom how she had gone from hiding in the woods to being protected by a group of Queen Elara's elite warriors. However, her mind drifted to thoughts of Will, who thought she should return to Durmak. She swallowed and tried to push his face out of her mind.

"It's our pleasure, milady," Rigel said, bowing his head.

Crystal jabbed him in the ribs. He stumbled back a step but laughed. "Rigel," she said, "stop that. You're making Serena uncomfortable." Then she rolled her eyes. "I still think we should leave you or Cole behind. It would be beneficial to have another spy on this side of the border."

At that moment, Serena sensed someone standing behind her in the doorway, and a deep voice said, "Come now, sister. Is that any way to treat your kin?"

The man was taller than Rigel with familiar light skin and platinum hair. He scrutinized Serena with icy sapphire orbs, and she stepped back nervously until she bumped into Xandra.

Crystal raised an eyebrow and crossed her arms. "Alarcole."

"Crystalira," he said with a nod, and the edge of his lips curled up. "I was starting to wonder if I'd ever see you again."

Serena snorted and covered her mouth with one hand. "Sorry? Crystalira? Such a... unique name."

"My name is Crystal," the guardian replied, her scowl searing into her older brother.

Rigel covered his mouth in a futile attempt to hold back his snickering. Glancing at her fuming friend, Xandra quickly said, "Their parents were quite original! It really is no wonder they both shorten their names." She approached

Alarcole, touched his arm, and said, "Cole, this is Serena Finch. Try not to scare her."

Alarcole pulled his arm away from Xandra and stepped closer to Serena. He looked down at her. "So you're the reason we're here. The family worth the gamble of coming all this way."

Crystal stepped forward and tossed an arm over her brother's shoulders. "Brother, you are as cold as ever. May I remind you that you volunteered for this mission?"

They exchanged frigid looks, and Cole said, "I am only here to make sure you three do not get yourselves killed."

"Then you should have stayed in Envyre because we are all well past the age of needing guardianship."

Cole smirked at his sister. "And let you have all the fun?" He turned his attention back to Serena and asked, "So where's the rest of the Finch brood? Were there not six of you?"

"Mary Finch and her two youngest were killed weeks ago," Crystal said. "The eldest is in Murmont. Her father's traveled somewhere north; she does not know where. She'll be the only Finch to make the crossing with us. The least you can do is be kind."

"Kindness is a luxury in wartime," the stoic warrior replied, and his sister growled under her breath and buried her face in one hand.

Serena stared into his steel eyes, unsure why he was still studying her. The hard look threatened to slice her deeper than any blade. Then she realized how unkempt she looked. Her cheeks flushed as she frantically ran her fingers through her tangled hair, wishing that the floor would swallow her up and out of sight.

Cole remained fixed on Serena as he said, "Even the strongest fall when grief clouds their judgment. Our enemies look for that sort of weakness. It's easy to snuff out. You must put aside your self-pity and focus on your future, lest you join the dead."

Xandra and Rigel dared not respond to this bitter sentiment, but Crystal lunged toward her brother. The other two guardians were quick to block her path, preventing her from punching him. "I'm sorry, Serena," Crystal said with a huff. "My brother stopped having common courtesy long ago. If only he could burn our enemies with his careless words."

But the apology meant nothing. His words had already pierced Serena's heart, and she struggled to keep her bearing. "Alarcole, was it?" she asked, taking in the spectacle of the frustrated warriors from New Hyrosencia. "Obviously, you have never lost someone you loved, or you would know such pain cannot be forgotten."

Something flashed in Cole's eyes, and the muscles in his jaw tightened as he turned away from her, stalking over to the window. "You know nothing about me," he muttered, peering down at the people in the streets below. Serena thought perhaps her words had meant something to him, but she dared not ask.

Crystal stepped toward her and interrupted. "Serena, you don't have to—"

"No," she said, holding out one palm to stop Crystal. "I must." The guardians stood in silence, waiting while she swiped at tears under her eyes. Turning back to the cold stranger, Serena said, "I held my mother as she passed from this world, and there was nothing I could do to save her. I shall forever be in mourning. But do not mistake my grief for weakness. This pain is what keeps me going. I thought I lost everything. Then someone reminded me I still have my life, and that is everything. I will not stop fighting for it." Serena lowered her trembling hand.

Cole clomped out from behind the guardians and stepped closer, looking down his nose at her. When he leaned forward, he paused a few inches from her face and said, "You are unusually confident for someone so broken. One day you will realize you cannot mourn forever and truly live. I advise you to find strength and purpose in something other than your dead. Love and grief cause blind spots. It's all a distraction meant to make you dependent on others. That's why I do not allow silly feelings like love to dictate my actions."

Rigel and Xandra frowned at his words, glancing at each other.

Crystal took her quiver and hurled it at her brother. Arrows scattered across the floor. "Father would be so proud of you, Alarcole," she said. "You are a stiff bastard just like him."

"Maybe one day Rigel's empathy will rub off on him," Xandra said with a grin.

Serena said, "I do not know you, Alarcole, but I think I know your sister well enough. I was not raised to be a warrior, yet she still sees value in me—despite my emotions. She saved my life. She does not care that I am grieving. She cares that I am still breathing. If you think normal people to be so frail, why have you come here?"

"Elara did not just task us with bringing the Finches to Symptee," Cole said. "She insisted you be taught to defend yourselves. That is why I am here. I am not here to be kind to you nor pity you. I am here to teach you how to protect yourself."

Serena looked to Crystal, who nodded. "That is true. You should learn how to protect yourself. The four of us will guard you with our lives, but we shall also be your mentors. Soon, we hope you will not need anyone to save you. Maybe you shall even save us."

"Maidens are such delicate creatures," Cole moaned. "It's much better to train younglings. They learn to heed only their training."

"That's not true!" Xandra argued. "I was an excellent student, and I have never been blind to my feelings or those around me."

Cole's gaze lingered on the woman for a moment. Just as he opened his mouth to respond to Xandra, Serena cut in.

"Missing my family doesn't make me delicate. If anything, it gives me strength. Anyone who has known love would suffer when they have lost it," she said. "I believe our feelings can change the course of this war. Ordinary people like me only fight because love gives us something to fight for."

Cole rolled his eyes and walked over to the window, gazing down at the busy street. "I care not how long you grieve, as long as you learn to wield the sword you carry. You should at least make your family proud."

"I know my mother is proud of me already," Serena hissed. "I can live with the pain of losing them. I shall not be fighting this war in a blind rage. I want to protect myself and anyone else who is in danger."

Placing a reassuring hand on Serena's back, Crystal said, "We all wish to bring an end to the unnecessary bloodshed. The guardians have made vows to protect the Hyrosencians while we work to restore the rightful heir to the throne."

Serena nodded. "I am grateful you've given yourselves to this cause. I hope you are able to succeed in your goals."

"Right now, our main goal is to get you to Symptee alive," Rigel said.

"I don't want any of you to die trying to protect me," she mumbled, picking at her fingernails. "I should rather die than see another fall before my eyes."

"The maiden is a martyr," said Cole, unsheathing his sword. "Fret not. Once I'm finished training you, you won't need anyone to take the edge of a sword for you."

Crystal grunted and tossed up her arms. "I think we have had enough of you for one day, brother. Let her rest. There shall be time for training in the coming weeks."

Rigel approached Cole and plopped a hand on his shoulder. "Come. Let us spar while the women rest," the guardian said. "You're more frustrated than usual today."

"Come to our room," Xandra chirped, grasping Crystal and Serena each by one arm and pulling them toward the hallway with a smile. "You'll stay with me until we leave Morlerae."

Crystal nodded and followed her friend out of the room. From the doorway, Serena glanced back at Rigel and Cole, who were practicing their sword skills.

She watched in awe as the two warriors crossed blades. The gleaming metal flashed and clanged like lightning. Rigel noticed Serena watching, and Cole used this distraction to his advantage, kicking the redhead roughly. He stumbled backward into a wall, and Cole swung his blade swiftly toward Rigel. Serena gasped as Cole stopped his sword less than an inch from his throat. "You lose again," Cole said with a grin.

Rigel chuckled. "That doesn't count. She distracted me." He looked at Serena and smiled, pushing Cole's sword away from his neck.

Turning to look at her, Cole said, "Never let anyone catch you off guard."

"The indignity," said Rigel, dropping his sword onto the floor and holding up his hands in surrender. "One day, I shall best you, friend."

Reaching out a hand to help Rigel to his feet, Cole said, "I doubt that, but you can try."

Crystal called from the hallway, "Serena! Come join us."

Leaving the men behind, Serena walked down the hall until she found the women in a bedroom to the left. Crystal and Xandra laughed and smiled as if there were no dangers ahead of them. Serena crossed the threshold and sat on the edge of a modest bed next to Crystal. She was quiet for a while, listening while the warriors spoke of their time apart. As she listened to them discuss their journey into Hyrosencia, Serena was reminded of just how different she was from them. She wondered if she would ever be capable of defending herself from people as skilled as the guardians.

OLD FRIENDS

Cameron descended the steep steps into the dark and damp dungeon of Graynor Castle. He nodded as they greeted the guards on duty, and Captain Pelham informed them they were there to question the girl from Durmak. Something in Cameron's chest tightened as he wondered who it might be.

When they reached the end of a long hallway, one of the guards jammed a thick key into the door. The mechanism clicked loudly as he turned it. As the guard pulled the door open, Cameron squinted into the dimly lit cell, his eyes widening as they focused on the girl hunched in the corner. He'd recognize her red hair anywhere.

"Talitha?" he breathed, stepping forward.

His captain stuck an arm out to stop him. "So, you do know her." Pelham grinned.

Cameron saw something menacing flicker through the captain's eyes and swallowed hard. "Yes, sir," he mumbled, turning back toward the cell.

Tired eyes blinked at him from the dark corner, her brow furrowed as she stared at him. "Prince Anteros?" she asked, her voice gravely as she pushed herself upright. As she shifted into the torch light, Cameron sucked in a breath. She was paler and thinner than he remembered, her cream frock tattered and stained.

Pelham stepped into Cameron's line of sight and leaned in, murmuring, "She's been very secretive. See what you can find out."

The captain turned and headed back down the hall. The guard motioned one thumb over his shoulder and said, "Best get in there. Time is ticking. Don't waste it." His lips curled up as he went back to patrolling the dungeon hall, shooting a wink over his shoulder.

Cameron stepped through the doorway, filling his lungs with the musty air as he approached his old neighbor. "Hey," he said quietly, noticing the way she clutched her legs tight against her chest. "It's me, Cameron."

She relaxed a bit as her eyes focused on his face, widening with realization. "Cameron?" she stuttered. "What are you doing here?"

He squatted in front of her, reaching out for her arm, but she squirmed and shoved her back against the wall. "Don't," she said.

He followed the line of freckles down her neck to her bare shoulder, wondering how she had more freckles than before. He had been gone less than a year. But as he looked her over for wounds, he realized those weren't all freckles; some spots were dried flecks of blood.

"What happened to you?" he pressed, resting his arms on his thighs. His calves burned, but he didn't want to sit on the grimy dungeon floor in his uniform.

Talitha turned to look at him, her jaw tensing as she glared at his uniform. "Maybe you should ask what hasn't happened to me," she muttered, leaning her head back against the wall as she exhaled. "Do you know? About what happened?"

Cameron looked down, fixating on a deep crack in the floor. "Yes. Will came to Murmont. He told me everything. At least, everything he knew."

Talitha nodded. "I should have gone with him. If I hadn't been in the woods alone, they wouldn't have harassed me and brought me here." She swung her arm out, gesturing around the cell.

"Why have they imprisoned you? What did you do? You must have done something, upset someone," he tried to reason.

Her brows raised as she pressed her lips together, scoffing quietly. "What did I do?" she repeated with an edge to her voice. "I didn't do anything. I was out looking for your sister!"

Cameron sighed and lifted his hands in surrender. "Look, I'm sorry. I didn't mean to—"

"I know what you think, Cameron," she said. Her eyes were more gray than blue now, reflecting the bleak interior of the cell. He had never seen such hostility in her gaze growing up. Now she reminded him of a feral cat, teeth bared and ready to tear him apart at the slightest misstep. "I have nothing to say to you. You're one of them now."

"What's that supposed to mean?" he asked, his voice defensive as he leaned in.

"If you're on Rexton's side, I'm done talking to you," Talitha roared, her voice echoing down the hall. Realizing her error, she shrank down, eyes wide as she waited to be punished.

Cameron blinked at her, uncertain how she had come to be a prisoner in the king's castle. From the sound of it, she wasn't willing to talk to any of Rexton's men about the incident in Durmak. "Tal, I don't know what happened to you, but I need your help to find Serena. Wherever she is, she isn't safe."

"No woman is safe in Hyrosencia," she hissed, turning her body to face the lone window in her cell.

Her accusation caught him off guard for only a moment before he remembered the king's words. Graynor was safe. If he brought Serena there, she would be protected from whoever was out there hurting innocent people. "If there's anything you can think of from the day she disappeared, I need you to tell me," he pleaded, stepping out on one foot so he could see her face better.

Talitha closed her eyes as a thin beam of sunlight cast its golden glow on a small strip of her face. "Get me out of here, Cam. Get me out, and I'll go with you. I'll tell you everything I saw, everything others have said. Just get me out. Please." She grabbed his forearm and squeezed, though her grip was meager, her strength diminished.

Cameron yanked his arm out of her grasp, inspecting his sleeve for traces of dirt. With a heavy exhale, he stood and shook his head. "You don't know anything, do you? You're about as useful to me as Will was."

Tears glistened in the corners of her eyes as she hugged her arms against her chest. "I've told a dozen men that. No one listens to me. They keep asking questions that I don't have any answers to. I don't know where Serena is!"

He scoffed, stepping closer until his shadow fell over her trembling frame. "Some friend you are, letting Serena run off like that," Cameron said through his teeth. He could hear the guard's heavy footfall coming down the hallway, and he wanted them to know he was on the king's side, not Talitha's. "As long as she's out there on her own, I won't be risking my neck to get you out of here."

"Don't leave me here," Talitha choked on her sobs, covering her face with her filthy hands.

Cameron's lips twisted in disgust as he took in her pathetic state one last time before heading toward the door. In the doorway, he locked eyes with the guard and shook his head. "It's time you and Serena learn to get out of your own messes," he said to her without looking back. Whoever she had angered, it did not matter; there was no way he could help her as a lowly foot soldier. The king would not be pleased that he didn't get any new information out of her, yet he wondered why the king's men were so sure she was hiding something. He marched down the hall past full cells filled with starving men, clenching his fists at his sides as the clink of a lock chased after him.

SERENA CLOSED HER EYES and allowed her mind to drift back to Durmak as Crystal and Xandra continued in deep conversation. Despite Rexton's tyrannical reign over Hyrosencia, she had never felt unsafe in her hometown. Her family lived, loved, and never wanted for anything. It seemed like ages ago when her greatest concern was whether Will Burroughs might start looking at her differently. Now when she thought of returning to Durmak with him, she was haunted by the memory of her family's massacre.

"Wasn't it, Serena?" Crystal asked.

"Wasn't what?" She looked up to see Crystal and Xandra staring at her.

"I said that the attack was so sudden, we barely had time to react. It was so bloody dark," Crystal repeated, shaking her head. "It was fortunate we managed to escape with our lives."

"Fortunate," Serena said with a faint laugh, touching her shoulder gingerly.

Xandra insisted on seeing the wound herself, despite Serena's uneasiness. Xandra inspected the wound, running her fingers gingerly along the healing gash. "It has healed quite well in such a short time. Crystal has quite the talent for healing. She has helped me out in a pinch a time or two."

Crystal laid back on the bed. "It really is nothing. Xandra exaggerates. She has never been so severely injured as you were, Serena."

They continued their conversation until Serena's stomach grumbled, drawing their attention. "I suppose we ought to feed the poor girl before she faints," Xandra said. She laughed, stood up, and stretched her arms overhead. "The Mocking Fox has an excellent cook. It's been nice to have a taste of home these past few weeks."

Crystal and Serena followed her down the narrow stairwell to the busy tavern, where they quietly enjoyed a hot meal. Serena scanned the room but did not recognize any of the faces in the tavern. When they returned upstairs, the rest of the afternoon was more of the same casual chatter. Crystal and Xandra proved to be the closest of friends, picking up as if no time had passed. This time Serena listened, eager to learn more about the warriors who were to accompany her to New Hyrosencia. She learned that after Sir Alexander Stanton took his daughter to Symptee at the start of the war, he was promoted to Commander of the Guard for recruiting several new allies.

"Queen Elara knew it was essential that she solidify alliances in order to fight the threat of Rexton's growing armies," Xandra said. "The dwarfs were surprisingly supportive during our journey over the mountains. Living between feuding kingdoms, they saw it best to pledge their loyalty to Elara since they had a longtime understanding with the Garricks."

"Of course, the elves were a different story entirely," said Crystal, rolling her eyes. She pulled her legs up onto the bed and crossed them.

"Elves? I thought they never left their territory," said Serena. "I know so little of the dwarfs and the elves. My father said neither would dare to enter Hyrosencia."

"There is a dark history that divides humans and elves," said Crystal. "Long ago, some humans sought the source of the elves' longevity in the most cunning ways. They thought if they drank or even bathed in Elven blood, they could achieve immortality."

"Gross," Xandra and Serena said in unison, their mouths wrinkling in disgust.

"One particularly stupid man thought he could learn Elven secrets by seducing their princess," Crystal said. "That was disastrous, of course."

"What happened?" Serena asked, leaning in.

"That oaf learned the hard way that there is no way for humans to achieve immortality. The princess was distraught, of course. She mourned him for a century before releasing her soul from this cruel world."

"She killed herself?" Serena whispered.

"Though elves may resemble humans outwardly, they are an altogether separate race," Xandra said. "They outlive humans by hundreds of years, and they only take one companion in their lifetime. His was the highest form of betrayal. She could never move on, never have a babe of her own. I imagine she was heartbroken."

Crystal added, "The queen spent nearly a century stewing in her bitterness toward humans, especially men. The current queen and Elders harbor the same resentment. It's considered the highest offense for an elf to choose a human companion to this day. The penalty is banishment from the lands of plenty."

"Lands of plenty? Is that where Symptee was built?" asked Serena.

"No. I speak of Ord Metsiilva, the homelands of the Elven clans," Crystal replied.

"They are known to think quite highly of themselves. They have the most beautiful faces and richest lands that you could ever imagine," Xandra said, chuckling and looking at the quiet girl sitting across from her. "Have you never heard any stories of them, Serena?"

Serena shook her head. "My father told a few tales of the other races, but we were skeptical. I've never met a soul who has seen either. I assumed if elves were real, their lands must be quite far from our kingdom."

Xandra laughed. "The four of us—well, all guardians—were trained by elves. That's why we're considered elite members of the Guard."

Serena blinked, leaned back, and inspected Xandra and Crystal. Then she asked, "How could you not tell me that? That is outstanding!"

"You never asked," Crystal muttered. She leaned her back against the wall and shrugged. Seeing Serena's interest, she added, "We were in the first class of warriors trained at the Envyre Academy, which included both elves and humans."

Xandra beamed as she said, "My father brought me with him to negotiate with the Elven queen when I was a child. She agreed to welcome humans into two cities and allowed her warriors to train any Hyrosencians who wished to learn to fight. I began my training nearly 14 years ago."

"Fourteen? But you are so young," Serena said, horrified. "You would have been a child then."

"Aye, I was, but my father wanted me to be able to protect myself. I was hesitant at first, but I wanted to learn. He left me in the care of the Academy. Dozens of young Hyrosencians were raised by elves, learning how to fight as they do. Perhaps the ferocity of the elves rubbed off on me a bit. It certainly surprised my father when I decided to join the Guard."

"Wow," Serena said. Looking at Crystal, she said jokingly, "I thought you said Elara did not enlist children."

Xandra's eyes went wide, and she shook her head. "She doesn't. I shall be twenty-four soon, and I have been in the Guard under three years."

Crystal sucked her teeth loudly. "The Guard does not accept anyone under eighteen. The elves train anyone who wants to learn. They do not discriminate by age as they begin training their own children young. It made sense to offer asylum and training to a generation of scared children. Most parents were quite eager to have their children learn for their own safety. It's a great honor to learn—and not easy to do. We would not be so skilled if we had not begun training as children."

"The elves took good care of us in Envyre," Xandra said. "They train children until they turn eighteen. After that, select trainees can continue their training with elite tutors if they wish. I began training when I was nine and left the Academy when I turned twenty-one. We went to the City of Mercy to compete for our positions as guardians."

"You had to compete to become a guardian?" Serena asked.

Xandra nodded. "Yes, only the best can become guardians," she said with a smug smile. "There are different levels to the Garrick Guard. Men like my father were trained decades ago to be knights, protectors of the royal family. The few knights who remain now serve as the queen's most trusted advisors on the War Council. Then there are those who were trained by the knights at the start of the war. Those officers deal with the security of Symptee and the adjacent city of Lexilor. Then there are those of us who have spent ten or more years training with the elves. We are considered the most skilled—besides the Elven warriors, of course. In action, elves are unlike anything you could imagine."

Crystal and Xandra exchanged a glimpse and grinned at each other. Serena was intrigued by the brief history she had heard.

"Crystal, why didn't you tell me about Envyre earlier? I should have loved to hear more about your training with the elves," Serena said.

The blonde woman swung her legs over the side of the bed and slammed her bare feet on the floor. "It's not safe to speak of such things—not out in the open. Do not be so naïve as to think the people in Hyrosencia would take such a story lightly. Rexton would have our heads if the wrong people heard of it."

"He could try," Xandra said with a confident grin. Serena did not understand how someone who was raised as a warrior during a time of great anguish in her kingdom could laugh so much. Then again, she and her brothers had once laughed, smiled, and given little thought to those struggling elsewhere.

"If the elves resent humans, why did they start allowing you into their land and training you?" Serena asked.

Crystal thought seriously for a moment before she said, "I shall tell you a bit more about the Elven history, but only a little. It would be impossible to teach you everything I've learned over the years, but I can tell you more about why the elves have hated humans for over a century, and what has changed since then."

Serena beamed as Crystal moved to sit beside her. Xandra spread herself out on the other bed.

"For centuries, the Elven clan of Silveryl has prospered in the forests of Ord Metsiilva, indifferent to the existence of humans," said Crystal. "But one day long ago, an Elven princess was tricked by a man. He made her believe he loved her. He lay with her. Then one night, he slit her throat while she slept. He believed that if he drank her blood, he too would live for centuries. The princess was nearly lost. Healers were able to save her, but she was never the same again. From then on, the Elders felt that humans were too selfish and violent to be trusted. The princess' niece, Queen Daephyra— High Queen of the Elves—has scorned humans all her life for their betrayal."

"But when my father and I traveled to meet with the elves," Xandra said, "Queen Daephyra took pity on Queen Elara for having been betrayed by a brutal man, as her aunt had once been. It was the first time she had given humans an audience during her reign. Even though the elves look down on the humans, they were willing to teach us how to fight for ourselves because the Garricks had never sought to harm them."

"I also think Queen Daephyra feared that if she refused, Antoine Rexton would kill the refugees and advance on her own kingdom," Crystal added.

"Whatever the case, the elves have been a crucial ally to us," Xandra said. "Perhaps one day you shall meet a member of the Silveryl Clan and witness their immense abilities."

Crystal nudged Xandra, who laid back and laughed.

"Perhaps we should retire early this evening. It has been a long journey," said Crystal.

"I'm not yet tired, but you should rest," Xandra said, standing up and patting the bed. "I'll be right down the hall if you need anything."

Crystal and Serena sat in silence for a few minutes after Xandra left. "I'm sorry I didn't tell you more these prior weeks," Crystal said. "It was important to know we were somewhere safe. I hope you can understand that."

"I can," said Serena. "How do you know we are truly safe here?" She thought back to the soldiers who manned the gates and kept the streets orderly.

"This half of The Mocking Fox is reserved for loyalists. The owner, Francis, is the son of a guardsman who died long before the war began," said Crystal. "It's protected by powerful magic—as the cabin is. We may sleep, spar, and speak in privacy."

Crystal settled into one bed, facing away from Serena. She pulled a blanket up over her arms and sighed. When Serena heard Crystal's breathing change, she knew the guardian was finally asleep, and she would soon be able to sneak downstairs to look for Will. Less than an hour later, Serena took the opportunity to head down to the tavern while Crystal snored faintly. As she crept into the hallway, she bumped into someone.

"Where do you think you're going?"

She turned to see Cole, who scowled at her like a father scolding his child. Taking a deep breath, Serena stammered, "I thought I would go down for a quick supper. Crystal is sleeping, and I would hate to wake her."

Cole nodded, quirking up one eyebrow as he said, "Suppose I shall join you then. Can't leave you unattended after all the trouble my sister went through saving your life." Placing a hand firmly on her back, he nudged her forward, following close behind as they descended the stairway.

When the barkeep came to their table, Cole ordered the evening special for both of them, as well as two pints of ale.

"Oh, no, thank you. I do not drink ale," Serena said quickly.

"Good... because both are for me," he said, dropping some coins in the barkeep's hand. "She'll have water."

Serena felt a sudden heat spread through her face, and she scanned the tavern for signs of her friend. Cole chuckled and asked, "Are you displeased by my company?"

Turning her face toward the arrogant guardian, she frowned and said, "Well, Alarcole, you would not have been my first choice."

Cole's smirk faded into a stern expression. "Who were you hoping to see?" he asked. His eyes shifted to scan the faces in the tavern. It was busy, nearly every table was packed with boisterous patrons.

"I thought perhaps Xandra might be—"

"Don't bother lying. I can tell when a foolish girl is hiding something," Cole said. The intensity with which he stared at her face was unnerving, and Serena swallowed hard, shifting on the bench. She feared his gaze would burn straight into her mind and discover Will lurking in an alley. Shaking his head, Cole leaned back and crossed his arms over his chest. "Xandra is upstairs, but we both know you already knew that."

Serena shifted again, allowing her eyes to scan the faces behind Cole. Will was not among the dinner patrons. She exhaled in frustration as the barkeep returned carrying three mugs and placed them on the table. Turning her gaze back to the guardian, she realized he was studying her as he sipped his ale. Cole narrowed his eyes as Serena grasped her cup and started chugging from it, thankful for the distraction from her new guardian.

She was relieved when the barkeep returned with their dinner. They sat in silence for half an hour eating their supper. When Cole finished downing his ale, he looked her in the eyes and asked again, "Who are you looking for?"

Serena held her breath as she scanned the faces in the pub once more. Unable to spot Will among the sea of strange faces, she said, "My father. He never came home. I look for him everywhere. You would not understand." Serena stood. "I'm going back upstairs. I should rather sleep than be interrogated by you."

As she stormed back up the stairwell, she felt a tightness in her chest and wondered if Will had seen her eating with yet another stranger—this time, a handsome man—and decided to finally return home without her. She heard Cole coming up the stairs behind her and quickly ducked into Xandra's room. Closing the door, she pressed an ear against it and listened as he strode past their door. She sat on the edge of the empty bed and waited, listening carefully. Muffled voices talked in the room next door, but she could not make out who it was or what they were discussing. Carefully opening the door, Serena poked her head out and peered down the hall. She found it was empty, and all the doors were closed. Without hesitating, Serena exited the room, quietly closed the door, and crept back down the staircase.

As she rounded the corner, Serena saw Will sitting alone in the far corner of the room. She started toward him while he looked out the window. There were few patrons in the tavern, mostly men enjoying the ale. None paid attention as she crossed the tavern. Serena was cautious with each step as she crossed the room, not making eye contact with anyone at the tables she passed.

When she reached the table where Will sat, she startled him. He stumbled onto his feet. "Ser—"

She shushed him, rushing forward to cover his mouth. "Will, please," she said. "Do not call me by my name here. It's too dangerous."

His forehead knitted together in wrinkled confusion as she stepped back and slid onto the wooden bench across from him. Will returned to his seat and clasped his hands together on the table next to an untouched pint of ale. Locking eyes with her, he asked, "Who are you running from?"

Serena placed her hands on the table and fidgeted as she watched Will's knuckles turn white. She whispered, "Will, my family was executed—I think by the king's men. With her dying breath, Mama told me to run and never return."

"I'm sorry, Serena. I was there. I still see Samuel and Daniel when I close my eyes. I cannot imagine what you are going through. You must be so scared." He reached for her hand. "But Durmak is safe. The attackers are sure to be long gone by now. Everyone will look out for you. I will look out for you. Talitha's been worried sick."

"It is not safe," she snapped, pulling her hand away. Closing her eyes, she breathed deeply, feeling a familiar heaviness rising in her chest. "It's more complicated than you know. Just know I'm going where my mother wanted me to go. Far from here."

"You still have people who care for you in Durmak."

"Everyone is safer now that I left," she said, picking at her cuticles.

"And what about you? Do you call this safe, wandering the world with someone you barely know? And who knows where your family's killers are or what they want. You know something—Did you find out who did this?"

She realized now that he had been talking about himself—that he still cared for her. "My family wasn't safe there, and I'm not either. I know you don't want to go home without some explanation for everyone, but I'm sorry."

"You're right about that," he said, balling one hand into a fist on top of the table. He ran a hand through his hair, brushing it back from his forehead and eyes. "I promised your father I would look out for you when he left town. All of you. And I failed miserably."

"What happened to them is not your fault," she said, "but I can't go back with you. When I think of Durmak, all I see is blood now. To live there, to be constantly reminded of that pain, would be cruel."

Will clenched his jaw and gritted his teeth, studying her face as she peered out the window. "There were many good times, too," he whispered. Desperation drenched his words. "Can you not remember those? Playing in the fields and climbing trees in the forest. Racing horses and getting scolded by our mothers. I still remember the day Talitha made you laugh so hard your face turned red as an apple."

She almost lost herself in his wistful eyes as the memories of childhood swelled between them. She closed her eyes and took a deep breath to get her senses back. "I shall never forget the joy we all shared as children," she said, reaching for his hand. "But we are not children anymore." He opened his mouth to protest, but she lifted a hand to hush him. "It was kind of you to come looking for me, Will. It means more than you know. Really. I wish things were different, but my mother told me to leave Durmak. You will not change my mind."

"Where will you go then? And who's the woman you've been traveling with?" Will asked. Serena turned in her seat; her eyes flitted about the room anxiously. Will cared too much for his own good. What could she tell him that wouldn't get him or her into trouble? He leaned closer to her, grasped her hand, and squeezed it. "Look at me."

Serena turned her face toward him. His eyes were like pools of warm honey, and she focused on his tousled hair, trying to avoid his gaze lest she find herself stuck in his comforting orbit. Hesitantly, she leaned closer and whispered, almost inaudibly, "Crystal and the others are from the east. They are taking me to seek asylum in Symptee."

"Symptee? Are you mad? What is going on?" Will asked, his voice and brows raised. Serena leaned forward and shushed him, but he went on, saying, "Is the king after you? This is crazy! There's no way to cross the border. You know that."

"I can't tell you anything else, Will. Just go home, please." Serena stared into his eyes. His face was inches from hers. She could feel the warmth of his breath on her hands. It sent a wave of shivers through her arms, making her squeeze his hand even tighter.

Will quickly withdrew his hand. "Everyone misses you, especially Talitha. We spoke before I left. We just could not live with the idea of never seeing you again."

"It's hard for me to imagine as well," Serena whispered, biting her bottom lip.

She stood and stepped away from the table. There were only three men in the far corner of the room, drinking and not paying them any attention. Will stood, too, and grabbed her arm. "Wait," he pleaded.

Serena paused, clenching her fists in a futile effort to hold herself together.

"At least let me say goodbye," Will said, pulling her closer to him with no warning. Serena stumbled forward, and he wrapped his strong arms around her thin frame. She nodded and gently leaned her cheek against his chest. It had been weeks since she had hugged anyone. The warmth spreading through her made her chest tighten, but she welcomed it. Closing her eyes, she thought of her brothers.

"If you ever see Cameron, tell him I love him, and I'll be alright," she whispered.

"Will you?"

She sniffled and hesitated. She didn't know how to answer that. Tears welled up in her eyes as she shrugged helplessly. He nodded as he released her and stepped back, clearing his throat. They walked to the door of the tavern together.

"I wish we could go back to before anyone left," Will said at the door.

Serena swiped away a tear before it could drip down her cheek. She steeled herself as she reached for the tavern's door and pushed it open. "I do, too. But you're making me homesick for a memory. There's nothing there for me anymore. I have let that place go."

They stood in the open doorway of the tavern staring at each other uneasily until Will broke the silence. "Suppose this is goodbye then."

Serena nodded. It was time to go before she was noticed. She reached out a hand, and he raised an eyebrow. Rolling her eyes, she took his hand and shook it. "I wish you safe travels on your way home. Tell Talitha I'm sorry I didn't say goodbye to her. I miss her terribly." Releasing his hand, Serena stepped back from him, putting distance between them. "Goodbye, Will."

Serena turned and retreated into the tavern, allowing the door to swing shut behind her. She imagined him standing there, his cloak billowing in the wind, before turning to trudge away from the tavern, fading from her life into the night.

10
WICKED PLANS

Captain Charles Thurwynn of Rexton's Enforcing Army had overseen encrypted correspondence from spies in several enemy kingdoms for the past decade. His most recent project had been decrypting a letter containing urgent news about Elara Garrick from one of their spies in Symptee. After a decade living as a Hyrosencian refugee, Rexton's spy had been promoted from second-lieutenant to a higher position within the Garrick Guard, finally getting his feet inside the inner citadel walls. Years of hard work earned him a place among Elara's most trusted advisors, and the subsequent intel from his last two messages proved crucial.

Since learning that Elara Garrick was engaged to be married again, the king was more determined than ever to strike Symptee from within. When the highest-ranking officers from his Enforcing Army arrived at Graynor from their posts, the king commanded an important assembly, addressing them passionately from the head of a grand oval table in his conference room.

"It is past time we infiltrate the fortress where Elara hides," Antoine said, spreading out the dozen maps their spies had sent over the years. "Our man has finally infiltrated her inner circle. What else has he to say, Thurwynn?"

Thurwynn hesitated, "As we anticipated, the Eastern Isles have aligned with the Hyrosencians, welcoming trade and travelers. One of their lords has grown quite close to Elara. They are expected to wed by summer's end."

Antoine slammed his fist on the desk. The wooden structure rattled violently. Snatching up a map of Elara's citadel, he glared at the parchment and said, "I have allowed that pathetic woman to live in hiding far too long. If she weds again, the Garrick bloodline could persist. An heir would renew hope among the loyalists—give the star-worshippers reason to believe their precious prophecy could be true."

A vase full of flowers rested near the center of the grand table. The king reached for the blooms, taking several stems in the palm of his hand, and plucked them up. He paused to admire their beauty; then in one savage motion, he crushed the fresh blooms in his clenched fist. "We must crush their hope before it has a chance to grow." Opening his hand, he brushed the crumpled petals from his palm onto the table.

Thurwynn said, "Our forces have been unable to cross into her territory for years thanks to her allies in the mountains and the elves in the south. As our spies are in important positions, it would be advantageous if they remain concealed and continue providing insight into the Guard's battle plans."

"And do you have an alternative plan if we do not use the spy to strike her?" the king demanded.

"I have conferred with Commander Bechtel. His best men prepare to travel under the guise of refugees and unleash your wrath upon Elara's stronghold."

Bechtel stood and said, "My men are armed with concealed weapons and poisons. They shall travel in small groups wearing common clothes and bearing no emblems. They shall cite their faith in the Hyrosencians' 'Divinity' to gain the confidence of the guardsmen."

"You seem to have made excellent preparations, commander," Antoine said, a sinister smile looming on his lips. "How many men form this brigade?"

"Fifteen, Your Majesty. They are our finest," Bechtel said proudly. "Eight were sent south to Norlee last week, where they have papers to get them across the borders. The other seven shall be ready to cross the valley within a fortnight."

"You authorized all this without my approval?" Antoine asked, clenching his jaw.

"Yes, Your Majesty," Bechtel said, lifting his chin with pride. "It was in the interest of gaining greater advantage in Symptee. I believed it best to split the group and stagger their arrival at the gates."

"And the other seven wait at the stronghold for orders?"

"Yes, they continue training in Murmont until you give orders," Bechtel said.

"Well, we must send them orders immediately." Antoine cracked his knuckles. "They must leave at once, for they have a wedding to attend."

"Your Majesty, the journey around the mountains shall take them over a month," said Bechtel. "There is no way to know exactly when the princess shall wed the Islander. Even the group I sent in advance may not reach the city until after their nuptials."

"Not if the second lot takes the direct route," Antoine said firmly, jabbing his finger into the Athamar Mountains on the map before him.

"But, Your Majesty, the mountains are far too dangerous. We stopped sending men that way when only two survived the initial crossing to join Elara." The protesting commander swung his arms about in an exaggerated way. "The dwarfs have pledged their loyalty to Elara from the start, but most humans perish by beasts or the frigid cold long before they reach any city. That's why we have yet to invade Symptee. Our plan was for them to cross the valley, where we control the border."

"You think yourself wiser than your king?"

"No, Your Majesty," Bechtel stuttered, taking a step back from the table and bowing low. "I only meant—"

"I am the high commander of my army. Only I give orders," Antoine said, his voice reverberating off the walls and down the hallway. "My men will leave for the Athamar Mountains at first light tomorrow."

"Yes, my king. As you wish," Bechtel sniveled, bowing repeatedly.

Antoine turned his attention back to Thurwynn, who stood inexpressive. Nodding his head, the captain asked, "How shall I aid you in this task, sire?"

"Hand me your sword," ordered Antoine, holding out an open hand. Thurwynn complied, concealing his unease by bowing his head. The king ran his fingertips along the blade. Keeping his eyes on the gleaming metal, he said, "We must cleanse this land of all who question my authority."

Antoine gripped the hilt tightly in his right hand, lowering the blade to his side. He scrutinized his officers one by one until his eyes returned to Thurwynn.

Without hesitation, the captain dropped onto a knee, bowing his head as he said, "Your power is absolute." Bechtel and the other men followed suit; the room filled with muffled echoes of their desperate declarations of loyalty to the king.

Pleased, the tyrant paced around them, tapping the blade gently on each of their shoulders as a child would play a game. Beads of sweat pooled on their foreheads as he repeated the motion, and they all held their breath in silence.

Thurwynn swallowed and declared, "Long live Antoine Rexton, King of Hyrosencia."

Immediately, the officers on their knees chimed in with: "Long may he reign."

Antoine reveled in their fear, a broad and malicious grin spread across his unshaven face. He paused with the blade on one captain's shoulder and said, "Today is your lucky day, Levraea. You have been promoted." The captain blinked up at the king in uncertainty.

With a knowing smile, Antoine grasped the hilt of the sword with his second hand, swinging the blade over Levraea's head and slicing into his target. Bechtel's head hit the floor with a thud and rolled a few inches, leaving a small blood trail from his body to his replacement. Captain Thurwynn's eyes widened as he looked down upon the lifeless face, its shocked eyes open and unmoving. The rest of the officers clamped their eyes closed, pointing their faces toward the floor.

"Rise, Commander Levraea. Let's see if you're capable of better planning than your predecessor," said Antoine, gripping the terrified man's shoulder.

He rose slowly, glancing at the other men, who remained on their knees, staring at him. Levraea turned to the king and said, "It is an honor to serve you in such a capacity, Your Majesty. I shall ride to Murmont myself to ensure the preparations are made. The soldiers will leave for Symptee as soon as supplies can be readied."

"The day after tomorrow," Antoine said, and Levraea winced. The king grinned as he added, "They are to sabotage Elara's wedding by any means. Kill every traitor in her fortress if they must."

"Yes, of course, Your Majesty," the new commander said. Blood dripped from the king's sword onto the cream-colored tiles as he stepped toward the man.

Inches from Levraea, Antoine leaned in and said, "Should they find the princess unguarded, execute her. If not, anyone she cares for shall suffice. I don't care how. The message should be clear: There is nowhere the Garricks can hide from my grasp."

"As you wish, Your Majesty," Levraea said, bowing his head. "I shall proceed to Murmont with haste."

"Not yet, commander," Antoine said before the man reached the door.

Levraea paused and turned to face the king once more. Antoine stepped over Bechtel's torso and took a seat in his chair, propping his feet up on his desk.

"May Bechtel serve as a reminder to always run your ideas by your king. Sometimes I have better plans in mind," Antoine said, his cold eyes flicking from the headless commander back to his skittish replacement. "With obedient men executing my orders, we may soon bring the Garrick bloodline to an end."

"Yes, Your Majesty," the commander said, clearing his throat. "I am but your humble servant. You are the mastermind."

Antoine's eyes gleamed with pride. "Take a seat." As Levraea walked over to the table, the king glanced back at his other men, who were still quaking on their knees. "Get up already. There's more work to be done, you pathetic lot." The captains clambered onto their feet and encircled the table once more.

As they were getting settled in their seats, Prince Anteros moseyed through the door, and the king stood to bid him a hardy welcome. "Ah, my son joins us at last!" All members of the king's assembly hurried to their feet, briefly bowing their heads to the prince. Anteros took a deep breath in, shoved his hands into his pants pockets, and walked around the table to his father's right side. His long-sleeved shirt was only halfway tucked into his black pants; his hair disheveled as if he had just awoken. Catching a glimpse of Commander Bechtel's body, he grimaced, averting his gaze from the corpse's unmoving eyes. "Was that necessary, Father? I quite liked Bechtel."

"He initiated a foolish plan without consulting with his king," Antoine growled.

"His mistake," the young man replied wistfully, brows raised as he gulped. "Someone remove the body."

Antoine nodded and snapped his fingers, pointing at the corpse. A pair of second-lieutenants rushed forward, their chair legs scraping loudly against the stone floor. One grasped Bechtel's torso while the other took hold of the man's severed head. Holding their breath, the two men shuffled out of the meeting room without delay. All that remained was a small pool of blood on the floor.

"Pleased?" Antoine asked his son, dropping back into his seat at the head of the table.

Anteros scoffed and plopped onto the chair beside his father's. "I will never understand your need to kill someone every time you call an assembly."

"My son, incompetence knows no bounds, and there is no place for imbeciles in this assembly," Antoine said as a servant stepped forward to silently refill his goblet with wine. He frowned, took the cup, and drank from it. "Have you anything new to share with us, boy? Or are you only here to test my patience?"

"The girl's name is Talitha," his son said with a smirk. Antoine nodded, his hands urging his son to continue. "She is from Durmak, as we suspected, and she did know the Finch family. She swears no one knew of their loyalty to the Garrick family, including their own children."

"I find that hard to believe," the king muttered, placing a firm hand on Anteros's shoulder and squeezing.

"I believe her," his son said without missing a beat. "She has no reason to lie. She is terrified, but she will not make up lies to appease you. We should just let her go."

Antoine scoffed, smacking his son roughly on the back. "You jest! Anteros, flesh of my flesh...This girl has admitted to knowing enemies of the crown, several of whom continue to elude us. She could know where to find them. She could go looking for them, give them intel on Graynor. Now that she has been brought here, we cannot just let her leave."

Anteros nodded. "Yes, of course, Father. You're right."

"I always am," Antoine said boisterously. Turning toward the captains and commanders of his Enforcing Army, he asked, "Can anyone produce the names of the soldiers who await my orders?"

"That should be in his documents, Your Majesty. Give me but a moment to find it," pleaded Commander Levraea, frantically shuffling through several of Bechtel's papers on the table. Thurwynn snatched several pages from him and began skimming the contents. Antoine exchanged an irritated glance with his son and sighed loudly in exasperation. He tapped his pointer finger against the wooden table, the pace quickening as a minute inched by.

"Here it is!" Thurwynn said with a smile as he hoisted the papers in the air.

Antoine reviewed the papers and barked orders at his men. Then he stood and rested both hands on the table, leaning toward the assembly. All but Anteros scrambled to stand as well, leaning toward their king as if anticipating a whispered secret. "Make the preparations and have them leave within a fortnight," Antoine said decidedly with a triumphant grin.

"As you order it, Your Majesty," Levraea answered, and all of the men in burgundy regalia bowed in unison to their king. Then, turning on their heels, the men quickly filed out of the room to begin the preparations for a grueling journey, leaving Antoine alone with his uninterested son.

Antoine smacked Anteros's feet off the table and scowled at him. "Would it kill you to conduct yourself like a crown prince? We are at war as long as the Garrick line persists," the king said, cocking his head to one side and clenching his fists.

"I am quite aware, Father." Anteros rolled his eyes. "Your men have ample experience and ideas. I don't know why you need me here."

Jolting forward, Antoine grasped his son by the shirt collar and yanked him forward until their noses were nearly touching. "Because I am the king, and if you do not shape up, the enemy will put your head on a pike long before you ever wear my crown," Antoine said, his breath hot against his son's cheeks.

"Yes, Father. I apologize for my foolishness."

"You seem unsettled today," Antoine said. "Why don't you call on a friend to join you at fencing this afternoon?"

Anteros nodded and took a step back the second his father released his grasp. "I suppose I have not seen James in a while," he said with a shrug.

"To be so young and energetic," the king said, shaking his head. "If only you would put that energy to good use!"

"I shall do my best, Father." Anteros glanced toward the doorway.

"Fear not, Anteros. The first hunt of the season approaches, and soon thereafter, the Solstice festival," Antoine said, wrapping one arm around his son's shoulders as a grin spread through his cheeks. "There will soon be an abundance of activities to entertain us both!"

EMBERS & ASHES

Serena snarled in protest at the edge of slumber as the guardians chattered noisily, eager to begin the grueling journey to Norlee. Sitting up sluggishly, she rubbed one cheek with her palm, scowling at the two hazy figures hovering over her. Dressed in fresh garments, Crystal and Xandra glowed, refreshed and ready to take on the treacherous quest before them.

"Serena! You look ill," Xandra said, taking one step back. "Did you not sleep well?"

"No," she muttered as she scrutinized the early risers. Crystal wore brown trousers as usual, but these appeared new—or at least freshly washed. She wore a pale green tunic that fluttered down to her mid thighs. At her waist, the guardian clasped a brown leather cinch belt with two buckles in the front, which matched her leather arm bracers and the quiver slung across her back. Squinting, Serena thought there was even a faint outline of leaves embroidered on the belt. Woven in the long blonde hair that cascaded over Crystal's shoulders were several tiny braids.

"I'm sorry to hear that," Xandra said, patting the mess of hair atop her head. Serena turned her attention and was surprised by how dark Xandra's attire was compared to Crystal's. The guardian wore opaque black tights with a burnt orange tunic dress, the sleeves of which spilled out from under a black leather corset. Two thick straps crisscrossed above her bosom, connecting the corset to the leather pauldrons on her shoulders.

"You look even more like warriors now," Serena commented, still feeling sour as she turned her body and touched her feet to the floorboards.

"I take that as high praise," said Xandra smiling. Her bouncy curls flopped over her face as she worked to attach short swords to her thighs with leather straps. Then she leaned back on the bed, balancing on one leg as she pulled on tall black boots. When she was done, she stood and brushed her hands over her dress. The fabric fluttered down to her midcalves, easily concealing her weapons.

"I'd have never thought to wear a sword like that," Serena said, gulping nervously.

The guardians chuckled. "Are you sure you feel well?" Crystal asked, pursing her lips.

"Perhaps we should wait a few more days?" Xandra asked, stooping down to examine Serena's eyes and press her hand to her forehead.

"I'm not sick. 'Twas just a bad night of sleep," Serena said, averting her eyes. "We should go. I'm ready to put this wretched kingdom behind me."

As Crystal reached for her shoulder, Serena stood and brushed past her, searching for her boots. Crystal and Xandra exchanged a concerned look but did not question her mood. As Serena shifted the bags on the floor in search of her boots, Xandra called out, "Wait! I have something for you."

Serena turned right as the warrior tossed something to her. She jumped, barely catching it, and raised her eyebrows. "Never worn one of these before," Serena said as she held the leather corset to her bosom and cocked her head to one side. "These were never in style back home. We just wear fur cloaks."

"I picked it out just for you," said Xandra, beaming with pride. "It matches your boots nicely. Besides, it's for more than warmth. It lends an extra layer of protection as well."

"And with your luck, you need that," Crystal said. Tossing a new pair of thick tights and dark brown pants on the bed, the guardian added, "We can't have you wandering about in torn, bloodied clothes. Wear these with your new blouse."

Lifting the pants, Serena ran her fingers over the thick, soft material. "I appreciate the gesture, really. But you did not need to do all this. It's too much."

"Worry not about the cost," Crystal said sternly. "It's best you blend in with us. We don't want to draw needless attention to you."

"And the only way to pass the border is to convince the Enforcing Army we are traders or part of the usual rabble that resides in No Man's Land," Xandra said, patting the weapons on her legs through the sides of her dress.

"I see. So, all this leather is meant to make us look like thieves," Serena said.

Xandra chuckled. "It's common attire among warriors and the mercenaries in Norlee. Anyone who dares try to cross the borders must always be ready for a fight. I'm surprised Sir Nathan didn't have you carrying a weapon at all times."

"My parents believed Durmak was safe," Serena said, second-guessing herself and begrudgingly stripping off her ragged pants. Sitting on the edge of her bed, she yanked on the tights, followed by the trousers. She needed Crystal's help lacing the back of her corset, which covered her bust and midsection nearly to her hips. Crystal laced the dark-colored ribbons gently over the blue blouse, tightening each but leaving ample room for movement. Serena took a deep breath, allowing the musty air to fill her lungs slowly. Smiling, she exhaled in relief.

Xandra approached, leaning around Serena to attach a thick leather belt just above her hips. "Take your sword and attach it like so," Xandra said, helping the overwhelmed girl. "Now it shall always be within reach should you need it."

"'Tis not like the reach should matter. I am no fighter," Serena muttered.

"We move within enemy territory," Crystal reminded her. "I require everyone to have a weapon on their person at all times. You never know what could happen. Stay close and stay alert. It's for your own good."

"You sound like a mother," Xandra cackled, slinging her own bag over her shoulder.

"She needs to understand that she won't survive unless she listens to us," Crystal replied, her clear eyes cutting over to her comrade.

"I changed into these uncomfortable clothes, did I not?" Frustrated, Serena dug her hand in the pocket of her tattered old pants, fishing out her hidden treasure before shoving the old pants into her bag. Slinging the sack over her good shoulder, Serena said, "If you're done constricting me in layers of leather, let's go."

"Is that all of your things?" Xandra asked.

"I didn't have time to pack. I just ran," Serena said frankly. She clenched her right hand, feeling the circle of cool metal press into her palm. Xandra bit her lip and nodded.

"Things can be replaced," Crystal said, putting a hand on Serena's right shoulder.

Serena was up now so she thought she might as well get moving. She went out the door to the hallway and walked right into Cole, bumping her forehead on his bare chest. Realizing he was shirtless, she blushed furiously, avoiding his eyes as she stammered, "Oh my stars... Excuse me. I did not see you."

She retreated farther down the hall and waited for the guardians, covering her face with a hand as her ears burned. She could hear Cole chuckle, no doubt amused by her mortification.

"When Rigel is ready, we can go. Should not be much longer," he said.

"I'm coming," grumbled the redhead as he exited another bedchamber sluggishly, towing several bags with him. "Ye know I hate mornings."

Crystal sauntered into the hall without sparing her brother a glance. She quickly approached Rigel, who was leaning against the wall a few feet from where Serena waited. With no warning, the blonde guardian slapped Rigel hard on the right cheek. Suddenly, he looked much more awake, and Crystal turned away looking rather pleased with herself.

"Anyone else need my help waking up?" she asked, locking eyes with Serena, who shook her head in stunned silence.

Rigel picked up his bags, rubbing his right cheek. Serena glanced at him as they fell in step following Crystal down the hall. "Are you all right?" Serena asked.

"Me? Yeah, that was nothing. If she really wanted to hurt me, I'd be on the ground," Rigel said, grinning broadly. "Oddly enough, I've missed her."

Serena chuckled, and Cole and Xandra fell in step behind them as they descended the stairs and crept through the tavern. Once outside, Xandra smiled and said, "It is so nice having everyone together again."

Crystal veered them off the main road onto an empty street barely illuminated by the celestial light. "We'll exit through the east gate. There are only two guards at this hour. They are quite tolerant of people leaving. They care more about who enters."

The small ensemble quietly guided their horses down the empty streets of Morlerae as the sun peeked over the horizon. At the east gate, the guards waved them by with hardly a second glance. Rigel even enthusiastically declared, "Long live the king," which elicited a halfhearted response from the guards.

As they disappeared into the trees once more, Serena took one last glance at the city of Morlerae and wondered whether Will was asleep there or already on his way back to Durmak.

"Come on," said Rigel, patting Serena gently on the shoulder. "You should not linger behind us."

Serena hastened her steps until she caught up to Crystal and Xandra, who moved to make space for her to walk between them. Rigel and Cole brought up the rear, exchanging pleasantries while watching the trees. "Hyrosencia shall be far behind us soon," Serena muttered to herself.

Though the trees provided ample shade, the temperature was stifling. They snaked through the forest for hours, resting their horses often. They remained in the thick of the woods, traveling southeast of the short path between Morlerae and the border of Norlee. Serena's legs were dragging by midday. Weakened by the pain and blood loss from her wound, she struggled to keep pace with the four agile fighters flanking her.

Crystal ordered them to halt again, noticing the sweat pooling on Serena's forehead. The guardian thrust a canteen into her hands and said, "Drink. We do not need you fainting."

Serena sipped from a canteen, aware it was already half-empty. Three of the guardians' horses toted thick satchels containing large canisters of water for the journey. Still, Serena drank sparingly from her personal supply.

Once the sun began to set and the sky became speckled with the white lights of hope, Crystal called for them to set up a campsite for the night.

"Daylight should not be wasted, Crystal. We should press onward," Cole argued.

"Serena is not accustomed to such strenuous travel," Crystal said, motioning toward the girl who was already laying on the ground. "A week ago, she nearly died. She is not yet fully recovered. It's crucial we allow her ample time to rest."

"If she were to go to sleep at a decent hour, that would aid her recovery," he said, fixing his piercing gaze on Serena. She fiddled with the ends of her hair that hung over her right shoulder. She pleaded with her eyes for him to say no more.

"We went to sleep quite early last night," said Crystal, rolling her eyes. "Perhaps if you had done the same, you wouldn't be so ill-tempered."

Serena's eyes flicked away from Cole's stern gaze, feeling a knot form in her stomach. "I'll help Xandra with the kindling," she said, brushing past Crystal.

"You move quick for someone still recovering," Cole said. One corner of his mouth quirked up in a grin.

"Come on, Cole. Leave the poor girl alone," Rigel called from behind a tree.

"What's your problem with Serena?" Xandra asked, glancing between them.

Cole shrugged, patting his horse on the side of its face. "Go on. Tell them how I caught you sneaking downstairs," he said, his pointed glare burning into Serena as she froze.

Crystal turned to Serena and asked, "You snuck out of our room last night? Why?"

Serena's eyes widened as she blinked at the stern warrior. "I didn't—"

"Don't lie to me, Serena," Crystal said, clenching her jaw.

Serena bit her bottom lip and looked down at her feet. "I'm sorry."

"Look. We're your guardians, not your parents," Xandra said, dropping a hand on her shoulder. "Just tell us the truth."

Glancing toward Crystal, Serena could see how irritated she was by the revelation. Crystal prompted, "Well? Who was it then?"

Serena fidgeted with the edges of her blouse, which poked out from under the thick leather corset she was trapped in. "It was someone from back home," she said, digging the toe of her boot into the dirt. "It doesn't even matter now. He's gone back, and I stayed with you."

Rigel and Xandra turned back to making the fire, breaking the tense quiet that followed. "It's our duty to protect you, but we cannot do that if you wander off," said Xandra, crouching and gently blowing on the hissing red embers.

In an instant, the fire ignited, the flames quickly devouring the kindling and rising toward the sky. Serena retreated behind the fire and sat; her face was red-hot from their interrogation. She could not comprehend why Elara's fighters were concerned about her meeting with a boy from Durmak. No one was injured. She said goodbye and told him to go home.

Cole rolled his eyes and barked from across the fire, "I saw you with him. He looked about your age. You seemed awfully close."

"You were watching me?" Serena asked warily.

"Of course," Cole said. "When I caught you leaving the first time, I knew you would try again, so I followed you. I thought you were trying to leave. Maybe you missed home. From the looks of it, I was right. Seemed to be quite a heated chat."

"You had no right to spy on me," Serena said, gritting her teeth.

"He has every right as your guardian," Crystal said flatly. She scowled at Serena, giving her a look that reminded her of the time her mother scolded her for staying out past sunset. "You could have been captured or killed. What you did was foolish, and it will not happen again while you are under our protection. Is that clear?"

Serena could not believe this warrior, who couldn't be more than ten years her senior, was chastising her as if she were a child. "Yes, mother," she said scathingly. Turning her back on the Windaef siblings, Serena plopped on the ground and glowered as the last glimpse of golden light disappeared behind the trees, shrouding the forest in darkness. Beads of sweat formed on her forehead, trickling down her face as the fire behind her intensified. For a moment, she grasped her bag tightly in one hand and considered running. She clenched her jaw, glancing at the guardians. All four were gathered across the fire from her, whispering and casting her an occasional glance.

Finally, Crystal walked over to her and laid a blanket out beside her. Sitting down, she cleared her throat to get Serena's attention. "Serena, I'm not trying to be your mother," Crystal said, pausing to consider her next words. Serena looked away from her, staring at the animal in the tree instead. "We're just trying to keep you safe. Hyrosencia is dangerous, especially near the border. It's not just soldiers. Slave traders wouldn't hesitate to snatch a pretty girl. Nobody wants that to happen to you."

Serena nodded. Once again, her mother's dying words echoed through her mind, cutting through the silence between them. The queen had also urged her to cross the border as quickly as possible. "You're right," she said, locking eyes with Crystal. "I don't know what dangers lurk out there."

"And we don't want you to find out," Xandra said, settling on the dirt to her other side.

"Just trust us, all right?" Crystal said, shoving her shoulder gently.

Her mother's voice weighed heavy on her heart as Serena snuggled under her cloak. For seventeen years, all she had known was the safety of her family's farm in Durmak. In two months' time, her family had been murdered, and she had been attacked more than once. She knew the guardians were right. The dangers would not end here. "I do trust you," she muttered. But even under the watchful eyes of the queen's guardians, she feared nowhere would ever be safe.

THE NEXT DAY THEY continued southeast in the wilderness between Morlerae and the Valley of Norlee. They were heading for a border town called Noomï, at the northern edge of Norlee and the foot of the Athamar Mountains. It was going to be risky to enter the valley, but it was the only way to reach the pass through the mountains. They journeyed in silence for much of the day, but as evening fell and they made camp, Xandra remarked that they were near to the City of Cinders, a place of which Serena had never heard.

"I didn't think there were any cities between Morlerae and the border?" Serena said.

"Not anymore," Cole said, cocking one eyebrow.

"There is only what we call the 'City of Cinders.' It hasn't been occupied for well over a decade," said Xandra grimly. "The loyalists rallied there, but Rexton's forces overwhelmed them. His men surrounded the city, and the rebellion was annihilated overnight."

"Rexton's generals set everything ablaze, hence the name," said Crystal. "They made an example of the city. The streets ran red with blood. The buildings were burned. His message was clear. The people on this side of the border have been too afraid to fight back ever since."

"What remains is said to be cursed," Rigel said.

Crystal rolled her eyes. "It is not cursed."

"People are afraid to walk among the ruins," Xandra said. "Some say you can still hear the wails of the dead."

Serena's eyes widened. "That's horrific."

"On occasion, a stupid thief will go looking for something of value, but they'll have a difficult time finding anything useful among the ashes," said Cole, staring intensely at her as the fire danced between them.

"So, the City of Cinders was never rebuilt," Serena whispered. "I suppose it makes sense why Morlerae grew into such a great city then. The survivors must have fled there?"

The warriors fell silent as they listened to the crackle of the fire before them. Everyone was visibly tense, especially Rigel. He clenched his fists, his knuckles turning bright white.

"What?" Serena asked.

"It was a senseless slaughter," said Crystal. "Men, women, children..."

"There were no survivors," said Cole, staring into the flames. "Rexton's army surrounded the city and made sure not one soul escaped."

Serena gasped. The air suddenly felt thick and hot. She whispered, "Who would do such a thing to children?" Her cheeks burned. She stood and kicked at the ground, sending the loose dirt at her feet flying into the air. Gruesome images of Samuel and Daniel flashed in her head. "It's not right," she said through angry tears.

"This land was once my home," Xandra said. "Rexton has scorned, taxed, and slain our people for far too long. He cares not for anyone, only for power. That's why we fight."

"We hold out hope that someone will end his reign," Rigel said.

Serena clenched her hand around the hilt of her father's sword as anger rose within her. "Is that what you shall do next? After we reach Symptee, will you come back and kill that wicked bastard?"

Xandra and Rigel exchanged a grim glance. Rigel said without looking at her, "He shall not die by my sword, but I should gladly give my life to aid the one destined to defeat him."

"Elara has a plan in place," said Crystal. "We are certain the person who is destined to bring about his downfall shall take a stand soon, when they are ready."

"What do you mean *destined*? Is it one of the guardians?" Serena asked, a glimmer of hope in her eyes.

Xandra laughed nervously and said, "Actually, many years ago, the last oracle of this generation, Idonea Cinderfell, foretold the way to take back Hyrosencia."

"Her prophecy specified that only the true heir to the throne could succeed in leading the uprising against Rexton. That is why none has attempted such a task yet," said Crystal. "The one who must face him is still not ready. They need more time."

"More time?" Serena shouted. "It's been seventeen years! Our people are being slaughtered. My family included! And this supposed savior waits in safety and does nothing?"

Xandra clamped her hand over Serena's mouth. "Please, keep your voice down," the guardian whispered. She gave Serena a stern look before releasing her.

"There are many things you do not yet know, things that are unsafe to speak of here," warned Crystal.

"Well, I should like to know the full story behind that prophecy when you see fit," Serena said, sitting next to Crystal in front of the fire. "As you said, there is still much I do not know of my own homeland." Serena frowned as she ran her fingers through the dirt.

"Perhaps you do not want to know," Rigel said.

Serena shrugged, biting her lip. Maybe he was right. Maybe she did not want to know more of the atrocities done to her own people. She shifted uncomfortably, the campfire making her break into a sweat. They sat in silence for a while before Crystal said, "You should all try to get some sleep. I'll take the first watch."

"I'll join you," Rigel said, stretching his arms and legs.

"Very well," Crystal said, exhaling. She moved to the opposite end of their camp, placing a dagger and her bow and quiver beside her.

Serena pushed herself onto her feet and went over to where Xandra laid a few feet away from the fire. Flinging her bag on the ground, Serena stooped down to run her fingers across the grass. When she found the area was dry, she sprawled out next to the woman, who gave her a little smile. Covering her entire body with her cloak, Serena sighed, unable to shake the tightness in her chest.

When Serena finally succumbed to the darkness, she tossed wildly in her sleep. Her skin itched as the night air grew thicker, the heat threatening to suffocate her. She ran down an unfamiliar street, searching for a way out, but there was none. She was trapped in a city on fire.

SERENA WAS AWAKENED BY a loud clap of thunder. They collected their things in haste under a deep gray sky, and the Windaefs led the way through thick fog, hoping to find shelter from the incoming storm. They reached the edge of the fallen city. The tumbled ruins of the silent city rose up from the mist like tombstones. With a solemn expression, Crystal suggested they stick to the outskirts as they passed.

Serena and Rigel stopped where the tall grass became peppered with molten remnants, looking into the remains of the once-active city. Haunted by her dreams, Serena shivered, clenching her fists at her sides. "You have to stop him," she said as she took in the desolate scene. She imagined children running through the streets, like phantoms in the mist. "There must be retribution for what he has done. For the lives he has destroyed."

Rigel squeezed her shoulder, but it brought her no comfort. "We'll do all we can to bring justice to Hyrosencia."

"There will be justice when Antoine Rexton loses his head," said Serena.

Serena glanced at the others. The other three guardians walked their horses ahead, keeping to the edge of the fallen city. Cole scouted the route ahead of them while Xandra was especially chatty, telling Crystal that she was looking forward to being back across the border soon. While Xandra spoke of seeing the Dwarven cities again, Crystal scanned the forest to their right and the ruins to their left, watchful as they neared the border. How could the guardians just move on? Serena looked back on the ruins. And how could she move on? She had not stopped moving ever since she lost her family; she had had no choice. But their deaths were always at the edge of her mind. Staring at the scorched remnants of Rexton's wrath, their spirits beckoned her to face them. And now she couldn't turn away.

Serena handed Midnight's reins to Rigel, who was lost in his own thoughts. She stepped forward into the scorched city. She crossed what seemed to once be the city's marketplace. She stepped around charred skeletal remains sprawled out in the road as she made her way toward a cluster of large brick buildings that had weathered the test of time.

"Serena!" Rigel called, hesitantly stepping forward. He winced at the crunching noise that came from under his boot. "This is no place for the living."

She waved for him to follow her as the rain trickled down, but he stood still as if he might be cursed for taking another step. The clouds burst and released a torrent of rain. Serena ran and ducked through the doorway to one of the crumbling homes. She thought maybe she heard her name being called under the roar of the rain, but the heavy downpour now walled her from the rest of the world. She wandered the house and wondered who might have lived here years ago. Memories of walking through her own home and finding her family killed swept through her mind, mixed with happier memories in the same space. As much as she had wanted to, now that she had the chance, she could not weep. She waited as the sky poured down.

A dazzling array of lightning flashed throughout the home. Thunder cracked and crashed throughout the sky. Serena thought she heard footsteps approaching, but before she could turn around, she heard another thud and slumped onto the ground.

SERENA'S HEAD THROBBED AS she came to; she had blacked out for a spell. Now a ball of damp fabric was shoved in her mouth, gagging her, and her hands were tied behind her back with rough lengths of rope.

A rugged middle-aged man carried her through the labyrinth of half-burned buildings in silence. Crystal and Cole called her name in the distance, the sound of their voices nearly drowned out by the downpour as the man trudged farther from them with each step.

"Serena. That you? Not a common name around here," the man said. "I wonder how much that pretty face would be worth to some lonely soldiers?"

Serena squirmed on his shoulder. Her head hung down behind him, and his warm breath against her bare arm made her skin crawl. She attempted to scream, hoping the guardians would discover them before her attacker managed to escape the scorched city, but her attempts were to no avail.

Though he had managed to snatch her quickly and quietly, Serena knew she couldn't let him take her without a fight. She thrashed, nearly rolling off his shoulder. Agitated, the man stopped and tossed her onto a jagged stone floor through the open doorway of an old dwelling. Her injured shoulder stung with excruciating pain.

"Got me a fighter," he said, chuckling as he popped his knuckles. Her eyes widened as she stared into the dark, wicked eyes of her attacker. He had tangled black hair that faded into his scraggly beard and a scar across his right eye and cheek. The man grabbed her by the chin and said, "Some men like a girl who puts up a fight." His lips twisted to reveal a crooked grin with one missing tooth.

The man gripped the hilt of her father's sword in his right hand and unsheathed it. Inspecting the sword, he said, "Now this is quite a blade. Ye don't see this every day." Serena glared at him as she mumbled. The man shook his head and squatted before her, grabbing a fistful of her hair to get a closer look at her face. When she squirmed, he pulled harder, pressing her father's blade against her throat. She froze as the cold steel grazed her heated skin.

Thunder cracked overhead, and a blinding white light flashed over his face. Serena jumped. The blade nicked her, sending a warm trickle of blood down the side of her neck. Her eyes brimmed with tears, and she squeezed them shut. Her entire body ached; pain pulsed through her shoulder. She wondered if her wound had reopened when she hit the ground.

The man released her face and stood towering over her trembling frame. Serena's eyes darted about the dust-covered room, searching for an escape. The rain rattled even louder, and Serena realized she could no longer hear the guardians calling for her. Her stomach twisted at the thought. Her kidnapper grinned as if he could read her mind, shoving the sword back into its leather case.

He searched Serena's clothes for concealed weapons. He snickered at her muffled cries as his hands skimmed over her. Without warning, a hooded figure dove through a hole in the wall, rolled across the floor, and stabbed the man in the thigh with a small dagger. The kidnapper winced and stumbled back in surprise. He yanked the dagger from his leg, grimacing as blood sprayed across the floor.

The cloaked man stepped between the kidnapper and Serena. Raindrops trickled off his cloak, sprinkling against her cheeks. She blinked up at him.

Her attacker struggled to balance on his injured leg. "She's mine!" he seethed, lurching toward her with both hands outstretched.

The man under the cloak reared back one arm, landing a heavy blow to the injured man's jaw. Serena jolted as his body slammed onto the ground beside her. From this close, she could see the blood pouring from the gash in his thigh, seeping through his pants. The attacker wheezed, pressing a hand to his wound as he struggled to sit up. Her rescuer kicked the man in the face. The scarred man slumped back, unmoving, and Serena turned to peer up at her savior.

The hooded man dropped onto his knees. "Thank heavens I found you!"

Serena's strength ebbed away, and she collapsed onto the ground. The last thing she felt was the man cradling her in his arms. Exhaling, he said, "Let's get out of here." She vaguely sensed movement as he exited the structure and retreated to the edge of the forest.

12

FRESH BLOOD

The hooded man trudged through the forest, his body hunched over to shield Serena's face from the rain as they moved farther from the ruins. Her breathing had steadied, he noticed, and he smiled when she nestled deep into his chest. When the rainfall slowed to a trickle, he gently laid her in the grass and examined her for injuries. The hair that clung to her face was sticky with blood. He brushed it back gently, revealing a small gash in her hairline above her right eye. The wound had stopped bleeding while he held her against his chest. Next, he noticed the cut on the side of her throat, though the trail of blood had been washed away by the rain. He slumped onto the saturated ground next to Serena and groaned. Glancing over at the unconscious girl, he reached over to brush the remaining hair back from her face.

Her eyelashes fluttered, and she blinked up at the sky. "Rigel?" she whispered hoarsely, squinting at him as she tried to push herself up. Unable to muster the strength, she slouched back, wincing.

He pulled back his hand and scoffed, "Who in the blue blazes is Rigel?"

Serena's eyes widened, and she turned her head to look at him. "Will?"

Will swiped his hood back, revealing an indignant frown. "I risked my neck fighting that raider, you know. I can't believe you assumed I was someone else."

Serena leaned on her right arm, facing him, and winced as she tried to sit up. Will moved on instinct, wrapping an arm under her back and helping her get situated. She searched his face and asked, "Will, what are you doing here? You should be on your way home."

He shook his head. "You told me to go home, but we both know I can't go back without you. Your brother would kill me if I left you in the care of complete strangers."

"So you followed me?" Serena asked, shoving his arm away. "What was your plan? To drag me back to Durmak?"

"That wouldn't work. You'd take off the second I fall asleep," he teased.

"You're right about that," she said with a sidelong grin.

"Actually, I forgot to give you something the other night." Will reached into his pocket. He pulled out a small rabbit's foot, and her breath hitched.

"Samuel's lucky charm! You have it? You kept it with you all this time?" she asked. She took it between her thumb and forefinger and clutched it to her chest. "Thank you."

"Was no trouble," he said, cocking his head to one side. "I thought you might miss home."

"I do," she said quietly. "But I can't go back with you."

"I know. If I can't change your mind, I suppose I'll have to go with you, make sure you don't get yourself killed," Will said with a resigned shrug. He stared off into the woods as if those words wouldn't change the course of his entire life.

"You can't," Serena whispered, studying him. "Think about your family, Will. They'd be worried sick if you didn't come back."

"They'll be fine," he said, swiping his hand through the air. "I sent word from Morlerae that I wouldn't return without you. They won't be expecting me."

"Searching the woods is not the same as leaving the kingdom," she argued, crossing her arms. "If we make it to Symptee, there's no coming back—not so long as Rexton is in power. You might never see your family again."

"I'm well aware," Will snipped, turning to face her. "These people couldn't protect you from one raider. What makes you so certain they can get you to Symptee?"

"That was no fault but my own. I shouldn't have wandered off," Serena said, biting the inside of her lip. She touched the top of her head near her latest wound and winced. "I know they can get us there because they've already crossed the border once. Queen Elara sent them in search of loyalists—my family included."

"Well, they're a little late in that regard. There were once six of you, yet they're only bringing one Finch back," Will said, "and somehow four of them managed to lose you in a matter of minutes."

"You have yet to see them in action," she said. "Crystal saved my life. I'm not even sure how she managed it, but I would be dead if not for her."

She reached for her left shoulder, and Will leaned closer. "Back in the city, you said you had been attacked, but you seemed well. What happened?"

"We were ambushed," she said, pulling her legs up to her chest and planting her boots flat on the ground. "When Crystal and I left Kypno, someone followed us. In the dead of night, they attacked us. I was stabbed in the shoulder... here." She reached her right hand across her body to point at her left shoulder. "The stars favored me that night. I am blessed to still be alive."

Will rolled onto his knees and reached for her shoulder, but she recoiled at the slightest touch. He pulled back his arm and sank into the tall grass feeling helpless. "We should get you to a healer," he mumbled.

"It's not that bad," she insisted. She brushed her fingers over the small incision on her neck. "I'm just a bit sore from that oaf dropping me on the ground." She laughed halfheartedly. "Perhaps in Symptee I will know safety again."

"If we can survive the crossing," Will said, his eyes cutting back to hers.

"Crystal has earned my trust," Serena said. She glanced sideways into the trees. "I need to get back to the guardians, Will. They must be worried."

Serena shifted onto her knees and wobbled a bit. Then her arms shot out in need of support. Will moved fast and caught her outstretched arms. Lowering her back to the ground, he said, "You're far more stubborn than I remember. You need rest. You took a nasty blow to the head. Who knows what vile things that man would have done to you if I hadn't come along." His forehead wrinkled and jaw clenched as he forced himself to look away, glaring into the forest.

"Don't think like that. I'm fine," Serena said, squeezing his arms before letting go. "Thank you—for showing up when you did."

"I would do it again too," Will said with a half smile and nudged her gently with his elbow. "But do try not to get snatched again."

"I will try my hardest," she said, crossing her heart. "Crystal will probably shackle herself to me for the rest of the journey after today's incident. If she wasn't sworn to protect me, she'd kill me."

"I'll make sure she doesn't," he said. "I'll help you find your guardians, but first you must rest. You're too weak to be ambling about the woods on foot."

Serena sighed but nodded. "If you insist. But only for a little while."

Will placed a hand behind her head and back, supporting her until the gentle cushion of the tall grass embraced her. Then he laid on his stomach beside her, resting his head on his folded arms. They laid shoulder to shoulder in silence for a time. When Will turned his head to look at her, she was staring up at the pale blue sky. "What are you thinking about?"

Serena turned her head to look at him, and the wet grass tickled her cheek. "This is the same sky we once played under in Durmak. The same blue, the same rain clouds—yet everything is different now."

Pressing his hands into the grass and craning his back, Will glanced up and smirked. "Suppose you're right about that. Some things are beautiful, no matter where you go." When he looked back at her, she was staring, her eyes searching his face for something. Will leaned closer, as if her eyes held a secret. Her face flushed red, and she turned her eyes back to the sky.

"Did you ever think about leaving Durmak?" she asked, ringing her hands over her stomach.

"I never gave it a thought until you ran off." Will folded his arms behind his head. He took notice of her staring as his shirt strained against his biceps and grinned. "Now that I'm here, I realize I have no reason to go back."

Serena's eyebrows knit together. "That's absurd. You have your parents, your sister, your friends. I can list over a dozen reasons for you to go back."

"They'll all go on with their lives, with or without me," Will said, plucking bits of grass out of the ground one by one. "I have no prospects in Durmak. Your father left so abruptly, I was unable to finish my apprenticeship."

"You learn quickly. Surely you could find another mentor in Morlerae or Kypno—"

"Or Symptee," Will suggested.

"Are you sure you can live with never returning home?"

Will laid on his side facing Serena, his head propped up on his fist. Studying her face, he replied, "My father is doing better now. My family doesn't need me anymore. We said our goodbyes. They encouraged me to go. They'd be happy for me to find my own path."

"You don't mean that," Serena said, her head slumping to the side to look at him crossly. "Your family loves you, Will. Don't ever take them for granted."

He could read the melancholy in her emerald eyes and knew she was right. Dropping his chin to stare at the ground, he whispered, "I'm sorry about your family, Serena. Daniel and Samuel, they were little brothers to me. I wish I could have done something—"

Serena moved her right arm and brushed her fingers against the back of his hand. "You need not say it. They saw you as a brother, too. I am not selfish enough to believe myself the only person mourning them."

Will nodded. "So you understand why I came after you?"

Easing herself onto her right side, Serena looked him in the eyes. "You are all family to me. I couldn't rest without knowing you were safe."

Serena's lips parted, and she took an unsteady breath.

Will reached out and cupped the side of her face with a warm, calloused hand. "Are you sure you're all right?" he asked, pressing the back of his hand to her forehead.

Serena leaned into his touch. "I'm fine. Just thinking about home," she said. Her lips curved into a bittersweet smile. Will nodded as he withdrew his hand. Though terrible circumstances had led them far from home, they could not forget that all the best days of their youth were intertwined and always would be.

"Get away from her, or I will end your life," snarled Crystal.

The pair turned their heads to find the fierce blonde warrior scowling down at them with a sword pointed directly at Will's throat. Without moving, Crystal whistled. The shrill tune echoed through the forest.

Serena winced as she reached her arm across Will. "Don't hurt him," she pleaded. "Will is my friend. He's from back home."

"You're bleeding," Crystal said to Serena without looking away from Will. "Is that your doing?" she asked him.

"No!" they both shouted.

"He would never hurt me," Serena insisted. "I was struck by another man, a raider, and Will saved me. He was going to help me find you once I recovered."

"That is not how it appeared," Crystal said, lowering the sword to her side. "Is this the friend you snuck out to meet in Morlerae?"

Will noticed Serena's cheeks redden as she glanced at him and nodded. "This is Will, William Burroughs of Durmak. We grew up together. He has been searching for me since—"

"Since your family was murdered," Crystal said callously, stepping over Will's legs to help Serena onto her feet. "That much I gathered. While I appreciate his aid, he should have returned you to the protection of your guardians instead of carrying you a mile into the forest."

"Sorry," Will said with a shrug.

Crystal ignored him and wrapped an arm around Serena. "Say goodbye to your friend. We must be going." She tried to pull the girl away from him, but Serena recoiled, planting her boots firmly on the ground.

"No," she said, pushing Crystal away. "Who do you think you are? I have known Will my entire life. I barely know you."

Crystal's face softened; her lips parted in astonishment. Taking a deep breath, the guardian said, "I feared you were dead the second we lost eyes on you."

Serena covered her eyes with a hand and exhaled. "But I am not dead yet. You need not be so hostile. Will is a good friend, as are you. I should like to introduce you properly—without any weapons between you."

Crystal nodded and turned to Will, who scrutinized her through skeptical eyes. The guardian sheathed the sword before extending her hand to help him up. When he stood facing her, Will was but a couple inches taller than the fierce woman. They stared at each other intensely for a moment before Crystal said, "Thank you for coming to Serena's aid. I promise she shall not wander from my sight again."

Will chuckled, glancing from the intimidating blonde to his friend. "It's quite all right. I shall be there to protect her should you and your comrades be distracted again."

Crystal raised her eyebrows, and Serena moved between the two, placing a firm hand on each of them. Serena said, "This was my fault! I wandered into the ruins recklessly, but I'm safe now. You have both fought very hard to keep me alive. The enemy has not won on this day. Try to remember that."

A sharp whistle rang out, and Will glanced around aimlessly for the culprit. Crystal gave Will a reproachful look before rolling her eyes. Grabbing Serena by the forearm, the warrior turned and started leading her away. "My duty is to guard those under the queen's protection," she said. "He is not a loyalist or a soldier. It's difficult enough to keep one person alive. He should return home."

"I can take care of myself," Will insisted. "Just allow me to accompany you."

"The path will only be more treacherous once we cross the border. We could not guarantee your safety," Crystal argued.

Serena stopped abruptly. "You can if you wish for me to remain in your care."

Crystal released her arm and snarled. She turned and glared at Will. "He belongs on a farm. He is untrained and unprepared for what is to come. He knows nothing of the dangers we have faced, nor what lies ahead."

"The same could be said of me," Serena said, raising her voice. "I am but a blacksmith's daughter. I have far less survival skills than Will. Why am I entitled to the City of Mercy, and he is not?"

"We were sent for the Finch family," Crystal said, balling her hands into fists. "We need not be burdened by a stranger with no ties to the queen. Your friend should return home."

"You were ordered to protect my family, but you only found me. If you expected to protect my entire family, surely you can accommodate one more person." Then Serena added, "Will is family."

Crystal paused for a moment and looked down at her boots, which had sunken into the wet earth. Her wide eyes glanced about as if in search of a logical answer. "When I returned with you alone, they only procured the supplies for five to make the journey. There will not be another city until we cross into the valley."

"I can feed myself." Will held up his ragged rucksack.

"Crystal, you saved my life, and I may never be able to repay that debt," Serena said, placing a hand on the guardian's shoulder. "But you are not my mother nor my master. It's my choice where I go and with whom I travel. If you won't allow Will to join us, then maybe we'll take our chances without you."

The guardian clicked her tongue loudly against the roof of her mouth as her eyes shot daggers at the unwelcome addition. "It's not that simple. We pledged to guard you with our lives, and you accepted our protection. We cannot just leave you behind now. We gave our word to Queen Elara. We must bring you to Symptee. Did Mary Finch not beg for you to flee this realm before you end up dead?"

Serena lowered her chin, looking down at her wounded shoulder, and damp hair fell in front of her face. "I want to go to Symptee with you." Then her eyes flicked toward Will. "And I want him to come with us. We shouldn't have to ask permission. Last I heard, all refugees are welcome in Symptee."

Without giving Crystal time to argue, Serena marched past her, fiery resolve gleaming in her eyes. Crystal and Will stared at each other dumfounded for a moment before striding after her.

Walking alongside Serena, Crystal whistled again. The sound of another shrill whistle echoed from the northwest. "That way," Crystal said, pointing, and they followed her in silence.

Within minutes, they came upon the rest of the guardians. Xandra raced toward them, threw her arms around Serena's neck, and exclaimed, "Serena! Oh, thank the stars! You're alive! We were so worried."

"Who the blazes is that?" asked Cole, pointing a sword at Will, who hung behind them and watched from the shadows.

Holding both arms out at his sides, Will asked, "Who the blazes are you?"

Serena stepped toward him and said, "Will, these are the other guardians." Addressing the small band of warriors, she smiled as she announced, "This is Will Burroughs of Durmak. He shall be coming to Symptee with us."

"Absolutely not," Cole said, turning toward his sister for support. "I doubt this boy has ever wielded a weapon in his life. He shall only be more dead weight."

"I can fend for myself. I managed to save Serena without any help," Will said, examining the aggressive blond guardian through narrowed eyes. Leaning closer to Serena, he asked, "Are those two related? They have the same hostility in their eyes."

Xandra and Rigel cackled, leaning on each other for support. Crystal rolled her eyes and said, "If you must know, Cole is my elder brother." Pointing toward the others, she added, "That's Xandra and Rigel. The four of us were sent to protect the Finch family with our lives."

"Excellent work today," Will said, his voice dripping with disdain. "If you're the queen's best, then perhaps I'll join the Guard. Seems they'll hire anyone."

Serena slapped a hand over his mouth. Will's lips curled upward in a broad smile as she shook her head. "Don't push it," she muttered, removing her hand. He rolled his eyes, and she shuffled over to Rigel, who held several horses by the reins. She greeted Midnight with a pat on the cheek.

Cole approached her, scowling as he loomed over her. Serena swallowed, her entire body shrouded by his shadow. "Your recklessness has thrown off our entire day. Might we ride while there is still some daylight left?"

"She has a head wound," Will piped up, standing beside Cole.

Xandra joined them, elbowing her way between the men to get a look at Serena. She was careful as she wiped the blood on Serena's forehead with a piece of damp cloth. "Your friend makes quite the impression," she said with a sly grin. "I like him." Serena smiled, glancing over her shoulder at Will. He winked but knew he looked out of place as he stood in the middle of the camp clutching his bag in one hand.

"I must agree with my brother," said Crystal, taking Cinnamon's bridles from Cole and mounting the horse gracefully. "This area is not safe, and the journey shall not grow easier as we near the border. How is your head?"

"I'll be all right," Serena replied, placing one foot in a stirrup as she grasped the reins in her hand. Will stretched one arm out in front of her to block the saddle. "Are you sure you should be riding alone?"

"Perhaps you should ride with one of us for now," Xandra suggested as she and Rigel mounted their horses. The four guardians circled around Serena and Will.

"Will does not have a horse," Serena said. "Perhaps he should ride with me?"

"No," Crystal said. "Let Will ride alone. You can ride with me. My steed can handle both of us." She smirked. She pulled back the reins and stopped next to Serena.

Will glanced from the warriors to Serena, and she nodded, handing him the bridles. "Here. This is Midnight. Follow close behind us." She squeezed his hand as he took the reins. He exhaled and stepped onto the stirrup, easily swinging his leg over Midnight and positioning himself on the saddle.

Crystal dismounted, steadying Cinnamon with her hands. She helped Serena climb onto the horse first. Then the warrior gracefully settled behind her.

"You should not lose her so easily this way," Will said, smirking.

Serena cocked her head to one side and gave him a reproachful look, trying not to break into a smile.

"Try to keep up, Burroughs." Crystal said. She nudged her horse in the side with her boot, gently tugging the reins. Cinnamon trotted in a semicircle before charging forward, and they led the group eastward.

Will kept a watchful eye on the back of Crystal's head as he followed them, and when Serena turned back and caught his eye, her wide smile was enough to calm his nerves. He was happy to join the party of unfriendly and unfamiliar warriors for the difficult task of escaping Hyrosencia.

WHEN CAMERON AND HIS captain reached the gates at Murmont, they dismounted from their horses, exhausted from the quick trip to Graynor and back. They rode fiercely through the night, shrouded beneath the blurred tree lines. They waved to the night watch as they made their way through, and the heavy gates crashed back to a close, secluding them from the surrounding wilderness. Pelham handed off his steed's reins and called over his shoulder, "Tie these up, then get some rest, Finch. You have quite the journey ahead of you." The soldier's eyelids sagged as he led the horses to the stables alone.

He quietly shuffled into the barracks, aware that most of his comrades were already in their beds, worn out from a full day of intensive training activities. A dim lantern near the room's entrance illuminated the space just enough for him to find his bunk, but before he could sink into his sheets, he spotted a folded letter propped up against his pillow. "What's this?" he muttered to himself, picking it up and flipping it over to read the address.

To Cameron Finch
From William Burroughs

He frowned, wondering what his old friend could possibly have written about so soon after his visit. At first, Cameron crumpled the letter up between his hands, resolving not to be bothered by it. He stuffed it under his pillow, curious why the army would even give him a letter from anyone but his kin. But as he laid in bed staring at the wooden bottom of the bunk above his, a thought occurred to him. Perhaps something had happened since their meeting.

Rolling onto his stomach, Cameron reached under his pillow and pulled out the wrinkled sheet. He unfolded the parchment and smoothed it over with his hand. Then he scanned the brief note from his friend. Serena's alive. Morlerae... Traveling east toward the mountains. With others... A blonde archer. Refuses to return home. *Stubborn as always.*

A broad grin spread across his face. This was the lead he needed to start his search for Serena. And if she was heading toward the mountains, was she going to the enemy? She couldn't pass through the valley; she had no credentials. But he could.

He reread the letter, slowing at the mention of her traveling companions. Who was this group Will mentioned? And were they involved in his family's murders? He clenched his jaw at the thought. Suppressed rage started to bubble up in his chest.

Why would Serena choose to travel with these strangers? She was far too trusting, and it was going to get her killed. If these were Elara's assassins, the ones the king had said killed their kin, Cameron would do everything in his power to hunt them down and avenge his family's senseless murders.

He flopped over and pressed the letter to his chest, his fingers splayed out over the parchment as if it were precious treasure. Though he didn't always see eye to eye with his best friend, he couldn't help but be thankful for Will's keen eye in that moment. With any luck, Cameron would be able to track down Serena and intercept these mysterious fighters in Noomï before they headed north into the mountains.

Invigorated by this news, Cameron shot out of his bunk and went over to the desk in the front corner of the room. In the lantern's light, he leaned over the desk and scrawled a brief message for his superiors on a blank piece of parchment in his best script. His captain was already aware that the king had tasked him with tracking down Serena, and he would be thrilled to know his soldier was already chasing down a promising lead the following morning.

Crawling back into his bed, Cameron sighed with content, drifting to sleep with ease. In his dreams, he pictured the king bestowing him with a promotion for his unwavering loyalty to the crown. All he had to do was catch the little bird who always flew too far from home.

CRYSTAL DECLARED THEY SHOULD set up camp for the night, and Serena sighed in relief. But when Crystal asked to speak to Rigel for a moment, telling him to bring his sack of weapons, her curiosity made her heart race. What did the guardian have in mind?

"Perhaps she wishes to kill me with my own sword," Rigel joked as he dismounted his steed. The others began securing the horses to the trees as Crystal led Rigel a short distance away from the camp.

Will helped Serena tie up Cinnamon. Together, they began removing the bags and piling them up on the ground a few feet away from the horses. Though Serena could only use her right arm, he was more than willing to help her lift the heavy bags and remove the saddles from both horses, and she appreciated his help.

Not far from them, Cole and Xandra tended to the other horses. As Xandra removed the heavy saddle from hers, her arm brushed against Cole's, and the saddle flopped hard on the ground. Picking it up, the steely warrior avoided her gaze and moved away from her, searching for a dry area to place their things.

"Thank you," she muttered. Ambling after him, Xandra bit her bottom lip and asked quietly, "Cole, are you angry at me?"

"No," he said impassively, lowering the saddle onto the grass.

"You have been avoiding me."

"We lost the girl today, Xandra. We were all distracted. That cannot happen again," Cole said firmly, removing the saddle from his horse and laying it in the grass.

"You have barely spoken to me all week. I wish you would—"

"Xandra," Crystal called out, walking in their direction, "would you see if there is any wood dry enough for the fire? I have a special task for Cole."

Serena, who had been helping Will collect fallen branches, watched Cole and Xandra disburse. She could feel tension between the guardians and wondered what was going on as she watched Cole meet his sister. "What do you require?" he asked.

Crystal turned toward Serena and smirked at Will. "You said you know how to wield a sword, correct?" Crystal's eyes shifted toward her brother, and she declared, "I should like Will to spar with you. Let's see what he can do."

Serena protested, "Crystal, that's absurd." Turning to Will, she grasped his forearm and looked into his eyes. "You do not have to prove anything. Not right now."

Cole pulled his sword from its sheath and examined it, seemingly ignoring their conversation. Serena furrowed her brows and frowned as he said, "Whether he can wield a sword is of no importance to me. But you—" Cole pointed his sword at Serena. "You, Miss Finch, should learn how to handle the sword you carry before you get killed."

"He's right," Crystal said. "It's past time Serena begins training."

Serena opened her mouth to object, but Will interjected, "I agree with them."

Cole scoffed, and Crystal chuckled. "So, the southern boy agrees with the experienced warriors now?" she asked, folding her arms over her chest.

"Yes," Will said. He put a hand on Serena's shoulder. "We should both train with them. The enemy shall be ready for a fight. So should we."

Serena gripped the hilt of her father's sword but felt uncertain. She stared at Will, finding no consolation in his resolve, but hesitantly nodded. Crystal clapped her hands together, drawing Serena's attention away from her friend.

"Excellent. Cole shall work with Serena, and Rigel shall teach William," Crystal said.

"It's just Will," he corrected, his eyes cutting sideways.

"And what shall you do?" Serena asked the guardian.

"Tonight, I shall work on our dinner," she said, pulling a small bag of potatoes out of one of their bags. "With luck, I'll snag a few rabbits or a stag while you're occupied." Grabbing her quiver, she ducked her head and one arm through the strap, gripping her bow in one hand. "See if he can handle beginner's sword play," she added, waving as she departed their camp.

Cole rummaged through Rigel's bag of weapons and fished out two narrow wooden swords. "I thought Rigel was foolish for carrying these. Now they shall prove handy."

Serena noticed Rigel's hearty tone and the pride beaming from his face as he said, "Thank you."

Cole tossed one of them toward Serena, but Will caught it right in front of her. "I believe your sister wanted you to test my skills first," he said with a confident smirk. Serena reached out and grabbed the staff, but Will refused to let it go. "It's fine, Serena. We're only sparring. It's not a fight to the death," he said.

"I'm not so sure Cole knows how to spar without aiming for the kill," Serena said, making Rigel laugh.

"Cole will behave himself," Xandra said from beside Serena, smiling at the brooding warrior. "But he shall not go easy on you either." Dropping an armful of sticks at her feet, she pointed toward an open patch of dead grass a few feet away and said, "Go practice over there."

Will and Cole walked in the direction of the broad opening between the trees with Serena and Rigel trailing behind.

"Sticks are for children," Will said boldly. "I can handle a real sword."

Cole's eyes turned an even brighter blue as a mischievous grin settled on his cheeks. "I welcome the challenge," Cole said, unsheathing a massive blade. Will tossed the wooden practice stick to Rigel, who caught it in one hand.

Serena leaned into Rigel and murmured, "Are you sure Cole will not hurt him?"

Will rolled his eyes as he tested the weight of a sword in his hand, swiping it through the air. "I can handle whatever he throws my way."

"We shall see about that." Cole planted his feet firmly in the dirt, his legs wide and his knees bent slightly as he gripped the black hilt of his sword with both hands. The blade was dark gray, glistening as rays of sunlight peeked through the canopy above.

Rigel looked at Will and held up both of his hands in jest. "You asked for it. Was nice knowing you." He grinned as he urged Serena to step back out of the way.

Will lined up a few feet away from Cole and took a similar stance, bending his knees and grasping the hilt of the sword in both hands. Rigel motioned for Serena to step further back, saying, "Better get out of their way. If your friend is any good, this could get interesting."

"I've never seen you with a sword before," Serena said to Will. Her pulse hammered in her ears as she watched Cole pace. The intensity in his eyes terrified her.

Will thrummed his fingers across the sword's hilt and smirked. "Your father taught us a thing or two during our apprenticeship. We didn't stand around and watch him all day."

"Apprenticeship?" Rigel asked.

"Papa was a blacksmith. Will trained with him until Papa left town," Serena said, closing her eyes. The image of her father hunched over a project in the smith sprung to her mind, the heat of the room hitting her as if they were there. She had not seen him for several months, but she would never forget his face, not the intensity in his eyes while working nor the love that radiated from his smile when he walked through the doors of their home.

"In wartime, that is a much-needed profession," Rigel said, leaning his back against a tree and anticipating the action with a grin.

"Too bad Mister Finch left before I could master it," Will said, turning his focus toward Cole. The dueling men stared each other down for a minute, circling each other like vultures sizing up their prey. Without warning, Cole sprinted forward, swinging his blade quickly at Will's left shoulder. Will stepped back on his left leg, rolling back his shoulder and swinging his sword around in defense. The metal clashed together with a loud clank, causing Serena to flinch.

Rigel laughed and called out, "Nice move, Will!"

Xandra placed a hand on Serena's uninjured shoulder and whispered, "It will be all right. Cole won't hurt him. He was our advanced swordsmanship instructor at the Academy for a few years. He just wants to see how Will handles himself."

Will stepped forward with his left leg, using his blade to push Cole back a few steps. Pulling their blades apart, they each stepped forward, swinging their swords in front of them. Will lifted his blade high, and Cole held his sword sideways above his head to block the impending blow. Their swords collided again and again, both grunting with each clang of steel.

Suddenly, Will swung his sword at Cole's head. Without missing a beat, Cole dropped his sword and hit the ground on his hands. Swinging his legs in one swift movement, he swiped Will's feet out from under him. Will hit the ground on his side.

"Will!" Serena shouted, lunging forward, but Xandra and Rigel each seized an arm, holding her back.

Grasping his sword in one hand, Cole leapt onto his feet. Standing over Will, Cole planted a boot on his opponent's abdomen, chuckled, and said, "Never forget your feet, boy." Then, lifting his weapon, Cole plunged it down toward the ground where Will lay, unable to move. Serena shrieked.

"Your friend is fine," Cole said, removing his leg from Will's chest. As he sauntered past his audience, Serena whipped her head around to see Will frozen on the ground, one hand over his heart. Cole's sword protruded from the ground mere inches from Will's left eye, but Will didn't have a scratch on him.

Serena raced over and threw herself on the ground near his head, asking, "Are you all right? That was quite a fall." She examined him. "Are you injured?"

Will sat up slowly, rubbed his elbow, and touched his side. "I'm fine," he muttered through his teeth, looking in the direction of their camp, where his opponent sat before the fire with a big smile on his smug face. Rubbing his side, Will said, "He knows how to fight dirty."

Rigel and Xandra laughed. "You cannot expect the enemy to play fair," Rigel said, extending a hand and helping pull Will to his feet. "You have learned your first lesson: Never underestimate your opponent. Even while sparring a comrade, one should always be prepared for the unexpected."

"Rigel forgets his own advice at times," Xandra said with a chuckle, wrapping an arm around Serena's back and guiding her toward the camp. There, Cole had already ignited a fire. Xandra whispered, "See, I told you he would live."

Serena glanced over at Will, who was quietly tending to his arm. Blood had soaked through his sleeves in several places between his elbows and forearms. Xandra approached him, offering a small jar full of colorless ointment. "One advantage of being a guardian is access to the royal herbalist, Ismenia. Her medicine is quite useful in our line of work. Let's clean your wounds and apply this. It helps prevent infection."

Drawing closer, Serena watched over Will's shoulder as Xandra carefully rolled his sleeves to check his scraped forearms. She poured some water from a canteen over the wounds, and the reddened water trickled down, soaking into the ground. Then, swiping two fingers through the ointment, Xandra applied it directly to the abrasions.

"Done practicing so soon?" Crystal asked, approaching the fire with three bloody rabbits in hand. "I expected you to last longer in a fight, Burroughs. I thought you knew how to handle a blade?" She grinned, appearing quite pleased to have a reason to mock him.

"I know how to defend myself, but your brother is something else," Will said crossly, glaring down at the gash on his left arm.

"Remarkably, he fared quite well, for a farmer. He remained on his feet longer than I anticipated," Cole said, glancing over the fire at Will.

"For one thing, I am no farmer," Will said with a glare. "I apprenticed as a blacksmith. We always tested the weapons we made."

"Perhaps with some training, he could prove useful."

"I am impressed," Crystal admitted, looking at Will with her brows raised. "My brother does not easily pay such a compliment."

"Perhaps you both underestimated him," Xandra said.

"Perhaps I did," the archer replied.

Rigel said, "Elara holds an annual competition to recruit new blood for the Guard. If you train enough, I'm sure you could qualify."

"He shall have ample time to prove himself on our journey," Crystal said, taking a seat.

Serena smiled. "I think he's up for the challenge."

When Crystal began skinning the first rabbit, the sight of the knife scraping against flesh caused Serena's stomach to tense. She turned away, desperate for distraction, and focused on the conversation between Will and the other guardians.

"Your blade is unlike any I've ever seen," Will said, motioning toward the sheath resting beside Cole on the ground. Will caught it in both hands when Cole tossed it his way. He studied the jeweled hilt before pulling the sword out of its black sheath. The deep gray metal gleamed in the dim sunset light, and he admired the weapon as if it were a work of art. "The craftsmanship is superb," he said, his smile reflecting in the cool metal.

"It's Elven-made," Cole replied with a smirk.

Crystal's eyes flicked up, immediately locking on her brother. "It's standard for those who train in Envyre," she said before returning to her work.

"I would love to learn how to make one like this," Will said, flexing his fingers around the hilt. Serena watched as the red rubies above his hand caught the light, casting a diffuse reflection all around the camp.

"You hoping to find a new master in Symptee?" Rigel asked, taking the sword from Will and admiring it with far less enthusiasm.

"Possibly," Will said, stealing a quick glance at Serena.

"And if not, they're always looking for able-bodied soldiers," Rigel noted, sheathing Cole's sword and returning it to him.

"Symptee will be a fresh start," Xandra said. "You can be anything you want there."

"I like the sound of that," he said with a half smile.

Serena's gaze lingered on the sword, the rubies' glow fading as the campfire flickered. A fresh start in Symptee... A mixture of hope and uncertainty stirred within her as she pondered the possibilities that lay ahead, a faint smile playing on her lips.

DARK CORNERS

The queen awoke with a shrill scream; her sweat-drenched nightgown clung to her body as she pressed a hand against her chest. Her heart pounded, and she was disoriented. Elara sat up and swiped a clammy hand over her damp forehead. Squinting from the sunlight streaming into her chambers, she peered around the room. As she realized where she was, relief rushed over her.

Two guards clamored through her chamber door, swords in hand, and Elara clutched at the blankets, quick to cover herself.

"What is the meaning of this?" she demanded.

The guards slowly lowered their weapons as their eyes swept the room. Seeing the queen alone and unharmed, one said, "Our apologies, Your Majesty. We thought we heard you scream." He bowed before her, face flushed.

Elara breathed a heavy sigh, burying her face in the bedding. Her face burned as if she sat too close to the hearth, and her muscles ached. "Perhaps I did. Nightmare," she said with a shrug. "I'm fine. You may return to your post."

"It nears midday, milady. Are you not well?"

"No, I suppose not. Please summon Ismenia to my chambers."

The knights bowed and turned to exit her chambers. Before the doors closed, she called out, "And send for the oracle as well. I should like to speak with them both."

"Yes, Your Majesty," the knights replied in unison.

"Thank you," she whispered as they pulled the heavy doors closed, leaving her alone once again. Laying back on her pillow, Elara pushed the damp tangled curls back from her face and sighed. She longed for company, be it her lover or her friends, as she could not shake the fear that had crept into her heart. She lay awake until a creaking noise drew her attention.

The door to the servant's corridor opened, and one of her maidservants poked her head in. "Are you ill, milady? I tried to wake you earlier, but you asked me to leave," the mousy young woman said.

"Bea!" Elara said, raising her head. "Come! Don't be shy."

The maid twiddled with her waist-length hair, the chestnut locks taking on a red shade as she stepped into the sunlight. Approaching the queen's bed timidly, she asked, "How may I help you, Your Majesty?"

Elara reached a weak hand up to her and said, "I am feeling unwell."

The maid's eyes were an unusual kaleidoscope of innocence and concern. "Allow me to fetch Lady Ismenia."

"I have sent for her already. Thank you, Bea. If you could bring me some water—"

"Yes, milady," the maid said, racing across the room to where a large ceramic pitcher rested atop a grand desk. Returning to the queen's side, she carefully helped Elara sit up, stuffing extra pillows behind her for support. As Elara gulped from a gold-rimmed goblet, the women heard three urgent knocks on the main door. Bea darted to the door and opened it, and Ismenia rushed past the maid to Elara's bedside, pressing the back of her hand to the queen's slick forehead.

"Dear, what poor luck," Ismenia muttered, pushing up the queen's loose sleeves and inspecting her arms. "No sores or signs of pox. That is good at least." Turning to Bea, the herbalist said, "Have the cook prepare a light soup and my special lavender tea. And be discreet regarding our lady's illness."

"Yes'm," Beatrice said, nodding and scurrying for the servants' entrance.

"I felt fine yesterday," Elara said, blinking groggily.

"Tell me of everything you ate and everyone you saw. Perhaps we can find the source of your illness," Ismenia said, a spark of determination glistening in her dark eyes. The herbalist dipped a cloth into the wash basin on the dresser near Elara's bed, wringing the excess water out before pressing the cool rag to Elara's forehead. The queen breathed a sigh of relief.

"It could not have been from my meals. Everything went through food tasters. If they were to fall ill, I would know it," said Elara. "I am sure 'tis nothing serious."

"Perhaps, milady, but I advise caution, nonetheless," Ismenia said, dabbing the cool rag against the queen's neck. "Do you trust your maids?"

"Absolutely. Beatrice has been with us since the crossing. In Graynor, her mother was a loyal maidservant to mine," Elara said. "Bea, Hazel, and Mina have all grown up in the citadel. They have always been quite helpful. I have no doubt of their loyalty."

"I hope your trust is well placed," said her friend with a frown. Ismenia wiped her hands down her thighs.

The pale pink fabric of Ismenia's silk gown reminded Elara of the gardens, making her long for the shade of her beloved wisteria trees. "Perhaps fresh air would do me some good," the queen said, lifting her head as her gaze drifted toward the balcony.

Ismenia placed a hand on the queen's shoulder and pressed down, forcing her to lay back on the bed. "I must object, milady. You have a fever," the herbalist said, dipping the cloth into the basin once more. Sitting on the edge of the queen's bed, she continued dabbing the wet cloth to Elara's face, repeating the motion as she worked down the other side of her face to her neck.

"Bea is trustworthy," Elara mumbled in a daze, her thoughts elsewhere. She lifted a hand to touch Ismenia's wrist, and the herbalist paused. "I had a horrid dream last night. It felt so real. Serena was here, and—"

"Elara, you know dreams are my specialty," Idonea said from the doorway, her lips curved in a knowing smile. As Idonea approached the queen's bedside, the monarch froze, her eyes filled with fear. The oracle donned a dark crimson dress that made Elara think of fresh blood. When she reached her sister's side, Idonea bowed her head to the queen and asked, "Is that why you summoned me?"

"Can you not see she is ill? She has a fever," Ismenia said, rolling her eyes.

Next to each other, the ebony-skinned sisters looked otherworldly in their flowing frocks. Elara closed her eyes, feeling uneasy, and said, "I summoned both of you. I need to know what my dream means. It was so real—so horrifying."

Ismenia nodded, drawing her hand back from the queen's face. "Suppose I should go down to the kitchen and see about your tea." Rising and looking directly at her sister, the herbalist added, "Do not get her worked up over nightmares."

"I shan't," the oracle said, wiggling her fingers in the air. When her sister was gone, Idonea perched on the end of the queen's bed and said, "Now tell me of your dream."

Elara took a deep breath, recalling the horrors she had seen. "I heard a woman scream, and then I saw her, a woman collapsed on the floor in a puddle of blood. I think she was dead. I could not see her face but—"

"Slow down, Your Majesty. Close your eyes and breathe," Idonea instructed. Elara complied, closing her eyes and taking a calming breath. She folded her hands over her stomach and replayed the dream in her head. The oracle said, "Start at the beginning. Where are you?"

"I am in the doorway of a sitting room," Elara answered, wrinkles appearing on her forehead as the dream replayed in her mind. "Guards rush in and surround me. I can see the blood pooling from the body, but her hair hides her face. It's long, dark brown. She's wearing formal attire. She could be anyone."

"Is anyone else with you?"

"I believe so, but I did not see any other faces," Elara said, wringing her hands together. "For a moment, I thought I was looking upon my own body. Perhaps she is younger. I am unsure."

"That's all right," Idonea said, reaching to grasp Elara's hands. "Did any colors stand out to you?"

"I cannot remember anything but red. The blood was seeping between the stones in the floor. The mere thought of it is nauseating. It was so gruesome." Although Elara squeezed her eyes shut and covered her face, she still saw flashes of red dancing behind her lids.

"What happened after your men surrounded you?"

"They ushered me into another room, elsewhere in the citadel," Elara said. Idonea nodded at her observation. "Serena stood on the balcony. There was a man with her—I only saw the back of his head—but her eyes? She was afraid of him. He lunged at her and I screamed at him, but neither looked toward me. I wanted to help her, but my feet were frozen in place. I could not move. He was choking her, trying to push her over—"

"You have only seen Serena's face once," the oracle said, raising an eyebrow. Elara nodded. "And you are absolutely certain it was her?"

"I have no doubts. It was her."

"And you do not think it was Serena in the beginning?"

Elara moved her hand, opened her eyes, and blinked at Idonea. "No. Not for a second did I think that was her. It could not be. It was someone else," Elara said unconvincingly.

"If that is your intuition, that is good," Idonea said, cocking her head to one side.

Looking into the oracle's eyes, the queen said, "I've never had a dream feel quite so real. Is it possible it was something more?"

"You think it could have been a vision," Idonea said, nodding her head with a faraway look in her eyes. "It's possible. There was a full moon last night. Perhaps you were blessed with a momentous gift."

Elara propped herself up on one elbow, grimacing in revulsion. Leaning forward, she cried out, "Blessed? It was the most horrific thing I have ever seen!"

"It could be a warning." Idonea placed a hand on Elara's arm. "Both incidents took place within the citadel. Perhaps it is not as safe here as we believe?"

"Everyone within these walls has been here for over a decade. None of the guards have reason to be disloyal," Elara contended, furrowing her brows.

Idonea lowered her chin, fixing her gaze on the queen's hands. "I cannot be certain in this instance, milady. But I would advise you to take extra precautions, especially when Serena arrives."

Elara covered her face with her hands. "I do not know what more can be done. Guards escort me everywhere. They watch the entrance to my chambers day and night, and the guardians shall do the same when Serena arrives."

"I still believe you to be safe, milady. Do not fret. We shall ensure you are both kept safe. I am sure your dreams are no cause to be alarmed," Idonea said, rising from the bed. "Momentous gifts are quite rare. But if it was so, we cannot change what is destined."

Elara sighed in exasperation, turning to look through the window at the Athamar Mountains. Soon, Serena would join her in the City of Mercy. Soon, the girl would know everything, and they would begin preparations to take back Hyrosencia.

AFTER AN UNUSUALLY QUIET dinner with his family, Anteros snuck into the kitchen to fill a basket with food before creeping down the stairwell to the dungeon. As he pushed open the door to her cell, Talitha approached him cautiously. Torches mounted to all four walls cast flickering light throughout the dim cell. Her eyes narrowed at the bottle of wine in his hand, and she asked, "What are your intentions?"

"Thought you might enjoy a drink with your dinner."

"Dinner? Have you brought me another apple?"

"I was feeling generous," Anteros said, stooping to put the bottle of wine on the ground. Leaning back on one hand, he lowered his body to the floor. "Sit," he ordered as he lifted the woven top of the basket and pulled out a dish with a silver dome over it. Lifting the metal lid, he revealed a filet, two large rolls, and an assortment of cheese.

Talitha's jaw dropped; ravenous, her mouth watered as she eyed the plate. "Is this all for me?" She dropped to her knees and reached for the bread with a shaky hand.

"That is not all," Anteros said excitedly, reaching back into the basket. He turned from the basket with a bright red apple in hand, the sight of which made Talitha smile.

"Eat up," he said, winking as he tossed the apple her way.

She caught the fruit in both hands and wasted no time sinking her teeth into it. Juice trickled down her chin as she closed her eyes, savoring the first bite of the sweet, juicy treat. Then, gazing at the apple, Talitha's face contorted, and tears spilled out of her eyes as she squeezed her eyelids closed.

Anteros reached for her. As his fingers brushed her knee, she flinched and scooted away, increasing the distance between them. "Please don't touch me," she whispered without looking at him.

"My apologies," the prince said, pulling back his hand and holding both up in the air. "Have I insulted you? Or is something wrong with the food? I can fetch something else if you would like."

"No. It's delicious," Talitha said, taking another bite and chomping indignantly. Wiping at her dirt-streaked face with the back of her hand, she sniffled and muttered, "Thank you."

Anteros stared in silence as the girl regained her composure. When the cell became too quiet, he asked, "Are you all right?"

"I'm the king's prisoner. This meal," Talitha said with a grand gesture of her hand, "this is the greatest kindness I have been shown in weeks. There are no words to properly express how much this means to me."

"Then say no more, Red," he said, running a hand through his hair.

Talitha watched his shadow move on the dingy floor and frowned. "Why do you still call me that? I have told you my name."

"But Red suits you," Anteros teased with a sly grin.

Talitha rolled her eyes and took another large bite out of the apple, asking with her mouth full, "And your name is?"

"Anteros."

"Anteros Rexton," she said reflectively, pulling the plate of food closer. The ceramic trembled loudly against the tiles until she came to a stop. "So regal. You must have better things to do with your evening than feed the prisoners."

Anteros scrunched his nose and shook his head. "You would be surprised. The nobles keep to themselves, as do the officers. Father limits the frivolous parties to weekly engagements. Otherwise, there is little to entertain us."

"In the South we had heard stories of the elaborate parties of the palace. But we had harvest festivals, bonfires... sometimes a wedding. Those were always fun," she said, ripping a large bite from a chunk of bread with her teeth.

"Thankfully, we have had none of those as of late," Anteros said. "Though my sister shall be sixteen by summer's end, and my mother shall insist on a grand ball to present her to the noble families properly. I dread the day."

"She is not much younger than I," Talitha said, pulling her knees up to her chin. The prince studied her face. "May I ask your age?"

"I am seventeen," whispered Talitha, biting her lip. "Eighteen in autumn."

"I am seventeen as well," Anteros said, his gaze raking over her lightly freckled face.

Talitha swallowed and turned her eyes to inspect the meat on the plate before her. Anteros imagined it was a finer cut than she was accustomed to eating. "Do you have a knife?"

"Ah, allow me," he said, scooting closer to the plate. Pulling a fork and knife from the basket, he carefully cut the meat into bite-sized pieces. While he worked, he asked, "Do you have siblings?"

"I do not wish to speak of my family," Talitha said, focusing on Anteros' hands as he worked the knife through her dinner. "Tell me more of your sister. What is her name?"

"Sabine. She is something..."

"What? I am sure she's a nice girl. She is related to you, and you're not so bad," Talitha said, hiding her shy smile behind the second piece of bread.

Anteros held a piece of meat out on a fork. A hint of color spread through her pale cheeks as she leaned forward and ate it. The prince grinned, and she averted her gaze and her ears turned red. "Sabine does not have many friends at court," Anteros said. "When she enters a room, all eyes are on her. The ladies who stand beside her can only hope one of the noblemen she casts aside will notice them."

"Heavens," Talitha murmured. "She must be quite beautiful then."

Anteros chuckled. "I suppose she is," he said, shaking his head. "She would like you. You both have a certain fire about you. It is rare to behold."

Her face flushed as her eyes met his. "So that is why you're here? You like my hair?"

Anteros stabbed another piece of meat with the fork and held it out to her, saying, "I was not referencing your hair, though it compliments your personality."

"You act as if you know me so well," Talitha said in indignation and leaned forward for another bite. "You barely know my first name."

"I know that despite being tortured, you didn't speak a word to my father's men," said Anteros. "I have seen far tougher men cave to their methods of torture, yet you stood firm. That's quite remarkable."

"Once you have been kissed by flames, drowning feels refreshing," Talitha said, resting one of her temples against her knee. There was a haunted look about her face as she stared at the floor.

"Water may feel better than fire, but that does not mean it cannot kill you the same."

Talitha lifted her head and scowled as she snapped, "Do not think me so strong. I prayed for death when they brutalized me. I begged Divinity to spare me from any more pain, yet here I am. As if He could not hear my desperation. Or maybe He thinks I deserve this."

"You're an Estrelle?"

"Of course," she said. "Most Hyrosencians are."

"Not in Graynor," Anteros said, folding his hands behind his head. "Since my father took over, most of the northern area converted. They worship Solaire among other deities."

"And in the south, Estrelles persist," she said. "You're the first Solairian I have met."

"How do you know what I believe?" Anteros jested.

Talitha's head cocked to one side, and she scoffed loudly. "You are the king's son. You're a Solairian. I have no doubt of that."

Anteros grinned. "I've always been curious about the Estrelles," he whispered. "Do you truly believe there is one higher being that rules us all?"

"Yes," Talitha answered firmly, nodding her head. "Though I question why I still bother praying to Him. Clearly Divinity is not concerned about what's happening to me."

"What a fool He would be to ignore you," Anteros said, leveling her with a hooded gaze.

Talitha's eyes widened, and she shook her head vigorously. "Do not say such things," she insisted, her chest rising and falling rapidly. She turned her face toward the barred window and said, "My mum told me when we suffer, it is reparation for our wrongdoings."

"Tell me, what could you have done in your seventeen years to deserve such a fate?" he asked in earnest.

Talitha shrank back against the rough stone wall. "I'm still trying to figure that out," she muttered with a lifeless shrug.

Anteros rested his head against the wall and stared forward, realizing just how bleak the cell looked. "I do not think there is anything you could have done to deserve what's been done to you," he said, resting his hand on the floor beside her. His fingertips barely brushed against hers, and they both sucked in a deep breath.

"Thanks," she mumbled. "You're the nicest person I've met since I got here."

He slammed back into the wall and snickered. "That's terrible. I'm not even that nice."

"Well, you're a gem compared to your father," she countered, shoving his arm.

"My father is complicated. But you're still alive, so that's a good thing," Anteros said with a shrug. "He could have done worse."

"I can only imagine. His ruthlessness is known far and wide."

"He might have let you go if you had answered his questions the first time," the prince said, leaning closer to her.

"Silence was the only way to protect my family and friends. That's all I could do," she said and yanked up one sleeve of her shirt to reveal scabbed cuts and healing scars. "These remind me to be silent. I would not wish this suffering on anyone else. My family and friends should not incur your father's wrath just because he fears a few loyalists in hiding." Talitha turned away from him.

Her words lingered in their ears as the silence dragged on, threatening to drag Anteros down into the darkest corner of his mind. "You're right," he whispered as the lifeless eyes of several corpses flashed through his head. He had seen all too many times what his father was capable of in a fit of rage.

Anteros was taken back by the pools of sorrow staring back as she turned to face him. Looking at her red-rimmed eyes suddenly made him uncomfortable, as if she could drown him with a pointed stare. His eyes dropped to the plate beside him, and he stabbed another slice of meat, saying, "You should eat. You need to regain your strength."

Talitha breathed slow and steady, shifting her focus from his face to the fork. She parted her lips and leaned forward. When the fork was right in front of her, she quickly snatched it from him and said, "I promise I shall not stab you with it. 'Tis not like I could get far."

Anteros pushed the plate closer to her and rolled his eyes. "You're a smart girl, Talitha. Smarter than most."

She swallowed another bite, cleared her throat, and said, "I shall take that as a compliment."

"Thirsty?" he asked, reaching for the bottle of wine. Looking at the label, he added, "It's from the year my father took the throne—the year I was born. There are a hundred bottles of this year in the wine cellar. Figured no one would miss this one."

He took the key to her cell and jammed it deep into the cork. Holding the bottle still with one hand, Anteros took hold of the top of the key and slowly began twisting it around. The cork slowly wriggled upwards as he twisted the key until the cork emerged from the bottle.

"I daresay that was impressive," she said, raising her eyebrows in surprise. Swiping the bottle from his hands, she took several generous gulps. When she was finished, Talitha placed the bottle down between them and wiped her lips with the back of her hand. "Who knew wine could be so sweet?"

"Have you not had wine before?"

"Don't look so shocked. I did not grow up in a castle. Durmak is a simple place with bitter spirits. You drink from the vineyard of bliss; we drink of your father's wrath."

"Do you miss it?" he asked, searching her face.

Talitha brushed a frizzy strand of hair behind her right ear and sighed. "It's home. Of course I miss it. I would give anything to be there now."

"I think you'll see it again one day," Anteros said coolly. He took a swig of wine and placed the bottle back on the ground. "I would give anything for this prison to be less dreary."

"Unlike me, you are not required to be here," Talitha said, scrunching her nose. She glared at him as she shoved a piece of cheese in her mouth.

"I did not mean the dungeon. I meant the castle in general. It's so dull. Everyone is afraid of my father," Anteros said. "It's hard to find genuine friends around here. Everyone is either scared of me or desperate to use me to advance their position at court."

"I can understand their fear. You're not what I would have expected of Antoine Rexton's son. Keep bringing me food, and I may even consider you a friend."

Anteros laughed heartily, which made one corner of her mouth twitch upward. "I have never had a female friend before," he said. "My sister may get jealous."

"I could be her friend, too," Talitha said. "It's not like I am going anywhere."

"I may be able to arrange that. She certainly needs more friends."

"Friends with two royals? Perhaps my situation is taking a turn for the better," Talitha said wryly, tilting the wine bottle up and chugging from it.

Anteros reached out to stop her, and his fingers brushed against hers as he took hold of it. "Perhaps you shall breathe life into this dismal fortress we call home," he said softly and took another swig from the bottle.

When they finished the bottle, Anteros stacked the plate and bottle back into the basket. Turning to her, he held out a hand and said, "Fork, please."

Talitha reddened as she pulled it out of her pocket. "I was hoping you would not notice."

"Planning to stab me on my next visit?" Anteros asked, raising an eyebrow as he took it.

"Not you," she blurted, wrapping her arms around her legs. "I just wanted it for protection. From the guards."

Immediately, Anteros leaned closer to her and leveled his face with hers. "Did anything happen after my last visit?"

"No. Nothing has happened in my cell," she said. "But I wish to be prepared."

"None are to enter your cell without direct orders from me or my father. Should anyone defy my orders, I will kill them myself," he said. Her eyes widened at his intensity; her lips parted, but she remained silent. Anteros pushed himself off the floor and onto his feet, slowly stepping backward toward the door. "Get some rest. I'll return tomorrow." He locked the door behind him, stealing one last glance through the small opening in it before disappearing down the hall.

As the prince rounded the corner to ascend the stairs, he bumped into a figure in a black velvet cloak. The basket hit the floor; the empty wine bottle clamored out of it and rolled away from them. Anteros scrambled to swipe the bottle, stuffing it into the basket as he asked, "Who are you? Why are you lurking in the dark?"

"Do you not recognize your own sister?" Sabine asked as she dropped her hood, her dazzling smile a stark contrast from the dark, damp dungeon. "And I do not lurk. I was waiting for you. Were you visiting the new prisoner again?"

Anteros gave her a stern look. "That is not your concern, Sabine. Did you follow me down here? The dungeons are no place for a lady."

"Is there not a young lady imprisoned down here? The servants talk, you know," Sabine said, twirling her hair. "I heard she endured torture for a week and did not utter a word. Perhaps she is mute!"

Anteros trudged past his sister and began the ascent upstairs, giving her no answer. Sabine turned, lifted her plum-colored skirt, and chased after him. "Anteros, slow down! I am right, am I not?"

"I was following Father's orders," Anteros said crossly without stopping. "Why have you followed me? You should not be in this part of the castle."

"As if Father cares where I am," Sabine said, falling in step with her brother as they climbed the stairs. "I noticed you were not returning to your chambers after dinner, and I was intrigued, especially when you left the kitchen with a basket full of food. Did you bring it to bribe the guards?"

"Yes," he said, clenching his jaw.

"Liar! I know you brought it to that girl," Sabine said, shoving him playfully as they reached the next floor. "Why are you visiting her twice in one day? I didn't know you were so desperate for a romp." She pressed her hand to her chest, her entire body shaking as she laughed.

Anteros whirled around to face his sister, glaring as he stepped up to her. Sabine bit her lip as his shadow swallowed her petite frame. He dared her with his eyes to make another joke. "She has been beaten and starved. She's terrified of Father's men. I'm sure you can imagine why."

Something dark flashed in his sister's eyes as she realized what he meant, and she quickly looked down at the floor. "How uncivilized," Sabine said, wrinkling her nose and shaking her head. "That poor girl."

"Despite all that's been done to her, she is unbroken, so I tried kindness instead," Anteros said, gesturing to the basket. "Turns out she'd rather chat with someone she can trust."

Laughter echoed up the stairs, and Sabine shivered, wrapping her arms around herself. "Must be hard to sleep with those scoundrels cackling down the hall," she said, glancing back as they walked away from the stairwell. "If only someone could make her situation better. She would likely throw herself at him."

"Must you always be so crass, sister? She isn't one of your floozy friends," Anteros said, rubbing a hand over his face. His eyelids drooped as he plodded on toward his bedchamber. "And I would bet Red is smarter than both of us."

"Red? That's an odd name," the princess muttered, once again falling in step beside her brother as they reached a different stairwell. She lifted her billowing skirt and clamored up the steps after him.

"It's a nickname," Anteros said, taking the steps two at a time.

"I thought she told you her real name?" Sabine huffed, struggling to keep up.

"She did, but only her first name. And I prefer Red. It irks her," the prince said. He grinned mischievously.

"There are dozens of young ladies ready to throw themselves at you, the crown prince, yet you're only intrigued by the girl accused of treason? Father would explode at the thought." She smirked impishly.

Anteros caught his sister by the wrist and slapped a hand over her mouth. Peering down at the small savage girl, he said, "Do not interfere. This is my assignment. Father entrusted me with it—told me to get information out of her by whatever means necessary. Since torture was useless, I am doing the opposite. I brought her a proper meal, and she seemed quite taken by the gesture. I may learn something useful if I gain her trust."

Sabine yanked her arm out of his grasp and raised her eyebrows. "I must say, Anteros, that is quite brilliant. Father might not agree with your methods, but I do not doubt it shall work," she said, brushing past his shoulder and continuing up the stairs. "What made you think to take that approach?"

"The hunt. Prey is often lured into a trap with food."

The Rexton siblings entered the main corridor on the second floor and continued walking side-by-side. Sabine peered up and down the empty hall before whispering, "Did you learn anything new from her tonight?"

"Nothing useful. I believe some of the guards abused her on the journey to Graynor. She is skittish, scared to be touched, but she has not lost her nerve. She tried to steal a fork from me," Anteros said, shaking his head.

Sabine's cheeks deflated as her smile melted into a look of concern. "That is barbaric. Perhaps you should bring a healer to examine her? If she was mistreated, she could die from infection—or worse, she could be with child!"

Anteros glanced at his sister and said, "That is not a bad idea."

Sabine smirked, pleased with the compliment. "I could arrange for new clothes to be sent down tomorrow."

"Nothing fancy, Sabine. She sleeps in the dungeon."

"Perhaps we could arrange a more civilized area for her, especially if she grows more comfortable with you," the young lady said, freeing her skirts to sweep across the floor.

As two servants walked toward them, Anteros placed a finger to his lips in warning. He nodded curtly as they walked by without a word. When they reached the hall where their private chambers were located, Anteros said, "You should bring the clothes personally. Tell the guards I sent you. Perhaps a female companion would make her more comfortable."

"I loathe the dungeon," Sabine said, dropping her head back in a melodramatic fashion. Returning upright, she added, "But I suppose I should get a look at this girl you admire."

"I do not admire her. I am trying to gain information from her," Anteros said, avoiding his sister's eyes. "If I am unsuccessful, Father will have her head, and I shall never hear the end of it from either of you."

Sabine paused in front of her bedchamber door and frowned. "There have been more than enough deaths in Graynor in our lifetime," she noted. "Do what you must to save this one."

He nodded. He would try.

COUNTING THE DAYS

Gerard Stirling bounded toward the Cinderfell sisters, who stood outside the doorway chattering in hushed tones. "Is Elara all right? I was not permitted to see her yesterday," he said with a frown, glancing past them at the queen's guards. "They said she was ill."

"Her Majesty has been terribly ill, but her fever has broken at last," Ismenia said. She wiped her own sweaty forehead with the back of her hand. "The maidservant and guards shall keep watch over her while she sleeps, and I shall return in a few hours."

"Have you any idea what ails her?"

The herbalist stepped back from him, and the oracle pushed off from the wall to address him. "It is neither pox nor plague. Whatever it was, we are optimistic she shall soon recover. You need not worry."

"I cannot help but worry. I love her," Gerard said. "May I see her now?"

"She just fell asleep, my lord. Perhaps you should return later," Ismenia suggested.

Gerard ran a hand through his silvery hair and exhaled in agitation. "I worried all night after the guards turned me away. I promise I will not wake her. I only wish to be there when she awakes. She should know I am here for her."

Ismenia looked at her sister unsure, but Idonea nodded. "I suppose that would be acceptable."

The tension in his face disbursed, and Gerard quickly cleared the distance between them, placing a hand on Ismenia's shoulder. "Thank you. I am grateful you were here to care for her. Please rest knowing she will not be alone. We shall call for you if her condition changes."

"I know you will." Ismenia produced a tired smile.

Idonea stepped forward and looped her arm through her sister's. "Let us retire, Ismenia." Nodding her head, the herbalist joined her sister, and the queen's caretakers trudged off toward their personal chambers to recover from their hard night's work.

The guards allowed Gerard to enter Elara's chambers. Beatrice, the maidservant, softly asked, "Should you wish to be alone, my lord?"

"That is not necessary," he whispered, approaching Elara's bedside. "Pretend I am not here." Looking down at his betrothed, a wave of relief washed over him. Her face was serene, as if she had not been suffering. Gerard kissed her forehead before taking a seat on the cream-colored chaise lounge a few feet from her bed.

Beatrice tidied up the room in silence, taking the wash basin by Elara's bedside and dumping the water over the balcony. Using a pitcher, she refilled the basin, as well as the glass on Elara's bedside table. Without asking, she fetched a second glass, filled it, and handed it to Lord Stirling, who thanked her with a faint smile.

Elara slept for several hours with little movement, and Gerard remained by her side. Beatrice left once around midday, returning a half hour later with a plate of food for the Islander. He was pushing the food around with a fork, his forehead wrinkled in displeasure, when a hoarse voice whispered, "You should eat that."

Gerard's eyes shot up from the plate to meet Elara's drowsy eyes and weak smile. Leaping from the chair and stumbling over to her bed, he grasped her hand and asked, "Did I wake you?"

"I do not believe so," she said, taking a deep breath. "How long have you been here?"

Gerard ran a hand through her matted curls. Gazing into her eyes, he replied, "Just a few hours. I spoke with the Cinderfells as they were leaving. Your condition was improved, but they were reluctant to leave you."

"Yes, I vaguely remember. They were here most of yesterday and well into the night. I am glad they are resting now. I feel much better already." Elara tried to push herself up into a seated position.

Gerard wrapped his arm around her and helped her sit upright. Staring into her sunken eyes, he said sternly, "You may feel better, but you still need rest. Do not attempt too much too soon."

Elara patted his cheek gently; his fingers grazed his coarse, unshaven face. She rolled her eyes and said, "How could I? You or the Cinderfells will scold me if I get out of bed."

"That we shall." He perched on the edge of the bed, and with resolve, he said, "We should postpone wedding preparations until you are recovered."

"Absolutely not," Elara snapped, wrinkles appearing between her eyebrows. Grasping his arm, Elara stared him down as she said, "That is not necessary. I shall be recovered in a day or two. There is no need to cease preparations—unless you have another reason to delay."

He shook his head. "I am ready to wed you, my love. I have been counting the days," Gerard said, squeezing her hand. "But you must be in good health. Our wedding is in a fortnight. I do not wish to carry you down the aisle."

"Perhaps I would enjoy that," the queen countered. A bright smile spread across her rosy cheeks. Squeezing his hands back, she said, "Gerard, don't delay our nuptials. Your guests should arrive any day. It would not be wise to wait any longer."

Gerard smiled and bent down to plant a kiss on her head. Elara placed a hand on his chest. "You should not get too close. My illness could be infectious."

"Your friends spent all night by your side. I am willing to risk it for you," he said, pecking her on the lips. "Is there any way I can help while you recover?"

"The War Council. We need to review the latest correspondence from our allies and the loyalists. Would you oversee the meeting in my absence? I trust you to act in Hyrosencia's best interest."

"If that is where you need me, it's my honor to represent you," he said. He was pleased with the assignment of this task. When Elara covered her mouth with one hand and yawned, Gerard turned his eyes away from her, focusing on the water glasses on the end table. "You need to rest," he said. "I should go. Ismenia will fuss if she learns I disturbed you." He rose from her bed and peered out her window toward the Athamar Mountains with his back facing her.

"I do not want you to leave. Your presence has lifted my spirits. Please stay—at least a few minutes more."

Turning back toward her, Gerard smiled, shook his head at her stubbornness, and said, "I shall stay, but only if you go back to sleep."

"I have had enough fever dreams for a lifetime." Elara peered through the open window at the snowcapped mountains.

"There is nothing to fear from dreams. Besides, your fever is gone."

"You do not understand. I told Idonea of them, and she—she thought perhaps they were visions," Elara said with hesitation, looking down at her hands and fidgeting.

Gerard scrutinized her face. He expected to hear more. Elara avoided his gaze and sighed. "Perhaps I am losing my mind from the stress of it all," she muttered.

Seeing her discomfort, he stepped forward, placing a hand over hers. "What do you believe? Do you think you saw something of the future?"

"I do not know what to believe. In one dream, there was a dead woman in my sitting room. In the other, Serena..." She paused, and Gerard knew she was recalling something dreadful as her eyes watered.

"You do not have to tell me," he said, taking a seat next to her. "It may have been a fever dream, as you said before. It may not come to pass."

A single tear slid down her right cheek. Elara breathed in sharply, blinking back her tears, and said, "If it does, I fear Serena shall be in danger when she arrives in Symptee. What if we cannot protect her? She has been through so much already."

"The Guard is prepared for anything. I am certain she'll be as safe as you have been all these years. We shall not allow any harm to come to her," Gerard said confidently. "She is far too important to you—and your people."

Gerard grabbed the blankets and pulled them up to her waist, saying, "I must insist you try to rest. I'll be right beside you should you have any more bad dreams."

Elara scooted down until she laid flat on her back with her head cushioned by a feather pillow. Turning on her side, she muttered, "If you insist," and closed her eyes.

SERENA WINCED AS SHE landed hard on the ground. For several days, Cole had been teaching her the basics of swordsmanship, but she moved much slower than the guardians. She glared up at him and said, "I shall never be able to fight you. This is unfair."

Her mentor rolled his eyes as he offered her a hand, and she took it unenthusiastically. As Cole helped Serena up, he said, "You must remember to plant your feet properly. If your weight is evenly dispersed, it will be harder for your opponent to knock you down. Even when you step forward or back, you must remain balanced."

"I have never had to practice standing before," Serena grumbled. She picked up the wooden training staff from the ground.

"You'll get used to it. It takes time, but you are picking up the defensive moves quickly," Xandra said with an optimistic smile. "It takes everyone time to adapt to the fluidity of sword fighting."

"Don't lie to her, Xan. You were a natural, even as a child. That is why you wield two," Rigel said, unsheathing his sword. He turned toward Serena and demonstrated a swift motion with his blade as he said, "You have to master control of your body. The sword must become an extension of your arm. Once the movements become natural, you must learn to predict your opponent's next move. Fighting is like chess. You must think three moves ahead."

"I was never great at chess," Serena moaned, burying her face in her hands. "Could I at least switch instructors? Will is picking this up faster than I am. He should be the one working with Cole."

"Have I scared you off already?" Cole turned but not in time to hide the hint of a smirk on the edge of his lips. Serena didn't miss his mocking tone and stuck her tongue out while his back was turned. Xandra muffled a chuckle, pretending to cough into her hand as Cole glanced her way. He turned toward his sister and said, "Noomï will be crawling with soldiers. One of us should stay back with Serena while the rest make the supply run."

"I can stay with her," Will said without hesitation.

Cole's icy eyes penetrated Will. "I meant a guardian." Then he looked at his sister and said, "But it's your call, Crys."

"Rigel will stay with Serena. They can practice while the rest of us go into the city. We shall only be gone an hour or so, and then we head north into the mountains. The dwarfs should be anticipating us," she said.

Serena pouted, crossing her arms over her chest. "I should have liked to see Noomï."

"We barely got past the border with stolen papers. Cole and Rigel had to pretend they were going to deliver us to a brothel," Crystal said, wrinkling her nose. "I should prefer not to have my weapons taken and my hands bound again."

Will's eyes bounced between Serena and Crystal. "Are you sure it's safe to leave them alone out here? Perhaps I should stay as well."

"I take great offense at what you're insinuating," Rigel said, stepping closer and puffing out his chest.

"I didn't mean that you would do anything." Will held up his hands in surrender as his face reddened. "I meant what if someone stumbles across the camp?"

"Give it a rest, boys." Xandra nudged the ginger guardian with an elbow. "Rigel can handle any issues. We shall need your help carrying supplies. The four of us shall have to carry enough supplies for six to reach Estivor."

"How long will that take?" Serena asked. She plopped on the ground beside them.

"Perhaps a week, if you can manage the pace," Crystal answered.

"Depends how the altitude affects everyone," Xandra added. "Crys and Cole were unaffected by the change, but it slowed me down quite a bit. Perhaps the journey back shall be better though."

"It's not an easy venture," Rigel said. "We are less likely to run into soldiers in the mountains, but there are far worse dangers."

"Then why don't we cross into the unsettled land sooner?" Will asked, sheathing the practice sword in his hands and dropping it back into the supply bag.

"Because it is far easier to cross the border between Norlee and Hyrosencia. The guards at the eastern border do not allow anyone to pass either way," said Cole. "We have planned our route quite carefully. The dwarfs have been incredibly accommodating, so we shall have time to rest and recover between our travels."

"I still cannot believe we're going to see dwarfs in person," Will said, nudging Serena's shoulder. "Who would have thought we should see the other realms in our lifetime?"

Serena shook her head and whispered, "I certainly did not."

Crystal emptied her bag of all its contents. Taking her canteen, she chugged its contents, water dripping down the side of her mouth and neck. "Ah," she sighed when her supply was emptied. "Drink up everyone. We shall refill all the canteens at the well in town."

They followed Crystal's orders, drinking swiftly from their water supply. Then Crystal and Xandra collected their array of canteens, placing them into nearly empty rucksacks. Without further delay, Crystal waved for her comrades to follow her out of camp.

"Take care of her," Will called over his shoulder to Rigel.

Serena wrinkled her nose and called back, "I can take care of myself!"

As soon as Will and the other three guardians left, Rigel and Serena resumed sparring. He went easier on her than Cole did, which was a great respite from the brutal intensity of her previous training. Serena planted her feet firmly in the thick grass, her left foot forward, and grasped her sword's hilt in both hands, holding it over her right shoulder. Rigel stepped forward and swung his blade toward her. Immediately, Serena stepped to the right and rolled her left shoulder back away from the strike zone before swinging her sword to block his.

"Good," Rigel said. "Now counterattack."

Serena applied force with her blade, and Rigel stepped back from her. Advancing with her right foot, she lifted her sword high and swung it down toward his left shoulder, which he quickly blocked. He held his sword up over his head. Remembering one of Cole's favorite moves, she stepped forward and kicked Rigel in the abdomen while he was open.

Stumbling backward, Rigel coughed and scrambled to regain his footing. "I see you have learned some tricks from Cole. That could be useful in a real battle."

"You said I was learning from the best," Serena said. She grinned as she charged closer to him. Swinging the blade once more, Rigel shifted his body to his right, blocking her sword and using his blade to shove hers away. He spun quickly before swinging his blade back at her, stopping short at Serena's wrist.

"Cole may be unbeatable, but you still have a way to go before you surpass me," Rigel said with a triumphant smirk. "He trained Xandra and I both in advanced skills, after all."

Puffing in disappointment, Serena whined, "I'll never be as good as you. You're guardians! You grew up fighting. I am just a normal girl. I should be fetching eggs and sneaking off to bonfires."

"You should be. We all should be. But everything changes when your homeland becomes a warzone," Rigel said solemnly, lowering his sword. "You have worked hard today. Let's take a break while the others aren't here to hassle us."

Serena smiled and nodded. They turned to the remnants of their makeshift camp and sat by the supplies near their grazing horses.

"You seldom speak of your life before the Academy," Serena noticed.

"It's not a fun story." Serena watched as Rigel stared into the distance. "I was born in Axys. My father was an armorer, and my mother was a midwife. My elder brother Silas wanted to join the Guard. He won the joust in the Garrick Games and earned a position as a royal knight the summer before Rexton invaded."

"Do you know what happened to him when the king invaded?"

"He had been posted in Morlerae when Rexton's army invaded. Since he never registered in Symptee, I assume he was killed in battle. When word of King Scorpius's demise reached Axys, my mother wanted us to get out of the kingdom. I was only a child then. My mother begged my father to take me to Symptee, but she refused to leave behind the women in her care. I have not seen her since the night we fled."

"Oh, Rigel, I am so sorry you had to grow up without her." Serena reached out and touched his arm. "She could still be alive. You never know."

"That's why I went to Axys with Cole while Crystal went south to retrieve your family." He picked at the blades of grass near his feet. "Another family lived in our old home. The midwife was a younger woman my mother had trained before she left town. She didn't know where my mother went. I will probably never know."

Serena looked down as she remembered the loss of her own mother, and she squeezed his hand supportively before drawing it back into her lap. "My mother was killed violently. Part of me wishes I never found her that way, but at least she died knowing I was alive. I suppose that was a small comfort in her final moments. She told me to go to Symptee, to Queen Elara, just as your mother did."

"Mothers always know best," Rigel said with a sad smile. Serena joined him in plucking grass from the ground. "Do you know where your father is?"

"I have not the slightest idea. He left months ago, and only my mother knew where he was going. I was told he needed new tools. He was the only blacksmith in Durmak. Will worked very closely with him."

"That explains that." Rigel smiled.

"What?"

"It's obvious there are some deeper feelings there." His knowing smirk grew bigger. "You like him, don't you?"

Serena felt the heat in her cheeks. "No. Of course not! Will is just a friend!" She thought of him traveling all the way from Durmak in search of her and how he pleaded for her to return home with him. She thought of the warmth in his eyes when they met in the forest mere hours before her life unraveled.

"Just a friend?" the guardian repeated, his eyebrows raised as he studied the deep flush of her face.

Serena shifted uneasily and turned to face the endless woods that surrounded them. "He was closer to my older brother. When Cameron left to join the king's army, he asked Will to watch out for us," she said. "I think he feels guilty for what happened."

"Perhaps he does, though it's no fault of his own," Rigel said, shaking his head. "I get the feeling he would die protecting you if it came to that."

"Don't say that! I could not bear to lose anyone else. I have already lost too much." Serena clenched her fists. Her dirty fingernails dug into her palms as her hands trembled. "Rexton might as well have ripped out my heart and crushed it in his fist. I have never felt such hatred for another person."

Rigel shifted and placed his hand in the center of Serena's back. "We are similar, you and me. We might as well be orphans of war. Both of our lives were torn apart by Rexton, and we lost the people we loved most."

The joy faded from Rigel's bright blue eyes, and Serena worried there was more he was not telling her. In hopes of changing the subject, she said, "Tell me what happened when you and your father left Axys. How did you escape before Rexton took control of the borders?" Rigel tensed. His face turned pale. Placing his elbows atop his knees, he pressed his lips against his intertwined hands. Serena waited; she was afraid she had asked something too personal. "You don't have to answer that," she added.

"My father took me northeast to Murmont for supplies," Rigel said at last. His eyes glazed over as he recalled the memory. "Rumor was the queen had been taken east to the citadel, so my father wanted to cross the mountains instead of going south toward the valley. At the time, we knew that the valley was home to insatiable characters, but few knew what lay on the other side of it. My father put his faith in the dwarfs, believing they would have pity on refugees."

"And did they?"

"Yes, though they were reluctant at first," he said. "Luckily, Elara had made an alliance with the Dwarf King when she crossed, and their people agreed to shepherd refugees through their tunnels to safety."

"So, you went through the mountains and were among the first to reach Symptee?" Serena asked excitedly.

"No," Rigel said quietly, the skin over his knuckles taut as he clenched his hands together. "My father became ill on the journey. When we reached the city of Jordis, the dwarfs were kind. They provided food and shelter when we had nothing to offer. As my father's condition worsened, the dwarfs made sure he was comfortable. He died in our room in the tunnels."

Serena reached toward him again, moved by compassion for her new friend. "Rigel, I did not realize—"

"I don't discuss the past with just anyone," he explained. "It took years for me to open up to Xandra and, much later, the Windaefs. But I wanted you to know you're not alone in your suffering."

"Well, thank you," Serena said with a grim smile.

"The moment we left Axys, my life became plagued by death and chaos. I was nine years old when the dwarfs escorted me through the tunnels to Silvermane. It was built on the highest peak of the mountain, and the view of Symptee is just incredible. I still remember the first time I laid eyes upon the City of Mercy. It gave me hope for a better future."

"It sounds magnificent," Serena whispered. "I hope it shall give me the same feeling. I could use something to hope for right now."

Rigel glanced sideways at her before speaking. "These are difficult times, Serena. Our homeland lies under a storm cloud which rains down blood without end. Symptee has become a beacon of hope for our people. That's why we call it the City of Mercy. Those who abandoned their homes and fled to East Hyro have a fierce belief that we shall take back our kingdom one day."

"I want to believe that," Serena said. "But after all these years, it's hard to imagine anyone defeating Rexton. As you said, the rebellion in Hyrosencia was crushed years ago. Rexton's reign is all I have ever known. It's hard to imagine Elara ever having the numbers to win a war when it's so hard for our people to cross the borders."

"Do you believe in Estrellogy?" he asked abruptly, and Serena could see the expectation in his eyes.

Hesitantly, Serena looked to the sky, bright blue with puffy white clouds overhead. "I did," she muttered. She wished she could see the stars that reminded her of her lost loved ones. "Lately, I am not sure what to believe."

"I felt the same after my father's death. I wanted to know why Divinity had me lose both of my parents and enter a strange new world on my own."

"Did you find an answer in Symptee?"

"Several Estrelists escaped to Symptee when the invasion occurred—among them was Idonea, the oracle. She prophesized that the true heir of Hyrosencia would rise to face Antoine Rexton. The promise of the prophecy was enough to give our people hope again."

"The true heir of Hyrosencia," Serena repeated, wrinkling her brow. "Would that be Elara?"

"She does not believe so," Rigel said flatly, averting his gaze. "We knew the Garrick heir would need an army of their own, so many of the orphaned refugees enrolled at the Academy. When the heir is ready to strike back against Rexton, hundreds will be ready to follow them."

"I am glad you found your purpose. I hope the City of Mercy shall guide me to mine," Serena said. She laid back in the grass. She pondered the oracle's prophecy as she watched the clouds inch by. One reminded her of a fluffy white rabbit. At first, her thoughts drifted back to her encounter with Will in the woods beyond Durmak. Death is unsightly. He was right. While she was on her own, she had no choice but to kill a small white rabbit for food. It was her first kill; the sight of bright red blood on her hands caused her to vomit. She hated that the most harmless creatures were the easiest to catch. It felt cruel to cut their lives short. She squeezed her eyes closed and shook the memory out of her mind, praying she would forget the dead eyes and putrid smell of blood that tainted her memories.

"Don't worry. Divinity will show you your path," Rigel said.

Serena opened her eyes and found the rabbit-shaped cloud was gone. She stared at the pale blue sky and wondered if Divinity was really up there guiding them. "If there's a higher power out there, I could use a grand gesture about now," she said skeptically.

Rigel chuckled. "Maybe once we reach Symptee, you can visit the observatory. There's something incredibly comforting about stargazing and praying in the holy place. I'm sure the Estrelists would gladly offer you advice."

"What is an Estrelist?" she said, turning to frown at him. "I thought believers were called Estrelles?"

"Yes, believers, like you and I, are Estrelles. Most Hyrosencians are Estrelles, but very few are capable of reading the stars and deciphering celestial signs from Divinity," Rigel said. "Those who dedicate their lives to the study of the stars and teaching the ways of Estrellogy are called Estrelists. They function as priests, spiritual counselors, dream interpreters. Idonea is blessed with the gift of sight, so she focuses on interpreting her divine visions of the future."

"I should like to meet an Estrelist. I have so many questions," she said. "My father said all worthy souls rise to join the stars upon their death. My mother always said, 'Do good, and you shall be rewarded.' She was the kindest soul. I cannot help but wonder why she had to suffer in the end."

"I believe the souls who suffer an unjust death are rewarded," Rigel interjected. He too laid in the grass, watching the clouds roll by. "The same for souls who make the ultimate sacrifice."

Serena gazed at a cloud that reminded her of a bird. "We have all suffered great losses."

"But to die for your kingdom—to sacrifice your body to save another—that is an honorable death. Something worthy of a place among the stars."

"I do not want anyone to die for me," Serena muttered. "I should rather die myself than lose one more person I care for."

"You do realize our positions as your guardians require us to protect you?" Rigel propped himself up on one elbow, and looked down at her. "Should a situation arise where you are in danger, we must intervene."

Serena pushed herself up and stood. She offered an outstretched arm to the guardian. "Then we should resume training. Should the situation arise, I want to fight alongside you, not cower behind you. Perhaps one day I'll be strong enough to save one of you!"

Rigel smirked, took her hand, and pushed off the ground. Picking up both of their swords, he handed Serena her father's blade and said, "We shall make a warrior of you yet."

THE WELL

As they approached Noomï, Crystal grabbed Will by the arm and led him ahead of Cole and Xandra. Once there was distance between them, she turned to Will and said, "You need to put distance between you and Serena. She has been through an ordeal none of us can begin to understand—except perhaps Rigel."

"Excuse me?"

"Serena has trauma to process. Training should be her focus. Don't complicate her life by playing with her feelings right now."

Will looked down, watching the toes of his boots as he marched through the grass. "I can assure you, I don't intend to complicate anything," he said. "I'm only here because she refused to go back home, and Cameron would kill me for letting her run off with strangers."

"She told me of the horrors she witnessed in her home. I can understand why she did not wish to return there," Crystal said. Her expression softened as she continued. "Serena was sheltered from the brutality of this war and her family's connection to it. There is much she still does not know."

"Then why have you not told her?"

"It is not that simple," the archer said, looking forward as they continued trudging through the woods. "She is not ready. She could not handle the truth. Not all at once. And there is too much at stake."

"Yes, we all know our lives are in danger with each step," Will said scornfully. "I made the choice to come along as her friend. Who are you to push me away? You are of no relation to her, yet I have known her longer than any of you."

She stopped abruptly and whipped her head around to face him. "May I remind you that you are of no relation to her either," Crystal said, her icy gaze bringing him to a sudden halt. "I mean to save you both from more heartache. Serena has family in Symptee. Family of noble position. She will be placed in their charge when we reach the city. There will be high expectations and strict rules to follow. Everything shall be different."

"She has living relatives, and you have yet to tell her this?"

"It is something the Finches kept secret for a good reason," Crystal said, taking a slow, deep breath. "I am trusting you with this information, Will. Do not tell her before the time is right. She was shocked when she learned her parents worked for the Garricks before the war, and that is the least shocking of their secrets."

"They what?" Will asked, grasping the guardian by her forearm. "But how? How could they be loyalists and not tell their own children?"

"Mary was never involved in the rebellion. She had children to care for. They hid the truth from their children to keep them safe," Crystal said.

"Is that why they were killed?" Will asked gravely.

Crystal nodded. "There is more, but this is not the place. I merely hope you understand how unstable this entire situation is."

"I know Serena is grieving. I mourn the same people," Will said. "I've seen people spiral after a loss like this. Grief can make people do reckless things. That's why I can't just abandon her."

"At least there's logic in your reason for being here," Crystal said. "Our objective is to reunite Serena with her family. In Symptee, she'll be safe and have the space to process everything. Can I entrust you to keep this to yourself for now?"

He nodded.

"Thank you," she said, locking eyes with him.

"I hope her family will be able to help her find peace."

"We have a long journey ahead of us," Crystal said, relaxing her shoulders and leaning back her head to look at the bright blue sky. "I've felt the weight of a brutal loss myself. That grief will wrap around you like a snake if you let it."

"We can't allow it to squeeze the life out of her. She has so much life left to live. She shouldn't live in fear and sorrow."

"Her heart is broken, her joy drowned in blood. The future she once pictured is a dream that can never be." Crystal brushed past him to continue their trek toward Noomï just as Xandra and Cole reached them.

"Crystal seems more tense than normal," Xandra said with a chuckle. "Will is an excellent addition to the group. I don't understand why she gives him such a hard time." She patted Will twice on the shoulder, but Cole shoved his way between them, forcing each to step back.

"Because the path we're on is incredibly dangerous," Cole said, his frosty gaze locking with Will as he passed him. "And he's only going to make it harder—for both of them."

"Hey," Will called out, turning to charge after him.

Xandra's smile melted away as she grabbed Will's arm to stop him. "Don't," she whispered. Will cocked his head to one side and clenched his jaw, cutting his eyes sideways. He knew Xandra was right. There was no point starting a fight he could not win.

Xandra glowered at Cole as she jogged back to his side. "Give him a break. He cares for her. Is that really so wrong?"

Cole sighed and then stopped, turning to face her. Will watched her eyes bore into Cole's, glistening with anger and expectation. "You know exactly why she's concerned," Cole said. "Elara would not approve."

"Since when do you care what Elara thinks?"

"Since I took the guardian oath. Her path is dangerous enough without the added distraction."

Xandra let out an exasperated sigh and stepped closer to Cole with a gaze that locked him in place. "Sometimes a little danger is worth the risk." Then she sprinted ahead of them and joined Crystal.

Cole huffed as Will caught up to him. "What did you say to anger her?" Will asked, pretending not to have heard.

"She thinks Crystal and I are too hard on you," the warrior said passively. "She will get over it."

"At least I have one guardian on my side," Will muttered. Looking ahead at the two female warriors, he noticed how different their moods were when they were together. Crystal and Xandra were engrossed in spirited conversation; Crystal's lips curled into a rare and dazzling smile. Glancing sideways at Cole as they walked toward the women, he asked, "They have been friends for a long time, haven't they?"

"They may as well be sisters," Cole replied, his eyes lingering on Xandra's profile. "They were in the same class at the Academy. Crystal is my flesh and blood, and we were never so close as they are."

"I wonder why," Will said with a sly grin.

Cole shot a quick, bitter glance at him. "I have always followed the laws of my people. Everything I am is because of the path my father chose for me."

"You and your sister have that in common, I suppose," Will said nonchalantly.

"Not at all." Cole chuckled, glancing at his sister. "Crystal has always been quite serious about what she wants. Even as a child, she wanted to be a warrior like most of our lineage. Our father wanted to keep her safe. With her natural ability to use magic, he urged her to become a healer. She went behind his back to enter the Academy. He was displeased, to say the least."

"I can imagine most fathers would rather keep their daughters close until the right suitor comes along," Will said. "My father treats my sister like one of the rare flowers in his garden."

"My sister is no flower. She is all thorns," the guardian said, one corner of his lips curving upward. Will wondered what would make a young woman with a talent for healing choose a harsh life of combat instead.

Crystal glanced back at them over her shoulder and called out, "We are almost there! Try not to wander, Burroughs. This is not the place to get lost."

Will nodded, and the men quickly caught up to the women. Within minutes, they emerged from the cover of the dark, lush forest into a bustling market. "Welcome to Noomï," Crystal said, outstretching an arm.

The guardians were unfazed by their proximity to many unsavory characters, but Will noticed them all. He looked from one vendor to another, inspecting their tattooed skin and stolen wares with wide eyes.

Cole grasped Will by his forearm and dragged him after Crystal. The guardians did not look out of place in their leather attire with weapons strapped to their bodies, but Will drew a few suspicious glimpses from unpleasant looking traders. He quickly averted his gaze each time it met a pair of squinting eyes.

"Will, come with me to the well. Xandra, go with Cole to find food," Crystal ordered.

Xandra eyed her partner uncertainly and sighed, resolving to follow orders without protest. Turning toward him, she said, "Come on, Cole. The sooner we gather supplies, the sooner we can get out of here." He nodded and followed her into the market.

Suddenly uneasy, Will walked painstakingly close to Crystal, who led the way down a crowded street. She nudged him and said, "Loosen up, farm boy. Your eyes should never show fear. Hold it in your heart and push it down. If you look nervous, the soldiers are sure to notice."

Will breathed in slowly, closing his eyes for a second. In his mind, he pictured Serena in the forest, holding a live rabbit by the ears and smiling up at him. The memory calmed him, and he opened his eyes feeling bolstered by the thought that someone needed him.

They weaved through tangled streets filled with leather-clad and scar-covered bodies. Will kept his eyes focused on Crystal, who waltzed through the crowds with fierce determination. As they rounded a corner, they came upon a dozen weary travelers and beady-eyed merchants clustered around a large well.

Falling into the lopsided line to use the well's pulley, they were silent for several minutes while they waited. Crystal was discreetly observing their surroundings. Will watched as one stranger after another stepped up and pulled the ropes, lowering the bucket into the well and pulling it back to the top. As the bosomy woman in front of them used the bucket to fill a large jug, Will leaned closer to Crystal and muttered, "We are finally next."

When the woman flounced off, Will stepped forward and reached for the bucket perched on the edge of the well. Before he could grab it, another set of hands came from their right and took hold of the half-full bucket. Crystal hurled her arm out to the side, slamming into Will's midsection. He turned toward her, his face twisted in confusion, and asked, "What are you—"

Crystal shook her head slightly, her steady blue eyes shooting him a warning. Turning back toward the well, Will realized four soldiers in deep burgundy jackets had cut them off. Jackets emblazoned with Rexton's crest—the silhouette of a bear stitched in gold thread.

"See, they don't mind," a dark-haired soldier with bulging arms said, winking at Crystal.

Feigning a smile, she lowered her arm and said, "No problem. We gladly give way for the king's men." She bowed her head and motioned for the men to continue.

Will eyed his travel companion suspiciously but remained silent. As the soldiers took their time filling their canteens, a few merchants grumbled from the back of the crowd. Another of Rexton's men peered out over the crowd and said pompously, "You will all have your turn in good time. Surely you do not wish to interfere in the king's business?" The crowd hushed, and two agitated men left the line, storming off in the direction of the market.

Crystal turned toward Will and ruffled his hair, the same smile plastered to her face. He grasped her hand, pulling it away from his hair. "What has gotten into you?" he muttered.

She laughed, placing a hand on his chest, and said, "Honey, wait until we get back to the room." Will felt his face burn as he brushed her hand away from his body, and Crystal winked, mischief reflecting in her sparkling sapphire eyes.

The closest soldier eyed them, smirked, and turned back to the other soldiers, saying, "What I'd give for a woman like her."

Another grinned and said, "Not so hard to find in these parts. Brothel's up the road."

Screwing the cap onto his canteen, another hushed them and said, "Keep it in your pants. There is no time for folly. We have an important task ahead."

"Yeah, soon we shall rid this world of the last Garrick monarch," a tall, beady-eyed soldier said, cackling. One of his comrades whacked him over the head.

Will stared at Crystal with wide eyes, but the warrior remained in character, a pleasant smile on her lips while her eyes revealed her awareness of their conversation. She glanced down at the sword on Will's hip, and he breathed in shakily.

Suddenly a hand slammed him on the back of the shoulder, and a voice declared, "It's all yours, boy. Have fun for us." Will blinked at the scruffy soldier, his hand instinctively gripping the hilt of his sword, and the soldiers chuckled as they trod away from the well.

Exhaling loudly, Will wiped the beads of sweat from his face with his sleeve. Stepping forward, he braced both hands against the edge of the well, his stomach twisted in knots.

"We must hurry," Crystal said, pulling her knapsack off her shoulders and fishing the first canteen out.

Will nodded, grasped the rope, and dropped the bucket into the well. As he hoisted the bucket back to the surface, he whispered, "Should we do something?"

"We are doing something," she interrupted, glancing out over the crowded streets. There was no sign of the uniformed men, and she gripped her canteen tightly.

Taking the full bucket and balancing it on the edge of the well, Will took the first canteen from her and filled it. Crystal did the same, her eyes darting behind them with each bottle. "I should find the others," she said. "Can you handle the rest on your own?"

His eyes widened, and he looked up at her slowly, disbelief all over his face. "You're going to leave me alone?"

"Yes," Crystal said without blinking. "I know you can manage it. When you're finished, find us in the market. We will not leave without you. I promise." She handed over her knapsack with the other empty canteens, and he reached out hesitantly.

He watched her through narrowed eyes as she turned and retreated for the marketplace, leaving him bustling to fill their bottles while the throng of strangers surrounding him chattered impatiently.

"Need a hand, handsome?"

Will turned and was shocked. A familiar face grinned at him. "Natalia?"

"In the flesh," the young woman said with a wink. "I must say, I never expected to see you in these parts, pretty boy. Quite far from home."

He shushed her, panicked eyes glancing about the crowd, and the woman laughed. Natalia was only a year older than Will. She wore a tattered brown dress with a plunging neckline, and her dirty-blonde hair was pinned out of her face in a messy bun. "I could say the same for you. How did a nice girl like you end up in Norlee?"

"How else," Natalia said, swinging her skirt around brazenly. "A handsome soldier decided I was pretty enough to bring along. I've been here nearly a year. It's not so bad as it looks."

"Is that so?" he muttered, focused on filling a canteen.

Natalia snatched one of the empty canteens out of Crystal's bag, which rested near their feet, and began filling it. "How does a blacksmith's apprentice end up in Norlee?"

"I am no longer an apprentice," he said. "Mister Finch left town shortly after you did and never returned. I left home in search of work. Fell in with some merchants."

She scrutinized him, her brilliant turquoise eyes taking in the state of his clothing and his freshly-calloused hands. One corner of her mouth twitched upward, and she said, "That's good to hear. As long as you leave Norlee the way you entered, there is nothing to fear."

"I'm not afraid," Will countered, glancing bashfully at her.

"You seem nervous. First time across the border?" she asked with a chuckle.

"Is it so obvious?" Will speedily screwed the cap onto another bottle and deposited it in Crystal's bag. "I can admit I haven't seen much outside of Durmak, but the realm is vast and beautiful. I see a bright future ahead."

"With your new lady friend? I must admit I'm surprised to see you with a beauty like her. I always thought you might end up with the blacksmith's daughter," Natalia teased, grabbing him by the chin. "What was her name again?"

"Serena?" he asked in bewilderment, brushing her hand off his face and averting his eyes. "She's practically my sister. Nothing more."

"If you say so," she replied as she slowly sealed the bottle in her hands and offered it to him.

He took it from her hesitantly. "Thanks for the help." Lifting the bag full of canteens, Will slung it over his shoulder and moaned at the weight of it smashing his back. "I must be off. My comrades await," he said, turning away from her. "Take care of yourself."

As he marched toward the marketplace, Natalia treaded close behind him. A mischievous smile spread across her lips as she said, "I would love to meet your friends. Bring them up to The Pleasant Peacock. We have the best ale around, and the ladies are always open to entertaining hardworking young men like yourself."

"No thanks, we're just passing through," Will said, pausing at the next intersection. Without turning toward her, he added, "You should go home, Natalia. This is no place for a young lady to live."

Her lips puckered, and she placed her hands on her hips. "There be nothing wrong with how I live. I need not and want not."

"It's not safe out here for a lady," he said, clenching his jaw. He couldn't see any of the guardians, and for a second, he wondered whether they had abandoned him.

"It's perfectly safe if you aren't an enemy of the king," Natalia hissed, crossing her arms.

"If you say so," he muttered. "I really must be off." He stepped into the crowded street in an attempt to elude her.

She lurched forward and grabbed him by the arm. Leaning into his shoulder, Natalia whispered in his ear, "The valley belongs to Rexton now. His men have eyes everywhere. They're looking for loyalists, including John Finch and his brood. If you find them, you had best turn 'em in. If you're harboring fugitives, you won't make it far."

The hairs on the back of his neck pricked up, and Will stared into her knowing eyes for a moment. His stomach twisted at the thought that Natalia might have overheard something about Serena. He snatched his arm from her grasp, holding Crystal's bag closer to his body. "I don't travel with any fugitives," he said, hoping the hammering of his heart wasn't obvious to her. His eyes flicked between her and the busy street, desperate for one of the guardians to stumble upon him. "I haven't seen any of Finches in weeks. But they would never dare try to cross the border."

Natalia chuckled. "Well, wherever they are, they shan't get far. There's a hefty price on their heads. The king is determined to find them—dead or alive, doesn't matter."

Will scrunched his brows, turning his eyes toward the crowded road before them. "I cannot imagine why the children of old loyalists would be of any importance to the king," he said. "They likely didn't know of their parents' allegiance."

The young woman from his hometown shrugged. "Who knows? I simply thought I should bring it to your attention in case you run into them on your travels. It would be a mistake to help them. You know how the king feels: guilty by association." Natalia smiled, stepping back from him. "'Twas good seeing you, Will. Stop by The Pleasant Peacock sometime."

With a parting grin, she turned and disappeared into the throng of people in the road. Will remained frozen, his boots digging into the muddy dirt road as his eyes searched in vain for his comrades. With each flash of dark brown hair, he pictured Serena's face, her bright eyes fading as a sense of dread filled his heart. *I must get back to her*, he thought, pushing his way into the crowd. *The valley isn't safe.*

He spotted a merchant whose brightly colored feathers and beads looked familiar and knew this was where they had emerged from the woods. Glancing around, Will saw no trace of the guardians and opted to carefully creep into the cover of the trees. He had only gone a few steps through the trees when Crystal grabbed him and slammed him against a tree, knocking the breath from his lungs.

"Who was that woman? What did you say to her?" she demanded, pressing a cold blade against his throat.

"Nothing! Her name is Natalia. I knew her from Durmak. She recognized me, asked about the Finches. I told her I left home weeks ago and have not seen them. That's all," Will insisted, pressing his head back against the tree bark.

"Calm down, Crys. He clearly cares for Serena. Why would he say anything to endanger her?" Xandra asked, placing a hand over Crystal's, and forcing her to lower the blade.

"He should not have said anything at all. No one can be trusted," Crystal snapped, her hostile eyes piercing through him. She grabbed her bag from him and slung it over her shoulder, disregarding its weight. Then she turned and said, "Come on," before marching off into the forest.

"I'm sorry I said anything. I was surprised to see her. She wanted me to bring my friends to The Pleasant Peacock for drinks," Will said.

Xandra and Crystal glanced at each other before bursting into thunderous laughter. Xandra slapped Will on the back and said, "Wouldn't that be a sight!"

"What?" Will asked, glancing between them. "Are the queen's guards not allowed to drink?"

"Oh, no, we can drink," Xandra said with a grin.

"But The Pleasant Peacock is for lonely fellows," Crystal said.

Stopping suddenly, Will's eyes widened as he asked, "It's a whore house?"

"Are you surprised? She was falling out of her dress," Crystal snickered. Will's cheeks burned as he pushed the image of Natalia out of his mind. The archer shook her head and continued toward their camp, where Rigel and Serena awaited.

"Where's Cole?" Will asked, gripping the straps of his knapsack tightly.

"He managed to acquire another horse, so he rode it back to the camp. It was best not to linger with all the soldiers prowling about," Xandra said.

Will stuffed his hands into his pockets and inhaled. "Natalia said the valley belongs to Rexton now."

"I wish there was a way to send word to Elara," Xandra said, biting her bottom lip.

"She knows," Crystal said. "He's controlled the border for years. It was only a matter of time before he occupied it."

They walked quickly as they went deeper into the forest, the thick canopy casting shadows across their faces as they marched on. Will followed behind Xandra, his eyes fixed on the wild grass underfoot. He wrung his hands together, unable to shake the uneasy feeling in the pit of his stomach. The bizarre conversation with Natalia replayed in his mind, and he wondered what more the wench at the well might have known about Serena Finch's whereabouts.

CRIMSON TEARS

As they approached the camp, one of their horses burst through the trees, nearly running over Xandra. Diving out of its way, she whistled loudly, and the horse slowed to a stop, whinnying as it circled around her. "Why are you loose?" she wondered aloud as Will helped her back to her feet.

Crystal stopped and shushed them, turning her head slightly and focusing on the sound of clashing metal.

"Serena sounds like she's faring better against Rigel," Will said.

"No. Something's wrong!" Crystal took off running, and Xandra and Will raced after her. As they closed in on their camp, the clash of several swords rang out through the woods. "We have company," Crystal called back, dropping her bags and picking up speed.

The king's soldiers outnumbered them eight to six. An injured soldier writhed on the ground a few feet away from Cole, who was busy fighting off a second man with a broad sword. On the opposite side of the camp were Rigel and Serena, surrounded by five men. Serena gripped her father's sword in shaking hands, deflecting blows from the nearest attacker.

Xandra raced toward Rigel but was cut off by a brawny soldier in the middle of their camp. Crystal snatched up her bow, nocked an arrow, and turned toward the soldiers clustered around Rigel and Serena. Drawing back the string to the corner of her mouth, she focused on her first target and loosed the arrow. The tip pierced through the shoulder of the burgundy jacket nearest Serena. The shaft embedded deep in the back of her target, who howled in pain. The soldier dropped to his knees and coughed; blood spurted from his mouth as he attempted to remove the arrow without success.

The distraction proved beneficial as Rigel seized the opportunity to slash through another assailant's throat. Blood splattered across Serena's face as the soldier slumped onto the ground between them. Crystal watched Serena step back as the man wheezed his final breath. Serena shuddered.

"Serena, focus!" Rigel shouted, snapping her attention back to their chaotic camp. She barely steadied herself before another soldier charged at her. They parried each other in a test of skills. The repetitive clanking drew everyone's attention, but Serena managed to hold her own. Rigel slowly worked his way around her until he was directly behind her. He engaged two of the soldiers at once, moving swiftly and skillfully to deflect each swing.

"Serena!" Will called from across the camp, gripping the reins of a nervous mare.

Crystal glared at him from across the camp. He had been frozen in place. "Be useful and tie up the horses," she demanded. Will quickly corralled the other horses and tied their cut-up reins together with shaking hands. Then he glanced toward the fighters, sweat making his dark hair cling to his forehead as he watched Serena defend herself.

Crystal pulled another arrow from her quiver and positioned herself in the center of their camp. Nocking the arrow, her eyes fell on Rigel, who was struggling to fight off two soldiers and protect Serena. Locking eyes on her next target, she drew back her arm, relaxed it, and loosed another shaft. The arrow pierced her target through the side of the head.

The other soldiers near Rigel and Serena narrowed their eyes and dug their heels in. Will sprinted in their direction, snatching a sword off the ground on his way to help Serena. Crystal turned her attention to Cole and Xandra. She was surprised to see both were having trouble overcoming their opponents. These men's sword skills rivaled that of their own elite training in Envyre. Crystal wavered as her eyes darted between the dueling combatants who moved in quick, fluid motion.

Cole continued the aggressive confrontation with the same bearded soldier while Xandra used two short swords against a large, powerful opponent. Crystal's attempt to find a target was futile as the warriors kept their bodies moving, entwined in a dangerous dance. She could not risk hitting one of her own.

Xandra cried out as her opponent kicked her, and she stumbled backward onto the ground. "This one's pretty," the brawny soldier said, kicking one sword away from her hand. Her opponent dropped onto his knees on top of her. Crystal watched as he placed one arm over her wrist. Struggling in vain, Xandra reached desperately with her left hand toward her other sword, but it was inches out of reach. "Feisty. Just my type," the soldier snickered. He took a small dagger and ran it along her left cheekbone. The sharp metal barely touched Xandra, yet it sliced through her delicate skin with ease. Her amber eyes glistened furiously, and she spit in the man's face. He growled, tightening his grip on her arm before driving the knife into her left palm.

Xandra's outcry could be heard throughout the camp and ignited a fire in Cole. As his opponent swung his blade straight down, Cole slid to the side, sending a cloud of dust puffing up around them. When the soldier stepped toward him, he sliced through the man's shins. Screaming in anguish, the bearded soldier fell to the side, his body slamming into the ground. Cole pushed himself up with one hand and sliced his sword through the man's chest.

Crystal watched as her brother raced to Xandra's aid. The soldier's free hand was roaming under her shirt. He did not see it coming when Cole kicked him in the side, sending him flying off Xandra. Her horrified, tearful eyes locked on him, but he stepped right over her and pinned his steely gaze on his next target.

Turning back toward the others, Crystal realized Rigel was still fighting the same soldier, distracted by the man swinging viciously at Serena. He towered over the girl, his strength and stature dominating her slender frame.

Even from a distance, Crystal could hear the man taunting Serena. "Our friends have been looking for you. The king sent us to crash a wedding—perhaps we can kill two birds on our excursion." The soldier swung his blade down from above. Serena countered quickly, but she was outmatched. Turning swiftly on his heels, the crimson-clothed soldier swiped at her, the blade slicing across her right thigh. Serena cried out as blood immediately began trickling from her grazed skin. She winced, eyes squeezing shut in agony as one hand dropped from her sword to her wound.

As quickly as Crystal nocked an arrow and drew back her arm, Will stepped into her path, rushing to Serena's aid. The guardian lowered her arm and cursed under her breath, edging closer in search of a better shot. The man fighting Will shoved him away, causing him to trip backward and fall to the ground. As Crystal lifted the bow and drew it to her mouth, Serena's voice echoed through the camp, "No!"

As the assailant whipped around to face her, Serena drove her sword upward into his abdomen. The soldier's lips parted in astonishment. Serena blinked in shock as she withdrew the sword, stepping back on her uninjured leg. The soldier dropped onto his knees, gasping as his blood poured out like a red waterfall. Shuddering at the sight of her blood-smeared blade, Serena dropped the sword, covering her mouth with one hand.

Glaring at her, the injured man sputtered, "Death to the Garricks."

Will bounded onto his feet, coming to Rigel's aid against the last of the soldiers. As Will deflected a blow, the guardian seized the opportunity to finish off the man, piercing his neck. Serena flinched as more blood splattered her face, and she let out a horrified shriek that echoed through the still forest.

"What did I do?" she murmured, tears flowing from her red-rimmed eyes as she wiped her face with her hands. Serena looked down at her hands and shook her head. "I—I killed him." Her knees buckled, and she dropped to the ground next to the lifeless man she had just slain.

Crystal rushed over and knelt next to her, examining Serena for injuries. "So much blood. Were you struck on the head?" she asked. She could find no wounds on the girl's head.

"No." Serena's voice was barely a whisper. "It isn't mine. I never meant to—"

"Serena, never apologize for defending yourself," Crystal said. She checked the laceration on Serena's thigh. "They attacked us."

"Crystal is right. You have nothing to be sorry for," Rigel said, digging his blade into the dirt to remove the blood. When he pulled it from the ground, he took a dirty cloth and finished cleaning it before returning it to the sheath on his belt.

The other guardians and Will encircled Crystal and Serena. Cole had a supportive arm around Xandra's back. She winced, leaning into his shoulder. Her left hand was wrapped in a torn rag that was already saturated in blood.

"If you had not killed him, he would have killed you," Cole reminded Serena, helping Xandra take a seat next to Crystal.

Serena sniffled, wiping at her cheeks with the back of her hand. "My family died by the sword. What if he had a family? Children?"

"He disgraced his family the moment he raised his sword against an innocent girl. If he had any family, they are better off without him," said Xandra, who grimaced as Cole peeled back the fabric to examine her injured hand.

Rigel appeared with two canteens he had retrieved from Will's bag near the camp. Serena stared into the forest. Crystal turned, took a canteen, and used her teeth to pop the top off it. She poured water onto the gash on Serena's leg, washing away the excess blood. "Though I'm sure it hurts, 'tis not fatal," Crystal said. She carefully cleaned the wound and applied their special healing salve to it. Then she wet a spare cloth and started wiping Serena's face until there was no more blood smeared on it. "I am proud of you for protecting yourself," said Crystal as she worked to clean the last of the blood from Serena's hands. "Your quick-thinking saved Will as well."

"Killing someone is nothing to be proud of," Serena snapped. She yanked her hands away from the guardian. Her green eyes bore into Crystal as she struggled to regain her footing. Will reached forward to offer her a hand, but Serena shook her head. Wincing with each step, she limped away from her companions.

Though Crystal moved to follow her, Xandra reached across her friend and said, "Let her go. The first kill is not always easy to stomach."

"Clearly, it is not safe out here," Crystal said, motioning to the dead soldiers around them. "She needs to stay close."

"I'll keep an eye on her," Rigel said as he wiped his sweaty face with his sleeve.

"Let me go," Will said. His eyes never left the back of Serena's head. "Maybe I can reason with her."

"Go. Both of you," Crystal said with a nod of her chin. "Stay close and keep an eye out for any more trouble."

"We won't let anything happen to her," Rigel said, patting Xandra on the shoulder as he passed her. Will nodded, and they both dashed after Serena, who hadn't gotten far. Crystal watched Rigel slip an arm around her shoulders, offering support for her hurt leg. Serena's head drooped.

The three settled and sat there in silence, not far from camp. At times, Crystal could hear the girl sobbing but kept her distance. As the sun sunk lower on the horizon, she continued to nervously glance back at them, unsure how to move forward. It didn't help that Xandra and Cole remained silent.

At dusk, Rigel urged Serena to go back to their camp. When she did not respond, he scooped her up in his arms and carried her back with ease. Serena glowered, her sour face a perfect picture of protest, though she didn't argue with him.

"Let me see your hand," Crystal said to Xandra as she pulled a small bag of supplies out. Xandra nodded and offered her bound hand to her friend, who unwrapped it and generously applied Ismenia's salve onto the oozing wound. As Crystal murmured incomprehensibly, her friend groaned and leaned her back against Cole's side for support. Crystal couldn't help but notice the way Cole glared at her friend's wounds. The warrior clenched his jaw and turned his eyes toward the fire, cracking his knuckles one by one.

"Do you think I'll ever be able to dual wield again?" Xandra asked, biting the inside of her lip as she stared at the glittering ointment that filled the hole in her hand.

"Of course you will," Crystal said without meeting her eyes. "But it will take time to fully heal. Could be weeks or months." She placed her hands over Xandra's palm and closed her eyes, murmuring to herself.

Not far from the guardians, Serena lay with her back facing them. Crystal noticed the way Will's tired eyes rested on her, watching her shoulders move slightly as she breathed. She had cried to the point of exhaustion, refusing to eat or speak to anyone for the rest of the day. Despite the haunting darkness of the forest after sunset, the fire cast the faintest light over them, and everyone kept a watchful eye on Serena in their peripheral vision. After a while, Crystal went over and insisted on reapplying the salve on her leg wound. Serena rolled onto her back and moaned, barely whispering, "Go ahead."

When Crystal was done treating her patient, she wiped her hands on a cloth and settled on the ground between Serena and her comrades. Rigel passed out bread and dried meat to everyone, which Serena accepted without words. She nibbled and picked at the bread for a while before wrapping it up and putting it to the side. Laying back on her cloak, she stared up at the twinkling sky peeking through the dark canopy of leaves high above them. "How do you all do this over and over again and stay strong?" she asked.

"Lots of training," Rigel said with a faint chuckle.

"You mean mentally?" Xandra asked, tilting her head to the side. "When I asked to enter the Academy, I was terrified, but I put on a brave face every day, pretended I was brave until one day I wasn't pretending anymore."

"I want to be brave. I'm tired of being scared for my life," she said, biting the inside of her bottom lip. "I don't think I'll ever feel safe again as long as Rexton is in power."

Crystal sat up and stared at the sad girl. "We will never let him get to you, Serena." Her resolve was unwavering. The guardian had vowed a sacred oath, and she would honor it with her life. No matter the cost.

Serena tugged her cloak around her arms when the cold wind picked up. "You cannot promise such," she whispered without looking at the guardian. "I thought once we crossed the border, we'd be out of his reach, but I was wrong. The farther we go, the closer he seems. Maybe there is no escaping him for he is the very darkness itself."

With a half-grin, Rigel folded his arms behind his head. He watched as a star flew across the purple-hued black sky. "Though it's hard to find our way at night, there's no reason to be afraid of the dark, for Divinity has scattered a million stars across the sky to light our way," he said.

Quiet followed as everyone pondered his words. Serena stared at a cluster of bright shining stars directly above them, and her eyes brimmed with tears. "Oddly enough, I feel most at peace in the moments before I drift to sleep. The stars somehow make me feel less alone out here."

"This path is treacherous, but we never walk it alone," Xandra said, wrapping a loose curl around one of her fingers. "How could we not find comfort in our loved ones keeping watch as we rest? It's almost as if they're still here."

Serena nodded, wiping away a tear from the corner of her eye.

Will glanced sideways at her and frowned. He reached out, his fingertips barely able to brush against her cloak from where he laid. "They are still here," he whispered. "Just in a different way."

Serena let her head roll to the side, her eyes locking onto his.

Cole rolled onto his stomach and propped his head up on one hand, asking, "Do you really believe you will end up a flickering speck in the sky when it's all over?"

"I don't just believe it," Rigel answered, drawing everyone's attention as he sat up. "I know it's true. They're up there. And one day we all will be, too."

"We're all just stars on earth waiting to ascend to a more peaceful place," Xandra said with a half smile. She looked back and forth between the Windaef siblings, who both looked skeptical. "Even those who doubt it."

"That's really beautiful," Serena said as she fingered the enchanted gold ring in her pocket. "I like that."

"If that's what brings you peace," Cole said with a shrug. He rolled over to face the forest.

"We should all get some sleep," Crystal said.

"I've got first guard." Rigel moved to sit on the tree trunk close to the fire. They listened to the quiet hum of the forest until they were sure Serena and Will were finally asleep. Then the other guardians sat up, scooching closer to the fire. Rigel leaned in and whispered, "Do you think she'll be ready to move on tomorrow?"

"She will not have a choice. We must keep moving," Crystal said. She glanced over her shoulder at the sleeping girl.

"Are you certain she is the one?" Cole asked, staring through the fire at Serena.

"Of course she is." Xandra motioned with one hand toward the girl. "Look at her. The resemblance is uncanny."

"I do not question her bloodline. I question whether she is capable of fulfilling this prophecy your people cling to," Cole said. He caught Xandra's eye, and she pursed her lips.

"Surely even you can see how quickly she is learning. She certainly surprised me today," Rigel said, recalling the way she hurried to Will's rescue.

"Surprise is not enough. Hyrosencia needs a warrior," Cole said. "That girl may have killed to protect her friend today, but she does not have the heart of a warrior."

"Despite all she's seen and done, she still has a pure heart," Crystal said, looking down at her hands. They were calloused and faintly scarred from her years of training. "We were all young and naïve once, yet here we are now. We are among Elara's best warriors. Once she builds up her strength, she will want to fight. She will not be able to sit by and watch anymore."

"Pure hearts hesitate," Cole said. He folded his arms behind his head. "We were outnumbered today. We could have easily lost someone. We nearly did. What happens the next time we are attacked if Serena hesitates to kill again?"

"That's why she has us. To keep her safe until she is ready. I will give my life protecting her if it comes down to it," Rigel said proudly. Crystal grinned as his blue eyes pierced through her cynical brother.

"As would I," Xandra said, closing her eyes with the faintest smile on her lips.

Crystal stared up at the stars through the tree branches. She wished she could see the oracle's prophecy for herself. "I should die for her as well if that is what it takes," she said. "We are all she has right now. We must prepare her for what is to come. The entire kingdom is counting on us."

Cole rolled his eyes and said, "I shall fight with all in me to get her to Symptee, but I have no intention of dying on the way there. We must all do better. What happened today cannot happen again. It was too close." His eyes rested on Xandra, who laid a few feet away from him with her eyes still closed.

"I agree. It cannot happen again," Crystal said, pulling her cloak over her body. "Rigel, are you still up for the first watch?"

"I can handle it," Cole said.

"I welcome your company," he said, going to sit beside his friend on the log. When he sat down, Crystal's eyelids started drooping. "Get some sleep, Crys."

The archer nodded sleepily, rolling and resting the side of her head on one arm. "Thanks, boys," she muttered. It didn't take long for sleep to take her.

Shortly after dawn, Crystal went over to Serena and carefully rolled her onto her back. Using her fingers to push aside Serena's torn pants, the archer examined the cut on her thigh, relieved to see the wound had already begun healing. Taking some of their salve, she lightly ran two fingers over the laceration, leaving a smear of ointment on it. Serena stirred and her eyelids fluttered as she adjusted to the dim morning light.

Crystal placed a hand on the girl's shoulder, gently pinning her to the ground, and said, "Just be still for a moment. I am treating your wounds." She hovered her hand over Serena's leg as she closed her eyes.

Serena laid flat and stared at the tree limbs overhead. Faint flecks of stars were still visible as the bright orange sunrise chased away the darkness. She sighed. "I hate mornings. Sometimes I wish I'd fall asleep and never wake up." Serena's bright green eyes brimmed with remorse.

Crystal's hands dropped onto her thighs, and she loomed over Serena with her forehead wrinkled. "You're far too young to give up on life." Her voice was soft, like she was speaking to herself and not the girl. "What would your mother say if she could hear you?"

"Well, she can't. She's dead," Serena snapped, thrusting herself upright. "I've asked the stars a million bloody questions, but they never answer me. Day or night, stars or light, it doesn't matter. My mother is gone, and I'm still here."

"But you're not alone," Crystal replied, her voice firmer than before. "And she is still here. You may believe her soul rests among stars, but she is with you, even in the daytime. You loved her, and she loved you, so a piece of her remains tethered to your soul. She is there to guide you, to make you stronger. She's why you keep fighting."

"I'm tired of pretending to be strong," said Serena. She glared off into the woods. "Everything feels heavy, like I'm being pulled underwater."

Crystal exhaled, resting one hand on Serena's arm. "My mother was killed when I was even younger than you."

Serena's jaw dropped as she turned to face her friend. "You never told me that," Serena said, searching Crystal's face. "How old were you?" The guardian's eyes gleamed clear and dry as she stared back, a skill she mastered ages ago to give no hints to her tragic history.

"Too young to be without a mother," Crystal said with a shrug, pretending to inspect Serena's battered hands. "It was a very long time ago."

Serena nodded, watching her intently. "Tell me: Does it get any easier?"

Crystal paused, and her eyes drifted upward to meet Serena's. She bit her bottom lip and took a long, deep breath before answering. "Yes. With time, all wounds lessen."

Serena took a deep breath and glanced toward the others sleeping near them. "How long did it take you to move past it?"

The guardian blinked at her, contemplating the right answer. "I don't know if you ever truly move past losing your mother," she finally said, turning to put the ointment away in her bag. "The loss I experienced will always be part of me, but one day I woke up, and it no longer felt like a knife in my chest. That's when I took up archery. It made me feel strong."

Serena's eyebrows knitted together. "I don't want to feel weak anymore either," she muttered, turning her attention to her injured leg. The swelling around the wound had gone down, and the gash did not seem as deep as the day prior, Crystal observed. She was quite pleased with her work. "You are lucky you heal so quickly," she said, feigning surprise. "Luckily, this wound was not as severe as the last one."

Serena reached to touch her left shoulder and said, "Or perhaps we have a great healer in our midst."

Crystal, reaching out a hand to help Serena up, chuckled and said, "I am not a trained healer. I merely learned a few tricks in the Academy. Think you can walk?"

Serena stretched her arms lazily before taking a few hesitant steps toward Will. She flashed Crystal a grim smile and said, "It's not too bad. I can manage."

Crystal was proud of Serena's resilience. "Let's wake the others," she said. "We should try to get as far as we can while there's daylight."

Serena nodded and continued toward Will, who slept near the base of a tree.

Together they awakened the rest of their party. The men saddled the horses, knotting together the torn-up reins as best as they could manage. Then they loaded their bags onto the horses and began slowly ascending the Athamar Mountains.

PREDATORS & PREY

Anteros ran a hand through his unkempt black hair as he trekked through the tall grass; his boots crushed the weeds and wildflowers with each step. Stopping to survey the area, he used a hand to shield his eyes from the unforgiving sun as he squinted at the guards ahead of them. Sighing, he wiped the sweat from his forehead before taking a swig of water. Glancing sideways, the prince asked, "Thirsty, Father?"

Antoine nodded and took the canteen from his son. "Always," the king replied with a smirk. As he chugged from the bottle, a tiny stream of water trickled from the corner of his mouth through his short, dark stubble onto his shirt.

Anteros noticed a patch of small orange flowers and paused, immediately reminded of the prisoner in the dungeon. Turning back toward the castle, the prince grinned to himself, considering what he could bring Talitha on his next visit.

"Who's the girl?" his father asked, continuing the hike toward the forest north of Graynor Castle. "I have seen that look many times before, but never on your face."

Anteros's eyes widened, and he suddenly picked up speed, striding past his father as he cooly responded, "Girl? You are mistaken, Father."

"Then what puts a smile on your face? You rarely smile unless you are up to no good," Antoine said.

Anteros chuckled, kicking a pinecone and sending it bouncing away from them. "You think so poorly of your only son. I am offended," he said, placing a hand over his heart.

"I was your age once," the king said with a broad smile, stroking his chin. "Perhaps you have more than one girl on your mind. There is certainly no limit for a handsome, young prince."

Anteros scoffed. "The girls at court are dull. Nearly all of Sabine's ladies-in-waiting have thrown themselves at me. All they want is a title and a crown. They do not care who I am."

"I shall let you in on a secret, son," Antoine said, catching up to his son and gripping his shoulder tightly as he leaned in. "Women are fools desperate to find rich husbands to care for them. We are lucky to be in such desirable positions."

"It's all fair in love, right?" Anteros chuckled, brushing off his father's arm, and trudged forth into the woods.

Antoine scoffed. "I don't speak of love, boy. Love is drivel fed to women to make them open their legs," his father said, rolling his eyes as they entered the forest. The lush canopy of leaves overhead shielded them from the intensity of the sun. Every few feet, beams of sunlight shone through the leaves, illuminating their path. The sound of dry grass crunching under their feet echoed eerily through the darkened landscape.

"So, just toy with any woman desperate enough to throw herself at me?" Anteros asked with an uneasy chuckle. The idea did not sit well with him.

"Precisely. All women want is romance," Antoine said. "That's the easy part. Say the right words, and they'll bed you quite willingly. But I should think I don't have to tell you that."

"No, you certainly do not," Anteros said, grinning as he recalled his past few dalliances. Then the thought of bright orange hair flashed through his mind, and he bit his lip, forcing the image of her out of his mind.

"You're young. I don't expect you to tell your old man everything," his father said wistfully. "I had a great deal of fun at your age. Sometimes too much fun. I felt the strongest desire when I met your mother. I was not much older than you are now."

"Did you ever love her?"

Antoine hesitated, his forehead wrinkling as he debated his answer. His relationship with his wife Chelsea was less than ideal now. They lived in separate bedchambers with Antoine often inviting other women from court to visit him.

"Perhaps I did for a time. When you were born, particularly. That was a chaotic but glorious year," he reminisced. Anteros thought he saw his father's lips curve upward in a fleeting smile. "I do not regret any of my decisions, nor the fact that I married your mother, if that is what you're asking. But I would advise you not to impregnate the first woman you have feelings for."

His son nodded, scowling at the thought of having a child at his age. "No, thank you. I have no interest in that anytime soon," Anteros said.

"I did you a favor by not arranging your betrothal when you were a boy, as my father did," Antoine said, giving him a nudge. "Enjoy your youth. I daresay you haven't been yourself the past few weeks. Perhaps you need to loosen up."

"I have had plenty of fun, Father," Anteros said, squatting down to study a pile of animal feces on the ground. "Smells fresh. Boars must be nearby."

Antoine grinned as he took a large crossbow from one of the soldiers who were accompanying them and continued onward. "I told you today would be a glorious day for a hunt. If the king says so—"

"Then it must be so," Anteros chimed in. He turned to another of the lieutenants accompanying them, who handed a longbow to the young prince.

"Just remember, you do not owe anyone anything. You are the crown prince," Antoine said. "Do whatever you want with whoever you want and know that any lady is lucky to have you—be it once or for a lifetime. One day you shall inherit my kingdom."

Taking notice of an animal grunting nearby, the king held up the crossbow. His dark eyes gleamed impishly as he glanced at his son and said, "Let the hunt begin."

Little time passed before the king made the first kill of the hunt—a massive boar—and sent his son to survey their prey. As Anteros knelt down to remove the arrow from its midsection, a lavender-blue flower with an extra-long stem and multiple leaves caught his eye. Just as he reached for it, Antoine rushed forward and stomped on the plant. His son's eyes widened in surprise as he glared up at his father from the ground, "Why did you do that?"

Antoine squatted beside his son and plopped a heavy hand on his shoulder. Using the handkerchief from his pocket, the king picked up the half-crushed flower by the stem. A terrifying smile spread across his face as he stared at the flower, informing his son, "This is larkshade. While it is quite beautiful, it is not the sort of flower you give a loved one—unless you are looking to kill them."

Anteros fell back in the grass, his brow furrowed as he stared at the delicate flower in his father's grasp. "It's poisonous?" he asked, wondering how he had never seen it before on their previous hunts.

Antoine stood abruptly and folded the flower safely inside his handkerchief before tucking it into his pocket. "It's an import from our allies in Denorfia," the king said. "With this, our trouble with the loyalists may soon be over."

Antoine reached out a hand to his son and yanked him back onto his feet. Anteros brushed the dirt off his pants as he followed after his father, wondering how something so delicate and beautiful could have such a fatal function.

WITH HER ILLNESS BEHIND her, Queen Elara Garrick marched down the hallway, a fistful of her heavy silver-beaded skirt in each hand as her heels clacked loudly on the stone floor. The War Council was set to convene for their weekly assembly that morning, and she awoke determined not to miss another meeting with her advisors. Escorted by four armed lieutenants, Elara rounded the corner and ascended the stairwell, excited to return to her routine. Stopping in front of the grand gold double doors to her conference room on the third floor, the queen breathed in, released her skirt, and ran her hands over the embroidered bodice of her teal gown.

"Enter, Her Majesty, Queen Elara Garrick!" one of her lieutenants declared as two of her men pulled open the heavy doors.

His booming declaration startled Elara, causing her to jump, but she quickly composed herself, clasping her hands in front of her waist and entering through the doorway. Seven men in navy uniforms adorned with silver pins and chains and three lords in sharp suits instantly rose to their feet, bowing their heads to greet her.

Among them was Lord Gerard Stirling, who donned a cobalt blue dress jacket over navy pants. Stepping toward her, Gerard reached out, took hold of his betrothed's right hand, and pressed his lips to her knuckles. "How are you feeling today, my queen?"

"As right as ever," she said, flashing her brilliant smile for all to see. "My apologies for my tardiness, gentlemen. Please be seated."

The assembly found their chairs, which circled a large round meeting table. Gerard led Elara by the hand to a throne-like chair at the head of the table, and after pushing her chair closer to the table, he sat to her right. "You have not missed anything," he whispered, squeezing Elara's hand in his.

"We are so pleased to have you back with us, Your Majesty," Alexander said, smiling. "With your nuptials in but a fortnight, we have been preparing for the arrival of the foreign ambassadors."

"Lord Stirling's guests from the Eastern Isles have been reviewed and confirmed," Captain Sirius Levick noted. Prescreening guests to the citadel was challenging work. Though he was nearest Elara in age, Levick's face seemed much older. His dark hair was clearly receding; the wrinkles on his forehead and deep bags under his eyes gave way to the many nights he worked late. "His lordship has been a vital help communicating with the crown prince of the Isles and determining who shall accompany him to this special occasion."

"That is wonderful to hear. Excellent work, both of you," Elara said, squeezing Gerard's hand before pulling back from his grasp. Leaning forward in her chair, she pressed her hands into the table and asked, "And what extra measures will be in place once Prince Kailan and his ambassadors arrive?"

"All guest chambers on the third floor have been prepared, as well as four additional rooms on your residential floor for your most distinguished guests, the prince included," Captain Zeke Evigan said.

The sweat glistened on Captain Fairhurst's bald head, and he dabbed at his forehead anxiously with a handkerchief. "We have already shifted assignments to include extra guards within the citadel for the next month," he added.

"Extend those arrangements indefinitely," Elara said, nearly cutting him off. "I have a feeling that something terrible is imminent. I have been unable to shake it since my illness."

"Your Majesty, I can assure you, the citadel is quite safe," Alexander insisted. Elara stared at the patches of chocolate skin showing through his short hair and sighed, leaning back in her chair. Then the commander added, "I mean no offense, Your Majesty. We all hold your safety at the highest level of importance."

"I am well aware, Commander," she said tartly. "However, I have reason to believe the arrival of a most special guest will make us question the security of this stronghold."

"Your royal guests will be guarded with the utmost grace and caution," one of the captains said, leaning over the table to meet her eyes.

"I don't mean a wedding guest," Elara muttered, side-glancing at the commander.

The Council members glanced between themselves, their wide eyes pleading for Alexander to address their queen's concerns. Hesitantly, he said, "Should the true heir find their way to Symptee, they will be well protected. None need know of their true identity, should you deem it unsafe."

"Regardless of age, the heir will require the utmost care, for it is their divine destiny to return us to our homeland one day," Elara said. "For that reason, only the best and most trusted of guards shall be placed in their protection detail. Understood?"

The commander bowed his head and replied, "Yes, Your Majesty. We shall ensure none but the best watch over our esteemed guests. All will be as safe as you have been these many years."

"I have grown tired of playing this role I was never meant to inherit," Elara whispered, exhaling loudly through her teeth. "Perhaps someday the rightful heir shall take this burden off my shoulders."

"Heavy is the burden, yet you have done a fine job, Your Majesty," Levick said. "And you shall remain our queen for many years to come."

Elara felt a tightness in her chest, and she gripped the beaded fabric in her lap under the table. "I appreciate the sentiment, captain. It has been a long time for all of us," she said. "I hope we shall all live to see our kingdom restored."

"We shall," Alexander said, his chin held high. "Under your guidance, the true heir will strike when the time is right, and Hyrosencia will be ours once more."

The uniformed men all cheered as if victory were already in their grasp, but Elara did not share their confidence. She wondered if either of her brother's lost heirs would ever come to their aid. The thought of serving as a queen without a kingdom for another decade made her stomach twist, and she yearned for the peaceful stillness of her private chambers.

"There is much to be done before then, but I have faith in the oracle's prophecy," Elara said, rubbing her temple as she shifted uncomfortably in her seat. As she glanced out of the nearest window, she frowned, wishing her corset was not tied so tightly.

"Milady, if I may," Gerard began, leaning toward her. "Are you certain you feel well enough to convene?"

Elara met her fiancé's cerulean irises and smiled reassuringly. His eyes reminded her of the calmness of the ocean she once laid eyes upon years ago. She squeezed his hand and whispered, "I am fine. Just a tad tired. There is no rest for a queen."

Turning her attention back to the War Council, she locked eyes on Zeke. Not one of the white-blond hairs in his ponytail was out of place. "Could we go over the timeline for the week of the wedding once more?" she asked, straightening her spine.

"Yes, Your Majesty," the captain replied, opening the file folder on the table before him. "We anticipate the Islanders' party will arrive May 30, and the

Denorfian convoy should arrive by the following day. The welcome dinner is set for the eve of June 1. This should allow everyone ample time for rest."

Elara nodded. "Perfect. This will be the first time royals from our three kingdoms shall break bread together in twenty years. We must put forth our best effort to welcome them."

"And the first time since the treaty was broken," Commander Moorfield added. His short auburn hair and thick matching beard made him look a decade younger than he was, and his bone structure was striking, his jaw wider than usual. Elara wondered what his secret was.

"It shall be an evening befitting royals," Gerard said with a confident smile. "My cousin and I are looking forward to meeting the King of Denorfia. It is quite an honor he intends to come all this way."

"King Boreas was quite familiar with my father in their youth," Elara said wistfully. "He has always been a good friend and ally to the Garrick family."

"Yet he has remained neutral in the war thus far," said Moorfield. "We should use this opportunity to recruit Denorfia's military aid. That could turn the war in our favor."

"You and I both know Boreas has no interest in losing any of his men fighting our war," Elara bit. "No argument could convince that old goat to put his own people at risk. It is why he has maintained trade with both Rexton and us."

"I must agree with Elara on this," Gerard said. "It took a great deal of reassurance to convince Denorfia that Symptee would be safe for an ambassador, and a great deal more to convince the king he should come personally. This is no small matter to them, and we should not pressure him to do any more for us than he already has. Angering Boreas could cost us crops and other imports that are vital to surviving the winter months."

"We are barely in summer, Lord Stirling," scoffed Captain Richard Bramley as he sauntered through the doorway.

Everyone turned their heads toward the cocky young captain as he made his way to an empty seat. His light-brown hair was shaved short, his facial hair trimmed close and tidy. His eyes flitted irritably from Lord Stirling to his queen, and his lips curled into a faint smile. "Your Majesty," he said, bowing his head low in a stately manner. "I must apologize for the delay. I received a letter from Captain Smedley this morning with an update on the upcoming tournament."

Richard's supervisor, Commander Jacob Maynard, clenched his jaw as he scowled at the captain. Maynard's bronze face glistened with tiny beads of sweat as it caught rays of sunlight coming through the window. "That is not our priority on this day," Maynard said.

"It's all right. I should like to hear his update today," Elara said, cutting off the commander. She gestured for Richard to join them at the table, which he happily did. "Please, go on. What is the latest from Envyre?"

Smirking, Richard held up a single sheet of folded parchment, flashing Smedley's exquisite cursive handwriting toward the Council before reading aloud:

My Dearest Queen and Comrades,

I trust all is well in Symptee. That is most excellent, if so. All is quite well in Envyre as well, though I must admit I feel quite the ache for the beautiful city we have grown to call home and for the face of our beloved Queen on this fine day.

We have elected to permit only two students to graduate from the Academy this year as they have demonstrated most excellent skills— Wesley Ironside and Heath Grange. They have matured into fine young men over their 12 years of training.

For the tournament, we have selected ten applicants. Preparations are underway for their return to Symptee. Expect their arrival toward the end of July. Among them are a few familiar faces from previous tournaments, including three who were not selected last year. We hope you will be impressed with their improved skills and find several worthy of employment in your most esteemed Guard. I have seen these fighters through their childhood and adolescent years and can attest to their ambition and determination to serve their Queen.

I sincerely wish my Queen and his lordship a most pleasing wedding day. May ye be blessed by Divinity with a long and most fruitful marriage.

Your Humble Servant,
Captain Aspen Smedley

When Richard looked up from the pages, Elara was facing the window in an attempt to hide the burning blush on her cheeks. "Bless Captain Smedley. Always such a way with his words," she said with a chuckle.

"It is good to hear there are two more graduates from the Academy. Last year there was only one," Maynard said. "I expect quite the crowd for the tournament this year. The returning favorites should draw quite an audience. Perhaps you will be impressed enough to select more than two for the Guard this year."

"I should like to. We need fresh faces in the Guard, especially with war on the horizon. It's not like any of you are getting younger," Elara joked, flashing her advisors a grin.

"I thought that was why I was promoted," Richard said brazenly.

Looking around the room, she realized that, although joking, all of the commanders and several of the captains were middle-aged and older. In his early thirties, Richard was the youngest to attain his rank, and the closest in the room to her age.

"We selected you because you have worked hard and proven your worth for over a decade," Alexander said, eyeing the young captain wearily. "Not because the rest of us are incapable in our advanced age."

"Advanced," Elara repeated, laughing heartily. "Good heavens. None of you are any older than my father would be today. You are the finest and most capable advisors I could ask for. I only ask that we continue to increase our numbers when the right students are ready. Soon we hope there will be new Garricks to protect."

Her men nodded, and Moorfield said, "We shall do all we can to protect any heir bearing the Garrick name, milady. You included."

"Aye," the other men agreed in unison, bowing their heads briefly to their queen.

Despite her men's confidence, Elara could not fight the dread that filled her heart, for she knew someone wicked was plotting against her. Even her fiancé's smile could not put her at ease. She looked around at the men on her War Council and realized that none of them took her warning seriously. None believed there was any danger lurking within the fortress walls, waiting for the perfect moment to strike.

TALITHA VISE SAT WITH her back against the cool stone walls of her cell in the Graynor Castle dungeon, daydreaming her warden might return for a visit, when she heard an unusual sound. The rhythmic clacking of heeled shoes was unfamiliar to her. The sound seemed louder with every step down the dungeon hallway, making her tense. Goosebumps spread up her arms and through the back of her neck, and she uncrossed her arms, bracing for trouble.

"You can relax," said a female voice, causing Talitha to jump. The terrified prisoner locked eyes with a beautiful, dainty girl no older than herself. Her black curled hair was pinned up in the back, but a few loose tendrils fell over her pale shoulders, covering the pastel pink gown embellished with a tiny floral pattern. Eyeing Talitha, Sabine said, "I am here as a friend."

"A friend?" Talitha asked, wrinkling her forehead as she inspected her new visitor.

Sabine smiled and snapped her fingers gleefully, prompting a guard to unlock the cell door. Talitha shrank back as the guard stepped inside before allowing

Princess Sabine to enter. Stepping through the doorway, the girl wrinkled her nose as her eyes scanned the dingy floor and walls. "How...quaint," she said, lifting her billowing skirts off the floor. Talitha ogled the girl's ornate heels, which looked like they were painted with liquid gold.

"Who are you?" Talitha asked. "Does the prince know you're here?"

"I am Princess Sabine Aileen Rexton, beloved sister of your keeper," she said, grinning mischievously as she tossed a wad of cream-colored fabric to Talitha.

Talitha's eyes widened as she caught the garment. Unrolling and inspecting the plain dress, she frowned and whispered, "You're the king's daughter?"

"Obviously," Sabine drawled in boredom. "What I do not know is who you are."

"I don't see why that's any of your concern. We are of two different worlds."

"I cannot imagine why you should withhold such a thing from me," the princess pouted, clomping across the room. "Stand up. Let me get a better look at you." Sabine came to a halt a few inches away from the irritated prisoner, who reluctantly stood so they were at eye level.

"Because it is mine to tell who I choose," Talitha said, crossing her arms over her chest as the princess circled around her. "Am I supposed to bow to you?"

Sabine scoffed. "Normally, yes, but not on this day. There is certainly nothing formal about this place."

"Then why are you here? This is no place for a princess."

"I wanted to see the girl my brother sneaks off to visit nearly every evening," Sabine said, running her delicate fingers through a strand of Talitha's red hair. "Even covered in filth, I can see why he keeps coming back."

Talitha recoiled, lacing her fingers through her hair protectively as her cheeks burned. "His father ordered him to get information out of me."

Sabine produced a juicy red apple from a small beaded handbag. "The guards talk. I heard you said nothing while being tortured, yet you told my brother your name for something so small as this," Sabine teased, taking a bite from the apple.

"I was starving, and he was kind to me," she said. Her stomach rumbled, and her eyes focused on the juice dripping down the side of Sabine's mouth as she chewed loudly.

"Sure there isn't some other reason?" Sabine asked, batting her eyelashes.

"I'm not sure what you're insinuating. I'm not here by choice," Talitha snapped, holding her head higher. "Why don't you get to your point?"

"Half of my friends have thrown themselves into Anteros's bed. Obviously, I don't see the appeal as he is my brother," Sabine said with a grimace. "He is the crown prince, of course, but it's not like he's looking for a wife."

"I am not throwing myself at the king's son," Talitha said sharply.

"And maybe that's why," the princess said to herself, gesturing emphatically toward the girl with both hands.

"Why what?"

"You don't worship him like every other girl around here," Sabine said with a triumphant twinkle in her eyes. "He's not used to a challenge."

"If you haven't noticed, I am a prisoner here," Talitha quipped, gesturing around the cell. "I had been treated like a dog up until Anteros—"

Sabine's eyebrows raised as she giggled, clapping her hands together. "Anteros! You call him Anteros. How informal! Father would fume over that." She pretended to swipe a tear from the corner of her eye.

Talitha shrank back, turning her blushing cheeks away from the young lady. Facing the tiny window high in the corner of her cell, she took a deep breath to clear her head, but instead, her lungs were overpowered by the scent of jasmine. "The prince asked me to call him by his forename. I meant no disrespect," she whispered.

"Oh, I am not offended, not at all!" Sabine said. Her eyes trailed downward, inspecting the girl's bony figure. "I am thrilled. My brother had grown cold and miserable over the past year. Ever since you arrived, he has opened up again. He's seeing his friends, telling jokes—even smiling! He's back to being the boy I grew up with."

"What does that have to do with me? He just brings me food, and we talk."

"I think it has everything to do with you, my dear," the young girl said, patting Talitha on the cheek. "You are the only new toy he's had to play with in months, and he's clearly smitten."

"You're crazy," Talitha muttered.

"We could be great friends, you know," Sabine said, inching closer. "We could have such fun this summer."

"Fun?" Talitha scowled, cautiously side-eyeing the princess. "Look around, princess. You are the only one living in a fairy tale."

"Fairy tale? Hardly," the princess scoffed. "There is a reason my brother looks forward to life again, and I can assure you it isn't any of the girls at court."

"I don't wish for any such attention—not from the prince or any other man," the prisoner snapped, shoving the princess back and scowling at her.

"Hey!" The guard stepped closer, grasping the hilt of his sword in warning. Talitha shrank back from the princess, her eyes wide.

"It's fine," Sabine said, waving him off with one hand as she dusted off her gown. She turned around to face the prisoner and offered a gentle smile. Talitha eyed the girl in the pink ball gown suspiciously. Their entire conversation had been unusual, and she was ready to be locked up alone.

"I am so tired of being treated like a chess piece," Talitha spat, sliding down the wall until she was seated on the stone floor. "I don't know what you're getting at, but I do not appreciate being toyed with. My life is not a game. It matters."

"Talitha," the princess said gently, grasping her hands together in front of her waist. The surprised glance from the prisoner prompted her to add, "Yes, Anteros told us your name. He did not have much choice. Our father ordered him to get information from you using whatever means necessary. The first thing they did was check the census records."

Talitha ran her fingers through her hair. She knew he must have told his father her name, but she had not thought they would be able to learn much from her first name alone. "What else do you know of me?"

"That you are from South Hyrosencia. Seventeen, same as my brother," Sabine said, cocking her head to one side. "Your father's family has been in Durmak for five generations, correct?"

"Six, actually," the prisoner corrected.

"So, you are Talitha Esther Vise then?"

The prisoner lowered her head, and her hair fell over her eyes as she nodded.

"Do not be upset," the girl pleaded. "If anything, learning your identity has helped us keep you alive. That is no easy feat when dealing with our father."

Gazing longingly at the tiny open slit high on the wall, Talitha whispered, "Do you think I shall ever feel the sun on my face again?"

Sabine paused, a pang of sympathy for the weary girl briefly crossing her face as she examined Talitha's pale face and the frail arms wrapped around her legs. "I do not know." She slowly stepped forward and placed a gentle hand on the prisoner's shoulder.

Talitha nodded without looking at the princess.

Looking at her guard, Sabine snapped, "Wait outside." At first, the guard opened his mouth to protest, but Sabine lifted a finger to silence him, asking, "You have a younger sister, do you not?"

"Yes, princess," the guard replied, his forehead wrinkling in confusion.

"And is she a lady?"

"Well, er, I sent her to the Refining School for Orphaned Ladies outside of Jessiraé. Did me best to give her an education," the guard said, scratching his chin.

"Is she young, pretty?"

"Uh, she is pretty enough, though still unwed at two-and-twenty, milady," the guard stuttered. "None will take her as she has no dowry."

"Excellent," Sabine said with a smile. "Is she in Graynor now? Can you bring her to me the day after tomorrow? She can be my new lady-in-waiting. I have lost two to marriage already this year."

"She is not in Graynor but nearby. Emmaline helps at the orphanage in Lettras," the guard said. "It would be the highest honor for her to become your lady-in-waiting, princess. We are not worthy."

"Oh, nonsense. One does not need money nor high title to be a lady," Sabine said, holding her nose high. "With any luck, I shall find her a proper match during the Solstice festival."

"I have not the money to wed her to a noble, milady," the guard protested. Talitha eyed the man in the crimson uniform and found his confusion amusing.

"Uh-uh, do not fuss over such a trivial thing. For if she is willing to be my lady for a short time, I shall cover the dowry myself, and none need be the wiser," Sabine said proudly.

Surprised, the guard glanced nervously at Talitha, then back to the princess before bowing his head. "Thank you, milady. I thank ye kindly for your generosity of spirit."

"Pish-posh, she is one of my subjects. Surely, charity is good for the heart—and the skin!" Sabine said thoughtfully. "Now go wait in the hall. We can discuss the arrangements when I am done here."

The guard bowed repeatedly as he exited the cell, taking a stand just outside of the open doorway. Sabine chuckled heartily, telling Talitha, "I do love playing matchmaker at court. I live to watch the drama unfold."

Curious, Talitha looked up at the beaming young lady and asked, "What made you want to do such a thing?"

"A mastermind never reveals her secrets," Sabine replied with a wink. Sabine reached into her little purse and pulled out a second apple, offering it to Talitha in her outstretched hand. "You shall see why soon enough. And you may see the sun as well."

Talitha smiled for a moment before bowing to the princess's feet. "I should be most grateful, princess, but would your father not frown upon such a thing?" Hesitant, she bit her lip, remembering the soldier he decapitated before her as she reached for the apple.

"Worry not about the king," the young lady replied, cupping a hand under Talitha's chin and lifting her face. "There are many things Anteros and I have gotten away with while our father was preoccupied with women and his war. Rest assured, the last thing our father shall be thinking about is you."

Talitha nodded. Though she felt uncertain following her brief interaction with the princess, she was left feeling hopeful that she might soon see the outside of her cell.

THE CRAGS OF VIGILANCE

The trek northeast into the Athamar Mountains was difficult. The landscape was craggy, the foliage barely sprung back to life after a long, harsh winter. Crystal rode in front of the group with Serena close behind, Xandra and Will on either side of her. Cole and Rigel lingered behind them, observing their surroundings.

"We near Estivor," said Crystal. "We should walk from here."

"It would be a pity to scare the mountain goblins," Cole called out, dismounting from his gray stallion. Crystal grinned.

"Goblins?" Serena asked, nearly falling off her horse.

Rigel laughed, slapping Cole on the back of the shoulder. "He means the dwarfs—but I wouldn't use that term around them unless you have a death wish."

They ascended the hills, leading their weary, apprehensive horses on foot. Serena breathed heavily, pausing to gasp for air as they climbed higher. Will rushed to offer her support, slipping one arm around her back. "We should take a break," he insisted, looking to Crystal for assistance.

"She is fine. This is normal." Crystal brushed Will's arm off the girl and thrust a canteen into Serena's hands. "Drink. You must keep your strength up."

"As we climb higher, the air grows thinner, making it harder to breathe, but she will adjust, as we all have," Xandra said.

"Halt!" a thunderous voice bellowed from above them.

Cole and Rigel sprinted forward, drawing their swords. Before Serena could speak, the four guardians surrounded her. Crystal caught Serena's eye and tapped her pointer finger against her lips. Turning her face, their fierce leader whistled, the sound echoing off the cliffs in the distance. A moment later, the shrill deep sound of a horn resounded.

The guardians relaxed, putting away their weapons. Will furrowed his brow, grasping at the sword on his belt, and asked, "What are you doing? Who is that?"

"Bevakors, the watchers of the mountain," Cole said.

Xandra touched Will's arm as if to reassure him. "They are dwarfs who guard the southernmost city from invaders. The horn means it's safe to approach."

Cole glanced sideways at them and added, "Without weapons in hand."

"Yes, if we go any further with weapons drawn, they will attack us without question." Rigel wiggled his eyebrows up and down.

"They sound dangerous," Serena whispered. She peered through the trees.

Will still gripped the hilt of the sword at his hip. "Are you certain we can trust them?"

"Yes. They are allies," Crystal explained. "The Bevakors have awaited our return for weeks." She led her horse forward, and the guardians fell in line behind their leader. Cole placed a hand on the small of Serena's back, urging her forward. As they slowly trudged ahead, the trees thinned out until they stood before a massive stone wall that towered miles above them. At the wall stood countless dwarfs in gleaming steel armor. They were shorter and stockier than the average human. Their faces were smeared with black lines, and they all brandished a large axe or hammer. As the two closest to them approached, their matted black beards and long hair blew in the breeze.

"Who seeks safe passage?" A blue-eyed dwarf pointed his axe in their direction and eyed them suspiciously.

Crystal bowed her head. "The falcons lead the sparrow home."

"We knew it be you fair folk. Could smell you a mile away," a brown-eyed dwarf said, lowering his weapon. Several of the Bevakors chuckled.

"We could smell you from three," Cole said with no hint of a smile. No one laughed, and Serena wondered why his comment sounded more like an insult than a lighthearted jest.

Rigel extended his hand to the closest dwarf. "Miss me?"

The dwarf shook his head and grinned, slapping away Rigel's hand with a meaty arm. "Did ye yet forget 'twas I who beat ye in combat?"

Rigel chuckled and threw an arm around the dwarf. "I could never forget the great Bortir Whitmane! I was ill prepared for our first match, but I have been practicing. Allow me a chance to win back my honor. Best two out of three?"

"We are only staying one night," Crystal interjected, brushing past Bortir. Waving her hand for them to follow, she approached the wall with her chin held high.

Rigel frowned as he watched their leader sashay toward their haven for the evening. "Only one? But it's another week to Faswyn," Rigel argued. "You can hardly call one night a proper rest."

Crystal stopped, turning on her heels to face Rigel and the rest of their group. Placing one hand on her hip, her piercing blue eyes locked on the red-haired guardian, and she said, "Our journey has already taken longer than anticipated. We are behind schedule, and the queen must be worried sick."

Serena cleared her throat, and Crystal turned to look at her. "Actually, I've spoken to her, to Elara." She stepped out from behind Will and Cole. "I told her when we reached Morlerae, so she's already aware the journey is taking longer than expected."

Crystal and the slew of dwarfs around them turned their eyes on Serena. The archer furrowed her brows and asked, "You've spoken to Elara? How?"

"Yes. Twice since we met." Serena averted her eyes.

Crystal's eyes widened and she whispered, "You have an enchanted object."

Serena nodded, tucking one hand in her pants pocket. She pressed the cold metal ring against her fingertips and bit her lip, unwilling to show them the last thing her mother had given her. "Perhaps we should speak in private."

"Yes, it seems you have been keeping secrets," Crystal shot. Serena felt small as the guardian's narrowed eyes searched her dubiously.

"Perhaps she does not trust ye," one of the dwarfs mumbled just loud enough for them to hear, earning hearty laughter from his people.

Another dwarf added, "Everyone be hiding somethin', but the mountains reveal all."

Crystal clenched her jaw as her cheeks reddened, the deep flush stark on her pale skin. Serena wondered why their cryptic words had angered her. Turning to face the closest dwarf, Crystal asked, "May we now enter Estivor?"

The dwarfs closed in on their party, looking over their appearances and weapons. The brown-eyed dwarf was but a few inches shorter than Serena yet carried himself as if he were ten feet tall and indestructible. "Aye, but first we have questions. We were expectin' a much larger party, ye see. Who be this, and where be the others?"

"This is Serena Finch. She was the only one of her kin we could save," Cole said, drawing displeased glances from the nearby Bevakors.

The dwarf narrowed his eyes, scrutinizing the exhausted girl. "Welcome to Estivor, Miss Finch. I am Glomir Whitmane, high member of the Bevakors. I shall grant you and your party asylum—should you ask for it."

Serena squinted as sunlight reflected off Glomir's bronze helmet, making it difficult for her to meet the kind eyes peeking through it. His hair was long and black, cascading out from beneath his helmet, and he had a long, fuzzy beard to match. "We would greatly appreciate your hospitality, Glomir," she said. The corners of her mouth curled up in a gracious smile. Glomir grinned, extending a hand to her, and she cautiously placed hers on it. "I'm surprised I've never heard of the dwarfs' generosity before," Serena added as he led her toward the wall.

"The other races seldom describe us well," Glomir said with a glower.

Cole rolled his eyes and fell in step beside his sister, who was only a breath behind Serena. Rigel, Will, and Xandra brought up the rear, leading the rest of their horses toward the towering stone barrier. "That's not true," Rigel said from behind them. "Queen Elara sings your praises."

Glomir stopped next to Bortir and gestured with one arm toward the wall. "Reveal the way, brother," he said with a slight tilt of his head. Standing before a seven-foot-tall door, Bortir tapped the metal three times with the handle of his axe, each clang ringing out melodically. When the echo faded, he repeated the motion thrice more before attaching his axe to his belt. Then a loud clunk rang out, making Serena step back from the wall in alarm. The sound of metal grinding against metal made the guardians and their companions grimace. The door opened, revealing a cluster of Bevakors as the sunlight pierced through the dark doorway into a dimly lit tunnel.

Bortir turned and said, "After you, brave Hyrosencians."

Serena peered nervously into the cavern, unable to see what waited on the other side. While she stood frozen in place, Rigel and Xandra pushed forward and stepped into the tunnel. Xandra exclaimed, "Come on, Serena! They have proper beds! We shall feast and sleep well tonight."

"I have missed their venison stew. None compared in Hyrosencia, sadly," said Rigel as his stomach gurgled loudly.

Will brushed the back of his hand against Serena's, and she inhaled swiftly. "It's all right," he muttered. Serena swallowed and hesitantly followed him into the darkness.

One of the dwarfs pulled a flickering torch from the rock wall and walked in front of them. Bortir did the same, lighting the way from the center of their group. Their horses stirred anxiously, and the guardians patted their cheeks. As they strode through a maze of twisting tunnels, Will stared at the torch ahead of them, which illuminated the thick, frizzy red hair of the dwarf leading them. Serena noticed him smirking and whispered, "What are you smiling at?"

Will nodded his head toward the men in front of them and murmured, "We may have found Rigel's long-lost brother."

Serena snorted before slapping one hand over her mouth and slapping Will's arm with the other. "Will! You shouldn't say that!" But she was unable to stop grinning long enough to properly scold him.

The dwarf in front of them stopped and turned to look at them. "Best not be causin' any trouble while yer here," he said before turning back to the door. He tapped on the metal in a deliberate pattern; each clang resounded loudly, startling the horses. While the guardians rushed to soothe them, Serena used both hands to cover her ears, but the dwarfs were unfazed by the sound. Seconds later, the door opened, and sunlight blinded them as the Bevakors ushered them through the doorway into an open area. They blinked, shielding their eyes while they adjusted to the midday sun.

When Serena's vision cleared, she looked around the city in wonder. "This is Estivor?" She took in the stone pathways which led to small steel-studded brick buildings built into the side of the mountain.

"This is not half of it, miss," Glomir said, throwing his arms wide. "Most of these structures lead down to homes within the mountains."

"You sleep underground?" Will asked, stepping toward the closest structure.

"Aye, 'tis our way. The mountains protect us from invaders," Bortir said, gesturing toward one of the nearest buildings.

Other dwarfs paused to watch as the Whitmanes led the group to a tiny barn on the right, where their horses would be safe overnight. After securing the mares, they crossed the path and walked until the dwarfs stopped before a sturdy brick building with an intricate metal door. Bortir fiddled with multiple wheels and levers, causing three loud clicks as the mechanism unlocked. Hoisting the heavy door open, the dwarfs stood to the side. "We have long expected your return," said Glomir. "Two chambers were prepared for your party. We shall let you put away your things and freshen up before ye meet with Aigon."

"Is Aigon the king?" Will asked. Some of the dwarfs scoffed and shook their heads; others chuckled at his question.

"He wishes," Bortir said gruffly. "Aigon Flintfeet is but the Elder of Estivor. Our king resides the next city over. You'll meet him soon enough, if you're lucky."

Glomir disappeared down the stairwell, and the guardians moved to follow him. Serena hesitated, but Rigel extended a hand to her and said, "Don't worry. We stayed here two nights on the journey to Hyrosencia. The dwarfs were quite accommodating, and the city is beautiful. Did you not wish to see it?"

Serena inhaled and nodded. Taking his hand, she descended the stairwell into Estivor beside Rigel, whose reassuring smile never wavered. "You seem happy to be back here. Meet a girl last time?" Serena asked with a grin.

Rigel chuckled, shaking his head. "Women are rare among the dwarfs. There is one for every two men, and they are so selective many never marry. They certainly never look outside their race. They are much like the elves in that regard."

"I suppose I never thought of it that way, but it makes sense. All of the races keep to their own lands, so it would be hard to meld any two together," Serena thought aloud.

From behind them, Xandra said, "The elves and humans work in harmony at the Academy. I daresay elves are not that much different from us."

"Folly!" spat Glomir, turning to scowl at them. "They may have agreed to train your kind, but they still believe themselves superior to us all. Ludicrous. We dwarfs live long lives as well and fight twice as hard!"

Rigel and Xandra smirked at his spirited response. Will looked to the guardians and asked, "How much longer do elves and dwarfs live than us?"

"We may live 250 to 300 years if we do not first perish in battle," Glomir answered. "And they—"

"Elves can live up to 1,000 years if war or disease do not take them," Cole said from behind them.

"But 1,000 years is certainly a rarity," Xandra added.

"Even still, most elves live 400 years or more," said Crystal, who lowered her chin and stared down her friend.

"Those righteous devils may look more humanlike than we, but their smell gives them away. Their sweat puts off a sweet stench. Pointy-eared bastards cannot even smell like real men," Bortir said from the steps above them.

Rigel belly-laughed. "You exaggerate, Bortir."

"Though the elves may appear human, their ears are only the first giveaway. There are far more differences than you could imagine. Their development, reflexes, instincts—it is entirely unlike humans," Crystal said.

"Whatever the case, the guardians chose to pleasantly disagree with the dwarfs on the matter, seeing as the elves were also kind enough to shelter and teach us." Xandra gently urged Glomir to turn and continue walking.

At the base of the stairs, Glomir took a right and led them through a large room loaded with aged weapons and indistinguishable artifacts. Light from endless torches illuminated the room, reflecting off the multi-colored metal pieces as they walked past. Serena reached toward the rusting hilt of an ancient sword; the blade was thicker than any she had ever seen.

"I would not touch that," Glomir said without turning to look behind himself.

Serena pulled back her hand, fumbling to clasp her fingers together. Soon they branched off from the hall of artifacts. Glomir led them down another hall past a dozen metal doors. Near the end of the hall, he stopped near an open door and motioned, "For the lasses."

Xandra and Serena entered the room first. The walls were rough and dark, chiseled from the very mountains in which the dwarfs resided. On the floor were four straw-stuffed beds on stone bases. Draped over each bed was a blanket made from animal fur topped with a feather-stuffed pillow. Xandra went to the second bed, dropped her bag onto the floor, and collapsed onto the fur blanket with a big smile on her face. "Oh, how I have missed this," she said.

"I should like you both to remain here while Rigel and I meet with the Elder," Crystal said, dipping down to place her knapsack on the floor beside the bed closest to the door. "Rest for now. We shall return shortly," she said before stepping back into the hallway.

RIGEL AND THE WINDAEF siblings quietly followed the dwarfs through a series of passageways. When they entered a room with gleaming weapons adorning the walls, they were greeted by a gray-haired dwarf sitting upon an ornate gold chair so large it seemed like a throne.

"The mighty leaf-lickers have returned at last," the Elder said, eyeing them sharply. "I was beginnin' to think ye had perished."

"Aigon Flintfeet, must you be so vulgar toward your allies?" Rigel asked, crossing his arms. "Your king agreed to the safe harbor of our queen's guardians—all of us."

"Thank you, Rigel, but there is no need to defend us," Crystal said. "We are all on Hyrosencia's side, but that does not make the pint-sized gold diggers allies of our kind."

"Sharp ears and sharper tongues," Aigon Flintfeet said. "I remember you two." He pointed a meaty finger toward Crystal and Cole. "You may look human to the human fools, but we dwarfs—we know the truth. You cannot mask your true self, even with your ancient magic."

"You do not have to like us nor our presence here. Believe me, I would feel safer in the woods than underground with your kind," Crystal sneered.

Cole stretched his arm out in front of his sister and lowered his chin to meet her eyes. "That is enough. The illusion was necessary to keep a low profile."

"If we are only here for one night, can we not be civilized until morning?" Rigel asked in earnest.

The dwarf tapped his chubby fingers against the arms of his chair, watching them through watery black eyes. Then he stood abruptly and hobbled down a few steps until he stood at eye level with the warriors. Addressing Rigel, Aigon said, "For the sake of your people, we are being civil. Allowing outsiders into Estivor goes against our ways, but I permit it under my king's orders. I trust you shall keep your fair friends in check during your stay."

Crystal narrowed her eyes at the Elder as he glanced her way, but Cole kept a sturdy grip on her shoulder, holding her in place. He bowed his head diplomatically and said, "We shall cause no disturbance among your kin, Aigon."

"We only ask that your men discontinue their comments toward our race." Crystal's ruthless eyes locked on the Elder. "The humans we protect, Serena and William, are presently unaware of our truth, as you called it."

"Deceitful as usual," Aigon said, shaking his head, and clacked his tongue against his teeth. "The mountains have a way of revealing all in due time. Remember that."

"We have heard the tales of your kind before," Cole said, wrapping an arm around Crystal's back and drawing her away from Aigon. "Should you require anything more from us?"

"I should like to ask permission for something," Rigel said hastily.

Aigon reared his head to glare at the human. "Permission? We have already offered shelter and food. What more could you want?"

"I would like to bring Serena and Will to spar this eve, with your permission, of course."

"This one dueled with Thomli and myself last they stayed in Estivor," Bortir said, grinning at the Elder. "He believes he could beat me in a rematch!"

Aigon chuckled, poking Rigel in a bicep, and said, "You are quite a courageous human. No wonder your queen chose you for such a dangerous task." Turning his nose up and puffing out his chest, the old dwarf hobbled back up to his chair. "Bortir, I trust you shall show the humans the sheer power of a dwarf's axe."

"With pleasure, Aigon," Bortir replied, bumping his chest twice with his fist.

The Elder waved his hand nonchalantly. "You may return to your friends. Rest assured none of my men shall reveal your secrets on this day—a favor returned to your dear queen."

Crystal clenched her jaw, and Cole replied, "We thank you, Elder."

Aigon rolled his eyes as he plopped into his grand seat. "The cooks will have dinner ready for the clan in a few hours. See to it our newest guests do not wander about without an escort."

"We shall keep an eye on 'em," Glomir said.

Crystal exhaled as she turned to exit the room and muttered, "I'm sure these oafs shall watch us as vigilantly as their precious wall."

Rigel stepped in front of Crystal. As they locked eyes, he placed a hand on her shoulder and said, "We are guests in this realm. It is no insult to have guardians of our own."

Crystal shrugged her shoulder, causing his hand to slip off. "They are no guardians. They hate my kind, maybe even fear us. But they do not care what happens to us. And they never will." Rigel sighed dejectedly as she shoved her way past him. "Could someone please show us back to our rooms? I should like to rest before dinner," Crystal said, batting her eyelashes as a sickly-sweet fake smile spread across her enflamed cheeks.

"As you wish, pointy-ears," Glomir said, chuckling as he turned toward the doorway.

The Elder sighed loudly and hollered, "That's enough, men! Keep your comments to yourself around the humans."

The Bevakors bowed their heads to the Elder before leading the guardians out of the room. Rigel chattered away, desperate to keep his friends' attention off the degrading comments the Bevakors ahead mumbled. Though Cole engaged in the banter, Crystal continued to fume. When they reached the hall where their bed chambers were located, Crystal quickly shoved past the dwarfs and entered her room, slamming the door shut without a word.

Giving their leader a moment to compose herself, Rigel and Cole entered their own room. Rigel greeted their eager companion. Will swung his legs off the bed and planted his boots on the rocky floor. He rested his elbows on his knees, propping his chin on his fists. "That was quick. How was your meeting?"

"The same as our first visit," Cole said. He flopped onto the bed in the far corner of the room. "They are not exactly keen on us being here."

"Their king made a promise to Elara, so they are tolerating us for the sake of the alliance," Rigel added. "That's why we cannot overstay our welcome."

"Why must we stay here if they are unfriendly?" Will asked.

"It's not as if we have many options." Rigel rubbed the back of his neck with one hand. "Some of the dwarfs are especially displeased with our alliance with the elves. Their two races have never been sociable."

"But the elves only trained you!"

Cole unsheathed his sword and inspected the cold black metal. "That is the point."

Rigel sat on the empty bed across from Will and leaned forward. "It's fine. They can be quite pleasant once you find a way to bond with them. Cole is not the sociable type, so they have no reason to like him. I, on the other hand, introduced them to the art of sparring, and they quite enjoy it."

"You did not introduce it, but they do enjoy beating you," Cole said with a smirk.

"Did they not spar before?" When Rigel shook his head, Will asked, "Then how do they become such legendary warriors?"

"Typically, they are taught to use a variety of weapons in their youth, and they give what they call demonstrations as they learn new skills. They can live 300 years or more, so many learned from the greatest fighters to ever walk the land," explained Rigel.

"On occasion they will partake in duels. With their proclivity toward angry outbursts and a shortage of women, it is a wonder the entire race has not perished in civil squabbles," Cole said.

"Anyway," Rigel interjected, regaining Will's attention. "We're allowed to spar in the designated area where they practice. Would you care to join us? I was going to invite Serena to come along as well."

"I would love to," Will replied, standing abruptly. "What should I bring?"

"Grab a couple swords, and we can go. I'm sure the Bevs are still outside." As Rigel expected, when he opened the door, he saw Bortir and Glomir Whitmane leaning against the jagged walls in the narrow hallway. The dwarfs were snickering among themselves. Rigel nodded to the Whitmane brothers as he marched past them to knock on the ladies' door. He knocked three times.

Xandra called out, "You may enter!"

He slowly opened the door and leaned his head into their room. All three of the young women turned to stare at him as he said, "Will and I are off to browse the weaponry and show off our skills. Should any of you like to join us?"

Serena looked away from Rigel and bit her lip. She had barely practiced sparring since Rexton's soldiers attacked them outside Noomï.

"Serena, you should go," Crystal said. "It is time you stop grieving the loss of our enemy and resume your training. Go. The Bevakors are vigilant watchmen. Use this haven to your advantage."

Though she hesitated at first, Serena rose from her bed, snatching her sword's casing from the floor near her feet. Attaching the weapon to her belt, she trudged past Crystal. Rigel stepped back out of her way as she stomped through the doorway and into the corridor without protest.

"I think I shall join you. Clearly, I could use the practice myself," Xandra said as she grabbed a broad sword.

"How is it?" Crystal asked, sitting up and reaching toward her friend's bandaged hand.

"It's fine, thanks to you." Xandra pulled her hand away from Crystal's prying eyes. "It's not my dominant hand anyway."

"Well, don't overdo it. Wouldn't want the wound to reopen," Crystal said, plopping back on the bed.

"You're not joining us?" Rigel asked.

"You know how I loathe being underground. With all the late-night watches recently, I think it best I sleep." To Xandra, she said, "Wake me when it is time for dinner."

"Of course," Xandra nodded.

"Thank you. Perhaps you can get through to Serena? Find out what she meant when she said she spoke to Elara. She clearly doesn't trust me as much as I thought." She rolled onto her side, facing the wall.

"I can try," Xandra replied with a shrug before closing the door behind her.

SECRETS

Serena and Will followed the Bevakors, peeking through each doorway as they traveled through the winding passageways. The underground city was greater in size and population than any city they had seen in the southern part of Hyrosencia. Everywhere they looked, the walls were carved several feet high, creating a vast cavern nestled safely within the depths of the mountain.

Glomir led them down thick steps deeper into the mountain. They crossed through another hall, this one with dwarfs bartering in a crowded marketplace. Though Serena found the dwarfs fascinating, she felt as if her stomach was going to rip out of her body. She tensed as they moved through yet another tunnel, taking them farther and farther from the hall where they left Crystal and Cole.

Finally, they trickled into the Bevakor hall. To their left were several basic cots—two of which had dwarfs lounging on them. Before them was a wide open area where two dwarfs were engaged in a heated duel with large battle axes. The sound of their war cries drew the attention of every man in the room, but the violent sound of metal clashing rang in Serena's ears, causing her to step back and bump into Xandra.

Xandra put an arm around her and whispered, "There is nothing to fear here. These men are merely competing for sport." Then, with a chuckle, she added, "They take great pride in their skills. Like human men, they too enjoy showing off." She took Serena's hand and led her over to a wooden bench, where they sat shoulder to shoulder, watching the dwarfs and reacting to their exchanges.

"Intense, is it not?" Rigel asked. He roared and cheered for one of the dueling fighters who just gained the upper hand with a swift blow.

"Quite so," Serena muttered, staring at the wet black drops on the ground where the warriors tussled. "Do the dwarfs often get injured while sparring?"

"Lass, ye call it sparring; we call it dueling," Glomir corrected her, nodding toward the clashing dwarfs. "In Estivor, he who draws first blood wins the duel."

Serena swallowed, her mouth suddenly feeling dry. She looked over to Will, who was stealing a glance at her as they watched the duel. He shot his eyes back on the dueling dwarfs.

"Still believe you can beat me, human?" Bortir asked with a chuckle.

The dwarf slapped Rigel on his lower back, and he stumbled forward but quickly regained his footing. He turned to flash the dwarf a cocky smirk as he pulled his sword from its sheath. "I was born ready," he said with a wink.

Serena watched as the firelight reflected off the cool metal, sending streaks of white light into her eyes. Clenching them shut, she pleaded, "You shouldn't fight him, Rigel. It's too dangerous." The Bevakors snickered at the fear on her face.

He knelt beside her, placed a gentle hand on her knee, and said, "You need not worry, Serena. We are safe here. Sparring is meant to be fun, educational. You can learn a great deal just by watching others."

"I should prefer not to watch any more fighting. But one week ago, I witnessed enough bloodshed for a lifetime," she said, brushing his hand from her knee. "Blood shed by my own hands."

Xandra stood at once and said, "Enough. I cannot have you drowning in sorrow on my watch."

Will stepped closer to them. "Leave her be. She has the right to be sad."

"I don't need your help, Will," Serena yelled. She gawked at him with misty eyes. "I may be weak, but I'm not helpless." He blinked at her, incredulous. Serena's cheeks burned, and she turned her face away from him. She clenched her fists as her chest tightened.

When Will stepped toward her, Xandra put an arm out in front of him and assured Serena, "You're not weak. Exhausted, perhaps, but not weak. Come. Let's leave the men to their duels." Serena exhaled and nodded slowly, whispering words of gratitude to her new friend. Xandra patted her on the cheek, smiled, and said, "Sparring was not my idea anyway. I should much rather be resting."

In the tunnel, Serena paused and dropped her head back. Frowning at the closeness of the mountain walls, she sighed and squeezed her eyes shut. "How do you do it? How are you always so confident? So hopeful?"

"It was not always so. I was not unlike you as a child," Xandra said. "After my mother passed, I felt lost. When I began training, I leaned into my anger. I wanted others to feel the pain I felt."

Serena could not imagine the cheerful guardian angry. She seemed to defuse conflict with ease. Cocking her head to one side, she asked what had changed.

Xandra pursed her lips and looked at the ground, breathing out slowly. "I accidentally injured someone while sparring. It was pretty severe," she admitted. "Luckily, there's always a healer or two around, so he was fine."

Serena nodded. "Did you get in trouble with the elves?"

Xandra turned her big amber eyes on Serena and smiled. "Absolutely. But after a firm scolding, they were understanding. They used me as an example in class, taught us that anger holds us back. It stifles our ability to make clear decisions in a fight."

"That may be so, but how do you just let it go? It's not easy," Serena said with a shrug. "Anger, sadness, fear. How is it the elves manage not to feel any of it?"

"Oh, they feel it. Those emotions cannot be avoided." Xandra glanced behind herself. She lowered her voice and continued, "Elves are taught to regulate their negative emotions from a young age. They always go into a fight with a clear mind."

"My mind hasn't been clear for months, and I'm afraid it never will be again." Serena turned away from Xandra and continued down the hallway.

Xandra jogged back to her side and then slowed beside her. "You're not weak for being sad or angry, you know. You've lost so much. But you must learn how to work around your anger and fear. When you rush into a fight overwhelmed by those intense feelings, you're not in complete control of yourself. That's when mistakes happen."

"When I thought that soldier was going to hurt Will, I moved without thinking. I was so scared, I completely forgot what Cole and Rigel had taught me." Serena covered her eyes with one hand. "I'm lucky that soldier didn't gut me. Then I would have been the one you buried in the woods, and your entire journey would have been for nothing."

"We would never have let that happen to you, Serena. Crystal would have shot him before he got any closer, but you held your own. That is nothing to hold against yourself. You saved Will's life, and we are proud of you for it." Xandra patted Serena on her back, but it did little to comfort her.

"I'm trying to move past it, truly, but it's not easy. When my sword pierced into him, all I could think about was my family's final moments—and how I wasn't there for them," Serena said somberly, pressing her lips together as brutal images flashed through her mind.

"It is a tragedy that you had to witness such violence, but you cannot allow sadness to consume your light. Your family is gone, but they would want you to be happy, even in their absence. Your mother would want you to move forward."

"I know," Serena muttered as Xandra guided her down a different hall. Serena tensed, staring at the chiseled floor as they continued walking. "I don't know how to forget all the blood I have seen spilled. How do you live with killing another person?"

"You ask whoever or whatever you believe in to forgive you. If you truly mean it, I believe they will," Xandra said thoughtfully. "Then comes the hardest part: Forgiving yourself. You must accept the choices you had to make to survive and move forward with the intention of being better. Defending yourself and those you love from the wickedness of our world is not wrong."

"It does not feel that simple."

"This is a mental battle that only you can conquer," Xandra said. "As the elves say: 'Do not linger upon the anguish of yesterday. Focus on making tomorrow better.' We must release the things that cloud our judgment. It makes us better warriors and better people."

"Have you ever asked Divinity for forgiveness?" Serena asked, turning her eyes upon the guardian.

Xandra smirked, turning her eyes forward, and said, "I have—and I am no spiritual fanatic. Estrellogy was the faith of my parents, and my mother spoke fondly of joining Divinity from her deathbed. I like to believe she got her wish. Though I was raised among the elves, I enjoyed hearing other humans speak of the faith. The thought of good souls finding eternal peace in their afterlife among the stars? It's comforting."

Serena nodded and said, "It brings me comfort as well." Somehow, the twinkle in Xandra's eyes gave her hope.

Turning away, the guardian cleared her throat. "The Garrick family were devout Estrelles. To this day Queen Elara encourages her people to look to the stars for answers and to cast their worries on Divinity. There's a beautiful Estrellogy temple in Symptee open to everyone."

"I would really like to see that," Serena said, smiling. To her surprise, she found herself looking forward to seeing the City of Mercy. And not just for the refuge it offered.

"Are you nervous to meet Queen Elara?"

Serena immediately pictured the queen's face. Her bouncy brown curls and piercing green eyes were burned into her memory. "I do not feel worthy to be in her presence," Serena muttered. "She is a remarkable woman, is she not? Her kindness and love toward her servants and guardsmen—"

"She is a queen who loves all her subjects and is beloved by them in return," Xandra said.

"I gathered so much," Serena whispered, her sad smile fading as fast as it appeared.

Xandra paused in the middle of the tunnel. "When we left Symptee, we were told Queen Elara had never had any contact with you, only with Mary Finch. When did you speak to her?"

Serena hesitated. Then she stuffed her hand into her pocket. The ring was still there, a cold reminder of the dangerous secrets her parents had kept from her. "On the day my mother died, she gave me an enchanted ring. She told me to only wear it when I was alone and safe." Serena held out the golden band for Xandra to see. "When we were safe at the cabin near the reservoir, I put on the ring while Crystal was asleep. I had no idea of the power it possessed. Elara had been waiting to hear from my mother. She cried when I told her Mama was gone."

"Elara spoke very fondly of Mary while the guardians prepared for this mission. She must have been devastated by the news," Xandra said. "Why did you not tell us about the ring? Surely Elara would have told you we are trustworthy. We are your guardians."

"I do not know why I hid it from you."

"Do you not trust us?" Xandra looked defeated as silence stretched between them.

Serena swallowed, shifting her feet uneasily. "No, I do. I trust you all wholeheartedly, even Cole. I meant to tell you... I did. But there never seemed a good time or place. It's been one thing after another since we met." Serena leaned her back against the jagged rock wall and buried her face in her hands, whispering, "Is Crystal really upset with me?"

"She's disappointed. Confused perhaps? None of us knew what to think of your sudden revelation. She's tough and not always easy to read. I think she's most concerned that after all you've been through together, you still may not trust her. It's imperative that you do."

"I trust her!" Serena's frantic eyes fell upon her companion as she lowered her hands.

Xandra rested a hand on her hip and asked, "But have you ever told her that?"

"No. I thought it was obvious," Serena muttered as motion down the hall caught her attention. A shorter-than-average dwarf peered around the corner, and she caught a glimpse of a beardless face with a round red nose. When their eyes met, the face disappeared behind the dark stone wall, and Serena asked, "Did you see that? There is someone watching us."

Xandra glanced down the hall, catching a peek of the inquisitive little one. She smiled and waved, and the little face disappeared again. Turning to Serena, the guardian said, "He is but a youngling! He probably wandered down here looking for his father." She crept down the hall, and when she neared a fork in the hallway, whispered, "Come out, little one. There is nothing to fear."

She bent her knees and stared at the corner until a pair of curious brown eyes reemerged. "You're tall," the youngling said shyly.

"I'd say we're average for humans," Xandra said with a chuckle. "Have you met a human before?"

"No. They do not allow visitors often," the child said, stepping toward her. He crinkled his round nose and examined her face. "You are women?"

They laughed, and Serena stepped closer. "Of course we are."

Xandra turned toward her and said, "Women are not so common among dwarfs. Neither are children. This is a special occasion for us all."

"Your skin is darker than hers," the boy said, poking Xandra's arm.

"That can happen among our kind. Mine absorbs the sunlight more than others." She smiled and patted him on the head.

"I have never been to the surface," he said. The youngling's eyes sparkled with a million questions. "Is it nice outside?"

"It is beautiful but quite dangerous," Xandra said. "Can you tell us your name?"

"Dangi."

"Dangi, what brings you down here? Surely you are too young for dueling."

"My father is a Bevakor. I like to watch him fight. I want to be strong as him one day." Dangi beamed, his big brown eyes brimming with pride.

Serena crouched down before him and said, "If you work hard, you will be."

"How about we help you find your father then?" Xandra asked. She stood and offered her hand to the boy. He reached his chubby hand up to grasp her fingers, and they began tracing their steps back through the tunnels.

ON THE FAR SIDE of the corridor, Will and Rigel sparred as a warm-up for his rematch against Bortir Whitmane. As they parried, Will thought it was the perfect opportunity to talk about the ladies.

"Rigel, you're not trying to gain Serena's affections, are you?" he teased, slicing through the air as the warrior stepped backward.

"William Burroughs, are you jealous of me?" Rigel chuckled as he countered the move. Their blades met with a heavy clank. The guardian slid his blade against Will's, and the metal inched closer to his opponent's face.

"Never." Will thrust his blade forward, pushing Rigel back a step, and they twisted away from each other. Both pulled their swords back briefly.

"Good. You have nothing to worry about there. I am no more than Serena's guardian. Besides, I would not dare look at her in such a way. Queen Elara would have my head!" Rigel smirked and thrust his blade toward Will.

The cold metal sliced through a sleeve of Will's cream-colored tunic, and he frowned as blood began seeping through the torn fabric. Will asked, "Is that meant to intimidate me? Because I already have Crystal breathing down my neck every time I so much as look at Serena. I don't understand why she hates me so much."

"She's just being protective," Rigel said, immediately getting to work wiping the blood off his sword. "But perhaps she's right to hold you back. It's best not to start a courtship in the middle of a crossing."

"Courtship?" Will repeated loudly, dropping his sword with a heavy clank against the ground. "Is that what she's worried about? That's ludicrous."

Rigel smiled at his reflection in the clean blade before sheathing it. Turning back to Will, he asked, "Is it really? The two of you are quite close."

Will felt his cheeks flush and turned his head away. He feigned inspecting the burning slash on his arm. "She's my best friend's sister," he muttered. "I don't have a death wish."

Rigel laughed and rubbed the back of his neck. "Well, maybe that's for the best then." Then he walked over and helped Will tie a cloth around his bleeding arm. "Your skills have improved, but it'll take months for it to become second nature."

"I cannot say it shall be as easy against your dwarf comrade," Will said, nodding toward the off-duty Bevakors gathered across the room. Bortir was watching Rigel with an intense gaze. When they locked eyes, Rigel's smile disappeared, replaced by a fixed jaw.

Rigel hollered across the hall, "For fairness' sake, we duel with swords this time!"

Attempting to ease Rigel's nerves, Will teased, "In case you die today, do you have any last words for me to pass on?"

The guardian raised one brow. "To whom? I have no kin left."

"I don't know. A girl back home?" Will quipped.

Rigel guffawed and slapped Will on the back of his shoulder. "No. There is no lady awaiting me."

"There must be someone who has caught your eye. Someone you'd like to spend time with when you return home?"

"Perhaps, but I don't know if anything shall come of it," Rigel said, his cheeks and ears turning nearly as red as his hair. "She is quite hard to read."

Suddenly, their eyes fell upon Serena and Xandra as they reentered the military hall with a dwarf child in tow. The little boy was dragging Xandra toward the Bevakors while Serena's eyes scanned the room for familiar faces. When she spotted Will, she beamed and waved at him.

Rigel stepped closer to Will and nudged his side. "Now that girl, she's easy to read," the guardian teased, waving back to Serena. "Are you truly so daft?"

Will grinned and shook his head. "She's always looked at me like that." He thought back to their last encounter in Durmak. "She's just being friendly. I'm the only person here she really knows."

"Sure, pal," the guardian said, rolling his eyes. "I'm just sayin' what everyone can see. It's plain as day."

"You're crazy." Will shoved Rigel back a step. "Tell me more about your lady friend."

Rigel caught his balance and glanced at the hall's entrance. Serena snickered at their antics as she headed toward them. "There's not much to tell. She's a spitfire. She could easily put me on my back in a duel," Rigel said, grinning. "And I'd let her."

Will couldn't suppress his grin at that snippet of information. "You've got it bad," he said, glancing over at the Bevakors. He narrowed his eyes as he focused on Xandra interacting with the excited youngling. "Did you meet at the Academy?"

"Yes, we did," Rigel confirmed. "We have a great deal in common, and yet there is so much we don't speak of. There's hardly time when you're on a mission."

"Try to spend some time alone with her."

"You suggest the impossible," Rigel replied, shaking his head. "We are on a mission that requires constant focus."

"It may be easier to surpass the shackles of friendship if you can steal her away from the others," Will suggested. "Try to talk about something other than sparring. Perhaps you can find a way to help her or teach her something new."

"I doubt there is anything I could teach her. If anything, there are things she could teach me," Rigel said with a mischievous grin. "But I shall heed your advice in the future should the opportunity arise."

"Sometimes the smallest moments are the most important," Will said. "I wish I could speak to Serena again without the kill-joy siblings looming over us."

"We all know why leaving you two alone might not be the best idea," Rigel teased, nudging Will with his elbow.

"Not for anything improper," Will disputed. He pushed Rigel playfully. "I just wish we could have a normal conversation about what happened back home. I miss her brothers, so I can't begin to imagine how she must feel."

"Give her time. When she's ready to talk, she'll head straight for you," he said in earnest.

Will grinned, clapping his friend on the shoulder. "Thanks, Rigel. I think your chances are promising as well—in love and in battle."

"Thanks for the pep talk," Rigel said. "I can't speak to Cole about women. He would not be so understanding of my feelings. He believes we should be hyper-focused on our mission. I trust you shall keep this between us?"

"Yes, of course."

Rigel started walking toward the Bevakors, and Will followed close behind. Confidently, Rigel turned to face his new friend and continued walking backward, saying, "Who knew Durmak could produce a man of such wisdom?"

"I have known it all my life," Serena said with a chuckle, startling Will.

Will turned to look at her, his lips parted in surprise. Rigel nudged him forward, saying, "Your friend Will is a smart man, is he not?"

"Yes, he is, and kind as well," she replied, smiling as she withdrew her gaze from Will. "But I was actually thinking of my father when you said that. He was the wisest man I ever met."

Will nodded. "I must agree with you on that."

"Well, you two can keep each other company. The duel is about to start, and I am going to show Bortir Whitmane that human guardians are no weaklings," Rigel piped up. Turning on his heels, he marched toward his opponent.

Serena glanced down at her boots. "I really don't wish to watch them duel. Crystal wanted me to practice, but I would much rather rest before dinner. It has been such a long journey, and my feet ache."

Xandra came up behind Serena and draped an arm over her shoulders. "Mine as well. I could walk you back to the room if you'd like."

"I'll walk back with her. I could use some rest as well," Will said. "You should stay and cheer on Rigel. You know him better than we do."

Xandra eyed Will and tried to stifle a smile, but he caught it. Rigel's words replayed in his mind. "Are you certain you know the way? The tunnels all look the same, you know."

"I paid attention. I promise to get her back without delay. Be sure to cheer loud enough for all of us."

"Oh, I shall," Xandra said, laying a hand on each of their shoulders. Looking at Serena, Xandra leaned closer and whispered, "You better take care of this one. He just lost to Rigel. We could lose him if you don't tend to his wound."

Serena laughed. Reaching toward Will, she grasped him by the wrist and said, "Don't worry about Will. He shall not die on my watch." Then she turned and walked toward the exit, pulling Will alongside her. They walked quietly through the first tunnel. Serena's fingers were stuffed in her pocket, fiddling with her mother's ring as she stared ahead. Will stole glances at the solemn girl lost in thought.

"You seem distracted," he said at last. "What did Xandra say to you on your walk?"

Serena's eyes shifted toward him, and she sighed. "She asked if I do not trust them. Crystal is upset I kept a secret from her."

"And do you? Trust them? They were only strangers a few weeks ago."

"Yes, but they have saved my life two times over. I could never thank them enough for that," she said. Wrinkles appeared on her forehead as she scrunched her nose. "I need to explain myself to Crystal. She has done so much for me. I would hate for her to think—"

"You don't owe your secrets to strangers, Serena. Whatever you kept from them, it was personal. You have a right to some privacy."

She shook her head. "Not this. I should have told Crystal the morning after I first spoke to the queen. She confirmed Crystal was one of her guardians. All this time, the guardians could have updated her, but they had no idea of the power I possessed."

"Power?" he asked.

Serena quickened her pace and didn't answer at first. Will hurried to keep up with her until he managed to grasp her free hand by the wrist. Serena avoided his eyes, clenching the cold metal in her other hand as she pulled her fist from her pocket. She opened her palm to show him the ring. "This belonged to my mother, and Elara has its match. They're enchanted. When we both wear the rings at the same time, we can speak to each other."

Will's eyes widened as he looked from the ring back to Serena's face. "That's incredible," he whispered, relinquishing her arm and reaching toward her open hand.

Serena pulled back her hand, quickly closing her fingers around the ring. "My mother gave this to me before she died. It's all I have of hers. That's why I didn't tell Crystal. I didn't want to share it. It's mine, and I can't part with it."

"Surely she would take no offense if she knew your reason. It is your property, after all," he said, watching as she slipped the ring back into her pocket.

"I hope you're right."

"I am always right," Will chuckled, and they began moving through the tunnels once more.

Serena rolled her eyes and held back a grin. "At the very least, I owe Crystal an explanation."

"Just tell her what you told me. She'll understand."

"We'll find out soon enough," Serena muttered. "I think I know the rest of the way from here. You should go back and watch Rigel's duel. You two have become fast friends."

"Rigel is a good man," Will said, turning around to face her. "But he shall be fine in my absence. He has Xandra to cheer him on."

"I hope he's not offended we both left," Serena said. Will watched her scrunch her face, lost in concentration as she tried to remember the route back to their rooms. She wavered at a fork in their path, and he motioned toward the left.

"Stop worrying about offending everyone. They're warriors. They're not so easy to offend," Will said. "Besides, I believe Rigel will enjoy Xandra's company more than ours."

"Xandra?" Serena asked, turning toward him with her brows raised. It was clear the thought surprised her. "You suppose he likes her?"

"He all but said her name," Will grinned. "And I daresay she knows of his feelings already."

"How should you know all this?"

"Suppose I have a trustworthy face," he said, his grin broadening.

"Perhaps you do, but is that all it took to coax such information from an elite warrior?" Serena asked. "Maybe I was right to keep the ring a secret. They sure like to talk."

Will laughed and said, "They certainly do. When we arrived in Estivor, I asked Xandra if Rigel was interested in you, but she shut down that idea quickly."

Serena slowed down and cocked her head to one side. "What would make you ask such a thing?"

Their arms brushed against each other as they walked. Looking her in the eye, he replied, "Because you've been spending a great deal of time together."

"Yes. Training. Were you jealous?"

Will kept his eyes forward as he said, "Of course not. I'm just looking out for you."

"Oh, of course you were. You always act like one of my brothers. Would you have gotten into a fight if Rigel was interested in me?"

"I don't know. Perhaps." Will stopped and turned his body to face her. "Not everyone is your friend, Serena. And not all men are nice. Someone must look out for you."

Serena squeezed her hands into fists and clenched her teeth. "I don't need you to protect me, Will. I'm not a child." Her cheeks burned a rosy pink, and her green eyes gleamed as the torch light reflected off her irises. Will thought for a moment that Serena might burst into tears before she turned and walked away from him.

He dropped his head and stuffed his hands into his pants pockets. "I know you're not," he muttered. They ventured through an empty hall and up many stairs in unnerving silence. Will could not help stealing glances at the beautiful brokenhearted girl from his hometown. He had seen sadness in her eyes too many days, and he hoped her life would take a turn for the better when they reached Symptee.

When they reached their rooms, Serena leaned back against her door and stared at Will. He found her shy expression adorable. "I'm sorry I snapped at you," she said, tucking a stray hair behind her ear. "I am really glad you came with us, Will."

"I'll always be here if you need me." He braced one hand against the jagged rock wall beside her. Just as he considered leaning closer, the door to Serena's room flew open, and she stumbled back into Crystal's arms.

"What are you two doing? You're supposed to be practicing," she said crossly, glaring at Will through narrowed eyes. Serena scrambled out of Crystal's arms onto her feet. She frantically smoothed the hair back from her face.

"Serena wasn't feeling up to it, so I walked back with her," Will said, pushing off the wall and standing tall.

Serena stepped between them and turned toward Crystal. "I was hoping to speak with you while the others are busy," she said, staring at the guardian expectantly. Crystal nodded, turning and strutting toward her bed.

Turning to Will, Serena added, "Thank you for walking with me. I'll see you at supper?" Will nodded, his gaze locked on her until she closed the door.

THAT EVENING, THEY RECONVENED for supper in the dining hall. Long wooden tables covered in overflowing platters lined the room, and dwarfs sat elbow to elbow on benches, their thick, stumpy arms reaching for hunks of cured meat. Though the dwarfs were boisterous during their communal mealtime, the guardians tried to eat quietly. Cole feasted in silence, sipping ale from an overflowing mug while keeping a watchful eye on their surroundings. His eyes kept drifting back to Xandra as she gave a dramatic retelling of Rigel's duel and his latest wounds.

Though they attempted to avoid interaction with the drunken dwarfs, Bortir wandered over to their table, bragging loudly about his latest triumph over Rigel. When he had taken his fill of the plentiful food, Cole chugged the remainder of his ale. Then standing abruptly, the swordsman said, "We should leave at dawn."

Crystal rose and nodded. "We should all retire. The journey to Faswyn shall be difficult and the nights bitter. Enjoy the beds while you can."

As Serena shuffled after her guardians, a dwarf grabbed her by the upper arm, stopping her abruptly. She turned toward the red-haired dwarf, her forehead wrinkled in surprise, and asked, "May I help you?"

The dwarf had a knee-length beard sprinkled with bits of breadcrumbs and a dazed look in his eyes. Leaning closer, he professed, "Secrets never keep in the mountains. Soon even you shall know the whole truth."

"How should you know any of our secrets?" Serena asked. She jerked her arm away from the dwarf, but his grip remained firm on her.

Crystal intervened, removing the dwarf's hand from Serena's arm and shoving him away from her. Taking Serena by the hand, the archer dragged her toward the door and said, "Pay him no mind. He is drunk." As she marched Serena toward one of the dining hall's exits, many of the dwarfs watched them through narrowed eyes, murmuring as they passed each table.

When they entered the tunnel, Crystal released her grasp on Serena's arm but remained by her side. As the guardians ushered Serena and Will further from the dining hall, they could hear the echo of the dwarf exclaiming, "The mountains reveal all!" The snickering of unruly dwarfs rang after them.

"What on earth could they mean by that?" Serena asked, glancing behind them as the taunts became harder to hear.

"They're all crazy," Crystal said. Serena thought she saw a hint of nerves flash in the guardian's blue eyes, but just as quickly, Crystal steeled herself. "We can't be out of here quick enough."

When they reached their room, Crystal and Xandra nudged Serena through the doorway, barely muttering goodnight as they closed the door behind them.

REPUTATION

Ismenia and Idonea were engrossed in deep conversation in the citadel apothecary. The royal herbalist's eyes flicked toward the queen, standing in the doorway, and her voice trailed off midsentence.

Stepping toward Elara, Ismenia threw her arms up and said sternly, "Milady! You are barely recovered. I told you to rest a few days more. You should summon me if you need something."

"Nonsense. I am well," Elara insisted. "The wedding is next week. With guests arriving every hour, there is hardly time for rest."

Ismenia puckered her lips, and her forehead creased in displeasure. "I still think you should postpone the ceremony. A couple weeks more would not hurt. We can accommodate your guests, and perhaps by then the guardians will have returned."

The queen shook her head and sighed. "There are no guarantees, Ismenia. You and I both know that," Elara said. "My first husband passed such a short time after our nuptials. There was hardly time for us to grow acquainted, much less produce an heir."

"Come now, Elara. You know Lord Stirling well, and he is in excellent health. Not to mention, you are quite familiar with each other already." Ismenia raised her eyebrows knowingly. Turning toward her sister, she pleaded, "Idonea, tell her there is no reason to rush the ceremony."

The oracle shrugged, picking up a vial off the counter and studying it. "Her Majesty has valid reasons for concern. People whisper. It's best she wed quickly for her own reputation." She placed the bottle back on the counter.

"Don't be ridiculous!" Elara said with a hearty chuckle. "I was never to be a virgin bride. It is my second marriage after all. Gerard makes me happy, and it has been a remarkably long time since I've been so."

"We are pleased that you managed a love match, and with the nephew of King Marinus at that," Ismenia smiled.

"Yes, but do not allow love to cloud your judgment," Idonea warned. "With all the new faces coming in and out of the castle for your wedding, I fear danger looms within these walls."

"See—danger looms," Elara repeated, looking back and forth between the two women. Wrinkling her brow, the queen locked her eyes on the oracle and asked, "What have you seen? Is Antoine to attack the city?"

"I'm afraid that is unclear, Elara. I have had visions every night this week, each different. More like flashes. The pictures are incomplete. In one, blood spread across the floor, but I could not see the source." Idonea crossed her arms over her chest. "I've already asked Commander Stanton to initiate extra precautions."

"That would explain it," the queen said. She glanced at the two extra guards standing close behind her. In the hall, another six waited. "But I cannot live in fear forever. Gerard and I shall wed as we originally planned. We can wait no longer. Not even for my kin. It is past time I wed again. I need to have an heir while it's still possible."

"You have no need to worry in that regard, Elara," Idonea said to the others' surprise. "You will announce that you are with child with your niece standing at your side."

Elara closed her eyes, and Ismenia noticed the way she breathed shakily. "All this time, my greatest fear has been having a child of my own before this war concludes. Would our people look to my child to save them? Could we even survive another two decades of waiting?"

"But we three know the truth. You have been the steadfast leader our people needed throughout these difficult years, but this burden should never have befallen you," Ismenia whispered, crushing herbs in a small bowl. "Soon our people will come to know the true heir, and all will be made right."

"I worry over how they will react," Elara murmured.

Idonea nodded and said, "Heavy is the burden to be placed on the hidden heir of Hyrosencia. Rexton is to blame for all our suffering. We must pray that the heir will rise to meet her destiny."

"Perhaps Antoine is not the only one to blame?" Elara wondered aloud. "I made promises to Mary I could not keep. Though we tried ten times over, we could not reach them in time. We could not save Mary or her poor sons. I will always regret that. If we had reached them sooner, I could have spared Serena so much pain."

Ismenia recognized the grim look on Elara's face and placed a gentle hand on her shoulder. "Everyone has lost greatly to this war, none more than you or Serena. But I believe we are on the path to reclaiming our kingdom. Be patient when the guardians return. Their part in this war has barely begun."

Idonea pressed her lips together and hummed to herself, drawing their attention. "I have had a recurring dream of a man being bested by two swords," the oracle hesitantly admitted. "Though I have never seen him, my intuition was that it was Antoine. And though I did not see the face of his challenger, they must be alive for such a vision to occur. We must have faith in the celestial plan."

"Are you sure it was a dream and not a vision?"

Idonea nodded and whispered, "It feels different from my past visions, but it may yet come to be true. I have always felt in my bones that we can win."

"It brings me so little comfort to know victory could be within reach," Elara said, pressing a hand to her abdomen. "Long have we worried over this war. All this waiting and wondering makes me feel ill."

Ismenia raised her eyebrows. Her face lit up as she turned and scoured the shelves full of plants and medicine vials. "I have just the thing for that." Plucking a narrow vial of oil from a shelf, the herbalist offered it to her. "This is Artemisia absinthium. It eases stomach pains. Put a drop or two in some mint tea. It should help with your nerves."

Elara eyed the vial of bright yellow oil and said, "Thank you. I don't know what I would do without your expertise."

"You would have perished long ago," Ismenia said lightheartedly, touching Elara's back and gently nudging her toward the door. "Now I must insist you return to your chambers and rest for at least an hour."

"An hour?" the queen moaned, rolling her eyes. She clenched her fingers around the vial, then turned toward the door and said, "If you insist. But you must visit me when you are less busy. You as well, Idonea—especially if you have any more visions."

The Cinderfell sisters bowed their heads, and Idonea said, "We shall come by your chambers an hour before dinner."

As the queen nodded and ducked out of the apothecary, Ismenia slapped the back of her hand on her sister's arm and said, "You give her more to worry about than anyone else. Why mention a vision to her if it isn't clear as day?"

"Sister, she seeks our friendship for our candor and good sense. If I told her of every fragment I envisioned, she would soon learn that seeing the future can be more of a burden than a gift," Idonea said.

"What more have you kept from her?"

"I sense a bad omen. Serena will make it to Symptee, of that I am certain, but at what cost? I fear more blood shall be spilled on her path, blood which will haunt her," Idonea whispered.

"The guardians knew the mountains would not be easy to cross," said Ismenia, inspecting her stockpile of freshly-picked herbs.

"They all know it, but that does not mean a loss will affect them any less."

"I am more worried about what shall happen once she arrives. Everything she was ever told about her family has been a lie." Ismenia bit her lip. "We have prayed and worried over that girl for seventeen years, and she has not the faintest idea."

"When she finally learns the truth, it will change everything. The fate of Hyrosencia rests in her hands." The solemnity of Idonea's words left Ismenia feeling unsettled.

"Perhaps it's best Elara does marry before they arrive," she said with a grim smile. "It could be weeks more before they return, and who knows what state they'll arrive in."

"I must agree. The wedding should not be put off any longer," the oracle said. "We cannot have nobles questioning the legitimacy of our queen's pregnancy."

Ismenia's eyes widened in realization, and she began fumbling through her stash of colorful vials. "You believe she is already with child? Why did you not say such when she was here?"

"There were extra eyes and ears around," Idonea replied with a shrug. "I trust our queen should like us to use the utmost discretion until after the wedding."

Ismenia paused and turned to stare at her sister. "Right. Good thinking." Then she returned to her task.

Idonea laughed, rubbing her hand over her shaved head. "I always am right, even when I do not know it."

The herbalist pulled two vials from the shelf. "Vitamins! She will need vitamins! And I must make her a special tea at once for the nausea." With an elated shriek, Ismenia raced for the door, leaving her sister behind.

Halfway out the door, Ismenia paused, turned back toward her sister, and called, "Come, sister! We must go to her at once!"

With a satisfied smirk, Idonea nodded and ambled slowly to join her sister, who eagerly laced one arm through hers. Then the Cinderfell sisters made their way down the hall to deliver medicine and good news to their cherished friend in her private chambers.

RELIEF WASHED OVER TALITHA'S face the moment Anteros appeared in the opening on her cell door. "Good eve, Red," he said with gusto as he turned the key in the lock. The metal clicked, echoing down the hall. It was the fifth night in a row Anteros had visited her in the dungeon right after dinner with his family. Throwing open the door, he sauntered over to her spot against the farthest wall with his usual basket of goodies in hand.

For the first time, he noticed that Talitha did not tense when he approached. "Good as can be expected in here," she said, raising her eyebrows and sighing. "What's got you feeling so chipper?"

Placing his back against the rough brick wall, he leaned against it, bending his knees and sliding down until he landed on his rear beside her. Glancing sideways at her, Anteros's lips curled up in a mischievous smile, and he said, "We made it through dinner without my father yelling or flipping the table, so that's quite the cause for celebration."

Talitha snickered. "That sounds miraculous, indeed."

"It's nice to see you smiling," Anteros said, locking eyes with her.

Talitha blushed and averted her eyes. "The food you bring is all I have to look forward to. It's actually quite sad."

The prince reached a hand into the basket to his left, chuffed by her comment. "I don't think you will be sad tonight." He turned to face Talitha with a triumphant grin spread from ear to ear. In his hands was a large plate with a sizable round divot in the center containing a flat pasta with a thick sauce made from chicken stock. On the side of the plate sat a fresh roll with a dark crust on the outside.

Talitha inhaled deeply, closing her eyes. "Is that chicken stock soup?" she whispered.

"Whatever you're used to, I promise this is even better," Anteros said. "Here." He placed the stark white plate on the ground between them, and the dish clanked against the uneven dark tile. Reaching into the basket once more, he produced a small fork and held it out to her. "This is vermicelli pasta in the chef's special sauce. Have you had anything like it before?"

Talitha took the fork from his hand; her fingertips gently grazed his palm as she clasped the cool metal utensil in her hand. Leaning over the dish, she said, "We never had pasta in Durmak, but I have heard of it. What is it made of?"

Anteros chuckled. "Well, I am no chef, but I believe it's made similarly to bread. They make a dough out of eggs and flour and form it into a shape, then cook it in hot water. It pairs well with a number of meats and sauces."

Talitha nodded, stabbing a couple pieces of the pasta with the fork. Lifting it to eye level, she noticed orange shredded bits in the sauce. "I love carrots," she muttered before taking a bite.

"As do I." The prince leaned his head back against the wall with his eyes trained on her while she chewed. Her eyes closed as she savored it. "Well, what do you think?"

"You were right," Talitha said, stabbing at her meal and shoving another bite into her mouth. While still chewing, she held her hand up to cover her mouth and said, "It's delicious!"

Anteros shook his head but smirked. "I had hoped you would like it. It is my favorite dish. The chef makes it at least once a month at my request."

"You are blessed to have such plentiful options in the North," Talitha said, clearing her throat. "Lucky, really."

Anteros leaned over and reached into the basket again. This time he produced a small flask. Popping the top off, he passed it over to her, saying, "I have never thought of this type of food being a rarity. I thought everyone ate as well as this."

"Certainly not," she said. She reached forward to accept the flask. She narrowed her eyes as she sniffed at the contents, seeming surprised by the fruity scent.

"Mulled wine," Anteros said. "Pairs well with the meal. Go on."

Talitha took a quick swig of the dry wine. Coughing briefly, she handed the flask back to Anteros and wrinkled her nose. "I shall never understand how you drink something so bitter." She wiped the corner of her mouth with the back of her hand. "Next time bring water."

"If you insist, Red," he said, shaking his head as he lifted the flask to his own lips. Anteros took two swigs before returning the flask to his basket.

"I insist you stop calling me that," she said tartly, narrowing her eyes while she chewed another bite of her dinner. "Otherwise, I shall have to give you a nickname."

"Make it a good one, then."

Talitha hummed contemplatively. Finishing off the last bite of her meal, she swiped her roll through the remaining sauce on her plate and ripped off a sizable bite with her front teeth. "Lucky," she said with a delighted smile.

"Lucky? Luck had no part in this!" he protested, gesturing toward his body.

Talitha looked away from him and rolled her eyes. "You're the crown prince of Hyrosencia, which affords you luxuries commoners only dream of. You never have to work, yet you eat and sleep like a king."

"Oh, I work plenty," Anteros argued. "My father forces me to partake in everything—history lessons, meetings with the military, family dinners, festivals, balls, socializing with the right noble families. You may think I have a great deal of free time, but I can assure you otherwise."

"Then how do you have time to come down here?" Talitha pulled her knees up to her chest. She rested one rosy cheek against them as she studied his face.

Anteros exhaled, leaning back against the wall. He focused on the blank cell wall across from them. "I make time because this is the only place where I can relax. I can breathe down here. I don't have to worry about my reputation or having a dozen eyes on me. I can just—I can be myself."

"You don't have any friends you would rather spend time with?" Talitha asked.

Anteros frowned. "There's a couple who are decent fellows, but I see them enough. We spar and play cards now and then. We all spent two weeks in Jessiraé for my birthday. I had just returned when you arrived here."

"What's Jessiraé like?" Talitha asked. The sun coming from the small window in the corner illuminated her red hair from behind, producing a halo around her face. "I think we passed through there on our way here, but I wasn't there to sight-see."

Anteros recalled many drunken nights going between the gambling tables and the private rooms of The Untamed Mare and smirked, averting his eyes from the prisoner. "It's," he searched for the right word, "lively. It has a reputation for entertaining gentlemen of all backgrounds."

"Oh," Talitha said, her eyes widening. She blinked repeatedly, avoiding his. "I may not be a proper lady, but I know you're implying something indecent."

"Don't be alarmed. It's not all whores," Anteros said with a chuckle.

"Well, I should hope not!" Talitha turned her back to him. "Two weeks," she mumbled to herself.

"It sounds bad, I know, but I promise I'm no scoundrel," Anteros said. He reached out a hand to touch her arm. "Not anymore."

She flinched and drew back from his touch. "I'm surprised you feel the need to leave court to look for women to bed. Your sister implied the young ladies of Graynor throw themselves at you."

He growled under his breath. "That girl. I still cannot believe my prim and proper sister came down here in a frilly ball gown to get a look at you," he said. "Our mother would kill her for showing her face down here. It is no place for a lady!"

Talitha tensed. "I guess that means I am not a lady," she whispered. "Perhaps you should find someone more respectable to spend your time with."

"I have enough sense to decide who I wish to spend time with," he said, waving off her comment. "The ladies at court are all the same. If you have met one, you have met them all. But you're different, Talitha."

"I am. I'm forced to be here, a commoner turned prisoner left to rot in a cell for no good reason." She pushed herself up onto her feet. "I'm sure the ladies at court look and smell better than I do."

The prince turned his eyes upon her. The pale light of the sunset coming through the barred window illuminated her face, bathing her in a golden orange glow that made her look ethereal. Anteros swallowed hard, stumbling to his feet as he countered, "Some, perhaps, but not all of them."

She snorted, covering her mouth with a hand as she laughed. Her hearty laughter was a sound he enjoyed hearing and hoped to hear more. "You're quite the liar."

"You do not look bad at all," he said. "I'm sure a bath would make you look and feel good as new."

She crossed her arms over her chest. "A bath would be nice," she muttered. "I feel so grimy, like I've been sleeping on the ground for ages."

"It's only been a few weeks," he replied. Immediately, he twisted his mouth in regret.

"A few weeks to you is a lifetime to me," she snapped back, her pale eyes full of hostility. "You're not the one locked in a dungeon."

"I know. I'm sorry." He said dropped his chin as he shoved his hands into his pockets. Then his eyes lit up with an idea. "Care for dessert?"

Talitha's eyes flicked from the prince to the basket on the ground. "There's more?" Their arms brushed against each other as she pushed past him to search the basket. With a quiet gasp, she whipped her head around with her mouth agape, a small berry tart cupped in her hand. "Blueberries? We don't normally see these until later in the summer!"

Anteros grinned in triumph. "They are in season a bit earlier this year. Lucky us."

"Lucky, indeed!" she said, taking a large bite from the pastry. She moaned in satisfaction as tears welled in the corners of her eyes. "'Tis absolute perfection."

The prince opened his mouth to remind her about the fork but decided against it. She was already three bites into the petite dessert and loving every crumb of it. "I wanted to bring you something special since I won't be able to come by as often," Anteros admitted.

Talitha paused, one last bite of the blueberry tart perched between two fingers halfway to her mouth. Lowering her hand, she locked eyes with him and asked, "Why? I thought you said you make time for it because you like it down here."

"I do," he said slowly. "But with the Summer Solstice approaching, I shall have to aid my mother and father in the preparations. There's a festival with games outside and a ball in the evening. My father always invites nobles from outside of Graynor, even from other kingdoms. It's quite important to him."

"Huh. We never celebrated the Solstice back home. It's just a reminder that the hottest days of the year have begun," Talitha said, popping the final morsel in her mouth.

"With my parents both originating from Nyzenard, they brought the festival over some years ago," he said. "It's mostly celebrated in the capital. It's just another excuse to throw an extravagant party."

"I bet your sister enjoys that." Talitha chuckled. "She was an interesting girl. Quite bubbly. Certainly not what I was expecting of the king's child. Neither of you are."

Anteros smiled broadly. He leaned his body back against the brick wall. "I shall take that as high praise."

Talitha blushed as Anteros stared at her. She glanced toward the window, taking in the last of the pink and orange sky as the sun retreated for the night. "Perhaps your sister can come by again in your absence?"

Anteros grimaced and shrugged his shoulders. "Perhaps. I can put in your request."

The corner of her mouth twitched upward, almost a smile. "Well, I hope you enjoy your party planning. I look forward to hearing all about that another day." She leaned against the wall next to him.

"I will not leave a shred of detail out," Anteros said. He pushed himself upright, and then leaned over and caught the basket by the handle. Taking slow, deliberate steps backward toward the cell door, he added, "I best be off now. 'Til next time, Red."

"'Til next time, Lucky," she replied quietly. Holding up one hand, she wiggled her fingers as he locked the door and ambled off, leaving her alone in the dark once more.

AS THE BUSTLING MARKET of Noomï came into view, Cameron dismounted from his horse, leading it by the reins through the hordes of people toward the city's center. As he went, he paused to ask several merchants if they had seen his sister, describing her in as much detail as he could. But each merchant shied away from his questions, having nothing to say about a runaway from Hyrosencia. He glanced down and wondered if wearing his uniform was a mistake.

Seeing a flash of crimson pass in his periphery, he whipped around and zeroed in on two young men who were wearing the same uniform as him. "Hey!" he called out, rushing after them. The soldiers paused and turned to greet him, and the paler one said, "Never seen you before. New to the valley?"

"I'm actually looking for someone," Cameron informed them. "My sister's gone and run off. Her name is Serena Finch. She's eighteen, about this tall," he held up his hand to his eye level, "dark wavy hair, green eyes, probably wearing a plain frock. Seen anyone like that?"

The men exchanged a look before shaking their heads. The taller soldier said, "Sorry, pal. Don't think we've come across her. But you should check the Peacock."

"That's where most of the runaway girls end up if they make it across the border," the other added, his eyes twinkling. "They have the best ale around. Come on. Join us for a pint." The man threw an arm over his shoulder and began leading him down the busy street.

"I'm afraid I don't have time for a pint," Cameron replied, trying to free himself from the soldier's grasp.

"Nonsense. There's no point going anywhere without a lead. That's like chasing a ghost," the tall one said, snickering.

He couldn't fight with that logic. Around the corner was a rust-colored two-story brick building that had seen better days. Broken shingles littered the ground outside, and a massive crack ripped through the middle of the front window.

The sign above the door read "The Pleasant Peacock," the words accented by garish paintings of overflowing mugs and womanly silhouettes.

"This isn't just an alehouse," Cameron commented as the pale soldier yanked open the front door and gestured for them to enter first.

The two soldiers chuckled, slapping him on the back as they ushered him inside. "No, it is not. It's much better," the pale one replied.

Cameron took a deep breath before starting to scan the faces in the small, crowded pub. For the first time since leaving Murmont, he prayed to Divinity that he wouldn't find what he was looking for at The Pleasant Peacock. If he found Serena here, he'd lose his lunch.

With a sigh of relief, he determined she was not among any of the bosomy women handing out pints of ale downstairs. Sinking onto a stool at the bar, he lifted two fingers to flag down the bartender. He suddenly found the sound of ale enticing. The man slammed three mugs down on the bar top, sending frothy liquid splashing across the counter. Cameron nodded as the three men each claimed their mug.

"I don't believe it!" a woman's voice exclaimed from behind them, and Cameron turned his head to see what the woman was yelling for. His eyes fixed on a woman he knew all too well in his youth, for he had spent many nights in Durmak sneaking off to dance at bonfires and make out in the woods with Natalia Thorne.

"Nat? What the blazes are you doing here?" Cameron asked. He slipped off the barstool and stepped toward her.

She closed the gap between them and thrust her arms around his neck, wasting no time planting a deep kiss on his lips as she pressed her chest into him. "Cameron Finch! I never thought I'd see the likes of you again!" she said with a grin.

Trying not to let her risqué attire distract him, he asked, "Why would you come to Noomï?"

Natalia rolled her eyes, pretending to pat down her messy blonde wisps while her eyes raked over his uniform. "After you left town, I didn't have much reason to stick around," she said, dragging her hands down his chest and adjusting his name badge. "What brings you out here, soldier boy? Missed me?"

He could feel the eyes of his new friends watching them while they drank their ale. Cameron wrapped an arm around her waist and leaned closer, whispering, "Is there somewhere more private we can talk?"

Natalia grinned, grabbing him by the shirt and whispering against his lips, "You'll have to make it convincing for my boss."

He nodded, and her smile broadened as she turned on her heels, grabbing him by the hand and dragging him to the stairs. In the upstairs corridor, she ushered him through the third door on the left and closed the door behind him.

"Now will you tell me what brought you to Noomï?" she asked, pulling him by the hand over to the bed.

Cameron swallowed hard as she ran her hands over his chest, pulling off his crimson coat. Then she pressed down on his shoulders to make him sit. "Serena's missing," he barely managed. He was distracted by Natalia unbuttoning his shirt.

"I heard," she said, standing upright to look him in the eye.

"The king's other men have been passing around her description. There's a high price on that girl's head," she noted. Her fingers worked quickly to remove his shirt.

He clenched his jaw, his thoughts slipping back to one hot August night a few years ago when his father interrupted their fun to get him to help track down Serena. She and Talitha had gone out late in the evening and hadn't returned by nightfall. Cameron begrudgingly sent his date back to the bonfire alone. His frustration ignited into an explosive argument with his father while they searched the woods, only to come across the girls making their way home fifteen minutes later. That was the day he decided he wanted to leave. No, he needed to leave. He needed to be free from the responsibility of always looking after his family, and enlisting was his shot at freedom.

Natalia pressed her lips against the side of his neck, giggling as he wrapped his arms around her thighs and pulled her onto his lap. "I missed you," she said just before he pressed his lips to hers.

"At least one good thing came out of her running off this time," Cameron muttered breathlessly between kisses.

"Maybe you can get stationed here, in the valley," Natalia said optimistically, raking her teeth against his bottom lip. "You never know who you'll see out here. I saw your old pal Will just the other day."

"What?" Cameron asked, grabbing her by the upper arms and forcing her back. Her hair was even messier than when he first saw her, her full lips swollen from kissing him. "You've seen Will? In Noomï? Did he come here? To the Peacock?"

Natalia chuckled, causing her cleavage to bounce as she shook her head. "Heavens no. That boy was on a mission of his own. Wouldn't surprise me if he was out looking for Serena, too."

Cameron grabbed her by the hips and hoisted her to one side, letting her flop on the bed beside him. She pouted and stared up at him as he went in search of his shirt. "He wrote to let me know she was crossing. He didn't say anything about going after her," the soldier tried to rationalize, pacing back and forth on the dusty wood floor. "And you're sure you didn't see Serena with him?"

She sat up and shook her head. "Definitely not. Just this tall, blonde woman who looked like she knew how to put up a fight," Natalia said, raising her eyebrows. "Didn't know that was his type." She chuckled.

"Blonde?" Cameron asked, pulling Will's letter out of his pocket and reading over it. Serena had been with a group traveling east. Could the blonde have been one of them? The archer? "Maybe he's already found her," he muttered, folding the letter back up.

The young woman stood and went over to him. She grabbed him by the cheeks and looked into his eyes. "Then let him find her for once," she whispered, her eyes dropping to his lips.

He inhaled, breathing out slowly while he stared at the girl he had grown up with. She was everything he had wanted as a teenager before his entire focus shifted toward the army. He hardly gave her a second thought when he put Durmak behind him. He never once thought maybe she'd wanted to get out of there, too.

"I can't, Nat," he said, his voice cracking. "I wish I could, but these are the king's orders. I have to go after her." She nodded, and he noticed a familiar sadness in her eyes. He knew what she was thinking. He'd always had to put Serena before himself, and he still did now. The thought made his muscles tense. Cameron grasped the young woman by the waist and pulled her a step closer. "But right now, I'm yours," he said, pressing his lips to hers with renewed zeal. This was his life, and he was going to put himself and his desires first from now on.

REFLECTIONS

Crystal had led the travelers for two long, difficult days into the mountains beyond Estivor, where the trees became sparse and the mountain air cooled as gusts blew down from the white peaks. As the sun descended behind the trees on the second day, they reached the hot springs, a spot the guardians had relished when they first passed through the mountains on their way to Hyrosencia. They were grateful for the respite to enjoy the healing waters of the mountains.

Crystal settled their campsite while the others got ready to dip in the springs. Cole had already gone off to a pool on his own. "I could use a break from all of you. Try not to need my help," he had said. Xandra and Serena went to another pool, and Will went after them. Crystal decided to dip into the one near the camp. Rigel was already there in the water.

"Mind if I join you?" she asked Rigel, barely glancing up at him. "I think Xandra can handle watching those two for a while."

"I welcome your company," he said. She turned her back toward him and began removing her outer garments. She heard Rigel suck in a deep breath and slip off the wet rocks, plunging the rest of his body into the pool and coming back up again.

Crystal turned her head and chuckled. She approached the pool wearing only a fitted tank top made of cream wool and thick brown tights. She sat on the ledge and dipped her legs into the pool, relieved by the warmth as the water soaked through her tights. Aware of Rigel's lingering gaze, Crystal shivered and quickly pushed herself off the rocks, allowing the warm water to engulf her. Then, slinging her hair back from her face, she closed her eyes, sighed, and leaned back against the edge of the hot spring.

She saw Rigel stealing glances as the comfortable silence stretched on. He drifted closer to her. "It's a beautiful night out," he said.

Crystal sighed softly. "Sometimes silence is more pleasant than small talk," she said as she squeezed her eyes closed.

"Sorry," he replied, holding up his arms in submission. "I just thought it would be nice to talk about something other than training for once."

"This mission is too important for us to lose focus," she snapped, lifting her head to sneer at him. "It seems like every other day we encounter hostiles, and we have had too many close calls for my comfort."

Rigel leaned back and looked up at the sky. Crystal closed her eyes again to relax. "Stop worrying about Serena," Rigel said. "The others are with her, and nobody can get to them without passing us first." She nodded and took a deep breath, her eyes remaining closed. Rigel sighed and said, "Open your eyes, Crys. You're missing quite the view."

She leaned her head back and opened her eyes, taking in the dazzling view of the night sky, where orange and pink shifted to a deep star-speckled blue. All the stars seemed closer from the mountains, and she reached out her fingers as if she could touch them. "Do you really believe the stars are the souls of your dead?"

"I do," Rigel said, staring at the expansive scene above them. "Perhaps not everyone who dies is so blessed, but I do believe that all who die with honor earn their eternal rest among the infinite sky."

"Maybe you are onto something," she whispered, smiling faintly.

"Does our mighty Elven warrior question her beliefs? What would your Elders say?" Rigel joked, glancing across the pool at her.

"Our Elders believe they have it all figured out," she said, catching his eye. Crystal often pondered what they had been taught from a young age—that upon an elf's death, they can appeal to the Emissaries of Life to grant them rebirth in another body. It was a belief her people held fast to for thousands of years, yet her doubts were firm. Why would anyone want to live hundreds of years, only to start over again?

"You don't sound convinced," he noted, a hint of surprise in his voice as he stroked his arms back and forth in the water.

Crystal cut her gaze toward him; she pulled her lips in a tight line. "If I had lived a previous life, I should think I would remember something of it—of who I was before. If not, can you really say you're the same soul?"

"I agree," he said with a smirk. "That's the interesting thing about death. Nobody knows what really happens until it doesn't matter anymore."

She scoffed. "That's the most difficult part—not knowing."

"You really cannot stand not having every step planned out, can you?" Rigel asked, straightening his spine. "Do you ever plan on actually living?"

Crystal turned her back on him and frowned, fixing her gaze on Xandra, Serena, and Will in the next pool over. If she focused, she could hear their voices, though they were not talking about anything serious. "This is living," she muttered, certain he did not hear her.

As the silence stretched on, Rigel chuckled to himself and mused, "Do you suppose I could have been an elf in a past life?"

"I doubt it. Perhaps a dwarf," Crystal said, snickering. According to the Silveryl Clan's teachings, reincarnation was reserved for the greatest of elves, none of whom would ever choose life as a human. Her shoulders tensed, thinking about her father's poor opinion of the very people she called her friends.

Rigel shook his head quietly, grinning as he gazed over their camp into the vast darkness of the forest. Turning solemn eyes on her, he asked, "Crystal, if I were an elf, would you be less tense around me?"

Her forehead scrunched up as she looked at him. "I don't know what you mean by that."

"You're always on edge. I wondered if you regret selecting me for this mission. My skills shall never be as advanced as yours or your brother's," Rigel said, looking down at the water. "It's a wonder someone like me was even allowed to join the Guard—much less selected for such an important task."

"Rigel, do not doubt your own competency," Crystal said sternly. "We recommended you and Xandra because you could hold your own against others with advanced skills. You both proved that at the tournament. I have great respect for your aptitude."

"You flatter me," he said, his grin broadening. "I don't hold a candle to the Windaef siblings. We all know the pair of you could have handled this operation without any human aid."

"You are mistaken," she said firmly, pushing away from the rocky ledge. Looking him directly in the eyes, Crystal said, "There has been a great need for all six of us to fight—even Burroughs. I am certainly thankful Elara agreed that it would take a strong group to accomplish our task. The Hyrosencians are not my people—as you know. We all agreed to be Serena's guardians, but you and Xandra—you are the heart of our quest. Cole and I would not be here had you not convinced us to join your cause."

Rigel's smile faltered as he stared at Crystal. "The heart, huh? I shall take that as the highest compliment," he said, bowing his head.

Suddenly he submerged his head in the water and exhaled, an explosion of bubbles floating rapidly to the surface. Crystal watched him through the curtain of clear water and frowned as she considered his original question. She stared at her reflection on the water and pondered what it would be like if she had been born of the tragically beautiful and fragile humanity of her companions. No sane elf would choose to come back for a measly hundred years, and humans weren't guaranteed that long.

Rigel gasped when he resurfaced, filling his lungs with the chilly night air. Crystal turned away from him, willing herself not to focus on the fact that she would one day lose these humans she had come to consider family.

"You are one of the best of your kind," she said. Immediately, Rigel's cheeks flushed as his jaw dropped. Crystal's eyes widened as she dropped her chin to her chest and added, "At swordsmanship, I mean. You should be very proud of yourself."

He coughed, scrubbing his wet hands over his burning face. "Hmm," he grunted, mulling over her words. "I wouldn't say I'm the best, but thanks."

"Of course," she said coolly. Using her toes to push off the bottom of the pool, she drifted further from him. "If you had been born an elf, you would still be in Ord Metsiilva. You never would have become entangled in this war."

"If I had not been born in Hyro, I may not have felt the desire to fight for it," he said. Swimming closer, Rigel cocked his head to the side and pointed out, "Then again, you were not born in Hyrosencia. You did not have to leave your home to fight for the fate of mine. What made you pledge your allegiance to a human queen?"

Crystal tipped her head backward and studied the stars twinkling above them. "Is it not obvious?" She let out a halfhearted chuckle. "We watched as countless refugees crossed the valley—starving, wounded, afraid. Some fled to Ord Metsiilva first, and my people just sent them north to Elara. It was not until our queens came to an agreement that the clan leaders reluctantly allowed humans to enter our territory. Before, they had been so cold, so distant. Your people were suffering, and my people did not show them compassion. Their attitude was callous. Even if they were humans, they were people who needed help."

"We did, but that still does not explain why you chose this path," Rigel said, surging forward to close the gap between them.

"When my parents learned I had healing abilities, they were so proud. Though I would have made an excellent healer, I longed for a less peaceful profession," she said, moving her arms through the warm water. "My father wanted me to be quiet and obedient—like my mother."

"That doesn't sound like the Crystal Windaef I know," her comrade said, raising his eyebrows.

Crystal shook her head. "You're right about that," she whispered. Her eyes twinkled as she stared out across the mountains at the canopy of stars. "He hoped finding me a respectable husband would somehow make me fall in line. How wrong he was."

"A husband?" Rigel asked, his brows furrowed. "But you're barely an adult by Elven standards."

The elf shrugged her shoulders, pursing her lips. "What can I say? My father is old-fashioned. But luckily for me, no Elder would approve a marriage before I turned eighty."

Rigel whistled, his eyes raking over her face before drifting lower. "I still cannot believe you're so old."

"Only by human standards," Crystal said, pressing a wet palm against her forehead.

"So, you joined us for the Guardian Tournament to get away from your father then?" he asked in earnest.

"Him and others," she admitted.

Rigel watched as she swam clear across the pool. When she reached the other end, he said, "That still doesn't tell me why you took the most dangerous job possible."

"Because I wanted to," Crystal said sharply. "Despite what everyone else wanted me to do and be, I wanted to be a warrior and a leader, so I made it happen. I have the skills to protect people. It would be selfish to sit by and wait to tend the injured."

"And that makes you the best of your kind," Rigel said with a thankful smile. "That's why you were the best choice to lead us. You aren't Hyrosencian, yet you care about my people as much as I do."

"People are people. They deserve to be safe and happy, not living in fear under a ruthless monster," she replied.

"With your help, I think they will be one day," he said, wading in the center of the pool. "But I must admit, your father wasn't completely wrong." She scowled at him as he continued, "Your healing ability has come in handy more than once on this mission. It's incredible what you can do without having trained with a master."

"It may be one of my gifts, but that does not mean I wanted to dedicate my entire existence to it," Crystal said as she ran her fingers along the pool's jagged edge. "I learned about herbs, salves, and healing spells, but I never felt a passion for it. Not the way I feel with a bow in my hands."

"I'm glad you entered the Academy when you did," Rigel said. "It wouldn't have been the same without you. You and the other elves always pushed us to be our absolute best. I still remember Mad-Eye's face when you beat her in the final archery exam in '66, and they chose you over her to graduate. I'm quite certain smoke came out of her ears."

Crystal smiled with pride at the fond memory. "I sort of miss that girl. The competition between us was certainly entertaining. I hope she finally graduated. She was a great shot."

"Just not quite as great as you," he said with a grin. "Why do you prefer the bow? You could have easily beaten any human with the sword."

"In truth, it was the first weapon I ever held," she said, smiling faintly at the memory. "After our mother was killed, Cole brought home a bow he had made at the Academy. He wanted me to be able to protect myself if we were ever attacked again. From a safe distance, of course." Her smile grew as she remembered the first time she wrapped her fingers around the bow and drew the string back. "Using the bow felt natural, like an extension of my arm."

Crystal had never mentioned her mother to him, but she knew Xandra had told him what she knew of the story. Lyrisanna Windaef had been murdered by humans who invaded Ord Metsiilva from the south decades ago.

"I'm sorry about your mum," he said quietly.

She fiddled with the wet ends of her platinum hair, avoiding his eyes. "I do not need your pity, Rigel. It was long ago. Well before Rexton invaded Hyrosencia," she said.

Rigel swallowed hard and rubbed the back of his neck with one hand. "How can you fight alongside humans after what they did?"

"I once hated the people who took my mother from me, but they are all dead. Our warriors ensured they would never hurt any of our most vulnerable again." She paused, seeing her solemn face reflected in Rigel's eyes, and shook her head. "When Rexton invaded, many of your people fled through Norlee. I saw how terrified they were, and I remembered the raids. I saw suffering like I had seen in my own people once, and I could not hate them, even if I had wanted to."

"How you managed to have empathy for us after everything you experienced back then, I'll never understand," Rigel said.

"While I was learning about healing, I could not put that feeling out of my head—the desperate longing to help the oppressed," Crystal said. "I wanted be a warrior just like my brother, and I knew I had to get to Envyre to become one, even if my father didn't approve." She laughed softly, remembering the day she rode south to make her dream happen.

"That sounds like the Crystal Windaef I've come to know well," Rigel said, swimming around the edge of the pool and attempting to close the distance between them.

She closed her eyes and dipped her head under the water for a moment, pushing back a flood of emotions. When she came up for air, he was only a few inches from her. He stared at her face, studying her in the moonlight. Crystal caught his eyes momentarily glancing down at her slender frame wading in the pool. He quickly looked back at her face. Anger brewed in his eyes. "I'm sorry your father could not accept what you wanted," he said, brushing his fingers up her bare arm. "Everyone else knows your skills with a bow are unmatched. If he couldn't see that, he is nothing but an arrogant piece of—"

"I am alright, Rigel. I do not need my father's love or permission to be who I am. I chose my own path, and I have come to terms with his disapproval." She stared blankly at him, barely brushing her fingers over the top of his hand. With a deep breath, her hand slipped back into the water, and Rigel pulled his back from her shoulder, searching her face. She hoped he could not see the anguish she kept beneath the surface.

Looking back to the sky, Crystal said, "My father always said I was much too headstrong of a girl. He was not wrong. I got my way in the end. Once word spread that I was enrolled in the Academy, he could not force me to withdraw. That would have reflected poorly on him." She smiled at the thought of her small victory.

"So that is why you lived with the humans in the Academy bunker?"

"Yes, at that point I had already become acquainted with Xandra. She was a few years younger in appearance but had a fire in her eyes like I had never seen before. She was determined to follow in her father's footsteps. I suppose that fire rubbed off on me a bit."

"I suspect you had a fire of your own from your start," Rigel said. "If anything, you found a kindred spirit in her."

"I suppose you are right," Crystal said. "Both of our fathers had such high expectations. Our late-night sparring sessions were the best for getting out our frustrations."

"I was there some of those nights, but I never realized your father disapproved," Rigel said, shaking his head. He clenched his jaw and added, "For someone with so much life left to live, you certainly chose a hazardous profession. Surely you must have a death wish to pursue such an undertaking as this."

"Perhaps I did once," she admitted. "Though my kind are far less fragile than yours, I envy your mortality some days."

Rigel placed his hands on her shoulders and asked, "Why are you being so candid? You have never been one for sharing anything personal. At least not with me."

"I blame you," Crystal said, laughing softly. Realizing how close he was to her, she tensed. Averting her eyes, she added, "I think you forget that I am not human like you. Perhaps I hide it too well."

Rigel released her, glaring into the darkness. "I have never forgotten that you are an elf," he said, his voice deepening. "Actually, I miss those pointy tips of yours. They suited you."

Crystal tucked some of her drenched tresses behind one ear. "They are still there. You just cannot see them. The power of a good illusion spell."

Rigel examined her exposed ear, which appeared rounded like a human's. "I know it's only magic." Reaching toward it, he paused and asked, "May I?"

Crystal took a deep breath and said, "I suppose it shall not hurt anything. Go ahead."

Using only his thumb, he gingerly touched the side of her ear, tracing the edge upward until he touched something he could not see: a pointed tip invisible to the human eye. Rigel shook his head and grinned, rubbing the point between his thumb and forefinger.

"See? Still an elf," Crystal said with a grin, propelling her body backward and swimming away from him. Chills racked her body, despite being submerged in the hot spring.

SERENA SAT IN THE warm waters of the pool with Xandra, answering the guardian's many questions about growing up in Durmak, as Xandra's grandmother had been born there. After a only few minutes Will emerged from around the corner where jagged rocks obstructed their view of the other hot springs.

"May I join you ladies?" Will asked, curling his fingers against the back of his neck as he avoided looking at the women in their undergarments. "Cole insisted I not join him."

"Oh, he is such a grump sometimes," Xandra said.

"I assume Crystal would not welcome my company either," Will said, laying his dagger next to Xandra's swords.

"Well, you're welcome to join us," Serena said, crossing her arms over her chest.

"Come on in," Xandra said with a reassuring smile.

Will perched on the edge of the pool on the opposite side from them. Slowly, he entered the water, and they waded in awkward silence for several minutes.

Then Xandra climbed out of the pool, saying, "I think I'll leave Serena in your care for now, Will. Clearly Cole needs someone to set him straight." She turned and quickly tip-toed down the path until she was out of their sight, leaving a trail of wet footprints on the stone path.

Serena looked across the water at Will and swallowed, her mouth suddenly feeling dry. "I still cannot believe how far we have come from home," she said quietly.

"Neither can I," Will replied. "Seems like we left ages ago."

"It does. I wonder what everyone is up to," Serena thought aloud. "I think of Cameron and Talitha often. Do you suppose they think about us?"

"I know it," Will said, wading toward the center of the spring. "Talitha was so worried after what happened. She feared something horrible would happen to you too. We all did."

"Some days I wish you had stayed home. I'm sure Talitha misses us both terribly," Serena said, turning her back on him. "I always thought you two would be a good match."

"Talitha?" He scrunched his brow. "She was like an annoying little sister to me. Sometimes I think our parents mixed up their babies." They laughed. Will inched closer to her. "To be honest, I only ever thought of one girl as more than a sister, but I never had the nerve to ask if she might feel the same."

"Oh," Serena said. She leaned her arms over the edge of the pool and peeked over her shoulder at him. "Was it Meganne Devereaux? All the boys whispered about her in school." She smirked, remembering the mischief they had caused growing up.

"No, definitely not Meganne," he said with a chuckle. "I never liked blondes. A bit too full of themselves if you ask me." He winked, and the motion sent butterflies fluttering through her stomach.

Then she snorted and slapped a hand over her mouth as she pictured their two strong but serious companions. "Will, you cannot say that! They're not all the same."

"Whatever you say." Will's smile broadened as he stroked his tan arms through the water. "I speak from experience, of course. I'm trying to protect this girl from back home, but an angry blond is constantly getting in my way."

Serena grinned and asked, "Which do you mean?" When she turned back to face him, she realized just how close Will had drifted. He was close enough to reach out and feel the fabric of her shirt as it puffed up in the water. She turned and pushed it down determinedly.

He chuckled. "If it isn't one, it's the other. I know they mean well. They have also fought hard to keep you safe, but I'm sick of them treating me like I'm such a burden. Xandra and Rigel are the only ones who believe me capable of helping."

Serena leaned her back against the rock wall and allowed her arms to float just under the water's surface. The cold air tingled in her lungs as she drew a deep breath. "I've asked them to stop treating you so poorly. I really don't know what their problem is. You may not have been trained by elves, but that doesn't mean you cannot handle the hazards of the journey."

"I suspect Cole's distaste for my presence is not limited to my sword skills," he said. A lock of her hair floated between them, and he reached out to coil it around his fingers, saying, "Perhaps Cole also favors brunettes."

"Will!" Serena pulled back from him, jamming her right elbow into the rocky edge of the pool. Wincing, she fussed, "You should not say such things."

"Are you alright?" he asked, glancing down at her arm in the water.

Serena's cheeks heated as she followed his gaze. The moonlight illuminated her pale arms, and she suddenly became conscious of how visible her curves were through her soaked garments. "I'm fine," she said crossly, rubbing her elbow gingerly. "You surprised me, is all. I don't think what you're insinuating—No, definitely not. You're wrong."

He shrugged, and he leaned against the wall a few inches beside her. "Maybe I am. Maybe I'm not. All I know is those two are incredibly hostile over how close we are. They forget we have known each other for a long time."

"We have. When I picture my brothers, you're always right beside them, causing mischief," Serena said. A swell of emotions rose in her chest. It surprised her the way the pain she kept buried suddenly broke through the surface, crashing into her like a violent wave against the shore. She felt as though she were being pulled down into the depths of the pool, unable to pull herself out of a heart-shattering memory. She gasped for air.

"Serena? What's wrong?" Will asked, his voice dipping lower as he reached out to comfort her.

She softened as he stared at her, his honey eyes glowing with concern, and she ran her hands through her hair as she turned away, desperate not to let him see her break down. "I miss them. So much, I can hardly stand it," she choked out, sniffling as she tried her best to force back the weight of all she had lost. But some days it was far too heavy to push down.

Will reached out and gently wrapped one arm around her back, drawing her closer. Serena thought she could hear her heartbeat pulsing loudly in her ears, or maybe it was the bubbling of the hot spring. She pressed her lips together and slowly turned to face him, bracing her hands against his chest to keep her distance.

"I miss them, too," Will said with a hushed voice as he rested a cheek on top of her head. "I wish we had gotten to enjoy one last bonfire, all of us together."

"I do, too," she whispered back, nuzzling her face into his chest as she sobbed.

"Please don't cry," he murmured, stroking her hair. "You're going to survive this. All of it. You'll be safe again soon."

"But at what cost?" she whispered, shoving him away. "Do you even realize you almost died because you came with us?"

"I knew the risk when I went after you, Serena," he said, allowing her to slip out of his hold. "I'm here because it was the right thing to do. Because I thought you needed me."

"I don't need you to get killed!" Serena yelled, her voice cracking as she swiped at the tears streaking her cheeks. "I care about you, and I don't want to see you die because of me."

"I care about you, too," Will said, wading closer. "That's why I—"

"I know. Like a sister," she spat, interrupting him. "You have no idea how difficult this has been for me. I am always worried for you and for the guardians. Everyone is risking their lives to protect me because I'm weak."

"You're not weak," he asserted.

"I'm trying my hardest not to be," Serena said. "You could have died right in front of me. I killed someone to save you, Will. I never wanted to do that."

He looked down, shaking his head. "I didn't want you to have to make that choice for me, Rena."

"How could I not?" She sighed and closed her eyes. "The only thing more terrifying than those soldiers is the thought that I almost lost you. You're all I have left of home, Will. I've lost everyone else."

Her hands trembled as she tried in vain to suppress sobs, but empty eyes and blood splatter flooded her mind, the cold corpses threatening to drown her in warm waters. Will approached tentatively, grabbing her by the waist and pulling her into the safety of his warm embrace. Serena sobbed as he held her close, her body trembling as her tears merged with the oasis.

"I feel the weight of that loss, Serena. I share your pain."

"It's not the same for you," she replied, pressing one side of her face against his chest so she could look out at the blurry landscape. "They were my family. That's a heaviness that cannot be matched."

"I would take all your pain on myself if I could," Will whispered, gently kissing the top of her hair.

Serena sniffled. "That's not how grief works."

"I wish I could do more," he murmured. "All I can do is be here when you need me."

"I'm thankful for that," Serena said and looked up at him. Touching his cheek, she stared into his deep brown eyes full of empathy and uncertainty. "I can't lose anyone else, Will. It will break me." She wiped anxiously at her tear-filled eyes, anguish overtaking her delicate face once more. She cursed herself for crying in front of him, for being weak and scared and unable to protect anyone she loved.

"You won't," Will said, wrapping his arms around her slim frame. "You have been through so much. I thought I could make this journey easier for you, but it seems I've made it even harder. I'm sorry."

"Don't apologize," she whispered. "None of this is your fault. I've just—I've held this pain in my heart for too long. I don't know how much more I can take."

"I know you're scared. I am too. But I'm not going anywhere," Will said quietly. "I will train every day until I'm as strong and skilled as Cole. Then you'll have no reason to worry about me."

"That could take a while." She almost managed a smile.

"I chose this route, as did the guardians. Put your faith in us. We can protect you and each other," Will insisted. "We'll reach the City of Mercy. Together, we're strong enough."

Serena wrapped her arms around his neck and squeezed tight, wishing that their arms were made of an armor strong enough to protect them both. "I hope so," she said, the rhythm of his breathing calming her.

She lifted her head, desperate for Divinity, or whatever was out there, to give her a sign, some encouragement that they were going to make it. Longing for distraction, she gazed up at their surroundings in awe. The sky was marvelous. High above them, a deep blue backdrop flecked with shimmering silver stars faded into a golden orange sunset over the mountains.

Serena pressed her lips together, mortified that Will was staring at her. Her face felt numb from her emotional outburst, and she felt the urge to swim away. Will stroked her tear-streaked cheek with his thumb, her tears washing away with a smear of spring water, and she smiled bleakly. "Thanks," she muttered, breathing in the cold air as she drifted further from him.

"Anytime," Will said, one dimple appearing with his slight grin. He moved to lean his head back against the edge of the pool and closed his eyes.

Serena couldn't help but stare as the starlight illuminated his face. Her heart swelled remembering how close he had held her moments before, and she accepted that she had done the right thing in killing the soldier, because it saved Will. He was a good friend—a good man—one her family already loved. Perhaps he could be more in time, she dreamed. Then as quickly as the thought struck, she shoved it deep down. The only thing that mattered now was keeping him alive.

22

EXPOSED

Cole tensed at the sound of footsteps coming down the path. Without turning his head, he knew who it was, and there was no avoiding her now. He sighed. "I am not so easy to sneak up on. What do you want, Xandra?"

She smiled mischievously, allowing the cloak to drop onto the ground as she tip-toed toward the edge of the pool. "You scared Will off, so I came to see what's got you in such a foul mood," she said and took a seat on the edge of the pool to his left.

"Maybe I wish to be alone," Cole said, stretching his arms behind his head. He did not turn his head to look at her, but he could feel her eyes on him, as they so often were.

Xandra dipped her legs into the warm waters. "No one wants to be alone," she said. She reached for his shoulder. As her fingertips brushed against his bare skin, Cole dunked his head underwater, stroking his pale arms through the pool to put distance between them.

When he emerged, Cole wiped his hands over his dripping face and slowly inhaled the cold night air, weighing his next words in silence. Then he turned his head to the side slightly so she could see his profile and said, "Your hands are cold. Get in before you freeze to death."

She grinned as she gripped the edge of the pool with both hands and pushed off, her entire body shooting forward and submerging in the warmth of the oasis. Bursting through the water, Xandra gasped for air as she tossed her curls back from her face. Just as their eyes met, Cole quickly averted his gaze, turning his chiseled face back toward the breathtaking view of the Athamar Mountains.

"You're avoiding me," she said, wading in his direction. "I hate when you do this."

Cole rested both of his elbows on the far edge of the pool, noticing his lightly tanned skin somehow glowing in the light of the two full moons. "You're staring," he said, turning his searing gaze on her.

Xandra rolled her eyes, wading along the rough edge of the pool until she was inches from him. "I'm certain I've caught you staring a few times yourself," she replied, raising her eyebrows. Their eyes locked in a silent standoff for a moment, both stubborn and unyielding.

"You should have stayed with Serena," Cole said. He shook his head and turned back toward the sky. The last of the sun's rays painted the sky a glorious orange. He hated that he knew it was Xandra's favorite color.

"We need to talk about—"

"There is nothing to discuss." Cole's jaw clenched as he frowned at her. "You had too much to drink and did something foolish. You slept it off."

Xandra tensed, then whispered, "I can't believe I thought we were getting on well. You must think me an idiot."

Cole huffed and rubbed the bridge of his nose, knowing she would not let him run away from her this time. "Have I given you any indication that I reciprocate your feelings?" he asked without looking at her.

"I thought so," Xandra stuttered, her forehead creasing as he denied his part. "You stayed in the tavern long after Rigel went to bed."

"To protect you!" Cole growled, balling his hands into fists. "You may be a warrior, but that doesn't mean some drunken oaf wouldn't try to take advantage of you."

"Why should you care? I'm a grown woman," Xandra snarled. "I never asked you to protect me."

"You certainly needed me the other day," Cole snapped. "You're reckless. You're going to get yourself killed one of these days if someone isn't there to watch out for you."

Xandra breathed rapidly, her chest rising and falling quickly as she bobbed in the pool. She glared back at him. "If you think me so incapable, how did I pass the final test?"

"You should not—" he started, pausing to reconsider his first thought. He rubbed his face with his hands, growling under his breath before he finished, "You excelled in Envyre, but we are not there anymore. Out here is different. We have all seen that. Even the most highly trained can make mistakes in the heat of a real battle."

"We're human. Mistakes are part of us," she argued. "You've always thought you were so much better than us. I still don't understand why you're here."

"I told you. I came because Crystal asked if I would join the unit," Cole said with a sigh. "She's my only sibling, Xan. I couldn't refuse."

"We both know she can handle herself. She does not need you to save her."

"Perhaps she does not," he said, "But she also cannot protect a dozen humans on her own."

Xandra slapped the water's surface. "Stop treating me like I'm one of your wards."

Cole didn't flinch as the water splashed him in the face, but his muscles tightened as he closed his eyes and exhaled, wiping his face with one hand. "Stop acting like a child."

Xandra scoffed, pushing her arms through the water swiftly until her hands bumped into his arm. "You first," she said. Her amber eyes glowed, the fire in them challenging his next move.

"What do you want from me?" Cole asked. He saw the anger in his tone startle her.

"The truth," she said. "Tell me I imagined how you acted that night at the tavern. That it wasn't you laughing at my stories, leaning closer, pushing the hair out of my face. Tell me that was all in my head."

Cole tensed as his eyes shifted down to the water. His insides twisted, knowing he couldn't deny any of it. He had let his guard down, allowed himself to be sucked into her orbit, and it had been as easy as breathing. So easy, he hadn't even realized what was happening until she leaned in for a kiss. "I didn't ask you to make things complicated," he said quietly. "I was not trying to come onto you at the tavern. You threw yourself at me without a second thought for the trouble that would cause me."

"At least I'm honest about what I want," she said, pinching her nose and slowly dunking her upper body under the water.

Cole scowled as he waited for her to resurface. As soon as she did, he argued, "I know your feelings for me. You made them abundantly clear that night. But nothing can happen between us. We are of two different worlds."

"Then why do I always catch you watching me?" Xandra asked dismally, leaning her head against the rock ledge.

Cole cursed inwardly, frustrated by her sharp instincts and refusal to walk away from a challenge. "I don't just watch you. I watch everyone," he said, his voice trailing off. "Besides, Crystal would kill me if she caught me looking at you."

"Since when do you give a damn what your sister thinks?" she asked, her lips curling upward in a satisfied grin. "That would only matter if you entertained the possibility."

"There is no possibility. It's forbidden," Cole insisted. Xandra averted her eyes, fighting back the tears that brimmed along her bottom lashes. His heart ached as she turned away to compose herself. Steam rose off the water between them, and they both exhaled in frustration. He stared at her golden-brown skin, admiring how it soaked up the last rays of sunlight as she bobbed in the clear water. Running a hand through his hair, he said, "This is why I did not want to talk about it. You are getting all worked up. We should be focused on our mission."

"I am focused. This has no impact on Serena. It's about us and us alone," Xandra snapped, swiping her arm across the water and splashing him again. "I may have been inebriated, but you were not. You knew who I was—what I am—yet you did not push me away. Not at first. You wanted to kiss me. Or do you deny it?"

"I never intended to cross that line. You threw yourself at me," Cole said, raising his voice. "It was a mistake letting you get that close." He shook his head, sullen eyes flicking toward the trees.

"The mistake was all mine. I never should have fallen for a heartless elf," Xandra said, her words hitting him like a sucker-punch in the abs.

"Your kingdom is at war. We made a commitment to your queen. She wouldn't want us distracting each other," he said, immediately regretting his choice of words. They weren't a denial of feelings, merely more excuses. "Our duty is to protect Serena. When our task is complete, my father expects me to return to Ord Metsiilva. There are expectations I must uphold, duties I must resume."

"What about your duty to your heart?" she asked, shielding her exposed upper arms from the wind with her hands. He longed to reach out and shield her from the cold but instead turned away from her to stare at the fast fading sunset. The sky glowed a beautiful golden orange behind the silhouette of the mountains, the color reminding him of her eyes. Cole clenched his jaw. He was unable to escape her radiant presence no matter where he looked. The feelings she stirred in him were a nauseating mix of longing and loathing.

"You're not wrong," he said, his voice low and coarse. "Somewhere along the way I did come to care for you. But that does not change who we are. Some lines are not meant to be crossed."

"Is the only thing that deters you my mortality?" Xandra asked, dropping her chin to her chest in defeat. "You look at me as though I could break from the slightest touch. I may be human, but I am not so fragile."

He shook his head as he moved toward her, his gaze unyielding. "I know you aren't," Cole said as his fingers barely grazed under her chin. She lifted her face to look at him with every ounce of stubbornness she could muster. "I do not think you are fragile. You are a fighter, one of the best of your kind. You have more fire in your eyes than anyone else I've met, human or elf." He held eye contact for a moment more before withdrawing his hand, flexing his fingers in the water as he turned away.

"Yet that fire doesn't keep you from icing me out," she said, scowling as she crossed her arms.

Cole lurched to a stop, inhaling shakily. "Do you even realize what you are asking of me? What I would lose if I chose you?"

A single tear slipped silently down her cheek. Though the elf could not see it, he knew it was there. He felt the same pain in his chest he had been fighting since the night she drunkenly kissed him at the tavern. Though he repeated to himself all the reasons they could not work, it did not quiet the feelings she had stirred within him. He wondered if anything ever could.

"Our people have lived apart for centuries—and with good reason. We are incompatible races," Cole said sullenly. "Love is fleeting for humans. Half the time your kind don't even marry for love. Humans have a history brimming with affairs and second marriages, things my people do not do."

"Am I really so far beneath your standards?" she asked, the words rushing out of her like an angry snarl.

"Of course not," he said, whipping around to face her. "You are exquisite and incredibly strong. You deserve someone who can give you everything you deserve. Someone who can grow old with you. That is not in the cards for us."

She nodded silently. "I wish I had feelings for someone else, anyone else. It would have made this journey so much easier," Xandra said, wiping her wet hands over her tear-streaked cheeks.

"I am certain you'll find another if only you look elsewhere," he said dejectedly. "We would never work. Our lifetimes are vastly different. Human lives are but a fraction of elves'."

"I know all about the elves, Cole. You forget I grew up among them," Xandra said. "Though I am starting to regret that decision."

"I never intended to give you false hope," he said, grinding his teeth. "I wanted to ensure you would all survive, my sister and Rigel and you."

"That is an insult to all three of us," Xandra said, shoving him. Though her hands pressed firmly against his chest, Cole hardly flinched. He gently took hold of her wrists and pried them off his body as she continued berating him. "You shouldn't have come with us. You should have stayed in Ord Metsiilva."

"Then you would be dead," Cole growled, releasing her wrists. The two locked eyes in a fierce standoff. Though darkness had descended on the mountains, her irises blazed as bright and fierce as the midday sun. He knew if he looked too long, that fire would burn a hole in his heart that would never heal.

Cole swiped a hand over his eyes and said, "I wish you hadn't come looking for me. I wanted to spare your feelings. But you are quite relentless." Drawing his gaze across her cheekbones to her lips, he tensed, looking away and taking a deep breath. "Every second you're near me is agonizing. Can you not see that?"

Xandra flinched. She laid back until she was floating atop the water, clenching her eyes closed. "Will you ever look at me without such sorrow in your eyes?" she asked quietly.

"Perhaps one day," Cole answered. Xandra sunk under the water. She swam closer, and as she crashed through the surface, right in front of Cole, the edge of her blouse brushed against his bare abdomen. A wave of chills swam down his spine. Cole leaned back away from her as she inhaled deeply. An intoxicating aroma hit him like a furious wave, the mingled scent of crushed flowers and the tree sap that she used to tame her curls. "Heavens help me," Cole said. "You smell like home."

Her eyes widened and her cheeks flushed as a glimmer of hope returned to her eyes, and he realized he should not have said that. Xandra bit her lip and looked down, spotting the faint white scar that crept up his forearm. She gently traced the scar with her fingertip. "You make that sound like a bad thing."

Cole yanked his arm away from her, eager to distance himself from her scent. He swam toward the edge of the pool. "It taunts me." He fumed as he looked up at the twinkling stars. They winked at him as though they knew his heart and dared him to follow it. "To be with you, I would have to give up the only home I have ever known. I shall never be able to have both."

Xandra frowned. "I should never have asked that of you," she whispered. "I'm sorry, Cole."

He looked down at the scar on his arm and remembered the day Xandra gave it to him. Xandra and Rigel had to face off against Cole in their final test before graduating from the Academy, and they somehow managed to surprise him, which was not an easy feat. Together, they managed to disarm him, which was how their instructors knew they were ready for the Guardian Tournament. He had never been prouder of his students than the moment she made his blood trickle down his arm.

"I am sorry if I have treated you as anything less than a skilled fighter," he said, grinning at the vivid memory of Xandra's beaming face as everyone cheered for their victory.

"If?" she scoffed, swiping the water between them.

As the drops of water pebbled against his face and chest, he shook his head, shaking loose the wet hair that clung to the nape of his neck. "I admit my fault, okay," he said, splashing her back.

Xandra cocked her head to one side and laughed. "I suppose you were not wrong. I now have a scar of my own to prove you were right to worry," she said, lifting her hand to show him the pink and white starburst scar on her palm. "I may be strong, but that doesn't mean I will win every fight."

Cole pressed his lips together in a fine line. "I wish I could bring that oaf back so I could kill him a second time," he grumbled. "He did not deserve such a swift end."

Xandra gasped. "You shouldn't say such things! I thought elves were supposed to be calm and composed. What would your Elders say?"

"They, too, would kill anyone who threatened one of our people," Cole said, staring at her hand as his breathing quickened.

"It's just a scar, Alarcole," she said. "I'm fine. You don't have to get upset about it."

"It makes me angry every time I think about it. The nerve of him to touch you," the elf said, turning his back on her.

"You're so dramatic," Xandra said, "just like your sister."

"I am not," he grumbled, and stared at the vast array of constellations above them. He wondered for a moment if his human friends would end up joining the stars by the end of the war. He knew one day he would lose them, and a world without any of them would be far darker. "It will never be just a scar. It is a mark of my failure. I hate that you must wear it."

"A couple more scars, and perhaps I'll be more bearable to look at by the time this war is over," she joked.

Cole turned around to face her. "I'm afraid no scar could ever dull your radiance," he said before turning away again. "You might as well be the damn sun."

"Alarcole," Xandra breathed out, surprised by his words. Approaching the edge of the pool, she balanced one arm on top of the slick rocks and faced him. "Are you quite sure of your choice?"

"Xandra, you're a human, and I'm an elf. There is no choice to make." With a tired sigh, Cole leaned back against the edge of the pool, and he folded his arms over his chest. "I was raised to respect the laws of my queen."

Xandra grabbed him by both forearms and plunged his arms down into the water with a scoff. "You cower behind the laws of a scorned old woman who has never known love."

Cole jerked free of her grasp and grabbed her by the wrists, holding her at arm's length. "You don't understand! You're not an elf."

Their faces were mere inches apart, the heat from their breath cutting through the crisp mountain air as they scowled into each other's eyes. Xandra averted her gaze and whispered, "I'll always wish I was." Cole released her arms, surprised as he realized what she had said.

They were silent for a minute. Then Xandra reached forward and wrapped her arms around his midsection, pressing a cold cheek against his bare chest. She sighed, basking in his warmth. Cole suppressed a shiver at her touch and closed his eyes, wishing she didn't fit quite so right nestled against his chest.

"Why must you make this so difficult? You know I cannot do this," he whispered, reaching his hands down to break free of her hold. He fell back, stroking through the water until she was a safe distance from him. When he reached the edge of the pool, he shifted upright and leaned his arms over the edge to observe the constellations that stretched over the dark expanse of the Athamar Mountains.

"You look most miserable," Xandra said. She propped her arms on the ledge beside him. "Are you angry with me?"

"No. There is no reason to be cross with you. I just cannot give you what you want, what you deserve. I'm sorry for that."

"I know," Xandra whispered back, gnawing on her bottom lip. Cole stared at the trees in the distance, jagged and black against the deep blue sky. "Tell me what you're thinking."

"Each day we face new dangers, and I fear I won't be able to protect everyone," said Cole solemnly, glancing sideways at her. Reaching out, he gingerly pressed one calloused hand against her cheek. "I do not wish to see anyone else cut down by the enemy. Should we lose anyone, I shall return a failure."

"I can handle myself. You don't have to worry about me," she said, touching the hand that caressed her cheek.

His eyes darkened as he pulled his hand back and shook his head. "Last week you were assaulted. That brute could have easily killed you," Cole said, swallowing hard.

"I survived. And it won't happen again," she insisted, looking at the scar on her palm. She flexed her fingers, and it was almost like she could still feel her sword stabbing through it. "I'm grateful that you stepped in. You saved my life, but Serena is more important. If you have to choose between us, you must choose her."

"She may be more important to you, but not to all of us," he said. "I still do not believe this girl is anything special. To be a true warrior requires intensive training. There's a reason we train for a decade at the Academy."

"You're a great instructor," Xandra said, resting her hands on the ledge. "Serena has learned so much from you already. I believe she'll be ready in time."

"We'll see soon enough," he said. "I hope you'll be satisfied when the war finally ends." Cole frowned, feeling restless as Xandra gazed up, her eyes dancing between the stars as if she was searching for one in particular. Putting distance between them, he laid on his back and floated, using his feet to push off the side of the pool. The water bubbled, and a thin veil of steam swirled in the air between them.

"I have faith in the prophecy," Xandra said. "Many souls have been lost in pursuit of our victory, but I know one day we shall see our queen restored to her throne."

"Try not to join them," he said. "The world would be far less bright without you."

After a pause, Xandra cleared her throat. "I could say the same of you." Her voice came out hoarse. Turning her back on him, Xandra grasped the edge of the pool with both hands and whispered, "I should go."

Cole took a sharp breath and submerged himself, moving swiftly through the water. When he emerged, he was right in front of her. As he took in a haggard breath, Xandra turned her misty eyes on him. Cole placed his hand over hers and said, "Don't." Slowly, she let her hands slip from the rock ledge into the hot spring as she turned her body to face his.

Wrapping one arm around her waist, the cold warrior pressed his palm against the small of her back and pulled her closer. Xandra blinked in surprise as he leaned his face in, his smooth cheek barely brushing against hers as he hugged her, breathing in her sweet scent. She swallowed hard, and he could feel her body tremble against him. "You are extremely close for someone who keeps pushing me away," she whispered.

Cole shook his head, the corners of his lips curling upward as he locked eyes with her, and asked, "Why are you so infuriatingly perfect?"

Her eyes widened, and she blinked wordlessly for a moment. Opening her mouth, she stuttered, "I'm far from perfect. You're the one who looks like a piece of art."

He chuckled. "Looks aren't everything. Is that all you like about me?"

"No," she said, her cheeks flushed as she stared at his bare chest. "I like the things you try to hide from everyone, like the love you have for your sister, how you want to look out for her, even though you act like you loathe each other. How you act stern and heartless, but once people get to know you, you can't help but be kind and encouraging, especially to your students." She tensed in his arms.

"You're the only person who has ever seen me that way," he said, smiling grimly. "I don't know how to let you go."

"Then don't," she whispered.

He leaned forward, grabbing the back of her neck with one hand and drawing her head toward him. His lips crashed into hers, and Xandra braced her hands against his bare chest, leaning into his embrace. He kissed her as if the steam could shroud their forbidden desire from the rest of the world.

Their lips parted briefly, and both inhaled sharply before kissing each other more fervently. Cole slid one hand down from her waist, pressing his fingers into the curve of her hip as he pulled her closer. Breathing heavily, Xandra pulled her face back and smiled in a blissful daze. "I thought you said this could never happen," she muttered, tracing a finger along his cheek.

Cole pressed his forehead against hers, one hand still entangled in the coiled hair at the base of her neck. Holding her close, he whispered, "I can't bear the look in your eyes every time you walk away disappointed. It kills me."

"Then stop pushing me away," Xandra whispered against his lips, wrapping her arms around his neck just as he pressed his lips against hers again. This time was more tender than the first; Cole wanted to savor the feel of her lips on his, the way their bodies fit perfectly together despite all the reasons he had thought they couldn't possibly. He wrapped his arms around her as his lips gently made their way down the side of her cheek to the fine line of her neck. With every touch of their skin, Cole felt a fire unlike anything he had ever experienced, and he knew that she was the sun his world would revolve around until long after she left him. With one kiss, their souls entwined. He would rather burn up in the sun's radiance than spend another second alone in the darkness.

"What the blazes is this?"

Their eyes snapped open as the stunned lovebirds froze. They turned their heads to find Crystal standing near the edge of the pool, glaring down at them. If looks could kill, Crystal's glare would have drowned them both in the hot spring.

"Sorry, did I interrupt you defiling the hot spring?" Crystal asked.

Horrified, they detached from their impassioned embrace. Xandra rushed to the edge of the pool, her rapid movement unsettling the peaceful water. As she crawled out of the pool, Crystal turned and marched back down the path, not waiting for an explanation. Xandra grabbed her cloak and ran after her friend, calling, "Crys, wait!"

Cole remained in the hot springs, watching as the two women disappeared. He cupped his hands over his face, lacing his fingertips in his hair, and cursed. "What have I done?"

When he willed himself at last to return to the group, he approached just as he heard Crystal murmuring the ancient enchantment, "*Revelare.*"

"What the blazes are you doing?" Cole asked as he stormed into their camp dripping wet, staring at his sister's pointed ears. "We never agreed to show her that in the middle of the bloody mountains."

Crystal turned her nose up at her brother, ignoring his comment. Looking at Serena, whose eyes were wide with confusion, she sighed and said, "It isn't safe for elves in Hyrosencia or Norlee. I'm sorry we had to hide it from you."

Serena pinched her own arm, blinking as if Crystal's ears were an illusion. While she scanned over the other guardians, eyeing their ears suspiciously, Rigel and Will approached the camp. Narrowing her eyes, Serena asked, "And what of Rigel and Xandra?"

"We're both human," Xandra said quickly, her eyes momentarily flashing toward Cole.

"And interracial relations are strictly forbidden by Daephyra, High Queen of the Elves," Crystal said, shooting a hostile look at her brother. Overhearing her, Rigel kept his eyes down, searching for his bag by the firelight.

"Wait, you're not human?" Will exclaimed, gaping at Crystal's ears.

She ignored his remark, her wrath still fixed on her brother. As Crystal opened her mouth to continue scolding him, Cole lifted a hand and shook his head. "I will not argue with you about private matters in front of an audience. We are on a mission," Cole snapped at his sister. "Compose yourself. You are being juvenile." Grabbing his bag, he retreated into the privacy of the woods to change into dry clothes.

Xandra quietly sat near her things, mere feet away from Crystal. When Cole returned, he wrapped a blanket around her shoulders before sitting beside her. "We'll take the first watch," he said calmly, nodding at Rigel. "Get some rest."

23
WARM WELCOME

Three guards escorted Talitha up several stairwells until they reached the second floor of the castle. The girl clutched at her soiled dress, aware of how uncivilized she looked among the pristine details of the castle. Her escorts did not address her, nor did they shackle her hands. These guards were unfamiliar; they were not the men who Anteros threatened while they guarded the dungeon. As they marched through a large foyer, Talitha kept her eyes to the ground, watching the shiny shoes of the few servants who passed them, murmuring amongst themselves.

The prisoner stumbled along between the guards, wondering to which part of the castle she was being taken. It was alarmingly quiet for midafternoon, and she felt like a ghost roaming the halls. They rounded a corner and entered a residential hallway. Talitha counted silently as they passed each closed door. One... Two... Three...

The guard in front of her stopped abruptly, and she bumped into him. Alarmed, she crossed her arms in front of her body and apologized profusely. The guard grunted, and she stared as he reached to open a large gold door. Another guard gave her a shove and ordered her to enter. The guards slammed the door shut behind her but remained out in the hall.

In the room, two maids wearing plain clothes and pleasant smiles greeted her. Between them was a large porcelain bathtub with the faintest steam rising from the soapy water. Talitha glanced back at the closed door for a second before turning to look at the two maids with a most puzzled expression. She remained frozen in place, unwilling to go any closer to these strangers.

"Good afternoon, miss," one said cheerfully. "Our lady asked us to help clean you up."

The wary prisoner eyed them, taking a step back toward the door. "Why?" she whispered, her voice breaking as she touched her cold fingers to her throat.

"To help you feel human again," Sabine replied, entering through another doorway in the room. "You've been in that dungeon for weeks. Thought you might like a bath and some tea."

Talitha scrutinized the bathtub and asked, "Are your maids to hold me underwater? Hate to tell you, but your father's men already tried that."

Sabine snorted gleefully, quickly covering her mouth. "Heavens, no! I only mean to offer you the hospitality my father severely lacks. You need not worry. I'll return you to that dreary dungeon before dinner."

"And you're certain we will not get caught?" Talitha asked, stepping toward the bath and swiping her fingers through the plentiful bubbles. The soap was smelled of jasmine, and the water looked cleaner than any she had seen back home.

"Absolutely certain. Trust me," Sabine said with a grin.

Talitha nodded.

"Amelia, Clara, you know what to do," the princess said as quickly as Talitha agreed. "I shall leave you to it. Once you're all cleaned up, come to my chambers. I have a few dresses pulled from the wardrobe."

Before Talitha could protest, the two maids busied themselves pulling her tattered clothes over her head. Attempting to cover herself with her arms, Talitha looked around and realized Sabine had already disappeared through the same doorway she had entered. The maids reached for her arms, supporting her as she stepped over the rim of the bathtub and lowered her body into the warm waters. The maidservants worked in silence. One scrubbed at the dirt caked onto Talitha's skin and under her fingernails while the other massaged her head with the floral-scented cleanser. When they had finished, the water was murky, muddled with the filthy remnants of her weeks spent on the dungeon floor. The maids helped her to stand before pouring a pitcher of clean water over her shoulders. If they noticed her bruising, they dared not ask about it. They helped Talitha step out of the tub, quickly dried her off, and helped her into a silk robe before leading her through the door that did not connect to the main hallway.

In Sabine's bedchamber, two more maids in plain frocks were busy dressing the princess in a stunning ball gown. One tugged her corset strings tight, cinching her waist so that Talitha wondered how the girl breathed. The sweetheart bodice was a lovely carnation pink silk covered in tiny iridescent beads that reflected the light. Thick silk straps fell over her upper arms, exposing her tan shoulders. The maids adjusted the full skirt made from a darker pink silk, which jutted out from just above her hips. Accentuating the skirt were the silhouettes of butterflies cleverly created by the same iridescent beads.

"It's perfect," the princess said, smiling at her reflection in an oblong mirror. Taking notice of her audience, Sabine turned and exclaimed, "Look at you all cleaned up! I knew you would look lovely without all that dirt." The princess grasped her skirt in both hands, lifted it off the floor, and rushed across her room to her guest. Sabine took Talitha by the hands and led her over to a grand bed with a canopy of delicate white fabric hanging above it. There three exquisite gowns were laid out. "Which do you prefer?"

Talitha ran her hands over the flowing material, each a different texture and color. The first was a beaded burgundy gown, far too dark and revealing for her taste. The second was a vibrant emerald ball gown with a matching lace overlay on the bodice. The shape of the green gown matched Sabine's current ensemble, except the edges of the neckline were scalloped. Her eyes barely skimmed over the third gown, an azure blue chiffon, before going back to the second one. "They're all beautiful," Talitha said, running her fingers along the smooth emerald satin.

"That is an excellent choice," the princess noted. "Green compliments your complexion very well. And your hair."

The detainee bit her lip and withdrew her hand. "Oh, I could never wear this. It's too elegant. It's meant for a princess."

"Don't you worry about that. I don't intend to send you back to the dungeon in satin," Sabine said. With a wave of her hand, two maids scooped all three gowns up and scurried off with them. "We'll save that one for a special occasion."

The maids who bathed Talitha returned with an ivory slip dress and matching overskirt, yanking at the silk robe without a word. Talitha frowned, averting her eyes as two other maids began changing Sabine into a lavender frock with a tulle skirt. As the maid gently tightened the corset back, Sabine breathed in and smiled. "Daytime gowns are so much more breathable."

When all the maids had finished and scurried into a line up against the wall, Sabine looked her new friend over and nodded. "This will suffice for today," the princess said. "Now join us for tea before I have to sneak you back downstairs."

"Us?" Talitha's heart pounded. What was Sabine thinking?

Sabine took Talitha by the hand and led her into yet another room. In the small sitting room attached to her chambers awaited Sabine's newest lady-in-waiting, whose pleasant smile revealed she had no idea about Talitha's identity. One of the maidservants stacked teacups with a lovely gold trim along the edges—the finest porcelain Talitha had ever seen—in front of each place setting. Sabine jumped right into polite conversation with their companion, wasting no time introducing Talitha.

"Emmaline, this is Lady Adelaide Winslow of Denorfia," Sabine said. She blinked playfully at Talitha. "Her father often trades goods with Graynor. Fine silks and beautiful jewelry in exchange for tea and sugar. She has come all this way to attend our Solstice celebration. Can you believe it?"

"Welcome to Hyrosencia," Emmaline said. She lifted the piping hot tea pot and poured each a cup. "I hope you will enjoy your time here as much as I do. Graynor is the loveliest place, and Sabine is such a wonderful host. Oh, just wait until the ball! Sabine cannot stop talking about it."

"When will that be?" Talitha asked curiously. She picked up her teacup and took a sip. Making a face, she set the teacup down on a matching saucer and added, "I'm afraid I have lost track of the days since I left home. Long journey."

The princess laughed as if she were joking. Emmaline and Talitha joined her, chortling weakly. "Dear girl, it is the first of June," Sabine said. "As the people of the sun, we celebrate the Solstice when the days of sun are longest. Festivities are held all week leading up to the ball on the twenty-first."

"Only three weeks to wait! It will be here before we know it," Emmaline said excitedly. Sabine shot the young lady a warning glance, and Emmaline sat back in her chair, taking a quiet sip from her teacup.

Another maidservant entered the sitting room carrying a three-tiered tray covered with finger sandwiches, miniature cakes, and macarons. Talitha's eyes widened as her stomach gurgled. She salivated at the sight. Glancing at Sabine, she pressed her lips together, awaiting instruction.

"Please, help yourselves." Sabine lifted her cup to her lips and took a silent sip. Talitha reached forward and grasped one of the little sandwiches. Skipping over the tiny porcelain plate in front of her place setting, she brought it straight to her mouth and was greeted by an unfamiliar but refreshing flavor.

"I also love cucumber sandwiches," Emmaline said with a smile as she plucked one from the middle tier of the tray and placed it on her plate.

"If this excites you, just wait for the feast we have planned for the Solstice," Sabine teased, raising her eyebrows and locking eyes with Talitha. "Try the lavender macarons. They're my favorite."

Talitha helped herself to one of the tiny desserts, enjoying the crunchy shells filled with caramel crème. At that moment, she knew her days as a prisoner were numbered. She had a taste of freedom for the first time in over two months, and it tasted sweet. If befriending the princess meant getting out of the dungeon and filling her belly, Talitha resolved to smile and play dress up as many times as needed until she could find a way out of the castle for good.

QUEEN ELARA ROUNDED THE corner into the main hallway with her royal purple gown clutched delicately between her fingers. As the clacking of her heels announced her presence, Gerard turned away from the two guards he had been addressing and greeted her with a brilliant smile. The guards between them stepped aside, clearing their path.

Taking her hand, Gerard kissed it and said, "Milady, you have outdone yourself. You are positively glowing. I could marry you right here, right now, and be the happiest man for the rest of my life." He pulled her closer, and she stumbled forward into his embrace. Elara smiled, blushing as she found her footing.

"But then you would miss out on seeing my wedding gown," she teased. Placing a hand on his chest, she leaned forward and pressed her cheek to his, careful not to leave any lipstick on his clean-shaven face.

She turned and asked the captain waiting in the doorway, "Have all our guests made their way to the dining hall?"

"All are accounted for, Your Majesty," the man said, striking his breast with one fist. When he bowed to his queen, his combed-over black hair flopped forward to reveal a bald spot. Elara made a muted snorting sound, but she quickly cleared her throat to cover it up. Gerard grinned as he took her left hand and laced it through his right arm. Patting the hand that rested atop his arm, he asked, "Shall we join them?"

"Lead the way," Elara said, gesturing with her free hand.

When they reached the dining hall, two guards opened the doors, and one announced, "All hail Her Majesty Elara Garrick, Queen of Hyrosencia. Long may she reign!" The room fell silent as everyone turned to bow their heads to her, repeating, "Long may she reign."

As Gerard escorted Elara to the head of the table, they stopped to greet each of their guests. Elara bowed her head and offered her hand to the gentleman closest to the doors, as Gerard whispered close to her ear, "My elder sister and her husband." Elara smiled and offered her hand to the lanky bald man first, shaking it briefly.

"Duke and Duchess Beckett," Elara said cheerfully. "We are so pleased you were able to come. I hope the journey was kind to you."

"It was splendid once we reached land," Duke Edmund Beckett III said, adjusting his spectacles.

Then Elara extended her hand to Gerard's sister, whose wavy black hair was streaked with silver strands just like his. "Please, call me Daria," Gerard's sister insisted, gently squeezing Elara's hand. "We are to be sisters, after all."

The queen beamed, restraining herself from pulling the woman into a tight embrace. She had not been welcomed this warmly by her previous husband's sisters. "Daria, I should be so delighted if you would call me Elara."

"We were honored to be invited, Your Majesty," the Duke said. His nose pointed upward.

"We never thought we'd see our dear brother marry, much less marry a queen," another gentleman said from behind the Duke and Duchess. Stepping to the side, they revealed a man in a fine navy suit who looked like a younger, more relaxed version of Gerard.

"Wade!" Gerard bellowed. He stepped forward to vigorously shake his younger brother's hand. "The way Mother spoke in her last letter, I assumed you would not be joining us."

"I am as surprised as you are," Daria said with a grin. Turning back to the queen, she added, "Wade spends all his time sailing, searching for new islands on behalf of our king. It is always a surprise when he shows up."

"You think I would miss such an event?" Wade said, hand on his chest. Laying eyes on Elara, he grinned as she reached out her hand to him. Kissing the top of it, he said, "When I heard my brother was betrothed to the Garrick queen, I could hardly believe it. But laying my eyes upon you, I cannot say I am surprised."

"You are too kind," she said, glancing at the quiet woman behind him. "And is this your wife?"

The couple standing behind Wade Stirling chuckled, the young lady vigorously shaking her head. "No, no," Wade snorted. He peered sideways at them. "This is Kailan's new wife."

"Oh," Elara whispered, zeroing in on the crown prince of the Eastern Isles. "You must be Prince Kailan. What a pleasure it is to meet you in person at last." Stepping toward the dark-haired man, she extended her hand. He donned a royal blue jacket with gold embroidery and light pants. The gold crown atop his thick brown hair was embellished with colorful jewels and seashells. Upon closer inspection, she noticed that he also had gray hair on his sideburns and in his groomed beard. Despite the differences in facial hair, the similarity between the prince and his cousins was uncanny. They could have easily been mistaken for siblings.

"The pleasure is all mine, milady," Kailan said, accepting her hand and briefly kissing her knuckles. "I must say I agree with Wade. If I had seen your beauty for myself, I might not have permitted my cousin to pursue your hand."

Elara's ears burned, and she was suddenly thankful for the mass of dark brown curls covering her ears and neck. She averted her eyes from the handsome prince and said, "I am grateful you sent Gerard to me. It seems everything worked out quite well for both of us. I see you found another blushing bride with no delay."

"That I did, and within my own court," Kailan said, placing a hand on his wife's back. "This beautiful woman is my wife Imogen. It's her first time traveling beyond the Isles."

"We welcome you to Symptee, Lady Imogen." Elara smiled at the young lady. Her hair was platinum, her frame petite. She was at least a decade younger than Prince Kailan, who was nearing forty. While his face was freckled from decades spent in the sun among his people, Imogen's skin was smooth and lightly tanned, her cheeks retaining their youthful plumpness. She looked like a paper doll in her modest cornflower blue gown.

Imogen smiled, but Elara could see she was shy. "'Tis wonderful to meet you, milady. I am sure you shall make a most stunning bride." Elara reached out her hand to greet the feeble woman. Her suntanned skin seemed to glow next to Elara's pale hands.

"Thank you. I'm certain you were a most elegant bride on your own special day," the queen said softly. She patted the woman's hand before letting it go. "I would love to give you and the other ladies a proper tour of the citadel tomorrow. The gardens are quite a treat this time of year, being in full bloom."

Imogen nodded, her nervous energy dispelling, and Daria said from behind them, "What a marvelous idea! I would love to see that."

"My brother might like to join you," Kailan said, gesturing across the table at another dark-haired man who was chatting with Elara's former sisters-in-law, Princesses Norah and Myra of Denorfia. Kailan leaned closer to the queen and said in a hushed tone, "Maximus is on the prowl for a wife at long last, but I can assure you he shall be well-behaved during his time here."

"You would have to place that handsome dog on a leash to keep him in check," Gerard said, and the men laughed heartily.

Across the table, a tall and gruff older man with a hefty gold crown on his head cleared his throat. Glancing at their remaining guests, Elara lifted her skirt with two hands and marched gracefully around the end of the table to greet her ex-in-laws. King Boreas Rasalas of Denorfia had aged poorly in the past decade. His scraggly gray and white hair cascaded down his back and over his shoulders, blending into his long facial hair. Upon seven of his ten fingers were various rings of gold and fine jewels. Standing to his right was his wife, Queen Aneira, whose velvet-trimmed jade green gown looked exceptionally regal. Her light-brown hair was pinned in a tidy updo, and her face looked like it had been hand-painted by an artist.

"You shouldn't keep an old man waiting on his feet," King Boreas said, reaching out his hand. Giving a firm handshake, he added, "You are looking well."

"Thank you, Your Majesty," she said, yanking her aching hand free. "I appreciate you coming all this way."

She curtsied to his wife, who reluctantly returned the gesture. Then Queen Aneira turned her thin nose up in the air and said, "We were quite surprised to receive your invitation. The last time we came to your quaint citadel was to honor our dearly departed son." Glancing at Gerard, who now stood a few steps behind Elara, the older woman sneered, "You are a brave man to marry this headstrong girl. I hope you shall meet a better fate than my Caspian."

Elara's eyes widened briefly before she regained her composure. Taking a deep breath, she turned her attention back to King Boreas. "It is good of you to return here after so long."

Boreas was busy eyeballing Gerard inquisitively. "There is much we should like to discuss on our visit," he said, stroking his beard. "Such a gathering of crowns should not be wasted."

"I agree wholeheartedly," Elara said. Her eyes darted just past him to two young ladies about her age and an unfamiliar gentleman. "And I am happy to see your daughters were able to join you," she added, feigning enthusiasm as she approached the two women.

"Yes," Queen Aneira said tartly, stepping out of Elara's path. "You met our youngest at your last wedding."

"Yes, I remember Myra, though she's grown up since our last meeting." Elara smiled at the young lady.

Princess Myra twirled a strand of her light brown hair in her finger as she studied the woman who had long ago married her brother. Bowing her head, Myra said, "I remember you as well, milady. You have only grown more beautiful these many years."

"You have grown into a beautiful young lady yourself," Elara said. The girl wore a beautiful pink and orange silk gown that reminded Elara of the sunset. She recalled how Myra was only a small child when she had married Prince Caspian. She beamed at Elara's compliment, and her big brown eyes glimmered. "I see so much of your brother in you, especially your eyes. You have the same spark of kindness."

Myra smiled bleakly, glancing down at her fidgeting hands. "Thank you, Your Majesty. You were the last to see that spark in his eyes, so that means a great deal."

"Though his flame flickered out much too soon, he is always with us," Princess Norah said as she placed a gentle hand on her sister's exposed shoulder. Turning to look Elara directly in the eyes, she added, "I just wish our brother could have had his own child to carry on that trait."

Elara tensed, feeling a knot form in her stomach, and she placed one hand protectively on her abdomen. "I am sorry we were unable to bring a child into the world before his illness set in," she said. "Though our marriage was brief and riddled with hardship, I cared very much for Caspian. Fond memories of him remain with me, even after all these years."

"Do not fear. I have been able to produce several children for my family, including my eldest son, who was named in honor of our dear Caspian," Norah said with a sly smirk. She had a slender nose, which she pointed toward the ceiling as she pursed her lips. "At least his name shall live on within our family."

Elara flushed, clutching her skirt with tight fists. Gerard quickly came to her aid. He placed a gentle hand on the small of her back as he said, "Let us all have a seat. The kitchen should have our first course prepared." Gerard took Elara's hand and led her to the head of the table, where she was to sit between King Boreas Rasalas of Denorfia and Crown Prince Kailan Marinus of the Eastern Isles. Several servants stepped forward to pull out everyone's chairs simultaneously, pushing them in as each person took their seat. Once Elara was seated, Gerard squeezed her hand before making his way across the room to the opposite end of the table. He sat between Prince Maximus of the Eastern Isles and his brother-in-law, Duke Edmund Beckett. Stealing glances across the table at her future husband, who easily conversed with Prince Maximus, she wished she was seated beside him instead.

After some pleasant chatter over fresh garden salad and the roast duck entrée, King Boreas clinked his glass gruffly with a knife, pushing back his chair and standing. "I should like to make a toast to the bride and groom. I wish you a long, fruitful marriage in hopes that one day our kingdoms may once again be bound through matrimony."

Everyone glanced nervously at each other, lifting their glasses quietly. Elara swallowed, touching her stomach gingerly once again. "You—you speak of tying our future offspring to your own?" she asked, baffled. "There would be quite an unusual age difference."

"No, not my children," Boreas boomed with boisterous laughter. "My grandchildren. Kristopher and Norah have ample offspring, all still in their youth. Should you be so blessed, we would gladly welcome discussions of an arrangement that could be advantageous to all three of our kingdoms." He lifted his glass higher, locking eyes with Crown Prince Kailan.

"I would certainly be open to negotiating a marriage alliance with your nation, as well," Kailan said, standing and holding out his glass to the foreign king. "There is no reason all three of our kingdoms cannot come to an agreement which benefits us all."

Elara breathed out, a wave of relief washing over her as the tension in her stomach finally eased. "Long has it been since the Treaty of the Five Realms fell apart," Elara said, standing and holding out her own glass. "It would be wise for us to solidify our alliance in a tangible way, especially when Denorfia and Hyrosencia are both so vulnerable to Rexton's whims."

"You have all traveled here to witness the union of two individuals," Gerard said, rising to his feet. "May we not waste this precious opportunity to enter a new era of partnership between Hyrosencia, Denorfia, and the Eastern Isles."

"Here, here," Wade cheered enthusiastically, raising his glass from his seat. Myra chuckled, and her sister nudged her with an elbow, silencing her.

"Long before your engagement our nations cooperated for mutual benefit," Kailan said. "It would be a privilege to solidify our alliance in a new treaty on behalf of my father, King Aidan of the Eastern Isles. What say you, King Boreas?"

Boreas was quiet for a moment, taking a generous gulp from his wine glass. Glancing sideways at Elara, the old man grinned. "I shall sign a new treaty with you upon one condition."

Elara sipped from her wine glass to calm her nerves. Feigning a smile, she asked, "What are your terms?"

"I should like to arrange betrothals for two of my grandchildren, one with an heir of the Isles and one with your firstborn, should you be so blessed," he said again, staring down Elara.

Gerard coughed, patting his chest. "King Boreas, it seems a bit early to arrange the betrothals of small children, especially children who are not yet conceived."

Kailan placed his glass on the table, glancing down at Lady Imogen while thinking. "I will consider such discussions, although I will not send any of my children away to wed before they are of proper consenting age."

"I am a reasonable man," Boreas said, sitting back in his chair. Reluctantly, the rest of them followed, and several servants scurried forward to push them closer to the table.

"Let us schedule a time to discuss the terms of the treaty later this week," Elara said as the servants began taking the entrée plates away. "I fear our conversation is seriously lacking for our poor guests who are not here for diplomatic reasons."

"Nonsense," Maximus said. "I quite enjoyed watching the three of you banter about treaties and baby betrothals. Even more reason for me to select a bride and sire my own heir." Wade attempted to stifle his laughter, while Myra beamed up at the handsome prince, much to her parents' dismay. Kailan groaned and rolled his eyes at his younger brother, pressing his fingers to his temple.

As the servants began placing small cups of dessert in front of each guest, Norah said, "Lady Imogen." When the young woman turned her attention to the princess across from her, Norah continued, "It is so nice to meet someone with the same name as one of my daughters. It is such a beautiful moniker."

Imogen's cheeks reddened as she smiled wide and asked rather loudly, "You have a daughter named Imogen? What an amusing coincidence!"

From there, the conversation dissipated into less serious topics such as the weather and the perils of the long journey to Symptee. As their guests chattered away, Elara finally felt relaxed enough to enjoy the food before her. With a lively start to their weeks-long visit, she had even more to look forward to than her nuptials later in the week.

THE STEEL FORTRESS

Crystal sulked in silence for the remainder of their trek to Faswyn, the great capital of the dwarf nation. Serena walked alongside their stern-faced leader in the middle of the group, attempting to get her to speak by asking about her upbringing as an elf, but Crystal was succinct, seeming uninterested in detailing her past. Avoiding the eyes of her brother and comrades, she only spoke to bark orders at them.

Days had passed since they left the hot springs when they reached another great stone wall. The Bevakors who guarded Faswyn accosted them, scrutinizing the guardians' familiar faces before ushering them through a secret tunnel. Immediately, two of the dwarfs collected their horses and led them to a wider passage. Then they disappeared into the mountain wordlessly. These dwarfs were stoic warriors, not as talkative as the ones in Estivor had been. One of the dwarfs' beards dragged the dirt path as they led their guests by torchlight. Suddenly, the dwarfs in front of them descended into darkness, and Rigel followed them without pause. Serena stopped, peering into the dark abyss hesitantly.

"We're going underground again," Crystal said. She stepped forward and began the descent down the dark stairwell. "Watch your step. Your eyes will adjust." Will stepped forward, taking the archer's place beside Serena, and held his hand out to her. Relieved, she took it, and they carefully strode down the steep stone steps, followed by Cole, Xandra, and two other dwarfs.

The descent was long with no end in sight, and the humans began showing signs of fatigue after a few miles. When they finally reached a landing between flights of steps, the Bevakors at the forefront of their party turned left, ushering them down a narrow passageway. At the end of the hall, they emerged into a grand open space with high ceilings. Serena and Will gaped at the larger-than-life dwarf statues that lined both sides of the room, each carved directly into the mountain. An eerie green hue covered the room, and the air was unusually heavy and musty. This made it harder to breathe. As they walked through, Serena noticed several passageways that broke off from the main hall.

One of the Bevakors in front of Rigel and Crystal said, "The king has long awaited the return of you fey mongrels and your nervous human counterparts."

When Crystal gnashed her teeth and clenched her fists, Rigel said, "You insult us. You cannot speak to us in such a way. Your king chose to align with Queen Elara. If we are to be allies, you should show some respect, especially to her best guardians. We shall fight against a common enemy soon enough."

The Bevakors scoffed. "The elves have not shown our people respect in over a millennium. Respect must be earned," one said.

"I have the deepest respect for your king extending such courtesy to Queen Elara and her guardians, just as our queen did," Cole said diplomatically from behind them.

The Bevakor flanking their group paused to stare at Cole. "This one smells like fey, yet he does not share her appearance. Is this a trick?"

"It is no trick. We only use magic to conceal our race for safety while we travel. My sister reverted her enchantment a few days ago," Cole said, giving Crystal a warning glance.

Crystal turned her nose up. "Please lead us to your king. It has been a long journey, and we would all appreciate time to rest."

The Bevakors turned and marched onward in silence. When they finally reached their destination, two guards heaved open a set of towering steel doors, revealing the throne room. They shuffled into the room, joining several dwarfs who were engaged in a heated debate with their king. He sat upon an elaborate throne that had been carved out of the mountain. The back of the throne extended high above their heads in a rounded shape like stalagmites. Jewels were beset along the edges of the great throne, and the rubies and emeralds dazzled in the firelight.

"Who dares interrupt the High King? He confers with the council!" A fierce red-haired dwarf glared at the intruders.

Serena shrank back, clinging to Will's arm as she examined the quarrelsome group of dwarfs. The Bevakors moved to either side of the visitors and allowed the guardians to step into the forefront. "The human queen's soldiers have returned," one of them bellowed as they all dropped down on one knee before their king.

Crystal stepped forward and bowed before saying, "We are the guardians from Queen Elara Garrick's court on our way back to Symptee from our mission in Hyrosencia."

"How dare a pixie address His Majesty the High King in such a way!" the dwarf said, taking a hostile approach toward them with a hand on the hilt of his sword.

"That's enough, Eldvar," said the king. His yellow-tinged eyes stared down the raucous dwarf. Eldvar stopped, though his unfriendly eyes remained fixed on Crystal. The king scrutinized each of their faces, squinting his beady eyes as he stroked his long silver beard. "I see there are new faces among ye," he said. "May I assume your quest was a success?"

"Yes, but only in part. Your Majesty, please allow me to introduce our friends to you properly," Crystal said. She bowed her head graciously. He nodded and gestured. She turned toward Serena and extended a hand. The girl took it, timidly stepping out from behind the archer so the king could take a better look. "This is Serena Finch. Her family was one of our primary targets."

"Where be the rest of ye kin, Serena Finch?" the king asked, lifting one bushy eyebrow.

Serena's lips parted as her sad eyes darted between the king and her guardians.

"Unfortunately, we were unable to rescue any of her kin." Crystal squeezed Serena's shoulder before dropping her hand to her side.

"And who be the boy?" the old dwarf asked, nodding his chin at Will.

Crystal rolled her eyes and said, "He is no one of importance. Just a boy from Durmak who wanted to cross the border with us."

"Hey," Will began, but Rigel and Cole each dropped a heavy hand on his shoulders and pulled him back.

"Will is my friend," Serena said with a smile. "He's been a great help over the past few weeks."

"Our journey has not been an easy one thus far," Crystal said, turning her attention back to the king. "We were attacked by some of Rexton's men. We nearly lost Serena before we could cross the border. Quite frankly, she is lucky to stand before you."

"Yes, lucky, indeed," the king hummed. He stroked his mustache and stared deeply into Serena's eyes. "And do ye know who I am?"

Serena stared at his crown and bowed her head nervously. "The King of the Dwarfs?"

He grinned and said, "Rise, child. I am Dranir Steelcast, High King of the Dwarf Realm. Over a century have I ruled this mountain."

"It's a pleasure to meet you, Your Majesty," Serena said sheepishly, her gaze scanning the other bearded faces in the room.

"I welcome you to Faswyn. We were just discussing who shall make the journey to Symptee with you. Your queen has invited two from the Great Mountains and two from the Great Forest to represent the alliance on her War Council," King Dranir said. "At present, I intend to send Eldvar Cragjaw and Martock Smeltbranch, two of our most respected warriors."

The dwarf nodded his head, and they all eyed the muscular warrior who had addressed them with hostility moments before. "It shall be my honor to serve in your stead, my king," Eldvar said before knocking his chest with a fist.

A younger dwarf with dark hair and a waist-length beard stepped forward. "As the crown prince, you should send me in Eldvar's place," he argued. "None should make a better ambassador than your own blood."

King Dranir considered his son's interjection thoughtfully before turning his eyes upon their visitors. "Please, come forward. I should like your expertise on the matter," he insisted.

Serena's eyes widened as the four guardians stepped forward to fill in the empty spaces between the rowdy dwarf warriors. Cole placed a firm hand on Serena's back, nudging her to shuffle forward. Then he brushed past her and said, "Typically we would not advise the heir to the throne traveling unnecessarily, as these are dangerous times. However, as you all know, sometimes an heir is exactly who the people need."

"I hate to say it, but the elf is right," said the Dwarf Prince. "As Dugran Steelcast, sole heir to our nation, I wish to prove myself to our people through diplomacy. The humans deserve the strongest minds and bodies to answer their call."

"Your day shall come, my son, for we shall aid the humans when the impending invasion begins. On such a day, you shall lead our men into battle," King Dranir said. "Until then, I would like you to work closely with the other generals in Eldvar's absence."

"You could send me," a rather deep female voice said, drawing the attention of everyone in the room. Serena peeked around the guardians, catching a look at a black-haired, blue-eyed female dwarf, the first female of their race she had seen.

"As your daughter, I am familiar with our generals and strategies. Entrust me with this task, Father."

"Rilura, my child, you know well that women only journey to wed. As you have yet to select a bridegroom, I am unwilling to part with you. You are more valuable at my side, where you may safely greet suitors. A War Council is no place for you," King Dranir contended.

Rilura swept her hair over her shoulder and protested. "You cannot treat me as a stand-in queen forever. Mother is gone, and I can be useful in other ways. I know our men, our strategies. I have trained as a warrior. Allow me to join General Martock. The journey to Jordis is nothing I cannot handle, and it is safe from there on to Symptee."

The king examined his daughter for a moment. Then Dranir Steelcast turned to the eldest dwarf in the room and asked, "What be your thoughts, Magril?"

Magril had a stark white beard and receding hairline. He stepped forward and said, "It seems unwise to send a woman, especially of a noble bloodline, when so few are they amongst our kind."

"If I may," Martock interrupted, stroking his beard. "I personally trained Rilura in defensive strategy. She is quite well versed."

"And what say you, Eldvar? Do you also believe my daughter to be fit for the journey?" the king asked, raising his bushy brows.

Eldvar bowed his head as his lips curled in a cocky smirk. "Of course, Your Majesty. Your daughter is as strong as the Steelcasts before her. I am certain she can manage such a journey, but I should protect her with my life should it be necessary." As he lifted his head, he caught Rilura's eye and winked.

Rilura wrinkled her nose and narrowed her eyes at the captain. "I will not need your protection. I was trained as any other dwarf in Faswyn," she said. She climbed the remaining steps to her father's throne and knelt before him, Then, taking his hands, she looked up into his eyes. "I am strong enough, Father. Please allow me and the guards of my choosing to go."

King Dranir narrowed his eyes and nodded slowly. He patted the top of her hands. "Very well. My daughter shall accompany Martock, Eldvar, and two guards of her choosing. From Silvermane, she, Martock, and one guard will continue to Symptee. The other shall return with Eldvar."

"That's preposterous," Prince Dugran said, scowling at his father and sister. "Surely I would make a more suitable ambassador than Rilura."

"As my eldest, her experience rivals your own. Rilura has stood by my side, observing my rule, and learning from our best generals for half a century," Dranir said, placing both hands on the arms of the throne. Rilura quickly stood and shuffled to the side as her father stood up. "You have more yet to learn, my son. Be that the end of this foolish spectacle."

Every dwarf in the room dropped onto one knee, accepting his decree in silence. Then the High King of the Dwarfs hobbled down the steps toward his guests. Standing face-to-face with Serena, he was shorter than her by a foot, though he held his chin high. Dranir reached for Serena's hands, and she allowed his thick, calloused hands to engulf hers. "You are every bit as beautiful as Queen Elara was when she stumbled upon us many moons ago," he said. "She shall feel such relief to know of your safe passage. Be sure to send my regards."

"Yes, Elara will be very pleased, indeed," Crystal said, snaking an arm around Serena's shoulders as soon as the king relinquished her hands. "Now, if you please, we should all very much like to rest in the safety of your great city before we must be off."

"And safe you shall be in the protection of the Glovni," High King Dranir said. He clapped his hands together, and the sound echoed through the corridor. "Bandan Icebraid! Come forth." From the dozen dwarfs clustered around them stepped forward the tallest of them, a blond-haired, blue-eyed dwarf of slighter build. He quickly approached and took a knee before King Dranir. "Bandan, please escort our guests to their quarters," he said. When he turned back to the guardians, he added, "I must insist you stay and rest for a few days so your guides may prepare to accompany you."

"As you wish, Your Majesty," Cole said, bowing his head. "We are most grateful for your kindness once again. Call upon us if you require anything. This shall not be our first pass through the mountains."

"Of that, we are well aware," Eldvar said derisively from behind the king, cracking his knuckles all at once. "We require nothing from the likes of you. Be ready to leave in two days' time. You got lucky the beasts were still hibernating during your first passing. I can assure you it shall not be so easy going back."

"We are always ready," Crystal said, turning to face their guide. "Bandan? Please lead the way."

The dwarf waved a hand, and the six visitors followed close behind him. Falling in step behind their guide, Serena was surprised that Bandan Icebraid was several inches taller than the average dwarf. She was the shortest in their group, and Bandan was nearly her height.

When they reached a hall of bed chambers, Bandan informed them that three rooms had been prepared with three beds in each. "We anticipated more of you after your initial visit. I'm sorry to hear your mission was not a full success. Feel free to utilize this space to your content. I have no doubts it has been a long and difficult journey for all of you."

"Thank you, Bandan," Xandra said. "It has been long, indeed. We appreciate your hospitality."

"I can take no credit. Dranir is a most generous king," the dwarf said. "He took pity on the human queen when she pleaded for aid years ago. Many years our people have lived in peace. Our warriors were itching for battle."

"I did not realize Elara had asked the dwarfs for aid when Rexton invaded," Serena said.

"Yes, her guards led her into the mountains, and a group of Bevakors happened upon them before they wandered onto a more dangerous route," Bandan explained. "Women are quite a rarity among dwarfs, so I think our king was quite smitten with your queen. Elara became fast friends with his daughter as well. They convinced Dranir to offer food and shelter to passing refugees, and he sent men to build the walls around the citadel. From there, your people had somewhere truly safe to call home while they rebuilt to the east."

"I never realized the dwarfs were so vital to Hyrosencia's survival," Serena whispered. She glanced at Crystal, who shrugged and entered the first of the three rooms offered to them. Meanwhile, Cole entered the third room, the farthest from Crystal.

"You should rest. I'll return to escort you to dinner in a few hours," Bandan said. He bowed his head. "Tomorrow I can show you to the training grounds if you should like to spend some time training."

Rigel lifted his fingers in a faint gesture of farewell and said, "Thanks, friend. We shall certainly make use of it while we're here." Then he opened the third door and disappeared, followed closely by Will.

As Bandan turned to leave them, Serena cleared her throat to get his attention. Bashfully, she asked, "Could you answer a question before you go? What does *Glovni* mean?"

Xandra and Bandan chuckled. "The Glovni is the underground fortress. We are within it. While our great city is called Faswyn, the stronghold where the Steelcast bloodline and other important families reside is the Glovni. You have been granted a place of honor during your stay. They say the Glovni is impenetrable."

"Oh, that's quite generous of King Dranir," Serena said. She glanced down the hall at the warriors pacing on guard.

"He is a generous king, indeed," Bandan agreed. "And you are most deserving of reprieve after all you've gone through." Serena furrowed her brow, curious how the dwarfs could possibly know all she had experienced on her journey.

"Well, Bandan, thank you kindly for being our guide. With that, we should retire for a much-needed rest," Xandra said. She touched the back of her neck and rolled it.

"Anytime." Bandan smiled, then withdrew down the hall.

Serena turned to Xandra and asked, "Which room are you going in?"

Xandra frowned, glanced at the first door, and said, "I suppose the empty one. You're welcome to join me."

"She still hasn't spoken to you?" Serena asked, looking over her shoulder at the first door.

Xandra shook her head and grasped the handle to the second door. "I've tried. I've said what I could. She won't acknowledge either of us. Cole's quite torn up about it. He's so caught up in his own head; he's barely speaking to me."

Serena ran her hand up and down Xandra's arm in support and said, "I'm sure she'll come around. You're her closest friend."

Pushing the door open, Xandra said quietly, "You don't know Crys as well as I do. Nor do you know their laws. This is no small quarrel. Their people turn each other in for disloyalty to Queen Daephyra. I selfishly pushed Cole to admit his feelings for me, and in doing so, I've put them both in a terrible position."

"Wanting the person who could make you happy does not make you selfish. Not in my eyes. It makes you human," Serena said, stepping into the doorway. "Do you regret it? Kissing him?"

"I will never regret telling him how I feel. When he kissed me—nothing has ever felt so right," Xandra said, smiling at the recollection of that moment. "I don't care what the edict says. Long have we denied our feelings for each other for fear of what others would say, but our feelings never lessened. I don't think any queen nor law can dictate how we feel. We're drawn together like magnets. There's no ignoring the pull we feel toward each other."

"It sounds like you're meant for each other," Serena said. She couldn't help but smile at the flush of Xandra's cheeks. "Perhaps I can reason with Crystal. Remind her that you never meant any disrespect. Sometimes people are naturally drawn to each other, and they can't help it. Surely if Cole feels as strongly as you do, she could be happy for you. It's his choice, after all."

The lovestruck guardian smiled grimly. "You're not usually the optimist, Serena. It's refreshing that you think she'll come around. I wish you luck trying to convince her of that," Xandra said. "If she ices you out, you're welcome to hop rooms." Xandra laid back on one of the beds and pulled a pillow over her face.

Serena closed the door, alone in the hallway. Closing her eyes, she took a deep breath to steady her nerves before entering the first room, where Crystal still fumed in silence. When she thrust open the door, Crystal glanced up from her book, her jawline softening when she realized Serena was alone. "Hey," Serena said nervously, dropping her bag on the floor next to one of the beds. "You mind if we chat?"

"If it's not about anything controversial, then no; I don't mind," she said, flopping back on her bed.

"I never would have thought our fearless leader could be so juvenile," Serena said. Crystal glowered as she continued, "Cole may be your brother, but he is a grown man. His feelings cannot be ruled by baseless laws, nor should yours."

"Did he say that? Did he dare say the laws he has adhered to for almost a hundred years are suddenly baseless?" Crystal snapped. The hostility flaring in her cold eyes took Serena back, but only for a moment.

"No," she said, looking away. "That is my own opinion. I spoke to Xandra. I understand why you feel betrayed by their actions, as does she. She feels guilty enough for complicating your lives, but they could no longer ignore their feelings. Cole knows the laws of your people, and still he chose her. Must you fault him for following his heart?"

Crystal sat up and swung her legs over the side of the bed. Facing Serena, she fiddled with her dagger, unsheathing and sheathing it repeatedly. Finally, she returned the dagger to the scabbard and let it go. Lowering her voice, she said, "I saw the way he looked at her when he thought no one was watching. I knew something had changed. But I'll never understand how he could give up his place in Ord Metsiilva for a human—any human. I love Xandra; we have been friends for a decade. But catching them together like that... I just don't understand it."

"They surprised you," Serena said. She fiddled with the frayed ends of her hair. "Surprised me, too, to be honest." She chuckled.

But Crystal did not laugh. Her fingers dug into the thin mattress as she stared at Serena. "You have an older brother. How would you have felt if you caught him kissing your closest friend?"

Serena paused as an image of Cameron and Talitha sprang to her mind. It would not have shocked her if Talitha had been interested in him, but the thought of them kissing made her grimace. "I see your point."

"Exactly," Crystal said, flopping back on the bed. "If my brother had told me his true feelings, maybe he could have made me understand. I don't know. Home, our people—that's a part of who we are. How does one walk away from that?" She grabbed the sheathed dagger from the bed and twirled it between her fingers.

"Are you angry because you think he'll leave you behind?" Serena asked.

Crystal paused; the dagger slipped between her fingers and pegged her in the chest. She groaned, picking it up and chucking it off the bed, saying not a word.

"Would it kill you to talk to them?" Serena asked. "It kills me not being able to talk to my best friend or my brother—and here, you have both."

"Our situations are different," Crystal argued. She crossed her arms over her chest as she stared at the ceiling. The walls of the mountain were low and dark, and Serena could see the tension gripping her friend.

"I'm well aware." Serena pushed herself onto her feet so she could see Crystal's face. The guardian looked down, meeting her gaze. "I don't know how you can fault them when they aren't the only ones who have been lying."

Crystal jolted upright; her mouth twisted. "I had to lie to protect myself. We wouldn't have made it this far if we ran around the human realm with our ears exposed," she snapped.

"You still could have told me," Serena said, her words spewing forth like venom. "You think you were blindsided? Imagine how I felt."

The guardian relaxed, unclenching her jaw as she searched Serena's eyes. "We've all kept our own secrets." She took a deep breath as her eyes fell to her lap.

"That we have." Serena took a step back and perched on the edge of the bed. They sat wordlessly, both finding some spot in the room to observe. The deep clay-colored walls reminded Serena of the dirt south of Durmak, how it welcomed their dead more easily than it nurtured crops, and she wondered whether there were too many fractures in their relationships to repair.

"I have every right to be cross with them," Crystal whispered.

Serena wasn't sure if she was stating it as fact or trying to convince herself that it was true. "You do," she said. "But wouldn't you feel better if you talk about it instead of avoiding the problem?"

Crystal made a humming sound in the back of her throat, not bothering to look up. "I've only ever wished them both happiness," she said, shaking her head. "But it's going to take time to accept them finding that happiness together."

"He's still your family, Crys," Serena noted. "At least consider having a conversation with him about it?"

"I'll think about it," Crystal said, crinkling her nose. She rose, stretched her arms, and walked toward the door. Glancing over her shoulder, she added, "I need some fresh air. Don't go wandering off. I'll return before dinner."

"Take your time," Serena said as the door slammed shut behind the guardian. Alone at last, she closed her eyes with a satisfied smile on her face, hopeful that Crystal's walk would lead her to one of the other guest rooms.

25

SOMETHING BLUE

The blinding sunlight woke Elara early, but she didn't mind. She closed her eyes as she stretched her arms overhead. She pictured Gerard waiting for her at the end of a flower-strewn aisle. "Today is the day," she whispered to herself.

The queen rolled out of her bed, slipped on her favorite violet robe, and walked onto her balcony. She leaned against the railing and smiled as she overlooked the city beyond the inner citadel wall. A cool breeze tickled her rosy cheeks, and she pulled her robe tight at her collarbone. The streets were already bustling as last-minute arrivals trickled through the gates into the courtyard below. The wisteria trees were in full bloom; the trail of pastel petals on the lawn beckoned Elara to her favorite shaded spot.

"You're up early, milady," Bea said and she passed by the open door with a tray in her hands. She placed it on a small table at the center of the room and poured Elara a cup of hot tea.

"I am far too excited to stay in bed." The maid approached cautiously, handing the queen a saucer with a teacup filled nearly to the brim. "Thank you, Bea." The queen sipped carefully from her steaming cup, her eyes lingering on the Athamar Mountains. A mass of dark clouds swirled above them, making her uneasy. She hoped the storm would not interfere with Serena's journey or wreak havoc in Symptee.

As the maid turned to leave, Elara called out for her to wait. She had something she wanted to offer the sweet woman. She marched across her chambers, barely pausing to place her teacup on the table. Bea wrinkled her forehead as she followed the queen over to her wardrobe. Elara thrust open the double doors and stepped inside, running her fingers across the satin and lace gowns on each side. "These are some of my favorites," the queen said. She turned toward the maid with a pastel gown in hand. Holding it up, Elara squinted and said, "This shade of blue would suit you well."

"Me? That is much too fancy for a maid, milady," Bea said hastily. Her eyes shifted away from the queen. "I could never wear one of your gowns."

"Nonsense, you must dress to impress at a royal wedding," Elara said, forcing the gown into Bea's hands. "Take it. I shall need friendly faces among all those stuffy nobles this evening."

Wide-eyed, the maid blinked at the queen and stuttered, "You, milady, you cannot want me to attend the—the royal wedding? I am but a commoner."

"You are no mere commoner, Bea. You have been as loyal a servant as your mother before you. I do not see your status. I see your kindness and concern. You are just as worthy to be there as any noble, so I do hope you will accept my invitation." Elara pranced back over to the table and picked up her teacup.

Bea hugged the smooth satin to her bosom and grinned. "Yes, Your Majesty. Of course. It is the greatest honor to be included on this blessed occasion. Thank you."

"No need to thank me." Elara squeezed the maid's hand. "On this day, it would be my honor if you would serve as my friend. I have invited a few ladies to join me after lunch and help me prepare for the ceremony. It would please me if you would spend the afternoon with us."

"The pleasure would be all mine, milady," Bea said with a shy smile.

Elara perched on the edge of her favorite chair and plucked a scone from the tray Bea had brought in. She took a bite as she stared at the clouds over the snowcapped mountain peaks. She thought back to the kindness shown to her by the dwarfs when she crossed the mountains seventeen years ago and hoped they were showing the same kindness to Serena Finch and the guardians as they made their way to Symptee.

"Will you be wanting me to draw your bath soon, milady?"

Elara turned her head, realizing Bea was still in the room. "Oh... Yes, that would be excellent. I should like to enjoy some time alone while I can."

The maid bowed her head. "Yes, of course, Your Majesty. I shall ready it with haste." Bea laid the blue gown over an empty chair and hurried toward the queen's adjoining lavatory.

"Take your time," Elara called after her, taking another bite from her scone. Feeling a nervous queasiness, she plopped the pastry back onto the tray and placed a hand on her stomach. "After the wedding, we shall have one less reason to worry."

WHEN BEA AND ANOTHER maid entered Elara's chambers with her lunch, the queen was in the lavatory expelling her breakfast into a pan. Worried, Bea knocked on the door and asked, "Milady, how may I help you? Should I fetch the physician?"

"No," Elara said sharply, wiping the corner of her mouth. She slumped back on the cold tile floor and exhaled, brushing back stray hairs from her face. "I am quite all right. It's just a nervous stomach. Prepare for lunch. The guests shall be joining us shortly."

Hesitantly, the maids left through the servants' entrance. When Elara heard the door click shut, she slowly pushed herself onto her feet. Entering her bed chamber, she went to the desk where her bottles from Ismenia glistened in the sunlight. She picked up the nearly empty vial of yellow liquid and uncorked it. She turned the bottle upside down upon her lips, sipping desperately until there was none left. With a frown, Elara tossed the empty container on top of her desk and groaned.

Bea poked her head back into the room and asked, "Milady, would you like some tea?"

Elara whipped her head around in surprise. "Oh, Bea... Yes, ginger tea would be quite nice. Thank you. And could you send word to Ismenia that I require more medicine?"

"Are you ill again, milady?" Bea asked, stepping closer.

"It is nothing that will kill me," Elara said with a faint chuckle. "With all the wedding preparations, I have been quite stressed. If you tell Ismenia I am out of medicine, she will know what I need." She held out the empty vial to her maid.

Bea nodded as she took the vial and tucked it in her apron pocket. "Of course, milady. I will inform her right away."

Half an hour had passed when a guard knocked three times on the door to Elara's private chambers. "You may enter," Elara said. She took a sip of her ginger tea before standing to greet her visitor.

As soon as the guard opened her door, Ismenia squeezed her way past him. "Honestly, you would think they would not delay an herbalist from seeing you!" Ismenia looked radiant in a modest mauve gown as she approached Elara. Reaching the queen, she offered her a full vial and asked, "Has the ginger tea helped at all?"

"Only a smidgen," Elara said, wrinkling her nose. She leaned forward and grasped her friend's arms and kissed her cheek. "Thank you for coming to my aid. I fear my maids are growing suspicious. They found me sick in the lavatory this morning."

"You will be wed in mere hours, and then it will not matter," Ismenia insisted as they took a seat on a small couch. "It has been many years since a Garrick has been born. The kingdom will rejoice over your blessing."

"Where is your sister? I am surprised she did not accompany you," Elara said, sipping from her teacup once again.

"She assured me this morning she would not miss your luncheon," Ismenia said. Elara fiddled with the glass bottle, biting the inside of her lip, and her friend reached over to squeeze her hand. Taking the bottle, she unscrewed the cap and held it over Elara's tea. "Two drops of this in your tea should settle your nerves." She winked at the queen as a couple drops plopped from the bottle into the teacup, swirling around before disappearing in the black liquid.

Elara took a deep breath and nodded. "I hope you are right," she said before downing the rest of the cup's contents.

THE QUEEN'S PRIVATE SITTING room was staged with a large mahogany table and ten chairs for her bridal luncheon. When the guards opened the doors, Elara and Ismenia entered the sitting room arm in arm with big smiles on their faces. The ladies rose to greet her, and the guards closed the doors behind them. Elara noticed at once that Queen Aneira of Denorfia was nowhere to be seen, though she was not surprised by her absence. In fact, she was relieved.

Elara and Ismenia parted arms. The queen went left to the head of the table, while Ismenia went to greet her sister. When the queen had nearly reached her chair, a quiet servant stepped forward and pulled it out for her. She nodded her thanks and announced to her guests, "Please be seated. I must apologize for keeping you ladies waiting."

"The queen is never late. The rest are simply early," Norah said with a smile.

Servants stepped up to gently push in each lady's chair as they lifted their skirts to take a seat. Sitting closest to Elara were Gerard's sister, Daria Beckett, and Prince Kailan's wife, Imogen, who immediately returned to their discussion with the Denorfian princesses. Next to Lady Imogen sat Idonea, who quietly sipped from a water goblet as she listened to the nobles' gossip. At the far end of the table, two of Elara's ladies-in-waiting began chattering with Ismenia about her lady's health.

"Nervous?" Daria asked Elara. "I had known Edmund for several years, and I was still wracked with nerves on my wedding day."

"Why should she be nervous?" Myra asked her sister. "She has been married before. This time will be no different."

Elara chuckled, locking eyes with the unwed young lady. "You are right. I have been married before, but why should this time not be different? Every man is different."

"That is true," Myra said, turning down her chin bashfully. "But still, why should you be nervous? You're a queen!" Her sister discreetly nudged her arm, her serious eyes warning the naïve princess to stop questioning the bride.

Elara smiled and told Norah, "I don't mind her questions. It's no bother." Looking back at Myra, the bride-to-be said, "Though I cared very much for your brother, it was a marriage of necessity. I needed a strong ally at my side, and your father had long been eager to tie our kingdoms together. Despite the abrupt end to our union, I grew quite fond of Caspian, but it was not the same as what I feel now."

"You mean you were not in love with our brother," Myra whispered. The girl looked down at her hands.

Elara took a deep breath. "Not everyone is blessed to know true love when they wed—especially princesses," she said somberly.

"Even in an arranged marriage, you could fall in love with your spouse." Norah took a sip of water before she continued. "It takes work from both people, but it can happen."

Elara clenched her jaw faintly. "While we made our best effort, obviously it was not meant to be," she said, the inflection of her voice putting a rest to their unpleasant conversation. Turning to the servants who stood silently against the wall near her, Elara whispered, "Please bring the first course," and the servants filed out of the room.

"Do you think you will ever remarry, princess?" Lady Imogen asked the eldest Denorfian.

"Goodness, no. I am still in mourning," Norah said. She blinked repeatedly without making eye contact. Her cheeks tinged a slight pink as she took a sip from her water goblet.

"Perhaps I should be next," Myra said abruptly. "Prince Maximus seemed quite the gentleman. Perhaps Father will warm up to his charms at the wedding banquet this evening."

Norah suddenly started coughing, grabbing for the nearest napkin to cover her mouth. "My apologies," she sputtered. She dabbed her mouth as the coughing trailed off. "I did not know you were so eager to wed a foreigner."

"Knowing Father would make the selection, I never dared hope I would even like my future husband. Of course, I should much prefer to marry a man I have met who is close in age," Myra said with a shrug. "After meeting the two princes from the Isles and Lord Stirling, I would never oppose a union with the Marinus family."

Daria beamed as she raised her glass. "You have a high opinion of my relatives."

Imogen chuckled. "My husband would be thrilled to hear it."

Elara smiled, reminded of her foolish dreams of love growing up in Hyrosencia. The first time she felt a spark of interest in a potential suitor was the day she met Prince Antoine Rexton of Nyzenard. The foreign prince was tall and handsome, with a chiseled jaw, clean-shaven face, and raven hair. He was charming—too charming—though she did not know then that every word he would say to her would be a callous lie while he plotted to steal her father's throne. What youthful ignorance! She would have happily married him had he not invaded her kingdom and taken everything from her. She would not wish that kind of blissful ignorance on any other woman, be they an ally or enemy.

"Are you well, milady?" Ismenia asked.

Elara blinked and focused on her friend sitting at the other end of the table. "Oh, I'm fine. Just lost in thought," she said, shaking her head. Then she realized the servants had placed the salads on the table in front of them. She quickly picked up her fork and said, "This looks delectable."

As the ladies ate their salads in silence, one of the servants went around replenishing their wine glasses. Once they had finished their first course, the servants cleared the plates to make way for the main course. "The cook has prepared Her Majesty's favorite meal: roast duck with asparagus," Bea said as each server placed a hot plate in front of the ladies.

Though it was normally her favorite, the smell of the meat made Elara queasy at first, as it had for the past week. Although the medicine that Ismenia had given her helped, she opted for a bite of asparagus first. She then moved on to ripping bites off the roll of bread with her fingers. As the women laughed and discussed men's shortcomings and the joys of motherhood, Elara felt the knot in her stomach ease, and she finally dared to fill her stomach with a proper meal.

ELARA AND HER GUESTS moved their conversation into the sitting area on the other side of the room after their meal. Over an hour after the luncheon, Bea returned to the sitting room wearing the beautiful blue gown from Elara and holding a green bottle in her hands.

"You look wonderful," Elara whispered with a wide smile.

Bea blushed and looked down at the blue skirt. "Thank you kindly, milady." Lifting the bottle, she said, "This is a gift for Her Majesty for her wedding. I was asked to deliver it to you."

"Oh, how lovely," Elara said, smiling as she read the label. It was dated 1350, the year her beloved niece Elyse was born. It had been the last year of peace and happiness in Hyrosencia before Antoine invaded and occupied their kingdom. She felt a sting in her chest and wished her family could be there for her wedding. She had not allowed herself to feel such a longing to be with her kin in many years, but in that moment, their absence weighed heavily on her heart. Sniffling and blinking her eyes, she handed the bottle back to Bea and said, "We must drink in honor of my family and all others who cannot be with us on this day."

"Of course, milady," Bea said. A servant wheeled a small cart over with ten cloudy glass flutes on top. Taking the bottle from the maid, he popped the cork off the bottle with a flourish and waited a moment before pouring the bubbly alcohol in each glass. The white wine dazzled as they poured it, shimmering as if it were full of miniscule jewels. Bea brought a glass to each of the ladies, who waited patiently for everyone to receive theirs.

When Bea was done, Elara leaned over and whispered for the servant to pour one more glass and hand it to her maid. Surprised, Bea sheepishly took the glass and blushed. Norah eyed the maid but turned back toward her sister in disinterest.

Finally, Elara looked down at her glass and smiled at her reflection, trying to redirect her thoughts to her beloved fiancé. "It's hard to believe that when Gerard first came here, I was entertaining the possibility of marrying one of his cousins." Elara and her friends chuckled. "As he was a diplomat in a strange place, I invited him to join me on my morning stroll in the garden. I quickly understood why he was asked to be their ambassador. I asked him many questions, and he always had a thoughtful answer. He charmed me in the most natural way."

"Gerard has always had a way with words," Daria said with a smile.

"Yes, he does," Elara said. "I came to enjoy our promenades, which were not always business focused. His stories of growing up in the Eastern Isles were quite entertaining. One day I realized I was laughing and smiling for the first time in a very long time... and I knew I was in trouble. I fell in love with him as easily as we blink our eyes. I wish for all of you to know the depth of a love rooted in friendship and respect."

"To falling in love," Daria said, lifting her glass.

The other ladies lifted their glasses, and several repeated, "To falling in love."

Elara turned and clinked glasses with Bea. The shy servant beamed at the show of affection toward her. Norah turned to her sister first, clinking glasses with Myra before they both turned to Elara and Daria. As no one else moved toward Bea, she took a paltry sip from the glass. Then she took a large swig of the sweet wine and watched the other ladies from the side.

The Cinderfell sisters clinked glasses, though Idonea looked unamused by the toast itself. The herbalist then turned a friendly face to Imogen, who was quite pleased to be acknowledged by her. As the women continued to clink glasses and chatter cheerily, Idonea lifted her glass to her lips and took a small sip. She scrunched her face and lowered the flute, crossing one arm across her body.

The sound of glass shattering against the stone floor rang through the room, drawing everyone's attention to Bea. She laid writhing on the floor, a trickle of foam escaping from the corner of her mouth.

"Bea!" Elara shrieked. The queen threw herself onto the floor beside her maid. "What's happening?"

She turned to Ismenia, who was already kneeling beside them. The herbalist pointed at the frazzled servants and yelled, "Come here! Put her head in your lap and keep her still." The young man rushed over and did as he was ordered. As Ismenia began pulling open the girl's eyelids and examining her, she asked, "Does she have a history of spasms?" Wiping the foam from Bea's mouth with a handkerchief, she attempted to look around inside her mouth.

"Not that I have ever seen," Elara said, breathing shakily. The other servants shook their heads in astonishment.

The servant with Bea's head on his lap grimaced, lifting one hand to reveal a smear of blood. "She must have hit her head," he said. Another servant rushed for the door, alerting the guards in the hallway about the commotion.

Suddenly, Idonea collapsed, knocking into Imogen as she fell to the floor. "Oh!" Imogen cried out, covering her mouth in shock. She stepped back from the oracle, looking down at her writhing body in terror.

"Divinity on high. It's poison!" Ismenia said, her eyes wide as she looked across the room at her sister. "The wine. Don't drink the wine!"

Immediately, Norah knocked the frosted flute out of her sister Myra's trembling hand, and several glasses shattered on the floor. "This was an assassination attempt," Norah said. She carefully placed her glass down on the table. "I daresay someone did not want your wedding to proceed."

"No, no, no, this cannot be happening. It was just a dream," Elara whispered, her voice cracking as tears welled in her eyes. She remembered her nightmare from mere weeks ago. Now she recalled the blue dress from her unusual fever dream and the pool of blood soaking into her favorite maid's hair.

Bea sputtered blood, and the convulsions slowed. Elara squeezed her hand and whispered, "I'm so sorry. It—it should have been me."

As Bea's body stilled, her open eyes glazed over, and Elara sobbed. Ismenia shook her head and muttered, "I'm sorry, too." Then she crossed the room and cradled her sister's head on her lap. Blood from Idonea's head wound seeped out onto Ismenia's mauve dress. "Idonea? Idonea, say something. Stay conscious."

A dozen guards rushed into the sitting room, followed by a shocked physician. Glancing at Bea, he shook his head solemnly before turning his attention to the oracle. After a moment, he said, "This one has a weak pulse, but she is still with us." Ismenia shed tears of relief, and Elara sucked in a shaky breath. He asked, "What was the cause of their injuries?"

"I suspect the wine was poisoned. It caused them to seize almost immediately. They both fell and hit their heads. We should bring her to the physician's ward," said Ismenia.

"Agreed," the physician said, gesturing for his assistants to bring in a small gurney. He turned to the queen, whose cheeks were tearstained, and asked, "Did you drink any of the wine, milady? Even a little?"

"No," Elara whispered, her red, swollen eyes widening in fear as she clutched her abdomen.

"This young lady was your maidservant?" Alexander asked, stepping toward the queen. Elara nodded, staring at the corpse of her loyal friend. Sobbing, she sank down to the floor. Tremendous pain swelled in her chest as she reached for Bea's hand. "You cannot stay here, Your Majesty. We do not know the culprit, though we can assume you were the intended target. Do you know where the wine came from?" the commander asked.

"No," Elara answered through sobs. "Bea brought it up from the kitchen and said it was a gift for me. A wedding gift. She could not have known..."

"My deepest apologies, milady," he said, pursing his lips. "Idonea will be well cared for. We should escort you and the other ladies elsewhere for now."

Elara did not reply, but Alexander gave orders for two guards to escort each of her guests back to their respective chambers and remain posted outside. Hesitantly, the guests from Denorfia and the Eastern Isles shuffled out of the sitting room, and Ismenia left with Idonea and the physician.

"How did he manage this?" Elara demanded, peering up at the commander from the floor. "How? The citadel is supposed to be safe!"

Alexander stepped closer and offered the queen a hand, helping her up onto her feet. From close, she could see the worry lines on his forehead. He exhaled and said, "There could be a mole in the Guard or the staff. Unless one of the dignitaries visiting for your wedding is responsible."

"I want them found. Now!" Elara screeched, clenching her fists at her side. "I will have the head of every traitor involved in this."

"We will find them, Your Majesty," the commander replied. "I am relieved that this vulgar attempt on your life was unsuccessful, but I am sorry for the loss of your lady."

"And what of Gerard and the other dignitaries?" the queen asked. "We must ensure no food or drinks are accepted without a food taster. The citadel has been compromised."

"They are all being secured, milady," Alexander reassured her. "Our greatest concern is you. Allow us to escort you elsewhere. We will post additional guards. Can you manage to walk, Your Majesty?"

Elara glanced back at Bea and the blue chiffon gown soaked in blood. She was thankful the girl's freshly curled locks were concealing her pale face from view. Her stomach turned, and Elara turned her back to the commander as she became violently ill. Breathing heavily, the queen wiped the corner of her mouth with the back of her hand, grasping the edge of a chair to steady herself. "Oh, for heaven's sake, someone cover her," she spat.

"Let's get you out of here." Alexander offered an arm for support.

As the commander ushered her out of the sitting room, she looked down at her feet and realized she had some of her friend's blood on the hem of her gown. The color flooded her eyes, painting everything in sight crimson, and she felt a wave of rage swell in her chest. Pausing, she said, "Alexander, when you find the people responsible for this, bring them to me alive. I wish for them to witness their failure and feel the weight of it. I want to be the last face they see as they lose their heads."

The commander nodded silently and shared her wishes with the cluster of concerned guards awaiting orders. At that moment, Elara knew she could no longer hide in the citadel and wait. The enemy was in Symptee, and she would have to fight Antoine Rexton with everything she had if she wanted to win the war.

SHE HAD PACED BACK and forth in the marital bedchamber for half an hour, alone with her thoughts, when there was a knock at the door. Before she could answer, Gerard pushed his way in, chastising the guards. When they laid eyes on each other, a rush of relief washed over both of their faces, and they ran into each other's arms.

"Elara! Thank the sun and stars, you're alive," Gerard said, grasping her cheek and kissing her passionately. Looking her over, he asked, "Are you all right?"

The queen wrapped her thin arms around her fiancé and pressed her face into his chest. "I am so glad you're here. You're alive," she whispered into his shirt as tears filled her eyes. "I was so scared I might lose you too."

Gerard wrapped his arms tightly around her and kissed the top of her head. "I am unharmed. I am most concerned about you right now."

"It should have been me," Elara said mournfully, looking intently into Gerard's worried eyes. "The wine was meant for me. It would have killed me."

"Don't say that." Gerard caressed her cheek in his hand and kissed her forehead. "You are safe now, my love. The Guard has plans in place. Rexton will never get this close to hurting you again."

The queen buried her face in his shirt again and breathed slowly, trying to steady herself. Finally, she looked up at her betrothed with weary eyes. "I should have expected so much from Antoine. This is not his first attempt to hurt or scare me. I have received countless threats from his messenger hawks. He sent loyalists' heads here in baskets before my first wedding. It was dreadful," she moaned.

"No matter what comes next, we shall not be caught off guard again. We know he has someone within our walls, and we will not let them near you," Gerard insisted.

Elara was quiet, her eyes glazed over in sheer exhaustion. A maid entered the room with a modest day gown for her, and the couple stepped back from each other. Elara looked down, instinctively pressing her hand against her stomach, and Gerard asked the maid to step into the hallway and wait for further instructions. The maid looked to the queen, who nodded her approval, and the woman stepped out, leaving the two of them alone.

Looking over Elara's worried expression, Gerard stepped closer. He pulled her into a tight embrace and whispered against her neck, "I don't know what I would have done if I had lost you today."

"Go back to the Isles, I suppose," Elara said with a strained laugh. She wrapped her arms tightly around his neck. "That probably sounds like a good option now." Gerard carefully stroked her hair, and the subtle gesture helped calm her.

"I could never leave you behind." After a contemplative pause, he asked, "When were you going to tell me?"

"Tell you what?" she murmured, lifting her head to meet his eyes.

"Do not think I have not noticed your strange behavior this week. Were you getting cold feet... or are you hiding a delicate condition?" he asked. He moved one hand down to gently touch the fabric covering her midsection.

Her eyes flicked up in alarm as her face warmed. "I intended to tell you tonight after our wedding. I did not mean to keep it from you. The Cinderfells realized it was the cause of my nausea before I did, and we have been so busy with guests and—"

Gerard smiled and pressed his lips to hers. "I cannot be angry with you for waiting to tell me. I only wish our wedding could have gone as we had planned."

"As do I," Elara sighed. "We must be wed soon. There is no time to waste. Not now. People cannot know of my condition beforehand."

"No one will hear it from me, my dear," he said with a grin. "I did not think I could ever love you more, and yet somehow I do." He pressed his lips to hers eagerly, and the tension in her body slipped away.

"I wish we were saying our vows right now," Elara whined. "It is a shame all our preparations have gone to waste. All the dignitaries came here for nothing. All the negotiations will result in nothing. All the anticipation and excitement in the citadel, and for what? Now this shall be a dark day. He has cursed the date which should be sacred between us."

"It is still early in the day. Though tragedy has struck, it does not have to be our only memory of this day," Gerard said as he delicately pecked down her neck and collarbone.

Elara's lips twisted into a smile, and she shook her head, pushing him back gently. "Gerard, it is already scandalous that the two of us are here alone when we have not yet married. You should not stay for long."

"Rubbish! I cannot just leave you in distress." He released her from his grasp. "I am not Hyrosencian, but I have sworn a sacred oath of my own to you, as each of your guards do. You have been my queen since I first kissed you. I am devoted to you, determined to keep you, and our child, safe at all costs. I would declare my vows here and now in this room and forsake the entire elaborate charade if I could. I just want to hold you in my arms and make you feel safe."

"I would like that, too," Elara admitted, gently caressing his cheek. "I love you with all my soul, Gerard. I was quite looking forward to this being the best night of my life."

"Then let us be wed tonight," he whispered. "Could you bear it? Could you find it in your heart to enjoy our wedding after all that has happened?"

Elara blinked at him, speechless for a moment. Her lips parted, but she struggled to find words. "I want to. I really do. But Bea is dead. I watched her die. And it is not safe to gather a hundred people in the hall right now. Surely you must know that?"

Gerard stroked his beard. "If I can work something out with Commander Stanton, would you still marry me tonight?"

"Gerard, please," she protested, grasping one of his forearms. "How could we possibly do such a thing when the citadel has been breached?"

"All the dignitaries and royal guests are already here, and most are unaware of the incident," he pointed out. "Can we not have a ceremony with more guards and less guests? If not today, then tomorrow?"

"Not tonight, darling," Elara replied. "Perhaps tomorrow, if the Council approves."

"If Rexton hears our marriage took place, he will know he failed. He does not have to steal all your happiness today," Gerard said.

Elara smiled and nodded. "You are right. I will not let him win. Summon the Council and determine whether it can safely be done tomorrow."

"This union shall tie Hyrosencia to the Eastern Isles in a beautiful covenant," Gerard said as he interlaced their fingers. "Antoine is sure to be vexed when he learns of his failure."

"It would be the simplest revenge—doing what we already had planned, despite his vile actions. Go. Speak with the Guard and let me know what they say." Gerard planted an impassioned kiss on her lips, and for a moment, she pushed away the image of Bea sputtering blood beside her. She managed to smile at Gerard's gray eyes, glinting with resolve as he turned and exited the marital bedchamber with a skip in his step.

DAYLIGHT

The wedding of Queen Elara Garrick and Lord Gerard Stirling began just before sunset. As she peered through a small slat on the door, Elara's heart fluttered. Sunlight shone through the large glass windows of the main hall as if Divinity were illuminating the aisle for this moment. Standing at the center of the altar, Gerard shifted his footing. Royal guests, ambassadors, and noble families chattered, all eyeing his royal blue suit. When the pianist began playing a grand, sweeping melody, the guests fell quiet, and everyone rose to their feet, turning toward the double doors at the back of the hall.

Four of Elara's ladies-in-waiting fluffed the cathedral train of her ivory wedding gown. The satin skirt flowed parallel to the floor for a second before drifting to rest perfectly on the hallway floor. The train was embroidered with the silhouette of a massive golden oak tree, its branches stretching upward and mingling with sparkling accents that mimicked stars and waning moons. The oak tree was the symbol of the Garrick family, the stars a symbol of her people's belief in Divinity watching over their realm from the heavens. The gold and silver bursts of sequins and embroidery continued up and around the front of her dress, and at her waist was a thin cerulean belt with three flying birds in the center, the symbol of the Eastern Isles. Her gown also featured thick off-the-shoulder straps and a sweetheart neckline, which drew all eyes to the incredible blue diamond necklace that laid perfectly over her heart. Gerard had given her this heirloom, attached to a dainty gold chain, shortly after she accepted his marriage proposal.

Elara took a deep breath and smiled, pushing her nerves to the back of her mind as two guards in crisp violet uniforms opened the double doors. A rush of air hit her as the gentle sounds of the piano and harp filled her ears. The guests lining both sides of the aisle stood facing her. She knew their eyes were on her, but she chose to look past the staring nobles at Gerard, who waited for her halfway down the aisle. Reassured by his smile, Elara beamed as she began the slow promenade toward her beloved.

When she reached him, he took her hand and kissed it, murmuring for only her ears, "You look radiant."

Elara blushed as he wrapped her right hand around his left bicep. The deep blue velvet of his coat and tails was soft and warm against her delicate hand, reminding her of the time her brother escorted her downstairs for her first ball as a young lady. She could hardly picture their faces—her brother, father, and mother—it had been so many years without them. She blinked away the stinging in her eyes as they glided forward, nodding intermittently as they passed each row of guests. She met the tired eyes of Captain Sirius Levick and thought he might make a fine dignitary. Time in the Eastern Isles' sunshine would do his complexion some good. For a second, she wished she could escape there as well.

Near the front, they slowed their pace next to Ismenia, and Elara sorely missed the presence of Idonea. She knew her friend would have stood by her side had she not scarcely escaped death. *Death meant for me,* she thought. Elara reached out to squeeze Ismenia's hand, thankful she had taken the time away from the physician's ward to attend. Her dear friend's eyes brimmed with joyful tears as they exchanged smiles.

In the very front, to their left, were King Boreas and Queen Aneira Rasalas of Denorfia, as well as their two daughters who seemed awestruck by the exquisite couple approaching the raised platform. Gerard and Elara paused and bowed their heads in a show of respect to the visiting monarchs. As Elara lifted her face, she met the hardened gaze of Queen Aneira. It was the same displeased sneer on her lips as when she attended her son's funeral. Thinking of the child in her womb, Elara swallowed, feeling sympathy for the aging woman's loss and fear for her own child's life. How cruel was it to give a woman a child she could not protect?

To their right were Prince Kailan Marinus and Lady Imogen, Prince Maximus, Wade Stirling, Duke Edmund and Duchess Daria Beckett, who all bowed their heads in unison, and the couple returned the gesture. Elara forced a smile as

Wade winked at his brother. In truth, she felt ill at the thought of her brother missing yet another wedding.

Reaching the end of the aisle, Gerard held his left arm out with his palm facing down, and Elara rested her right hand on top of it as he escorted her up four steps onto the platform. Pausing before their officiant, the High Priest of the Estrellogy Temple, they both bowed their heads low in respect for his divine position. "Welcome, welcome," the priest greeted them and their guests. "We gather here today to celebrate a love which knows no bounds of borders or wars. This love has been witnessed by all who know them, and surely, it is a gift from the great Divinity to our most deserving Queen of Hyrosencia and this noble Islander. Fate brought him here, and today you bind your lives and your lands together through matrimony."

With each word, Elara tried to focus on Gerard; she fought to ignore her looming thoughts of lost family and friends. In a moment, he would become her life partner, and she would no longer be alone. They would begin the next chapter of their lives together, embracing the good days and carrying each other through the bad days as they started their own little family.

"Now, if you would please turn and face each other, it is time to profess your eternal vows before your distinguished guests," the priest declared, gesturing toward them with his wrinkled hands.

When Elara didn't move, Gerard ran his fingers up her forearm, the shivers ripping her out of her dark thoughts. Elara turned to her right and focused on him; his salt-and-pepper hair and lightly tanned skin called to her like the comfort of her bed after a long day. He took her right hand in his, and she wished he could wrap his strong arms around her and kiss her that very moment. That his embrace could shield her from the crushing crown she wore, protect her from Rexton's relentless attacks against her people—against their unborn child.

Gerard smiled at her, causing tiny wrinkles to appear at the corners of his eyes as he gently stroked the side of her hand with his thumb. "Elara, my love," he said, staring deeply into her eyes. "I came across the sea to your city as an envoy for my cousin and king, who sought a potential alliance. But from the moment I laid eyes on you, I knew my life would never be the same. Getting close to you was no easy task. You were all business and worry at first."

Everyone chuckled, nodding their heads at the jest.

Elara chuckled, too, knowing nothing had changed. She was still worried, still weighed down by the expectations of her people. A wedding would not change that.

"Then you stumbled upon me playing piano. The sound of you humming to my melody startled me—in the best way. Then I turned and saw your big, beautiful smile for the first time. That moment changed everything."

Elara remembered that day, how she had followed the beautiful sound of the music down the hall curiously. She peeked through the crack in the doors, quietly observing his concentration and skill. His song reminded her of sunlight on her skin while she sat under the wisteria trees. The melody made her heart flutter—a strange feeling she had not allowed herself to feel for ages. Without thinking, she whispered to her guards to remain in the hall before stepping through the doorway to get a better view. She could not help humming to the elegant tune.

She should have been humming with joy as her beloved warmed her hands in his, recalling the unfolding of their love story, but she could not forget that someone within these very walls had attempted to end her life—someone who might be sitting among her guests. She turned her eyes, catching glimpses of sparkling gowns and studded jackets, and wondered if the person responsible was watching her right now.

Gerard continued, "Once you let down your guard, it was quite easy finding more and more things to love about you. You are beautiful, of course, but you are also kind, patient, and determined to help your people. Your tenacity is a sight to behold. I had never met anyone like you, and I knew I never would again. That's why I had to win your heart."

Elara sniffled, dabbing at her eyes with the back of her hand. It was all too much—her hormones, his vows, the unwavering fear that Antoine Rexton could destroy everything at any moment—again. Without missing a beat, Gerard pulled a small ivory handkerchief from his coat pocket and handed it to her with a smile. "Thank you," she whispered in reply, grabbing the token from him.

"You are the strongest and most stunning woman I have ever met, and it is my greatest honor that you want to share your life with me," Gerard finished, reaching forward with his left hand to caress her cheek with his fingertips. Elara closed her eyes for a moment and leaned into the warmth of his hand, wishing such warmth could break through the coldness around her.

The hall grew quiet. Gerard waited for his bride to respond. When she didn't, the priest cleared his throat. The queen shook her head, glancing at the gathered guests and guards. One or more of these people were traitors, but who? She blinked, regaining her composure, then spoke.

"Gerard, if I could count the number of times your words have left me speechless," she said, looking down at their intertwined hands and smiling. "When you first arrived in Symptee, I was not looking forward to arranging a second marriage to a stranger, much less through an envoy, but I understood immediately why your cousin had appointed you for the task. You are quite charismatic, so much so that it vexed me at first. I felt you were too familiar in our early meetings. Now I know that is just the Islander way." Gerard grinned, squeezing her hand as his family chuckled behind them.

"The day I heard your song, you won my heart before I even knew it was you. Your music spoke to me in a way no song or person had in years. You made me want to sing in the gardens again, to do things to break up the mundane of my every day." Instead of singing in the gardens, she'd been fated to bark orders in War Council meetings and depend on food tasters. "Soon after, our evening strolls became a highlight of my day, and I could not help but look forward to the next time we would meet. You are the epitome of the very song which entranced my heart. You are the sun that warms my weary heart and the stars that guide me through the darkest nights. You are the sea crashing against the shore and the vastness of the mountains I now call home. It would be the greatest blessing if I could be in your presence infinitely because you are all I have ever wanted. Even in the chaos of this war, you bring my heart peace." At least that's what she told herself—and him.

Behind them, several of their guests were weeping, dabbing their saturated cheeks with handkerchiefs. Ismenia and Daria were among them, shedding happy tears at the couple's heartfelt vows.

"And I hope to always bring you peace," Gerard said. "You have given me a home and a life I never could have imagined. We may not be the youngest couple to get married, but we still make the best-looking pair in any room, and you've given me hope that, even in my old age, I might one day have a family of my own." A few of their guests chuckled.

The high priest pressed his fingertips together and declared, "Such beautiful words. Love is a divine gift which offers us the chance to share in our joys, sorrows, hopes, failures, and every mundane moment between. Now, if you could produce the rings." Gerard released Elara's hand to pull two rings out of his coat pocket. The priest mumbled prayers to himself with his hand hovered over the gold bands as he blessed the rings. Then he plucked Gerard's ring from his hand and said, "Lord Stirling, you may seal your oath by placing this ring upon Her Majesty's hand."

Gerard grasped the gold band carefully between two fingers and held it up to Elara, who presented her left hand to him. Carefully, he slid the band up her finger and over her knuckle until it rested perfectly at its new home. She noticed the intricate etchings in the gold—two tiny birds with a pair of stars above them.

Like the crown she wore, this gold emblem felt heavy, like a fetter binding her from the freedoms and serenity her people knew better than she.

She loved Gerard, of course, but she couldn't ignore how trapped she felt within the City of Mercy. She wanted to feel safe with him, but his presence didn't erase the knowledge that someone close to her wanted her dead.

"Now we ask Lord Stirling to declare his devotion to our queen and our people," the priest said, bringing Elara back to the present moment. "Lord Stirling, if you may."

Gerard grinned and whispered, "I believe we have already done that."

Elara stifled a chuckle, reprimanding his cheekiness with the slightest shake of her head.

He continued aloud, "Elara Garrick, Queen of Hyrosencia, with this ring I make a promise to live out the remainder of my days by your side. I vow to keep you safe and to work unceasingly to take back the kingdom that belongs to you and your people. With this ring, I give myself to you as a partner and a subject of your kingdom. I will support you as best as I can while you lead your people through this fight, and I promise to remain in awe of you through every second of it. You are the queen Hyrosencia deserves, and now you are the queen of my heart as well." Elara smiled, and this time, it was sincere. Releasing his hand, she turned and accepted the other ring from the minister. Gerard held up his left hand and gazed deeply into her eyes. He mouthed silently, "I can't wait to kiss you."

Elara blushed as she lowered her eyes and pushed his wedding band onto his ring finger. His thicker band also featured the same symbols representing both of their homelands, and she reminded herself she wasn't alone anymore. His allegiance had come at a grave cost; still, he accepted the target on his back to become hers. He wasn't receiving a kingdom to rule; he was inheriting a war.

Nervously, she parted her lips and said, "Lord Gerard Stirling of the Eastern Isles, with this ring I vow to spend every day of my life with you until Divinity calls us to the stars. Until then, you will be my guiding light on earth, the rock which lends me strength, and I will give you all the best parts of me in return. I will grant you whatever you desire in exchange for leaving your homeland behind to live out your days in a foreign land. I am no stranger to being displaced from home and the homesickness that comes with it," she said, swallowing hard. "Though some days shall be hard, I will ensure you are always safe and warm, and I shall strive to make wherever we are truly feel like home to you. One day, I hope I will get to show you the Hyrosencia of my youth—a peaceful kingdom of plentiful resources and caring people."

"I think we should all like to join you in that glorious future, Your Majesty," the priest declared, gesturing to the crowd. Many nobles in the audience erupted into applause, clapping at the prospect of returning to their homeland. Elara and Gerard glanced to the side, smiling at their guests as they gripped each other's hands tightly. Raising his hands, the minister silenced the crowd and concluded, "Your vows have paid a proper tribute to your love and hopes for the future. On behalf of the High Estrellogy Temple of Symptee, I declare your nuptials blessed by Divinity. What you have vowed before these witnesses may only be broken when Divinity calls you to rest. Until that day, I declare that our beloved Queen Elara Garrick be wed now and for evermore to Lord Gerard Stirling of the Eastern Isles. You may now seal your union by kissing your beloved."

Grinning broadly, Gerard pulled Elara closer, wrapped one arm around her waist, and kissed her lips with ardent passion. They closed their eyes, ignoring the applause from their many guests, and embraced as if they were the only ones in the room. Finally parting and smiling at each other in a daze, Gerard took her hand and raised it as they turned to face their guests, who continued clapping as they waltzed down the steps and the aisle until they exited the hall.

FOR THE FIFTH TIME in two weeks, Sabine snuck Talitha out of the dungeon for afternoon tea by telling her favorite guard the prisoner was working to earn her freedom. The castle was bustling with many eager visitors. Children ran down the hall past them as Sabine led them from the sitting room to a mystery destination. "You are going to love today's activities," she informed Talitha, grinning knowingly.

Talitha frowned and fiddled with the thin chiffon dress that Sabine had insisted she wear. It was clearly a dress designed and tailored for the princess, as it was very snug in the chest, making Talitha self-conscious of the deep square neckline. The beige bodice was fitted with thick straps over her shoulders, and halfway down the flowing skirt, the color faded into a gorgeous rose pink.

They were joined again by Emmaline. The girl wore a dress with hundreds of wispy strands of burnt orange chiffon hanging down at different lengths. She smiled as she scurried along behind the princess. "I must admit I have been looking forward to the masque more than today."

Sabine rolled her eyes and said, "You do not have to stay the entire time. We must make appearances, and I have a few introductions to make. Then you may do as you please after the games." The princess skipped in flat shoes and a unique two-tone dress; the bodice was bright yellow, and the skirt featured a multitude of pink, red, and orange layered fabrics. Together, the three of them looked like the phases of a marvelous sunset.

As they rounded a corner, they entered a hallway with tall, arched openings to their right. Sunlight streamed through and illuminated their path. Talitha stopped in her tracks. The sunbeams were warm against her pale, exposed skin. Tears sprang to her eyes, and she gasped in shock. It had been two months since she had been kissed by the sun.

Sabine turned her head to the side and called, "Don't get all emotional now! Come on. The games are about to begin." The princess turned and continued walking toward the large open door ahead of her. Talitha sniffled and nodded her head.

"Are you crying?" Emmaline eyed Talitha.

"I'm sorry." She dabbed her eyes with the back of one hand as she walked quickly to catch up to them. "It's been... a long season. I have been feeling quite..."

"Homesick," Sabine declared, placing a supportive hand on Talitha's arm. Glancing at Emmaline, she added, "I'm sure you must miss your family on occasion."

"You know it's just my brother, and I see him plenty enough."

"What about your parents?" Talitha asked, picturing her mother's red hair and her father's thick, dark beard. "Surely you miss them."

Emmaline shrugged. She ran her fingers through her long blonde waves. "It's hard to miss what you can hardly remember. I was a child when they passed from the pox. That's why my brother enlisted, so he could afford to send me to boarding school. Now that I've aged out of school, I need to find a suitable husband."

"And that is why I have carefully selected a few prospects to introduce you ladies to today." Sabine stopped and looked down, smoothing her dress with her hand. "Stay by my side and act as if you are having a good time. It will be hot, but you can bathe later. Today is the start of the games, and it is as much an opportunity for the women as it is for the men competing. When the time comes, I will give you the chance to mingle with several gentlemen under the appropriate supervision. No matter what, do not do anything to ruin your reputation while you are representing me. If you do, any chance you had of marrying a decent man will disappear."

Emmaline replied with haste, "Of course, Your Highness. You are doing me a great service. I would never dishonor you by sullying my reputation."

Talitha shook her head and muttered, "I have no interest in meeting any nobles nor finding a match. The few men from Graynor I've met have all been quite unfortunate characters."

"Surely not all of them, Adelaide," Emmaline said with a chuckle.

Sabine grinned at Talitha, who stuttered, "Well, perhaps there has been one decent fellow, but I still do not wish to court anyone."

"I understand your sentiments, truly," Sabine said with a flourish of her hand. "Most boys are complete fools who allow the most basic of physical urges to rule them, and they lack the maturity us ladies are expected to always exhibit. Luckily you have me to tell you who would make a tolerable husband." She smirked as she marched through the doorway.

Talitha and Emmaline exchanged a quick glance before following behind her. As they stepped through the doorway onto a stone path, it took a moment for Talitha's eyes to adjust to the harsh sunlight. There was not a cloud in the sky. In the distance past a small garden was a great field bustling with people. There were several colorful canopies set up in a large circle to offer the richest and most prestigious guests an optimal view of the games.

Under the largest tent stood King Antoine with his wife. It was clear she was trying desperately to hold her husband's attention in a low-cut dress of vivid red silk. Antoine glanced her way, his eyes dancing over her exposed bosom as he wrapped one arm around her waist. As Chelsea smiled at the attention, his eyes trailed off to admire that of two other women under the same tent. She fanned herself slowly, feigning her smile for their guests.

Meanwhile, Anteros was busy talking with a group of his peers. The young men were all dressed in light khaki trousers and loose-fitting white shirts. Their sleeves were rolled up to their elbows in preparation for the games ahead. Anteros ran his fingers through his raven locks, brushing it back from his eyes. He laughed and gesticulated wildly at something one of his friends said.

Sabine paused, and Talitha stumbled into her, ripping her gaze away from the prince. Talitha grasped Emmaline's arm to stabilize herself. "Oh, my apologies."

Sabine scoffed, straightened her skirt, and shook her head. "You're drooling," the princess muttered. "Pull yourself together." Emmaline snickered as Talitha tried to hide her burning cheeks from view.

Stepping close behind Sabine, she whispered, "Do you not fear that your father will recognize me?"

"Do you?" Sabine laughed hysterically. But Talitha did not find it funny. The princess placed a hand on her shoulder. "My father met you, what? Twice? You are no one to him, and I am certain he would not recognize you. But Lady Adelaide, I'm sure he would find you quite lovely. Your father is one of his favorite trade partners. He would likely try to find you a husband." Sabine chuckled.

"All the more reason for me to avoid him," Talitha murmured. The skin between Talitha's thin eyebrows wrinkled as she scowled at the king from afar and crossed her arms over her chest.

"What's with you today?" Emmaline brushed past her to stand at Sabine's side. "I, for one, should love to meet the king! If he were to select my husband, it would be the greatest honor. He has the best connections."

Sabine scoffed. "Sadly, my father is not on the list for introductions today. We will be joining the nobles' daughters over there." She gestured toward the red canopy to the right of her parents. Pivoting their path, they continued the trek through the grass toward the tents.

Talitha sighed. She brushed a strand of her long copper locks behind one of her ears. "What games shall they be playing?" she asked from behind them.

Sabine grinned and clapped her hands together. "Sword fighting," she replied.

Talitha tensed. "Is there really nothing better to do than watch soldiers fight for sport?"

"Oh, the soldiers do not compete today. Soldiers and commoners participate later in the week. The first two days of the games are for the nobles," Sabine said as they reached the crimson canopy.

"Well, well, he's rather handsome," Emmaline said, nodding her head.

Sabine glanced in the same direction then rolled her eyes. "That is my brother. He is well out of your league, Emmaline. Try his friend Terion. He is the firstborn son of a Duke."

Emmaline pouted, but shifted her gaze from Anteros to his friends. Meanwhile, Talitha studied the prince, who stood mingling with several young men and women close in age. He seemed at ease as he polished his sword, and his dazzling smirk made the girl next to him giddy. She used a paper fan to cool her face while gently touching his forearm. He leaned closer to her, brushed hair back from her cheek, and whispered something close to her ear. Talitha's ears burned, and she shook her head, focusing instead on Sabine, who was already being swarmed.

"These are my new friends, Emmaline and Adelaide," the princess said, gesturing to the two ladies behind her. "Emmaline recently graduated from finishing school, and Adelaide is visiting from Denorfia. Her father is a prominent trade partner."

Talitha feigned a smile as two ladies greeted her with a slight bow of their heads. One young man offered his hand, and she hesitantly took it. "Percival Bryant, son of Duke Alden Bryant of Lettras," the young man said, kissing the top of her hand. "I would be honored to present you with a token should I win today's competition."

"Leave her alone, Perce. You are the least likely to win today." Anteros pushed his way past his peers to get a look at her. When his eyes fell on Talitha, they widened, and he stuttered, "Red?" Talitha yanked her hand back from Percival Bryant, her eyes wide as she realized Sabine had not informed him that his ward would be attending the games.

"We can all see she has red hair, brother. There is no need to announce it," Sabine chortled, drawing a laugh from their peers.

Talitha's heart raced, and she felt as though her entire face were on fire. Her lips parted, but her voice caught in her throat as Anteros stepped closer. She bit her lip, trying to come up with something appropriate for Adelaide to respond. "Brother, you said?" Talitha asked after a moment. Her eyes pleaded with Sabine for assistance. "So, this is the infamous crown prince of Hyrosencia then?"

"I did not know he was infamous," Sabine said with a hearty laugh. "But yes, this is my brother Anteros. Brother, this is Adelaide Winslow of Denorfia. Try not to scare her away. I quite like her company." She winked at Talitha before turning her attention to another friend.

Talitha slowly turned back to look at Anteros, who was admiring her attire with his arms crossed. He looked confused but boasted a cocky smirk on his lips as he blinked. His eyes quickly returned to hers again. "You are looking quite well, if I may say so."

Talitha's cheeks flushed as she glanced down at her dress, suddenly aware of how much of her bosom was on display. "This—It was a gift. Your sister has exquisite taste."

"She has always enjoyed the finer things." Anteros shook his head. Taking a step closer, he offered his hand to her, and she placed hers on top of it, watching him warily. "I must admit I'm surprised to see you here of all places," he whispered for only her ears.

"That makes two of us," she muttered through her faint smile.

Anteros wrapped her hand around his arm and asked, "Shall we promenade?"

Talitha nodded, relieved to be taken away from the cluster of people under the tent who were eyeing her like vultures. Several of the noble ladies whispered as they passed arm-in-arm, exiting the tent. He led her through the grass behind the circle of canopies, careful to go in the opposite direction from his parents. Once they were far enough from others' ears, Anteros glanced to the side and asked, "Are you at ease? My sister has a knack for toying with her new friends. I can get you out of here if you like. You do not have to comply with her reckless plans."

"I know that," Talitha said, finally relaxing her shoulders. "She is an unusual girl, but I am enjoying the daylight while I am blessed with it. I should not complain."

Anteros grimaced, and Talitha could feel the muscles in his arm tighten. "I should have been the one to do this. To get you out of there. I'm sorry I have not done more for you."

She pressed her free hand to his fist and patted it. "You have done more than enough for me already, and I am grateful for you both."

"But I can do more," Anteros insisted. He stared deeply into her eyes, and Talitha noticed how his hazel eyes glistened with determination. "I will. I will find a way to help you. I will make it all up to you somehow."

"You are not the person who put me in that dungeon," she murmured, glancing around. "I cannot expect you to do anything that might get you in serious trouble. I certainly never expected this much from your sister."

"Sabine does not fear our father the way she should," the young prince said, clenching his jaw. "She has always been so desperate for his attention, any attention, even if it ends up impacting her negatively. Be wary of her schemes. She's young and foolish."

Talitha laughed and said teasingly, "She has similar things to say about you."

Anteros sneered, squinting at his sister in the tent some feet behind them. "Pay her no mind. She's my little sister. She will always know way too much about my personal life since everyone at court gossips. She does not know everything, nor should she."

"I agree," Talitha said. Peering ahead, she realized there was a lake that had been obscured by the canopies in the field. The colorful tents next to the lake and forest were a most unusual and breathtaking sight. Seeing the lake reminded her of the river that flowed near Durmak and the forest to the south where she spent many mornings doing chores and talking to Serena. She wondered where her friend was and if she was safe. If she was still alive.

"What vexes you?"

Talitha took a deep breath, filling her lungs with the warm summer air. Blinking to suppress her tears, she warded off her thoughts of home and said, "It's nothing. Just homesick."

Anteros turned Talitha to face him. Taking in her fresh face and the faint jasmine and vanilla scent of her washed hair, he brushed his fingers against her forehead, pushing a stray strand behind her ear. Stepping closer to her, he grasped her waist firmly with one hand and said in a hushed voice, "Talitha Vise, this will not be the last you see of the sun. That I promise you."

His face was inches from her ear; his breath tickled her neck, sending shivers down her spine. Every little hair on her arms stood up, despite the stifling heat. Talitha leaned her head back slightly to look him in the eyes and said slowly, "I believe you." She gulped nervously.

Smirking, the prince released his grip on her, and she stumbled back, nearly falling as she tried to catch her balance. She laughed as she steadied herself, and the sound made Anteros grin. For a moment, Talitha had let her guard down.

A horn sounded from within the circle of tents, and the smile faded from her lips. Anteros shook his head and said, "That'll be the start of the games. I have to go now."

"I wish you didn't," Talitha admitted, watching as the other young men left their families to enter the competition. "Suppose I should go find your sister."

Anteros reached out his hand to her, and she took it. "Will you cheer for me?" he asked with a smirk before pressing his lips to her knuckles.

Talitha rolled her eyes and exhaled. "I suppose I have no choice. I do not know any of the other competitors. Except for that Percival fellow," she teased.

The prince released her hand and scowled. "I would be quite offended if you rooted for anyone else. It would be no surprise if I were to dedicate my triumph to you after our long promenade, would it, Lady Adelaide?" His eyes met hers, and she held her breath, remembering that she was playing the role of a foreign noble's daughter. "Would you accept such a thing?"

"Accept?" Talitha asked, aware that he needed to head toward the competition grounds. "I am sure Denorfia would be quite flattered if you found favor in one of their ladies. How could I refuse such an honor?"

The horn sounded again, and she could see the muscles in his neck tense. His grimace revealed that his time with her was up. Anteros stepped closer and pecked her on the cheek before running into the competition ground, leaving Talitha with her jaw on the ground and a hand pressed softly to her cheek. Glancing about, she thought they might have been fortunate enough that no one had seen his sudden display of affection, and she smiled to herself as she walked back to the crimson canopy to find Sabine and cheer for the prince.

THE HEIR'S BLADE

After their morning meal, Bandan Icebraid showed Serena, Will, and the guardians the Faswyn training grounds, a massive cavern carved within the mountain. The rock floor, covered in dry leaves and dead grass, barely lessened the impact when combatants slammed into the ground during practice. Serena lounged on a bench next to Cole, who busied himself sharpening his blade. Rigel was itching to spar with a new opponent after his defeat in Estivor and wouldn't stop saying as much. Although Crystal and Xandra were speaking again, Serena felt it would take time before their friendship was fully restored.

A hand brushed against the back of Serena's, drawing her attention away from the guardians. "Will," she breathed, jumping slightly. "I thought you were going to spar with Rigel?"

He chuckled. "Didn't mean to scare you. I wanted to ask if you'd like to spar with me. I know you've been taking it easy the last few days."

"Then who shall help Rigel work off all his extra energy?" Serena asked, laughing as she watched the guardian and Bandan engage in a friendly discussion about their favorite weapons.

"Perhaps our new ally will?" he suggested.

Rigel caught his eye and waved to them. "Come over here!" When the rest of his friends surrounded them, Rigel clapped Bandan on the shoulder and announced, "Our friend here was selected as one of the guards for the journey to Jordis."

"You must be quite the warrior then," Will said.

A cluster of nearby dwarfs snickered, and one commented, "Look at Icebraid—finally among his own kind."

Bandan hung his head and said, "This is the first task entrusted to me in many moons. Long have I wanted to join the ranks of our greatest warriors, but none saw fit to give me the chance—until my lady Rilura."

"You must have proven yourself to King Dranir before," Cole interjected, rising to his feet. "Do you not guard the Glovni?"

The other dwarfs chuckled maliciously. "Half-breeds are unfit for such an honor," one shouted with a smug grin.

Bandan was much taller and leaner compared to the typical dwarf stoutness. He more closely resembled humans than his own people.

"I'm afraid not. I am but a lowly recruit of the Fifth Regiment, used as but a messenger," Bandan said bitterly. "My kind see me as unfit for battle because I am built differently. The axe was once too heavy for my arms to wield, so I dedicated myself to swordsmanship instead."

"That's hogwash," Rigel said. "You're the same build as I am. If your people won't give you a fair shot, Queen Elara will! The Tournament of Guardians takes place when the leaves turn shades. If you follow us to Symptee, you could join our ranks by year's end."

"That's right. Take the half-breed with you. He'd fit better among your kind," another said, gruffly shouldering past the melancholy dwarf and knocking him back a few steps.

"But I have no interest in leaving my kind, cruel as they may be," Bandan said, holding his head higher. "These are my people. Dwarf blood runs through my veins as much as it runs through theirs. This task is my opportunity to prove my skills. I will rise in their ranks."

"Bandan, why do they call you half-breed?" Serena asked, her voice sympathetic as she glowered at the uncouth dwarfs preparing to duel near them.

"They believe me to be the bastard of a human, but my father claimed me. He never questioned my mother's faithfulness. This is how I was born. Still, many dwarfs cannot accept those who are different," the blond dwarf said, his bangs overshadowing his eyes. "Does the same go for humankind? And the elves?"

Cole glanced at Xandra, lowering his eyes the moment they met hers. Clenching his jaw, the elf said, "It is not so easy to veer off the path others expect you to follow. Perhaps half the struggle is accepting our variances in our own minds."

"He's right," Crystal said grimly. "It is hard to accept those who walk a different path, but that does not mean those people are undeserving of a chance at happiness or glory."

Rigel added, "I was a frail, half-starved human child, but your people took pity on me. Once I regained my strength, I worked tirelessly to become worthy of the Guard. Your plight to become a warrior is not in vain so long as you never succumb to the empty words of those who wish to see you fail."

"Demonstrate your skills for us. We are all well versed in swordplay. Even Serena and Will, thanks to our most recent scuffles. Show us and everyone here what you're capable of," Cole challenged. He lifted his black blade as an invitation.

"You cannot challenge him, Cole. An injury could be seen as an act of war between your people. We cannot risk that," Rigel said. "Fortunately, we humans are now aligned with the dwarfs, so we may duel freely."

Bandan swallowed and pulled his sword from his hip, saying, "Perhaps it's best none of us duel today. We should all be well rested for our early departure tomorrow."

"Scared to face me?" Rigel teased, taking a battle stance.

"I could put you on your back in an instant," the dwarf said. He pulled back his long hair. "But there be no purpose in injuring my new comrades. As I have heard, you have faced many swords already. Consider these days of peace a gift."

"That's a pleasant sentiment, Icebraid, but I live to spar," Rigel said. "If you are not up to the task, then who shall I face?"

"I'll spar with you!" Serena drew the attention of all her companions.

"Really?" A puzzled look crossed his face, and he lowered his sword to his side. "You don't have to. I can spar with Cole."

"I can handle it."

Crystal grinned as she nodded her approval. "If the girl wants to spar, give her a shot. It's past time she took training seriously."

"I know," Serena said. She was quick to unsheathe her father's sword. "I'm ready."

"Where did you get that?" a familiar looking dwarf with long light-brown hair demanded. He charged toward her from across the room. Serena froze, her eyes wide as she watched the hostile dwarf barreling toward her, but Cole and Rigel stepped between them with their weapons drawn. Crystal's hand wrapped around the hilt of the knife on her belt, prepared for trouble.

"We have no quarrels with you," Rigel said.

"You were there when we met the Steelcasts yesterday," Cole noted, glaring at the seething dwarf. "Who are you?"

"I am Martock Smeltbranch, general over our armies. That sword is unmistakably Dwarven. How did a human child come to wield it?"

"Dwarven?" Serena rested the blade on her open hand and inspected it. "You must be mistaken. This belonged to my father. He was a member of the Garrick Guard, long before the invasion."

Looking up, she realized a dozen dwarfs had swarmed around them, trying to get a better glimpse of her weapon, and Will had joined the four guardians in forming a protective circle around her. "How are you so certain of its origin?" he asked.

"There is no cause for alarm," Martock said, urging the other dwarfs to back away from the apprehensive warriors. However, an armor-clad dwarf with thick, dark brown braids poking out of his helmet stepped closer, peering between Rigel and Xandra at Serena's sword.

Martock stuck out his arm in front of the dwarf and said sternly, "What have you to say, Thovur? Do you recognize it?"

"My father forged this blade nearly a century ago. I was a youngling, but I remember it well," Thovur said, his deep voice trailing off into a whisper.

"His father was Thorgin Opalsunder, one of the greatest weapon forgers of the age," Martock informed their clueless visitors. Turning to Thovur, he asked, "Do you know what became of it?"

"'Twas commissioned by King Duthiol Steelcast, who led us to victory in the Great War. He dubbed it Sannarvin, the Heir's Blade. It was a gift for King Elias Garrick of Hyrosencia when our people began to trade wares."

Several of the dwarfs gasped, shoving forward to get a closer look. Serena held the blade upright and inspected it, asking, "If it belonged to the King of Hyrosencia, how did my father end up with it? He was but a knight."

"The sword was meant to remain within the Garrick line. How a commoner came to possess it, I cannot begin to imagine," Thovur said. He crossed his bulky arms. "My father swore no other blade compared to it. Sannarvin was his greatest creation, meant to defend a nation without yielding. He believed its owner would be unbeatable. Had our kings not been amicable, we would have never given such a powerful weapon to a human."

Xandra and Rigel glanced at each other, and then Xandra said, "It's lucky we found it in Serena's possession. Whoever challenges Rexton might need it."

"If what he says is true, I will gladly give it to the queen when we reach the City of Mercy," Serena said. She frowned at her reflection in the shining metal. It was the last piece of her father she had, but if it belonged to the Garrick family, she would return it to its rightful owner.

"Sannarvin will always find its way into the hands of the true heir to Hyrosencia's throne," Thovur said, bowing his head to the girl. "'Tis the will of a blessed blade."

Serena placed a firm hand on Rigel's back, pushing him out of her way. "Then my destiny must be to deliver it to Elara," she said thoughtfully. "But until then, Sannarvin will remain in my hands, as it was entrusted to my father."

Martock held his nose in the air and asked, "Is a girl of your stature even able to wield such a powerful weapon?"

Serena grinned and gripped the jeweled hilt with both hands. Planting her feet with bended knees, she lifted her hands to her left cheekbone. The blade extended parallel to her eyes. Her heartbeat quickened as she said, "You dare insult my skills before you've seen them?"

The guardians widened their eyes at Serena's brazenness. Quickly, Bandan Icebraid stepped toward Serena and said, "I think we would all like to see the Heir's Blade in action, and your friend has been dying for a fight."

Rigel grinned as he glanced at the dwarfs around them. "Everybody back up please. It's time we show our hosts what humans of this age can do."

Everyone strode backward, forming a wide circle around Rigel and Serena in the center of the training grounds. She closed her eyes and breathed in deeply. Her heart raced as her lungs filled with the musty mountain air. When she opened her eyes, Rigel was circling her with a confident smile on his face.

"Certain you're up for this?" he teased.

She rolled her eyes, catching a view of Will in her peripheral. His eyes were locked on her, his jaw square and tense. Her lips curled upward as she turned her attention back to her opponent and said, "I am not so naïve as I once was. I killed one of Rexton's men. Remember? I know what it takes to be a warrior now. I won't hold back."

Rigel chuckled. "Hold back? I am your mentor. I'm the one who's been holding back."

Serena narrowed her eyes and sidestepped in the same direction as Rigel. As they moved in a circular motion, the two slowly closed the distance between them, both waiting for the other to go on the offensive. After a moment, Rigel sighed and said, "Suppose I'll go first then." Rushing forward, he swung his blade toward her arm, and Serena planted her feet firmly, lifting her blade to counter his move. Their swords clanged together repeatedly as Rigel swung his blade at her three times in succession. Each time, Serena moved swiftly to block his attack. The fourth time he swung at her, she bent at the waist, swooping down to avoid contact with his weapon.

"Nice reflexes," Xandra called out.

As she felt the whoosh of his blade passing her, Serena lifted her head and kicked out one leg, slamming Rigel in the stomach and sending him stumbling back. As he staggered, he released one hand from his sword's hilt.

In this moment, Serena seized the opportunity to go on the offensive, charging at him and swiping her blade at his right hand. Rigel leapt back, narrowly avoiding the strike, and grinned. "You fight with such zeal today."

"Scared?" Serena taunted. Then she stepped forward and thrust her weapon at him.

He laughed, rolling his shoulder back to evade the blow. "You wish," Rigel said with a grin. "But I am impressed."

Serena pivoted, turning in a full circle, and swung her sword around with full force. Rigel held his blade up, deflecting the powerful swing. She gripped the hilt of Sannarvin, pressing hard against the steel of his blade. "I appreciate the compliment," she said through gritted teeth.

Suddenly, her back slammed against the rock floor, knocking the breath out of her lungs. Serena gasped, blinking at the stalactites as she realized Rigel had swept her off her feet when she least expected it. Her head pounded, and she thought she heard her name being called in the distance. Feeling the vibration of Rigel's footsteps approaching, she pushed her head back to look behind her. Her eyes widened as she quickly rolled to the side, narrowly avoiding Rigel's blade as it came down. He missed, and his blade clanged onto the ground.

"Rigel!" Crystal yelled. "Don't hurt her!"

He chuckled, glancing back at the concerned elf, and said, "There isn't a scratch on her yet! She's stronger than you think."

While Rigel was distracted, Serena pressed both hands to the ground. She lifted her torso and swung her legs around, knocking her opponent off his feet. As his legs flew up and his body became parallel to the ground, Serena snatched her sword off the ground and hurled herself on top of Rigel right as he hit the ground. She dug one knee into his chest and held her sword against the side of his neck. "You have made a fatal error, my friend. Your distraction has led to my victory."

The guardian blinked up at her from his back, his eyes shifting from the blade over him to her. "You beat me," Rigel muttered incredulously, entranced by the girl hovering over him. Serena breathed heavy, sweat dripping down her face as she held her position, continuing to press the cold metal blade against his skin, despite his forfeit.

Feeling a hand on her shoulder, Serena snapped her head to look at its owner. Xandra squeezed her shoulder and said, "My, how you've improved, Serena! I cannot believe you defeated the magnificent Rigel DeVarr." She chuckled as she extended a hand to her.

Serena's face softened, and she unclenched her jaw. Slowly she pulled Sannarvin back from Rigel, taking Xandra's hand and rising to her feet.

"That's not fair," he muttered. He sat up and rubbed his sore neck. "My superior addressed me mid battle. I cannot believe Crys was so worried about her. She nearly took my head off."

"I would never," Serena replied with an eye roll. She sheathed her sword with a smile, feeling proud of her accomplishment. "I respect you too much to kill you."

"I am pleased to see your progress," Cole said, stepping toward Serena. "You held your own against the soldiers, but this is the first time you've bested any of us."

She nodded and whispered, "I was ashamed that I took a life, but now I know. It was necessary, and I would do it again. No one else is getting hurt trying to protect me. I can defend myself."

Will stepped beside Serena and traced his fingers along the back of her arm. "I didn't know you had that in you." She smiled a shy smile, happy to have impressed him.

"This is your idea of a duel?" Martock asked. He crossed his arms and glared disdainfully at the pleased humans.

Cole offered Rigel a hand getting up. Rigel glared at the Dwarf General. "When we found her, Serena was unable to protect herself. Now she has the strength and confidence to defend herself... and others. It has been a privilege to watch her grow into such a capable warrior in such a short time." Serena beamed. It was one thing to be proud of herself; it was another to know she had made the elite guardians proud.

"Sannarvin symbolizes the strength and honor of Hyrosencia," said Thovur. "This girl has proven herself worthy to carry such a weapon, even if it is borrowed for a time."

"Serena is worthy," Xandra said. "She's not just any refugee. She had to claw her way out of Hyrosencia. Despite all that tyrant took from her, she keeps fighting. She knew nothing when we met her, but now she is a fighter. If she is not worthy to carry Sannarvin, no one is."

The dwarfs began disbursing, some leaving the training grounds while others prepared for their own duels. Martock turned his back to them, engaging in private conversation with Thovur Opalsunder. Then a dwarf clad in head-to-toe armor entered the grounds, his eyes fixed on their visitors. He marched over to them, pausing a few feet away from Rigel and bowing briefly.

"May we help you?" Crystal asked, approaching the soldier.

Bandan turned to the dwarf and smiled. "Thomli! What brings you here? I thought you were preparing for our departure tomorrow."

"My things are prepared," Thomli said in a gravelly voice. "King Dranir wishes to speak with the Hyrosencians again. He would like to present them with a gift for their queen."

"A gift for Elara? Could his ambassadors not bring it themselves?" Cole asked.

"His Majesty wishes to bestow it upon her appointed guardians," Thomli said, and his black eyes showed no hint of emotion.

Bandan turned to the guardians and said, "Thomli Orefury is a member of the Steelguard, a selected protector of our royalty and the Glovni. It is an honored position. If they have sent him to fetch you, we should report to the king with haste."

"Rigel and I will go," Crystal said. "The rest of you can stay behind to practice."

"His Majesty requested that your ward be present," Thomli added.

"Me?" Serena asked in surprise. "But I'm not even a guardian. I'm no one, really."

"We are all someone, young lady. Please come with me," the guard insisted. The he turned and marched toward the exit.

Crystal waved a hand and said, "Come along then, Serena. I'm sure there is nothing to worry about. He seemed to like you in our meeting yesterday."

"He said she reminded him of Elara when she was that age," Rigel said. Crystal nudged him, glaring pointedly at her comrade.

Crystal, Rigel, and Serena left the others at the training grounds, following the Steelguard through the maze of underground tunnels until they reached the throne room. When they entered, they found King Dranir joined by his two children and Eldvar Cragjaw, Captain of the Second Regiment.

"Welcome," Dranir proclaimed, leaping down from his throne. "Come closer, please. I have an important task for you."

Rilura dipped her head as she said, "Thank you for fetching our guests, Thomli." The guard bowed his head, but his steady gaze never leaving the Dwarf Princess. She withdrew her eyes first and looked instead to their guests. "'Tis good to see you all once more. Be ye well rested?" Rilura eyed Rigel and Serena, both of whom had worked up a sweat.

"We are appreciative of your continued hospitality. We especially enjoyed the use of your training grounds this morning," Crystal said as she approached the royals with caution. "Your guard said you have a gift for Queen Elara?"

"Yes, she is soon to be wed, correct?" the Dwarf King asked, and Crystal nodded. "Good, good. This shall be a gift for the couple then. Long may they reign."

Dranir turned to his daughter, who handed him something large wrapped in a deep blue cloth. He unfolded it, revealing a sheathed broadsword. Grasping the hilt with the cloth, he drew the sword and held it up to the torchlight. The pristine metal reflected a beam of light across the room. "This is Mäkarlek, the Blade of Everlasting Devotion. Forged to match your queen in beauty and unwavering loyalty. Notice the sapphires and amethyst gemstones in the hilt, representing the alliance between your people and the Eastern Isles," Dranir said proudly.

Rigel smiled crookedly, stepping closer to gawk at the beautiful blade. "What a magnificent sword. Queen Elara is sure to be pleased with it, Your Majesty," he said.

"I should like the girl you rescued to present it to Elara personally," Dranir said, his steady eyes fixed on Serena. "You are familiar with the queen, correct?"

"Familiar?" Serena asked with uncertainty. "I have never met her in person, though she knew my parents long ago. That's why she sent guardians in search of us."

"I believe the guardians said Elara sent them to recover the last of those she called family," Rilura said with a smile.

"If she cares enough to send guardians after you, it should be by your hands that she receives this. That is my wish," the Dwarf King said, sheathing the sword and rewrapping it in the blue cloth. Stepping forward, he extended both hands toward Serena with the wrapped gift laying on his open palms.

Speechless, Serena looked to Crystal for encouragement, and the guardian said, "It would be our pleasure to present this to Queen Elara on your behalf. Serena shall take extra care of it, won't you?" She caught the girl's eyes and tilted her head forward.

"Yes, I am honored you place your trust in me," Serena said, accepting the sword from his hands. Holding it gingerly in both palms, she added, "Thank you for your hospitality toward us and our queen. Hyrosencia is eternally grateful for your friendship, King Dranir."

Pleased, the Dwarf King grinned as he waddled back to his throne. "We have been peaceful neighbors for over a century, and never did the Garricks move against us. For that, we owe our friendship and more."

Eldvar stepped closer to the king and said, "I ask that I be excused, my king. I should like to look over the preparations myself before we leave at dawn."

"Very well," Dranir said, waving the captain off with a chubby hand. "You may all leave me now. You as well, Thomli. Rest this eve, for you shall have no other rest until you reach the safety of the pass."

"Yes, Your Majesty," Thomli said, pounding his chest as he bowed. When he looked up, his intense gaze fell on Rilura before departing.

"I shall retire as well, Father," she said, stooping to kiss him on his cheek.

"I wish to look upon your face once more before you depart," the king whispered to his daughter. "Shall you join your brother and I for supper?"

Rilura smiled and nodded. "I would not miss it, Father."

As she turned and walked toward the rear exit of the throne room, Eldvar Cragjaw stomped after her. From the hall outside, they could hear her rebuke him, "I do not need an escort, Eldvar. Go your own way."

"We shall take our leave as well," Crystal said, bowing her head.

"This shall be the last I see of you," Dranir said. "Keep a sharp eye on the path to Jordis. Dangers far worse than men lie ahead. You would do well not to get distracted."

"We shall remain vigilant," Rigel said, giving a low bow.

Serena swallowed, feeling a sudden tightness in her chest, and she wondered what foul beasts awaited them in the thick of the Athamar Mountains. Gripping Mäkarlek in her fists, she followed the guardians out of the throne room with a look of uncertainty on her face.

"You look worried," Rigel said in the tunnels, nudging Serena.

"His warning," she whispered. "It feels like a bad omen. I fear something terrible awaits us."

"Nothing we cannot handle," Crystal assured. "You are far more adept with a sword than when we started this journey. The dwarfs will brief us when we leave tomorrow, and whatever lies ahead, we will face it."

"And we will not be alone," Rigel added. "We'll have five dwarfs with us. They know the land, and they're absolute legends in battle."

Serena nodded, loosening her grip on the sword. "I hope you're right," she murmured.

ELARA JOLTED UPRIGHT IN her bed. Her chest ached as she breathed heavily, her fingers digging into the bedsheets. Gerard grasped her hand and asked blearily, "What's happened? Are you okay, my love?"

"I think I had another vision," Elara whispered, pressing one hand to her abdomen. Though she was not yet showing, she felt the heaviness of carrying the next Garrick heir in her heart. With every ache of her tired bones, she wondered whether she would live to meet their child.

"It was likely just a nightmare," her husband said. He settled his head back onto the pillow.

Tossing back the covers, the queen swung her legs out of bed and stepped down, the floor cool against her bare feet as she padded across the room. "I need to see Idonea," she said, searching for something to wear over her nightdress.

As she clasped a violet cloak at the neck, Gerard threw the sheets back and leapt off the bed, running after her. "Elara, dearest, it's the middle of the night. The sun has yet to rise over the mountains." He grabbed her by the arm, gently pulling her back toward their bed.

"That does not matter now!" Elara tugged her arm from his grasp.

Gerard paused, realizing all the color had drained from her cheeks.

"Something is wrong," she whispered, her eyes glistening in the dim moonlight.

He sighed, his shoulders dropping as he gave up arguing with her. He could see the fear etched across her face. "If it cannot wait, at least allow me to accompany you," he said as he pulled a shirt over his head.

Elara propelled herself into his arms, pressing her cheek against his chest. "I'm sorry, my love. I do not wish to bother you."

"It is never a bother to be by your side."

"Thank you," she said, lifting her head to meet his gaze. "Ismenia said sometimes her sister is restless at night. As Idonea is the only person with this gift, I need her opinion, should she be capable of giving one."

"I'm not arguing," Gerard said with a tired smile, raising his hands in resignation. "You are the queen, after all."

Elara rolled her eyes. "I wish I wasn't," she mumbled irritably, drawing away from her husband. She slipped into a delicate pair of satin slippers before opening the bedroom door and ordering her night guards to escort them to the Infirmary.

When they reached the citadel's medicinal wing, Elara was surprised to find Ismenia asleep in a chair next to her sister's bed. Her eyes blinked open, and she licked her dry lips. "Your Majesty?"

"Is, what are you doing here? Surely you can't sleep here every night," Elara said, patting her friend on the back.

The herbalist stood and stretched her arms above her head, little popping noises coming from her tired body. Her brown eyes were bloodshot as though she had not slept all week. "I did not intend to fall asleep, milady," Ismenia said, rubbing her neck. "Is it morning?"

"No," Gerard said abruptly. "But Elara could not sleep without seeing your sister." He nodded toward Idonea, who was sound asleep on her back in the Infirmary bed, her bald head still wrapped in bandages.

Lines appeared between Ismenia's eyebrows as she glanced from the queen to her sister. "She is resting, milady. Perhaps it could wait until morning?" Ismenia suggested.

Elara sighed and nodded. "I am sorry we woke you," she whispered, grasping her friend's hand. "I do not think I shall manage to sleep again tonight. I could stay with her if you would like to retire to your chambers?"

Gerard's lips parted in protest, but before he could argue, Idonea whispered hoarsely, "I do not think I have ever been so popular in all my life."

They all turned their eyes to the oracle as she tried to sit up. Ismenia lurched forward, one hand on her sister and the other adjusting her pillow. "Be careful, Idonea! You are still recovering."

"You exaggerate my condition," Idonea said. Her familiar dry humor put them both at ease. "It's been well over a week."

"You have a head wound," Elara said, blinking at her friend. "Listen to your sister. If she says you should rest, rest."

Idonea rolled her eyes, leaning back against her pillow. "I've done nothing but sleep all week."

"And still no visions?" Ismenia asked quietly.

Elara glanced hesitantly at her guards and commanded, "You may wait in the hall." The guards bowed their heads before marching out of the Infirmary. The healer on night watch scurried after them, leaving Elara and Gerard to converse with the Cinderfell sisters in private. Gerard pulled another chair next to Ismenia and motioned for his wife to sit. Elara smiled, squeezed his hand, and situated herself beside her friends.

"I had another dream that felt real," Elara began, rubbing her hands together on her lap. "I can only compare it to what I saw when I fell sick with the fever weeks ago. I think it was a vision, something that will come to pass as Bea's death did."

Ismenia glanced nervously at her sister, who pursed her lips and nodded. "What did you see?" Idonea asked pensively.

Elara closed her eyes and inhaled deeply. "There was a large wolf. Fur white as the snow. It was charging toward me. As it leapt into the air, I thought surely it was about to kill me. Then I awoke."

"That could just be a nightmare," Gerard noted. He crossed his arms over his chest as he loomed behind them. "You know the guardians should be returning any day."

"I would not make a fuss if it was like any other dream. This was different," Elara scoffed. "It must have been a vision. I just do not understand. Why now? Have you ever known someone to attain a divine gift so late in life?"

"No," Idonea murmured, staring straight ahead at the far wall. "I suspect it is not your gift at all. Divine abilities take root in the pure of heart, most often children."

"That's right," Ismenia whispered, turning to look at Elara's abdomen.

Pressing a hand to her stomach, the queen asked, "You think our child has been blessed with the gift of sight? Then why would I—"

"Your child must be a great prophet of Divinity if their ability is coming through in your dreams," Idonea said with a grin. "Surely this child will be quite special."

"Of course," Gerard joked, squeezing his wife's shoulder. "A child of Garrick and Islander blood is doubly blessed."

Elara shook her head. "Have you ever known another oracle to have this prenatal effect on their mother?"

"I was taught that it was a possibility, that one woman once believed the same during her pregnancy. However, there was never any recorded evidence of it in our manuscripts," Idonea said. "This shall be a rare case, one for our history books."

"Why did it make me so ill the first time but not this time?" Elara wondered, rubbing her tiny bump through her nightgown.

Idonea closed her eyes and shrugged. "I can only guess, milady."

"Perhaps your body was adjusting to both the infant and the toll of its divine ability," Ismenia suggested. Her forehead wrinkled in dismay. "It's been a few weeks, so I suppose your body has built up the strength to maintain itself during visions."

"That is likely why these images come while you sleep. Essentially, you're unguarded as you rest," Idonea said. "The state of relaxation paves the way for divine visions. It's why most oracles spend so much time in quiet meditation in the sanctuary."

Gerard appeared cross at their assumptions. "Can this divine ability harm her?" He clenched his jaw, looking down at his wife.

"I do not believe so, my lord," Idonea said with confidence. "She seems perfectly well after this latest event."

Ismenia leaned over the arm of her chair and pressed the back of her hand to Elara's forehead. "No fever, thankfully." She flopped back into her seat with a relieved sigh.

"What can we do with this information?" Elara asked. "How can I see these terrible things and not try to stop them?"

"Sadly, there will be times when nothing can be done," Idonea said. "Especially if this vision involved the guardians crossing the mountains. We have no way to know where or when the event will transpire. The most you could do is send a squadron up to Silvermane to see if there's been any news of them. They could warn the dwarfs of an impending attack by the beasts."

Elara zeroed in on her friend and pushed herself onto her feet. "That's it! The Guard. We must send a knight's squadron at once."

"It's the middle of the night," Gerard reminded her. He pressed one hand firmly against the small of her back. "At first light, we can summon the Council and make the preparations."

Elara hung her head and leaned back against his shoulder. Her eyes drooped as she nodded. "Yes, in the morning," she mumbled.

Ismenia rose and bowed her head. "Please return to bed, Elara. You must be sure to rest as well. You carry the next heir to the throne. You must maintain your health for the baby's sake."

"I agree," her husband chimed in, giving her arm a light squeeze. "You need your rest." He pecked the top of her head with his lips. "So do both of your friends."

Idonea chuckled. "I should like to read for a while." Locking eyes with her sister, she added, "You should return to your chambers. I promise I shall be fine without your constant vigilance."

Ismenia's frown was interrupted by a drawn-out yawn, which she attempted to cover with her hands. "My apologies," she said. "I suppose you are right. My bed is much preferable to this chair."

"Good eve, ladies," Elara said with a gentle smile. Relief washed over her seeing the oracle on the mend after two difficult weeks.

"Good night," they both replied.

Elara left the Infirmary arm in arm with her husband, and Ismenia followed close behind them. The guards escorted them through the dimly lit hallway, and Ismenia parted ways with them when they reached her chambers. As Elara laid her head on her pillow, she sighed, the back of her eyelids imprinted with the image of the white wolf's fangs. She feared that it was already too late to warn the guardians of the danger lurking in the mountains, and her unease kept her from returning to sleep.

DARK CLOUDS ROLLED IN, casting a harsh shadow over the snowcapped peaks. Crystal stopped and said, "We have lost the light. We should set up camp for the night."

"There still be light. We keep moving," insisted Eldvar Cragjaw.

The leader of the guardians sighed loudly, plopping her bag into the thin layer of hard-packed snow underfoot. "No, we will not," Crystal spat at the dwarf. "Night has come early, and King Dranir warned of dangers in these mountains. We should start a fire."

"I do not take orders from the likes of you," Eldvar snapped. Clenching his fists at his side, he scowled at the elf.

"That's enough," said Martock sharply. He squeezed Eldvar's shoulder. "The guardian is right. Conditions are unfavorable. Let the women rest. We can resume our journey at first light."

Eldvar turned, yanking his arm out of his superior's grasp, and stormed away from the rest of the group. Rilura stepped closer to the faction of humans and elves, offering them an encouraging smile. "Please ignore Eldvar's brashness. He has never liked taking orders from anyone, dwarfs included," Rilura said, putting down a large knapsack.

Serena shivered and pulled her cloak tight around her body. She watched as Thomli pulled out a thick blanket and laid it down on the snow for Rilura to sit. She patted the blanket next to her and said, "Come join me, Serena. You must be freezing."

Serena approached the female dwarf, whose smile put her at ease. Taking a seat next to her, Serena looked up at the rest of their party: five dwarfs, four humans, and two elves in total. "Never in my life did I think I should travel among elves and dwarfs, and here I am outnumbered by them," she said with a chuckle.

"You are blessed indeed to be on such a journey. Few of your kind have the honor of meeting both our races in their lifetimes, much less seeing us work together," said Bandan as he began setting up a tent.

"Far fewer have the honor of traveling amongst royalty," Thomli said, draping another blanket over the princess' shoulders.

Crystal exhaled and said halfheartedly, "Yes, we are blessed to be in the presence of a great Steelcast descendant. Long may your kin reign over the mountain."

Rigel shook his head, smirking as he began unpacking supplies. Cole helped set up their temporary shelter, while Will kept his eyes locked on Serena.

"Do you know how far we are from Jordis?" Serena asked.

Rilura leaned closer and draped half of her blanket over Serena. As she relished in the extra warmth, the Dwarf Princess said, "Of that, I am uncertain. This is the first time I have left Faswyn or even the Glovni. I am still surprised my father allowed it."

"We should reach Jordis the day after tomorrow if the weather is in our favor," Martock said without looking at them. Behind Rilura and Serena, the Steelguard members were busy setting up pallets for the dwarfs to sleep on.

"We would have reached it tomorrow had we not been slowed down," scoffed Eldvar, who stood the farthest from their travel companions.

"What nonsense. I certainly could not have walked any faster," Rilura said, pursing her lips at the shrewd red-haired captain.

Once the sleeping arrangements were prepared, Thomli aided the humans in the difficult task of starting a fire in the snowy terrain. The dwarfs carried more than enough supplies to build a fire and eat a hearty meal on each night of their journey. The weary travelers quickly ate their provisions around the warmth of the fire, each relieved to know it would be their second-to-last night sleeping in the frigid mountain air.

As the humans bundled up and prepared to enter their tents, Thomli asked, "Have you been informed of what may lie ahead?"

Rilura glanced back at her guards to no reply.

"They have nothing to fear on this night. We are still too far," Eldvar said irritably. Turning to the Dwarf Princess, his demeanor softened, and he offered her a hand. "Should you need anything, you know where to find me."

She stared at his hand for a moment before looking him directly in the eyes and saying, "Eldvar, I do not believe I should have any further use of you tonight. You may leave us." His ears turned a deep crimson, and he stomped off into the darkness.

Serena watched Martock roll his eyes. Standing, the general stared into the dancing flames and stroked his beard thoughtfully. "Long ago, Ranor Steelcast rid the mountains of the last dragon. Free from this threat, the dragon's lair was made into Jordis, the greatest of the mountain cities. From Jordis, expansive tunnels offer safe passage to Silvermane, the last of the Stålfä-stad cities."

"Stålfä-stad? What does that mean?" Serena asked.

Rilura smiled. "Excuse Martock. It's easy to forget not everyone knows our people's rich history," said the princess. "Long ago there were eight dwarf clans. After the Great War, the five clans settled on this mountain merged into Stålfästad, forming one clan ruled over by the Steelcast heir."

"And what of the other three clans?" Will asked.

"The three in the southern mountains merged into clan Smält-rok. We are not in close contact with those brethren."

"They need only hear of our mountains for now," Martock said bluntly.

"Very well, General," the Dwarf Princess said with a sigh. Leaning forward, she added in a hushed tone, "I can tell you more another time if you'd like," and Serena nodded eagerly.

"The general is right. They need to know the dangers of this mount before they come face-to-face with the beasts," Thomli said, glancing at the princess with a grin.

"Beasts?" Serena asked, turning concerned eyes upon the guardians.

"After the fall of the last dragon, a pack of dire wolves moved in on the northern part of these mountains," Martock said. "These be no ordinary wolves. We call them the Mørkewulv."

"They are monstrous—large, lethal beasts with unrivaled strength," added Bandan. "Their teeth can tear through the thickest armor and rip flesh from bone. They prowl the land around Jordis in perpetual hunt."

"Why have your people not cleared the area of these beasts?" Crystal asked. "Surely an army of your best warriors could defeat a pack of dire wolves?"

"Many have tried, but all were outmatched," Thomli said. He lowered his head. "Some of the beasts have been killed, others injured. Ultimately, it was not worth sending more of our people to their deaths. The beasts hibernate when it's warmer. That's why you were fortunate not to cross them on your first crossing."

"So it's just our luck that it's snowing in June," Xandra said, shaking her head.

"How many could there be?" Cole asked, draping an arm around her.

"At least a dozen, though the Mørkewulv do not have a typical pack mentality. In the past, dwarfs have witnessed as few as two together," said Thomli. "If you reach Jordis without drawing the beasts' attention, you are among the lucky few."

"And there is no way around them?" Serena asked, her heart pounding as her mind raced.

"Not if you wish to go north. The underground pass is the safest route to your queen, if you can reach Jordis in one piece," Bandan said.

"Now, men, let's not scare them. The pass they roam is expansive, and years pass between incidents," Rilura interrupted, rising to her feet. "We should all sleep in peace knowing we are at a safe distance, and odds are we shall never face such foes."

"Agreed," Bandan said with a grim smile. "I'll take the first watch."

The remainder of the shivering bodies stood and slogged toward their respective beds. The guardians had set up two larger tents for their party of six—one for the women and one for the men. As they approached their cozy quarters for the evening, Rigel squeezed Serena's shoulder. "Don't be afraid. If we were to encounter anything on our way, they would never get near you. We would not allow it."

"Thanks," Serena muttered, ducking into the women's tent.

In their small shelter, Crystal and Xandra slept on either side of Serena, facing away from her. Though she was tired, Serena was restless, rolling back and forth in vain attempts to grow comfortable. "Serena," Crystal said with a heavy sigh. "Do not allow fear to deprive you of such vital rest. We still have two long days ahead."

"The dwarfs only meant to warn us. There is no cause for alarm. There are eleven among us, each with suitable skills. Should anything happen, we shall be fine," Xandra said.

Still, Serena was alarmed; nothing the guardians could say would change that. As they listened to the whirring wind batter their tent, they each succumbed to their exhaustion. The howling of the monsters lurking on the snowcapped hills ahead haunted Serena's slumber.

MASQUERADE

When the Solstice games were over, Sabine once again snuck Talitha up to her chambers with a suspicious smile painted across her carnation pink lips. "You certainly cannot be seen in this condition. The bath is being prepared, and the maids are waiting to tend to you. When they are done, I daresay my brother shall be speechless," Sabine said with a wink.

Talitha exhaled loudly as they entered the girl's personal quarters. "I am not a doll for you to play with. I am a prisoner. We should not be doing this. Your father will have my head," she said, turning back toward the door and reaching for the handle.

Sabine's heels clacked loudly against the tile floor as she rushed to intercept Talitha. Beating her to the door, Sabine turned the lock and sighed. Turning to face the detainee, the princess insisted, "Please indulge me. I offer you a night of freedom from that dismal dungeon. Would you not prefer clean clothes and a warm bed? I can give you that and more, and my father shall never know of our fun."

"Tonight is the ball you've been raving about?"

"Yes," Sabine said, twirling her long brunette curls with her pointer finger. "You must attend. Everyone expects Adelaide to be there."

"You are mad!"

"There is no need to worry," Sabine said. "Not even my father would cause a scene and ruin this night. The Summer Solstice is our most sacred day."

"I don't know the first thing about your holy days, Princess. My family does not worship the sun," Talitha said hastily, fiddling with the mangled slip dress she had slept in all week. "I don't know why you would even want me there. I have nothing to offer. I don't even know how to dance. Not the way a noble would."

"Oh, come on. Adelaide is from Denorfia. No one would expect her to know anything about our customs." Sabine rolled her eyes. "Besides, it would not make sense for Adelaide Winslow to have traveled all the way to Graynor and leave before the masque, so you must go."

Talitha crossed her arms. "If you insist. How do you intend to hide me from the king this time? Surely the guards will report my prolonged absence from the dungeon."

"You sweet, naïve girl. The guards have been handled. Stop worrying," Sabine said. "You are Adelaide Winslow of Denorfia. Act like you belong here."

"Someone will notice an imposter posing as a noble's daughter."

"Alas, Adelaide has never graced our court before," the princess said coolly. "The only people who know what she looks like are the ones you met earlier this week."

"And what if the real Adelaide shows up at court?"

Sabine reached for her wardrobe and held up a letter before reading it aloud. "Lord Soren Winslow sadly sends his deepest regrets to His Royal Highness King Antoine Rexton for being unable to attend his Solstice ball as his wife has become terribly ill." Sabine crumpled the letter up and chucked it over her shoulder, laughing. "The forgery my father received states that he is sending his daughter in his stead. He hopes the king shall allow her to befriend his children during her first time at court."

Talitha's eyes widened in horror. "If your father saw me, he would recognize me. He would know I'm not Adelaide. Anteros wouldn't possibly agree to this."

"Yet he did," Sabine said, rolling her eyes. "We are offering you a night of freedom. You can eat, drink, and socialize with no worries. You can sleep in a proper bed tonight. Then Adelaide shall leave in the morning, and all shall be as it was."

"Why do you want me there so badly? You must have friends at court."

"Because you do not deserve to be caged for loyalty to your friend. I would do anything to have a friend half as loyal as you," Sabine said, taking her by the hands. "The ladies at court are all untrustworthy gossips and whores. They cling to my side in hopes of catching my brother's eye."

"I wish that were the greatest of my problems. My closest friend disappeared without a word of goodbye, and your father is looking for her. I don't even know if she's still alive," Talitha whispered, plopping on a plush chaise.

Sabine squeezed onto the seat beside her, placing a hand on the girl's shoulder. "I'm sorry about your friend. I would help you find her if I could."

"Thanks," Talitha mumbled.

"You seem like a nice girl. I hate seeing you waste away in the dungeon for no good reason. I thought the party would help cheer you up," Sabine said. "Plus, Anteros will be happy to see you."

"Why should your brother's happiness matter to me?"

"It doesn't have to," Sabine stuttered. "I just thought you would like to see him, too. You both seemed so at ease with each other the other day." The princess shot a questioning look at Talitha.

"Your brother is charming, but I'm sure he is like that with all women," Talitha said. She avoided Sabine's bright eyes as memories from their promenade before the games flashed across her mind. "It doesn't matter if he finds me amusing. When I'm gone, he'll find someone else to entertain him. There is no future for me here. The longer I'm trapped in these walls, the more likely I am to lose my head."

The princess groaned. "I cannot free you tonight, but perhaps one day. For now, though, I can offer you a chance to be treated like a lady instead of a prisoner." She leapt up and extended her hand to Talitha, who brushed her grimy fingertips against the palm of Sabine's pale, delicate hand. "Could you at least pretend to trust me, Red?"

Talitha wrinkled her nose. "Please don't call me that. You know my name."

Sabine's shoulders drooped. "Sorry. That's all Anteros ever calls you."

Talitha ran her fingers through her greasy hair and took a deep breath. "If you can promise your plan is foolproof, then I suppose I can be Adelaide for one more night."

Sabine squealed in delight, dragging Talitha off the chaise and pulling her toward the lavatory where two maids and a warm bath awaited her. As the maids descended upon Talitha, Sabine slipped out of the room.

An hour later, the princess returned, clapping her hands with a pleased smile on her face. "You look stunning," she declared, approaching the mirror where Talitha gazed at her appearance.

Her hair was pinned up with only a few loose strands framing her face. Seeing herself in the emerald gown made her feel uneasy. "I may be dressed like a noble, but this shall not fool anyone up close." She traced her fingers over the faint white scars on her forearms, taking notice of a few fingernails that had yet to grow back. Then she inspected her dry elbows and cracked hands.

"Luckily for us, it's a masquerade ball," Sabine said, holding up long black silk gloves and a lace-covered mask that perfectly matched the gorgeous green gown.

Talitha shook her head slowly, grinning as she realized Sabine had planned for everything. "You really are a mastermind," she murmured. She accepted the accessories from her ally. Talitha made quick work of pulling the gloves on. Holding the mask up to her face, she inspected the complete ensemble in the mirror. With the mask, she could hardly recognize herself, which somehow eased the butterflies in her stomach. Now she was ready for what was sure to be the most interesting and extravagant night of her life.

ANTEROS REXTON ENTERED THE ballroom in an all-black ensemble. His dark hair was combed back from his face, and he wore a black mask made to resemble the face of a fox. Though it was not his first choice, Sabine had insisted he wear it. Scanning the room, he saw no trace of his sister, who would no doubt be the center of attention upon her arrival. Spotting his mother by the grotesque display of her chest, he approached her, kissing her cheek before saying, "This is quite a turnout. Did you bribe the ambassadors to attend?"

Chelsea Rexton pursed her lips, rubbed her hands against her champagne-colored chiffon gown, and ignored her son. Anteros tried not to laugh out loud at her mask, on which the great white neck of a swan wrapped around her left eye with its beak resting below her right eye. She turned up her nose and muttered through her fake smile, "Your sister knows how to socialize. Perhaps you could learn from her if you quit spending all your time with those imbeciles." She glared at the young men across the room shamelessly flirting with young noble ladies.

"Come now, Mother. My friends are harmless," Anteros said. He shoved his hands into his pants pockets. "Do not fault us for having fun while we are young. You once knew how to have fun yourself."

"I hope we can arrange a suitable match for you soon. Perhaps when you have a family of your own, you will take your responsibilities more seriously," she said without looking at him.

"I have no interest in anyone you would choose for me." His voice was hushed as he overlooked the many shrouded faces in the ballroom. Several heads were turned toward the main doors, where a group of young ladies had just entered. In the center was his sister Sabine; that was unmistakable. Her black curls were the first indication, followed by her bright pink dress. Her big blue eyes were perfectly framed within two magnificent golden butterfly wings.

As his eyes raked over her companions, he paused on the girl to Sabine's left. Her pale arms peeked through the gap between her long black gloves and the straps of her deep green gown. Though a black lace-covered mask concealed half her face, he immediately recognized the blue-gray eyes scanning the room in awe. Unexpectedly, her eyes met his, and Talitha pressed her pink-painted lips together.

Without another word to his mother, Anteros strode across the room. When he reached his sister, he greeted her. "My darling sister, you command the room as always. There is quite a turnout this year. Father should be pleased. Is everything to your liking?"

"Yes, Anteros, everything looks splendid, but we already knew I would do an excellent job," Sabine said. Then she smirked as she noticed his eyes fixed on Talitha. "I'm sure you did not walk all the way over here just to flatter me."

"You know me too well, sister," the prince said without taking his eyes off Talitha. "I have come to welcome your new friends."

"Of course you did. I believe you met Emmaline and Adelaide before the games," Sabine said, placing a gentle hand on the small of Talitha's back. "Adelaide joins us from Denorfia."

Emmaline bowed her head to Anteros, but he did not shift his gaze to acknowledge her. Instead, he reached for Talitha's hand and lifted it to his lips. Flashing his winning smile, he paused and said, "Yes, I remember Adelaide." Then he bowed his head and kissed the top of her hand. "It is a pleasure to see you again, miss." Emmaline tossed her blonde hair over one shoulder and charged off.

Talitha pulled back her hand, lowering her eyes as she curtsied to the prince. "The pleasure is all mine, Your Highness."

"Anteros, please," he said with haste. "No need to be so formal."

"This is her first visit to Graynor. We must show her the best time, so she will want to return," Sabine said, giving her brother a wicked grin. "You should take her for a turn later."

"No, thank you," Talitha blurted out, stepping back from him. "I don't know how. Dancing is so different where I am from. I should much prefer to watch."

"You worry for naught," the princess reassured her. She wrapped her thin fingers around Talitha's wrist and dragged her reluctant friend further into the ballroom. "I'm sure my brother would gladly teach you."

Talitha bit her lip, raising her eyes slowly as she glanced back at Anteros. "Please do not make a fuss over me. I really do not mind watching."

Sabine released her arm and exhaled. "If you insist." She rolled her eyes. "Have fun watching then." Then the princess curled her lips in a fake smile as she lifted her gown in both hands, turned on her heels, and charged toward the center of the room.

Anteros watched with furrowed brows as his friend led his sister away to dance, muttering "Julian" under his breath as he glared at their backs, cracking his knuckles one by one. Sabine and her partner took their positions for a processional dance, and several couples lined up on either side of them. The men bowed and the women curtsied before joining hands for a fast paced waltz.

"You seem quite protective of your sister," Talitha said as they watched the ladies twirl about the room.

"Someone has to be." Anteros slowly peeled his scrutinizing eyes from Sabine to look at Talitha. When their eyes met, his face softened.

Talitha stepped closer to Anteros. "You're a good brother." One corner of her mouth turned up in a faint smile.

"Not good enough." His eyes fell to the floor. "I try to keep her out of our father's wrath, but sometimes it's impossible to keep ahead of her."

Talitha reached out and grazed her hand against his forearm, the cool silk of her glove caused the hairs on the back of his neck to stand on edge. Her pleasant floral scent intoxicated him. She smelled like all the other girls at court, but when he closed his eyes, he pictured the girl sitting on the dungeon floor. "I am pleased she has befriended you, Red."

"Do not address me so informally," Talitha pleaded, her nervous eyes darting back to the dance floor. The beaming princess continued to promenade across the ballroom, oblivious to their conversation. "Tonight I am a lady. Lady Adelaide Winslow of Denorfia," she said. "Treat me as you would any lady that you have just met for the first time."

He grinned as his hungry eyes raked up her lace-covered gown, eating up the slight curve of her hips and chest. "Be careful what you ask for, Lady Adelaide," he said softly, grasping her waist. "Especially when you look like this."

Her eyes widened as he pulled her closer, and she quickly shoved his hand off her waist. "Anteros," she gasped, and her cheeks flushed as her eyes darted about the room. She glowered at him. Rubbing her hand along the front of her skirt, she whispered, "And here I thought you were better than all the other brutes I've met."

"Don't be angry. I was only teasing you," he said. His smile faded as he studied Talitha's cross expression.

"Well, you are certainly living up to your reputation, aren't you?"

"I fear I must apologize. I truly meant you no offense. Seeing you like this surprised me."

She fidgeted with the top of one of her gloves while watching the noble ladies and gentlemen twirl around. "You weren't expecting to see me here, were you?" she whispered. Though she grasped her hands together, Anteros noticed their trembling.

"I wasn't, but it was a welcome surprise," he admitted, his fist gently touching her under the chin. "Fortunately, my sister seems to have thought this through more than her usual schemes, and I am glad of that."

Talitha flinched away from his touch, sidestepping to put more space between them. "Blazing embers, that girl can tell a convincing lie," she muttered. She glowered at Sabine. "I certainly hope she did not learn that skill from you."

Anteros frowned, sulking for the remainder of the song. When everyone around them began clapping at the conclusion of the waltz, they both reluctantly joined in their applause. Another song began, and Sabine remained on the dance floor, selecting her next partner from the lines of swarming suitors. Anteros leaned closer to Talitha and asked, "Now that you have seen some of my world, what do you think of it?"

Talitha glanced at him uneasily. "Court is extravagant. There is so much richness here. The food, the fine clothes, the music. I'm surprised you waste any time in the dungeon." Talitha watched Sabine laugh at something her partner said.

"I have wasted time on many foolish people at this court, and I can assure you the girl in the dungeon is no waste of my time," he whispered back, smiling as he traced the back of his fingers against her bare forearm. She shivered but did not move away as he brushed a stray hair behind her ear. Her eyes danced between him and the people surrounding them.

"Do you not have your sights set on some unsuspecting noble's daughter? I hear you can be quite the charmer."

"I am quite content with the lady beside me," he said casually. Then he grinned when he noticed her ears were as red as her hair.

"Do not jest," Talitha pleaded, her voice dropping to the faintest whisper. "I cannot help but feel that this is the most dangerous place I've ever been. I daresay I felt safer in the dungeon."

"Are you still scared of me after all this time?" Anteros lowered his chin as he narrowed the gap between their faces. "I am greatly offended by that."

"Your sister is playing a dangerous game, and I do not like it," murmured Talitha. "What will happen when your father—"

"My father shall never know you were here," Anteros interrupted. He stared at her with great intensity. "He would never recognize you. He has seen you three times in so many months, and you're perfectly safe beneath this mask." He paused, brushing his fingers along the place where her mask cut off along her cheek. "Stop worrying. I promise you will be fine."

"Somehow that does not bring me comfort," she said with a scoff. "I feel like a child playing dress up."

"You play the part well."

The second song ended, and the ballroom erupted into applause once more. Anteros and Talitha both turned their attention back to Sabine, who was reveling in the attention she was receiving from two eager suitors. As an upbeat tune began, the princess rushed toward them and grabbed Talitha by the hands. "Adelaide, you must dance to this one! It's easy to follow. I can show you," she insisted. Talitha glanced back at the prince, her wide eyes pleading for help as his sister dragged her away.

He followed after them without hesitation. He grabbed his sister's arm to stop her. When she whipped around, he insisted, "Allow me. You have a trail of suitable partners waiting."

Sabine released the girl with a smug grin. As she turned away from them, she shouted back, "Try not to step on her toes!"

Anteros brushed his fingers lightly against Talitha's forearm, trailing down to hold her gloved hand. "Shall we?" he asked, and she nodded, allowing him to lead her to the middle of the ballroom. "Just breathe," Anteros whispered. He stopped once he was in line with the other men dancing. He guided Talitha to stand facing him at arms' distance and dropped her hand. She took a deep breath and nodded, biting her lip as her eyes glanced behind him. Many nobles in gilded masks stood watching the dancers from the outer edges of the great hall. Anteros cleared his throat as he bowed his head, bringing her attention back to him. The men took two steps toward their partners. Closing the gap between them, Anteros whispered to her, "Think of this dance like a mirror. Try to match my steps."

The other dancing ladies stepped forward, and each couple held their right hands up, pressing their palms together. Without hesitation, Talitha stepped forward and held up her right hand, meeting Anteros in the middle. For the first time, she did not shy away from his touch, and the prince counted this no small victory.

"Let me lead you," he whispered. He studied her pale face and focused expression with quiet intensity. She stood before him like stalked prey as they circled each other, their hands pressed firmly together.

Talitha whispered, "People are staring. I can feel their eyes on me."

"Pay them no mind. They watch all of us."

"Do they stare because I'm dancing with you?"

"They stare because you are the most stunning girl in the room," he said, pulling back his right hand from hers. Leaning closer, Anteros whispered, "Do not tell Sabine I said that."

Talitha chuckled, and her shy smile accentuated her flushed cheeks. "Prince Anteros, you are quite bold. Do you use that line often?"

"There is a first time for everything, milady," Anteros said, winking. He playfully lifted his eyebrows before grasping her waist and hoisting her in the air, spinning her around slowly. As he lowered Talitha back onto her feet, he noticed a change in her demeanor. She placed her hands on his chest as her feet hit the floor, and she didn't rush to step away from him. Her eyes twinkled in a way he had never seen before. "Am I mistaken or are you enjoying yourself?" he asked.

Anteros held up his left hand, and Talitha placed hers firmly against his. "You and your sister have been so welcoming. It's almost easy to forget I don't belong here."

"The way you look tonight, no one is saying that you do not belong here," he said, circling her counterclockwise.

"You shouldn't say such things."

"You should know I'm harmless," he said. "Do you still not trust me after all this time?"

"As a foreigner and a lady, I must be careful who I trust," she struggled to say. He wrapped his fingers around her hand and pulled her close to his chest. Staring at him, Talitha swallowed and said, "I want to trust you. There is no one else I could possibly trust in Graynor."

Anteros quickly twirled her around. "That is untrue. You somehow made a second friend at court," he said, nodding toward his sister dancing beside them.

"I'm not so certain I can trust her. Her motives remain unclear," Talitha said.

The prince leaned close and whispered, "I question her motives as well, but rest assured, she is harmless. Knowing she has brought you here in secret must give her a thrill." He nodded for her to turn and face the back of the couple next to them, and the couples began to move in a circle around the ballroom.

"Well, it has put my stomach in knots," Talitha said. "The king would have my head if he discovered I was here."

"I would never allow that." He paused in the middle of their promenade to address her concern. "You are my responsibility. If I take the blame, you will be spared. I can get away with far worse than my sister."

"And your sister would get away blameless," Talitha whispered, nodding her head for them to keep moving. "You should not take the brunt of your father's anger for her games."

"Sabine brought you here on her own, but I have allowed you to remain because I trust you will not do anything foolish. My sister enjoys causing trouble because our father is unkind to her. She finds pleasure in his failures, as do I at times."

"Failures? He assassinated the prior king and has ruled this land ever since."

Anteros wrinkled his forehead, and he squeezed her hand tighter. "I am aware of how the commoners feel, Tal—Adelaide, but you should not say such things aloud. Not here. We cannot change the past."

"But you have more power than any commoner. You could change things now."

"There is not much that can be done without my father's knowledge," Anteros said swiftly.

"And yet here I am," Talitha said through her teeth.

The couples stopped, and the men faced their partners, taking them by both hands. With one hand, the prince entwined their fingers. With his other, he placed Talitha's hand on his shoulder before taking hold of her waist. Anteros stepped forward, and she took a wobbly step backward, squeezing his hand and upper arm apprehensively. "Relax," he whispered. "I've got you. Just follow my lead."

Bright, colorful skirts swept across the floor as the men led the women in circles. As the music quickened, the men pulled their hands back from their partners' waists. Holding their clasped hands up, they led the ladies to the side and strolled in two lines around the center of the ballroom. The women turned until their backs faced their partners, and the men wrapped their arms around their waists from behind.

Anteros breathed in the sweet scent lingering on her skin. Her breathing became heavy as the prince brought his left hand up to brush her bare shoulder, tracing down her skin, over the strap to her gown and the elbow-high silk gloves until he met her hand. For a moment, they swayed to the romantic melody. Talitha closed her eyes, taking a deep breath as they moved together. Releasing her waist, Anteros lifted her arm toward the heavens, turning her twice in front of him. When she was facing him again, he released her hand, grasping her by the waist with both hands. Then she was in the air again. The men lowered their partners to the floor in a smooth display of strength.

Applause erupted as the music concluded, and the couples on the dance floor began to disburse. Talitha clutched his jacket for support. Anteros leaned closer, his cheek brushing against hers as he whispered, "Are you all right?" She nodded, loosening her grip on his clothes.

"That was divine!" Sabine exclaimed, bouncing up to them. Anteros relinquished his hold on Talitha, though his eyes remained fixed on her. "I knew you should be able to follow that one. It is one of my favorites. Makes you feel alive. Am I right, Adelaide?"

Talitha gradually dragged her gaze from Anteros to his sister. She blinked at the giddy girl. "Yes, that was—It was unlike any dancing I ever experienced back home," she whispered. "Thank you."

Sabine clapped her hands gleefully and said to her brother, "I am so happy you led Adelaide in her first dance at court. Perhaps it shall not be her last." Pleased with herself, the princess rushed off to speak with a group of her friends.

"Let's find something to drink," Anteros said, pressing one hand against the small of her back. Talitha nodded again, allowing him to lead her toward the horde of other guests at the ball. Anteros procured two goblets of wine from a servant, then watched as she scanned the room. Handing a glass to her, the prince said, "My father has not yet arrived. You will know when he does. They shall announce his grand entrance, and everyone will bow to their king. We can find a quiet corner in the back of the room if you would like."

"I would appreciate that," she murmured, taking a small sip from her cup. "Even if he did not recognize me, I would not like to come face-to-face with him again anytime soon. He is far more terrifying than the rest of your family."

Anteros laughed and said, "You have yet to meet my mother." He grinned as he took a large swig from his goblet. Creases appeared on Talitha's forehead, and she took another sip of the bitter red wine.

As the prince had warned, trumpets heralded King Antoine's entrance moments later, and a hush fell over the crowd as everyone turned to bow at the doorway. A massive jewel-encrusted crown perched atop his jet-back hair, and a white fur-lined cape dragged the floor behind him. Even from afar, the king's powerful presence was palpable. "Welcome, my distinguished guests, to our Solstice celebration," his voice boomed throughout the hall.

Chelsea was the first to rise and rushed to greet the king, but he remained cold and unmoving in the woman's presence. "There's my mother," Anteros said, taking another large sip. His father nonchalantly browsed the room. Talitha shrank back. She stepped into the shadows behind Anteros. Recognizing the fear in her eyes, he turned and touched her waist gently. "I must greet my father, shake a few hands. Then I can get you out of here. Stay back here, and I shall return soon."

She nodded, biting her lip as the prince turned and worked his way through the guests. Minutes later, another servant came by offering hors d'oeuvres. Talitha took one of the thin bread slices topped with cured meat and cheese and popped the entire morsel into her mouth. She grabbed two more from the tray, earning an odd look from the servant. "She had a long journey from Denorfia," Anteros told the servant as he reappeared by her side. "You must be starved," he said as Talitha covered her mouth with a hand. She nodded sheepishly. Turning back to the server, the prince said, "When you return to the kitchen, have someone bring a few plates from the feast to my chambers." The servant nodded and walked away from them, offering the last few pieces on his tray to guests before hurrying from the ballroom.

"Your chambers?" Talitha's voice was hushed. She crossed her arms in front of her body.

"I thought you did not wish to stick around with my father here?"

"What shall your sister say if I disappear?"

"She knows you are with me." He glanced back at his sister. The young princess was beaming as she spoke to two young men dressed in fine suits. "I suspect that was her intention all along."

Once Antoine and Chelsea had made their way to the massive thrones at the front of the ballroom, Anteros took Talitha by the hand and led her along the edge of the room to the exit. Slipping through the doorway, he could feel the searing gazes of scorned women and knew Talitha must, as well. In the hall were a few nobles and their teenaged children. They were all wrapped up in a heated discussion of who had the best chances of a marriage with the king's heirs. Anteros gritted his teeth and quickly stormed past them. He slowed his pace as they entered a quiet hallway, and then they rounded a corner and walked until they reached a grand stairwell. Talitha paused, and Anteros turned back to look down at her from the second step. "Come, Adelaide. Food awaits," he said, squeezing her hand. She nodded and followed close behind.

The second floor was silent; not a soul passed them in the hall. Anteros slowed his pace to wait for Talitha to catch up. She reluctantly walked faster, falling in step by his side as they passed several doors. "It seems everyone is at the masque," he said with a grin.

"Everyone?" She dropped his hand and stood frozen in the middle of the hallway.

"Yes." Anteros stopped just shy of a large door embellished with gold filigree to look at her. "Come on. You are safe with me. I promise." He held out his hand, urging her to trust him.

She stared at him, seemingly uncertain for a moment, but his hand never wavered. Finally, she placed her hand on top of his and allowed him to lead her into his chambers. He closed the door behind them with a loud clack of the lock. Talitha slowly stepped deeper into his private chambers, caught sight of the grand bed on the far side of the room, and turned pale.

Anteros sauntered across the room to a chest of drawers, atop which was a slew of crystal decanters filled with wine and other spirits. "Would you like another drink?" he asked as he held up two empty chalices.

Talitha watched as he poured a glass of crimson wine. When he glanced back at her expecting an answer, she stuttered, "Whatever you recommend."

Anteros handed her the first glass, and she took a long sip from it. As he poured his own glass, he said, "This is from the year Stellan Garrick was born. They would have opened these when he was crowned king, but now there is no use holding onto it." Talitha coughed, lowering her glass to stare at the sanguine liquid. Breathing in shakily, she charged for the glass doors to Anteros' balcony and peered through them, gripping the stem of the goblet with white knuckles. The prince joined her, grasping the handle and thrusting the door open. "The view is far greater from out here," he said, leading her out onto the balcony. He leaned against the thick stones of the parapet overlooking the castle grounds.

Talitha inched forward with slow and hesitant steps. "How can you look down on the world and not be afraid of falling?"

Anteros turned toward her. He rested one arm against the stone ledge and smirked. "Because when the stone is strong, there is nothing to fear. From where I'm standing, I see only beauty." Talitha flushed, taking another swig of the dead prince's wine.

Anteros set his glass down on the chest-high stone barrier before taking hold of the fabric concealing half of his face and finally removing it. He sighed as he laid the fox mask on the edge of the balcony, the black ribbons cascading off the side. Talitha studied his bare face and smiled. Taking a few steps toward him, she reached out and traced the faint red lines on his cheeks with her fingertips. "There's the face I've come to know," she said. "You look far kinder without the fox looming over you."

Anteros grinned, his eyes focused on her cracked lips. It was a shame, he thought, that someone so beautiful could be doomed to that dismal dungeon. He'd have to ask Sabine to see to it that Talitha received some ointment for her dry skin. "Allow me," he said, taking her glass and placing it next to his on the balcony ledge. Then he grasped the sides of her mask and gently pulled it up over her head. His hands dropped back to his sides, and he held the mask loosely in his left hand. Staring into her eyes, Anteros brushed his thumb against her cheek and said, "Somehow, you continue to surprise me, Talitha."

Her mask fluttered to the ground as he slipped his fingers into her hair and pulled her body against his. Talitha tensed at first, bracing her hands against his chest. But he felt her melt into his arms as his lips touched hers. He kissed her softly at first. Then, as she leaned in and kissed him back, he could rein in his passion no more.

For a second, their lips parted, letting the humid summer air fill their lungs as his heart beat wildly in his ears. They gazed at each other wordlessly through half-hooded eyes. Anteros took in every strand of her beautiful hair and fair skin, reveling in having her close. When she did not push him away, he pulled her closer and kissed her with even more ardent passion.

Then, Talitha's eyes snapped open. She pressed her hands firmly against the prince's chest, forcing him to pull apart from her. Pushing his chest away, she pleaded, "Anteros, wait. I—I can't—"

"Just kiss me," he said with a grin as he brought his lips back to hers. But he felt her body stiffen as he lifted her off her feet. With no warning, she bit down hard on his bottom lip. He cursed, dropping her abruptly, but she managed to land on her feet. He pressed a hand to his lips and glanced at the blood on his fingertips in disbelief. "Blazing embers, Red. That hurt."

"Is this why your sister cleaned me up? So you can pretend I'm one of your whores for a night?" she asked furiously, and he saw the way her body shook with anger or fear. Perhaps both.

"No. It's not like that," he said, wincing as he dabbed his shirt against his bleeding lip. "I thought there was something between us. You kissed me back." Watching her shrink away from him, he sighed and said, "I'm sorry if I scared you. You should know by now I would never force anything on you. I thought you knew that."

"I shouldn't have come here," Talitha said, blinking as tears filled her eyes. "You don't know the pain I've endured or the dread that lingers. Those men took so much from me. They stole my peace of mind, and I'm afraid I'll never get it back. Not so long as I'm trapped here."

"I'm sorry I've upset you." Anteros stepped closer. Talitha shrank back against the balcony wall, and he stopped short, his arms falling to his sides.

"You will never know who I truly am because even I can't find her. But I can assure you that ball gowns and castles are not me." Tears trickled down her rosy cheeks. "This is all a façade. You only want me because you know you shouldn't. No part of me belongs here."

"That is not true," he said, stepping closer. "How can you say I do not know you? Never have I known anyone as well as you. You are brave, loyal, and resilient. The strongest woman I have ever met. I have seen you at your lowest, and all I saw was your strength. Ball gown or rags, you enchant me just the same. It is you that I know, and it is you that I want, Talitha."

She sniffled. "That cannot be true. I am your father's prisoner."

"But it is," he said, stepping closer and cupping her face in his hands. "Please don't cry. I did not mean to upset you. I only wanted you to have a good night."

"I have lost count of the days I've been here, Anteros." She clenched her eyes shut. "You and your sister have shown me kindness, but that is not enough. The dungeon, that is no place to live. I cannot keep living like this. I don't belong in a dungeon, nor in your bedchamber. I belong on a farm in Durmak. I belong with my family."

"I know. You're right," Anteros said. He brushed a streak of tears across her cheek. "I asked earlier if you trust me. Is your answer the same?"

Talitha considered the question as she gazed into his eyes. She shook her head and whispered, "I'm trying to."

"I will find a way to free you. I promise. I just need more time." He wrapped his arms protectively around her. "Don't fret. I will figure something out. I always do," he whispered, resting his hand on the back of her head.

Talitha blinked, then wiped her cheek with the back of her hand. "I feel like I am losing my mind."

"I am quite experienced with crazy people, and I promise you aren't there yet," Anteros said. Talitha chuckled faintly as she pulled back from him. "Here," he said, handing her a small white handkerchief with a red letter *A* embroidered on the corner.

Talitha's eyes glistened as she looked up at him. "You keep surprising me." One corner of her mouth curved upward in an uneasy smile.

"I hope that's a good thing." He leaned his head closer and paused inches from her face. His eyes glanced longingly at her lips. She squeezed her eyes closed, gasping in surprise as he pressed his swollen lips against her forehead. "You should eat. You need your strength." He scooped up both of their glasses in one hand, their masks with his other, and walked them over to the bar counter. He downed the rest of his wine before asking, "Water?"

"Yes, please," Talitha said, shuffling back into his chambers and quietly closing the balcony doors behind them. She followed the mouthwatering scent of baked ham and roasted vegetables over to Anteros' sitting area, where two plates awaited them. Her stomach gurgled, and she pressed a hand to her abdomen.

Anteros joined her, setting two glasses of water on the table as he perched in a chair. "Please help yourself, milady," he said, gesturing with one hand toward their dinner.

Talitha tried to hold back a smile as she rolled her eyes and took a seat in the chair beside him. They ate in silence, stealing glances while they enjoyed the food that had been carefully prepared for the Solstice ball. "Your cook really is magnificent," Talitha said as she stuffed her mouth with another bite of rich, creamy pasta.

Anteros chuckled, then washed down the meal with the rest of his water. As the last bit of sunlight dipped below the tree line outside, he got up and lit the lantern on the table nearest the sofa. He turned to find Talitha swiping her last piece of bread through the remnants on her plate. She popped it into her mouth with a satisfied sigh.

"You have had quite the eventful day," he said with a grin and shoved his hands in his pockets. "Tell me, did you enjoy your first Solstice ball? I enjoyed taking you for a turn around the dance floor."

Talitha shook her head. "I did enjoy the dancing, though it would have been much more enjoyable if your father had not attended."

Anteros sputtered, and his grin grew broader. "I think the entire castle would agree with you on that," he said. "It's getting late. We should probably get some sleep."

Talitha swallowed, and her eyes shifted to the massive canopy bed behind them. Seeing the uncertainty in her cool eyes, Anteros said, "You can have my bed. I will not disturb you." He took her hand and dragged her over to it. She avoided his eyes, but he could see the blush spreading across her face. "You're safe with me," he whispered, brushing his thumb over her cheek before hoisting her up onto his bed.

She flopped back on his mattress, sighing as his bedding cushioned her back. "Have I died?" she asked as she spread her arms out on the soft linen. "Surely I have known no such comfort as this in all my life."

Anteros frowned as he helped draw the sheets over her legs. "I am doing everything in my power to keep you alive." His eyes raked over her gown. "Will you be comfortable in that? I can call for a maid if you should wish to change."

Talitha flushed as his heated gaze met hers. "Anything is better than the dungeon—even a corset," she said, turning away from him. "If you could loosen the laces, I should sleep just fine."

Anteros swallowed as he stepped closer, slowly reaching for her corset strings. Sabine's maids had done an excellent job of tying her in, and he bumbled with the knots for a few minutes before successfully untying them. As he pulled the back of her gown loose, Talitha inhaled and said, "That's better." She rolled onto her back to look at him; her arms crossed over the top of her dress to keep it in place. "Thank you, Anteros."

He licked his bottom lip and nodded, his eyes dropping to the floor as he stepped back from his bed. "Of course. Get some sleep. I'll have to sneak you back downstairs before breakfast."

Talitha nodded, situating herself so she had an unhindered view of the sitting area. The prince peeled off his embroidered suit jacket and vest, tossing them over a chair on his way to the sofa. Aware she was watching him, Anteros made a show of slowly pulling his black shirt over his head, and he grinned when she squeezed her eyes shut. He fluffed a small pillow and stuffed it under his head. Then, the prince winked as he said, "Good night, Talitha."

He blew out the lantern that sat on the table beside him as she whispered back, "Good night." Though it was pitch black, he stared intently at his guest, fighting the urge to crawl in bed beside her. If anyone could save her from Antoine Rexton's clutches, it was him. As he watched her drift to sleep, he knew he had to find a way.

29
TRAITORS

Lowering the two papers to meet Richard's bloodshot eyes, Elara asked, "How did you find this, Captain?"

He clasped his hands behind his back. He looked her in the eyes as he answered, "It was in the middle of a stack of papers I was given to post. He must have included it by mistake."

"Can we be certain it's his handwriting?" Elara asked, lowering her chin as she compared the swoop of each *g* and the curve of each *m*. The writing was the same as the first time she looked down—a perfect match. Her jaw was clenched so tight her teeth ached; her stomach twisted in knots. She closed her eyes, letting the papers float to rest on the desk between them, but the letters continued dancing behind her eyelids, making her head spin.

The captain swallowed, his somber expression matching the hefty accusation he was making. "I was not certain," Richard admitted. "That's why I brought it to the commander."

Alexander hummed as he leaned over the desk, drawing the handwriting samples and the letter in question closer. While some pages featured notes from prior War Council meetings, one was more damning. Though not addressed to anyone, the report detailed weaknesses at the citadel, ways men could sneak in undetected. Alexander rubbed a hand over his face and exhaled. "It seems to be a perfect match," he proclaimed. His eyes cut to the man standing behind the queen. "What do you think, Lord Stirling?"

Gerard leaned over his wife's shoulder and dragged the letters closer with two fingers. His eyes danced over the letters in search of any discrepancy but found none. "I would also believe these were written by the same man," he said. He shifted his hand from the dry parchment onto Elara's shoulder. Alexander nodded, refocusing on the queen.

She stared at the commander; her eyes were wide with worry as she took in shallow breaths. "How could we not have known? Zeke has been with us from the start." Her words trailed off as she pictured the man in question's sleek blond ponytail.

"I do not know, milady. But this evidence is quite damning," Alexander said as he straightened his spine. "How do you wish to approach this, Your Majesty?"

Elara's head spun. One of her own captains might have betrayed them. Betrayed her. He was likely the one behind the attempted assassination. A man who had lived within her refuge and advised her every decision for years. Her stomach lurched, and she barely whirled away from the desk in time to vomit in the corner, her shoulders shuddering as she pressed a clammy palm into the wall for support.

"Elara," Gerard exclaimed as all three men stepped toward her.

"Are you all right, my queen?" Richard asked hesitantly.

Gerard shouldered past the captain and rubbed her back as she breathed heavily, still hunched over the putrid evidence of her anxiety. "You should lay down." He attempted to coax her toward the door.

Elara turned slowly, wiping the corner of her mouth with her wrist. "No," she said firmly. "Zeke must be dealt with before he realizes his error." She turned to face the commander and captain. "Convene the Council in the great hall in half an hour."

The men blinked at her with pity and concern in their eyes. Alexander unclasped his hands and said, "Perhaps we should determine a course of action. Investigate his chambers for further evidence first?"

"No need. The letter is evidence enough. All four of us can attest that the handwriting matches," she said, pausing to take a deep breath. "Gather the Council. We shall hear what he has to say."

"Yes, Your Majesty," Alexander and Richard said in tandem. The bowed then marched from the room.

As she brushed off her skirt, searching it for signs of her illness, Gerard stepped in front of her and blocked her path to the door. "Do not stress yourself over this, darling. It's not good for the baby. The commander can handle this nasty business. You need only rest."

She glared at him. "I am queen. I must be the one to deal with this gross betrayal." Brushing his arm aside, she lifted her skirt in a white-knuckle grip and started toward the doorway.

Gerard scoffed, grabbing her arm to stop her from walking away. "I may not be king, but I'm still your husband. And the father of the child growing within you. I don't want you taking on any more than you must. You know well what stress can do in this situation."

Elara flinched. She felt the blood drain from her face and turned to stare at her husband. Though he meant well, his words were like a dagger to her chest—a reminder that she had been inadequate in her prime and not all blessings are meant to remain. "You may be my husband, but I am Queen of Hyrosencia. I do not need to be coddled." She yanked her arm away from him.

Gerard's face fell as she turned away from him. "Elara, I didn't mean—"

"You have said enough," she said, her voice cracking. The beading on her skirt dug into her palm as she clenched her fists tighter. She breathed heavily, and her heart ached from old and fresh wounds alike. "This man tried to assassinate me, Gerard. He nearly succeeded," she said more quietly.

"I know," he whispered. He stepped toward her. "I just want you to take care of yourself, my love. You don't have to do this alone." Gerard stooped to kiss her neck, but she shrank away from his touch.

She cast her eyes over her shoulder as she replied, "Yes, I do. That is the burden of my blood—something you will never understand."

Her ears rang as she entered the hall, faintly aware that her husband replied, though she did not care to hear it. She charged toward the throne room flanked by a gaggle of armed guards. She pressed one hand to her abdomen, blinking back the tears threatening to fall. There was no time for desolation or coddling. She was queen, and she would protect her child and her people as best she could.

Elara gripped the arm rests on her gilded throne as the members of her Council trickled into the hall. She tapped her fingernails against the carved wood, faintly narrowing her eyes at everyone who entered. Any one of them could have been a traitor, a spy for her enemy awaiting the opportune moment to strike. No one could be trusted.

As Zeke entered the hall, her stomach tightened; her breath hitched in her throat as she watched the man laugh at a colleague's comment. The action made something snap within her, and she thrust herself onto her feet, clapping her hands to get their attention. "Doors," she ordered. She motioned with two fingers to the guards. They moved swiftly to close the doors and posted themselves in front so no one could exit. Her audience silenced, stepping into a line before the raised platform and bowing to their queen. Elara gnawed at the inside of her cheek, disgusted by their expectant faces, a mix of curiosity and concern. Zeke looked calm, not the least bit nervous as he looked her directly in the eyes and offered a warm smile. Elara cut her eyes away, scanning the faces until she settled on Alexander and Richard. She motioned silently for them to approach, and they did, coming to stand to her left.

"How do you wish to address this?" Alexander asked, his voice low enough so others could not hear him.

"There is a traitor among us," Elara declared, her jaw set as she lifted her chin high.

Some of the high-ranking officers gasped. Their eyes widened as they peered between their colleagues suspiciously. Zeke was among them, whispering to a peer as he eyed Richard standing beside the high commander.

"We have become aware of a spy in our ranks. I shall give you but one chance to earn my mercy. Step forward now," she demanded. The men glanced between themselves, their foreheads furrowed in dismay, but none stepped forward. "I should have known you would not turn yourself over willingly," Elara muttered. She turned to Alexander and nodded her head. "Please apprehend the spy, Commander." He nodded, his ebony skin glistening with tiny beads of sweat as he dismounted from the platform, trailed closely by Richard, and marched straight to Zeke.

"What is the meaning of this?" Zeke asked, his face going pale. The commander seized both of his arms while the young captain quickly set to work binding his wrists together with a thin rope.

Elara took each step down the platform with the grace and speed of a lioness stalking its prey. "Evidence has implicated your direct involvement in espionage for our enemy. You stand accused of treason against your queen and kingdom. What have you to say?"

Richard kicked the back of the man's knees, forcing him to kneel. Zeke stared up at the queen in horror, stuttering, "Your Majesty! What could I have done to make you think such a thing? I have been your loyal servant all these years. I would never betray you!"

Elara sneered down at him, the sight of his sniveling causing bile to rise in the back of her throat. He was right. He had been a loyal, hardworking member of the Guard for as long as she could remember. That is what made this even more painful. "A letter was found detailing the citadel's weaknesses. Ways for people to get inside undetected. The fact that such a document was ever made—"

"I would never be so foolish!" Zeke interrupted, throwing himself forward. Richard grasped the man by his pristine ponytail and yanked him back from her. "You must believe me, Your Majesty! I am innocent!"

Elara looked up to find the rest of the War Council staring at her. Wiping her sweaty hands against her skirt, she took a deep breath and said, "We have compared the handwriting to his notes from our prior meetings. Alexander and I have no doubt the letter in question matches Zeke's writing."

"I can explain," the captive argued, his eyes wide and wild. "I would never help our enemy. My family has served the Garricks for four generations!"

Elara turned on her heels and strutted back to her throne. Perching on the edge of her seat, she stared down her nose at the man who had once served her well and frowned. "Show them the papers, Commander," she ordered.

Alexander walked in a circle so all the men could see the letter in question and Zeke's notes. As he passed each man, they began to whisper, staring at their comrade in confusion. Finally, Alexander paused in front of the man they had apprehended, allowing him to view the evidence against him. "Why would you do this, Captain?" the commander asked.

"Do not address him so. He is undeserving of such a title," Elara said sternly. She pushed her body further back on her throne.

"I can explain," he said again. "Those are my notes, yes. I did write that report, but it's not what you think!"

The men began murmuring, but Elara silenced them. "You admit these are indeed your letters, then?"

"Yes, Your Majesty. But I'm no spy! I only meant to find the vulnerabilities of the citadel, not for the enemy but for you! After the assassination attempt, I feared what danger might still loom within these walls. I thought if I could identify our weak points, I could strategize greater protection."

Elara looked at the commander for a response.

"Your Majesty," Alexander said, "what he says may well be true, though I knew nothing of it." Then, turning toward Zeke, "Why is that? Why wouldn't you discuss this with me first?"

The detainee looked down, his face burning red, but he didn't speak.

"Well?" the commander probed.

"I wanted to impress you, sir. I—I wanted to impress Your Majesty," his eyes slowly trailed up to look at the queen, "by finding the problems and presenting solutions. I wanted to make you both proud." He sighed. "I wanted to be considered for promotion," he admitted.

Elara clutched her abdomen, closing her eyes. She was so weary of others aiming to impress her. And for what? If they only knew how their beloved queen truly felt, buried beneath a crown she never wanted. Now she didn't know what to believe. Before, she had no reason to distrust the captain. Never had he shown disloyalty toward any of the Garrick family. What he said could be true. Still, a traitor remained. Someone had attempted to kill her, and in turn, her unborn child. In truth, she couldn't imagine any of the men before her capable of such betrayal. But that's the nature of betrayal. She let out a despairing chuckle at the thought.

"What are we to do with him?" Richard asked, his gaze locked on the queen.

She stared at the face of the accused and steeled herself, forcing back a lifetime of memories that included his family. With a heavy sigh, she declared, "Zeke Evigan, I declare you guilty... of being reckless. Had your report fallen into the wrong hands, the City of Mercy would have been jeopardized. For your crime, you are hereby sentenced to..." She swallowed, forcing down the lump in her throat, unsure how to proceed. To show mercy would show the true traitor her own weakness, but to show no mercy would be a betrayal to her own people— to herself. "You are sentenced to be detained in the dungeon pending a more thorough investigation and following a trial."

Gasps rang out in the hall, and the men began their murmuring again. The commander rushed to restore order. Tears streamed down Zeke's reddened cheeks as he resigned against Richard's grasp, and Elara averted her eyes. When the commander approached her, she blinked at him in a daze. "What of his family, milady?" he asked quietly.

Elara watched as Richard and two other guards dragged Zeke from the hall. It was the only time she had ever seen his pristine coif unkempt. Tearing her eyes from him, her thoughts drifted to the man's wife and daughter. "Have them moved to housing in the outer ring." Alexander nodded, and she noticed his exhaustion. There were bags underneath his eyes, and wrinkles were set deep in his forehead, though he would never argue with her brash judgment. He couldn't understand her position, she knew, and didn't fault him for that. "And commander," she said, "Isolate him. Only you and I are to visit him." Though she wasn't convinced of his guilt, she wasn't convinced of his innocence, either. The commander nodded and walked away.

Rubbing her stomach gingerly, she muttered to herself, "I will do whatever it takes to keep you safe." And she meant it. If she was not safe in Symptee, no one was.

SUN RAYS PEEKED THROUGH the thick array of gray clouds, awakening the warriors on the third day of their grueling trek to Jordis. Packing their things quickly, they resumed the uphill hike through the snow. Hours passed before they stopped to eat midday, and the dwarfs urged them to eat quickly as they were near the edge of Mørkewulv territory. Serena wearily ate her meal and listened as the dwarfs and Crystal deliberated.

"Think we can reach Jordis by nightfall?" Crystal asked Bandan. The dwarfs were already loading their bags to resume the trek. The rest of the travelers arose and started making ready to go.

"If you lot can move your feet any faster," Eldvar said, brushing past the elves to join Martock at the head of the group.

"Yes, we should make it," Bandan said, handing the guardian her quiver.

"How are you feeling, Princess?" Thomli asked with a grin.

Rilura smiled coyly and said, "I am faring well. Thank you for your concern." The princess looked over to Serena with her smile. Serena giggled.

"Allow me," Thomli said, reaching for the bag in her hands.

"Thanks," Rilura whispered, promptly turning away as her cheeks reddened.

Eldvar glared back at them. "Princess, stay close to the general and me, as we are the most seasoned warriors here. Your chosen guards may take up the rear."

"If you insist, Captain," Rilura said and trudged toward him.

Serena shoved the last of her things back into their bags, wishing to catch up with Rilura. Bandan nudged Thomli, and Serena was close enough to hear his loud whisper. "Eldvar seems jealous. That is a compliment, my friend. He has been vying for her hand for decades."

"I'm not worried about Eldvar. Rilura has never cared for his advances. She is much too strong-willed for a brute like him," Thomli said, watching her march past Eldvar to speak with the general.

"Luckily, 'tis her choice alone. Not even King Dranir can force her to wed that brute," Bandan reminded his friend.

Serena glanced over and caught Thomli's dark eyes glistening as he braided a small section of his black hair. "And for that, I am quite thankful," he said.

Bandan shook his head as they approached their waiting comrades. The guardians started up the path. Serena tied up her bag and trailed ahead to catch up.

WILL TRAILED SERENA AND saw her steps falter again and again. "Let me take that," Will said, catching up to her and reaching for her bag. "You look exhausted."

Serena glared as she shoved her bag into his hands. "Thanks," she said. Then she shuffled ahead of her friends to speak to Rilura.

Rigel cackled, slapping Will on the back. "Never tell a woman they look poorly, Will. Next time try: 'Your eyes are so bright this morning.' Even a simple 'Good morning' would suffice."

"And what makes you an expert on speaking to women?" Xandra asked with a snicker.

"Hey, I have always encouraged my female comrades, in the most respectful way," he said defensively.

"That you have," Crystal agreed, patting Rigel on the back as she walked by him. "Now come on. We have dawdled long enough. The quicker we move, the sooner we can rest in the comfort and safety of Jordis."

"The last underground city of our tour," Cole added loudly, one corner of his mouth curled in a half smile. "I never thought I would miss Symptee so much."

"I knew I would! Outside of the Academy, Symptee is home. It's so exciting to think we shall be home again within a fortnight," Xandra said, practically skipping off after Serena.

Watching their Elven comrades trudge ahead, Rigel urged Will forward. "Best we catch up to them, friend. Hate to fall behind and miss any of the action."

"Don't joke. We've seen enough action already," Will said, his forehead wrinkling as he marched toward the others. As they ascended the mountain, Will kept his eyes locked on the back of Serena's head. For hours, he remained focused on her, watching closely as she spoke with their female companions. Occasionally, she turned to wave and offer him a reassuring smile.

GRAY STORM CLOUDS ROLLED overhead, casting a dark shadow over the mountain. The wind blew haphazardly, the harsh gusts battering their freezing cheeks as they braved the ever-increasing altitude. Serena gripped her cloak tight around her body and face, wincing as they worked against the wind. As the humans struggled against the inclement weather, the guardians and half of the dwarfs slowed their pace, offering their arms for support.

"It's getting worse," Crystal said, adjusting her cloak. "Are snowstorms normal for this time of year?"

"It's not unheard of," Thomli said, pointing toward the thinning trees to their left. "Use the trees to shield yourselves from the wind."

Approaching from ahead, Cole said, "Martock thinks we are almost to the city wall. We should keep going." Serena squinted her eyes, as though she could see the wall ahead, but she quickly squeezed them shut as the blistery wind blew against her face. She grumbled, feeling defeated, when she realized it was no use. She'd have to take the dwarf's word.

"Don't give up, Serena. Warm beds await," Rigel said, his voice muffled by the cloak wrapped around his neck and face. She offered Rigel a weak smile, not that he could see it with her cloak pulled so tightly around her face. She marched forward, losing her footing here and there in the deep snow.

"Here, eat." Xandra pulled a piece of jerky out of her bag. "It will give you a bit of strength."

Serena took it begrudgingly, ripping a large bite out of the jerky with her teeth. "Thanks," she said, turning so the harsh wind whipped against her back while she scarfed down her snack.

"Thank heavens we shall be out of the elements soon," Crystal said. "I loathe snow."

"Never thought you would long to be underground," Rigel teased, glancing over his shoulder with a grin.

Serena shook her head, gnawing on the last bite of jerky. As she glanced toward Will, a gentle flurry of snow fell over them. She gasped, gazing skyward and wrinkling her nose as flakes landed on her frozen cheeks. "Is this...?"

"Snow!" Xandra exclaimed. She twirled with her arms spread wide.

"It's nothing to celebrate," Crystal said irritably. "There was plenty of it on the ground already. How can anyone possibly enjoy being this cold?" She stomped over to Serena and yanked the girl's hood over her head to protect her face from the snow.

"They live underground," Cole snipped, drawing his own hood over his head. Just as quickly, the wind blew it back off, and the elf groaned, tossing his arms in the air.

The humans snickered. Their spirits were lifted by the soft flurries. Rigel scooped a ball of snow from the ground and pelted Cole in the back of the head, instigating a lighthearted war between the weary travelers. Serena squealed in surprise as Will snuck up behind her, smashing a snowball on top of her hood.

Their fun was cut short by the lead dwarfs' yelling. The smiles quickly faded from the guardians' faces as they readied their weapons. Crystal locked eyes with Serena and said, "Ready yourself. There's trouble ahead." Complying with her order, Serena and Will drew their swords, and the guardians formed a tight circle around them.

Will clenched his sword in his shaking hands and asked, "Is it the Mørkewulv?"

"Possibly," Crystal said, gripping her bow tightly in her gloved hands. "Cole and I will scout ahead. The rest of you, stick to the trees and be watchful. Get to Jordis if you can."

"I can defend myself. You don't have to treat me like a child." Serena gripped the hilt of Sannarvin with both hands.

"Do not allow your pride to overshadow the danger ahead," Cole said. "You may be a match for some men, but you are not invincible."

As Crystal and Cole rushed to the leading dwarfs' aid, Xandra called after them, "Be careful! You're not immortal either."

They could see the scuffle up ahead in an opening between the trees, and a dwarf cried out in pain. It was difficult to make out, but they saw huge fearsome shapes tearing at their comrades swift as lightning. The beasts from the legend were unmistakable, their stature staggering compared to the dwarfs. Serena saw dark fur flash past, their glowing yellow-green eyes burning between the branches of the trees, and their snarling snouts filled with fangs. Their howls were haunting, echoing miles across the snowy plain and reverberating off the frozen trees, as if there were dozens of them lying in wait. Xandra grabbed Serena's arm and dragged her deeper into the forest, away from the danger. Rigel and Will followed closely behind. Both glanced back through the veil of snow until they were too far to see.

CAMERON CROUCHED BEHIND A cluster of pine trees, the setting sun casting shadows all around as he watched the group ahead. For weeks, he had been tracking them, desperate to find his sister. Now he had found her at last. He clenched his fists, fighting the urge to rush forward when he heard her voice from afar, but he needed to assess the situation first. Serena was with Will and two of the runaway princess's assassins, but she wasn't restrained. In fact, he was certain she followed them freely. His heart pounded in his chest, his anxious energy making it hard to think clearly. He couldn't fail to bring Serena to the king. That was the only way to keep her safe.

From his vantage point, Cameron watched them slow to a halt. They all raised weapons and took a defensive stance around Serena. He had heard the bellowing howls echo throughout the mountains, but his eyes widened when he realized these were not wolves. Instead, several hooded figures emerged from the thick of the forest. At first, he thought they were refugees, but something in their demeanor seemed off. They moved with a predatory grace that set his nerves on edge. Then his breath caught in his throat as the first man swung a blade at Will's neck. The refugee barked an order to his comrades, "Kill them!"

Cameron's grip tightened on his sword as he watched the one called Rigel thrust himself between Serena and another attacker, deflecting the strike aimed at her. He pushed the man back with a forceful shove. Clashing metal echoed through the cold mountain air. Serena was watching them parry, holding her sword up to her shoulder as her eyes followed their movement.

Cameron rushed closer, careful to remain concealed behind the trees. Peering around a massive pine, he focused on the closest fighters. Another ruffian was engaging the one Serena had called Xandra. The wind whipped the man's cloak around, hindering his motion. She took advantage, her twin blades moving in a swift, lethal dance. She forced the attacker back until he stumbled, entangled in his own cloak. With a fierce flourish, she crossed her arms and sliced outward, her blades cutting deep into his chest. Blood sprayed, staining the snow and her face. Judging by Rigel and Xandra's skills, these were the assassins the king had mentioned. Serena had no clue the amount of danger she was in.

More attackers emerged from the trees just a few yards north of Cameron, and he searched the area for signs of any others, gripping the hilt of his own blade. Who were they, raiders? The dwarf hurled his axe, embedding it in the head of one assailant. Two others stalked toward Serena, grinning with malicious intent. Cameron's heart raced as he watched Will step up beside her, his sword dragging through the snow. The dwarf retrieved his axe and moved to aid the humans.

"You can do this," he heard Will say to Serena, his voice lacking its usual confidence. Cameron could see the uncertainty in both of them and wondered what made Will think he could wield a sword. Not that long ago, his friend swore he had no interest in becoming a soldier. Serena, determined not to cower, lunged at one of the attackers. Cameron recognized that same stubbornness he'd inherited from their father and cursed it. She was going to get herself killed.

The man dodged her initial strike, laughing at her effort. His amusement turned to rage as Xandra positioned herself on his other side, her cheeks smeared with blood. Distracted, the man slashed out at Serena again, but she blocked the hit with her blade. The amethyst in its hilt glistened in the light of the moon. Where had Serena found such a regal sword? Their father had never forged something so elaborate at the smith. The man kicked her in the middle, sending her sprawling. Cameron should have intervened then, but he had to time his appearance just right. His sister's company was holding their own, he hated to admit. He wasn't sure how he felt about his old friend's defensive stance as he fought to protect Serena. He should have been grateful, but the sight of Will and Serena together angered him.

"Weakling," the attacker sneered as he spat on the ground beside her.

"Try me," Xandra growled. Her blades spun around her fingers before she charged. As they clashed, Serena unfastened her cloak and scrambled to her feet. She crept closer, using the man's distraction to her advantage. Just as Xandra used her blades to lock the man in place, Serena threw herself to her knees and slashed through the back of his legs.

He shrieked, collapsing in pain but still managing to point his weapon at Serena with a shaking hand. "You'll die for that," he hissed.

Xandra snarled, lunging forward and driving one of her blades through his back. Blood bubbled from his mouth as he fell face first into the snow. "Not on my watch," she muttered, her eyes fierce. Cameron could only assume that Elara Garrick must have promised a reward for his sister to be brought in alive, seeing the way the assassins rallied around her. But why Serena and not the rest of his family?

Cameron's blood boiled as he watched Will block another man's swing. Their blades clashed, and Will shoved the man back, his teeth gritted in anticipation. The attacker charged again, aiming low, but the dwarf intercepted with his axe. As he pinned the man's sword, Will lifted his own, ready to strike. Before he could, Xandra intervened, slashing through the aggressor.

"Leave it to the warriors if you can, Will," Cameron heard her say as she wiped her bloodied blades through the snow.

Rigel let out a victorious howl, cutting his opponent's hand and sending his weapon flying. The man fell to his knees, clutching his bleeding hand to his middle. "Do it," he challenged the redhead.

Rigel glanced at his comrades, then back at the defeated man. "No. Unlike you, I would never kill an unarmed man," he declared. Xandra picked up the captive's sword and pressed it to his throat while Rigel bound his hands with a leather strap. "But don't think I wasn't tempted," he added, shoving the man onto his side with his foot.

Cameron found it odd that they didn't kill the man outright, but he was quickly distracted when he heard Xandra call out, "Hurry up, Rige. We have company."

Cameron's heart pounded as more attackers charged into the fray. The dwarf withdrew to help an injured comrade, lifting him to his feet despite his wailing. "We must get to Jordis! Can you walk?" the dwarf urged.

"Will, help them!" Xandra shouted.

Will and the dwarf hoisted the injured man. "We will send reinforcements!" the dwarf promised.

"Serena, go with them," Rigel commanded, stepping protectively in front of her.

She raised her sword. "I'm not leaving anyone behind," Serena insisted.

Will hesitated, his gaze fixed on her. "Serena..."

But there was no time to argue. The last of the ruffians emerged. The clash of swords rang through the mountains, and Will stepped away from the dwarfs, heading for Serena with his sword in hand.

"Where's Cole when we need him?" Rigel muttered, kicking an opponent in the gut.

Cameron wondered who Cole was. Another assassin, no doubt.

"Getting tired already?" Xandra taunted as she parried rapid blows. "I thought you could do this all day."

"I never tire of this," Rigel replied, his grin infuriating his opponent. With a somersault, he slashed out, severing the man's hand.

Cameron watched, holding his breath. His heart pounded as Xandra struggled against a dominating foe. Serena gritted her teeth, raising her sword as she anticipated her opponent's next move. With the others occupied, she was on her own. One wrong move, and all his time spent tracking her would be for nothing.

He could stand it no longer. His sister was in danger, and the sight of her fighting for her life pushed him into action. As much as she frustrated him, Cameron wanted to protect his sister, but more than that, he wanted to please his king. He imagined the satisfied grin on Antoine Rexton's face when he not only brought in Serena but eliminated Elara's assassins as well. To do that, he would have to help them fight off the hostiles first.

With a roar, Cameron charged into the battle, his sword clashing with the first attacker he reached. The need to protect Serena overpowered his senses, and he fought with a ferocity that surprised even himself. He was determined to save his sister, no matter the cost. As the oldest child, he was always the one who had to rescue her. Now, he couldn't just stand by and risk losing her to the assailants. She had important information the king required, and he wouldn't let him down.

He easily cut down one attacker after another, his mind a blur of adrenaline and fear. It wasn't until the last man fell that he recognized the rugged face of Lieutenant Emrick, an officer in the Enforcing Army. Emrick had visited Murmont at the beginning of Cameron's training, giving an engaging lecture on the importance of stealth and endurance on covert missions. He had stopped to chat with Cameron after the talk, pleased to hear how the young soldier could relate the lecture to his history of hunting in the woods near Durmak. "If you are a skilled hunter," Emrick had said, "then you already know the importance of stealth. Never forget, my boy, every place your foot treads is a battleground." The lieutenant had winked at the recruit before joining Captain Pelham for a smoke.

Looking at his lifeless body in the snow, Cameron's stomach churned as he realized the implications of his actions. If Emrick was among the attackers, these were no refugees at all. Breathing heavily, Cameron looked around at the fallen bodies. He had just killed his own comrades. The weight of his actions settled on him like a stone. He had defied the king in his attempt to save his sister. Had he not saved his sister, he'd still have failed the king. There had been no winning outcome here.

Cameron turned to Serena, feeling all the color drain from his frozen cheeks. "You shouldn't be out here, Rena," he said trembling.

Serena gasped, recognizing her brother's voice. As he pulled his black hood down to reveal his face, confusion and relief mingled in her eyes. "Cameron? How'd you find us?"

"I always find you," he said, his voice strained. "You need to come with me. The king has offered you protection. These people," he gestured to Rigel and Xandra with his blade, "they are not your friends. They're the ones responsible for tearing our family apart."

Serena shook her head. "No, Cameron. You're wrong. These people have protected me. They've saved me. The king is our enemy." The wind whipped stray strands of her hair around her head as she stared at her brother.

Cameron's eyes flashed with frustration. "You don't understand. The king is not our enemy. These people are."

"Mum told me to go to Elara with her dying breath," she said, crossing her arms over her chest. "She knew it wasn't safe to stay in Hyrosencia. Not with Rexton's men hunting us."

"The army never would have harmed you. I bought your safety with my service," Cameron argued, stepping closer to his sister. "It was traitors who killed them. Loyalists. The likes of these." He sneered at Rigel and Xandra.

"Our parents were loyalists," Serena yelled, her heavy breaths coming out in white puffs.

Cameron scrunched his face, his eyes dancing between Serena and the others. Rigel clenched his jaw and nodded, affirming her words. "It's true," he said.

"You're lying!" the young soldier shrieked, blood rushing to his cheeks.

"It's the truth, Cameron." Serena's voice was low and steady. "I know these people. They're not cold-blooded killers. They never fight unprovoked. It's Rexton's men who kill senselessly."

He remembered Rigel refusing to kill the unarmed captive. But showing one man mercy did not make him a friend. Not when they were surrounded by corpses.

"It's true," Will said, taking a protective step toward Serena. "Your sister is telling the truth. You need to listen to her."

"Stay out of this, Will," Cameron spat at his friend. "Your letter said you were going home. You're the last person I expected to cross the border. And with my sister?"

"What letter?" Serena asked, turning toward Will as his muscles relaxed.

His hand moved to cover his forehead as he replied, "I wrote to him after I saw you in Morlerae. Before I knew what was going on. Just to let him know you were alive and safe. I didn't think—"

"What? That I would come after my own sister?" Cameron snapped at his friend, gripping the hilt of his blade tighter. Blood dripped from his blade and tainted the pure snow with dark red. Turning back toward his sister, he barked, "This is over. You're coming with me. Your friends, too."

Serena stepped back. She tightened her grip on her own weapon. "I'm not going back with you, Cameron. You don't understand what you're proposing! Rexton will kill us all. You really think he's going to let you live? You're his pawn!"

His face twisted with anger and desperation. "You're coming with me, Serena," he said again. This time he reached out and grabbed her arm. "I'm not letting the king down."

Rigel stepped forward. His eyes blazed with determination. "Let her go. She's not going anywhere with you."

Cameron narrowed his eyes; his grip tightened on Serena's arm. "Stay out of this. This is between me and my sister."

Rigel drew his sword, wedging himself between Cameron and Serena. The men were nose to nose, glaring at each other as Rigel said, "I've pledged an oath to protect her with my life. I won't let you take her."

Cameron's eyes flicked to the fallen soldiers around them and swallowed down the rising bile. He had just killed the king's men, and now he was faced with the reality of his situation. He was the king's only man left on the mountain, and he had to make a choice.

With a growl of frustration, Cameron released Serena's arm and stepped back. He turned toward Rigel, lifting his sword to grasp it with both hands. "This was a family matter," he said. "You should have stayed out of it."

"That's the first true thing you've said. This *is* a family matter." Rigel wielded his own sword, digging his heels into the snow.

Cameron clenched his jaw. Anger coursed through him, fueling his erratic movements. He attacked with fierce power, each swing of his sword driven by adrenaline. He could see the calm determination in the redhead's eyes as he blocked each strike with skill. But Cameron's fury was overwhelming, and with one mighty swing, he shattered Rigel's blade, his own sword continuing through to slash his opponent's arm.

Rigel groaned loudly as he stumbled back and fell. His breathing was haggard. Cameron's chest heaved as he glared down at the fallen man. In his periphery, he saw Will holding Serena back from the fight. Her voice was a desperate plea. "Cameron, don't do this. He isn't the enemy."

But her words were drowned out by the rage and betrayal he felt. His mind was set. Rigel had to pay for his treachery against the crown. "On my honor, I declare you a traitor of His Majesty King Antoine Rexton and hereby deliver swift justice in the name of the king." Cameron leveled his sword at one side of Rigel's neck.

Rigel's expression shifted from defiance to acceptance as he closed his eyes and readied himself for the final blow. "Divinity knows my allegiance," he said with a half smile.

Cameron smiled, knowing one blow would avenge his family's murders and earn him the king's favor.

PERILOUS PATH

Serena lurched forward and screamed. Her voice echoed through the vast space as she dove between her brother and Rigel, swinging her arm and willing Sannarvin to stop her brother's strike.

Cameron glanced to the side, his grin dissipating as Serena thrust her body between them. He hesitated mid swing, and the Heir's Blade crashed into his with unexpected force. The move dislodged the weapon from his grasp. "Serena!" he yelled. His nostrils flared. The only time she had ever seen him this angry was when he fought with their father over joining the army. But now, his hostility was directed at her.

"What happened to you?" Serena asked. "If you would kill an unarmed man, you're not the brother I remember. You're just another one of the king's minions."

Her words did nothing to dissipate the tension in Cameron's body. He cast his narrowed eyes to the snow, taking two long strides and scooping up his weapon from the ground. "You would choose a stranger over your own kin? After all I've done for you?"

Serena scoffed. "What have you done for me lately? You left, and I'm the one who had to pick up the pieces! Mum was distraught, Papa was angry, and I'm the one who had to take on all your extra work."

"Oh, really?" Cameron asked, twirling the hilt of his sword around his knuckles absently. "Did Papa ask you to man the forge, too?"

Serena stared at him. The darkness in his eyes was unrecognizable. With each venom-laced word, he felt more like a stranger. "Did you not feel a hint of guilt for leaving us?" she whispered. "If you had been home, you could have protected us." Serena stepped back, aware of Will helping Rigel to his feet behind her. Her palms ached from fighting, but her instincts told her not to let go of her weapon.

"That's always my job, isn't it? To protect you," her brother snapped. He gripped his weapon in a tight fist as he stepped toward her. "You wander off; I find you. That's how it always is. Did it ever occur to you that maybe I left because I didn't want to spend the rest of my life responsible for your failures?"

She froze, and her chest tightened as if the air had been knocked out of her. Could her own brother really feel so much resentment toward her?

"That's not fair, and you know it," Will said from behind her.

Serena took a deep breath, fighting back the stinging in her eyes. This was no time to cry.

Her brother stalked in a semicircle around her, dragging the tip of his bloodied blade through the snow. Cameron replied, "She knows I'm right. Just look around." He threw his arms out and gestured to their surroundings. "We're all here on this damned mountain because of her." With a swift movement, his blade pointed at her, the threatening motion forcing Serena to lift her own weapon in defense. He was so close now, she could feel the rage emanating off of him like a bad omen. Serena gripped Sannarvin in both hands; the cool metal dug into her raw palms as if it were an extension of her arms. She pressed slightly, contacting Cameron's sword, and the shrill sound of metal scraping metal made her wince as she pushed the blade away from her face.

"If you hate me so much, why go through the trouble of tracking me all the way out here?" She took one step back and grounded herself. If this was the Cameron she had grown up with, she knew an explosion was coming any moment.

Cameron inspected her stance, dragging his gaze up her form and cocking his head to one side. "When did you learn how to fight, sister?" he asked with a taunting grin.

"It's been a few weeks," she replied.

"And you think you can take me?" he asked smugly, flexing his fingers and adjusting his grip.

"I'm stronger than I look," she said. Her confidence wavered as she stared at him, the only brother she had left. "We don't have to do this, Cameron.

You can go back to playing soldier and forget I exist. I don't have to be your problem anymore."

Something cold flashed in his gaze, and Serena steeled herself. "I can't do that, sis. The king wants you brought in for questioning. I can't just let you disappear."

"You would side against your own blood?" Her stomach tightened. Of all the enemies they had faced on the path to Symptee, she never anticipated her own brother getting in the way of her safety.

"I am a soldier first. My duty is to the king," Cameron answered, lunging forward. The snow slowed him, an advantage for Serena as she braced in place for his first strike. The hilt cut through her gloves as she gripped it tighter, and she blocked his strike with ease. Cameron sneered as she pushed with all her strength, forcing him two steps back. A gap in the clouds allowed the light from the full moon to cast harsh shadows across Cameron's face. Anger possessed him, making his movements erratic. He swiped back and forth at Serena, and she matched his movements with a speed and sheer power that stunned them both. "Give up already," he demanded through clenched teeth.

Serena parried another powerful blow, her strength only seeming to enrage him further. "Never," she hissed, aware that with each step the distance between them and her friends was growing. Serena leaned in as they pushed their swords against each other, locked in an intense standoff. She remembered Cole's lessons—never get distracted, focus on your opponent, always be one step ahead. She tuned out the voices of her concerned companions, forgetting everyone else. In this standoff, Cameron Finch was the only man between her and the safety she so desperately desired.

Her brother's gaze shifted over her shoulder, focusing on her comrades. The momentary distraction was enough to give Serena an edge. She thrust her body forward, driving her knee into Cameron's groin with force. He sucked in a shuddering breath, mortification and pain overtaking his features as he went down on his knees, dropping his blade.

Serena stepped back, looking down her nose at him. "Give up already," she said, her voice dripping with disdain as Cameron writhed in the snow. She shook her head, certain their fight was over, and turned toward her friends. Rigel had lifted the hostage to his feet while Will supported Xandra. They all stared at her, their relief apparent as she smiled and started toward them.

But she did not get far. Cameron threw himself forward and grasped her by the ankle. She slammed onto the ground, padded by the snow. "I will not fail because of you," he hissed, army crawling closer as Serena rolled onto her back. Her heart raced faster as she realized she had dropped her blade. Cameron loomed over her, pressing a knee into her thigh and pinning her in place.

"Serena!"

She heard voices call from behind them, but all she could see was her brother crowned in a halo of twinkling stars against the deep purple sky. His bloodshot eyes bore down on her as cold leather gloves curled around her delicate throat without hesitation. As Cameron squeezed, his nose crinkled in anger and concentration, and the stars around his face blurred in a blinding spectacle of light until she could no longer see the details of his face, only the shadow of Death threatening to rip her soul from her physical being. "Give up," he demanded, his voice strained. Serena clawed at his fingers, trying to make him loosen his grip, but it was no use. Cameron scoffed, glancing at her friends before leaning close to her ear. "Once I'm done with you, I'm going to kill the assassins and bring their heads back to the king."

Serena stopped struggling, and her body became dangerously still. Sannarvin was too far to reach, which left her only one other option. She dragged a limp arm to Cameron's hip, fumbling along his belt until her numbing fingers closed around the hilt of a small dagger. The blade he used to kill and skin animals, no doubt.

"Please," she croaked, almost inaudibly, but his grip did not slacken. Serena closed her eyes, knowing her time was almost up. She thought back to her brothers' bodies already cold and limp when she found them. Mama dying in her lap. Papa's smile when he'd come home from a long day at the forge. Will's strong arms wrapped around her as she sobbed for all she had lost. She couldn't have been through all that pain just to die on this mountain.

She heard voices ring out again, this time closer, but she didn't want Rigel or Will to interfere and face her brother's wrath. This was her blood—her fight—and she had to be the one to save herself this time. Tears stung her eyes as Serena thrust her left hand upward, and Cameron released her throat, sitting back on his legs.

Her eyes jolted open as she inhaled the crisp night air, her heartbeat pounding in her ears. She blinked, her vision still hazy as she rolled her neck to look around. Her body ached all over, but she was alive.

As she pushed herself up on her elbows, Serena gasped. She realized then what she had done to the boy who used to love and protect her. Cameron looked down at his abdomen with a furrowed brow. "Rena?" he breathed as he touched the dagger protruding from his stomach. They stared at each other, their haggard breath intermingling in the frigid air between them as blood leaked out onto his shirt. "How could you? We are kin."

Serena sucked in as she squirmed backward, the sight of her brother's torn flesh making her stomach turn. "No, no, no. I didn't mean to," she stammered hoarsely. Her throat burned as she struggled to speak. Despite the cold, her cheeks burned as she took in shallow breaths. She reached out for him, but paused midway, realizing there was nothing she could possibly do to fix this. "I never wanted—"

Cameron yanked the dagger out, and blood sprayed from the gash, spilling onto the white powder between them. Blood seeped through his garments, soaking through his gloves as he pressed his frozen hands to the wound. Serena watched her brother gasp for air, unable to drag herself off the ground. "Cam," she choked. He slumped over, his body coming to an eerie stillness, and she knew it was over. She had traded her own life for her brother's, an offering to appease fate that could not be undone. The Finch name would die on the mountains, the aftermath of a tyrant's war with no winners.

The hum of approaching voices mingled with a haunting wail echoed around her. Rigel, Will, and the tied-up soldier looked past Serena across the open terrain, and their mouths dropped when they spotted people running toward them. The ground rumbled under their feet, and then they finally heard it. Crystal and Cole were both shouting, "Run! Get to the wall!"

A massive Mørkewulv with fur that matched the snow and glowing red eyes bounded after them. This beast was much larger than any wolf Serena had seen in the southern woods; seeing their fearless companions fleeing for their lives made it even more frightening.

"Serena, run!" Crystal shrieked, still several yards away.

Two of the dwarfs charged for the wall, not coming near Serena and the other guardians. When their allies reached them, they barely slowed their speed as the Mørkewulv was right on their heels. Cole ran right past Serena, making a beeline for Will. When he reached him, Cole quickly scooped Xandra up in his arms and rushed for the wall. A small horde of dwarfs were waiting outside the gates; all they had to do was make it that far.

Rigel rushed to Serena's side, shaking her as she stared down at her brother's corpse. "He's gone, Serena. And we're next if we don't beat that thing to the wall." He pointed at the vicious beast stalking toward them, swiping Sannarvin off the ground near her feet. Serena's body froze with fear. "Come on," Rigel said, grabbing her by the wrist and forcing her to run toward the wall. As Crystal caught up to them, she grabbed Serena's other arm, willing her to move quicker.

"Over there!" Rigel screamed, following the direction Cole and Will were heading in. They were close enough to the wall to see the intricate symbols in the dark metal and the dwarfs lined up along the top with heavy crossbows in hand.

Serena glanced back as the monster picked up the body of one of Rexton's men in its teeth and chomped down, the crunch of bones sending bile up the back of her throat. She shuddered as a few of the soldier's limbs dropped back onto the ground, resting among the other dead men. Turning its head, the beast whipped around, its blood-red eyes fixing on them as it surged forward.

Serena tripped and tumbled to the ground, sending a puff of snow into the air around them. "Rigel!" she shouted. She could feel the ground vibrate as the beast vaulted toward them.

Rigel slowed down. He looked back with a horrific expression on his face. "Serena!"

Serena leaned back, a flood of memories flashing through her mind as she anticipated a fatal blow. The guardians called her name. Their voices grew closer as the beast launched itself into the air. Crystal loosed two arrows at once, both of which implanted in the underbelly of the mighty Mørkewulv. The beast landed on its feet a few yards from Serena, shaking the mountain with force as it let out a booming roar.

Serena clamped her eyes closed, feeling the hot breath of the beast blow against her face, and thought she must be fated to die on the mountain like her brother. As the beast launched for her, Serena felt something brush her arm, running past her at the monster. When she heard the squelch of teeth ripping flesh, Serena opened her eyes to find Rigel had thrown himself in the beast's path. The white monster snarled at her, its jaws clamped tightly on Rigel's upper arm. Her sword was plunged in the side of the Mørkewulv's mouth, yet the beast did not relinquish its hold on him. Jerking its head, the wolf lifted Rigel off the ground and tossed him aside as if he weighed nothing.

"Rigel!" she screamed, reaching toward the guardian. He struggled to stand up, his face twisted in agony. The beast had shredded through his shoulder and nearly ripped his arm off.

While the Mørkewulv bared its razor-sharp teeth at its victim, Crystal bombarded the monster with a barrage of arrows. "Over here," she taunted, shooting the beast in the neck.

"Get up," Cole ordered as he ran past Serena and launched himself at the monster. He slashed through the beast's side, injuring one of its hind legs. The Mørkewulv howled as the guardian circled it, and black blood dripped from the blade into the snow.

Serena pushed herself onto her feet and asked, "What can I do?"

"Get out of here!" Crystal ordered.

Several dwarfs ran past Serena to their aid. One lifted a silver whistle to his lips and blew into it. The high-pitched sound made the Mørkewulv shrink low to the ground and bare its teeth. Crystal and Cole poised themselves between the beast and Rigel. This gave Serena a chance to get to him. The guardian pressed a hand to his injury, but blood continued to pour through his clenched fingers. He winced as Serena ducked under his good arm to offer support.

"Don't worry about me," Rigel gaped, stumbling forward as his wound gushed.

"I'm not leaving you behind now!" She struggled to support him on her own but wouldn't leave him behind. As she lugged him forward, they left behind a trail of blood on the ground.

The dwarfs helped the Windaefs hold the Mørkewulv's attention, battering it with everything they had. The beast howled and reared its head in search of its attackers.

"Right here," Cole said, pulling a large knife from his belt and launching it like a spear. The wolf turned its face, and the knife embedded deep in its cheek.

A few steps behind him, Crystal let loose her last arrow. This time, she hit the Mørkewulv in one of its glowing eyes. The beast whimpered, staggering back until it slumped over. When the beast heaved its final breath, the dwarfs began cheering. Crystal found Sannarvin on the ground and picked it up before running for the wall.

As Serena dragged Rigel through the gates to Jordis, Will rushed to her aid. "You've made it," he said, glancing back through the open gates. "What of the others?"

"They fight the white Mørkewulv," Serena said. She looked around at the bustling crowd. Many dwarfs crowded around Rilura Steelcast and her guards from Faswyn, fussing over their wounds. Thomli, the worst of the four, laid on the ground with two dwarf healers tending to the deep gashes he had received from a Mørkewulv.

Xandra rushed over to them, relief alight on her face for a moment. "Heavens," Xandra said, her chest rising and falling fast as she peered between Serena's bruised neck and Rigel's open wounds.

"We need a healer," Serena said, grimacing as Rigel collapsed, too weak to stand on his own any longer.

The dwarf healers yelled orders as they examined their battered visitors' wounds. Bandan came up behind them and winced when he saw Rigel's mangled arm bleeding profusely. "That looks painful." He turned away from the guardian and called out to the others, "We need a healer over here!"

The Windaef siblings shoved their way through the crowd at the gate. When Crystal reached them, she dumped her bow and quiver in the snow and dropped to her knees next to Rigel. She examined the deep wounds where the Mørkewulv's teeth had torn through his flesh and tendons. Taking a deep breath, she shook her head and shouted, "I need water and towels. Now!"

Bandan nodded, departing to hunt down what she needed.

"You're alive," Xandra choked out as Cole enveloped her in a tight embrace.

"Are you all right?" he asked, holding her at arm's length to get a better look at her bloody face and torn clothes. "Where else are you hurt?"

Burying her face in his shirt, Xandra said, "I'll live, but Rigel—He's bleeding out."

Crystal yanked her gloves off and ripped a large strip off her cloak. "You do not have permission to die today," she said. She pressed the balled-up fabric into his bicep. Her hands glowed white as she started muttering chants in the ancient language.

"Crys," Rigel whispered deliriously. "We all made it. I told you we would." He writhed in pain as she pressed the fabric firmly against the injury that spanned across his shoulder and down his side.

Blood gushed forth. It seeped through the material and pooled around her pale fingers. "Hold still, Rige. I can fix you," she said, tossing the soaked strip of cloak aside. She pressed the rest of her cloak to his wound. "*Minuo subsisto*," she commanded louder, her palms glowing white as she put pressure on his wounds.

He gasped, and his sluggish eyes glanced from his friends' worried faces to his wound. Taking a haggard breath, Rigel whispered, "I'm going to be with my father again."

"The stars cannot have you yet," Crystal said angrily, tossing aside the blood-soaked cloak. Drawing back her bloody hands, she assessed the damage. The Mørkewulv's teeth had pierced through his bicep and shoulder; two dozen deep puncture wounds continued to bleed and made it nearly impossible to see through the sea of red. Peeling away his shredded shirt, she pressed her hands against his mangled flesh and screamed, "*Minuo subsisto!*"

Crystal looked up from the wound and froze. His face was turning gray, his eyes drooping tiredly. Will stepped toward her and asked, "What can we do, Crys?"

"Just stay back," she snapped at him.

Serena stood behind them. Her legs trembled as she flashed back to their battle on the mountain. "No," she whispered. "This isn't real. This isn't happening. Not again."

Will grasped her by the shoulders and looked her square in the eyes. "Serena, snap out of it," he said, shaking her gently. "We made it to Jordis. We're safe now."

Serena focused on Will for a moment, her sadness dissolving away as anger washed over her. She pushed Will away and stomped over to Rigel. Then she screamed through tears, "Why did you do it? Why did you throw yourself in front of me?"

"The princess," Rigel mumbled. "We... must save... the princess."

The other guardians' eyes widened as Rigel squeezed his eyes closed. Crystal took one of his hands and squeezed it. She whispered, "Do not quit on me. We are not home yet."

"Rilura?" Serena asked in confusion. "She was not even there! Where is she anyway? Did she not make it?"

Cole exhaled. "Rilura is safe. The captain made sure of that."

"And what of Martock?" Bandan asked, passing Crystal a pail of water and a handful of cloth.

"He is dead," Cole said.

"The general? But how? He was the strongest of all of us," Bandan said.

"Martock and Eldvar were protecting the princess. Two of the beasts charged at him, and he was wounded. I tried to divert one of the beasts' attention, but it was too late. The Mørkewulv swarmed Martock, and Eldvar used the distraction to get Rilura away," Cole explained.

"That bastard abandoned us," Thomli spat. "I should have known Eldvar would only think of himself. We are lucky he saved Rilura. Had it been out of the two of them, he would have sacrificed her to save himself."

Bandan said, "That's enough, Thomli."

Serena leaned over Rigel, touching his pale face with her trembling hands.

"Get her out of my way!" Crystal yelled, knocking her arm away. Xandra stepped forward to help Serena off the ground. She wrapped an arm around her waist.

Taking a clean rag, Crystal wiped her friend's sweaty brow and whispered, "Stay with me, Rige. I will get you all healed up. I just need you to be strong for a little longer." Crystal continued whispering enchantments while pressing her glowing hands to his wound. "*Minuo subsisto.*" After a few minutes, the elf lifted the blood-soaked rags from his wounds and exhaled. His face was gaunt; his lips drained of their usual pink hue. "The bleeding has stopped," Crystal said at last. She wiped her sweaty forehead with the back of her arm. "But I am not sure if that is a good thing. He lost so much blood."

"Will he survive?" asked Will.

"I cannot be sure." Crystal looked down at her trembling hands. "I can close a wound, but I cannot create more blood for him. It's up to his body to fight now."

A few yards to their right, the gates opened, and several dwarfs rushed inside. Verifying their identities, two of the Bevakors of Jordis lifted Thomli off the ground as if he weighed nothing and placed him on a stretcher. The healer caring for him told Bandan, "We will take him to the Infirmary now. The humans might wish to do the same."

"There's no use. That poor bastard already has one foot in the grave," said one of the Bevakors walking past them.

"Hush your mouth," snapped Crystal. Her menacing eyes shot arrows at the dwarf. Turning back to Rigel, she pressed her bloody palms to his cheeks and said, "Don't listen to them, Rigel. You are the strongest man here, and we still need you."

He opened his eyes, and a faint smirk appeared on his lips. "I like the sound of that." His faint chuckle quickly turned into a dry cough.

"Now is not the time for jokes," she argued, gripping his cold hands as a tear trickled down her cheek.

Rigel opened his mouth to speak but paused. He inhaled slowly, deliberately, as if he was struggling for each breath. He stared into Crystal's eyes and murmured, "Your eyes are my favorite sky."

Xandra and Will struggled to stifle their laughter.

"He's delirious," Crystal said, pushing herself onto her feet. "Let's move him to the Infirmary. I'll try to heal him more after I rest."

"You saved my life," Rigel said, wincing as two dwarfs lifted him onto a stretcher. Smiling drowsily at the blonde guardian, he whispered, "Thanks, boss."

As they hauled Rigel away, Serena turned to the guardians with an icy glare. "The beast wanted me. Why did he get in the way? He could have died."

"Because you have not met your fate. Try being grateful," Cole said coldly. Then his boots crunched against the ground as he sauntered after his friend. He paused next to his sister. He placed a gentle hand on her shoulder and squeezed it. "You did well today. You're the only reason he's still here."

Crystal nodded, and her brother marched after his wounded friend. Her shoulders quivered as she buried her face in her ensanguined hands. Xandra shook her head, wrapping her arms around her friend. "It's all right, Crys. He's all right. We all made it," she murmured, patting the back of her head. "Let's go. We all could use some rest."

A dwarf stepped toward them and said, "The Bevakors will recover as many bodies as they can. Tomorrow you can determine how we should honor your fallen friends."

"Friends?" Crystal snarled. "Thankfully none of our friends perished to those monsters."

Serena looked up and called out, "Cameron! My brother. His body is out there. Can they recover it?"

Crystal glanced at her in surprise. The Bevakor looked from the weary guardians back to her. "My sympathies, young lady," he said. "I will ensure he is brought in for you. The body can be tended tonight. We will ensure you have whatever you need to send off his spirit in the morn."

"Thank you," Will said, bowing his head.

Xandra dusted the snow off her tattered clothes; then she turned and did the same for Crystal, whose drooping eyes indicated her exhaustion. A female dwarf stepped forward, offering them water and blankets. "I am Megrena Greydigger," she said. "Please, allow me to show you inside."

She led the shaken humans and their Elven comrade down a grand stairwell into the underground city. When she showed them into a large room with four sets of bunk beds carved out of the mountain rock, they each traipsed inside and collapsed onto a feather-stuffed mattress.

"You all look exhausted. Do get some rest," Megrena said.

"Where are Rilura and Bandan?" Serena asked as she settled against a pillow.

"Oh, the princess is in special chambers kept for the Steelcast family, and her guards are resting. We have Bevakors posted outside her room, so you need not worry for her," Megrena assured them. "I'll be back to escort you to the morning meal. We should see them there."

"When can we see Rigel?" Crystal asked, sitting up on the edge of her bed.

"The man they brought to the Infirmary?" Megrena asked, and they nodded. "After we break fast, if he is up for the company."

Cole joined them later and reassured them that Rigel was in stable condition. Despite their exhaustion, none slept soundly. Their drained bodies were on edge after the grueling battle, their hearts missing their cherished friend's company. It was hours before the room grew quiet, each succumbing to their exhaustion one by one.

HAUNTED

When Serena entered the Infirmary a couple days later, it was easy to spot Rigel's red hair in the second bed on the left side. He sat propped up with pillows, clumsily attempting to eat left-handed from the tray on his lap while Crystal snoozed on the cot beside his. She had spent all her time there since the night they arrived, alternating between sleeping, healing, and warding off unnecessary visitors.

As Serena approached his bedside, Rigel glanced up at her, greeting her with the same crooked grin as usual. "Good morning," he said before taking a swig of the fruity concoction the dwarf healer had brought him. "I was starting to worry when no one came to see me."

"You can blame her for that," Serena said with a nod toward Crystal. "She told us to leave you to rest."

"While she's been in here night and day?" Rigel asked, his eyebrows raised as he glanced over at her. He shook his head, but a broad smile broke through. Then he quickly redirected his attention to Serena. "How are you?"

Serena scoffed as she stared at his injured arm. "I should be asking you that," she said. She shook her head as her eyes scanned the dressings on his body. There were no signs of blood on his bandages today, and the pallor of his face was much improved. Seeing his usual lopsided grin made the heaviness in her chest dissipate for the first time in days. She settled in the chair next to his bed and heaved a sigh of relief.

"I'm alive, as you can see," he replied with a devilish grin and hocked a handful of roasted potatoes into his mouth. "Thanks to her." He nodded his head toward their sleeping friend. "Were you worried for me?"

Serena leaned forward and slapped the side of his leg, scowling as she loomed over his bed. "Of course I was! We all were. What kind of idiot jumps in front of a Mørkewulv?" Serena asked, throwing her hands up in the air.

"An idiot who was trying to save you," Rigel said. He looked away. "I didn't have time to think about it. I saw it running for you, and my feet moved on their own."

Her eyes trained on the beads of sweat forming along his forehead, not quite concealed by his wild hair. She understood what he meant. Flashes of Cameron's final moments took her breath away, and she shut her eyes tight. She had never meant to kill her brother, but when her life was on the line, her instincts took over—blood be damned. "You're one lucky bastard," she muttered when she shoved the memories down and opened her eyes again. Serena sat back and folded her arms over her chest.

"Suppose you're right," Rigel said, looking at her. "I also have you to thank. If you had not intervened—"

"Did my sacrifice mean nothing to you?" Serena interrupted. She saw Rigel's face tighten, almost as if her words had physically struck him.

"Of course not," he stuttered. He attempted to move his right and grimaced from the pain. "I know you made an impossible decision in the moment, and I hate that it came to that."

"I didn't have time to think about it; he was about to kill you, and my body moved on its own," she threw his words back at him. "I had to save you. I had so little family left, and yet I sent Cameron to the stars with my own hands."

"I never asked that of you. It's my job to protect you, not the other way around," Rigel said, his voice projecting through the room. They both looked around, realizing the dwarfs on the other side of the room were staring at them.

"You didn't have to ask," she whispered. She stared at her hands. The skin was dry, cracked from their grueling battle on the mountain. She could have asked the dwarfs for something to help, but after surveying everyone else's injuries, her own felt trivial in comparison.

Rubbing his hand over his eyes, Rigel exhaled and lowered his voice when he said, "I will forever be grateful you thought my life worth saving, Serena. I know all too well what that choice cost you."

"It would have been for nothing if you had died," Serena said, the stinging in her eyes threatening to upend her composure. "Had I known you had a death wish, I—"

"I'm not sorry I saved you." Rigel's voice was loud and clipped. "I made a vow to Elara to save the people she cares about. I would have failed my queen had I not tried to save you."

Silence settled around the two friends. Finally, Serena asked the question that had been burning within her for months. "Why does my life matter so much? She knew my parents, not me."

Rigel groaned. He didn't answer right away, but when he did, he said, "You're the only person on her list we recovered." They both glanced at Crystal then, who'd begun tossing and turning and panting in her sleep. "Our entire journey would have been for nothing if we had lost you." His eyes held raging waves that threatened to drown her in that moment, but she still didn't understand the depth of his sorrow or his devotion to the queen.

"Maybe surviving isn't worth it, not if it turns you into the very thing you're running away from," Serena quipped as she rose to her feet.

"That's enough," Crystal said. Her bloodshot eyes stared them down from her resting place. "None of us is a heartless monster for defending ourselves. You are both here, alive, because we fought together—all of us. That's what matters."

"Serena," Rigel said, reaching for her hand, but she was already on her way out of the Infirmary. Passing Will in the doorway, Serena made a beeline down the hall as hot tears burned a trail down her face.

ELARA JOLTED AWAKE, HER heart pounding in her chest. The remnants of another vivid nightmare clung to the edges of her mind. She shot up in bed, clutching her swelling abdomen. Her breath came in ragged gasps. Beside her, Gerard stirred, his eyes blinking open in alarm.

"What's wrong?" he asked. Sleep and concern mingled in his voice, causing it to sound deeper and more rugged than usual.

"It happened again," she whispered, her voice trembling. "The vision... It was the same as the first time, but this time... this time I saw more."

Gerard sat up, his expression turning serious as he placed a comforting hand on her back. "Breathe, my love. In," he said, taking a deep breath in himself. "Out... Good. Now tell me what you saw."

Elara closed her eyes and tried to steady her racing heart. The scene from her dream replayed in her mind with haunting clarity. "It was Serena. She was being attacked, choked by a man with dark hair."

"Dark hair? That's not Zeke. Did you recognize him?" Gerard asked, leaning closer. He stroked his hand up her back and into her hair, gently massaging the back of her neck.

"No, but he was in uniform—a Guard uniform," the queen said. She gripped her bedsheets in tight fists. Her chest constricted, and she gasped for air as tears welled in her eyes. "He is in the citadel, Gerard. The man who tried to kill me. He's still here."

Her husband's brow furrowed as he pulled her onto his lap, wrapping his arms around her as she trembled. "If he's in the Guard, we'll find him," he whispered. Then he kissed the top of her head. "Don't worry, love. I won't let anything happen to you."

"He's eluded us for heaven knows how long," Elara whispered. She sniffled as she wiped at her cheeks. "I couldn't see his face, but the band on his arm was visible. One of my officers is a traitor." She nuzzled closer to his chest, thankful for his warmth, yet his embrace could not dispel the chills racking her body as the vision replayed in her mind.

Gerard's grip on her tightened, his jaw set in determination. "We need to act quickly. If he is one of our own, we must capture him before the guardians return."

Elara took a deep breath as her mind raced. "Summon the Cinderfell sisters. They need to know about this vision. Idonea's insight might help us."

Gerard nodded and rose from the bed, quickly donning his robe. "I'll send for them immediately. Stay in bed and try to remain calm, Elara. We'll get to the bottom of this. I'll be just outside the door speaking with the guards. An officer, you say?"

Elara nodded, her heart heavy with dread as he slipped out the door. She pressed a hand to her belly, feeling the flutter of her unborn child within. "I will protect you," she whispered, her resolve strengthening.

It wasn't long before Gerard returned with Ismenia and Idonea, their expressions a mixture of exhaustion and concern. They had been woken from their slumber, but the urgency of the situation left no room for complaints.

"Tell us everything," Idonea urged. Her eyes were intense with focus as she perched on the bed beside the queen. Elara recounted the vision in detail, her voice steady despite the fear gnawing at her. When she finished, Idonea closed her eyes, deep in thought.

"This is significant," she confirmed after a long pause. "Your visions have been growing clearer, more precise. It's a warning. As if Divinity is urging you to uncover the truth. Discover the culprit, and you could stop what you've seen from happening."

Elara felt another flutter, this time followed by a sharp pain. She gasped, clutching her stomach. Gerard rushed to her side, his face pale with worry.

"Elara, what's wrong?" he asked, his voice trembling. "Is it the baby?"

"I don't know," she whispered, tears streaming down her face. "The baby... What if it's reacting to the vision?"

Gerard held her close, and Elara could read the fear in his face. "Ismenia?"

Her face was etched with concern. She examined her carefully with gentle but firm hands. "You need to rest, Elara. The stress is too much for you and the baby."

"But we can't ignore this," Elara insisted. "If someone within our ranks is a traitor, we need to act now. Idonea said we could stop this from happening! We must protect Serena." She sucked in a sharp breath, pressing a hand to her chest.

Idonea placed a hand on Elara's arm. "Your health and the health of your child are paramount. We will help you, but you must promise to take care of yourself."

Elara nodded, feeling useless as she sank back into the bed. "I promise. But we must uncover the traitor. With haste. No one is safe."

Idonea offered her friend a comforting smile. "We will find him. Let's focus on the details of your vision. Even the smallest details could be crucial." Then, she looked at her sister. "Can you steep some lavender and chamomile tea for the queen?" Ismenia nodded and left the room at once.

Idonea and Gerard pulled a couple chairs beside the bed, and Elara described the insignia on the arm band she had seen in her vision. "It was a crest with two crossed swords beneath a crown. I remember that much."

"That's the insignia of the high-ranking captains in the Guard," Idonea said. "We need to get the commander in here. He would know which captains wear that specific emblem."

Gerard added, "And we should keep a close eye on anyone who might act suspiciously or out of character. We still do not know if we are dealing with one rogue captain or a group."

Elara felt a wave of dizziness and leaned back, pressing a hand to her forehead. "When will this nightmare end?"

He took her hand, and she found comfort in his strong grip. "We'll get through this, Elara. Together."

Elara closed her eyes, feeling the weight of exhaustion settle over her. "Promise me you'll find him," she whispered.

Gerard kissed her forehead. "I promise. Now rest, my love. Leave it to us."

Just then, Ismenia returned with several steaming cups of tea. Elara took hers eagerly, slowly sipping the scolding herbal concoction, and soon, she felt her muscles relax, one by one. Within minutes, her eyelids grew heavier, and Gerard pulled the blankets up to her chest. Cradled in the comfort of her bed, Elara felt a flicker of hope. The path ahead was fraught with danger and uncertainty, but she was ready to face it with her husband and allies by her side.

Rexton may have ripped her birth family away from her, but she would not let him hurt this new family she had found—or her child. For the future of Hyrosencia, she would not rest until the shadows were banished and peace restored.

COLE STRUCK TWO BLADES against each other until they produced sparks. As the kindling surrounding Cameron Finch's body ignited, Serena took two steps back from it. Her eyes flooded as the fire engulfed his corpse, blurring her vision as his burning body faded into memories from happier times. They had spent countless mornings tackling their morning chores together—feeding the chickens before they trekked into the woods to check the animal traps, laughing and teasing along the way. Cameron's smile had held such warmth for her in his youth, the fuzzy memory of his love for her only causing her more heartache. She tried to pinpoint a specific time when that love turned to resentment.

"May his soul ascend to the heavens, joining the stars which guide us through the darkness," Xandra said. One of her eyes was still swollen from the beating she had taken, and her blouse concealed a multitude of bruises and broken ribs. Cole walked over to the bench and sat beside her, allowing her to lean against his shoulder.

Will stood beside Serena, his arms clasped in front of his body as they watched her brother become one with the flames. In Hyrosencia, the practice of cremation was not uncommon, especially for soldiers, traveling merchants, and those taken by disease. Still, many chose to bury their dead together on their family's land. Serena scoffed, remembering she had no family and no home now, just a sword and a shattered heart.

Will asked Megrena something, but Serena ignored them, concentrating on the inferno before her. The heat coming off the fire was stifling, but she could not step away. She clamped her eyes shut and tried to remember one of the prayers her mother had taught her as a child. "Blessed be the souls who believe in Divinity, fight for a righteous cause, and die with a sword in their hand. May they be granted divine mercy and find peace among the heavens."

"Though his cause differed from ours, he stayed his convictions to the end." She opened her eyes, startled by Will's quiet voice.

"He should have stayed home with us," she muttered. "He should have stayed in Hyrosencia. He could have been buried with the rest of them."

"We both know how stubborn he was," Will said, touching the small of her back. She pulled away from him as if touching her might doom him to the same fiery end. Sweat pooled on her forehead as she stared at the flames, wishing that it was her body on the pyre, not her brother's.

It should have been me, she thought. Her cheeks burned from the sweltering heat of the burial chamber. "Cam was always the fighter in our family, even as a child. He fantasized about sword fighting and epic battles," she said. She thought about the times they snuck away with wooden swords. The boys had pretended they had to slay a dragon to save her, the helpless damsel in distress. She was no actress and would giggle throughout their dramatics. But every time, Cameron vanquished the enemy, beaming with pride as she leapt out of the trees into his arms. "I suppose he was destined to meet a warrior's end." Now she feared she had turned into the final dragon in his life, a monstrous twist of fate they both never saw coming.

"His crazy quests kept our lives interesting," Will said with a reminiscent smile.

"He was always looking for a fight," Serena agreed with a faint chuckle. "As he got older, he couldn't help butting heads with our parents. Papa wanted all the boys to work the smith or the farm, but Cameron couldn't wait to leave Durmak behind for bigger things." Serena grimaced as she thought about how Cameron always sought something more. Durmak was never enough for her older brother, and she couldn't forget how easily he had left their family behind.

"I can't fault him for wanting to forge his own path," Xandra said. "My father was not supportive the first time I said I wanted to join the Guard. He threatened to lock me in the highest tower at the citadel." Her friends chuckled.

Crystal added, "My father felt the same. Though the rest of our family were prominent warriors, he latched onto the idea of me being a healer."

"I think he just wanted to keep you safe," Cole said. "I think that's what all parents want."

Serena closed her eyes and whispered, "That's why my mother told me to leave Hyrosencia. She knew I would never be safe there. The king would find me just as he's found everyone else."

"But he did not win this time," Xandra said, lifting her chin proudly. "You're still here."

"Barely," Will muttered.

"This does not feel like a victory," Serena said. Her stomach turned as the smell of burning flesh hit her. She turned away from the pit and breathed deeply through her mouth. "I might make it to Symptee, but I have lost everything—my parents, my brothers, the only home I've ever known. At every turn, Rexton has been there, ready to take what little I have left."

"You have been so brave through these trying days, Serena," Crystal said.

"But you do not have to carry these burdens alone," Xandra added. Shifting shadows shrouded her face as the fire flickered before them. "We have faced these hardships together, and we will continue to lend you our strength until your spirits are lifted and your strength regained."

"Just keep your head up," Cole said. "Loss is difficult, but it lessens with time. We all know that much to be true."

"He's right," Xandra said, reaching for his hand.

"It's just not fair," Serena whispered over the crackling fire. "Cameron gave his life in service to the king. Our family should have been safe. How could Rexton think we were a threat all these years later?"

"Because Rexton has lost all sense of morality," Crystal said. "He has allowed his lust for power to overshadow his humanity. There is nothing redeeming left of him."

"He is a beast who must be slain, just as we put down the Mørkewulv," Cole said.

Serena swallowed hard and nodded. Her throat felt scratchy from crying earlier that day; her voice coming out in a rasp. "You're right. Rexton and his men are animals," she said crossly, tiny beads of sweat mingling with the tear streaks on her face. "Cameron was so loyal that he was blind to what that man was capable of. I didn't want to hurt him, but he refused to listen."

"It is truly a shame you were put in such a terrible position," Cole said, the sympathy in his voice catching her by surprise. Serena knew he was sincere. "But it's a testament to your strength that you chose to save Rigel and yourself."

"I shall never forget the look on his face," she whispered. "Neither of us thought I could hurt him. I suppose I've changed more than I ever thought possible."

"You're still the Serena Finch I've always known," Will said, nudging her with his shoulder.

"You're wrong," she said. She turned her gaze from the fire to her friend. The light from the flames danced across the side of his face as he stared at her. "I am not the same. I never will be."

Will's lips parted, but there were no right words in that moment. The guardians stayed quiet, respecting her space as she sulked under her heavy loss. Her brother was dead, and she would have to live with the insurmountable guilt she felt for the rest of her days.

"I wish we could have buried him back home," Serena said with a sigh. "Papa always said to give the dead back to the earth."

"He may burn here, but this need not be his final resting place," Crystal said softly. "My people believe the vessel must deteriorate before the spirit can find its next home. Fire does quickly what the earth does slowly. Cremation is how many honor their loved ones. The ashes can be collected and buried wherever you desire."

Serena nodded her head. "At least I won't be the only Finch buried in Symptee."

"Oh, don't say that," Xandra said, her brows knitting together. "You have much more life to live before anybody will be burying you. We have all fought hard to make sure of that."

Something in her words triggered a wave of anger that shot through Serena like a bolt of lightning in her veins, and she scoffed. "Yes, you have," she said. The questions swirling through her head caused an unbearable heaviness in her chest. Turning to face the three guardians sitting behind her, she scanned their solemn faces and asked, "Why is my life so important to you? To Elara? My life is not worth more than that of her best guardians. Maybe my parents were—but even that's a stretch."

"Don't say that, Serena. Your life is important," Xandra insisted.

"We were sent on a classified mission to search for a number of people," Crystal said. "Classified as in we do not have all the facts, nor would we be allowed to tell you. That is not our place as your guardians."

"When are you going to stop lying to me?" Serena asked, looking Crystal square in the eyes. "I thought I could trust you, yet you've been keeping secrets from me this entire time. And not just your bloody ears!" Crystal looked away. Serena glared at them for a moment, moving her eyes from one guardian to the next. Fear of the unknown crushed her chest like a rock. Her lungs ached, and she just wanted to scream. Instead, she sank to the floor and rested her head upon her knees. "Rigel threw himself into the jaws of a Mørkewulv for me," Serena said quietly. "What on earth would make him do that?"

"He did what any of us would do," Cole said.

"He protected his family," Crystal added.

"Family?" Will asked, doubt painted across his tired face.

"We are his family," Crystal said, raising her voice, "the two of you included."

Cole gripped his sister's shoulder supportively and said, "That we are."

"I've already lost one family," Serena said bitterly. "I don't want to lose any of you."

Nobody said a word until Will cleared his throat and asked, "How is Rigel doing?"

Tucking a strand of hair behind a pointed ear, Crystal shrugged. "He was pleased to see Serena this morning, but it will be a while before he regains his strength. He'll need more rest before we can move on."

"At least it wasn't one of his legs," Cole muttered.

"Will your magic help him heal faster?" asked Serena

Crystal bit her lip and scrunched her nose. "The muscles and skin, yes, but he will remain tired and in pain while his internal wounds heal. I may be able to speed up the process, but not overnight. Magic has a heavy price. My own energy is depleted, so I fear I'm out of commission until tomorrow."

"We are so close to Symptee," Xandra said. "Once Rigel has the strength to walk, we can take the journey slowly. It will be good for him to be back home among our people."

Cole nodded. Then he looked at Serena. "When we return, Elara and the Guard will honor Rigel's courage and commitment to protecting you with his life."

"I would rather die than see anyone else run straight into danger like that," Serena said, "even you." She glared into the fire. "That was reckless. He would have died if Crystal didn't have magic."

"That's our job," Crystal reminded her. She shuffled over to sit on the floor beside Serena. "All guardians pledge an oath to protect the Garrick family—and anyone they deem important. The Finches were on Elara's list because they were among those most loyal to her. That's why she sent several units in search of them. She knew Rexton would find them if they were in his territory—and he did. She never wanted such a terrible fate for Mary or her sons."

Serena stared at the white-hot flames as they licked up high in the underground cavern, crackling loudly as they consumed her brother's flesh. The putrid stench permeated the room, making her hold her breath. She still could not believe what had happened. How under the stars had she ever gotten here? It felt like just yesterday Mama and her brothers gathered around the kitchen table to sing her "Happy Birthday." She clenched her fists as tears of frustration escaped from her bloodshot eyes. Her voice was steady as she said, "I don't understand how I'm still standing. Men and monsters have tried to kill me, yet I remain—the weakest of the Finches!"

Cole's boots crunched against the coarse ground as he walked toward Serena. Without looking at her, the swordsman said, "The humans believe your destiny is in the stars. I do not believe in such a thing as fate, but Rigel is quite sure of it."

"Cole," his sister warned, clenching her jaw.

Serena's eyes flicked toward Crystal. "What would he know of my destiny?"

"More than you can fathom," Xandra muttered. She closed her eyes and rubbed one of her temples. "We'll be in Symptee soon. Then they will tell you what you need to know."

"*They* who? Why are you all being so cryptic?"

They were silent for a moment; the guardians exchanged grievous looks. Finally, Crystal said, "We will tell you what we know tomorrow. But let us honor your brother now."

"Tell me what?" Serena asked, her eyes widening like a scared doe. Pushing herself off the ground, she snarled and kicked the gravel near her feet, which scattered through the air and sprinkled around Cameron's body. "I have grown tired of your countless secrets."

Cole exhaled slowly. "Elara ordered us not to tell you anything."

Xandra cocked her head to one side. "We never wanted to deceive you."

"What's changed then? Why tell me now? I've come this far in the dark," Serena muttered. She lifted her chin toward the ceiling. The sky was concealed by the mountain around them, making her feel utterly alone. She shook her head at the stalactites and wished she could be outside under the stars. Holding her hand out over the flames, she said, "I should be the one burning to ash right now." She pressed her palm against her aching heart, the warmth of her flesh just another reminder that she had her brother's blood on her hands.

"Serena!" Xandra gasped.

"Don't say that," Will pleaded, reaching toward her.

Then Serena turned and bolted for the hallway, leaving her friends behind in the burial chamber. Her heart felt as dark and clouded as the storm clouds rolling in over the mountains, threatening to burst at any moment. She had to get away from them—these people who had weaseled their way into her heart in such a brief time. *As easily as they've lied to my face every day*, she thought. The only person there who she could trust was Will, and after what she had done, Serena was certain he'd never look at her the same again.

32

HARD LESSONS

When Will found their sleeping quarters empty, he knew there was only one other place where Serena would find comfort on this most difficult day. He bounded up the stairs two at a time until he burst through the door, the chilly air hitting his face. The sun was low, bathing his skin in warmth as he searched for her. His boots sloshed through the half-melted snow as he paced down the cobblestone path in front of several dwellings until he spotted her.

Serena was shrouded by the branches of a mighty willow just off the path, and Will might not have noticed her if a passing breeze hadn't blown the drooping branches just enough to one side. Will paused, his chest swelling as he watched her tear bits off a fallen leaf. Her mind was clearly elsewhere, her eyes glazed over as she stared through the curtain of green leaves at the house across the path, oblivious to his presence.

When he mustered the courage to step off the path, he moved slowly, hoping not to scare her. "Nice spot," he said as he brushed aside two low-hanging branches to join her in the shade. "Mind if I hide with you?"

Serena snapped out of her trance and gawked at Will. "Oh," she said, allowing the last of the frayed leaf to float to the ground. "Depends who you're hiding from?"

He chuckled and leaned his back against the tree trunk as he tucked his hands into his pockets. "No one in particular," he mused. "Question is, who are you hiding from?"

She tugged at her bottom lip with her teeth, and her eyes searched between the hanging limbs for signs of someone. "The guardians, I suppose," she said quietly. "I haven't had a minute to myself in weeks," she added with a shrug.

Will's face fell, his eyes coming to rest on his worn boots as he nodded. "I understand," he murmured. He pushed his torso off the tree as if to leave. "If you want me to go—"

"No," Serena said hastily. She turned and pressed him back against the tree with her palm. Will stared into her eyes, laying a hand over hers. His hand lingered there as he watched realization dawn on her face, knowing she could feel the fast beating of his heart.

"I'm not going anywhere," he promised.

Serena cleared her throat as she stepped back, wringing her hands together. She thanked him, and a faint smile spread across her face. She turned and leaned back against the tree with her shoulder resting beside his. They were quiet for a while, until she broke the silence with her soft and solemn voice. "Why did you come looking for me?"

Will turned his head. He searched her melancholy face. He would do anything to bring back the light he'd come to love. "I was worried about you."

She looked down at her bandaged hands.

"You can talk to me, you know?"

It was then that Serena whispered, "I don't know how you can even look at me after what I did." As if ashamed of her confession, she buried her face in her dressed hands.

His boots sloshed in the slush on the ground as he straightened and looked at her. "You mean Cam?"

Serena nodded, sliding her hands down from her face to cross them at the waist as if that could somehow shield her from their conversation. "He was your best friend."

"I don't blame you for what happened," Will said. He leaned one hand against the tree trunk over her shoulder and looked into her eyes. He urged her to understand what he was saying. "He attacked you. He wasn't himself. You did what you had to do."

"Yet he was still my brother," Serena said, her voice dripping with malice. "What kind of a monster kills their own kin?"

"Serena," he said gently. He reached out to caress her cheek, and though she tried to look away, he turned her face until she dragged her eyes to meet his. "I know you, and you are no monster."

"But you don't know me." She pulled his hand away from her cheek. "I am but a shattered fragment of who I once was. This path has changed me, and not for the better."

Will stepped in front of Serena then, so she could not retreat. "You're wrong about that. You are much stronger than you used to be. You've proven you can survive anything, and I'm proud of you for that."

"I'm not!" Her sharp tone startled him. "I do not like what I have become. Death would have been kinder than this slow descent into madness."

Will rubbed his hands over his face and groaned. "Heavens help me." He tilted his head back to peer up through the branches. The sky was heavy with clouds, casting an ominous shadow over the mountains.

"He's not listening. He never does."

"What?"

"The Great Creator has ignored my every plea for aid. I must be damned for He has forsaken me."

"That does not sound like the Divinity our parents spoke of," Will said. "He hears you. But sometimes He answers us in unexpected ways."

Serena growled under her breath. "Do you think my brother showing up was an answered prayer?"

"Of course not," he began, but she shoved him a few steps back. "I don't know what His plan is, but He hasn't forsaken you. You're still alive for a reason."

"I should not be!" Serena kicked a puddle on the ground, and the filthy water sloshed upward and splattered across Will's clothes. "I should have closed my eyes and let Him take my soul back."

Will's lips parted in horror. "You can't mean that."

Serena turned. He had seen her cry before, but now her eyes were dry and puffy, void of any sadness. She was full of rage now, her fists flying at him.

"I do. I have done unspeakable things to survive. Things that cannot be undone," she said. Will grabbed hold of her wrists and held them down firmly to stop her from striking him.

Serena twisted defiantly; her face contorted in a displeased pout. "I don't know why you're out here arguing with me. You must hate me as much as I hate myself." Her voice broke, the fragile sound making his chest throb as he watched her crumble under her guilt.

"Is that what you think?" Will asked quietly. His heart ached as he released her arms. They slumped to her sides dejectedly as she chewed the inside of her lip and avoided his gaze. He stepped closer. "Look at me." When she glanced up, he cupped her face in his hands, forcing her to lock eyes with him. Leaning in, he whispered, "I could never hate you."

"Never?" Her eyes were the brightest green he had ever seen then, almost luminescent as if they held all the fire of her soul.

"Never," he affirmed, and he felt her heart rate steady.

She nodded and whispered, "I'm sorry." Her eyes dropped to his chest, and she brushed two fingers against the small area of pink skin peeking out of his shirt where she had punched him. "I'm so sorry, Will," she choked out, her face puckering. "I'm just so angry. At Cameron and Rigel. And myself."

Will tugged her against his chest, and she wrapped her arms around his middle. "I know," he whispered, stroking his fingers over her hair. "It's okay. Whatever you're feeling, just let it out." She sobbed into his chest, clutching the back of his shirt between her fingers, and he wished he could hold her like this on better terms. Maybe he'd try one day when she was ready.

After a while, Serena took a slow and deep breath. She had shed countless tears onto his shirt. A loud crack of thunder rumbled through the mountains, making her jump in his arms. Will chuckled, drawing his torso back to look at her face. "Don't laugh at me," Serena fussed, wiping the tears under her eyes on her shirt sleeve. Her gaze drifted down to the massive wet splotch in the middle of his shirt, and she grimaced.

The pitter patter of raindrops against the half-thawed ground grabbed their attention. Serena sighed and dropped her neck back, basking in the cool drops as they massaged her tired face. Will watched as the rain washed away the tension in her shoulders. Somehow the rain washed her sorrows away.

"You see? The stars weep for you," he said, stepping toward her. She lowered her chin and smiled faintly, cocking her head to one side. One strand of her dark tresses clung to the side of her face, and he smoothed it back with his palm. "I will stand here, basking in Divinity's tears, for as long as it takes you to stop hating yourself. Because you are not deserving of hatred, and you are not alone in your pain. You never will be."

Serena lurched forward, throwing her arms around his neck, and his eyes widened in surprise. Will stepped back, regaining his footing before wrapping his arms around her. She hugged him as if the warmth of his sturdy arms could shield her from what haunted her, and in that moment, he knew they did.

ANTEROS TWIRLED THE HILT of a thin parrying blade between his fingers and taunted his opponent with a crooked smile as he carefully selected his weapon. The young man with a long face sneered as he took off his jacket, tossing it into the arms of a friend before brandishing a much broader blade.

"Are you sure you can handle that, Julian?" the prince teased, earning a snicker from his sidelined friends.

"Scared, Your Highness?"

"In your dreams," Anteros jeered. He tossed the blade gently so another of his friends could catch it. Sauntering over to where several shining swords were mounted on the gray stone wall, the prince ran his fingertips along the cold metal of two before pausing to stare at his reflection in a third option. He knew his appearance was unkempt; he had rushed down to sneak food to Talitha between breakfast and his weapon studies. A flash of her red hair crossed his mind, and the memory of trading her breakfast for a deep kiss brought a broad grin to his face. Her lips tasted of the crisp red apples he always brought her; now the only way he desired the sweet fruit was from her kiss. He couldn't wait to get back to her after dinner.

"Where is your head at?" his instructor mused, furrowing his brow.

"With a girl, by the looks of it." His friend Calix punched him lightly on the shoulder.

The prince shook his head and took the sword off the wall, feeling its weight. "With far better company than you gents," he replied, pointing the sword at Calix and Julian.

"You're not usually one to be tight-lipped," Calix quipped. "Do not think your disappearance went unnoticed the other night. We all saw you slip out of the masque with a girl in tow. Was she better company in private?"

Anteros grinned as he recalled Talitha's transformation the night of the Solstice. The cut of her dress accentuated her figure while hiding the fact that she was still somewhat malnourished; the black lace mask made her blue-gray irises more alluring. It took everything not to crawl into his bed and kiss her all night long. If he had the chance to sneak her out again, that's precisely what he intended to do.

"A gentleman never tells," he said, giving the boys a wink as he crossed the room. Anteros positioned himself in the far corner of the sparring square outlined in black marble tiles and faced his opponent.

"But you are no gentleman," Julian scoffed, stepping into the square opposite Anteros.

Calix chuckled in agreement. He stood outside of the square beside their instructor. "Come on. Tell us how the lady was," he said, raising his eyebrows suggestively.

Anteros snickered, then ignored their taunts to focus on the fight. Julian grinned as he charged at him, going on the offensive with a swing from the side. The prince reacted quickly, their heavy swords clattering between them. Both pressed forward seeking an advantage, but their strength was evenly matched.

Julian wasted no time going at the prince with a barrage of moves. This forced Anteros three paces backward as he defended himself. The shrill sound of their scraping blades made everyone wince. As Julian reared back to assess his next move, Anteros took the opportunity to charge forward. The quick succession of strikes forced their bodies back to the center of the square.

Sweat dripped down the sides of their faces as they caught their breath. Only a few paces separated them. The prince lifted one arm and wiped his forehead on his billowing white sleeve, his watchful eyes never leaving Julian's.

"Keep going," their instructor demanded as he crossed his arms.

Anteros grinned as something familiar flashed in his friend's eyes, and he knew Julian's next move. While his friend was strong, he lacked originality, and that allowed the prince's intellect to shine. As Julian charged forward, swiping his sword at the prince's midsection, Anteros used his blade to deflect the blow. He shoved his friend's weapon to one side, and the move gave himself an opening to kick the boy square in the abdomen. Julian's eyes widened as he flew backward, his sword clattering on the ground as he landed on his rear.

"Not very gentlemanly," Julian said through clenched teeth. The disgruntled young man snatched his weapon off the floor.

Anteros chuckled as he stepped closer to loom over his opponent. "This is swordplay," the prince quipped. "There are no gentlemen. Only winners and losers."

One corner of Julian's mouth raised wickedly when Anteros extended a hand to help him up. "In that case..." His sword swiped low to the floor as he aimed for Anteros' ankles.

The prince narrowly leapt over the blade, the sudden move throwing him off balance. He staggered back a few steps, then reared up for round two. "Don't think my father would appreciate you marring the crown prince," he huffed.

"The king expects you to earn your victories," his instructor said.

Calix, energized by the stakes of their ongoing match, whooped, "You've got him, Anteros. Put him on his back like last time."

Anteros dug his heels in, holding his blade crosswise in front of his chest. "Your move, Jules." His lips pulled tight in a taunting smile.

"Oh, no," his opponent said. "I will not fall for that again. Your turn."

A thought crossed Calix's mind. "Tell me, Anteros, how would you feel if your sister were caught sneaking out of the masque as you did?"

"What?" Anteros said. His spine straightened as his eyes bounced from Calix back to Julian. He gnashed his teeth together and then glared at his opponent with resounding animosity. "Was it you?" he asked through his teeth before pointing his sword dead at Julian's chest.

Julian lifted his hands in surrender. "Anteros, my old friend," he grinned, "your concern for sister dearest is admirable." He adjusted his grip on the hilt of his sword. "But do not fret. I am a gentleman, after all."

Something in Anteros snapped, and he charged at his friend. Julian deflected his initial attack, leaning back on one leg as Anteros brought down a barrage of erratic hits in succession.

"Remember your feet, gents," the instructor said, his tone indifferent as he stepped around Calix for a closer view.

With their hands trembling as they pressed their blades together, both glanced down at their feet. Anteros grinned as he dragged his dark gaze to meet Julian's and asked, "Anything to say before I end you?"

Julian's knowing look made Anteros want to pummel him with his bare hands. "I wonder which of us had the better evening," he mused. His goading prompted the prince to force their blades upward so he could knee Julian in the groin. Both blades plunged to the floor, rattling loudly as they bounced against the black and white tiles. Calix winced as his friend dropped to his knees on the floor. Anteros loomed over him, panting heavily while he debated knocking out a few of Julian's perfect teeth. "I yield," the boy wheezed, moaning as he flopped over, clutching his groin.

Anteros stepped closer and dug the toes of his boots into his squirming friend's shirt. Bending over him, he grabbed Julian by a handful of his hair and said, "If you so much as look in Sabine's direction again, you will feel far worse pain by way of my blade."

A slow clap boomed from the doorway, and everyone whipped their heads around to find Antoine Rexton had been watching their match.

"Your Majesty," Calix and the instructor said in tandem, knocking their heels together and bowing at the waist. Julian scrambled onto his knees and bowed his head.

"Father," Anteros said, quickly bowing before stepping toward the king. "Come to watch me put these gents in their place?"

"Is that what you called that display?" One brow quirked up in curiosity.

"Yes! I won. I incapacitated him," he huffed. "What more should I have done?"

The king stroked his thick beard, eyeing his son thoughtfully before he said, "In my youth, the match did not end until blood was drawn."

The young men lifted their pretty faces in alarm as they looked between each other and the king. "But he yielded, Your Majesty," Calix stuttered, his eyes wide with concern. When the king whipped his head around to scowl at him, the boy bowed, his torso hovering perpendicular to the ground.

"If I may, Your Majesty," interrupted their instructor, "They are still mere boys with no real experience in battle."

"Then perhaps those more experienced should demonstrate," Antoine said, meandering his way to the wall of mounted weapons. He carefully inspected his options before selecting the broadest sword, giving no indication of its heaviness as he lifted it from the brackets with one hand.

Everyone grew quiet, for they knew Antoine Rexton with a sword in his hand was a man to avoid at all costs. No longer squirming, Julian swallowed hard. "Please, Your Majesty, I beg of you. Do not kill me." The frightened boy bowed his head.

"I have no quarrels with you, Julian." The king waved his free hand nonchalantly. "Get out of the square."

The boy stumbled onto his quivering legs and staggered over to hide behind the instructor. Calix sidestepped, trying to weasel his way behind the instructor as well. Antoine rolled his eyes at the pitiful boys.

The instructor cleared his throat and said, his voice changing octaves midway, "Should you need my assistance in this demonstration?" He clasped his gloved hands behind his back to keep the king from noticing their trembling, but Anteros need not look to know the fear his father provoked in others.

"Not today," Antoine said. His eyes glistened darkly as he eyed the sword in his son's hand.

Anteros scraped his sword against the tile as he started toward his father. "You want to fight me?"

"Who better to teach you how a real battle is won?" Antoine asked, holding his arms out wide. "You boys are lucky. When I was your age, my father sent my brothers and me off to fight in the war between Nyzenard and the neighboring kingdom of Idaris."

"I have never heard of Idaris." Anteros took a few steps back in the square.

The king stepped into the sparring square too. Anteros watched his lips quiver in a heinous grin. "Exactly."

As the boys' eyes widened, Antoine lifted his sword and stormed at his son. Anteros, who was unprepared for this sudden attack, barely managed to block his father's first strike. He gritted his teeth as the king bared down on the blade with his full force. Though Anteros was tall and athletic, his father dominated him in height and used his brawny build to his advantage. They drew their swords back briefly, only to thrust back into parrying, their blades clashing in swift sequence.

The prince thought he had a feel for his father's strategy and attempted to change up his own method. But when Anteros swung his blade for his father's left shoulder, Antoine was ready. He quickly blocked the move, interlocking their swords to where Anteros could not pull back his arm. The prince's eyes widened as his father tugged his arm to the side, and the king thrust his head forward to ram into Anteros' forehead with full force. The blow disarmed the boy, and he staggered back until he fell to the ground. His ears rang as he scrambled for his weapon, but it was too far out of reach. Antoine stepped lightly on his hand, somehow not breaking any of his son's bones under the heavy weight of his leather boots. He ticked his tongue thrice in his mouth before removing his foot, his black eyes full of disdain as he stared down at his son. "Is that it then? Are you done?" Anteros asked with hostility as he pressed his palm to his throbbing head.

His father eyed him for a moment before glancing around the room. Everyone in the room had stopped their training to take in the spectacle of the king teaching his son a lesson in swordplay. No one looked surprised by the outcome. Antoine Rexton had never lost a fight. Without warning, the king pressed one foot to Anteros' chest, forcing him to lie back. "We are done when I say so." He pointed his sword at his son's chest.

Anteros blinked up at his father from his back. The tip of a sword pressed against his clavicle, and for a moment, he panicked, wondering whether his father would go so far as to stab his only heir out of spite.

A triumphant smirk played on Antoine's lips as he savored his son's fright. "Now hear the greatest lesson I shall ever teach you: Never allow an adversary to walk away from you unscathed. If you do, you have not won."

Anteros tried to sit up, but Antoine forced him back down with the tip of his sword. The sharp steel pierced through his skin, and a trickle of hot blood dripped from Anteros' clavicle down his chest, the crimson streak disappearing into his shirt. The prince grimaced, slamming his head back against the hard tile. Anteros held his breath, waiting to see if his father's lesson had ended as his blood soaked through his shirt, sullying the once-pristine fabric.

With sinister eyes trained on his son, the king added, "I trust you will not fail me again." Then he tossed the sword onto the floor beside Anteros with a clatter before marching out of the room.

CRYSTAL SCRAPED A FORK against her plate, shuffling her breakfast potatoes about in a distracted manner while the others discussed how soon they might be able to travel through the tunnel to Silvermane. "Will he really be well enough to travel so soon?" Serena's eyes lit with hope as she turned toward Crystal.

When Crystal did not respond, Xandra scooted over on the bench where they sat and nudged her friend's shoulder. "Where is your head today, Crys?"

"Hm?" She blinked at her comrade, her azure eyes questioning what she had missed. "Did you say something?"

Cole shook his head and lifted his chalice off the table. "Serena asked about Rigel's condition," he said before taking a swill.

"Ah," Crystal looked back at her plate. "Yes, he gains strength every hour. It's making him restless. We shall see how he does on his feet today."

"I hope you will not push him too hard, too soon," Serena said.

"Knowing Rigel, he will do that to himself." Cole stood with his plate and cup in his hands.

"Where are you off to?" Will asked, scooping the last bite of his meal into his mouth.

Cole smirked. He balanced the chalice on top of his pewter plate. He patted Will roughly on the shoulder and said, "We have the weaponry for training this morning."

Will's face fell as he glanced over his shoulder at Serena. She sighed and muttered, "Suppose we should prepare for the worst. Who knows what else is out there?"

"Not you," Crystal said, finally locking eyes with Serena. "Rigel asked if you would visit him after breakfast."

Serena relaxed. She was relieved to avoid training. "Of course I will," she beamed.

"I would like to see him, too," Will said. He brushed his thick hair back from his eyes. It had grown quite long, and he was in desperate want of a haircut, Serena thought.

"As I require a partner and you require further training, we will have to visit our friend after luncheon," Cole said. Then he stepped over the bench and departed from their table. "Come, Burroughs."

Will huffed, glancing back at the ladies. "Give him my best then," he said with a shrug before trudging after the elf.

Serena frowned as they disappeared into the hallway. "Surely they could have stopped by the Infirmary before training."

"It's for the best that Will does not join us this time." Crystal reached across the table to take Serena's cup. Xandra took all their plates and stacked them up before following Crystal to return their dishes.

"What?" Serena scrambled off the bench and rushed after them.

The guardians deposited the dirty dishes in two bins, thanking the dwarfs on their way out the dining hall. Serena hurried into the hallway on their heels, a growing sense of unease settling in her chest as she followed them in silence. Something had changed in the guardians' demeanors this morning, and she feared whatever the guardians were trying to hide from Will.

When they reached the Infirmary, Crystal held open the door and beckoned Serena inside with a faint smile that did nothing to reassure her heavy heart.

"Good morning," Rigel greeted them. He exchanged a nervous glance with his comrades.

"Good morn," Xandra replied as she pulled an extra chair to Rigel's beside and motioned for Serena to take a seat. Crystal nodded to the only healer in the corner of the room, and he scurried for the door, leaving the four of them alone. The guardian then shoved a sword through the door handles, locking all others out of the room and Serena within.

Serena's eyes widened when she realized the other patients had been moved overnight. She lowered herself onto the chair, bracing her hands against its cold metal arms. "Why do I feel like I am about to be scolded?"

Rigel and Xandra chuckled, and Serena could tell they were uncomfortable by the uneasy smiles plastered on their faces. "You're not in trouble," Rigel said, his bandaged arm shifting a hair closer to her on the mattress. "But we have something important to tell you."

"Something Elara did not want us to tell you," Crystal added sharply, leaning against the foot of Rigel's bed. Serena held her breath as she stared at the ground, remembering all the unspoken and unanswered questions whirling within her the past three months. She reached into her pocket and pulled out the thin gold band that had given her the chance to speak to the queen, eyeing the enchanted piece of metal in her palm. She had spoken to Elara using the enchantment twice:

at the safe house near the reservoir and briefly in Morlerae while the guardians were sleeping. In both instances, the conversations left her with more questions than answers—and the perturbing feeling that Elara was keeping something from her. The last time she put her mother's ring on, Elara had not been wearing its match, which had only made her more suspicious. "I have spoken to Elara before," Serena reminded them, clenching the ring in her fist. "If there was something important I needed to know, why would she not tell me herself?"

Xandra sank into the chair beside her and rested her elbows on her knees. As she wrung her clammy hands together, she said, "It's a delicate matter. Something very few people are privy to," Light from the row of torches on the wall reflected off her brown skin and bright eyes, reminding Serena of the sun's golden rays. The honesty reflecting from Xandra's eyes would have put her at ease had the guardians not looked remorseful.

"And it's far too dangerous to be said out in the open," Rigel added. He took a steadying breath as Serena gnawed the inside of her lip and glanced around the empty room.

"Then why do you want to tell me now?" she asked as she leaned forward in her chair. Her knuckles were stark white as she gripped the arms.

Rigel's voice resounded throughout the Infirmary. "Because you deserve to know." The silence that followed was haunting, only interrupted by the sound of his haggard breathing. Xandra reached over and patted the top of his bound hand, and she nodded in agreement.

"He's right. We should have found a way to tell you sooner. It was not fair to keep this from you," she said.

"Keep what from me?" Serena yelled, pushing herself off the chair. The metal scraped against the floor as it skittered back, slamming into the next Infirmary bed. "Enough of the cloak and dagger. Tell me the truth. Now."

Crystal's voice was low but clear as she stared at Serena. "You are the lost heir to the Garrick throne." A sliver of sympathy flashed in the guardian's eyes as she pushed off the bed to block the girl's only exit.

Serena laughed, but Crystal maintained a straight face. This had to be a joke, Serena reasoned. Then, looking at the other guardians, she froze. No one else was laughing. She leaned back on her right leg, slowly shaking her head as the words replayed in her mind. "No," she said firmly. She inhaled, pressing one hand against her chest as it constricted. "That can't be. I'm a Finch. My parents were commoners."

"It's true, Serena," Xandra said, standing and reaching out to her. But Serena recoiled from her touch.

"And you are not just a blacksmith's daughter." Rigel's downcast eyes offered her no light.

"What are you saying? That John Finch was not my father?" Serena stuttered, struggling to form the words.

"John and Mary loved you very much," Xandra said. "But Mary did not give birth to you."

"I knew something was amiss when I first saw Elara, but I never dreamed..." Serena paused, closing her eyes. A jolt of pain like lightning stung her head, and she jammed her fingertips in her temples, hoping to relieve the swell of pain. "No. This can't be..."

"You know how Rexton feels about loyalists," Crystal said, taking a step forward. "He would stop at nothing to eradicate the last of the Garrick claim to his throne."

"Is she my mother?" Serena whispered, lowering her hands to her sides. Fragments of her life flashed through her mind and shattered like glass. The peaceful life she once knew was over. When the guardians did not answer quickly enough, she raised her voice and repeated her question: "Is Elara my mother?"

"No, dear girl," Xandra said. A glimmer of tears lined her lashes. "She is your aunt. Your real parents were killed in the siege."

The realization hit her like a brick to the skull. If Elara was not her mother, that meant the late Prince Stellan Garrick was her father. And she had lost not one but two families in her short life. Xandra reached out to comfort Serena, who was quivering in a vain attempt to suppress the sobs rising in her chest. Serena stumbled back into the bedside stand behind her, and Rigel's breakfast dishes clattered against each other. His glass tumbled over, shattering on the floor as the table continued rocking on its frail legs. Xandra grabbed Serena's arms to steady her, which only made Serena feel more hostile. "Don't touch me!" she said as she yanked her arms free.

Xandra stepped back and lifted her arms in surrender as her chin dipped. "We just want to help you," she whispered.

Crystal pushed past the empty chairs, taking a firm hold of Serena's shoulders and locking eyes with her. Something in the elf's eyes emanated serenity; was it another enchantment? Crystal pulled her chair forward and said, "I know this all feels like too much right now, but you are strong. You will overcome the shock. But for now, sit."

"Why?" she asked, swiping away her tears before they could forge a path down her flushed cheeks. Serena slumped dejectedly into the metal chair. A rush of questions burned in her mind; she ached with the fear that she would never have all the answers. "Why did they take Elara to the citadel and leave me behind?"

Rigel shifted his body to face her. "Rexton used his engagement to Elara as a means of gaining the king's trust. Once their guard was down, he was able to plan the perfect coup from the inside. When they attacked, there was no warning. Everyone dispersed and prayed they would somehow survive."

"How did I end up with John and Mary?" she asked, the knot in her throat dissipating.

"Mary was helping in the nursery when the siege began," Xandra explained. "There were half a dozen children there, you and your brother included. Everyone was told to take a child and get to safety."

"I had a brother?" Serena asked as hope beat in her chest. "What happened to him?"

The guardians lowered their heads, and none jumped to answer her question. Crystal looked as if she were about to say something when Xandra cleared her throat. "The little prince had just been born when Rexton attacked. His whereabouts are still unknown after all these years."

"So he may still be alive then?" Serena said, taking a shaky breath as she rose from her seat.

"It's true," Xandra said, but her head bowed as she said his survival was unlikely.

Serena gave way to abandoned hope, groaning. "Am I so undeserving of peace that Divinity had to rip not one but two families from me? Was it not enough that I lost the only family I can remember? Now I must also live with knowing I lost one I cannot."

"You have not lost everyone, Serena," Xandra tried to comfort her.

Rigel winced as he tried to sit up more. "We never meant to upset you," he pleaded. "Though life has dealt you a blow, you will overcome this pain."

"Did you think I would feel some sort of relief to learn Cameron Finch was not my own flesh and blood?" Serena asked bitterly, looking between Xandra and Rigel. "You were wrong."

"That was not the intention behind this," Rigel said sternly as he pounded a fist into his cot. "Cameron will always be your brother, just as much as the little prince was. It is not by blood alone that we claim people as family."

"But it is by my hands alone that he died," Serena said, turning on her heels. "I need to get some air. Alone."

Crystal stood still but said, "I do not think it wise for you to be alone right now."

"What are you so worried about?" Serena narrowed her eyes. She jabbed a finger in the guardian's chest and said, "It's not like there's anywhere for me to run."

"You are not thinking clearly." Crystal crossed her arms to put space between them. "And it's my job to keep you out of trouble."

Serena scoffed as she shoved past the guardian, almost knocking her on top of Rigel. "I'm not going to hurt myself, if that's what you're worried about," she seethed.

Serena paused. She stared at Rigel's limp arm before she made eye contact with him. "When you said we must protect the princess, you didn't mean Rilura." She said it without question as she knew in her heart it was fact, and for the first time she understood why he had risked his life to save her.

"When you came to see me yesterday and asked why I saved you, it took all the strength I had left not to tell you the truth."

"It was Rigel who convinced me we should tell you everything," Crystal said, patting him on the leg. "Cut him a break."

"I thought you were my friends," Serena whispered. "But this was always just a job. Save the lost princess, earn a reward, right?"

"Come now, Serena. We all care about you, and it has nothing to do with your status," Xandra argued.

"Friends don't keep such dangerous secrets from each other." Her fingernails dug crescent shapes into her palms. "Maybe guardians do, but not friends."

"We all did what we had to in order to keep you alive," Crystal said. "I will never apologize for that."

Serena rolled her eyes as she turned and stomped over to the doors. She pried the sword out of the handles, gripping the hilt tightly in one hand as she shoved open one door.

"Where are you going?"

"That's none of your business," Serena said as she lingered in the doorway.

"Yes, it is. Especially with that in your hands," Crystal argued, pointing at the blade.

"I'm going to find Will," Serena said. "He's the only one here who has never lied to me."

"Wait," Crystal called out suddenly, making Serena falter in the doorway. "Serena, you cannot tell him."

She faced them, overcome with animosity. "What?"

"You cannot tell Will who you really are." All traces of sympathy were gone, and the elf's blue eyes pierced Serena, daring her to defy the order.

"She's right," Rigel said. "Will is a commoner, and this is the secret of the century. As queen, Elara alone has the authority to decide who is privy to the truth."

Serena's eyebrows ticked up as the words settled uneasily between them. "You thrust this truth upon me and then dare ask me to lie to him?"

"Serena, I know you're upset," Xandra began, moving beside Crystal in the walkway.

"You don't know half of how I feel right now. You should have left me where you found me."

And with that, Serena turned and marched through the doorway. The door swung back and forth on its hinges as she disappeared into the hall. Now, Serena knew the truth of her lineage, and its implications left her head spinning. She pressed a hand against the stone wall, steadying herself as she tried to process what she'd been told. Though the guardians seemed certain that royal blood ran through her veins, Serena knew she was no princess. She knew how to feed chickens and catch rabbits, not how to walk in heels and dance with nobles. No, she was a girl who always got her hands dirty for the sake of helping the family she loved so dearly. Now, any hope she had of a peaceful life was long gone, left behind with the lifeless bodies of the Finches in the quaint village of Durmak.

MERCY

Anteros walked briskly in the direction of the courtyard with his hands clasped behind his back. He had been preparing to head down to the dungeon again when his father's aide knocked at his door. It was late afternoon, nearly dinnertime, and his father's urgent summons caught him off guard.

"Did Father send for you as well?" Sabine asked. Her heels clacked loudly against the tile floor as she rushed to catch up to him. "The courtyard is an unusual request."

"Highly suspicious," he replied, glancing sideways at his sister as she fell in step with him. She gripped her delicate cream-colored gown in each hand; a gold necklace made of glistening rubies bobbled against her collarbone.

Anteros combed through his hair with his fingers and inspected his attire, adjusting the rolled-up sleeves of his white shirt and fastening the top buttons. Sabine watched with a smirk. "How has Talitha been since the ball? I haven't been able to visit her," the princess quipped, a broad grin spreading across her face.

He clenched his jaw, trying to hide his face from her as his lips instinctively curved upward. "She's surviving," he said, feigning impassivity as he stuffed his hands into his pockets.

Sabine frowned.

Anteros sighed and added, "She enjoyed the ball and feast. She was very grateful for her night of freedom."

Her eyes lit up as she clapped her hands together. "Oh, wonderful! I am so glad I could oblige," she squealed. "I am already planning for the next one. It will be even better!"

Anteros shook his head. "Should the Solstice not be the best ball of the year? It's Father's favorite holiday."

Sabine rolled her eyes and declared, "It may be our greatest holiday, but surely, I deserve an extravagant celebration as well. After all, I am the only princess of Hyrosencia. And I'll only turn sixteen once."

"I am sure your next birthday will be just as elaborate," Anteros said with a chuckle.

They rounded a corner, and the sunlight streaming in through the courtyard entryway momentarily blinded Anteros. As they stepped onto the courtyard path, his eyes adjusted, finding their parents were waiting in the shade of the grand fountain.

"I do not care what you think. I am king!" Antoine roared, his foreboding presence looming over their mother. Chelsea recoiled, shrinking back against the fountain.

"Father, Mother!" Sabine called out, beaming at them as she outpaced her brother. "How lovely to see you this fine evening."

Seeing his children, Antoine narrowed his eyes and crossed his arms. The malice in his expression caused Anteros and Sabine to slow their pace, glancing at each other uneasily. There was no doubt their father was in a particularly foul mood this evening.

"Enough of your chatter," Antoine spat, his volume causing Sabine to flinch. Anteros watched her smile melt away, and he realized his mother's eyes were brimming with tears. He had never seen her tremble before, and the sight caused bile to rise in his throat.

"What is the meaning of this, Father?" Anteros asked frankly, mirroring his father's stance.

The king turned his back on his son and traced his fingertips along the stone on the fountain wall. "Have I not been a generous father to you both?" Antoine asked, rubbing his wet fingers together.

"Always, Father. Did I forget to thank you for something?" his son asked with a disdainful chuckle.

"You have always been so ungrateful!" Rage flashed in his eyes.

Anteros swallowed, shifting his footing as his smile fell. His father often tolerated his sarcastic quips and disheveled appearance. But something was amiss, and only one transgression came to his mind.

His father continued, "Both of you have. But I shall no longer tolerate such insolence from you."

"I'm sorry if I have been ungrateful, Father. Whatever you're angry at, I'm sorry," Sabine stammered, locking eyes with her mother. Chelsea gripped her daughter's hand, her breath hitching in her throat as she tried to shield her daughter with her own body.

The king whipped his head around to face Sabine, grabbing a fistful of her hair as he boomed, "Silence!" Anteros watched as his spittle splattered against her face, and she whimpered, unable to escape his grasp.

"Leave her alone," he shouted, storming toward his father. "I'm the ungrateful troublemaker. All she's ever wanted is your love."

Antoine released Sabine, and she stumbled back, falling onto the ground. He glared at his son as he yelled, "What has she ever done to earn my love?" Sabine began sobbing, and Chelsea pulled her daughter closer.

Anteros lurched toward his father, swinging his fist through the air. Antoine shifted his body and caught his son's fist in one palm. "You dare raise a hand against the king?" he asked through clenched teeth. "I knew you were defiant, but I never thought you would stoop so low." Squeezing his son's fist in his left hand, Antoine reared back his other arm and delivered a forceful blow to his son's face that sent him staggering back onto the ground.

The prince pressed tenderly on his left eye. He winced in pain. Antoine loomed over him, his nostrils flaring as he glared down at his son. "If you were not the crown prince and princess, I would string you both up in the dungeon for your treasonous actions," he said. Turning toward the courtyard entryway, Antoine snapped his fingers, and two guards marched into the square dragging a struggling girl between them.

Talitha thrashed desperately; her eyes filled with terror at the sight of the king.

"I hope you had your fun with this girl because none of you will be smiling when we are done here," Antoine said, turning his nose up to look down at Talitha. The guards threw Talitha down roughly beside Anteros. She kept her head down as her eyes flicked to the left, pleading with him for help. Antoine took slow, deliberate steps toward them. He stalked around his son and his prisoner like a predator circling its prey. "Did you really think I wouldn't find out about your indiscretions?"

"Father, she—Talitha—she is innocent in all this," Sabine stuttered helplessly. Her mother grasped her by the forearm and shot her a warning look.

"Innocent?" Antione laughed, the twisted sound instilling fear in them all. "This girl? This commoner my men plucked from the forest? The one who knew the Finch family—the traitors I have hunted for over a decade?" Kneeling in front of her, the king gripped her chin in his hand and surveyed her. "This temptress dared to sleep in my son's bed. How stupid of you all to think I would not notice. This is my castle, and all in it work for me." Talitha's body shuddered with fright, and Antoine dropped his hand.

One of the guards stepped forward and handed the king a thick black whip. Antoine felt the weight of the weapon in his hands before turning his attention toward Sabine. "I can only assume this idiocy was plotted by my foolish daughter," he said, slapping the whip against one palm.

Sabine trembled as she covered her mouth with one hand and sank further into the gravel. Chelsea shielded her daughter, crying out, "Antoine, please! She is your daughter! You cannot mean to—"

"It was my idea. All of it," Anteros said. When his father turned back to him, he was on his feet, standing in front of the shaking prisoner. "I asked Sabine to bring Talitha clothes and have her cleaned up. I wanted to give Talitha a taste of freedom. It was all me. I thought perhaps she would let her guard down and tell me something new."

Fuming, Antoine stomped toward his son until he was inches from his freshly bruised face. "Don't think I will ever trust your word again, boy," the king said. "Consider yourself lucky that I was not blessed with another son."

Two guards carried a massive wooden post to the center of the garden. With each strike of their mallets, Talitha flinched as the post sank deeper and deeper into the dirt. Sabine quivered, clutching onto her mother. She bit her lip, looking feeble as she watched from her mother's shadow.

"This is the one, the girl you're always thinking about?" Antoine asked. "Since you care so much about her, you can select her punishment." His lips curled in a malicious smile that sent chills up Anteros's spine.

"She deserves no further punishment, Father," Anteros said, standing his ground. "She should never have been brought here in the first place."

Antoine scoffed, ignoring his son's declaration. "It's high time you learn that every choice has consequences." He tapped the whip against his hand again and said, "I can give the girl twelve lashes. One for every week she has been here and failed to give up Serena Finch."

Talitha's eyes glossed over, and she pleaded, "No! Please, spare me. I don't know anything. This isn't right. I don't know where she is!"

Antoine ignored her desperate pleas. Pausing in front of his son, the king forced the whip into his son's hands. "Or you can give her five lashes yourself." His eyes gleamed like black holes, the darkness of his irises threatening to swallow them all up.

Anteros looked down at the whip in his hands and shook his head. "No. I will not. I'm not a monster like you," he spat, shoving the weapon back at his father. "This is barbaric. She isn't a traitor. She's just an ordinary girl. She doesn't know anything."

"She stopped being 'an ordinary girl' the moment you started caring about her," Antoine sneered at his son. "Since you refuse, you can stand there and watch how it's done." The king motioned for the guards to lift Talitha off the ground. The soldiers lugged her over to the post, her legs dragging behind.

"Wait!" Talitha pleaded breathlessly. The men bound her by the wrists and attached the rope to the top of the post with her back facing the Rextons. "Please, don't do this," Talitha begged. "Please! Help me, Anteros!"

"Anteros?" Antoine pulled a knife from his belt. Stomping toward her, he reached forward and slashed through the plain crepe gown she was wearing, exposing half of her back. Talitha cried out in terror. "You are to call him 'Your Highness' and nothing else, filthy peasant," Antoine whispered in her ear.

"Yes, Your Majesty," she stammered.

The king stomped a few paces from the girl. The end of the unraveled whip rested on the lawn. Anteros clenched his jaw and watched as his father reared it back, extending the braided leather weapon behind him. The prince's chest tightened; the rapid pace of his heartbeat boomed in his ears, drowning out the sound of Talitha's voice. He swayed, and speckles clouded his vision as he stepped back.

Suddenly, his mother's hand was on his shoulder, and he turned to stare at her, powerless. She leaned close enough for her husband not to hear and whispered, "She'll be dead before the tenth swing if your father does it. He will make sure of it."

Anteros tried to swallow, but his mouth had gone dry. His chest rose and fell rapidly, and he shook his head, knowing his father would inflict severe pain with every blow. Antoine practiced whipping the weapon against the pavement, the crack of the whip causing all of them to jump. As he positioned himself a few feet in front of Talitha, the king drew back his arm, a menacing grin blooming on his face as if he were about to conquer a kingdom with the flick of his wrist.

"Wait!" Anteros cried out, stepping forward. But it was too late. His father released the whip, ignoring his son as he drove the weapon at his victim. The whip cracked loudly before slapping against Talitha's exposed flesh. It left a deep gash in the center of her back. She cried out in agony, her knees buckling from the pain, and the guards urged her to stand back up. Anteros raced forward, throwing himself in between his father and the writhing girl. "That's enough," Anteros said, outstretching his hand. "I will do it. Give it to me."

Antoine leered as he handed the weapon off to his son, his dark expression turning smug. "There you are," he said, leaning closer. "Five to go."

"You already gave her one!" Anteros protested.

"And the deal was for you to give her five," Antoine said, slapping his son on the back of his shoulder with such force the prince stumbled forward.

Talitha sobbed, her muscles stretched taut as she anticipated the next blow.

Antoine tramped toward the fountain and pulled his daughter by the hair. He dragged her closer to the violent scene as Chelsea shuffled after them. "I want you to watch this." The king turned his daughter's chin in the direction of Anteros and Talitha. "Watch so you will always remember your place." Fresh tears slid down Sabine's cheeks as she forced open her eyes.

Anteros held his breath as he gripped the leather handle and watched his knuckles pale. He glanced toward his father, who urged him on with the nod of his head. Then, clenching his jaw, Anteros cracked the whip; the instrument slapped Talitha's flesh roughly, knocking the air from her lungs. She threw her head back and cried out, and the shrill sound pierced his heart like an arrow. Anteros sucked in sharply as he assessed the damage he had caused to the delicate skin that had haunted his dreams all week. Just to the right of his father's gash was a bright red streak where his first strike had hit her; he had somehow managed not to tear her flesh open. Anteros groaned. He blinked back tears, refusing to allow his father to witness the anguish caused by his cruel game.

"Another!" Antoine ordered. "Do not hesitate."

Talitha moaned. "Do it."

Anteros pulled the whip back, and his chest constricted as if his father's hands were wrapped tight around his heart. Watching the girl he cared for tremble, the prince pressed his lips together and propelled his arm forward. When the cracker struck her back, her cry resounded through the garden. Servants passing in the nearby halls went running, not daring to witness the scene. Anteros dropped the whip, horrified by the blood seeping from the fresh tear in her pale skin. The tattered remnants of her dress greedily absorbed the trickling blood.

"Please, Anteros. No more," she gasped. "Your Highness, please have mercy."

"If you stop, I will start the count over," Antoine snarled, crossing his arms. His eyes danced over her back; he seemed enthralled by her injuries. "Another. Now."

"I'm sorry, Red," Anteros said as he quickly scooped the whip off the ground.

"Please, I beg you. Have mercy!" Talitha cried.

"Do it now, or I will," his father bellowed, stepping closer.

Grinding his teeth, Anteros cracked the whip. All around him became a blur of red as he panted, his heartbeat pounding in his ears. Talitha's back was swollen, streaked with harsh red lines and brutal tears in her delicate flesh.

Sabine took a step forward, but her mother grabbed her arm and pulled her back. "There's nothing you can do for her," Chelsea whispered to her daughter. "Do nothing to draw your father's ire. This will soon be over."

Anteros wiped the sweat from his brow on his shirt sleeve. His ears burned as he held back a storm of rage, but he wore a mask of indifference for the sake of his father. The last thing he wanted was to hurt someone in this way. Chelsea nodded, urging him to return to his task. When he turned back to Talitha, she hung limply by her restraints, her knees bent and her muscles relaxed as if she had lost consciousness. Anteros paused, desperate to make sure she was still breathing.

"I believe you have two left to fulfill our bargain," his father noted with a smirk.

The prince gripped the whip tightly in his palm and silently cursed his father. He briefly considered turning the weapon loose on the king but chose not to for fear of further repercussions for Talitha. One wrong move, and Anteros knew his father would kill the poor girl just to prove a point. Anteros ground his teeth together as he pulled the weapon back once more. "I will never forgive you for this," he muttered, hoping his father heard him.

Antoine chuckled. "I do not need forgiveness, boy. I need you to be as ruthless as I am. Then you will be deserving of my crown."

After the whipping, the guards were ordered to dump Talitha in a smaller cell in the dungeon. Antoine made sure to tell his men that Anteros and Sabine were not allowed access to any prisoner. When they dragged her wilted body away, Anteros hurled the whip at his father's feet and stormed out of the courtyard. Antoine yelled from behind him, "Get to your rooms, both of you! You have not earned a place at my table."

Sabine scurried down the same path as her brother without making eye contact with her father. Anteros was already halfway up the stairs to the second floor when his sister reached the staircase. As she reached the top, she called out, "Anteros! Wait." But before she could reach him, he marched into his bedchamber, slamming the door shut.

He slammed his fist into the glass balcony door, the shattered shards reflecting resolve. When he let out a furious howl, Sabine thrust open the door and entered his room without a word. Though his back was turned, he could feel her presence in the room as he loomed over his collection of liquor bottles. He cradled his bloody hand against his abdomen and picked up a large bottle by the neck. "Anteros," she breathed, seeing the mess. "Are you all right?"

He pulled the silver stopper from the bottle with his teeth and spit it onto the floor. "Peachy," he said without looking her way. Using his unmarred hand, he lifted the spirit to his lips and gulped until it was half-empty, and a tiny trickle escaped out of the corner of his mouth. Breathing heavily, Anteros turned and rammed his back into the nearest wall, sliding down until he was sitting on the floor. His eyes glistened. "What sort of man am I?" he mused, giving his sister a tortured look.

"A foolish one," Sabine muttered as she lowered herself onto the floor by his side. "But also a caring one. You have so many excellent traits that our father lacks."

"I am a monster like him," Anteros replied, ignoring her sentiments. "He has always wanted me to revel in inflicting pain as he does." His face scrunched, and he pressed his bloody hands to his forehead. "I did not revel in it. Not for a second. I never wanted to hurt her."

"Brother, you are no monster." She pulled him into a gentle hug. "You were in an impossible situation. It was not fair. For you or for her."

"I could have killed her," Anteros said. "She begged me to stop, and I kept going."

"You saved her," Sabine reassured him. She patted the back of his head, and it felt motherly. "Father most certainly would have killed her, and he would have made it as painful as possible. What you did was the more merciful option."

"There was nothing merciful about it."

"You chose the lesser of two evils." Sabine stroked her brother's sweaty hair. "She will survive because of that. She's a strong one, remember?"

"Even strong people have a breaking point." They sat in silence for a moment with their heads leaned back against the wall. "We caused this, you know," Anteros said, taking another swig from the glass decanter beside him. "What were we thinking, parading her about the castle for all to see? She was vulnerable, and we—"

"I treated her like a paper doll," Sabine interrupted, covering her eyes with her dainty hands. "I am the one who should have been punished."

"Neither of you deserved a beating for what you did," Anteros said. "Father took things to a new extreme today. He will not tolerate disobedience anymore. We must be careful if we want to keep our heads."

Sabine scoffed. "You are his only heir. I doubt he would ever harm you."

"Have you seen my face?" he asked, turning to show off his swollen eye. He pressed the glass decanter to his temple and winced as he gave up and put it back on the floor. "It is not unheard of for a woman to take the throne," Anteros said. "I think you would be more suited to it than I."

"I should rather not have that kind of power. Too much responsibility," she said, pinching her lips as she studied her brother's face. "You may be his only heir, but that does not mean you have to lead by his example. When he is gone, you can change things. Make Graynor a dignified place again."

Anteros shook his head. "I would like to burn it all to the ground right now."

"That's rather dramatic," Sabine said, her laugh breaking through the tension. "He may be awful, but this is still our home. The only home we have ever known. I could never ruin this place, though I should like to rid it of certain people."

The prince's eyes glazed over as the traumatic incident in the courtyard replayed in his mind. "She must hate us both now," he muttered. "I would."

"If I was her, I would not hate you," his sister said quietly. "It was a difficult choice. But you spared her from far worse lashings by our father. You were much kinder than he would have been."

"I do not think she will see my actions as kind," Anteros scoffed. "I am just another man who has hurt her. She will never look at me the same again."

Sabine paused. "You love her," she said finally, her voice sad but certain.

Anteros looked away from her. Instead, he chose to gaze at the sky where his glass door used to be. "That does not matter now," he said, staring at the deep gray clouds that obscured the sun. "It was all a farce, just as she said."

"I don't think it was."

"Whatever it was, it's over now," Anteros said wistfully, picking at the shards of glass in his knuckles. "There was no point befriending that girl. She was marked for death the second she entered the gates."

"Don't give up on her so easily. She could forgive you."

The prince clenched his fist, resolving to release his attachment to the girl in the dungeon. "I do not deserve to be forgiven," he said. "I left marks on her that will never heal."

"None of this was your fault, Anteros. Father is a madman. He did this to hurt you. To hurt all of us. He does not love us. All he cares about is having indisputable power."

"And that he has," the prince said, taking another swig straight from the decanter. His bloody fist ached as he clenched it tight. He wished he could punch his father's face in, but no matter how he looked at it, one truth remained: Antoine Rexton held all the power in Graynor. The only way for Anteros to live the life of luxury he had come to enjoy was by playing the role for which he was born. "Going against Father was futile," the prince said. "I am his only heir. Any blood he spills mars my own hands. His enemies shall always see him in my face, whether I like it or not."

"How dismal," his sister said. She grabbed his hand and unfurled his fingers. "You have punished yourself enough. Stop moping! And no more punching walls. You look like death."

Anteros exhaled and pushed himself off the ground with one hand, quickly rising to his feet. "Yes, Your Highness," he said, pretending to curtsy as Sabine scowled up at him.

The plentiful layers of her skirt made it difficult to stand, and Anteros rolled his eyes and offered her a hand. "Thank you," she said, shaking bits of glass off her dress. "See, I told you, you are not all bad. That's just not you."

"I am not who I was yesterday," her brother quipped, picking up the bottle off the floor and staring at it sullenly.

"Neither am I," she replied. Sabine yanked the bottle out of his hands and swigged. She winced as the liquor went down. Anteros raised his eyebrows in surprise. "Ahh," she said, grinning as she deposited the bottle back among his collection. Anteros crossed the room; his shoes crunched on broken glass as he retrieved the bottle topper. Returning to the glistening cart, he deposited the silver stopper onto the bottle with a frown.

"Well, if you are done with your pity party, shall we start planning?" Sabine asked, dusting the dirt and glass fragments off her dress.

Anteros whipped his head around. "Planning what?"

"How to help Talitha, of course." She fluttered her eyelashes, feigning innocence. Anteros opened his mouth to protest, but she turned and flounced over to his sitting area. "Come, brother," she called back as she flopped onto an emerald green couch. "Do you not wish to help your beloved?"

"Do not call her that," he said sharply, reluctantly joining her on the couch. "What you are suggesting is high treason. Do you have a death wish?"

"Not at all," she laughed. "But since when do you care about the rules?"

Anteros carefully considered her words. "Sabine, we are clearly incapable of sneaking around without his knowledge." Closing his eyes, he pictured Talitha's face. He held the memory of her smile as they danced together in his mind. "We cannot risk her life again."

"Then we wait until Father has forgotten her," Sabine said, a glint of determination in her stubborn sky blue eyes. "She deserves a better life. We must set things right."

Anteros fixated on the balcony across from them; his mind wandered to the night of the Solstice when he dared to kiss her. One corner of his mouth curved upward before sinking back into a straight line. That memory was now tainted by the sounds of Talitha screaming, begging him to show her mercy.

"No," he said, much to his sister's shock. "It's over, Sabine. There is no saving her."

"I cannot believe you are giving up."

"The only way to keep her safe now is to stay far away." Anteros leaned back and crossed his ankles.

Sabine huffed as she rose to her feet, giving her brother a reproachful glance before she stormed for his door. "She will die if we do not help her."

Anteros rested his head on the back of the couch and sighed. "There's nothing we can do for her now, 'bine," he said. "Go back to your room and stop making trouble for everyone. I do not have it in me to keep cleaning up your messes."

Sabine sucked in a shallow breath. He didn't have to look at her to know the hurt in her eyes was his own doing. The sound of her heels clacking against the floor as she left told him all he needed to know. And he prayed that for once in her life, Sabine would listen to reason before ending up on the wrong side of their father's wrath.

UNITED AT LAST

Serena and company were joined by Elara's reinforcements in Jordis. After ten long days, Rigel had recovered enough to begin the last leg of the journey. Though Serena was still on edge around the guardians, her heart began to soften as they traveled. The guardians weren't the ones who had left her behind in Hyrosencia a lifetime ago; they were the ones who brought her back into the light, filling all the cracks in her broken heart with kindness and compassion. Maybe it was for the best that she knew the truth after all this time—and that she heard it from them.

Though she had fond memories of growing up with Cameron, Serena knew the man she faced in the snowstorm was no brother. Rigel, however, was a kind and loyal friend. He'd been willing to risk his life for her when Cameron sought to send them both to the stars. For that reason, she knew saving Rigel—and herself—had been the right decision.

Serena mourned the loss of her brother, but she realized Xandra had been right. She wasn't alone. Two families might have been taken from her, but she had managed to stumble into another type of family, the type that would fight beside, with, and for her. And after all they had been through, Serena would choose to protect each of them in the same way.

As they entered the tunnel to Silvermane, Serena ducked through the doorway, descending the steep steps into the dimly lit bowels of the Athamar Mountains. With each step, her eyes adjusted more to the darkness, but her heart raced knowing she was closer than ever to the City of Mercy and at last meeting her aunt in person.

After a brief respite in the starlit city, they bid their dwarf allies farewell and began the slow descent down the side of the Athamar Mountains through thick foliage. Everyone was eager to lay eyes on Elara's refuge; the guardians chattered with such enthusiasm about returning to their home-away-from-home, while Serena, Will, and the dwarfs were curious how the mysterious City of Mercy would compare to the stories they had heard.

A few hours into their trek, the trees thinned, allowing sunbeams to cast streaks of light and shadow across their faces until they emerged in a stunning field scattered with tiny lavender and yellow wildflowers. The distant sound of flowing water drew Serena's gaze, and her breath hitched as she looked out over the open field and beheld Symptee in its full glory for the first time.

A massive stone wall enclosed the city; armed guards paced the path along the top of the wall, their vigilant watch ensuring the safety of the refugees inside. From this height, they could also see the inner wall that protected the great citadel where Queen Elara and her most trusted allies resided. The citadel stood a floor taller than the walls, its rising towers offering the queen a breathtaking view of the enchanting landscape and the stars that dazzled over it at night.

"Welcome home," Xandra said, grinning at their astonished expressions.

Not far past the city was a harbor with two small ships docked in the river, their impressive white sails billowing in the summer breeze. Serena could almost smell the mineral-rich water as memories of the Eldawia River ensnared her senses, bringing her back to the day Crystal found her swimming in the river what felt like a lifetime ago.

"I didn't know there was a river so close to the city," Serena said, gleaming as she turned to Crystal on her left.

"It's magnificent," Will breathed. His gaze followed the mighty river that flowed southeast with no end in sight.

Serena blinked as she stared at the city that was nearly within reach. "Yes, it is," she murmured.

"I did not think to mention it," Crystal said with a shrug. "You cannot see much of it from within the walls."

"And after a while, you grow so accustomed to the sound that you can barely hear it," Rigel said, wiping his sweaty forehead on his left arm's sleeve. His breathing was labored, but he tried to hide his exhaustion.

"Are you faring well, Rigel?" Will asked as he stepped toward the guardian.

"I am most excellent. Best shape I've ever been in," Rigel said, waving his hand.

"Do you suppose we'll reach the wall before nightfall?" Serena asked, using her hand to shield the harsh sun from her eyes.

"Without a doubt," Gideon, a member of Elara's Guard, answered, turning to flash her a smile.

Xandra said, "We can slow down if you need a breather." She eased one pack off her shoulder. Pulling a green canteen out of the bag, she extended her arm to Rigel, who snatched it from her and immediately started chugging the contents.

"No more stops," another guard called from the front of the pack. He was at least two decades older than Gideon, and his face held a look of urgency. "You can squawk all you want once we're behind the wall."

Rigel sucked in a breath as he handed the canteen back to Xandra. "I won't be the one to slow us down. Not when we are this close."

Serena felt a flutter in her abdomen, and she clenched her fists as they marched onward. Will walked alongside her, reaching for her hand as the city wall became larger, and its shadow consumed them. He slowed his pace until Rigel fell in step to his right, and he asked, "What happens to refugees when they arrive? Will there be a safe place for us to live?"

Rigel stared at him for a moment before shifting his gaze to the flowers they were trampling. "There is always a place for everyone," he replied. He smiled as he looked at the city in the distance. "Don't worry, Will. We will vouch for you, and Elara will find you a position. And you can bunk in the Guard wing."

"Would that be a suitable place for Serena?"

Serena squeezed his hand, touched by his thoughtfulness.

Rigel paused, holding his stomach as he snickered. "Serena?" he asked, wiping a tear from his eye. "You don't have to worry about her. A cushy room in the main hall awaits. She'll be right around the corner from the queen and the nobles."

"Nobles? Why would she put up a Guard's daughter where the nobles live?" Will asked, his brow furrowed under his bushy hair. Rigel's eyes widened, and he faked a cough, falling back a few steps and shoving Cole in front of him. Serena released Will's hand and gently patted his elbow before taking a few quick steps ahead. She longed to tell him the truth and feared he could read her if she lingered nearby too long.

"Is he all right?" she heard Will ask Cole.

"He'll be fine, but if you keep asking, he may stab you."

"I would never," Rigel countered from behind them, and Serena laughed.

Rilura hurried up from behind them, her black braids slapping against her back as she suddenly slowed her pace beside Serena. Serena had been grateful for the princess's presence on the trek to the citadel, and she hoped she'd see her more in the days to come. She was pleased to know she'd have one more friend within the walls. "Would be quicker if we could race the whole way down," the Dwarf Princess said, smiling at her.

"I'm not sure my legs could handle that at this point," Serena replied, rubbing her hands on her sore thighs. "The next time I sit, I may never get up."

"Well, ye have traveled much farther than I," Rilura chuckled, taking a sip from her canteen.

"You're right about that," Serena said. She stared wistfully ahead of them. Gideon and the other guards took up the front of their party, their dark purple uniforms a constant reminder that she would soon be face to face with Queen Elara Garrick. Serena chewed her lip absentmindedly as she thought about all the things she wanted to say to the queen when they arrived.

"You seem lost in thought."

The dwarf's voice snapped Serena back to reality, and she turned her head to offer a sheepish smile. "Sorry. I was just thinking about what it will be like once we arrive."

"You have seemed perturbed the past few days. Care to talk about it?"

Serena exhaled, glancing around at the guardians. Cole had led Will ahead of them, sucking Gideon into a conversation about working for the outer wall, and Crystal chatted with Xandra to their left, both unconcerned with her speaking to the princess. "The guardians told me something the other day, a secret they had been keeping. A secret that changes everything," Serena admitted. She stooped down to pick a wildflower along their path.

Rilura nodded, patting Serena on the back as gently as possible with a broad hand. "We wondered when you would be made aware," the dwarf said quietly.

Serena stared at her. "You knew?" With her accusation, she cut away all past pleasantries. "Who else knew?"

One side of Rilura's face cocked a half-grin as she shook her head. "We knew nothing for certain. Your guardians were tight-lipped, even with my father." She leaned closer to Serena, so the guards would not hear them. "But they forgot Elara passed through the mountains many moons ago, and we dwarfs never forget a face."

"The first time I saw her, I thought I was crazy to see any sort of resemblance," Serena muttered.

"Your instincts were right," Rilura noted, squeezing Serena's hand. "You have the same eyes, like rare jewels, as my father always says."

"My father's eyes, I suppose," the girl whispered. She wished she could remember what Stellan Garrick looked like. "I wish they had told me the truth years ago."

"My people believe in absolute truth," the dwarf said. "But in your situation, I think the only reason you survived is because it was kept secret."

"Perhaps that is so, but it would not have been such a shock when I was younger," Serena supposed. She took a calming breath before continuing. "I do not know what Elara will expect of me when we arrive. All I have ever been is a blacksmith's daughter."

"I am certain that is not all," Rilura said with a laugh. "You are still good, despite being scarred by the most painful of losses."

"I don't feel good. I feel… frustrated? Angry. Like I want to scream at the sky until there is no air left in my lungs."

"Your feelings are valid," the princess said. "The moon is not always full, but in each phase, its might and beauty are the same. No matter how eclipsed it is by the darkness, it still has some sort of light to offer, as do you."

Serena stared at her, the words ruminating as she blinked slowly. Knowing where she came from did not change where she had been and who had done the better part of raising her. A part of her would always be Serena Finch, the determined but helpful daughter of a blacksmith and his wife, and she would cling to that part of herself when Elara asked her to step back into her identity as a member of the royal family.

THE SUN WAS LOW to the earth when they reached the city's entrance, two heavy metal doors that stretched several feet above their heads. The eldest of the guards escorting them tapped the hilt of his sword in a pattern on the metal, the clanging noises reverberating through the air and echoing in the distance.

"Who goes there?" a muddled voice called down to them.

"Sir Ian Clemmons of Guard Sector 7," Sir Ian declared loudly.

"Crystal Windaef and Guardian Unit 13."

"What is the name of the city bird with no fear?"

"The sparrow," Xandra called back.

"Tell Her Majesty that a missing sparrow and a Steelcast princess have come seeking shelter," Rigel said with a grin.

There was a pause while they waited. Then, they heard a loud click and the subsequent sound of a mechanism turning over. Serena and Will glanced at each other as the guards cranked open the doors to reveal a city bustling with life within the great wall. Serena's heart raced. This was it, the City of Mercy; she pictured Mama's proud smile.

"We made it," Serena gasped, watching their escorts head through the doorway. "We're finally here."

"Welcome to your new home," Gideon said, outstretching his arms as the guardians started after the other men.

"Come on," Rigel called out, walking backward as he waved for them to follow. "The queen awaits!" As she crossed the threshold into Symptee, Serena peered down at her frayed clothes and grimaced, cognizant that all eyes were locked on them as the guards led them down the main road through the bustling metropolis.

"We may look like vagabonds, but everyone in the citadel will recognize us," Xandra said with an excited grin. "Especially my father and the queen."

"I'm looking forward to meeting your father," Serena said with a shy smile. "He must be so proud of you."

"He always has been," Crystal said, draping an arm around her friend's back. "And everyone will be thrilled that we have brought *you* to Symptee."

Serena watched as more of the citadel disappeared behind the inner wall. When she looked up, the sun blinded her. She tried to focus on the dark silhouettes of several guards along the top of the inner wall. *All the answers are on the other side of this wall*, she thought. Her life was going to change forever the moment she crossed the threshold and entered the citadel.

QUEEN ELARA AND THE Cinderfell sisters were basking in the shade of the wisteria trees near the edge of the gardens when they heard a trumpet sound from the gates. The guards along the top of the wall looked like ants scurrying every which way in a frenzy. The queen pushed herself upright and whipped her head around as the gates opened.

"Your Majesty," a breathless middle-aged guard called out from the top of the wall. He must have run three miles from the entrance to report to her. But Elara did not need his report. She knew what the gates opening meant. She pushed herself onto her feet and quickly dusted the specks of grass off her fuchsia gown.

"Who has arrived?" she called back, gripping the chiffon fabric in her fists in anticipation of his answer.

"The guardians have returned, milady," the guard said with a bow. "With the Steelcast princess and a sparrow."

Elara gasped, staring into the distance as a cluster of men in Guard uniforms escorted a small group down the main path to the citadel. They were too far away for her to distinguish any faces, but she thought she recognized the blur of blonde hair leading the way. "Thank you, sir. You may return to your post," she said, bowing her head swiftly before turning to her friends. "I must greet our guests at once. Feel free to stay here and enjoy the rest of this glorious day."

"Oh, I would not dream of missing this occasion," Ismenia said. She and her sister were already on their feet, their arms looped together and expectant smiles spread across their faces.

Idonea nodded. "We will join you." Her head was wrapped in a vibrant silk cloth, hiding the remaining signs of her traumatic injury.

The queen nodded eagerly, lifted her dress an inch off the lawn, and walked briskly toward the closest set of doors. Ismenia and Idonea followed wordlessly like a pair of shadows. There was a buzz in the air as servants scurried by with giddy smiles on their faces. News of guardians returning from a dangerous mission was a rare and exciting occurrence. Most of the time, guardians were sent out and never returned.

As she rounded a corner, Elara collided with Commander Jacob Maynard, interrupting his deep conversation with Richard.

"Beg your pardon, milady," the commander said, bowing low at the waist. "It seems everyone is in a hurry today."

"All is well. No need for apologies," she said, sidestepping the gentlemen and continuing her charge toward the great hall.

Richard leaned toward Ismenia and asked, "Where is she off to in such a hurry?"

"Have you not heard? The guardians have returned," the herbalist said, coaxing her sister to follow the queen.

"That is most excellent news. We must greet them at once," Jacob said, turning back in the direction they had just come from.

By the time Elara reached the doors to the great hall, she was out of breath. Panting, she paused in the open doorway and scanned the room. Alexander was beaming as he lifted his daughter Xandra off the ground in a tight embrace. Their matching smiles brightened the entire room. As the commander put her down on the ground, he realized the queen was staring at them, and he straightened his stance, his smile fading as he smoothed down his uniform.

Elara wrung her hands together as she slowly entered the room, her eyes darting from person to person in search of the only face that mattered in that moment. She paused when she noticed Rigel's entire right arm was wrapped in taut bandages, a sense of dread filling her heart.

"Your Majesty," Rigel said, bowing as low as he could manage in his condition. The other guardians did the same, their movement revealing two young people who had been hidden behind the small crowd. Elara froze; her eyes locked on Serena Finch. The girl stared back, her familiar, dazzling emerald eyes nearly bringing the queen to her knees. The queen took a shaky step closer. It had been seventeen years since Elara had been in the same room as another member of the Garrick family; her heart could have burst right there from the mere sight of her long-lost kin.

"It's you," they whispered in unison.

Serena bit her lip, quickly bowing her head like the guardians and the boy beside her. The queen quickly stepped around the guardians and reached a hand toward her, her gentle fingers catching Serena's chin and guiding her face up. "No need to be so formal. You must be exhausted."

Serena straightened, glancing quietly at the guardians. Her wide eyes beckoned them for assistance, so Crystal stepped forward to address the queen. "Your Majesty, we are pleased to see you again. It has been a long journey, indeed, and I regret we were only able to retrieve one asset from your list."

"You owe me no apologies for that. You have done well," Elara said, grabbing the guardian's hand and patting the top of it. "If only one could be saved, then I thank the heavens for it being Serena."

"Why?" Serena asked, her voice ringing through the massive space.

Elara turned back toward Serena with a grim smile. "All life is precious," the queen said, her hands pressing against her abdomen. "Mary told me so much about you over the years. I can hardly believe you're finally here, where you belong."

Serena recoiled, stepping back at the mention of her mother. "You speak as if you knew her," the girl whispered, shaking her head. She clenched her fists at her sides and scoffed as she looked over Elara's ballgown and the ruby necklace resting against her collarbone. "You may have spoken to her, but you did not know her, and you certainly do not know me. You have no idea what my family has been through, all because they once served yours."

Elara flinched. Two guards stepped forward to intervene, but the queen held up a hand, signaling for them to stop. No one had ever spoken to Elara with such malice, but she understood the girl's frustration. She had once been in Serena's shoes, losing all she had ever loved and making the same arduous journey to escape the same power-hungry man. Studying Serena, it was as if she were staring at the younger version of herself who had been forced to run away—and then forced to wear a crown.

"We have all been through terrible hardships the past few months," Elara murmured.

"What hardships have you faced in your ivory castle?" Serena glared fiercely into the queen's soul.

"Serena," Crystal warned, reaching toward her.

"No," the girl replied, drawing away from the guardian. "You have all kept secrets from me. Secrets I all but died over. And I want to know why. Why didn't you tell me when you had the chance?"

The queen glanced around the great hall, taking notice of the members of the Guard listening to them. "I understand your anger, dear girl," Elara said, sighing. "We should take this to a more private location."

"After soldiers attacked us in the mountains, she had a lot of questions," Xandra said.

"We all felt she deserved answers to those questions," Rigel added, lifting his chin.

"And what have you told her?" the queen asked without looking at any of them. She did not need to hear their answer. The fire in Serena's eyes, hot and angry and scared, told her all she needed to know. Serena already knew the truth.

"She knows who she is, and why she matters to you," Rigel replied.

Elara's eyes widened and her lips parted in surprise. "I specifically asked you not to divulge anything until she was safe. I always intended to tell her everything, once she was secure within these walls."

"We have been her guardians for three months," Crystal said, her tone unabashed. "It was not easy to keep things from her after all she has been through. It was hardly fair to her. We needed her to trust us."

"She deserved to hear what we knew," Xandra said. "That much was long overdue."

Elara fumed, crumpling the delicate fabric of her dress in her fists. "I am indebted to you for bringing her here," she finally said, the sharpness of her tone revealing her irritation. "You have done your duties well, and I applaud you for overcoming every obstacle in your path. You may take your leave now."

The guardians bowed their heads out of respect, all reluctant to leave their friend behind with the queen in their equally enraged states.

"If I could have everyone clear the room, I should like to speak to Serena privately now," the queen finished, turning to face her.

Serena's chest swelled with pride hearing the guardians' support for her. "I should like them to stay," she stammered, her fearful eyes pleading for her allies to remain. "Please."

Elara exhaled, pursing her lips as she considered the request before nodding. "If that would make you more comfortable," she obliged, "then so be it. For now."

"Pardon me, milady," Jacob said, startling the queen. "Allow me to remind you, the Council convenes this morn."

"Oh, heavens," she said crossly. "Tell the Council we will have to postpone. This is more important. We can convene this afternoon or tomorrow."

Jacob nodded; his forehead wrinkling as his thin lips twisted in a stark frown. "And who should I tell them the guardians have brought to our great shelter?"

Elara hummed, her eyes scanning over her niece for a moment before she said, "Serena Finch, the daughter of Sir John Finch and his wife Mary."

Serena's lips parted in protest, but Crystal's fingers brushed her arm, drawing her attention away from the queen. She stared her down, the ice in her gaze warning the girl not to say anything amid strangers. Serena swallowed, her eyes dropping to the floor in submission.

"And the boy?" Richard asked, eyeing the young man next to Serena.

All eyes turned to Will, who had been quiet thus far. "Me? Uh, William Burroughs of Durmak, sir."

"He is a lifelong friend," Serena quickly added. "He apprenticed under my father."

"As a squire?"

"No. As a blacksmith," Crystal said. "But having an extra set of hands on our side did not hurt our odds in a fight."

Elara nodded, turning back to Jacob. "Tell them I will be hearing the firsthand account of their journey and seeing to it they have everything they need to settle in at the citadel."

"I shall inform the Council," Jacob said, bowing his head before promptly departing from the great hall. Richard stole a final glance at Serena Finch and William Burroughs, giving them a wink before following his superior out of the hall.

"I am to stay in the citadel?" Will asked. The glimmer of hope shining in his brown eyes tugged at Elara's heart.

She started toward him; the clack of her heels echoed through the hall as she eyed him over. "You look strong, capable. If Serena and the guardians speak so fondly of you, I am sure we can find a place and put your skills to good use."

"We vouch for him," Rigel said with no delay. "With a bit more training, he would make a fine member of the Guard, should he so wish."

Serena flinched. "Or perhaps you could find a blacksmith to finish his apprenticeship," she suggested, glancing anxiously between the queen and her friend.

Elara lifted her eyebrows as she eyed Will's boyish face. His warm brown eyes shifted toward Serena as his stubble-specked jawline broadened into a grateful grin, and Elara clenched her teeth when she saw the way the girl flushed. "What should you prefer?" she asked, stepping between Will and Serena.

Will swallowed, bowing low. "Please put me wherever I am needed, Your Majesty. I am but a willing servant of your crown." He placed one hand on his heart.

"I appreciate your willingness to adapt to our needs. The guardians are welcome to find you a bed in the Guard's wing."

Will and the guardians nodded, and for a moment, Elara softened, seeing their brilliant smiles across the room. Only Serena still seemed uncertain, her narrowed eyes studying the queen as though she did not trust her motives.

"Commander," Elara said, motioning for Alexander to approach. He marched past his daughter to Elara's side, where she whispered something inaudible to him. She offered a feeble smile to Serena when their eyes met, but the girl crossed her arms and cocked her head to one side, impatiently waiting for her chance to question the queen further.

"Let us show you to your chambers so you can freshen up," the commander said, motioning for Serena to follow him. She opened her mouth to protest, but the queen spoke before she could say anything.

"I will answer all your questions once you've bathed and had a proper meal." Elara placed a firm hand on the girl's shoulder.

"Go," Crystal whispered, nudging her forward. "You are safe here, so do not fret. We can see you in the morning following a much-needed rest."

Serena nodded and silently followed Elara and the commander out of the great hall and in the direction of a massive stairwell. On the steps, she stole one last glance at Will and the guardians as they disappeared down the hall, and part of her ached knowing they would all be living under the same gilded roof—so near, yet so far apart.

SERENA JUMPED WHEN TWO guards opened the doors to the sitting room, and one bellowed, "Enter, Her Majesty, Queen Elara Garrick." She scrambled onto her feet, the swathed sword from King Dranir clattering to the floor as she attempted a curtsy.

"No need for that, child," Elara said, smiling as she took in her niece's clean face and attire. The princess was adorned in an orchid-colored silk gown, and a fresh lilac scent lingered throughout the room. The queen's face fell when she noticed the Heir's Blade sheathed at Serena's hip. She hadn't seen the blessed blade since it was in Stellan's hands. Elara quickly recovered her smile as she stared into the eyes he had passed down to his beautiful daughter.

The queen crossed the room, taking Serena's hands in her own and squeezing them gently. "You look lovely." She sat next to the girl, glancing briefly at their reflection in the ornate mirror centered on the sea-green wall before them. Though they looked uneasy side-by-side, they also looked right; they looked like they belonged together, the resemblance remarkable.

"Thank you," Serena said, rubbing her hands together in her lap. "I must apologize. I should not have been cross with you before. My mother raised me better than that." She stared at an area on the rug as she clutched her skirt.

"No apology is needed," Elara said. She placed her hand under Serena's chin and gently lifting her face until their eyes met. "I understand your frustration." She lowered her hand, tracing the etchings on her wedding band absentmindedly. Serena's face softened as they stared into each other's eyes, the same rare gems that sparkled in her own reflection. "Antoine Rexton has taken much from us: our families, our homes, our peace. It maddens me knowing all the damage he has done. All the lives he has taken in his pursuit of power."

Serena's eyes widened as she whispered, "My father—I mean John Finch. Do you know where he is? What happened to him?"

Elara gave a tired nod. "Yes. He was my only contact in that region, so I had no choice but to send him north in search of other loyalists. We knew there were numbers over the border, awaiting contact."

"So, he may still be alive then?" Serena asked eagerly, leaning closer to the queen.

Elara could hear the hope in Serena's voice, and she considered how difficult it must have been for her niece to endure such hardship in his absence. She was better acquainted with that feeling than she liked. "As of last month, yes," she said with a grim smile. "There is an underground faction near Jessiraé preparing weapons for an uprising."

"I still can't believe Papa was—is—a knight," Serena said, her eyebrows raised as she flopped back. "Are they to storm Graynor? When?"

Elara stared at Serena, wrinkling her brow as she weighed her words. "Have you ever heard of the True Heir's Prophecy?"

Serena narrowed her eyes and shook her head. "I believe the guardians mentioned a prophecy, but I don't know much of it."

"*The kingdom overtaken shall mourn and wait as their children suffer and grow. The man who stole his crown shall meet his fate when the true heir fights for their rightful throne,*" the queen quoted from memory. "That was the last great prophecy given by the oracle, Idonea. You'll meet her. Our people have clung to these words with hope for many years, waiting for the heir's arrival."

Serena blinked at her aunt for a moment before terror ignited in her gaze. "You mean me? I'm the heir? But that does not make sense. I could never rule. I was not raised for this. Surely you are mistaken."

Elara bit the inside of her lip hard as she pictured her brother's face. Her memory of him had become more of a blur with each passing year, yet today his face was vivid. Serena resembled him so very much it made her heart ache. "I wish it were not so, but you are Elyse Serenity Garrick, firstborn child of Crown Prince Stellan Garrick. Your destiny is to inherit the throne Rexton now sits upon."

"No," Serena said, standing abruptly. She kicked the Dwarf King's gift with a simple satin shoe, and her mortified gaze fell to the floor. "No, the prophecy must be about someone else. I am sure of it."

"There is no other, Elyse," the queen said, rising to her feet. She swayed a bit, grabbing Serena's arm to steady herself.

Serena snatched her arm away, a savage glint in her eyes as she snapped, "Do not ever call me that. My name is Serena."

Elara pressed her fingers to the bridge of her nose as her head pounded. "My apologies. I know this must all be a shock."

"What about you? You have been called 'Queen' by our people all these years."

Elara sighed, flopping back down on the edge of the chaise. "That has been but a formality while you were hidden. I am but a regent in your absence." Serena's face went blank as she stared at Elara in sheer horror at the queen's brazen candor. "We are the last of the Garrick bloodline, Serena. If we do not fight for our kingdom, it will be lost to Rexton forevermore."

"Why should I be the one to fight for it?" Serena snapped, her ears searing a vivid red. "I am no prince and no warrior. I am just a girl. If I am what you say, then I have been lied to my entire life."

Elara frowned, pressing her hands against the seat of the chair. "It was for your own good," she insisted. "Everything I have done my entire life has been for the good of Hyrosencia. It was my job as the queen to protect my people, and that included you. That especially meant you. So long as you were in enemy territory, it was best none knew the truth."

"After all that effort to get me here, you plan to send me back over the mountains to fight this war for you?" Serena raised her voice with disgust. "You must be mad!"

"I am not," Elara said, raising her own voice. "Divinity blessed us with this prophecy, with hope for a better tomorrow. Hope that you may yet take our homeland back. Your destiny is written in the stars, Serena. There is no denying that."

"Your oracle was wrong. I will never be a warrior, not like the guardians. There must be another," Serena insisted. "Xandra said I had a brother. Where is he?"

"There has been no word of your brother's whereabouts since the siege," Elara said, lowering her eyes. "I fear he was killed when Rexton executed your parents and your grandfather, King Scorpius."

"This is absurd," Serena whispered. "I cannot save Hyrosencia. I can hardly protect myself. I am nothing but a beacon of death. Wherever I go, pain follows, and those nearest me are doomed."

"That is not true, Serena. You and your friend made it all the way here, along with all four guardians," the queen said.

"And it cost me everything," Serena shouted. She pushed off the teal couch and kicked the packaged gift across the room. She screamed, and the guards outside thrust open the doors in a panic to find the cause of the commotion.

Elara held up a hand to stop them, merely shaking her head as their eyes combed over the sitting room. Serena seethed, her breathing rapid as she glared daggers at the men in the doorway. "You don't have to do anything today. Or this week," her aunt said, slowly approaching her. She dismissed her guards with the wave of a hand, and they plodded out of the doors and closed them with a click. Turning back to Serena, Elara took her hand and said gently, "There is no rushing destiny, Serena. You will be safe here while you train with the guardians for as long as you need. We will make sure you feel ready before you return to Hyrosencia."

"If this destiny you speak of is unavoidable, then I will do my best to prepare for it," Serena resigned, drawing her hand back from her aunt's. "Not for you or your precious throne, but for Mary Finch—for Daniel and Samuel, and even Cameron. I will train because I want to ruin the man who ripped everyone I cared for away from me."

She stalked across the room, pausing to scoop up the package off the floor. When she turned back to Elara, she thrust the blade into the queen's hands. "A wedding gift from King Dranir Steelcast."

Elara peeled back the thick fabric wrappings, revealing the glistening blade of Mäkarlek. She admired the sapphire and amethyst gemstones in the hilt, sucking in a breath as sunlight from the window made a kaleidoscope of blue and purple refractions on the walls. "It's beautiful. I suppose I should give this to my husband."

"They called it the Blade of Everlasting Devotion," Serena said with an unamused huff. "Perhaps you, too, should learn how to protect yourself."

"Is that a threat?" Elara asked, glowering as she lowered the blade to her side.

Serena shook her head, staring down the queen. Her gaze was cold as the steel in Elara's hands, sending a chill down the queen's spine.

"Not from I," Serena said. She wrapped her fingers around the hilt of Sannarvin. "But I should think the head that wears the crown will always have its share of enemies."

"Yes," Elara said, lowering her eyes. "Yes, I suppose that is true."

"If I am to be a fighter, I will make you a promise," Serena said, unsheathing Sannarvin from her hip. She looked at the blade with fresh eyes, testing the feel of the hilt in her hand as she studied her reflection in the cool metal.

Elara stepped back, bumping into a chair as her eyes widened. Her niece snickered as she lifted the Heir's Blade high and plunged it straight down into the floor, cutting through the thick damask rug and implanting it in the wooden planks underneath. Elara's chest heaved as she stared wide-eyed at Serena, who dropped onto a knee before her, hands perched atop the hilt of her blade.

"I will vow to be the sword of justice for our people, if that is to be my destiny," Serena said. The ferocity in her eyes paralyzed the queen. "But I will never wear the crown. That will always be your burden to bear."

Before the queen could reply, Serena stood and yanked the blade out of the floor, the swift movement causing Elara to flinch back. Without another word, Serena turned and marched for the door, throwing it open haphazardly. As the door slammed into the wall, the gilded mirror shattered on the ground, sending glistening fragments flying across the room.

Elara fell back into one of the plush chairs and shuddered, allowing Mäkarlek to clatter onto the floor. Nothing could have prepared her for the anger Serena exhibited. Gone was the sweet girl Mary Finch had bragged about. That girl had been torn apart and pieced back together with steel for bones and fury in her blood—fury that was now directed at her aunt and anyone else who had stolen her promise of peace.

Acknowledgments

If you are reading this, thank you for taking a chance on a debut novelist. Writing and publishing *A Sparrow Among Stars* has been a wild ride. So many times I had ideas and didn't have the confidence or willpower to work on it. I stopped and started a dozen times, but by a miracle, I finally found the strength to push through and accomplish my life's goal thanks to the encouragement of some amazing people.

Thank you to my family for your continued support of this longtime dream, especially my mother Laura, sister Kelly, and husband Caleb.

Huge thanks to Samantha Carpenter Gregoire, editor extraordinaire, for being ruthless with a red pen while also bolstering my confidence every step of the way! Your expertise and friendship have been crucial throughout the editing process, and I will forever be grateful I get to partner with you on this series! Thanks to Jack Clarie for his editing contributions, as well. *A Sparrow Among Stars* would not be where it is today without this dynamic duo!

Special thanks to my earliest readers: Kelly, Isabella, Nikki, Harriet, and Victoria. Your positive feedback was exactly what I needed!

Thanks to my Sparrows, my wonderful street team, and my ARC team! Your enthusiasm toward my novel before you even got to read it was so greatly appreciated! I hope you each found something to love in this story.

Thank you to every teacher who ever encouraged my love of reading and writing my own stories. On the hard days, I remembered your encouragement and the yearbook signature that said: "Can't wait to see you publish a novel one day." I finally did it!

Lastly, thank you to all the friends and Internet strangers who have shown me support through social media during the process of independent publishing. I felt like I had my own virtual cheerleading squad. Special thanks to the Authors Supporting Authors group. You are all awesome, and I love being a part of our little community.

About the Author

Sara Puissegur lives in south Louisiana with her husband Caleb and their little boy. She has a Bachelor's degree in Communications and works full time as a Communication Specialist managing a website, newsletter, social media, and more. She has enjoyed taking her work experience and applying those skills toward her passion project, the labor of love that is her first novel.

Sara has enjoyed writing original stories since elementary school, and it has been her lifelong dream to publish a novel. The Celestial Destiny Series has been a work in progress for over a decade, and the first book in the series, *A Sparrow Among Stars*, is Sara's first published work. She is grateful that she gets to finally start her author career by sharing the epic saga that has been on her mind for many years.

Learn More & Subscribe

Sara Puissegur
www.sarapuissegur.com

Verse & Vine Publishing
www.verseandvinepublishing.com

Printed in the USA
CPSIA information can be obtained
at www.ICGtesting.com
LVHW041638230824
789012LV00004B/7